PATH OF
THE CAT

PATH OF THE CAT

VAMPIRE EARTH VOLUME 3:

FALL WITH HONOR

WINTER DUTY

E. E. Knight

SCIENCE
FICTION

FALL WITH HONOR   Copyright © 2008 by Eric Frisch
   Publication History: Roc mass market, December 2009
WINTER DUTY   Copyright © 2009 by Eric Frisch
   Publication History: Roc mass market, July 2010

First SFBC Printing: June 2014

Selected by Michael Phillips, SFBC Senior Editor

Published by arrangement with
The Penguin Group (USA), Inc./ The Berkley Publishing Group, Ace
375 Hudson Street
New York, NY 10014

Visit The SFBC online at http://www.sfbc.com

ISBN 978-1-62953-028-4

Printed in the United States of America.

Contents

FALL WITH HONOR

A NOVEL OF
THE VAMPIRE EARTH

E. E. KNIGHT

To the memory of Thomas Manning,
a fine artist and a finer friend

I have also remarked, fellow-soldiers, that such as are eager in the field to preserve their lives at any rate, for the most part perish wretchedly and ignominiously, while I see that such as reflect that death is to all men common and inevitable, and seek in battle only to fall with honor, more frequently, from whatever cause, arrive at old age, and live, while they live, with greater happiness.

—Xenophon, *Anabasis*

One

Forward Operating Base Rally, Missouri, September, the fifty-fourth year of the Kurian Order: the Show Me state has a flat bootheel stomping a corner of northeast Arkansas.

Those who pass through the region remember only a dullish stretch of Midwestern farm country running along the river, pierced by bayous and bisected by interstate. There's little to distinguish it on the surface. But beneath the good topsoil, the bootheel fascinates on a geologic scale. It is home of the New Madrid fault line that gave way in the chaos of 2022, causing the Mississippi to run backward as far north as St. Louis.

The destruction that resulted from the earth writhing like a heavy sea made the region ill-omened. Everyone who could move did, to the better-preserved areas of Missouri at first, and then south or farther west once the Grogs showed up.

Then came Southern Command.

The few Kurian Lords organizing the area fell rather easily, surprised by the strength and tenacity of the guerrillas. With the Kurians gone, the area became another fought-over piece of no-man's-land between the Mississippi and the Ozark Free Territory, not as well patrolled as the Tennessee–Little Rock corridor or as danger-filled as the bushwhack country in southern Missouri. A powerful smuggler named Shrivastava set up shop around an old fireworks warehouse, running whatever he could between the Kurian Zone, Grogs, and Free Territory. He's long since retired to the older family holdings on a remote piece of Carolina coastline, but a nephew still runs the business, now under the probing noses of Southern Command forces directed by the new United Free Republics.

*Rally Base, set up just down the road as though keeping the post
company, is only a couple of acres in size, including the killing ground
outside the wire and blockhouses.*

*Of course the business isn't quite as profitable these days. There's
no more smuggling of captive souls into the Kurian Zone or antitank
rockets capable of taking out small watercraft up to the Grogs. But
thanks to the soldiers at Rally Base, there's also less of a chance of a
team of Reapers coming through and killing everyone who doesn't make
it down the hidey-hole in time, or of Grogs looking to prove themselves
in battle, killing security men and stealing livestock. Shrivastava &
Family have shifted with the trade and opened a tiny brewery, soap
mill, and bakery, growing rich on a few dozen lesser transactions a day
rather than the bigger scores the old man saw.*

Civilization, after a fashion, has returned.

*The family business is well-off enough to hire hands to take care of
the endless outside labor that keeps the bake stove burning and the meat
locker filled.*

*One of their hands, a lean, bronze-skinned man with a thick head of
black hair tied back from his sweating face, works shirtless in the dust
of the firewood pile, reducing wholes to quarters with a shining ax. His
lower back is a topographical map of old burns, his face is scarred from
the right eye down, and there's something a bit off about his jaw. If he
were talking you'd guess he'd just said something ironic.*

*But he's not wasting breath, talking to himself or his surroundings.
He works with the easy, constant pace of an outdoor man who knows
the optimum operating speed of his body, picking up the wholes, splitting them, and then retrieving the quarters with a precise economy of
effort that would do a machine credit.*

*He moves with a hint of a limp as he retrieves another whole for the
splitting stock. He casts quick glances all around as he works, and his
momentary stiffening when one of the soft-stepping daughters of the
house comes out to throw potato peelings in the pig meal suggests that
he's a hard man to sneak up behind.*

*The slight, unconscious shift in his grip of the ax suggests that it
might even be dangerous.*

David Valentine would always remember it all beginning the day he
got his first gray hair.

Or, to be more accurate, the day he *noticed* his first gray hair. Three
of them, in fact. For some reason all of them decided to erupt on his right
temple. He'd used the mirror to shave that morning, as he had to go over
to the fort to teach, and picked them out as he combed his hair back.

PATH OF THE CAT: VAMPIRE EARTH VOL. 3   9

They reminded him of his father. His mother had never gone gray, but he had only a vague idea of her age when the Valentine clan died. His father had lots of them, which was natural for a man of fifty-six.

That's what Father Max had burned into the cross, anyway.

He'd chopped firewood for Father Max from the age of eleven until he joined up with the Cause at seventeen.

He split and stacked his last piece of firewood, wiped the ax clean with an oilcloth and hung it up in the toolshed.

YLPPUS YXALAG read the reversed letters running the roofline of the big trading post, bakery, diner, and repair shop. All the buildings of Galaxy Supply except the family home were painted in a durable barn red, though someone with an artist's eye had added white and green accents around the doors and barred windows, with smaller decorations depicting grape vines and cheery songbirds.

An unusually hot late-September day was working up. The sun was hardly blocked at all by decades-old particles riding the upper atmosphere. Some said the sky was washing itself; others maintained the haze had swirled off to the southern hemisphere for a few years and would be back, the way it had returned in '43.

He'd sweated enough to discard his shirt, both to preserve its condition—he had to teach at the base today—and keep himself cool. He used a bucket, a rag, and some of the milky Shrivastava soap to clean himself up in the outside sink before going in for his breakfast.

The two Shrivastava girls dodged nimbly around him in the back kitchen, giggling to each other with some private joke. There had to be more dodging these past few days in the baking kitchen than usual. Mr. Shrivastava had extracted an old pizza oven from an establishment up the interstate toward Cairo and was converting it to wood fire. Welding tools and tanks were interspersed with the usual bread racks.

The girls, rich black hair bound up in kerchiefs to keep the flour out, didn't give him a second look. They had teenage soldiers swaggering out their first forward duty to make eyes at daily, and Valentine was coming up on thirty-three, battered, and dragging a leg. Besides, he was hired help.

Not that it would have done him much good to be eighteen again. He'd been too shy to flirt back then. He would have just discreetly admired their caramel skin and wide, inviting eyes from the other side of the pastry case.

He had toast and eggs for breakfast, with a side of peppery okra leftover from last night's dinner. With real black tea. The family liked tea and through their trading connections had some strong blend that left a far more pleasant aftertaste than coffee.

The fresh food was why he worked for the Shrivastava clan rather than living in the civilian squats blistered off the base.

"Finished the firewood so fast?" Mrs. Shrivastava said, her quieter sister in tow, as always. Mrs. Shrivastava loved him to death, though in her case love manifested in cramming food down his throat. As soon as he cleared one plate she'd appear with another, and if he didn't dig into that with enough gusto he sometimes worried that she'd ram it in with one of the long wooden spoons she used to fill his dish. Then hold his nose until he swallowed.

"Out of timber. I'll take the mule team out tomorrow and get some more trees."

Pines and poplars had reclaimed the bootheel farmland, but the cleared ground around neighboring Rally Base meant a drag to fill the winter dry racks.

"Why not—oh, I forget. Today is one of your days at the fort."

"I should get cleaned up."

"Use the washroom with the running water. Nice to have the smell of a young man's shaving soap here," she said, frowning at her daughters.

"It is my fault Patrick would rather be a soldier than a storekeeper?" the elder of the sisters asked.

He slipped down the hall toward the full bath. "Patrick" was something of a tender spot in the family conversation. Letters from him had ceased altogether six months before. When he hired on with Shrivastava, giving an abbreviated version of his service history, the girl had quietly asked him how often men declared "missing in action" returned.

Fresh back from Kentucky, Valentine couldn't offer much hope. Especially since he'd just spent months in Kentucky seeking another missing soul.

Valentine relished the heated water in the family bathroom. The rest of the help had to make do with stove-warmed water in the bunkhouse. As he buttoned his shirt he searched the sink for stray hairs and soap residue. Mrs. Shrivastava might like the smell of this young man's shaving, but it would be rude to repay her graciousness with a dirty basin.

He grabbed his teaching satchel and walked over to the base, taking his time in the unseasonable heat.

"Argent, Max," the sentry at the gate identified him, stepping out from the shade of corrugated iron. Though he knew Valentine's face and alias, he still checked the ID provided by Styachowski's specialists. "Base is on alert. We've got a sidearm and carbine for you, if you don't have your own." The guard's eyes were unreadable behind his wraparound sunglasses.

"Thank you," Valentine said.

Valentine's weapons were arranged in netting hanging from the un-nailed floorboards of his bunkhouse. He visited the base as a civilian expert, and at the moment his boots and pocketknife were the only military-issue items he had.

"No drill," a sergeant who handed him a pistol belt with magazine harness said. He was heavy as a side of beef, and Valentine couldn't remember him pulling a shift in the guard hut before. "How's a model four?"

"I qualified. This serious?"

"River traffic reported. It may have landed."

Valentine had heard a largish patrol go out in the predawn but had thought nothing of it. Pizzaro was an experienced enough forward area base commander to make sure nothing left or entered his base by regular schedules.

"Message too," the sergeant added as the sentry made a notation of the gun's serial numbers. "The CO wants you to come by his office after your class."

"Can do," Valentine said, adjusting the pistol belt.

Valentine headed into the base, where windows were being filled with sandbags and extra men idled in the shade at the mortar positions, ready to get the tubes into action as soon as orders came down. The quick step of the men carrying the sandbags and the lack of joking put Valentine on edge.

He had militia today, mostly young men fresh from a year or two with Labor Regiment. Unless the boys or girls were lucky enough in their LR term to get apprenticed into a technical field, they were dumped into the militia pool and made miserable enough that joining the regulars seemed like an elevation to paradise. Some stuck out militia service for a four-, six-, or eight-year term in return for land and tools, a "stake" in some new community in land won from the Kurians.

Only six years, and the militias rotated a lot of soldiers through good vocational training. Texas had huge swaths of fallow land to fill with stakes. If the former militiamen were lucky, they never heard the words "or such time and duty as the needs of Southern Command require."

He had two classes, a basic literacy-and-science group fresh out of the bush and his "advanced" class, who was learning about Southern Command and how it hoped to disassemble the grim Kurian Order surrounding the embattled freeholds.

Today would be his advanced group. They met in a dining hall, a wood-framed building with a roof and canvas sides, pulled up now to admit the breeze.

Valentine had drawn a misshapen pyramid of figures on his black-board. It rather reminded him of the ranks of invading aliens he'd seen in a video game at the Outlook back in the Cascades.

He leaned against the front table.

"So that's it," he said. "There's a reason pyramids last so long: They're stable. Wide at the bottom and thin at the top."

The men and a sprinkling of women, mostly first-year recruits growing their hair back in save for a couple who went the other direction and shaved down to bald, took notes on loose paper. Because of the alert, each had his rifle on the table within reach, combat harness hanging off the back of the chair. The platoon sergeant could form them up in a few seconds.

"Bottom is the population in the Kurian Zone. Middle-level functionaries direct and take care of them. At the cream level you've got those trusted with weapons and the people watching the functionaries. Above them are the Reapers, the eyes and ears and appetites of the master Kurian at the top. What's the weak point?"

"The alien at the top."

"Physically, you're correct. If you've got your hands on him, it's about as easy to kill a Kurian as a chicken. A good stomping is all it takes. It's the getting at them that's dangerous."

Valentine turned, lifted his shirt, and showed some of the burns running his back.

"But they usually live in towers that are very hard to get into, complete with bolt holes and escape tubes that you can't fit down if you're bigger than a bobcat. They're about as easy to catch as running water."

"You got three," a second-yearer named Hoke said. "Or was it four?" Hoke had been an early doubting Thomas at his classes, wondering how a rather beat-up civilian worked up the nerve to lecture soldiers, until a lieutenant with an interest in the Hunters took the sophomore warrior aside during a break.

"But what is he: Wolf, Cat, or Bear?" Hoke had asked. Valentine's Wolf-sharp ears could pick up the conversation, but he intentionally softened his senses to avoid the rest of the conversation after the lieutenant said something about *He's dangerous, and that's enough. . . .*

"Three," Valentine said. "But the third's sort of unofficial." Then there was the one he wasn't sure of, in the sunken sub off Hispaniola.

"Getting back to my point, it's the Reapers we try to hit. Yeah, they're the most dangerous thing on two legs you're ever going to meet, but they're the connection between the Kurian and the Quislings. The Kurian feeds, gives orders, and judges, all through his pale-skinned avatar. If you can get one just after a feed or in a hole far from the Kurian avoiding daylight, you've got a chance, if you can put enough lead on target and get in with explosives. Or a well-swung ax."

"They run from sunlight, right?" a Missouri kid said.

"Sunlight doesn't hurt them one bit. It messes with the communication with its Master, though, like static. They sense us, because intelligent living beings give off something we call lifesign. They can home in on it at night. That's the whole point of those breathing exercises we've been doing at the beginning and end of each class: getting you guys trained so they might mistake you for a paddock of horses or a pack of wild pigs."

This elicited some quiet hog calls and chuckling.

Valentine felt jealous of their youthful confidence. *The first Reaper's easy. It's the second that makes you shit your pants*, went an old saw from the Wolves.

There was a time when Southern Command left killing Reapers to the Hunters. But the Lifeweavers, brothers to the otherworldly Kur but their mortal enemies who trained the Hunters, had been scattered during Solon's brief occupation of the Ozarks. Valentine was an advocate of giving more of the rank and file of Southern Command at least the basics of first avoiding and then dealing with the Reapers, and Pizzaro agreed, giving him an occupation until Highbeam could get going.

If Highbeam would ever win approval. It was one thing to raid into the Kurian Zone. Quite another to establish a new Freehold, especially one so close to the great nerve trunks of the Kurian Order.

Valentine brought himself back to the here and now of his class.

"There's another reason for going after the Reapers. A lot of times the Quislings aren't even sorry to see one offed. Sure, your die-hard churchmen will still damn you to the cleanup crew, but everyone else is walking around a little easier. On the other side of the river they don't have guns, don't have grenades, and a lot of times they aren't even allowed to have locks on their doors. If you're lucky, you'll see a couple Reapers before you muster out, at a distance, usually running away. Quislings see the Reapers all the time, poking around at night with the full authority of the KZ behind them. They've got to talk to them."

Valentine walked past a sandbagged observation point camouflaged to look like another water tank. A pair of soldiers had set up a twin-lensed range finder, just poking above the rim of the tank like the antennae of a lead ant checking the exit from the nest. Wires dangled from the phony tank, running to the underground PVC tube leading to the mortar pits.

The command building was two units of prefabricated housing, easily ported by trailer and then joined, its outline concealed under a mesh of netting and some young trees. A dugout stood just opposite, its door open and beckoning thanks to the alert.

He signed in with Colonel Pizzaro's admin and chitchatted over coffee until Pizzaro waved him in from the door. He had lined, leathery skin but very bright eyes that reminded Valentine of the comical little goggle-eyed walnuts the church youth groups sold as fund-raisers. A squawk box crackled in the corner. A flak jacket, combat harness, and carbine like Valentine's rested on a foldout extender on his desk.

"Let's take a walk," Pizzaro said, buckling his harness and picking up the carbine.

He led Valentine out to the two layers of perimeter wire. Most officers had a bit of military business that either irritated or obsessed them. Pizzaro's was base security. He didn't like the idea of anything leaving or coming into his station without his knowing about it. He liked to walk the wire as he talked rather than stay cooped up in his office. According to his staff, he'd been in an interrogation camp during Solon's occupation of the Ozarks, which was enough being boxed up for a lifetime.

"You want the good news or the bad?" Pizzaro asked. The shade of his slouch hat and the hard daylight dimmed his eyes somewhat.

"The good first. Otherwise it's like drinking bourbon out of a shaving mug."

Pizzaro licked his lips. "All I ever see you drink is milk or coffee. When we go off alert, stop by."

"Is that the good news? Alert called off?"

"You're messing up your ordering," Pizzaro said, checking some frayed wiring on a quartz lamp. Valentine looked at the manufacturing stamp. It had originated in Mexico City. "Let's stick to the good news. I got a courier packet. Highbeam is on—I have this from Lambert herself. I've got to punch your ticket and give you escort to the staging briefing. Even my staff doesn't know this yet, and I want to keep it that way, but this post will be Point Zero. You'll set off from here. If it wasn't for the alert, we'd already be laying plumbing for a new camp."

"Was that the good news or the bad?" Valentine asked.

"Thought you'd be pleased to hear that all that scouting you've been doing in Kentucky is about to pay off."

"I never found what I was looking for."

"Anne . . ."

"Ahn-Kha," Valentine supplied.

"Sorry, not much with Grog talk. Sounds like dogs snarling at each other to me."

"So what's the bad news?"

"I'm sealing the base. First recon reports are in: It's a strong Grog column out of Cairo area. It's those gangly, hunched-over ones with the pig-ugly faces. They're avoiding contact and mostly hunting and scavenging. There aren't many settlements up that way but I'm getting reports of thievery—stealing livestock and chickens and whatnot. Anything they can sneak off when no one's looking. Some folks have disappeared, but we're not sure if they've run or the Grogs got 'em."

"Doublebloods, they call themselves," Valentine said. "Odd of them to come across the river like that. They keep to themselves."

"You spent some time in Illinois. Anything else you can tell me?"

"The Illinois Guard has a lot of stations around Mount Vernon, keeping watch on the Doublebloods. I had someone in the Illinois Guard I wanted to meet."

Sergeant Heath Hopkins. *He died badly.*

"So they're neutrals."

Pizzaro had enough troubles with the big gray Grogs inhabiting the riverbanks on his side of the Mississippi, the lonely Kurian tower watching river traffic from Cairo, and the Kurians on the other side of the twisting river in Kentucky and Tennessee. Valentine wasn't that surprised he didn't know much about the Doublebloods. There were piss-worthy fires closer to the colonel's feet.

Valentine dredged up his very limited experience. "More like they hate everybody. Kurians tried to make a half Grog–half human and it didn't work out. They're ill-tempered, even for Grogs, so the Kurians planted them on the borders of Southern Command, hoping they'd be trouble for us. Problem is, they all remember which direction the trucks that brought them came from, and it wasn't southwest."

"Can you savvy their lingo?"

"No more than a few phrases they use to communicate with the other Grogs. But I'd rather not walk on into the camp. This could be a man raid."

"A what?"

"They're amazons. Something amiss with their reproductive system. Not many male embryos live to be birthed. The ratio is four or six to one or thereabouts, if the Illinois Guard has the numbers right. There're problems up and down the Doubleblood genetic line, and the only way they're sure of a live birth is with a human donor and a Doubleblood female. Inbreeding worsens the defect. They're smart enough to grab new males now and then."

"Good God."

"It's not so bad. I hear they stick two layers of bagging over your head. Insurance," Valentine said.

The colonel tapped down some wire pegging with his foot and made a note on a pocket-sized sheet of paper. Valentine wondered if it was about the Doublebloods or the wire.

"What kind of weaponry?"

"Just small arms for fighting. They hunt with bows or crossbows and slingshots. They'll carry explosives to blow open locked doors. Tell your patrols to keep their distance."

"I'd just as soon discourage raids. What kind of casualties do we have to inflict to turn them around?"

"It's not that simple. Like I said, they're ornery. If they spill blood down here, a feud will start, and a good feud can go on for years."

"They're invading us. What do they expect to happen?"

"Logic and tribal custom. Ne'er the twain shall meet."

Valentine sensed Pizzaro was wavering, so he spoke again: "Right now you're just *other*. Start skirmishing and you'll be *enemy*. Your other option is to kill every last one of them. Then they'll think the gods punished them for arrogance. But you know how hard it is to run down Grogs who've gone bush."

Pizzaro thought it over, flicking his thumb over a rusty barb in the wire. "I'd better get to the communication center, then. Anyway, this is your chance to get out, if you like. Nobody'll say anything if you show up for the Highbeam—or whatever the crap they're gonna call it— conference a week or so early. Otherwise it'll be Rally Base cooking for you for a few days until whatever business the Doublebloods want to start finishes."

Valentine couldn't see riding away from some of the kids he'd helped train in a crisis. *Or could he?* "Can you shelter the Shrivastava clan?"

"Shrivastava? Of course. But it'll take more than a bag over his head to get him hot to abandon his store and stock."

Trader Shrivastava may have been a civilian, but there was something of Valentine's old captain, LeHavre, in him. He had a gentle manner masking a pirate avarice, but it didn't make him any less outraged at the idea of hiding behind locked gates while the Doublebloods stole from his pens and coops.

Valentine spoke to him in front of the arms room, the one part of the store back in the family quarters. Racks of rifles and pistols lined the walls, and reloading tools filled a long workbench. There was only one other exit from the room, and it led down to a tunnel to a separate basement, the family "Reaper-proof" in an old underground gas tank.

"The fort? This building is tougher than it looks, young man. Both basement and attic have firing slits to cover my property."

His nine-year-old son sat behind, loading bullets from boxes into fresh new magazines. The whole family knew the story of Grandfather Durtee, who held two Reapers off with a shotgun while the rest of the clan fled to the vaultlike underground shelter. The grandfather had been the only loss that night.

"If you draw blood, they'll be back to avenge it."

"Then I will draw more blood, young man. Yes! Let them return! I welcome all at my store, provided they pay for what they take. These creatures will pay for my stock, one way or another."

Valentine wondered if it was too late to catch that transport to the conference.

Ray, the trading post's butcher, appeared, an old army flak jacket draped over a beefy arm. He accepted an old M16 from his employer. "You take the wall covering the back door, young man," Shrivastava said, and Ray nodded. The boy passed him a bag of magazines.

Shrivastava turned back to Valentine. "You taking a gun, young man, or will you stay in the Reaper-proof with the mothers and children?"

Maybe the Doublebloods would let him guide them to a bottom that contained a sizable herd of wild pigs. They could get all the side meat they wanted and carry off the young. "I'm going to go talk to the Doublebloods."

"No! Youn—David, do not waste yourself in that manner. My great-uncle went to set up a post with the Whitefangs up beyond the ridge. They ate him. I do not call you a coward. The children will be comforted—"

Whatever else Shrivastava said was lost in the rush of an idea. Was there enough daylight left to get over the ridge?

Maybe. With a fast enough pair of wheels.

Within an hour he'd convinced Pizzaro to loan him a driver and transport. Plus a big bag of supplies.

Scaring off coyotes with wolves? Pizzaro had said, liking the idea.

He arranged for a motorcycle, his best two-wheel man, fuel, survival gear, even priceless com gear. "We'll worry about the authorizations and paperwork later."

Valentine wanted to kiss him, remembering his days in the Wolves.

If Southern Command had a Pizzaro at every forward post, the Wolves would spend more time raising hell on Kurian Zone backroads and less cadging for supplies.

"You're not bad back there, sir," Callaslough, his driver, said from the front of the big Harley. Harley-Davidson still produced up in Milwaukee, and this specimen had found its way into Southern Command's motor pool. Fat-tired, with a high clearance and rugged brush breaks and plenty of horsepower and hookups for attachments. It was meant to hold a sidecar, maybe even one of the dark-canopied blisters for a Reaper, or to pull a one-body medical sled.

The motorcycle jumped and blatted along the old road, now not much more than a potholed deer trail, quickly enough under Callaslough's urging.

Valentine had tied two small staffs of pig iron to the rear backrest/ gear bar. A white flag fluttered at one, a netted bag of Texas oranges on the other. Though each man had a carbine, they'd slung them facing down and backward, further proof of peaceful intent.

Not that it would stop an ambitious young Whitefang from trying to knock them both off the bike with a single .50 caliber bullet, a thought much on Valentine's mind as they bumped up Badblood Ridge.

Valentine's active imagination felt the notched foresight of a rifle resting on his eye, wondered if some poor, horny, unmated Grog would ignore the signals for parley. The noise the bike made must be drawing Whitefang scouts like the musical ice cream wagons of the KZ lured children to the New Universal Church ice cream that had proselytizing cartoons and homilies on the wrappers.

Callaslough spotted them first as they came off Bad-blood, bouncing down a gravelly wash under the gaunt, nest-and-vine-draped skeletons of power pylons. A wind chime of bleached skulls alternating with femurs and tibias hung from one long arm, threaded on old wire.

A bent, loose-skinned old Whitefang stood atop a fallen hickory, his long rifle gripped in the exact center but held stiff-armed toward them. Some females watched from the other side of the log. One, younger or more daring, climbed even higher than her male guardian to get a better look. She bore a bulging harvesting bag.

Callaslough slowed the big motorcycle.

"Pull up," Valentine said. Their seating arrangement made it easy to communicate quietly, at the cost of having to smell each other's sun-baked sweat. "Point the bike so it's parallel to his rifle, not pointed into White-fang land."

Callaslough executed a neat stop, swinging the bike's rear tire so it sent a spray of pebbles toward Whitefang territory.

"Leathery old hangball," Callaslough commented. The old Grog's testicular sack was well below his loincloth line in the heat.

"That's good for us. Foragers mean one of the tribe's bigger camps are around."

Valentine stepped off the bike. He held up with his right hand some signaling mirrors given as trade goods, tough squares of chrome on lanyards. In his left he held a selection of Texas coast oranges in a net bag. He had several boxes of matches in reserve; he'd yet to meet a Grog that didn't love to strike a match, just for the pure dazzle and power of instant fire-creation.

"Foot pass! Parley!" Valentine called, in the lingua franca of St. Louis.

The females issued chirping noises, seeing what he had to offer. The male scratched an itch under his loincloth in thought, but his eyes didn't leave the oranges.

"I think we're good," Valentine said.

The nimble female plucked at his ears, urging.

The Grog planted his gunstock, hooted, and gave an unmistakable "get over here!" sweep of his arm. He licked his lips as he did so.

"Shit. I'd almost rather be shot at," Callaslough said.

They arrived about an hour before sunset.

The humans walked the bike in with the help of one of the females. They wore soup cans around their necks, indicating that they'd come in peace, and offered up tokens and gifts to be allowed on Whitefang lands—the "foot pass" of Grog commerce and diplomacy.

The Whitefang encampment stood in an old field with an irrigation trench on three sides and thick woods on the fourth. Water flowed in the trench. Clay pots stood upstream for drinking water, and laundry lines hung downstream. Old books hung on the bushes shielding the toilet area where the ditch drained off.

The Whitefang villagers lived in tents made of pulled-up carpeting and quilts of plastics, weatherproofed with beeswax or musky-smelling oil.

Human captives hewed wood, made charcoal, and carried water. They looked at the newcomers with pleading eyes.

Valentine avoided their gaze. *Nothing you can do about it at the moment.*

At first the tribe wanted nothing to do with Valentine and Callaslough. The young males, unblooded and untattooed, their long hair a testament to lack of wives, glared or hopped up and down in excitement, letting out little war cries. The younger females taunted by slapping their own backsides or spitting in the embassy's direction.

"Lots of unmated Groggies," Callaslough said as they walked the bike into the village. Pizzaro had sent along a man who knew something of the Grogs, but Valentine would have preferred a little less experience. Callaslough was just finding things to be nervous about, and the Grogs read body language better than words.

The chief lived in an old farmhouse, apparently. On the lower level, the walls had been mostly pulled away to admit air, but the upper rooms remained intact. Valentine wondered how many wives were crammed into the aluminum-sided seraglio.

Stripped old farm equipment stood in the center of the village, a playland-junkyard for the little Grogs. They swung and climbed and chased each other and an assortment of village dogs in and out of old harvesting tubing, control cabs, and engine housings. At the edge of the playland, a scrubbed and polished claw-foot bathtub served as a central drinking trough.

Their escort Grog pointed to a place for them to sit and went up the stone stairs to the skeleton of the house's first floor.

The chief remained huddled with his subchiefs and elders. Valentine extracted a two-pound bag from his trade goods, went to the big drinking cistern, and ripped open the packet.

An elderly female tried to stop him, hooting and slapping at his hands. Valentine ignored her and emptied the packet, full of granules that looked like sand, into the trough.

That got the attention of the elders and the chief.

Valentine mixed the water with a clay carrying pot, upending and dumping the water as it began to froth.

"What the hell's that?" Callaslough asked.

"Root beer mix."

Valentine took his canteen cup and drank. Then he refilled it and offered it to the grandmother. She sniffed suspiciously and turned her head away.

"Damn," Valentine said. He filled another cup and drank again. It wasn't very good—the mixture really needed to sit and chill to be truly tasty—but it was sweet.

The younger Grogs weren't so shy. They slurped and squealed, and their elders ran forward to pull them away. A squirmy youngster managed to break away from his mother and go back to the tub, drinking with both hands.

The chief came out on his steps to watch, eyes shaded under a heavy brow. He had huge, woolly thighs that looked like a pair of sheep standing close together in a field. One of the youngsters brought him a cup of the mixture, babbling.

The chief sniffed. He laughed and upended the mixture down his throat. He wiped his lips and laughed again.

"Good-humored guy," Callaslough ventured.

"I'm sure he'd laugh just as hard if his warriors were playing soccer with our heads."

"I am Whitefang," he barked at Valentine in the Grog trade tongue. He stamped on the old steps, hard, and Valentine heard a commotion from the upstairs.

"O Whitefang, this foot-passed stranger begs the powers of your ears and eyes and tongue."

Whitefang waved them over with a two-handed gesture that made it look like he was taking an appreciative whiff of his own flatulence.

"He didn't just cut one, did he?" Callaslough said.

"Try and look agreeable, no matter what," Valentine said as he stepped forward.

The chief bobbed and one of his subchiefs put a pillow-topped milking stool under his hindquarters, but he didn't sit until Valentine and Callaslough were both off their feet.

It took a while for the negotiations to commence. The subchiefs and elders and warriors had to arrange themselves in a semicircle around the visitors, bearing their best captured weapons, flak jackets, and helmets. The most battle scarred of all of them, both with intentional artistry and in random wound, held a massive surgical-tubing slingshot and two bandoliers of captured hand grenades.

Whitefang's dozen or so wives stood behind him, the two most heavily pregnant in front of the others, turning now and then to display swollen bellies as proof of the chief's potency. Others gripped their children by the ears to show them how their father conducted himself with strangers.

A splendid-looking teen female, almost attractive in her careless lounge, wore the white headband of an unmarried daughter as she rested against Whitefang's scarred shoulder. By the woolliness of her thighs, Valentine guessed her to be Whitefang's eldest daughter. She wore a long, modest skirt made out of old Disney bedsheets, but she managed to hike it up a little in the direction of the unblooded warriors.

Valentine heard splashes and slurps behind as the Grogs drank the root beer. A young warrior made for the tub, but his fellows held him back, grumbling and grunting.

"What do the strangers beg of Whitefang?" Whitefang asked. Valentine couldn't tell what had changed in the assembly that caused him to commence negotiations.

"Battle alliance," Valentine said.

The audience gasped or hooted.

"Battle alliance. With humans?" the veteran with the artistic battle scarring asked.

Whitefang laughed. His daughter rolled her eyes.

"Battle alliance is for against humans," a white-eyebrowed old male said.

"They insult," a younger warrior shouted from the crowd to the side. At least that's what Valentine thought he said. The youth's trade tongue was clumsy, either from emotion or lack of practice.

"Want battle!" another youth said.

Others shouted in their own tongue. Valentine thought he recognized the word for blood.

"Kill us and you will have battle with humans," Valentine said.

Whitefang laughed, finding the prospect of war as funny as the taste of root beer.

"Fuck you up," Whitefang said. In pretty fair English.

If the Whitefangs killed them, at least it would be over quick. Warrior enemies would be dispatched quickly and cleanly. The Grogs reserved torture for criminals.

"Means bad old times," Valentine said. "Come soldiers. Come artillery. Come armored car."

"Let armored car come," Whitefang laughed. He barked at his harem, and they disappeared into the basement of the chief's house. They reemerged bearing steering wheels and machine-gun turret rings, executing neat pirouettes in front of Valentine and Callaslough.

Callaslough was breathing fast, like a bull working up a charge. "Bas—"

"Easy," Valentine said.

"Humans beg help," Valentine said, loudly enough for all to hear.

That got them talking: humans begging. Whitefang slapped his callused, hairless kneecaps to silence them.

"Doublebloods attack humans," Valentine said. "Steal much. Capture many. Doublebloods worst enemy humans now."

Even more talk now, with some excited yips from the young warriors. Valentine suspected that the Double-bloods had done their share of raiding on Whitefang lands, being just across the river from southern Illinois. He suspected an old feud existed.

"Worse than Night-stalkers?" Whitefang asked, his eyes lit by the setting sun.

"Night-stalkers on other side of Great South river. Doublebloods on human side."

"Humans stop Night-stalkers," Valentine said. "Otherwise Night-stalkers raid Whitefangs."

This time Whitefang didn't laugh. The uneasy truce—not without the occasional raid and ambush—that had existed in southern Missouri between Grogs and mankind dated to the brief Kurian occupation of the Ozarks. Reapers had been loosed into Grog lands to drive them away from Solon's planned Trans-Mississippi empire. The Grogs were only too happy to see Southern Command return.

Callaslough, who'd evidently been able to follow at least some of the conversation, reached into his shirt and pulled up a pair of black Reaper teeth interlaced with his dog tags. They were only short ones from the back, but the Grogs recognized them. Callaslough held them high and rattled them.

Valentine remembered teaching Blake to clean teeth just like those, only smaller, with a brush and baking soda.

"Humans beg battle alliance," Valentine repeated. "What Double-bloods stole, Whitefangs keep. Who Doublebloods capture, Whitefangs release."

"Trophies?" Whitefang asked.

"All Whitefangs keep."

The young warriors stirred at that. Their prospective mates among the females started chattering to one another. A warrior returning home with the blood of an enemy on his blade, or even better, some skulls or scalps, could marry, having proved himself worthy of establishing a household and producing children.

Whitefang's daughter stared out into the crowd. Valentine followed her gaze to a tall, proud-looking warrior standing naked with only his weapons, splendidly lush hair hanging from his head and shoulders and upper back. He hadn't wanted to contaminate his clothing with human blood, should it come to that, evidently. He stared back at the girl.

She whispered in Whitefang's ear.

Whitefang elbowed her hard and she toppled backward. He grumbled something to the female who ran to her aid.

The chief tongued the remainders of root beer out of his cup. "Trade root beer?" he asked.

"If battle alliance is successful."

"Trade licorice?" Whitefang asked.

"Yes."

Whitefang licked his lips and the eyes under the heavy brow brightened. "Trade—*Soka-coli*?"

"All Coca-Cola same."

An entrepreneur was supposedly bottling RC down in the sugar farms near the Louisiana border. Valentine had seen some cases behind lock and key in Shrivastava's mercantile Galaxy. Whitefang wouldn't notice the difference. He hoped.

Whitefang held out his hand, and a senior wife placed a sawed-off, double-barreled shotgun in it. He extended the butt end toward Valentine.

Valentine wasn't sure what to do. He'd never observed a battle alliance; he just knew the term. But it never hurt to imitate the head honcho in any organization, human or Grog. He unslung his own carbine and held it toward Whitefang, butt end extended.

The oldster with the hand grenades cackled.

Valentine approached Whitefang, and the chief gripped the end of his gun. Valentine wrapped his fingers around the pistol grip of the shotgun.

The warriors cheered.

"Fuck Doublebloods up," Whitefang said in English, winking at Valentine. Then he laughed long and loud into the night.

The Mississippi, wild and untended since 2022, had carved little islands along its banks for most of its length. Within twenty-four hours of his promise of *Soka-coli* to Whitefang, Valentine was swatting mosquitoes and trying to keep from being splashed by the paddlers.

Grogs paddle as though they were at war with the river.

Grogs had an instinctive knack for warfare. Once they made up their minds, they did everything at the hurry-up. After a conference that lasted long into the night—most of it taken up by definitions of geographic points—Valentine sent Callaslough back to Rally Base with a written report. Whitefang called for his warriors, and Grogs loped off in every direction.

They left a substantial reserve at the camp, perhaps still fearing a human trick, and a core of veterans set off with the youngest warriors on the Doubleblood hunt.

The Grogs were proud of their weapons. They displayed their prowess to Valentine, sending steel-tipped arrows through entire trunks of trees from bows made out of truck leaf springs (Valentine couldn't even string the bow, let alone draw it, and felt very much like a sham Odysseus) or driving spears through practice dummies made of old kegs and barrels. The tall young Grog Whitefang's daughter had made eyes at had a big Grog gun and ten bullets probably donated by his entire family. The .50 caliber rounds were scarce on this patch of riverbank, and

Valentine suspected they represented an investment of his whole family in the warrior's future.

He used one to shatter an old bowling pin at a distance of a kilometer, making Valentine stand within ten paces of the target to show that no tricks were involved. For a split second between the shot (Valentine saw the Grog take the recoil) and the pin's destruction, he wondered if he'd be dead before he heard the sound of the report.

With the young males gathered, their chief led them to war, leaving the old fellow with the slingshot and the hand grenades behind.

Valentine felt like a war correspondent watching them hike off in loosely grouped bunches, formed into a diamond shape if you plotted them on a map at any particular point. A poor sort of war correspondent at that, because he could get only a vague sense of their intentions. At first he feared they were just going to plunge into Southern Command's territory and make straight for the Doubleblood trail, but they proved craftier than that and took big war canoes down a stream to the Mississippi.

The Grogs watched him sit down in the canoe and unroll a condom over the business end of his carbine. A warrior with six feet of lethal, single-shot steel-and-wood showed Valentine how he protected his piece: Valentine recognized a leathery testicular sack, undoubtedly human, closed by a tight drawstring.

The Grog had left the hairs intact, probably to help it bleed water.

Then, with a call from Whitefang, they paddled as though chased by living fire. One hundred and eighty-some Grogs moving fast with the current, canoes swerving and crossing like a school of excited fish.

They reached the islands opposite Cairo by dark, and Valentine saw smaller scout canoes hook to either side of Whitefang's. Valentine's canoe waited with several others under the metal remnants of an old interstate bridge.

They spotted the pulled-up canoes and flatboats and hulled pleasure boats and houseboats floating at anchor, shielded from Southern Command by a long strip of muddy island, tree roots fighting the Mississippi for possession of the soil.

With their objective in sight, Whitefang let his Grogs rest and feed, waiting for the moon to go down. Valentine found himself dozing, resting against a big warm Grog who smelled like brackish water.

Owl hoots from Whitefang's canoe woke him. Grogs slipped into the summer-warmed water.

Most of the canoes huddled against the banks, while scouts swam, or crawled, or slithered forward, depending on the depth of water.

Valentine's Cat-sharp eyes picked out a shadowy shape, glistening wet in the darkness, climb onto a sailboat and merge with something that looked like a bundle of canvas leaning against a mast. Others of the Whitefang tribe emerged from the riverbank and stalked into the trees.

Evidently the Doublebloods hadn't counted on an attack from upriver.

A flaming arrow, looking like a bum-winged firefly as it turned tight circles along its parabolic arc into the Mississippi, announced that the scouts had done their job.

Valentine splashed ashore with the veteran Grogs carrying belt-fed machine guns and laced-together Kevlar over their broad frames. Valentine felt sorry for anyone going against this contingent. It was hard enough to get a bullet through Grog hide around the shoulders and chest. Add Kevlar to the mix and you had something resembling a living tank.

The younger Grogs were showing each other gory trophies taken from the Doubleblood sentries.

The remaining unblooded Whitefangs prepared to win their own bloody prizes. The Grogs caked themselves with mud, dead leaves, and bracken. It would conceal them from the eyes of their enemies and be an earthy burial shroud should they die.

By dawn Doubleblood message runners showed up at the Southern Command bank. Valentine got a good look at one. She looked a little like a bloodhound, with short dark hair, lots of loose skin about the face, and a gangly, underfed look compared to the gray Grogs. But the Doublebloods could run like deer and climb like spiders—even with an arrow through her leg that one Grog shot through the brush on the riverbank like a snake.

Valentine didn't care to watch the questioning of the captured messengers, but it amounted to bringing the bigger boats around the south end of the island and setting up boarding ramps big enough for young cattle and pigs.

The Whitefangs happily followed the plan. They were setting up the inviting-looking boarding ramps (and brush blinds for snipers and archers flanking the landing) when a brown-water river patrol motored upriver and turned in to get a good look at the operation, covering the Grog boats with what looked like 20mm cannon while a squat mortar boat watched over matters from midriver.

Valentine slipped into the water off the side of one of the Doubleblood boats, just in case the Quislings stopped to search. He felt the deep Mississippi mud, cool and gritty, around his toes. But the patrol recognized the Whitefang warrior tattooing and gave the chief some boxes of

ammunition and a case of incendiary grenades in the interest of bringing a little extra misery to Southern Command and staying friendly
with Whitefang's people.

The tall young warrior who'd caught Whitefang's daughter's eye
was able to fill his bandolier with .50 rounds, and stick extras behind his
ears, braided in his long unmated warrior's mane, and up one cavernous
nostril.

The patrol sped away, not wanting to draw more attention to a Grog
raid than necessary. Valentine could still hear their motors from upriver—
they were making for the Ohio, seemed like—when the first of the
Doublebloods arrived.

Valentine stayed in the water with his carbine, waiting in the shadows beneath the gangplank, battle harness with his ammunition wrapped
around his neck and shoulders to keep it out of the water. The bullets
were supposed to be water-resistant, but Valentine had an old soldier's
mistrust for allowing muck and gear to mix.

A panting line of warriors loped up, waving to a couple Doubleblood bodies on the flatboat nailed to wooden staves, gruesome puppets
already thick with flies. Grogs hidden behind the gunwales worked the
arms with bits of cattail.

Valentine slipped the condom off his gun barrel. He'd used more of
the things keeping water out of his barrel than he'd had in sexual assig-
nations. Not that one of Southern Command's rough-and-ready prophy-
lactics could compete with the artfully wrapped, gossamer-skinned
little numbers smuggled in from Asia at great expense that he'd tried in
Fran Paoli's well-appointed bedroom back in Ohio.

The advance party fell to a hail of arrows. Two in the rear who figured out what was happening and shouldered carbines to shoot back
were brought down with well-placed shots. Valentine knew Grog sniper
check-downs all too well: obvious officers, then anyone giving signals
of any kind, then machine gunners. Sometimes they wouldn't even use
their precious bullets on ordinary soldiers.

One of the Doublebloods spun as he fell, and Valentine thought of
young Nishino on Big Rock Hill.

The time and miles that yawned between made him feel as old as
one of the riverbank willows.

Things went badly as the Grogs cleared away the bodies. The main
body of Doublebloods were close behind their guard, driving herds of
cattle, geese, and swine. Blindfolded human captives, linked by dowels
and collars at the neck, staggered under yokes with more bags of loot
attached or pushed wheelbarrows.

The west bank of the Mississippi went mad as the bullets began to fly, with animals fleeing every which way and the humans getting tangled, falling, dragging their fallen comrades, until they too tripped and fell hard.

More and more Doublebloods arrived, seemingly from all points west, and the arrival of their rear guard gave the Doublebloods the advantage. Now it was the Whitefangs who were pinned. The Doublebloods even managed to set up some knee mortars, raining shells on the riverbank.

Grogs hated artillery. Many of the younger warriors crept back to the water.

A crossbow bolt whispered past Valentine's ear and struck the transom of the flatboat with a loud *kunk*.

As the skirmish progressed a group of Doublebloods forced their way toward the boats, using cattle as bleeding, lowing shields, splitting the Whitefangs.

Valentine laid down a steady stream of single shots at the shapes moving in the cow dust, but the Grogs on the boats had a better plan. They cut the anchors and sent the boats nearest the bank off downstream.

Something splashed into the water near Valentine. *Grenade, mortar shell, or flung rock?* his brain wondered for a split second, waiting for an explosion.

It didn't come.

Seeing their salvation float away took the heart out of the Doublebloods. They broke and scattered for the riverbank, abandoning their prizes.

The Doublebood rear guard stayed together, fighting as they turned north instead of south after the boats. Whitefang sent his most experienced warriors after them. Valentine emerged from the river, shimmied up a thick trunk and got a chance to observe a Grog assault from the rear, with warriors avoiding superior firepower by exploding from cover to cover in short hops.

Whitefang shook his head in disgust at the slaughter of livestock. He kicked a shrapnel-scratched youngster to his feet and set him to work hanging and dressing some swine who'd been caught in the cross fire.

Someone had tossed an incendiary grenade in his excitement and started a small brush fire. Valentine gesticulated and pointed and a few Whitefangs stamped and kicked dirt on the smoldering wood.

It gave him a chance to go to the captives. Using his utility knife, he started cutting ropes and unhooking yokes.

"Much obliged, son," a man with four days of beard croaked.

"He's a renegade. He's with these other stoops," another said. "We're just out of the frying pan and into the fire."

Valentine showed the beat-up militia tag on the shoulder of his half-wet tunic. "No, sir. This is a joint operation, of sorts. Southern Command will be along in a bit to offer assistance."

"A bit" turned out to be about fifteen minutes. Valentine marked the approaching troops flitting from tree to tree up the trail of the departing, exchanging shots with the last of the Doubleblood rear guard, a pair of sappers so occupied in shooting at the humans and keeping from getting shot themselves that they probably didn't even feel the arrows striking between their shoulder blades.

Valentine stood among the freed captives, waving one of the men's grubby yellow cotton shirt.

Luckily someone recognized him from Rally Base and waved him forward as the Grogs collected and organized their loot.

"So you're the Grog lover," a corporal said.

Valentine heard the expression with a pang. He'd had it shouted to him now and then as he rode next to Ahn-Kha on the long drive into Texas after Archangel had freed the Ozarks. It had angered him then, Ahn-Kha being worth any three of Southern Command's men. Now it just made him miss Ahn-Kha.

He'd spent months in eastern Kentucky chasing rumors. No time to think about that, or the possibilities Highbeam presented . . .

"You call me sir, Corporal," Valentine snapped. "The Whitefangs just saved Southern Command another small war."

Someone snorted.

Valentine added, "This was just a raiding party. If the Doublebloods had come across the river with a couple of their warrior regiments, Rally Base would have been scratched."

"Sorry, sir," the corporal said, smart enough not to show that he doubted Valentine.

Of course, that younger Valentine who'd watched Nishino fall might have doubted this road-worn, tired Valentine too. He had willow leaves in his hair and his boots were drifting down the Mississippi on the flatboat.

A captain came up and Valentine gladly turned the captives over to him. Southern Command and the Whitefangs watched each other over a few dozen yards.

The smell of a roasting hog brought the two groups a little closer together. Valentine filled a birch-bark platter with a cooked haunch and presented it to the Ozark boys with the compliments of Whitefang. A few soldiers cautiously traded.

"Excuse me, son. Can I buy that off you?" Valentine said as he saw a private extract a bottle of RC from his sack, smacking his lips at the scent of hot pork fat and crispy skin.

"Dunno, sir. You don't look like you got—"

"Just give it to him, dummy," a sergeant said.

A Grog veteran probably would have grabbed the younger warrior by the long hair on his shoulders and given him a shake, but Valentine recognized correction when he heard it.

"Carry it all this damn way . . . ," the private said, handing it over.

Valentine trotted across the open space and presented the bottle to Whitefang, who smacked his lips as he held up the caramel-colored water to the sky, evaluating its color.

"Not *Soka-coli?*" Whitefang said, tapping the logo with a claw.

"Try," Valentine urged. He wondered if the Whitefangs would be up for a march on Atlanta. Most of the Cokes he'd had in his life bore an Atlanta Gunworks imprint.

The Grog flipped off the cap and took a generous swig. He rolled the liquid around in his mouth and gave a rather girlish giggle. Then he swallowed.

The chief belched. Now it was his warriors' turn to laugh.

"More, yes?" Whitefang asked.

"Soon," Valentine temporized, wondering if one of the Shrivastava clan would be brave enough to open a small post in Whitefang territory.

The tall young warrior who'd made eyes with Whitefang's daughter slapped Valentine on the back and gabbled. Valentine was pretty sure he was describing a victory over the Doubleblood rear guard but caught only a word here or there. The young Grog grabbed Valentine by the hair on the back of the neck and shook him, and Valentine felt his eyeballs rattle in their sockets.

The youth opened up a wet canvas case and extracted a Doubleblood head, yammering something that could only have been "Take one. I got plenty" as he tried to hand it to Valentine.

Valentine demurred as politely as he could.

The warrior pushed the blood-caked mess on him again, making a gesture with his forearm from his waist, clenched fist at the end, that Valentine found easy to interpret.

"No, you're right, still not married," Valentine said in English as the Grog pointed at his long hair. "But I don't think a skull will help."

A little cautious trading took place between the soldiers and their usual adversaries. Southern Command offered jars of honey or wrapped pieces of taffy or can openers or clasp knives in exchange for Grog machete sheaths and wrist protectors or earrings.

Valentine facilitated where he could, using a half-gnawed pork rib as a pointer. He found himself smiling more than he had at any time since that Fourth of July gathering.

It wouldn't last, of course. Some Grog would kill a pack trader, looking for loot and a trophy to show his prospective bride's family, or a hotheaded sergeant would teach cattle-rustling Grogs a lesson in the language of the noose. Then matters would flare up and not be calmed down until the next holiday or bad-weather season.

The past was done and the future would come soon enough. If better than thirty years on Vampire Earth had taught David Stuart Valentine anything, it was to enjoy the good moments for what they were.

Two

Stipple Field, Arkansas, October: The skeleton of Southern Command's short-lived Air Force School crawls with fresh activity.

There was a time when Southern Command had a substantial fleet of aircraft and helicopters. Accidents and lack of spares has reduced the fleet to a few choppers and long-wearing crop dusters or air shuttles, Frankenstein flyers operating on the parts of dozens of dead ships.

Twenty years ago the airfield, tower, hangars, and office space of Stipple Field had trained younger pilots and mechanics to handle and fix Southern Command's air wing, but with so few craft left, the school only operates for two months in the winter as experienced pilots and mechanics test and give initial training to the few recruits they need.

In the summer, Stipple hosts the cadet games, where promising youngsters compete in marksmanship, riding, and athletic and academic face-offs.

The rest of the year, a few custodial workers keep the place painted, cut back, and lit.

Because the location is remote and easily guarded, low-level conferences between political and military leaders in eastern Arkansas use the facility, mostly to give each side a chance to have grievances heard and smooth over the resulting ruffled feathers over alcohol in the "Flyer's Club."

Kurian spies don't pay much attention to Stipple. Nothing important ever was decided or planned there.

Which is why Colonel "Dots" Lambert chose it as the site for the Highbeam conference.

*   *   *

David Valentine hated Stipple Field's folding metal chairs. And the hangar lights turned the attendees' faces shades of blue, purple, or green, but that didn't bother him like the chairs. There was something exactly wrong about their design for his butt and lower back. Sitting in one for more than an hour made his bad leg ache and his kidneys hurt.

Most days of the Highbeam conference he was in it for six, wearing his rather ill-fitting militia uniform and a fine new pair of fatigue boots, Dallas-made no less, a present from Colonel Pizzaro to replace the ones lost to the Mississippi current—or a Grog scavenger looking for something he could fashion into knee pads.

The hateful chairs were arranged in a square in a big, cold hangar around a map drawn onto the floor in four colors of tape. White for topography, green for Southern Command's routes toward New Orleans, red for known Kurian strongholds and Quisling bases, and yellow for notations.

It was all bullshit. But well-thought-out bullshit, in Valentine's opinion. Lambert had probably kept a team of officers working in odd hours planning an operation that wouldn't take place. Maybe it was part of the General Staff training Valentine had once been set to enter.

Lambert did her briefings on whiteboards, which she and her staff worked on for hours each morning and then meticulously washed each night.

The sentries for the conference, all of whom were going on the trip, had every reason to be alert. But Kurian promises of eternal life had found willing ears before. Some maintenance person might figure out a way to get a picture of the map with a micro-digital camera.

The first day of the conference had been spent mostly in social activities, as officers got to know each other and inevitable late arrivals trickled in—Southern Command's rather rickety infrastructure did well if you arrived within twenty-four hours of the time on your travel orders.

Valentine played cards the first night with a craggy Wolf captain named Moytana. Moytana sported streaks of gray in his long, ropy hair and had once served as a junior lieutenant in LeHavre's old Zulu company, Valentine learned. The Gods of Poker chose not to favor Valentine that night, but Moytana consoled the losers by buying drinks.

He also received, and smoked, a cheroot with an agreeable young staff lieutenant named Pacare. He had a golden, round face, and Valentine thought he'd make a good sun king. Pacare was a communications specialist and told Valentine about the latest mesh that was supposed to keep the juice bugs out of the wiring. Pacare did enough talking for both of them.

Valentine turned in early.

After breakfast, everyone was directed into the hangar. Forty folding chairs, ten to a side, were arranged in a square around the chalked
map. Each chair had a name taped to the backrest. Each person stood in
front of his or her chair; a few of the regulars stiffly "at ease." A civilian
who'd sat stood up again when he realized no one else was sitting.

Everyone waited to take their cue from the general, who stood
chatting with some lieutenant colonels.

General Lehman, in charge of Southern Command's eastern approaches, opened the first day of the conference. The general had a famously heavy mustache that covered most of his lips. He was affectionately
known back at Rally as "The Big Dipper," as the ends of his mustache
visited soups and beverages before his taste buds. The moniker might
have also referred to his habit of dipping his little silver flea comb in his
water glass at the end of the meal.

Valentine's name had been put in the line with support and technical
staff, judging from the insignia around him. Opposite him sat Moytana
and a couple of his poker-playing Wolves. A lieutenant with a scarred
cheek and absent earlobes and who Valentine guessed to be a Bear
waited at the far end of the row. Only a Bear would come to a conference
wearing a crisp new uniform shirt with sleeves freshly snipped off. A
popeyed civilian in a natty sportcoat that looked about two sizes too
small fidgeted uncomfortably next to the Bear. The fresh sunburn and
two-wheeler full of reference binders gave Valentine a guess that a quick
look at his ID card confirmed—he was an expert from Miskatonic.

The row of chairs to Valentine's right held General Lehman and the
big bugs; to his left, Guard regulars.

The assembly was mostly officers, with a smattering of senior sergeants and neatly dressed civilians seated with the big bugs.

The chair with the name "Lambert" taped to it stood empty, as did
the one next to it with no name on it. Lambert was present; Valentine
had seen her in the hangar office with some other uniforms. She was the
closest thing he had to a commander in his ill-defined, ill-starred relationship with Southern Command.

Valentine also recognized one civilian to the other side of Lehman,
a well-dressed fixer named Sime. At this distance Valentine couldn't
tell if he still used that rich sandalwood soap or not. Valentine had last
smelled it when Sime came to visit him in prison, when he was offered
up as a sacrificial lamb to doubtful Kansas officials who were considering switching sides and feared reprisals. The Kansas uprising hadn't
gone as well as most hoped: The Kurians brought an army all the way
from Michigan across the Mississippi and Missouri rivers and smashed

most of the rebellious territories before Southern Command could get there.

Sime ignored him. Valentine, skin crawling as though trying to make a discreet exit, doubted it was out of embarrassment.

Lambert and her group arrived. A man on the hard side of middle age with a loose-skinned face that reminded Valentine of a woeful hound stood next to her at the unmarked chair. He wore a plainly cut black coat, trousers, and leather shoes that made him look like either a Mennonite or a backwoods undertaker. Valentine wondered if he was a Lifeweaver, relatives to the Kurians and mankind's most powerful allies in the war against the Kurians.

"Be seated," Lehman said. Lehman tightened his words before shooting them out of his mouth in little explosions of air, making his mustache ripple like a prodded caterpillar.

Valentine's relationship to the uncomfortable metal chair began well enough. He was glad to sit. Metallic creaks echoed in the empty hangar.

Lehman remained on his feet: "We're present at a historic moment. You've been brought together for an important campaign. What we have come here to plan is no ordinary op. A new Freehold is about to be born. You will all be midwives." The general unbent a little. "Let's just hope it's a live birth.

"Some of you have heard rumors of Highbeam being a move against New Orleans. That's still what it is as far as the various people in your commands who are going to help you organize the men and material are to think. I expect you all to go to sleep every night with a Creole phrasebook next to your bed and maps of swamps and bayous piled on your desk.

"Our true objective is an area in the Appalachians. Some of you may have heard what's happening in West Virginia and eastern Kentucky. A coal miners' revolt has grown into a thriving resistance. Usually uprisings like this are stamped out in a few months, but the fellows running the show there vanish every time the Kurians think they have them trapped. They've got popular support and friends on both sides of the mountains.

"We're going to cross the Mississippi and Kentucky in reinforced brigade strength and offer assistance."

He let that sink in.

Valentine felt a momentary loss of balance. He'd been working out a route of march but had only a couple companies of Wolves and perhaps a contingent of training and technical units in mind when he presented his ideas to Lambert.

Lehman gestured to the big bugs behind him. "And that's it for me.

I'm just here to sign and seal the op orders. You all are going to do the planning over the next two weeks. With forty of us I think we can get a little softball going on Wednesdays and Saturdays. I'll handle the rosters and decide who'll be playing and who'll be grilling and baking when. Unless you vote on basketball, that is. My headquarters, barring contingencies, will be located at the old motel just across the road. I've given most of my staff furlough or dispersed them for training. I'll try to get the pool filled so you can use it, if you like. Drop by if you want to sample the liquor and tobacco a general gets."

Valentine's heart warmed at that. It wasn't often you met a general who knew when to get out of the way.

Lambert took over the rest of the welcome briefing. She introduced the big bugs and allowed the other three sides of the squares to present themselves. Valentine was most interested in the first man introduced: Colonel Seng, who would be overall command of the expeditionary brigade. Seng had a flat face; indeed, he looked as though he'd spent some time using it as a battering ram, as it was heavily pocked and built around a big, pursed mouth suggesting he'd been tasting vinegar. After each introduction, Seng's chin dropped and he shifted his eyes to a blank space between his knees.

Seng had a lot to think about. A full regiment of two battalions of Guard regulars would be his responsibility, each with organic light artillery, plus a support battalion with more artillery and anti-armor—or anti-Reaper—weapons. Of course the men and gear couldn't travel without commissary, transport, and medical companies. Another smaller ad-hoc regiment included a full company of Wolves, three Bear teams under the sleeveless lieutenant, and logistics commandos—the scroungers. Seng's headquarters would have engineers, signals, and intelligence staff, and even a meteorologist and an agronomist.

Valentine hoped he had a good chief of staff.

When it came time for Valentine to introduce himself, Lambert nodded at him, giving him the go-ahead to use his real name. Valentine just stood and said: "David Valentine. Last held the rank of major, Hunters and Special Operations."

"I was wondering what a militia corporal was doing here," a civilian sitting next to Sime murmured, showing off the fact that she could read shoulder tabs and stripes. Sime didn't seem to hear her; he was busy refolding his handkerchief.

Some of the regular officers took another look at Valentine. For once, Seng didn't look down. Valentine nodded to Seng as he sat. The chair squeaked and the colonel returned his gaze to that spot between his knees.

"He's attached to my Special Operations Directory," Lambert said.
"Knew he was an SOD," someone in the regulars muttered.

Lambert moved on, beckoning to the woman next to Valentine, a captain with training and indoctrination who smelled faintly of boiled vegetables and butter.

Only one face hadn't been introduced, the person Valentine suspected was a Lifeweaver. If so, he—she—it? was an extraordinary specimen. In Valentine's limited experience they never mixed with so many humans at one time. He suspected they found all the thoughts and moods stressful, or perhaps frightening. The human imagination sometimes wandered into rather dark and nasty corners when not otherwise engaged.

"You've probably all noticed that I skipped someone," Lambert said, stepping forward again to give voice to Valentine's thoughts. "Brother Mark is an expert on the Kurian Zone. He's former New Universal Church with the rank of elector, I believe. He's serving as liaison between Southern Command and the rebels."

Valentine received his second shock of the meeting. An elector was a senior priest with voting privileges that allowed them to set Church policy—for all intents and purposes a bishop, though they were technically below bishops and the all-powerful archons. Most Quislings were expected to obey orders from the Kurians. Churchmen were trained from childhood to love doing so.

"He's also been prominent in the Kurian Order longer than I've been alive."

The sorrowful spaniel in black rose.

"I'm not sure the guerrillas rate a term like 'army' from such professionals," Brother Mark said. "May I call them partisans without offending anyone? Good. The partisan army in the Virginias–Kentucky borderland triangle isn't like the military as you understand it. It is a small cadre of leaders who go from place to place, where they temporarily swell their numbers in order to destroy a specific objective, be it a mine or a tunnel or a garrison house. With the job done the guerrillas return to their homes and remove all telltales of their participation. Still with me?"

Valentine could tell from the exchanged glances and squeaking shifts in weight the officers were uncomfortable being addressed by a churchman. Or maybe it was the patronizing tone.

"There's a potential in that part of the country for a true Freehold. With regular soldiers such as yourselves to handle external threats, the populace could organize its own defense on a county-by-county basis. I'd say the population is six-to-one in favor of the guerrillas, though they've seen enough reprisals to be chary of rising up en masse. Not the best specimens in that part of the country, either physical or mental."

He paused again to let his gaze rove over the room. He settled his stare on Captain Moytana, who had the thumb of his fist pressed to his mouth as if to keep his lips from opening.

"Yes, we all know what happened when a rising like this was attempted in Kansas. Unlike Kansas, we already have local fighters in place who've lost their fear of the Kurians. This time the rising won't take place until your forces arrive and are integrated with the locals."

Lambert spoke again: "It's not Kansas. The Kurians are holding on to their mines by their fingernails. A couple strikes on key Kurian-held centers, destruction of the local constabulary, and a few Reapers burned out of their basement lairs would greatly further the Cause in North America."

A hand went up, and Lambert nodded.

"That's awfully near Washington," a lieutenant colonel named Jolla with the big bugs said. He was perhaps the oldest man at the briefing other than General Lehman. Campaign ribbons under his name lay in neat rows like a brick wall. "They're tender about that, what with all those Church academies and colleges and such. The Kurians in New York and Philly and Pitts would unite."

"The Green Mountains are just as close," Lambert said. "There's a Freehold there. Smaller than ours, but they're managing."

"Can we count on them to take some of the heat off?" a youngish Guard major named Bloom asked.

"You won't be alone," Brother Mark said. "God sees to that."

Valentine glanced around the assembly. Some eyes were rolling, expecting a mossbacked homily.

"You'll have friends to the west," Brother Mark said. "The guerrillas are getting help from some of the legworm ranchers in Kentucky. About four years ago the Ordnance—that's the political organization north of the Ohio, for those of you unfamiliar with the area . . . as I said, the legworm ranchers have grown restive, especially since the Ordnance began conducting raids into their territory, coming after deserters and guerrillas."

Valentine, who had fled into Kentucky from the Ordnance as something between a guerrilla and a deserter, could tell the assembly didn't like their renegade churchman. The officers were keeping their faces too blank when they listened.

"Some of the troops won't like it," a Guard captain said. "That's a long way from home."

"Their forefathers went ten times as far against lesser evils," Brother Mark said.

This time General Lehman came to his rescue. "Tell 'em what the gals in Kentucky look like, brought up on milk and legworm barbecue. You know that area, Valentine."

"They're pretty enough. Tough too," Valentine said, thinking of Tikka from the Bulletproof. "All that time in the saddle. The backhill bourbon's smooth. Everybody and his cousin has a recipe. Some of the older ones will want to allot out and become whiskey barons."

"Whiskey barons," someone chuckled. "They'll like the sound of that."

The second day they broke into working groups. The big bugs from the one end divided the assembly into three groups: "combat," "support and liaison," and "hunter."

Valentine ended up in the support and liaison group, under the bald lieutenant colonel with the wall of campaign ribbons who'd asked the question about how the Kurians would react to a new Freehold. Valentine wondered if the question hadn't been prearranged by Lambert.

"Don't be fooled by all this," Jolla chuckled, tapping the campaign ribbons. "Just means I'm old. I don't know much more about Highbeam than you. They called me in because I know how to keep the soup pots full for an army on the march." Valentine couldn't help liking him. Some of the other officers who knew him from other campaigns called him "Jolly." Jolla told those in Valentine's team to do the same.

There were study guides to go through about Kentucky, the Virginias, and the surrounding areas. Every day Valentine lugged around two hundred or more pages of text and maps in Southern Command's battered three-ring binders, with tabs for future additions as the operational plans were developed. An artist, or maybe just a bored student, had sewn a denim cover on Valentine's binder at some point or other. Valentine smiled when he saw William Post's name as one of the intelligence staff who'd prepared background. Post was at Southern Command's general headquarters now, studying and tracking Quisling military formations and assessing their capabilities.

The appointment said a lot about his old number two, Will Post.

General headquarters wasn't a place for cushy assignments bought by politics, patronage, or a mixture of rank and bureaucratic skill. You had to be good to get an office at GHQ. Post was good.

They thumbed through the study guides until Lambert and Seng arrived. The big bugs had worked out a preliminary organizational chart before they even arrived, but gallstone surgery and the death of a major's spouse had meant a little last-minute juggling.

The pair met with Jolly first, relocating to a corner while everyone else read through their local study guides. Valentine was studying a history of the legworm ranchers—he recognized some phrasing from his own reports about the Bulletproof, one of the Kentucky clans—when Jolly told him Seng and Lambert wanted him next.

They shook hands and the triad sat down.

"Glad to meet you at last, Valentine," Seng said. His squashed-flat face was pulled down a bit at the corners, reminding Valentine of a catfish.

"Thank you, sir," Valentine said, a bit befuddled by the "at last."

"I had charge of the brigade in the Boston Mountains that was keeping Solon's boys busy while Southern Command was reorganizing in the swamps. They were getting set to roll over us when you derailed them in Little Rock."

Why in God's name isn't this man a general? Seng's history, prompted, came back to Valentine in a flash. He'd kept ten times his number tied down with a couple of regiments of regulars and some Wolf and Bear formations. He'd been at the Trans-Mississippi combat corps briefings.

"I should be thanking you, then," Valentine said. "They were so scared of you, they never shifted enough men to Little Rock to just roll over us. It's an honor to meet you, sir."

"If you two want to hug, I won't tell," Lambert put in. "We've got twelve more sit-downs today, Colonel."

"Terrible thought. Dots is off schedule," Seng said.

"Are you sorry you're not with the hunter or combat groups here?" Lambert asked Valentine.

"I'm just happy Highbeam is under way," Valentine said.

"I know. Ahn-Kha," Lambert said. "There's a picture of you and him up at GHQ, by the way. It's in the case with some mementos from the drive on Dallas. You guys are sleeping on the hood of a truck. He's sitting with his back against the windshield and you're pillowed on his thigh. It's rather sweet. His fur is all muddy and spiky. I recognized you by the hair."

"He was a good friend," Valentine said. If the rumors of a golden Grog leading the guerrilla army in the coal country had any truth to them, a piece of Valentine's soul knew it had to be Ahn-Kha.

"He's the one who brought in the heartroot tuber, right?" Seng said.

"It's more like a mushroom than a tuber," Valentine said. Heartroot was protein rich, with a nice balance of fats and carbohydrates. It was usually ground up and made into animal feed, or a hearty meal that could be boiled in water or baked, or a sweet paste that could be put on a biscuit, the last variant popularly called "Grog guck." "But we're putting Dots off schedule again."

"Thanks, Val," she said.

"Where's Styachowski?" Valentine asked. "I'd think she'd be involved in this."

Lambert's face blanked into a funereal mask. "Killed, two months ago. Plane crash in Mississippi. She was coordinating our Wolves with some guerrillas in Alabama."

"I'm sorry to hear that," Valentine said. Numb now, he would feel the shock sink in when he was alone at night, the way it always did. He was horribly used to this kind of news after a dozen years of fighting.

"That's why I try to avoid the bother of a personal life," she said. She opened the thick folder on her lap. Bookmarks with notations on it ran all around its three edges like a decorative fringe. She glanced at Seng and he spoke.

"We want you to put together a formation of company strength. You'll recruit them out of a pool of refugees at Camp Liberty. You know about Liberty?"

Valentine had heard of it. He'd even seen horse-drawn wagons full of people leaving for it. Just like Camp Freedom in the South, or Independence in the Northwest. What was the new one in north Texas called? Reliance. "That's where the rabbits picked up by Rally Base were sent."

"Rabbits" was Southern Command slang for people who made the run out of the Kurian Zone.

"Been there?"

"No."

"The commander's a good egg. He'll help you out," Lambert said. "He'll be ordered to assist, as a matter of fact."

"What has he been told?" Valentine asked.

"The bare minimum," Lambert said. "Keep using the Argent ID for now. 'Southern Command indulges war criminals' is one of the more popular Kurian propaganda points. They talked up your escape in Kansas, to show what Southern Command does with murderers. Even the *Clarion* still mentions you now and then, when they're picking at old scabs. 'Sham justice for real murder.' That sort of thing."

The *Clarion* was an antiwar paper. Most of the soldiers called it the *Clarinet*, because of the high, squealing tune its editorial page frequently played.

"What's the purpose of this company?" Valentine asked, though he was already guessing.

"We want a few locals who can speak to the folks in their own language," Lambert said. "Facilitation with trade, scouting, scavenging. Ideally, your men will later get promoted to lead squads and platoons of their own, once we're set up properly in the triangle. So think about that: One day your company could swell into a regiment."

"Officers?"

"We'll give you a lieutenant to take your place if something happens to you," Lambert said.

Lambert was a chilly little calculator at times. "Happy thought. NCOs?"

"Take your pick, though we'd rather you did it from the ready reserve. We'd hate to disturb frontline units too much. We've got some names if you feel like you're out of touch."

"I'd like to be able to offer a sergeant major star, sir."

"For a company?" Seng asked.

"You said it might grow."

"I don't see a problem with that," Lambert said. "I'll speak to the general."

"Where will we train?" Valentine asked.

"Haven't worked that out yet. It might be Rally Base, unless they decide that's too far forward. Highbeam will establish a separate depot, wherever they end up."

"I don't suppose you can tell me when we're going."

Lambert smiled. "You must be joking. But it won't be before next year. So if you want to take some time off to disappear into northern Missouri again, you can have a couple weeks once you've got your men assembled and they're training. Clear it with Seng and myself and we'll square things with the general. Just don't get yourself caught."

"Be terrible if they found out New Orleans was about to be hit," Valentine said.

"So, how does it sound?" Seng asked. "I know you've wanted a mission to aid the guerrillas in the coal country. Suit you?"

"It's back to the Kurian Zone. I like it there. I can shoot at my enemies."

"You'd like to take a shot at Sime, I bet," Lambert said.

Valentine shrugged. How did she know that? Well, not worth thinking about that. Lambert had taken an unusual interest in him. He wouldn't be surprised if she'd read the old letters from Molly Carlson, resting in some warehouse with his Cat claws and other souvenirs.

"One more thing. Do you mind being available for questions about conditions in Kentucky? I get the feeling Brother Mark isn't going over that well."

"New Church just sticks in some of these guys' throats," Seng added. "They're not swallowing what he says."

Valentine didn't like churchmen, even former ones. "My gag reflex has been acting up too."

"Speaking of swallowing, he only eats raw food. Nuts and milk and honey and stuff," Lambert said. "Gets odd looks at lunchtime and he never joins in for pizza or barbecue."

"I saw him eat a hard-boiled egg," Valentine put in.

"But you don't mind being called on for an opinion?" Seng asked.

"Not at all, sir."

"Go on to your next meeting," Seng said to Lambert. "I'll catch up in a minute."

Lambert glanced at Valentine. "It's going to be a busy ten days. We'll talk again."

"I'll look forward to that, Colonel," Valentine said.

She left and Seng shifted his chair so it faced Valentine directly.

"You were headed for staff training when they arrested you."

The shock and hurt had long since healed over. That was a different young man. "Yes."

"Sorry to hear that. I went through it, you know. I think we would have done it about the same time, right after Dallas."

"How was it?"

"Tough. Felt like I was being rotated through every unit in the command. I've got most of a footlocker filled with my texts and workbooks. I'd like to loan it to you. There's a lot of good training materials in there. I expect if Highbeam gets off the ground, it might be useful to you. Lambert wasn't kidding about that regiment. We're going to have to rely on the locals to supply most of our manpower. They'll need training from our best people."

Valentine fought down a stammer. "Thank you. I'd like that."

Seng wasn't a smiler, but his mouth relaxed. "You haven't had to decipher my handwriting yet. I know we've just met, but I'm glad you're with us on this trip. When I went over the list of names our sharp young colonel drew up and I saw yours, I remembered when we heard you'd blown up the Little Rock depot. You don't know what that meant to us, boxed up in those mountains."

Again, military formalities saved him embarrassment. "Thank you, sir."

Valentine spent the next ten days on double duty, working with the planners in his group and acting as a second opinion to Brother Mark, though he couldn't answer the questions about the guerrillas in the triangle, of course. He attended working meetings, helped write plans and orders, but mostly thought about the company he was to build. Some days he had little to do but listen and be grateful for the quiet time to get himself organized and draw up his own plans.

The officers bonded in meetings, at meals, and especially on the baseball diamond. Colonel Gage, in charge of the regulars, blew hot and cold, alternately charming and cutting. Gage's chief of staff was the rather pugnacious and compact Major Cleveland Bloom—an odd name for a woman, Valentine thought. She captained Valentine's team and went by the name Cleo on the baseball diamond, where she once pitched a shutout—not the easiest thing to do with softball. When her team was at bat she slapped each of them, man and woman, on the butt and ordered them to "get a hit." She didn't care about stolen bases, doubles, or walks—she wanted hits and more hits.

She had a similar reputation in the field as a fighter.

The Bear lieutenant, a scarred figure named Gamecock, only stayed a week and was the first to leave. "One of my team is in hospital," he said as they said good-bye at dinner. "I've got two places to fill, and there's few enough Bears about these days. I'm going to try to talk a couple out of retirement."

Valentine heartily wished him luck, thinking of his own plans after the departure date.

Gamecock hadn't been much involved in the meetings in any case. Bears didn't give a damn about planning. You put them up close to the enemy and turned them loose.

The civilians rotated in and out of the meetings unpredictably. Usually one or two were away, but never all three. Valentine began to think of them as a single organism that morphed, for they dressed and spoke remarkably alike.

One day a courier arrived bearing a package. Valentine unwrapped it in his Spartan quarters and found a basket containing a set of paper-wrapped soaps inside.

Glad things worked out for the best.
Please accept this peace offering.
Best of fortune and rewards of honor in the coming year—
—S

Valentine unwrapped one of the soaps and took a cautious sniff. Sandalwood. They even had elegant little labels written in French. Sime had remembered that Valentine had asked for a bar during their interview while he was incarcerated in the Nut awaiting trial.

At Valentine's shower that evening he spent an extra fifteen minutes wallowing in the silky feel of Sime's gift. It lathered up at the barest kiss of water and left his skin as smooth as an infant's.

He found Brother Mark silent, gloomy company during their meetings together. He was the one member of the group Valentine couldn't get a feel for one way or another. Of course, high-ranking members of the New Order were habitually standoffish, quiet, and reserved.

He sometimes wondered if Lambert just placed Brother Mark with the planning group to act as a lightning rod for discontent. In mistrusting the churchman, all the other officers grew closer together.

He grew fond of the unassuming Jolly. Valentine was looking forward to serving under him.

"Beats being called Jelly, my old playground nickname," Jolla said. "I was chunky as a kid. Don't know how I managed it—whole family was just about starving, thanks to the cold summers. At sixteen I became a letter boy and started biking around with mail, and it finally came off."

Meanwhile, Valentine's denim-covered file folder grew ever thicker as they worked out variants on the basic plan involving weather and enemy countermoves. Highbeam was taking shape, and Valentine approved. He learned there was even a network of Cats in place to wreck rail lines in Tennessee and a bridge or two across the Ohio to delay any countermoves with large formations of troops. There was only one functioning rail line through central Kentucky anyway, and it would be easy enough to disable it.

Then it was time for them to disperse. They'd meet again outside Rally Base in a gradual buildup. The regulars wouldn't arrive until the last moment. They'd marshal farther to the south to preserve the illusion of the move on New Orleans.

Lambert walked around the square one last time and handed each of them a folded sheet of paper the size of a small piece of stationery. Lambert's neat handwriting was a little blotchy. Obviously the ink she used to write the forty notes wasn't the best quality.

The note read:

> *The code name for this operation is now Javelin. Any changes to the blue-book plan will be marked Javelin. Everyday correspondence and orders will still be marked Highbeam, as will certain messages from me designed to bring confusion to the enemy. Please ignore any High-beam order from my office dated with an even number.*
>
> *This message is printed on sweet rice paper. It's tasty—enjoy.*

Valentine smiled. Confusion to the enemy.

* * *

A week later he stood before a house well outside Russellville, Arkansas, wearing civilian clothes and carrying his Maximillian Argent identification.

The imposing brick house had a rebuilt look to it, with a newer roof and windows added to something that had probably stood vacant and deteriorating since 2022. There was paper over the upstairs windows and Valentine saw a pile of sawdust in the garage. A big garden stood out back, and melon patches flanked the house. Household herbs grew under the sills.

Valentine scanned around with his ears and heard soft clicking out back.

He walked through the nearer of the two melon patches and found Nilay Patel next to a small mountain of stacked river-smooth rocks, digging what looked like a shallow trench connecting two foxholes but judging from the roll of waterproofing might be a sizable artificial pond. Patel had put on a little weight since he'd last seen him.

"Sergeant Patel!" Valentine called.

"No need to shout. I heard you come off the road," Patel said, fiddling with some tools in a bucket.

Valentine took a closer look. There was a revolver handle in there.

Patel's bushy eyebrows shot up. "Lieutenant Valentine!"

Valentine felt pleased to be recognized. He wondered if he'd recognize himself. "How are you, Sergeant?"

"Come across the hedge, just that away. Nadi," he called to the rear screen door. "Drinks! An old comrade is here to visit."

He picked up a curve-handled cane and limped to some garden furniture with hand-sewn cushions.

Nadja Patel, whom Valentine had once met as Nadja Mallow, emerged with a tray. Though she kept her glorious head of hair, she'd aged considerably, but then Solon's takeover of the Ozarks had taken her first husband.

She turned her back on Valentine as she set down the tray. Valentine smelled spicy mustard. "I thought I might as well bring you your lunch," she said to her husband. "Would you like something . . . ummm—"

"David," Valentine supplied. "Yes, it's a good walk from Russellville."

"I like it that way," Patel said. He used his cane to help himself sit. "Ahhh. The knees. I stayed too long a Wolf," Patel said.

"You're not listed as a disable."

"If there's a crisis, I don't want to be stuck behind a wheel or a desk," Patel said, rubbing his kneecaps. "I have good days and bad ones. I've been working since morning, so this will be a bad day."

Valentine heard a clatter from the kitchen and the woman's voice, quietly swearing.

"Can I help in there?" Valentine called.

"No," Nadja called back.

"I know this is not a social call," Patel said. "She has guessed too."

"Nilay, you were the best sergeant I ever knew in the Wolves, which makes you the best I ever knew, period. I saw you listed as inactive. I would have called, but—"

"We don't have a phone," Patel said, smiling. His teeth had yellowed. "I keep a radio. For emergencies."

Nadja Patel emerged and dropped a sandwich in front of Valentine. "You're welcome," she said, before Valentine could thank her. A quartered watermelon followed.

"Now, Nadi," Patel said.

"I know what he's here for. A sandwich he's welcome to. Another husband he's not."

Valentine thought it best to keep silent.

Nadja returned to the house.

Valentine didn't touch the sandwich. "I'll leave. You two enjoy your lunch. It's a beautiful garden, by the way."

"Sit down, sir! Let me hear what you have to say. You came all this way."

"It's an op. Outside the Free Terr—Republics. I can't say any more. But your legs—"

"Are still fit to carry me. David, I've been retired just long enough to feel the grave close in. With nothing to do I've started smoking again. I should like very much to help." Patel tossed the cane he'd been using into the diggings.

"Here I thought I'd have to convince you," Valentine said, getting up and retrieving the cane. "I've got warrant papers for a star to go in the middle of the stripes. You'll be my top."

"I do not need convincing. She does. That would help."

"Don't you want to talk it over with her first?"

"For three years I have done my best to give her whatever she wants. This, I want. She is upset because she knows me. I said no once before to Captain LeHavre and came to regret it."

"He's still alive, as far as I know. He made it to the Cascades. He's fighting out there now."

"I always suspected there was more to you."

"Tell her it would raise your pension. You'd get a sergeant major's land grant too. You could sell it or add to this spread."

"Thank you, sir. Not for the land; for the chance to get back to important work."

Valentine raised his voice, hoping the woman inside was listening. "It's just for a few months' work, all in the Free Territory. Training. When we step out, you'll come back here with your rank permanently raised. I'll promote someone else into your place."

"We shall see. You say you need men trained? Not Wolves?"

"Unfortunately, no. Regulars, more or less. I'm due at Camp Liberty in six days. Is that enough time to get your affairs in order?"

"Camp Liberty? Yes, if I have the written orders."

Valentine opened his rucksack and extracted his order book. "I prefilled out most of it. Except your . . ." He lowered his voice. "Next of kin. That kind of thing."

"I know where to submit the copies," Patel said.

"Thank you, Nilay. It'll only be a few months. I can promise her that, if you like."

"Don't. It would be better coming from me. She knows promises don't mean much where the Cause is concerned."

"I could find housing for her, you know. You wouldn't have to be separated so much."

"I think she would prefer to keep fixing this place. She's a better carpenter and painter than me anyway. When it comes to homely matters I'm fit only for ditch digging. Besides, she has a sister in Russellville. She will be better off here."

Valentine ate his sandwich, wondering whether she'd spit in the mustard. They talked about old friends until it was time to leave.

Patel's eyes shone with excitement as they shook hands. Odd that Valentine was now the reluctant one. Maybe it was the faint sobbing from inside the house.

Three

Camp Liberty, November: The word "camp" implies a certain bucolic simplicity, but Camp Liberty is anything but. It is in fact a small town once named Stuttgart: "The Rice and Duck Capital of the World."

A few old-timers remain in town, "making do" as the locals say with the constant influx and outflow of people picked up from the banks of the Mississippi. Everything from exhausted, half-starved families to rogue river patrol units who beached their boat and ran for it are funneled into Liberty.

The former Camp Liberty, which stood just south of town, headquartered at the old high school just off Route 79, was destroyed during Solon's takeover. Much of Stuttgart's housing was demolished and populace was herded into "temporaries"—prefabricated homes designed for easier concentration of a populace, a Kurian specialty. Solon had great plans for the rice-growing region, and construction materials were hauled in for apartment buildings, a New Universal Church Community Apex, even a theater. When Solon's Trans-Mississippi order collapsed, most of the residents fled the wire-bordered housing, happy to abandon the roof over their heads for wider horizons.

Southern Command was not about to let the construction gear, raw materials, and prefabricated housing go to waste, so Stuttgart became the new Camp Liberty and work began on a new hospital, training and orientation center, and combined primary/secondary school for children who escaped the KZ with their parents.

Meanwhile, their elders were put to work in the rice mills, when they weren't attending class to acclimate them to life in tougher, but freer, lands.

*When David Valentine visited Liberty, it was the finest facility of its
kind in the Texas and Ozark Free Republics—and it was still under
construction.*

After checking their luggage at the station, Valentine paid for a
horse cart so he and his new sergeant major could ride through town—or
the camp, rather—saving Patel's legs from the walk.

They passed through two checkpoints—there were no wire, towers,
or searchlights, at least not visible from Main Street, as Valentine learned.
There were guards watching from a balcony or two, and more mounted
officers riding horses chatted and swapped news with the locals.

They held handkerchiefs over their faces as they passed through
construction dust. Men in dungarees with sleeves and trouser legs of
different colors were digging a foundation.

"POWs?" Patel asked.

"Doesn't look like it. I don't see a single guard," Valentine said.

"Look at all the signage," Patel said, gesturing to a general store. A
universal white stick figure pushed a wheeled basket across a plain green
background. Iconography for beds, phones, and even babies and animals hung over other doors or were stuck into second-floor windows.
The streets, too, were color coded and marked with animal-cracker out-
lines.

Valentine had visited more Kurian Zones than even an experienced
soldier like Patel. He was used to signs both written and in iconography.
It hadn't registered this time for some reason.

"It's for illiterates," Valentine said. "Shopping cart for store, dollar
sign for bank, syringe for medical center . . ."

Of course in the Free Territory there wouldn't be a smiley face
for the NUC building.

They ate in a diner, killing time until Valentine's appointment with
the camp supervisor. Which was just as well, as the service was slow to
the point that Valentine got their own coffee refills.

Valentine helped the attendant at the register make change for his bill,
when Valentine threw him off by paying a $12.62 tab with $13.12.

"I'm all muddled up from multiplication and division, sir," the attendant said, tucking his head in that old Kurian Zone gesture of submission. "Clean forgot my subtraction."

"Take your time," Valentine said. "I just wanted a couple of dollars
to buy a paper."

"Always amazes me that they can even find their way to the Territory," Patel said once they were back on the street.

" 'West to the big river and freedom,' " Valentine said. "The underground helps some of them along."

Valentine turned a WET PAINT sign right side up as they walked down the sidewalk, and the gap-toothed painter gave them a Morse-code grin and a thumbs-up.

Liberty's administration building looked like an old town hall or possibly a courthouse. They got directions from a bright and attentive young woman in another strange dual-color outfit.

Supervisor Felshtinsky had a nice corner office with a view of the towering rice mills and a staff of three. One was arguing over the phone with someone about duck poaching and the other two were buried in paperwork.

"My name's Argent," Valentine said. "Southern Command. I've got a two o'clock appointment."

"The super is out on the grounds," an older woman said. "I can page him on the walkie-talkie."

"I'd appreciate that."

"Sorry he's out, but you never know with the trains," she said, smiling. "He's a very busy man."

The other put down his pencil and turned around and took a plastic bag off a bureau.

"Welcome to Camp Liberty. Visitor ID tags and a house key," he explained, handing the bag to Valentine. "You can use the ID tag to eat in any of the cafeterias. Your trailer's in the southeast quadrant, just behind this building. Go in through the green arch. You can see it from the south side of this building. You're lucky: As guests, you have a kitchen with a fridge and everything. We'd appreciate it if you didn't wear pistols, and you can check any other guns in at the armory. It's in this building's basement."

"Why no pistols?" Patel asked.

"Most of the folks here, they just wilt when they see someone with a gun," the older woman with the walkie-talkie said. She spoke into it again and then returned her attention to Patel. "Might as well put on a pair of lifts and a Reaper's hood."

Patel looked at Valentine and glanced heavenward.

Valentine changed the subject. "I'd asked for an index of your current residents who came out of Kentucky and Tennessee. Even the Virginias."

"And we haven't got to it yet," the man on the phone said, covering the mouthpiece. "We've got only one computer allocated to admin and only one man who knows how to work the database. Our old printer runs on curses and tears."

"Hot dog," Valentine said, letting out a deep breath. "Hammer's going to go red as a baboon's butt."

Patel's eyes widened, then he nodded. "Tell me about it."

"Who's Hammer?" the man with the key packet asked.

"My CO," Valentine said. "Ex-Bear." He tapped the scar running the side of his face for emphasis. "He'll probably be here by tomorrow to get things moving."

"You think the file cabinets will fit through that window?" Patel asked Valentine.

"Eventually," Valentine said.

"You'll have your list delivered to the trailer this evening," the man with the phone said, clicking off his call and dialing a new set of numbers.

They met Supervisor Felshtinsky out front. He had a tall, muscular assistant and rode in an electric golf cart.

Valentine had never seen a golf cart fitted out with a gun rack. A beautiful over/under shotgun rested in its locks, and Felshtinsky had flying ducks painted on the back of the low-riding vehicle. Its rear was filled with plastic file folders.

"You'll excuse me not standing," Felshtinsky said as he turned in his seat to shake their hands. He looked relaxed and tan in a polo shirt. "I've been on wheels since 'fifty-eight."

He had a strong grip and heavy shoulder muscles. Valentine guessed he lifted weights; you didn't get muscles like that just dragging your body around. Valentine felt humbled and apologetic, as he always did when meeting someone who'd lost a piece of himself.

"Hop in back there. I'll give you a tour."

As they drove around to the cart's smooth, almost silent engine whine, Felshtinsky told them about his post. He was proud of his operation. He had close to four thousand people under his charge, temporary residents acclimating to the Free Territory, or permanents who'd settled around Liberty.

"We've got as many teachers here as Little Rock or Dallas," Felshtinsky said.

"How long do they stay?" Valentine asked.

"Depends. Sometimes a young couple meets up here, decides to get married and start fresh, and leaves right away. We get some not much smarter than a well-trained horse. They count on their fingers and can recite a few Church verses about flushing only once a day. Try learning to write at forty-three."

Felshtinsky explained how all the residents earned "Liberty bucks" doing training. Liberty bucks could buy them furniture and appliances for their homes or beers at the camp's bowling alley, and most of the merchants in town let them use the scrip to buy from a limited selection of toiletries and merchandise provided by Southern Command's warehouses at a discount.

They passed the first wire Valentine had seen. It was ordinary fencing, and a military policeman with a pistol stood in a guardhouse at a gate.

The tightly packed trailers inside the fence looked too numerous for a prison compound, unless the residents of Liberty were unusually lawless.

"What's that?"

"That's for Quislings. They stay there until they're cleared by Southern Command. They're worried about another big sabotage outburst, like just before Solon showed up, so they make sure."

Valentine saw one of the residents pushing a wheel-barrow with a yellow plastic water keg in it. He wore that alternate-color scheme Valentine had seen here and there.

They drove around the hospital and the ethanol plant, the rice mill and the cane fields. Arrowheads of ducks and geese flew overhead.

"Lots of waterfowl in this part of Arkansas," Felshtinsky said. "If you want to get up early and go for a duck, I've got the best blind in the county. Privileges of rank."

"Sergeant Major?" Valentine asked Patel.

"I would like that. If I could have the loan of a birding gun. What about you, sir?"

"I'll spend the morning going over the printouts. Assuming they showed up and we don't have to sic the Hammer on our host's staff."

Everything about the next day, save for Patel's ducks—simmered in a homemade korma sauce all afternoon in their tiny cabin oven and served over (what else?) rice—disappointed.

Their first order of business, after dressing the morning ducks, was to check out Liberty's militia training camp. The young men and women were sad specimens, mostly undersized, undertrained, and undereducated. Valentine had never seen so many hollow chests, flat feet, bad eyes, and rickety knees.

"To think these are the ones with the ability to make it out," Patel said.

They stopped by the rifle range and saw a bored Southern Command corporal watching a couple of men in the two-tone Quisling fatigues training some kids to shoot.

"Hold it tight into your shoulder," one said, patting a recruit on the back. "It's not going to hurt you, 'less you hold it like a snake that's gonna bite."

"Kur's sake, keep your damn eyes open and on target when you pull the trigger," his companion bawled.

"Let me see that gun, um . . . ," Patel said.

" 'Probation,' " the Southern Command corporal supplied. "That's what we calls 'em."

"Sergeant," Patel barked. He still didn't have his stripes with the star in the middle for his old Wolf deerskins.

"That's what we call them, Sergeant," the corporal said, stiffening.

The "probation" came to his feet smartly, took out the magazine, and opened the breech, presenting the weapon to Patel.

"Sir," he said.

Patel placed his cane against his crotch and took the rifle, checked it barrel to butt. "They take good care of their weapons."

"They're not afraid to clean them, sir."

The other probation ignored the byplay. His recruit, firing from the prone position with the gun resting on a sandbag, shot across the field. The hidden range man in the trench flagged a miss.

"Them sights is all messed up," the militia recruit complained.

The probation/trainer next to him took up the weapon, put his cheek to it, and fired from the seated position. The spotter pulled the target down and pushed it up again with a bit of red tape at the edge of the ten-ring.

"You're right. The sights are off."

"These, I like," Patel said.

Valentine had announcements that called an evening meeting in one of the rec centers, but the meeting wasn't as crowded as Valentine would have liked. The basketball courts in the rec center could have held a thousand people, with more in the stands, but he got only a few hundred, and many of them were women with children.

Valentine didn't see a single person in the two-tone overalls or out-fits. He wasn't that surprised. A former Quisling could expect an instant death sentence if found bearing arms against the Kurians.

"You should have advertised free beer," Patel said, sotto voce.

"I'm looking for volunteers to go back into the Kurian Zone," Valentine announced. "To go back fighting. This time with an army of our people. I don't need riflemen so much as facilitators—people who know the locals and can interact with them."

Valentine saw a few at the back slip out and head for the washrooms or the exits.

"Service grants you all the benefits of OFR citizenship, pension benefits, retirement allotment, and combat service bonuses."

He was flopping. He felt the sweat running down his back. "Anyone interested, join Sergeant Major Patel here on the bleachers. We'll come around and get your information, meet, answer questions. Then we'll let you know in the next day or so if you'll be called back for a physical and a second interview."

A man with a Riceland cap laughed as the crowd dispersed. He smiled at Valentine and touched his cap. "First rule, johnny soldier, is don't volunteer for nothing. Goes same in Free Territory."

They got eleven. Valentine could tell right off that he wouldn't want three of them—way too young or far too old. They took down the details of them all anyway.

Later, over the duck and rice and a couple of beers Patel had had the foresight to buy as the day went south, Valentine looked over the "applications." They'd had to fill out the blanks for the four illiterates—well, they could write their names, but that was about it.

"Six or eight, depending on the physical," Valentine said in the dim light of the cramped trailer kitchen. "We might get another couple dozen out of the militia in training, and that's if we don't restrict it to those from Kentucky and Tennessee. Southern Command's already got the pick of the men passing through here. The ones eager to fight have already joined up."

"The only two I really liked were those Quislings on the rifle range," Patel said.

"I think those will be our first corporals," Valentine said.

"God help us," Patel said, reaching for two more beers. That was one nice thing about the prefabricated trailer home. You only had to turn around to reach the fridge.

Patel was slow getting up. He'd flex his legs and then get up on one elbow. Then he'd swing his legs down and raise and lower each shoulder.

Valentine brought him some hickory coffee. Though moving coffee beans between Kurian Zone and Free Territory wasn't illegal, at least as far as the UFR was concerned—just dangerous—and "smugglers" saw to it that such luxuries were available, Valentine couldn't afford the price. The only thing stimulating about the hickory coffee was the temperature. Whoever made this mix put just enough of the real thing in to remind you what it wasn't.

"I was thinking we could try having breakfast in that probation camp," Valentine said.

"You think we will do better with the Quislings," Patel said, massaging and rotating his knees. He paused, reached for the cup, and downed half his steaming coffee—his throat must be tough as his leathers, Valentine decided—and held out the mug for a refill.

The Quislings ate in an oversized Quonset hut. Every word, every *clunk* of cup being set upon table, every scrape of knife and fork in a tray was magnified and bounced around by the curving walls as though the diners were musicians in a concert shell. Valentine tried to turn off his ears.

Valentine looked across the group—mostly men; there were far fewer women and children in this group—with something like hunger. These specimens were straighter, fleshier, longer of limb, and more alert of eye. Some wore tool belts or had hard hats dangling from nearby hooks; others read or did crosswords over the remains of their breakfast. He shifted his feet and cleared his throat.

"Could I have your attention please?" Valentine said.

He'd misjudged the volume required. His words were lost in the breakfast clatter and chatter.

"Oi!" Patel shouted. Patel's voice was like a mortar round exploding beside him. It almost blew him out of his boots. "Who wants to kill a few Kurians?"

The room quieted admirably as better than a hundred faces turned their way in interest.

"Sorry, but you can't have 'em," Felshtinsky said from his office wheelchair early the next morning. He pushed the names of the probations back across his desk at Valentine and Patel, seated opposite.

"Why?" Valentine asked.

"Ex–Kurian Forces aren't allowed to just leave Liberty whenever they want. They have to be cleared by Southern Command."

"If you just need a signature, I'll take responsibility," Valentine said.

"Sorry, it's not that simple. I can't release them to you."

"What if General Lehman's HQ signs off for them?"

"It's not just Southern Command. The civilian authority has to sign off on them as well."

"Which civilian authority?" Valentine asked.

"Interstate Security Office."

Valentine knew little about the ISO, save that their field officers were called marshals. He'd once seen one come in to Rally Base to pick up two river patrol Quislings who'd gotten drunk and decided to fish from the wrong bank of the river. The marshal wore blue pants with a navy stripe down each side and had a badge, but other than that he looked like a typical hand on a horse farm.

"I don't suppose there's someone from the ISO here."

"As a matter of fact, there is. You've got a UFR/ISO district marshal just across the street at the station. He runs a one-man show. He's got an office off our regular police force. His name's Petrie and I wish you luck with him."

Ray Petrie had alcohol on his breath at ten thirty in the morning.

The duty sergeant at the small police station had advised them that he showed up anytime between eight and eleven, depending on how late the card games went.

You had to catch him quickly before he left for lunch, a uniformed woman struggling with a rusted padlock on an evidence cage added. So Valentine and Patel drank police-station coffee (and used the station washroom shortly thereafter; Liberty cops liked their smuggled-in beans strong) and waited for Petrie to appear.

There was already a waiting line. A couple, both in the two-tone dungarees, the woman swollen in pregnancy, waited.

"Not long now," Valentine said, looking at the mother-to-be.

"You don't know Petrie," the man said. "I was a librarian in a Youth Vanguard school. I've got a job here, filing, but our application still hasn't been approved. We don't even want to move out of town! And we met here; that's how long the wait's been."

"I meant not long for the child," Valentine said.

"It's our second," she added, closing her eyes and sighing.

Petrie came in yawning, a fleshy man with a heavy mustache and a growth of beard. He paused on the way in, a thoughtful look on his face, grabbed the edge of the duty sergeant's desk as though to keep himself from keeling over, and farted abundantly.

"Christ, Petrie," the duty sergeant said.

The marshal took a chained ring of keys and opened his side office.

"A minute," he said to them. Valentine had time to spot a dead houseplant atop a file cabinet before Petrie closed the office door behind him.

He reemerged only to go into the washroom carrying some items wrapped in a towel. He emerged again, shaved and combed.

"Just another minute," he said, nodding to them. This time the station cat managed to flash through the door.

A radio flicked on in the office. Valentine heard the keys employed again, a file cabinet open, the pop of a cork being pulled, and the marshal sit heavily. A minute passed, then the cabinet and keys sounded again.

The door opened. "C'mon in. Open for business," he said to Valentine.

"They were here first," Valentine said, gesturing to the couple.

"They can wait. They're used to it."

Petrie turned heavily away and went to his chair.

"Go ahead," Valentine said to the Quislings.

The couple went in. Petrie didn't bother greeting them. "Good news, Courage," Petrie said. Valentine watched the interaction. "Your application came back, provisionally approved."

"Provisionally?" the man and woman groaned, if not in unison, at least in harmony.

"Your list of references got misplaced somewhere between here and the office." Petrie got up and shut the door, but that didn't matter to Valentine's ears, or to Patel's for that matter.

"Believe you me, it might take a while. I could make sure they get found soon for another five hundred," Petrie said. "You want that kid born a regular citizen, right?"

Valentine flushed. Those poor people. This was how business was carried out in the Kurian Zone. Some combination of an office and a title with a bit of power, looking for his taste of sugar on the transactions crossing his desk.

He and Patel exchanged a look. Patel worked his jaw as though he wanted to spit.

"You'll have it in a week," the man called Courage said. Valentine suspected it was a first name.

"To show you two just how good I take care of you, I'll give you the provisional without waiting." Valentine heard a couple of resounding thumps on the desk as Petrie stamped paperwork. The couple left, the man holding a file folio as tightly as he did his wife.

Valentine and Patel stood up to enter, but Petrie was right behind the couple. He took his keys out and stuck them in the lock.

"Missed your chance," the marshal said. "I'm going to lunch."

Valentine extracted a bill. "I'm in a hurry. How about I buy you lunch in exchange for fifteen minutes of your valuable time."

"You got it, militia." The bill disappeared so smoothly Valentine thought Petrie an amateur magician. He held the door open and they entered his office.

The cat crouched, peering under a bookcase. Valentine suspected a mouse was down there. Maybe more than one. Enough crumbs and bits of paper-wrapped sandwich littered the desk and sat in the unemptied wastebasket to feed a family of mice.

A file cabinet with PENDING stenciled on it had another overflowing box of paperwork atop it marked "priority pending."

"What can I do for a militia major and a Wolf, by the looks of it?" Petrie asked.

"I'm going to need some paperwork processed quickly. I want to do some recruiting among the probations. About a hundred."

"A hundred?" Petrie ejaculated, showing more animation than he had all morning. "Probations? You mean, let them loose?"

"No, just released to Southern Command, through me."

"That would take months."

"You want to do this the easy way or the hard way, Petrie?" Valentine asked.

Petrie tested his newly shaven chin. "Meaning what?"

"Meaning you can say 'Anything for the Cause' and get off your duff. Figure out a way to get ISO sign-off on the men I want. Pick up the phone and talk to whoever you need to talk to in order to get them cleared to join the Command."

"What's the easy way?" Petrie asked.

"That was the easy way," Valentine said.

"I'm late for lunch," Petrie said.

"He wants the hard way," Patel sighed.

Valentine stood up and opened the door for him. "Go to lunch, Petrie. Make it a big one. By the time you get back, Sergeant Major Patel and I will have sworn out a warrant for your arrest. We both heard you extort a civilian on a Southern Command base. For five hundred dollars, to be exact. In case you don't know military law, that's a very big no-no."

Petrie looked around his office as if to see where they were hiding when they overhead the conversation.

"Lose your appetite?" Valentine said. He shut the door again and turned to address Petrie.

"You might think that being OSI, you're not subject to military law, but the people you've been juicing are certainly protected by it. You'll spend at least a night in the cells, probably more, as it'll take a bit of time to get you counsel. With our sworn statements, JAG investigators will be here tomorrow. I'll tell them to be sure to bring a good accountant to see just how your paperwork balances up for this little corner of ISO. I wonder why you don't have a clerk to help you with some of these files, Petrie. Or do you? Existing only on paper, maybe? In any case, maybe the jaggers can't prosecute, but they can tie up your case in a beautiful ribbon and present it to the circuit court."

Petrie glowered for a moment, and then his lips curled into a sneer. "You think you're so smart, militia. Didn't you read the name on the door? My uncle's the lieutenant governor of Texas. I'll make a couple of phone calls and whatever stink you made will get blown right out the window. You'll get busted down to private and you'll spend the next four years pumping out portajohns for the biodiesel plant."

"Thanks for the tidbit, Petrie. I don't follow politics, so I didn't recognize the name. But right after I talk to JAG I'll see if I can get a couple of newspapers interested. 'Recent arrest implicates Lieutenant Governor in corruption probe,' is how the *Clarion* will put it, I expect. Better yet, 'Governor's office tainted.' The papers love a good coat of taint. Be interesting to see if your uncle lifts a finger to help you. Hope you remembered to send him his birthday card."

"Two can play your game, militia," Petrie said, folding his arms. "I can fill out warrants of my own. You're threatening an ISO officer into malfeasance. Maybe they'll put us in adjoining cells."

"You're not a big fan of reason, are you, Petrie? You never should have hit me."

"I never put a hand on—"

"The nose, Patel, good and hard."

Patel made a fist and punched him hard across the bridge of his nose. White light shot through his brain, and when Valentine opened his eyes again, he tasted blood, felt it dripping.

"Patel," Valentine gasped. "Restrain the marshal. He's flipped."

Patel moved nimbly for a man of his bulk. Petrie tried to rise but Patel sat him back in his chair hard with a good shove. When he rose again, Patel spun him around and gripped him across the back of the head and his right arm.

The cat gave up on its mouse and hid.

Valentine recognized the grip; he'd been in it often enough. Patel had been the Second Wolf Regiment's premier wrestler for three years running. Valentine had once seen his new sergeant major dislocate a horse rustler's shoulder when he didn't like the tone of his answers under questioning.

Valentine turned up the radio. "Give him something to think about, Sergeant Major."

"Hel—" Petrie began to shout.

It was a tight fit, with the three of them behind Petrie's desk, Valentine keeping Petrie's mouth shut with a stiff-arm.

Petrie finally gave, his muscles turning from wood to oatmeal.

"We're going to take care of three pieces of business this morning, Petrie," Valentine said, wiping his bleeding nose and flicking the blood onto Petrie. "First, you're going to fill out a hundred releases for me with the names blank. Second, you're going to do whatever paperwork needs to be done for your central office. Patel and I both know how to write and type. We can do either to give you a hand. We'll even send out for sandwiches on my tab and have a working lunch. When I'm satisfied, we're going to write out your resignation from ISO. You can tell your uncle you got sick of rice.

"One slipup, one bit of paperwork slowed up, one questioning telegram—and you're going to jail, Petrie. I'd better see a postcard from whatever sinecure your uncle finds you. Yes?"

He removed his hand from Petrie's mouth.

"They're Quislings," Petrie said.

"That wasn't a yes. Dislocate his shoulder whenever you like, Patel."

"Who cares if they get squeezed? They've done plenty of squeezing across the river, believe you me."

"That's in the past."

"You're assaulting an ISO officer. You'll wind up—"

Valentine heard—and felt—the pop of Petrie's shoulder.

"Arrrrgh—" Petrie grunted, sagging. Patel shoved him back into his chair, his arm hanging.

"I didn't think you'd do it," Petrie said softly, his face white with pain.

"A dislocation's easy to fix," Valentine said. "Petrie! Keep your hand away from that phone. Broken fingers are a bitch while they heal."

"I could pop his jaw," Patel said, gripping either side of Petrie's head. "That'll cut his talking down to 'Ow.'"

Valentine let Petrie catch his breath.

"So, Marshal, have we reached a deeper understanding? You've got three more limbs. I don't want to have to leave you in a bathtub full of ice without any of them working, but I will."

"You can have 'em," Petrie said. "Hope one of them rolls a grenade into your tent for me. That's all the thanks you'll get from those mooks."

"You're a mean, stubborn bastard, Petrie," Valentine said. "If your uncle can't find anything for you, you're welcome to join my outfit."

Four

Highbeam Assembly Area, Arkansas, November: Just outside the city of Jonesboro, now notable only for its hospital, which is the only one in the northeastern corner of the state, a new camp is going up.

Southern Command believes that the best people to build a camp are the soldiers who have to eat, sleep, and train in it. Cartload after cartload of lumber, tenting, plumbing, and wiring arrives as the assembly area swells, hauled from the rail terminus to the camp by ox wagons and mule teams.

A tricky autumn dumped rain and a freak snowstorm on the soldiers as they hammered and tacked and strung. Now, with canvas roofing above their heads at last and corduroy roads made of scrub timber and wood chips, the rain blows out northeast and a cool, dry fall sets in, though the chill in the midnight-to-dawn air hints at worse to come.

Valentine's company arrived after the Wolf contingent and Bear teams but before most of the Guard forces of the expeditionary brigade. They got their own corner of the assembly area, a little blister near the camp's drainage.

As far as the men were concerned, they were preparing for a "long out." Lambert had planted rumors that their destination was New Orleans or a big raid on the river patrol base at Vicksburg. Consequently the men assumed that they'd be going in the opposite direction, perhaps to Omaha or another try at western Kansas. One Wolf swore that it would certainly be Omaha, as he knew for a fact that Major Valentine was familiar with the city, as his sister had served under him on Big Rock Hill and afterward on the drive into Texas. She knew all about him. Others bet him that it was Kansas, as Colonel Seng had buried a lot of soldiers there and was going back to reclaim old ground.

Each man both hopes for and fears the coming "long out." On the return from such a campaign, promotions and awards are handed out like Archangel Day candy. Quieter, dirtier stories of the women looking for an easy out of the Kurian Zone appeal to some; others talk of strange liquors and dishes. The best of them, writing letters home or making out the public paragraphs of their wills, refer to the gratification of liberating a town or county, the fear of the residents that slowly transforms to hope, and the hard work of making individuals out of cattle.

David Valentine, looking at his motley assortment of Camp Liberty volunteers (ninety-two former Quislings and twelve refugees, of which nine are women) drawn up on a freshly cleared field within their winter encampment for their first morning's exercises, readies himself for the strain of once again being responsible for men's lives— including, in the words of his old Wolf captain LeHavre, "burying your mistakes."

Patel was still the only NCO. Valentine's requests had disappeared into the maw of Southern Command's digestive process. What would emerge from the other end remained to be seen.

He was lined up with the other men, ahead of the massed ranks. Valentine wore his oldest militia fatigues and the men were still in their Liberty handouts. They'd divide the men into platoons later. For now they'd eat, sleep, and exercise in a big mass.

Even in the early days of their acquaintance he was already conditioning himself to the idea that some of them, even all of them, might die in the coming operation.

Valentine had made peace with his own death. He'd seen Kurian rule in all its fear and splatter. Faced with his experiences and the mixture of revulsion and hatred they inspired, he had only one option, the only option a man who wanted to call himself a man had: risking all in a fight that would end only with his death or the Kurian Order's destruction.

Why the men under him signed up wasn't strictly his concern. Whether they fought so they could look other soldiers in the eye, to take the place of a lost relative, to get an allotment, or because they thought of battle as the ultimate blood sport made no difference regarding the orders he would give: He'd do his duty the same whether a man signed for faith or money.

Speaking of duty, his first was creating a healthy environment for his men while they trained themselves into a fighting company.

The only improvement to their ground was a length of three-inch piping and some conduit extending out of the main camp. The rest of their materials were in the supply yard.

Patel stepped out of the little "command shack," the only structure standing in their blister at the end of the camp. His cane had disappeared and he looked as spry as ever.

He walked back and forth in front of the men once. He'd inked in a star on his old stripes and done a good job of it. Valentine could hardly tell the difference.

"My name is Sergeant Major Patel. You came here as a hundred and five individuals. Southern Command's going to make an army of one out of you. One well-trained, sharp brain that's always alert. One tough Reaper-eating body. One heart that fears only God and Sergeant Major Patel. You read me, slackers?"

"Sir yes sir!" Valentine shouted. A few voices behind joined in.

Patel put his hands on his hips and faced them. "Rest of you haven't finished evolving? Communication occurs when the transmitter broadcasts and the transmittee acknowledges. Try again!"

"Sir yes sir!" they shouted.

"I don't want to hear harmony—you're not a fuckin' chorus. All at once, and louder."

"Sir yes sir!" they shouted loud enough to be heard in Jonesboro. Georgia, not Arkansas.

"After morning exercise, we're going to build you all shelters. Ladies get theirs first, because we're in Southern Command. We're blessed with natural gallantry."

Morning exercises lasted until lunch. Patel took them through his "twelve labors." Again and again, he managed to find fault with the rhythm of their jumping jacks or the height of someone's buttocks during a push-up. He sent Valentine and four exhausted "slackers" off to get the meal while he finished with the rest.

There wasn't a chuck wagon available so they piled bread and beans and trays into a wheelbarrow and ate with spoons. Dessert was flaky pastry smeared with "Grog guck."

Valentine got tap detail. He turned on the spigot and filled cups and a couple of beat-up old canteens and bladders from the flow of water so the recruits had something to drink with their food.

With everyone sprawled on the cold, damp ground, eating and drinking, Valentine finally got his pan full of beans. The beans tasted as though they'd once shared a tin with some ham but divorced some time back, though the molasses in the sauce was sweet and welcome.

Patel gave them thirty minutes and then roused them to get to work on the frames for the tents. Valentine was the only one to notice that

Patel's breath smelled like aspirin as he bellowed. But they did manage to finish the women's tent and get a start on the showers.

That night they slept around fifty-five-gallon drum stoves burning scrap from the lumber they'd measured and cut.

The first day was nothing to the second. Everyone ached and groaned as they did the twelve labors. Some fool asked when they were going to get their uniforms and Patel showed them why they weren't yet fit to wear Southern Command issue by running across, covering in, and crawling through the noisome field where the camp's sanitary waters drained off.

"Too slow," Patel said each and every time they fell into the mud. Or crawled. Or got up. Or crossed the field. Or turned around to cross the field again.

They slept in a formidable stench that second night, thanks to the field and two (or more—the men had had a long trip on buses) days' worth of hard-sweat body odor. The next day, eating a breakfast of biscuits and greasy gravy out of wheelbarrows again, they learned all about democracy as they voted to finish the showers before the men's shelter.

Valentine liked the decision that they'd rather sleep rough and cold than dirty. Men who wanted to get clean had pride in themselves. He also liked being under Patel's orders. It got him out of Camp Highbeam meetings and working dinners that were more social than productive.

They had the floorboards laid, the sinks running, and the shower headings up when Patel stopped them and had them line up on the camp's main road to welcome three new companies of the Guards into camp.

They must have made a strange impression, hair spiky with mud, the odd multicolor dungarees of Camp Liberty filthy with a mixture of muck and sawdust.

"Better get back to wrangling them pigs, boys," one called.

"Whew! Someone's been on shit detail," another Guard soldier called as they walked in. Catcalls and jibes were part of the Command's proud tradition. The men stared off blankly into space or looked down. They didn't have the spirit to answer back.

Yet.

That was his job. And Patel's. And the rest of his NCOs', if he ever got any. To make up for the jokes, after dinner that night he told them a little more about what they would be doing in the Kurian Zone— scouting and trading for food, scrounging up replacement gear, and interacting with the local resistance.

Unfortunately for his company, he learned the next day that the second name stuck. Maybe it was their odd bubo placement in the camp's layout, but Valentine's company became known as the "shit detail" in everything but formal correspondence.

He discussed the problem the next morning with Patel in the little command shack as the men slept—clean now, thanks to the functioning showers but still in tiny field tents or bags in the cold dew—as they planned the day's training.

"What do you think of promoting from within?" Patel asked. "There are several ex-sergeants. You've even got a busted-down captain in your ranks."

"I'd like to see talent rewarded," Valentine said. "It's more of a mindset than technical and leadership skills that I'm worried about. In the Kurian Zone, it's enough to just issue an order. Here the men like to know the whys and hows so they feel a part of something larger. I'd like to see initiative—intelligent initiative—from privates on up."

"I don't think that's possible in a few months. If you want some sergeants taught to be Southern Command sergeants, I may be able to help. Can you get me any money?"

"I can try. What are you talking about?"

"About thirty thousand dollars."

"I don't have a pension to borrow against anymore, Patel. I'll try Lambert. She might have access to a slush fund. Tell me what you have in mind."

They worked out the deal with Lambert, the general, and Southern Command in three days. When Valentine pointed out that in the long run it would be cheaper than adding more men to the "long out" with bonuses and land grants and so forth, they agreed.

Plus it would be good for the "shit detail's" morale to be led by their own.

Naturally, there were staffing orders to cancel. As luck would have it, one position filled as the order was transmitted: a heavy weapons expert named Glass, rank of corporal and with a spotty record of wanting to do things his own way, showed up at camp and reported to the command shack as everyone was eating their lunches out of wheelbarrows again.

A small man with a big pack, he looked like some kind of beetle with an oversized carapace of pack and camp gear. He also sported the world's scraggliest beard. It looked like Spanish moss Valentine had seen in Louisiana.

Valentine stood up to welcome him and Patel trailed behind.

"Very glad to see you," Valentine said, shaking Glass' hand.

"Thank you, sir," he said rather sullenly.

"Don't want this assignment, Glass? You didn't get someone twisting your arm to volunteer, I hope."

"No. Nothing like that, Major. Tell the truth, I'm glad to be back under General Lehman. Just tired from the trip."

Glass was one of those compact, wiry men in what looked to be his late twenties. Judging from his qualifications list on his Q-file, he didn't look to be the type to wear down. Valentine let it rest.

"You're early, so you get to pick the most comfortable corner in the NCO tent. It's just you and Sergeant Major Patel for now."

They sized each other up, Patel in his Wolf leathers, hand sewn and patched, Glass in his ordinary Guard cammies. Glass stared vacantly at Patel, not so much challenging his superior as transmitting indifference.

"What's the company's support weaponry?" he asked.

"It's not here yet," Valentine said. "As you can see, everything's late to arrive, even uniforms. You might as well learn early, we're the shit detail of this outfit. Eat up."

"Will that be all, sir?"

"For the moment," Valentine replied.

"I'll get myself squared away, then," Glass said. He turned for the tent with Patel's name painted on the old bit of traffic sign next to the door.

"Brittle," Patel commented. "Just hope he's not about to break."

"He's got outstanding references for his competency. Leadership's lacking. His last CO called him 'prickly.'"

"Wonder how the guys who had to share a tent with him would have put it," Patel said.

"We're not going across the river to have a harvest bonfire and sing-along," Valentine replied. "I'm willing to wait and see."

Valentine's company's first lieutenant finally arrived late at night as Valentine caught up on paperwork in the one-bulb shack. He tripped on the doorstep coming in, straightened, saluted, and handed Valentine his orders.

They told a curious tale in the dates and checkboxes and comments. Valentine spent sixty seconds reading through.

Lieutenant (militia) Rowan Rand was Kentucky-bred; his parents made the run for Free Territory when he was fifteen. His father disappeared one night while scouting what looked like a vacant farmhouse and he'd helped his mother and sisters the rest of the way to the Ozarks, crossing the Mississippi on barrels à la Bilbo Baggins.

"Stint in the militia, and then right into Logistics Commandos?" Valentine asked, looking up from the file.

Rand blinked back at him through glasses that the ungenerous might call Coke bottle. "Bad eyesight. Astigmatism. I'm bat-blind without my eyewear plus I don't see so well in the dark. They never put it down on my record beyond 'needs glasses.'"

Southern Command's recruiters had the sense to weigh shortcomings against strengths, almost always in favor of giving a candidate a chance to prove his mettle. "You tore through the SC Intelligence and Aptitude tests. Your test scores make mine look like an illiterate's."

"Six years in a Church academy in Columbia District," Rand said.

"Church background? I'll introduce you to Brother Mark. How'd you like it?"

"The schoolwork was fun. And there were all the outings and marches and drives, singing the happy tunes as we worked. I'm embarrassed to think about it now."

"You were eleven. How could you know?" Valentine said.

"Same for you? You kind of choked up there, sir."

"I grew up in a different church, luckily."

"I would have run on my own during summer leave if my parents hadn't decided to try."

Valentine read over the file again. "Platoon leader and then a lieutenant in the militia. Five trips into Kentucky, three into Tennessee with the LCs. No combat?"

Rand shrugged. "Logistics Commandos think that if you get into a fight, you're a screwup."

The Logistics Commandos were odd units. They went into Kurian Zones to beg, borrow, or steal items Southern Command had difficulty manufacturing or maintaining. Mostly they were made up of veteran Hunter members, Wolves and Cats primarily, but Valentine had heard that with Hunter training slowed to a trickle, more and more regulars had been doing the hazardous duty.

Valentine read to the bottom of his assignment orders. Lambert herself had placed Rand with his company. If she believed in the man, there was no need to probe further.

"Welcome to Delta Company," Valentine said. "At the moment Sergeant Major Patel is running the show, turning the men into a team. When we're on the parade ground, he's in charge."

"Yes, sir," Rand said.

"I'll introduce you to the company. You'll stick close to me for a week or so until you find your feet, then you'll take over. I'm going north into Grog country. I'll be back in a few weeks, barring catastrophe."

*   *   *

Rand sank into his duties easily enough. To Valentine's delight, he soon swam lustily. He was all knees and elbows in the field and had a tendency to trip. After a sprawl he had a way of pushing his thick glasses back up his nose that disarmed the laughers and charmed the more sympathetic.

He accepted formal command of the company from Valentine with a nod and a yessir, then took off his glasses and cleaned them with his shirttail.

Valentine had a final word with Patel as the groom from the brigade stables held his horse, a sturdy Morgan named Raccoon. A packhorse stood just behind. Valentine hung his baggage and the odds and ends he'd been collecting on the packhorse.

"Keep up the good work, Sergeant Major," he said as Patel helped fix a clip.

"Enjoy your leave, sir."

"It won't all be fun. I'm going to see if I can do a little more recruiting in Missouri."

"You don't mean . . ."

"Yes. Grogs."

The horse holder snorted. Valentine took the reins and Patel shot the groom a look and growled: "Thank you, Private."

Valentine and Patel walked toward the gate. Well, not so much a gate as a big chain with a Southern Command postal number hanging from it and blocking the camp's entrance.

"Since you got out of the Wolves, sir . . . any head injuries?"

"The Cowardly Lion says it wasn't so much a head injury as Bud ringing my wake-up bell."

"Bud? Ah, yes, my old friend who tried to climb up a tree to God. Your memory's still on target. I was going to ask who was the first governor of the Ozark Free Territory."

"Kird Q. Pelgram," Valentine said. "I think you'll have to do better."

"If a Quisling troop train pulls out of New Orleans at twelve thirty, going twenty miles an hour toward Baton Rouge, and eight hours later their support train pulls out, going forty miles an hour, when will—"

"It won't. We'll blow up the bridge at Red River so the Quislings have to fight without artillery."

"When are you going to change out of that militia rag?"

"Near the border, at one of those shifty inns that does business with the Grogs out of a basement armory."

"Speaking of uniforms," Patel said. "There's a Kentucky gal in second platoon who used to be on some big bug's staff. Ediyak—Private Ediyak now. She knows Kurian auxiliary forces from the Gulf Coast to the Lakes. She's got a design for a uniform based on their priority labor. Moleskin, they call it, almost as tough as leather, with denim shirts, both dyed down to a foggy gray."

"I've seen something like that in the KZ. Those the guys who run phone lines?"

"Yes. Flying specialists that work their communications and electrical. Always moving from place to place, so strange faces won't raise eyebrows."

"Denim's easy to get. Labor troops. I dunno about the moleskin."

"Popular with ranchers. Rand says he can find some with his old LC connections."

"If she can modify them so they're Southern Command but still look KZ, that would be ideal."

"I'll speak to her about it."

Valentine decided to jump in with both feet. "Put Rand to work getting denim and dye and sewing supplies. He might as well get his baptism of fire with Supply or put his LC background to work in the UFR. Worst-case scenario is they'll be a fresh set of civvies for our guys."

"These leathers are getting a little gamey anyway."

"How are the knees holding up?"

"I'm now a confirmed aspirin addict, sir."

Valentine extended his hand and they shook. "Give yourself a break, Patel. Let Glass take them through the twelve labors. No one's going to think worse of you if you pick the cane back up after these last weeks."

With that he rode out of camp, turning north into a November wind.

For six gallons of root-beer syrup he got a Whitefang guide to take him up to St. Louis, the Grog clearing a path through the brush with a year-old legworm. His guide frequently stopped his mount to scout on foot, and at these rests Valentine would feed the horses and check their trail. The only thing that picked them up was a slight cold on their ride north. Both he and his guide took turns sneezing and blowing their noses, but it was better when they came into St. Louis three days later.

He traded a captured revolver—he'd tinkered with it on the journey and modified the grip and trigger guard for Grog-sized fingers—for a foot pass and toted his bag full of toys to Blake's home.

Not that Blake lacked toys. The old Jesuit researcher, Cutcher, had been observing him constantly as he played with various puzzles, games, and toys, gauging the young Reaper's mental development.

They'd built another coop and chicken run in the side yard of the prairie-style house located high on the bluffs above the Missouri. The

Owl-Eye Grogs had added a rock pile at either side of the driveway. According to the scratchings, this was a place of powerful good magic for the tribe.

He gave some bolts of cloth, seeds, and religious books to Narcisse. Along with her care of Blake, she'd started a little church for the human community in St. Louis. While the only holy spirit the human river traders took came in a square bottle, Narcisse had made it her specialty to invite human captives of the Grogs into her circle. She'd been traveling to a couple of different neighborhoods more or less strapped to a mule. Valentine would have to promote his packhorse to the carriage trade and find her a little two-wheel cart. He could acquire the kind of thing high-ranking Grog chieftain wives used to visit relatives in the complicated tribal family structure, curtained to prevent lowlier Grogs from gazing on the high and mighty.

Valentine pulled the bell rope that told Blake that it was okay to come out of his comfortable basement room.

Blake, at just under four years, was as tall as a boy on the cusp of his teens. *"papss,"* Blake hissed excitedly as he emerged. He wore an oversized jacket and jeans with the cuffs extended. Gloves dangled from his sleeves. When he'd go outside he'd add a scarf and a floppy old hat to disguise his appearance.

Wobble, Blake's little dog, picked up on the boy's excitement at having "paps" home and chased his tail in excitement.

"night games tonight?" Blake asked.

"Anything you like," Valentine said. "Fishing, a deer run, or I can read you stories."

Blake put up with stories only when he was very tired. He didn't like to sit and just listen or read along.

"night games!"

For night games Blake wore a football helmet with padding sewn in at the sides so it fit snugly on his rather narrow head.

The games took place in the old St. Louis children's museum, a warren of chutes and ladders and tunnels made out of assorted bits of industrial and artistic junk from the pre-2022 world. The Grogs used it to train young warriors. At night the Grogs loosed their young on each other, to chase and brawl.

Some of the tougher human children sometimes joined in, also suitably padded and helmeted. Blake's helmet had a mesh with eyeslits attached to the grill—Valentine once explained to another human parent that the Grogs sometimes gouged with their long fingers—and with leather gloves on it would be hard to distinguish him from any other skinny young boy.

He could even shriek like a prepubescent when the mood hit.

There were no human kids there the night he took Blake. Valentine relaxed a little. Blake sometimes liked to show off by executing a jump no human could make and sometimes when wrestling he reversed his arm joints.

The most common Grog game was for one of the less dominant males to run up and swat a tougher one and then try to get away. The Grog children clearly considered it something of a coup if they could get away from Blake; they would swing or dangle from climbing obstacles and hit him, or three would strike at once and run off in different directions. Blake took the punches and swats with good humor and pursued his attackers and threw and pinned them when he could.

The roughhousing resulted in surprisingly few injuries. Young Grogs bounced like basketballs.

Valentine had stiffened the mesh in front of Blake's chin. Blake had acquired a good deal of self-control, but no sense taking chances.

He sat, watching Blake play. When Blake disappeared into one of the ill-lit buildings filled with noise and shadow, he followed, carrying a mug of sweet tea hot from a thermos.

A second thermos waited in Valentine's pack for when Blake tired. It was filled with warm chicken blood.

They fished the next day, then crossed into the woods on the north side of the Missouri the night after that, going on a deer run in the early morning.

Blake didn't have his helmet this time, just a hat with earflaps.

Valentine and Blake had a unique manner of deer hunting. They'd cover their scent as best they could with deer droppings and then wait. The deer liked to forage at the edges of old roads and broken-up parking lots. When they decided a herd was close enough, Valentine tapped Blake and they took off after a deer.

Last time they'd gone on a deer run, Valentine had been able to sprint ahead of Blake, even with his stiff leg. This time Blake beat him early in their dash after the bouncing white tails.

Valentine had that moment most fathers had, much earlier in the quick-developing Blake's case, when the son outdoes the father physically. He pulled up and sheathed his knife, relegated to the role of watcher.

Sometimes the deer crisscrossed and Blake got confused. But this time he bounded onto a big young buck at the fringe. Valentine had a moment's doubt, wondering if Blake would be taken for a brief ride before he lost his grip, but he brought it down like a cougar, clawing his way onto its neck and biting.

By the time he trotted up to Blake, the deer's eyes had gone dead and sightless. Blake raised a blood-smeared smile to him.

"Clean kill, Blake. Let's dress it. Sissy will have venison for the whole winter now, or deer sausage to go with her eggs."

At noon—Blake liked to sleep through the days—Valentine settled him down for a nap. They'd return with the deer carried on a pole between them that night. He read to Blake a little from *Charlotte's Web*, but Blake seemed unimpressed by Wilbur's predicament.

"pigs don't talk," Blake said. *"story is not real."*

"It's a story. In stories pigs can talk. So can spiders and rats."

Blake didn't understand why, if the pig could talk to Templeton or Charlotte A. Cavatica, it couldn't talk to Fern.

Blake would rather watch the bugs moving in the grasses and find out what they were doing. Maybe he was just scientifically minded. Valentine still found it disturbing that he couldn't summon his imagination to aid him in understanding the story.

Or empathy.

Blake helped him with various repairs to the house. Valentine went into St. Louis and got kerosene and tallow for light, a big bag of rice, chicken feed, and tar for a couple of weak spots in the roof and drainspouts.

Valentine watched Blake with Narcisse. She touched Blake frequently, patting him on the head or shoulder or arm, and he smiled, but he rarely touched or returned hugs with much enthusiasm.

But then he loved to nap with his head pillowed on her lap or breast.

Once, while Blake was sleeping away the morning, Valentine asked Narcisse if she was ever afraid.

"Daveed, don't be silly. I am safer with the boy here than with a whole pack of guard dogs. He tells me when the Grogs come ten minutes before I hear them."

"No, I mean of Blake."

"He cares, in his way. He is like—he is like the cat who just takes affection on his terms. One time I fell from my wheel-stool and before I knew it he was beside me and righted it. After, I had a scrape on my arm and he got a cloth with vinegar for it."

Valentine gave voice to his doubts. "Maybe he just thought he was repairing you, the way he did the chicken wire."

"One night in August it was hot and I did not kiss him good night.

He asked me why I didn't as I left, and I told him I was worried that he was getting too big for a kiss good night. He said he liked it because it made him feel warm and sleepy. He has love and caring. Do not worry for me."

Valentine let the matter rest.

They said their good-byes in the driveway. The garage now had a two-wheeled rig for Valentine's packhorse. Wobble sniffed at the new feed trough Valentine had built.

Narcisse had shown herself adept at driving the trap and Blake found the challenge of driving a horse fascinating. Blake approved of simple action-result loops much more than E. B. White.

Valentine had acquired the rig by pledging to a loan of trade goods at the old church office in the city. He'd pay it back through the river rats.

"No sneaking blood out of that horse, now," Valentine said to Blake.

"no, papss," Blake said. Neither of the horses were happy about Blake's presence. They sidestepped and danced every time he moved. The carthorse would get used to him eventually.

"Help Sissy all you can. I may be gone for a while, so you've got to look out for her."

"no trouble for sissy," Blake said. Narcisse stroked his odd tufts of hair. It looked as though someone had glued old toothbrush heads in odd patterns on his scalp. It just grew in that way. He remembered one of the Miskatonic researchers saying something about it possibly being an identifying mark.

"Go with the magic of the right hand, Daveed," Narcisse said.

He plucked her out of her wheelchair and hugged her. She'd put on a little weight since he'd met her in Haiti.

"Can't thank you enough, Sissy," Valentine said.

"I go where the most need is. Blake needs someone to teach him. My whole life, I never fit in anywhere," she said. "That is something I can teach Blake. How not to fit in right. The people here, especially the captives of the Grogs, they need me too."

Valentine knew she'd been practicing her folkloric brand of medicine with the humans. She had turned a sunny south breakfast nook into a room devoted to growing herbs. How she got exotic peppers and roots in St. Louis was a marvel. Cutcher had probably helped her build her collection.

He was proud of the victories he'd won for the Cause, but he couldn't visit Big Rock Hill again without seeing faces of Beck and Kessey, knowing where they were buried and what they looked like before they'd been cleaned and shrouded.

Narcisse was also a victory, in a way. There'd never be a plaque to commemorate her, the way there was one on the old red-brick consular residence on Big Rock. Instead of brass lettering, this victory came with a shining smile, a colorful kerchief, and arms he could feel as they embraced.

He rode away from the house on the Missouri bluffs and into a cold wind. He didn't dare think of it as home, or else he'd never have left it.

Valentine's Whitefang guide must have had a fine old time in St. Louis. He'd acquired two wives, one for him and one for his brother, and a legworm's worth of trade goods.

It looked like his brother was getting the ugly one. But then Valentine wasn't current on Gray One aesthetics. While he waited for his guide to arrange the departure, Valentine fended off a trade Grog trying to buy his hair.

Luckily his guide didn't mind him hanging bags of horse grain from the legworm's dry, fleshy hide. First you had to sink a cargo hook into the thing, which took some judgment, as patches of skin were constantly sloughing off. Then there was the legworm's habit of crashing through thickets. You didn't want to put your load where it might get accidentally torn off as the legworm brushed a tree.

They passed south easily enough, the tough Morgan stepping easily in the legworm's wake, nibbling at bits of trampled greenery now in easy reach. Valentine only remembered wondering how big Blake would be the next time he saw him.

His efforts at recruiting a dozen or so Whitefangs met with a stern refusal from the chief:

"In the days of my grandfather, whisperers promised much and gave little. Little thinskins all same."

"Give good guns. Give good gear. Whitefangs share camp and food and battle, become friends to thinskins," Valentine said.

The young warrior who'd led the Whitefangs in battle against the Doublebloods snarled and displayed in front of Valentine, stamping his feet and tearing up ground with a ceremonial planting hook.

"Not need thinskins' guns put up plenty good fight," he said. Valentine got a nose-full of Grog breath.

"I saw Whitefangs in battle," Valentine said. It was hard not to flinch. One good swing of that hook and his brains would be leaking out of his nose. "Would want such warriors as friends against whisperers."

The young warrior squatted and looked to his chief.

The chief fingered his necklace. Valentine saw two Reaper fangs among the odds and ends of his trophy braiding, gearshift knobs and dog tags, mostly. "Whitefangs enemies enough. Not need seek more across river," the chief said.

That seemed to settle things.

Back at the Highbeam assembly, Valentine found his company hard at work sewing.

He changed back into the tired old militia uniform and ordered a powdered meal as he received Rand's report. A contingent of three aged Wolves had arrived. They were already known through the company as "Patel's Shepherds." Each had taken a platoon and were putting them through tough field training.

"Recon's hard work," Rand said, taking off his glasses and cleaning them with his shirttail when the formal report ended. "They've sniffed out six stills, two basement markets, three gambling dens, and a brothel and a smokehouse that does beefsticks you won't believe. They also located a mother and two talented widowed sisters in Jonesboro who enjoy giving formal dinner parties for the handsome, brave young officers of Southern Command. Handsome and young being key to an invitation to dinner."

"In other words, they're experienced soldiers."

Valentine found his desk unusually orderly. He'd been expecting an overflowing in-basket.

"Private Ediyak, the gal with the idea for the uniforms, helped me with some of the low-priority stuff. The rest is in the locked file cabinet."

They'd set up two sewing machines in a workshop next to the command tent. Someone had found a battery-operated radio and hung it high in the tent.

He met Private Ediyak, a small blonde with the delicately wide-eyed look of someone brought up on KZ rations, when she had a soldier model the new uniform.

It was made out of denim the color of an foggy evening. Baggy about the legs but easily bloused into boots and knee pads. She'd layered a denim jacket over an athletic sweatshirt, and put an olive canvas utility vest over that. The vest was trimmed with yellow reflective tape.

Valentine recognized the vests. They were Labor Regiment. He used to cram sandwiches and water bottles into the big pockets for a day in the fields or on the roads. There were D rings for holding more gear on this version.

He walked around the soldier modeling the uniform. He looked like a young, fit construction worker.

"The Day-Glo tape is almost out at Supply, sir," she said. "I backed it with fabric and Velcro. Removing the reflective stuff just takes a second. Speaking of Velcro, sir, the same goes for the arm patches. If it would be possible for us to get something made that looks KZish, we could swap between KZ and Southern Command as needed."

"I wondered about that, sir," Rand said. "The inspector general's office won't like flags not being sewn on. 'These colors don't run' and all that."

"The inspector general's never had to look inconspicuous in a KZ streetcar," Valentine said. "Who's the honcho there now?"

"General Martinez," Rand said. "Three Hots Martinez, the men call him."

Valentine's stomach went sour, but there was no need to pick at old scabs. He offered his hand to Ediyak.

"Good work, Ediyak. You just won yourself a promotion to corporal. You're also company clerk, if you want the job."

"Clerk, sir?" she said.

"It's a quick path up to lieutenant's bars, if you'd like to start that climb again."

She considered for a second. "I'll do it, sir."

"Good. Your first job will be to requisition whatever you need to finish these uniforms. I'll speak to someone about getting us some KZ patches." That someone being Lambert and staff. Valentine rather liked being able to dump such details off on someone who could be relied on to get it done.

"What about helmets and rain gear, sir?" Rand said.

"Typically these formations wear white or yellow hard hats, sir," Ediyak said.

Valentine's liquid dinner arrived. It tasted like a shake made out of strawberries and mud but it was fast and easy. "Let's see if we can scrounge up some civilian winter coats," he said as he sipped. "I don't ever remember seeing these guys in ponchos. As for helmets, maybe we can stuff some old hard hats with Kevlar. Get canvas covers for when we don't want the Day-Glo look."

"Patrol coming in," the company outdoor fire watch shouted.

"Patrol?" Valentine asked Rand.

"Patel's Shepherds have been taking them out, platoon at a time, on overnighters or three-dayers, sir. This should be first platoon coming back from a three-dayer."

Valentine went out to take a look.

The platoon looked dog tired and strained, rolling on their feet in the toe-in manner of footsore men as they carried sand-filled artillery shell casings instead of guns. The bearded old Wolf in charge straightened them up and they saluted as they marched past. Valentine saw some bandages across noses and a few blackened eyes.

"Sergeant, halt," he called.

"Line up for inspection," the bearded sergeant bawled. Valentine saw Corporal Glass at the other end discreetly check the line.

Valentine took a look at one of the bandages. "What happened here, Sergeant?"

"We paused at a roadside for fresh pretzel bread and beverages, sir," the old gray Wolf said. "The gentlemen owning the establishment didn't care for scrip. We convinced them otherwise."

"Anything serious?" Valentine asked. He doubted the road-stop in question would make a report. Everyone was required to take Southern Command scrip but some business owners didn't care for the exchange rates.

"One of them drew a knife, sir. The civilian in question will be working his fly with his left hand for a while. Corporal Glass has a good eye. He's quick or I might not be standing here."

"Good work, first platoon. Get some food and sleep."

Valentine fell back into the regime of training as the days turned grim and gray and the nights cold. They'd formalized the roster at last and had three balanced platoons. Valentine had known companies where there was a crack platoon that took the toughest jobs and two less-reliable ones to support it, but he'd rather distribute his best men where they could teach the others than rely too much on a single elite formation. The NCO slots were filled with ex-Quislings.

He gave them a brief speech about duty, as he saw it. In the KZ command flowed down, with a lurking "or else" implicit at the end of every order. While that was a fact of military life regardless of origin and uniform, Valentine would rather have those under his command following orders because they understood the stakes and consequences of failure.

Several of them turned down offers of promotion to leadership roles.

That was the big shortcoming of these men, he'd learned. They could use their equipment but not their minds. Everyone was terrified of making a bad decision, lest they be out a seat when the next round of musical chairs orchestrated by the Reapers came round. Soldiering wasn't for the dumb—not if you wanted good soldiers rather than gun-toting robots.

They held a company party at Christmas, with everyone in their smoky denim uniforms and the kind of glossy shine you could get with new boots. The base hall was being used by the Guards so Valentine spoke to the pastor of a local church and got the use of a big revival tent, complete with a deacon to open the ceremonies and offer a Christmas homily. The company made paper lanterns and fire balloons and put up a Christmas tree in front of the command shack. A distribution of quality flour, confectioner's sugar, and food coloring allowed the foodies in the company to make green- and red-iced cupcakes. With a couple of guitarists, a fiddler, and Rand, who turned out to be an accomplished hurdy-gurdy player (he claimed he was always too clumsy to dance, so he might as well play for others), they held a dance.

Valentine paid a visit to the hospital in Jonesboro to issue a general invitation to the nurses there. A handful were brave enough to show, and a few brought friends. Valentine issued strict orders not to talk about the "move south" no matter how pretty the face or how good the reason for future correspondence.

"We might as well get to know them. Some of us are going to end up seeing a lot of nurses before the operation is over," he finished.

Valentine enjoyed an opening waltz with the senior nurse chaperoning her charges—the nurse had a lot of experience dancing with a man with a stiff leg—and then settled down with Patel to watch the festivities and make sure the punch bowl wasn't spiked to over eighty proof.

The smiles on the men and the laughter of the nurses cheered him more than the music. The company had worked hard on their uniforms and decorations, and he liked seeing them show off a little.

A blat of a trumpet interrupted the music. There was some kind of stir at the door of the tent and then a group of Guards forced their way in, dragging what sounded like Marley's chains and lockboxes.

The dancing stopped and the men parted.

"We brung you a Christmas present, Major," one of the Guards said, with a rather drunken salute. "New recruits. You was looking for some Grogs."

Valentine heard a riding crop strike flesh and a "Go on." Two other Guards pulled on a chain, and Valentine smelled a zoolike stench.

"They'll fit right in with the shit detail," someone guffawed.

A Grog sprawled for a second, then stood up. Two more were pulled in behind. But Valentine couldn't take his eyes off the foremost. She was a female gray dressed in an oversized pink tutu and fake ballet slippers.

It was the Grog he'd once known as Bee.

"Bee!" Valentine said.

"Beeee," she said back, eyes open wide and staring. She tried to slink sideways up next to him.

The room fell silent. Most of the men there had never heard Grogs do anything but ook or cry out *graaaawg* when wounded and begging for assistance.

Valentine locked his gaze on the joker who'd called them the shit detail.

"What did you call this company?" he asked.

"Errr, nothing, sir," the Guard said, red-faced and counting the number of men coming to their feet. One of Patel's Shepherds snapped his teeth at them.

Patel thumped his cane on the floor. "Boys, these visitors seem to be confused as to the location of their barrack. Escort them back."

The party dissolved into chaos. Southern Command soldiers would probably have let out their trademark foxhunt shriek as they chased the Guards back to their regimental grounds. Valentine's company let out a deeper *uhuh!*

Patel's Shepherds used the confusion to dump a couple more preserve jars of busthead into the punch.

The Guards wisely dropped the Grog chains and ran, with half the company in hot pursuit, throwing Christmas cupcakes.

The male Grogs behind Bee fell to their knees and covered their heads with their hands as men hurdled them. Bee dragged herself up to Valentine and sniffed his hand.

Valentine took Bee, the other two, and a plate of cupcakes over to the workshop tent. As he issued cupcakes—most Grogs had a sweet tooth—he employed his rough-and-ready Grog but her dialect made it slow going. The other two Grogs understood him well enough, after a period of suspiciousness broken by Bee's emphatic thumping of Valentine's chest, a Grog version of saying "He's a stand-up guy," evidently.

Hoffman Price, the bounty hunter Bee traveled with, was dead, evidently of some illness. He'd made it into free territory and turned Bee over to an old friend before dying during a surgery Bee didn't begin to understand. The old friend, whom Bee called White Hair, promptly dropped dead a short time after Price. White Hair's family either gave or sold Bee to a circus.

That's where she met the other two Grogs, Ford and Chevy. They'd been warriors from a tribe in Mississippi who crossed the river in some incursion and were left behind, wounded. They were captured, defanged (they pointed to the big gaps in their teeth), and bought by the D.C. Marvels Circus.

They didn't know the name of the circus—Valentine had guessed it. He'd seen posters put up around the hospital giving the dates for the circus performances at the Jonesboro fairgrounds.

According to the men, it was mostly a set of rigged carnival games and bad ginger ales sold for three bucks a bottle. A beer that was all head cost six.

In the circus Bee performed what Valentine guessed to be a comic ballet in her tutu—all Valentine got from her was "make dance, make fall, make roll." The other two took turns standing in an empty kiddie pool while spectators threw rotten onions and tomatoes at them.

He ordered a couple buckets of warm soapy water, a sponge, and towels. First thing to do was get them cleaned up. And Bee out of that ridiculous tutu.

"You want finished circus?" he asked the three.

"Yes, yes," Ford and Chevy chorused. Bee used another word of her limited English vocabulary: "Pleease."

"Like join thinskins warrior tribe?"

Bee said her version of please again; Ford and Chevy pointed to the gaps in their dental work. "Not warriors. Us finished warriors."

"Not matter with thinskins," Valentine said.

They thumped Valentine's chest. This time Valentine relaxed into it, though he couldn't help taking a tender, experimental breath afterward to see if any ribs were broken.

The men didn't much care for having Grogs among them. The former Quislings considered the troops who fought using Grogs the lowest of the low, hardly human themselves. Discontent filtered up through the sergeants and to Patel.

"Yes," Valentine told Patel, who seemed a little discomfited himself. "The Kurian Zone despises them. Southern Command hates them. But a uniformed Grog can cross a bridge or stand at a crossroads without anyone looking at him twice in the Kurian Zone. I'm sure you can see the use of that."

"Yes, sir."

"We're going to have to put them under someone. Any ideas?"

"Why don't we just call them the major's bodyguard?"

"That's a bit Lawrence of Arabia for me. Anyone who wants to do it gets to be a corporal, quick promotion—that is how they entice people to do it in the KZ. I'll teach whoever volunteers the language."

Glass, their heavy weapons expert, took the job. "Not so much that he likes Grogs; I just think he hates people more," Patel said. They talked over how they'd juggle the platoons once again.

A messenger interrupted them. "You won't believe what's outside, Major. It's quite a show."

Valentine peeked out one of the many cracks in the shack, and believed it. A pair of civilians stood at the gate, a rather dazzling bronzed man in a purple tailcoat and oversized yellow bow tie and a black mountain of muscle in overalls.

He'd been half expecting this. He went to the corner of the shack and took a tin plate off a bucket he'd been saving for just such an occasion. He filled his pockets.

Valentine closed the top button on his old militia tunic—he wanted the men to have their uniforms finished before they made his—and stepped out to the top step of the command shack.

"Is that him?" the man in the purple asked.

"Yes, sir," the gate escort said.

"Hello, Major," the man in the purple said, flashing whiter-than-white teeth. "D.C. Marvels is the name. Dazzling cavalcades of marvels is my game. You've heard of me?"

"Not until recently."

"Then I'd like to extend a personal invitation to the show. You're aware that soldiers are entitled to a ten percent discount at my circus; twenty percent on food and beverages? For parties of three or more, that is."

"How can I help you, Mr. Marvels?"

"There's been some sort of misunderstanding. A few of your gallant comrades rented an attraction of mine, poor benighted Grogs I've taken under my wing, saving them from river dredging or worse. They never returned, and I'm due in Mountain Home by the end of the week."

Valentine was beginning to look forward to this. "I don't see where I fit in. Were they men under my command?"

Marvels planted his feet. "Didn't say you were responsible, Major. The soldiers in question said things got rather out of hand at your party, and they had to leave my attractions behind. Grogs can't be left in the hands of amateurs. They'll sicken and die, poor things."

"I'm afraid they've quit your circus, Mr. Marvels. They've enlisted with Southern Command."

"You're kidding, right? They're not competent. They're mine and I want them back. I'm trying to be nice here, but I'm perfectly willing to take legal action."

Valentine crossed his hands behind his back. "So am I. Get off this post."

"Corricks," Marvels said out of the side of his mouth.

The muscle inflated his chest. "Ford! Chevy! Bee! Here now!" He pulled a whistle from his pocket and the trilling filled the company tents.

Valentine felt the whistle as much as he heard it. It gave him a headache.

"Shut your man up, Marvels."

"When I see my property!"

Valentine hurled a ripe tomato at Marvels, striking him just under the yellow tie. He drew a rotten onion from his other back pocket. The whistling didn't stop until he bounced an onion off the handler's head.

The big man took a step toward him and Valentine matched his move, more than half hoping Marvels would throw a punch.

"That's assault! You've assaulted a civilian. I'll have your commission for this," Marvels said, extending his shirtfront as though it were a warrant for Valentine's arrest.

"Then I might as well enjoy myself," Valentine said, aiming an onion at his head. Marvels ducked under it.

"The gate's that way," Valentine said, throwing another tomato. This one hit Marvels square on the buttocks as he turned to run.

The expected summons to Colonel Seng's office came that very afternoon, courtesy of Seng's messenger, Tiddle. Tiddle reminded Valentine of the White Rabbit, or maybe the Road Runner, always in a hurry to get somewhere. He either ran or used a light motorbike rigged with tires for cross-country driving. His hair normally looked as though he'd had a recent close encounter with a live wire.

Valentine washed up with some of his French soap and put on his best uniform. Lieutenant Colonel Jolla didn't look particularly jolly.

"That Marvels fellow just left. He's in quite a temper."

Valentine shrugged. "Is he getting his Grogs back?"

Seng's frown deepened. "No. I pointed out that the practice of chattel slavery is against the law and is in fact a hanging offense. He said I could expect a letter from his lawyer. I don't need these headaches, Valentine."

"Sorry, sir. He had two of those Grogs in what amounts to a bear-baiting pit. Customers paid to throw fruit at them."

"Says as much about some of the customers as it does about Marvels," Jolla said.

"If he starts a legal fight, it might be worth someone's while to check his payroll accounts. When I had Ahn-Kha on my rolls, I kept up-to-date with policy. They're free to hire on or quit, and you have to pay them at least convict rate. According to the Grogs, they never saw so much as a dollar."

"Still not a defense for your behavior," Seng said. "Save it for the enemy."

Valentine smiled at that. Technically he was still a condemned man under Southern Command's fugitive law, though his face had long since been removed from the "Wanted" cabinets.

"Will that be all?"

"No," Seng said. "Lambert told me you were a little unorthodox but effective. Let's work on the effective and cut down on the unorthodox. Why aren't ordinary militia uniforms good enough for your men?"

"You want us to operate in the Kurian Zone. Southern Command militia uniforms might be a bit of a giveaway."

"Still, it's odd," Jolla put in.

"It's an odd unit with an odd role," Valentine said. "Supply in enemy territory, acting as liaison with the local resistance."

Jolla brushed back nonexistent hair with his palm. "Yet from what I've seen, you're training your company like you're part of the hunter battalion."

"You don't object to fitness trials, I hope."

"We'll see what kind of men you have when the real training starts in January," Seng said. "I'll look forward to seeing what you can do."

The guns arrived a few days after the unpleasant meeting. It was hard not to be disappointed.

They viewed them from the back of the wagon rig, three cases of rifles and one of pistols. A trio of Uzi-style submachine guns were in with the pistols, evidently meant for the officers.

The rest were mostly militia stuff: deer rifles and shotguns and a few venerable AR-15s. In the hands of a company of veteran Wolves, it could be a deadly enough assortment, but he wondered if they'd be heavy, expensive noisemakers in the hands of some of the greener members of his company. It would make familiarization and training a nightmare.

Plus there would be supply difficulties, trying to get everything from buckshot to .358 to .30-06 to .223 into individual hands.

Patel's cane tapped behind and Valentine turned to see his sergeant major shake his head sadly as he lifted a double-barreled bird gun. "It's like telling the men they can't be trusted with anything better," he said.

Valentine thought a couple of the Remingtons might make decent sniper rifles, if they could find optics. He had at least six trained scout/snipers out of the Kurian services—they had an easier time sneaking away than most. A shotgun or two distributed to each squad would be handy for urban use. The rest, not much more than rabbit guns, would be better off in the hands of the UFR's young Camp Scouts or backwoods raccoon hunters.

There was nothing to do but hand them out.

"They've got to be kidding," one of the former Quislings in line said. Valentine recognized him as one of the men he'd seen training the militia back at Liberty.

"Mebbe these are just to carry for practice weight, like the shells," another said.

"We should take a trip over to the river patrol reserve armory between the Tennessee and the Mississippi. They don't hardly guard that. Get us some real guns."

Valentine dredged up that last man's name: Robbins—no, Rollings. "Private Rollings. What's that?"

"Sorry, sir."

"No, you're not in trouble. Come over here."

Rollings gave his pants a subtle hitch up as he approached, his sergeant falling in beside like a protective dog. "The major wants something?"

"What did you say about an armory?"

"You're not in any trouble, Rollings," his sergeant said.

Rollings kept his gaze on Valentine's feet. "River patrol armory and motor pool, sir. The old western Kentucky number four. We used to gas up there when I was with the River Road Light Artillery of the Tennessee Troop. It's a crap—err, CRP—um, that's Combined River Patrol, sir. Reserve armory and warehouse for patrol and artillery boats on the Tennessee, Ohio, and Mississippi. Creepy place. There's those flappy gargoyles quartered in town and nests of harpies in the hills up by the Ohio."

"Explain what you meant about unguarded."

The man gulped. "Not unguarded. There's usually six or seven men about. It's just that the armory's for the river patrol, so the Tennessee Troop, they don't see it as their job to garrison it. The river patrol figures that since it's inland, it's the Troop's job to secure it. Nobody wants to be stationed there, exactly, with the harpies in the hills and the gargoyles in the empty town. Not much to do but play cards and come up with better nose plugs."

Rollings had five more uncomfortable minutes as Valentine quizzed him about the roads in the area, the terrain, the location of KZ settlements. . . .

When he finished the poor private was sweating.

Valentine gripped him on the shoulder. "Thank you, Rollings. You're the kind of complainer I like."

Rollings' eyes finally came up. "How's that, sir?"

"The kind that offers a solution."

Five

The wilderness of eastern Kentucky, New Year's Eve, the Fifty-fourth Year of the Kurian Order: With the sun an orange-and-purple bruise along the western skyline, harpy country wakes up.

There's something odd about this particular Grog territory. Bird and animal life seems more furtive, the insects tougher and more numerous—even in the winter chill big black flies drone by like thrown pebbles. The kudzu on old utility poles and lines grows thick on every sunstruck prominence in a twisted-tendril game of king of the hill that dares you to contest its ownership. Thicker stands of wood have a bat-cave smell with nothing thriving in the shade but thistle and thorn and tree-hugging fungus looking like suppurating wounds.

The few highways cutting through harpy lands are barely open, the vegetation kept back only by big machines clawing through the pot-holed roads. The devastation from the New Madrid quake has never been repaired. Whole communities are nothing but heaps of rubble with a vine-covered wall or chimney still standing.

Binoculars just made the warehouse and truck yard look worse. In the dark from a distance, Valentine could see the armory was only three buildings, two of cinder block linked by a nicer brick office forming an uneven U lit at the doors by tired bulbs that looked like they wanted to surrender to the night. With the aid of the binoculars, Valentine's night eyes picked out peeling paint, the tires and blocks holding down plastic sheeting on the roofs, and the plywood nailed over the windows.

Patel and Hoboken, the youngest of Patel's Shepherds, looked at it with him.

The ad-hoc raid had come together as though it were a natural, expected event, like a birth. When Valentine proposed the operation at a scheduled meeting, he met initial resistance in the form of a frown and a shake of Colonel Seng's head, but Moytana and the Bear lieutenant Gamecock both came to assistance, claiming that their men were fretting, wanting either leave or an operation. They could have both by joining in the raid, as Hunters back from the KZ traditionally enjoyed at least a three-day pass, if not a twenty-one, in Southern Command's vernacular.

Valentine argued that the rest of the brigade might be reassured by a quick successful strike into the Kurian Zone and a return across the Mississippi, and Seng gave his approval.

Valentine turned in his written plan that very evening and started on the orders for the company the next morning.

As Rand organized transport, Valentine received an unexpected visitor. The Bear lieutenant knocked on the open door of the command shack. Dust fell from the ceiling and the spiders hunkered down in their webs.

"Morning, Major," Gamecock said. He had thick hair on the arms projecting from his sleeveless shirt, and wore the first legworm leather pants Valentine had seen since he lost his rig in Pacific Command. Most officers in Southern Command knew better than to lecture Bears on proper attire. He had an ear of roasted corn in hand and a flour sack over his shoulder. He gave Valentine a casual salute with the roasted ear as he looked around the command shack. "Okay to talk about the op?"

"In here," Valentine said. The command shack had a divider now, so Valentine enjoyed the luxury and status of a knothole-windowed office.

They went into the back room.

Gamecock finished off the roasted ear and tossed it in the wastebasket. The basket wobbled briefly. "Sorry about that, suh. Had to eat breakfast on foot this morning. This scheme of yours: You're going to be a Quisling Grog officer."

"Yes," Valentine said.

He tossed the flour sack on Valentine's table-desk. "I was going to trade this to a sorry excuse of a Guard captain for a case of Canadian scotch, but it's turning my stomach to see the guy who held at Big Rock walking around with an old single-shot militia rifle.

"Go on, suh," Gamecock said. "Got it off a Quisling lieutenant colonel with matching tooling on his belt, hat, and boots. Even dead, he looked like a show-night fag, but he knew his hardware."

Valentine extracted a gleaming submachine gun and a screw-on tube as long as the gun itself. It had odd lines; the barrel was pitched on a bias different from the frame. He picked it up and extended the handle just under the muzzle.

"That's an Atlanta buzzsaw," Gamecock said. "Model 18 Select entry model. Limited production run, elites and officers only. That cockeyed barrel's there for a purpose. The bolt's at an angle so recoil keeps the muzzle from climbing off target. Pretty accurate one handed, even on full auto. No selector switch—you can tap them out single shot with light pulls. Goin' over to full auto, you just pull the trigger all the way. She'll group under a meter at a hundred paces. That silencer there is something I rigged."

Valentine looked at the magazines—two short and four long—and the twenty- and forty-round boxes. "Nine millimeter Parabellum."

"I know—a little light for stopping a Reaper in full charge," Gamecock said. "I threw in some boxes of silverpoints. Team Fumarole's had good results with them. They don't flatten out against Reaper cloth so much."

"I don't suppose you've got any Quickwood bullets."

"We got a box of 7.62 for the whole team, suh. One lousy box. Production problems. Wish they'd tell me where the trees were. I'd make myself some friggin' stakes."

"I'll show you one personally when we get back. Assuming some farmer hasn't cut it down for tomato stakes. By the way, where's the accent from?"

"South Carolina born. First name's Scottie, suh."

"Val will do from now on, when things are less formal. Grateful to you, Scottie."

"Grateful to you, suh. My boys are ready to kill each other. Only three things will keep a Bear quiet if there's no fighting going on: sleeping, eating, and . . . well—"

"Screwing," Valentine finished. "Lieutenant Nail in the old Razors put it a little more colorfully."

"Any case, suh, we've all put on ten pounds and everyone's caught up on sack time. I got all I can do to keep the women and chickens round here safe."

Pizzaro at Rally Base greased the entire operation, even setting up an escort by a contingent of the "Skeeter Fleet," Southern Command's own force of low-draft vessels that were employed in riverine combat. The SF's airboats and fast motorboats weren't a match for the bigger, cannon-mounted craft of the Quisling river patrol, but they could cause enough trouble somewhere else to draw off the forces guarding one set of loops in the twisting Mississippi.

Valentine practiced entry drills with the Bears and ran short patrols with the Wolves, always taking a few of the company with him. It did a little for their confidence and it was good to see the men getting over some of their wariness when it came to the Bears. Most of the men thought Bears would just as soon kill a man as look at him, and the day might come when members of the company would have to guide a Bear team to a target.

Valentine expensed three hundred rounds training with the new gun while Bee worked on sawing off the barrels and smoothing down the stocks on the old shotguns she'd been converting to pistol grip. Valentine practiced changing magazines until he could do it without thinking about it. Then he cleaned the weapon and test fired a couple more rounds to make sure he didn't foul something up.

The Bears and most of the Wolves were employed in a strike at a collection of river patrol docks and blockhouses on Island Ten, while a short platoon of Valentine's company, escorted by a striking team of Wolves, made for the armory. The rest of his command remained at either side of the Mississippi under Rand, blowing up rubber boats and improvised rafts called "Ping-Pong ball miracles" in preparation for the trip back.

The trip across and the movement to the armory had gone off well, with the Skeeter Fleet bringing them across just before dawn on New Year's Eve, their camouflage-painted twin-outboard boats growling into the muddy Mississippi waters like dogs giving the angry warning that comes before the leap.

Valentine's picked team of twenty, Bee, and the Wolves paralleled the east-west highway heading into Mayfield, Kentucky, and then turned north into the Grog country, the Wolves out front and behind and flanking, continually restoring contact like sheepdogs with a flock.

They took advantage of a chilling rain to make good time down the road, which had deteriorated into a rutted trail. According to Rollings no one "who counted" lived up this way, in a region of low, sandy hills and scrub forest. River patrol supply trucks and Grog recruiters were all that used the roads meeting at the armory.

They rested, ate, and observed while the skies cleared and the sun went down. Valentine taped a thin commando dagger to his forearm—it never hurt to have something in reserve. After giving everyone inside a chance to get deep into REM sleep, Valentine decided the time was ripe.

He, Rollings, and Bee approached from the east down the tree-throttled road, three Wolves trailing through cover behind. Valentine carried his 18 Select in a battered leather courier pouch filled with a meaningless assortment of captured paperwork. Valentine smelled harpies on the cold wind blowing down from the northwest.

As they approached the gate, he slipped on the brass ring he'd won in Seattle. He didn't like to wear the thing.

"No Kurian towers around here, right?" he asked Rollings, nervous as he felt the warmth of the ring when it contacted his skin.

The armory had old-fashioned bars around it, linking cement columns. Valentine wondered if something more ostentatious had once stood on the other side of the fence. This was like garlanding a turd.

"No, sir. Well, none that I know about. Never went into the harpy woods, though, or met any Reapers on the river road that way. Is that what I think it is, Major?"

"Yes."

"You take it off a—"

"It's a long story."

A dog barked as they approached, a mud-splattered, hungry-looking thing that seemed to be a mix of a German shepherd and a long-haired camel. It jumped atop its shelter to better sound the alarm.

Behind its house was a line of trucks and a wrecker. The trucks looked rusted and worn, though they had hedge-cutting blades fixed below the front bumper and iron bars welded across the windshield and windows.

Valentine approached the buzz box on the post outside the gate and opened the dirty glass door covering the buttons.

"Anything here indicate there's more men here than usual?" Valentine asked.

"No, sir."

Rollings nodded and Valentine hit the button marked CALL.

When Valentine didn't get a response in ten seconds, he pressed again, long and hard, the way an impatient Quisling ringwearer would when he wasn't getting service to his liking.

It took a full minute for a crackly voice to answer.

"Yes?" the voice crackled through the tarnished, oil-smeared speaker.

"This is Colonel Sanity Marks, Combat Tech Service. I've got a wiring team broken down three miles west of here and I need transport. I'll require one of your trucks and a motorcycle for at least forty-eight hours."

"Tell it to the Coastal Marines, sapper."

Valentine raised his eyebrows to Rollings.

"Is Sergeant Nelson in there?" Rollings said.

"Who wants to know?"

"Tell him it's Rollings, late of the River Road Light. This colonel is steamed, I shit you not, and he's got a brass ring and a crapped-out truck full of guys with computers and fiberoptic line."

"Someone will be out in a moment."

Valentine snapped: "I had a harpy swoop overhead not five minutes ago. Get out here before the damn thing comes back and shits on me. I hate those fucking things."

A corporal and a private appeared, looking like they'd just yanked their uniform shirts off of hangers: The shoulders were riding ridged and high.

"Sir," the corporal said. "I'm going to need to see some orders and identification."

Valentine shoved his ring fist through the bars. "I've got a broken-down truck and a wiring team that's six hours late now. Get us the hell inside."

The corporal bussed the ring with his lips. Valentine had made the obeisance often enough during his sojourn as a Coastal Marine in the Gulf. On a ring belonging to the proper wearer, it gave off a slight tingle.

"Not the Grog," the corporal protested.

If he folded once, he'd fold again. Valentine turned his gaze to the silent armsman.

"Private, you want to speed things up for me? You can have this corporal's stripes. I think by the time I've written my evaluation, he won't need them anymore."

"Sir, no disrespect, but I'll get into more trouble by not following procedures than you could ever bring down."

"I wonder. You know anything about distributed secure networks?"

"Uh—no, sir."

Which was just as well. Valentine didn't know anything about them either. The corporal silently allowed the group inside.

"Gas up two trucks. Put batteries in or whatever you have to do to get them going."

"Thought you said—"

"I'm going to listen to the engines of both," Valentine said. "I'll take the truck that sounds healthier."

Valentine didn't wait for an answer and headed toward the main office door between the two bigger buildings. Bee trailed behind.

He opened the door and wiped his feet. Two men in undershirts were lacing boots up. There was a duty desk, a mail sorter, and a long bureau with an electric coffeepot and pieces of weaponry, lighting, and com gear wearing yellow toe tags atop it beneath silvery letters reading:

HAPPY NEW YEAR—LOOK ALIVE IN 'FIFTY-FIVE

"Where's Sergeant Nelson?"

"Celebrating in Paducah, sir."

"They're having fireworks," the other added, gaping at Bee. She sniffed the warm, stale air. Valentine smelled a grilled cheese sandwich and coffee.

"Rollings!" Valentine called over his shoulder. He used the opportunity to scan the little office. There was a sort of wooden loft above with a water tank and boxes of supplies. He had a moment's startle—a shadow above pointed at him with an accusing finger. . . .

It turned out to be a mannequin of a nude female with a feather boa.

"Right here, Major."

Valentine thought quickly. "That's 'Colonel,' son. I'm not your old CO. You keep forgetting."

"Sorry, Colonel."

"You know any of these fellas? Who's in charge?"

"That would be me," a gruff voice came from the doorway to what looked like a residence room. A sergeant with a beer gut partially covering a pistol belt stood in the doorway. "What's the emergency, Colonel?"

"Worse than you know, Sergeant," Valentine said. He reached into his attaché and began extracting paperwork and placing it on the duty desk. He took out the gun and pointed it at the NCO.

"I'm sorry to inform you all that you're my prisoners. Rollings, that's a nice-looking .45 the sergeant has on his belt. Relieve him of it."

Bee stiffened and drew her own shotguns from her waistband. "Watch the door, Bee. Door," Valentine said.

"Turn your backs, gentlemen, and place your hands on the back of your head, fingers interlaced. Kneel."

Valentine made sure they complied, listening for other sounds of life in the dark warehouse next door. Out in the motor yard, he heard a truck turn over. "Now, if you're cooperative for the next hour or so, you'll be taken prisoner and brought back to a Southern Command base. You'll be surprised how nice the day-release POW camps are. If you give us any trouble, I'll leave you tied here for the Reapers. Decision time."

*   *   *

Valentine called the other two in. They gaped at their comrades kneeling with faces to the wall.

"What's with all this?"

That was the kind of quality manpower that pulled duty on New Year's Eve. Only after Valentine prodded the corporal with his barrel did the Quisling realize what was going on. He made them the same offer he did the others.

They cooperated.

Valentine snipped the telephone wires, hoping that if it activated a trouble alarm, there wouldn't be enough New Year's staff to investigate right away. He set Rollings to work unscrewing the station's radio from the shelf at the com desk. They did a quick sweep of the building while the Wolves watched both ends of the road, and then started looking through the armory.

The river patrol had good gear, including rocket-propelled grenades that Corporal Glass looked over and selected. Valentine found a case of four Type 3s—that had been the weapon issued to his Razors by Solon, who'd evidently had a bigger budget than the river patrol. The small arms were a little disappointing, mostly cut-down versions of the venerable M16. On the other hand, there was a plentitude of small support machine guns that could be carried or fixed to a boat mount. Most of the weapons were packed in protective lubricant—it would take hours to clean them—so the platoon would have to get back with what they brought.

They ended up filling two truck trailers with boxes of weapons and ammunition and other assorted pieces of lethality, plus as much com gear and medicines as they could find. As Valentine and Patel supervised the loading, the assigned drivers checked the tires and tested the lights and horns on their vehicles.

The men rode in the beds of the camouflaged service trucks with the prisoners secured to floor bolts. They'd even liberated some walkie-talkies so the drivers could communicate with each other. Condensed and dehydrated foodstuffs and extra gear was piled in bags hanging off the back and strapped to the hoods.

They even took the dog. Valentine didn't mind; he liked dogs. Though it was heartbreaking if you had to eat them.

As they pulled out and bumped west, witch fingers of tree branches scratched the sides of the truck.

In the dark, with the roads potholed and washed out, they couldn't go much faster than a man could trot. Patel had the Wolves lope ahead and behind, scouting and checking for pursuit.

All that marked their departure was noise, and that only briefly. A siren started up from the armory as soon as they were out of sight.

"What you figure that signifies, Major?" the man at the wheel asked.

"We'll find out soon enough," Valentine said.

Valentine shifted the machine pistol to his lap and checked the soldier's rifle and the bandolier resting on the dash. He and this version of Southern Command's single shot breechloaders were old, conflicted friends dating back to his days in the Labor Regiment. It was a fine gun, accurate with stopping power sufficient to knock a Reaper off its feet, if you didn't mind having to reload every time you fired a round.

Valentine opened the glass panel between the cabin and the back of the truck.

"Someone ask our prisoners what that noise is," Valentine said over the truck's protesting suspension.

"Alarm, sir."

"Was there someone there they didn't tell us about?"

Valentine waited a moment while Patel asked a few questions.

"Could be a gargoyle, Major. They overfly the area all the time. One might have seen the trucks leave. Could be he flew down to investigate. Gargoyles are smarter than harpies."

They're also smart enough to guide in a few Reapers.

Valentine opened the truck door, checking that he wouldn't be swept off, or worse, by the branches ahead. He searched the night sky.

The glare of the following truck's headlights made it difficult to see.

"Kill the lights," Valentine said to his driver, dropping back into the cab.

"Pass back to the following truck: Kill the lights," Valentine said to Patel. Patel lifted a brand-new walkie-talkie from the armory and spoke into it.

With the lights out on the rear truck, Valentine tried again, ducking under a branch that snapped and snipped as it broke along the truck's side.

A shadow hung behind the trucks, following the road. A shadow that closed in on itself, thickening as it followed their vehicles.

Harpies. Dirty, flapping—

Valentine wondered what they were carrying, apart from ugly. He wondered if the theoretical gargoyle had sent them after the trucks. They had enough cunning to know something was wrong and that they'd be rewarded for stopping the trucks.

Fixated by the shadow, Valentine started to pick out individual wings and short, skinny bowlegs. A branch slapped him out of his trance, and he ducked back into the cabin.

"Harpies," Valentine said. "Pass the word. Honk and bring the Wolves in."

He hated those snaggletoothed bastards. A sort of cold clarity took over as he stifled the urge to get one in his hands and dismember it like a well-cooked chicken.

"We could stop under thick trees, Major."

"No, that'll just give them more time to figure something out. And let them aim."

Valentine looked at the bungees holding the cargo on the roof. He detached a couple of the S hooks and fitted them on to his vest and belt. Testing his grip, he exited the cab, closed the truck door, and hooked another bungee to the bars covering the passenger window.

"Stop a sec and pass me up the gun and bandolier," Valentine said. "And try to keep to the left."

As the truck ground into motion again, Valentine, now hanging on the outside with his foot on a fuel tank, found that the side-view mirror protected him from the bigger branches. All it did for the smaller ones was bend them back to give them a little more energy for a swat.

The Wolf scouts returned and perched on the hood and front hedge cutter. At a turn Valentine saw the following truck also had Wolves atop the driver's cab.

"Pass the word: Wait until I shoot," Valentine ordered.

The shadow broke into individual forms as it neared. Valentine searched the flock for the bigger, longer-legged form of a gargoyle. The harpies darted and zigzagged as they flew; it was how their bodies kept aloft. He placed his foresight on one hurrying to get ahead of the trucks. Its course was a crazy mix of ups and downs, backs and forths. . . . But between the frantic beats of the wings you could sometimes track them on a glide—

BLAM!

Valentine had been so used to firing guns equipped with flash suppressors he'd forgotten the white-yellow photoflash. And he'd forgotten just how hard you had to press into the stock to absorb the shock.

Valentine worked the lever and ejected the little thimble of the shell casing, his shoulder smarting with the old mule kick.

Missed.

The Wolf on the hood had a combat shotgun, a sensible weapon for brush fighting. He tracked one of harpies above and fired.

Valentine heard a high, inhuman scream.

Time to get down with the sickness.

The sickness. The shadow half. The monster.

Valentine had a few names for it, depending on his mood. He'd learned long ago that a part of him rejoiced in the death of his enemies and his own survival. Whether it was a character flaw or some piece of strange heritage passed down from his Bear father didn't matter. The awful exhilaration he felt when he killed, triumphed, made him wonder whether he wasn't even more deserving of destruction for the good of the world, like some rabid dog.

But for now the sickness had its uses.

Valentine, remembering his early years in the Wolves, made an effort to thank those left behind at the landings and hear their accounts.

He shouldered the gun. One was diving right at the truck. Its feet rubbed together and a plastic strip fell—it had armed some kind of grenade. BLAM!

Damn cranky gun.

Maybe he put a bullet through its wing and spoiled the dive. It flapped off to the left and dropped its explosive.

It detonated, orange and loud, in a stand of brush. Valentine wondered what the birds and critters residing in the undergrowth thought.

Don't get weird now, mate. Job at hand.

Valentine heard canvas tearing. The men in the bed of the truck were hacking off the truck-bed cover to better employ their guns.

Valentine aimed again, but a twiggy smack in the back of the head spoiled his shot.

"Four o'clock!"

A line of harpies were coming in, bright plastic grenade tabs fluttering as they pulled the arming pins. They were flapping hard, each bat form describing a crazy knuckleball course.

"There's a good straightaway ahead, sir," yelled the driver.

"Put on some speed," Valentine said.

He fired, and the men in the trucks fired, and when the orange ball of light cleared there was only one harpy left. It dropped the stick grenade on the road and flapped hard to gain altitude, but someone in the second truck brought it down.

Their luck was in. The device didn't go off.

Another line of harpies had gotten around the front.

"Twelve high!" the Wolf hanging off the brush cutter called.

Now the small, questing branches could whack him on the cheek and bridge of Valentine's nose. A good deal more painfully, as the truck had picked up speed.

He tasted his own blood and felt something sticky on his neck, but he didn't feel anything worse than a scratch or two.

The night smelled like blood, wet leaves, and rotten eggs.

Valentine reloaded as the harpies made their run. He could see their beady eyes reflecting red in the moonlight.

One of his soldiers in misty denim, a big man with bushy sideburns, let loose with a double-barrel, dropped the gun to someone below, and took up a pump action. Valentine aimed and fired. He watched his target plunge, falling loopily as a kite with a cut string, but suspected the man resting his aiming arm on the cab hood had downed the beastie.

The others dropped their explosives. Grenades bounced all over the road. The man hanging off the brush cutter disappeared into flash and smoke, but when they emerged again from the blasts he was still there, blackened and frazzled but evidently intact.

Valentine, with the thick fuzzy head and the muffled hearing of someone who'd been a little too near a blast, saw another harpy fall, brought down by the truck behind. The flock, perhaps not liking the punishment being handed out with little to show for it, turned and gathered to the east, doing a sort of whirling corkscrew aerial conference.

"Eyes on the road," Patel bellowed at the driver.

A pushed-over tree blocked the road.

The driver braked hard, and the truck jumped to a tune of squealing brakes. The Wolf on the front, evidently uninjured but stunned by the explosion, was thrown by the sudden braking, struck the trunk of the downed tree, and went heels-over-head onto the other side of the trunk.

Valentine, more or less secured by the bungees, lost nothing but his dignity as he saw himself swinging, holding on to the bars over the passenger window.

Patel was already out of the truck, running with a first aid kit.

Valentine saw a big, wide-winged shape flapping away low. He raised his gun, aimed, and fired at the big target.

The gargoyle lurched but kept flapping.

Valentine swore. The big, soft-nosed bullet should have brought it down. His old marksmanship trainer in the Labor Regiment had promised the kick in the shoulder was nothing to what the target experienced. He'd seen a round take a softball-sized chunk of flesh out of a wild pig. He must have just clipped it on a limb.

It disappeared behind a line of trees.

Valentine looked at the roadblock.

What kind of super-gargoyle could push over a tree? Nothing short of a Reaper could. Valentine looked at the tangle of old, weatherworn roots. The tree had been downed some time ago and moved off the road. The gargoyle had simply moved it back. Still, an incredible display of strength. Their flying arms were supposed to be powerful.

Worse, the harpies were heartened by the stationary trucks. They formed a new shadow, and then an arrow, pointed straight at the delayed trucks.

"Get that tree out of the way," Valentine shouted.

The men piled out of the trucks while the other Wolf helped Patel with the injured man.

"Faster," Valentine urged. He rose up so he could shout to the truck behind. "Second squad, deploy. Let's keep those bastards off us."

The men, with their varmint and bird guns mixed in with the militia rifles, spread out.

Valentine fired into the flying mass without picking out a target. Hitting with the wonky old rifle was purely a matter of chance.

"Watch each other's backs—there's more coming around from eight o'clock," Valentine shouted.

The rest began to pepper the harpies with careful shots. One pair, Rutherford and DuSable, shifted position to give better covering fire to the men working on clearing the fallen log. Valentine made a note of it—the noise and confusion of gunfire short-circuited some and they forgot the bigger picture. A flier spun down; another followed intentionally, coming to its aid. Perhaps they were a mated pair.

Valentine fired three more times quickly, and then jammed the gun. The ejector had torn off the heat-softened brass rim on the casing. He grabbed the hot barrel at the other end. The ornery weapon would be more lethal as a club anyway. Then he remembered his machine pistol.

He flipped open the stock and extended the foregrip. It did group tightly, and the harpies were closing.

The prisoners in the trucks began to yell. They'd been left handcuffed inside.

The harpies swooped over the vehicles, dropping grenades and plastic arming tabs. Valentine watched a grenade bounce under the truck, realized that the same bungees that kept him secured to the passenger door were keeping him from jumping off—

All he could do was wait for it. He fired a burst at a harpy coming straight for the cab, watched with satisfaction as the bullets tore it into a blood-rain of gory pieces.

The grenade went off but didn't sound much louder than an overstuffed firecracker. Other explosions rocked the second truck.

Valentine brought down another harpy, who'd suddenly appeared from behind a tree as though he'd popped into existence just to aim a leg claw at Valentine's throat. He reloaded, but the sky had cleared. The harpies had had enough at last and the flock was keeping low.

The soldiers moved the obstacle and got on their way again.

The front truck was leaking coolant, and a couple of the mechanically minded did a bird-droppings-and-bubblegum fix that slowed the leak. They had to stop and refill with water. They'd destroy the engine before recrossing the Mississippi anyway.

It got them to the landing.

The men were in admirably high spirits. The only serious injury they'd suffered was to the Wolf from the front truck, who'd broken a wrist, hurt a knee, and taken a piece of shrapnel to his calf, though one of the prisoners had an ugly gash in his scalp and another had torn his wrist open trying to get out of his handcuffs as the trucks were bombed.

The injured Wolf rode back to the landing, scratching the dog's ears in good humor despite his injuries.

At the landing Valentine was happy to let Rand take over.

"Far shore says river watchers report clear river," the man at the radio said. "We've got the okay to cross."

A pair of the Skeeter Fleet roared downriver.

Valentine's head felt thick and the old gunsmoke smell was getting nauseating. "Get the swag loaded and the men on the boats and rafts. And—"

There it was. The cold spot on his mind, a bit of ball lightning lurking in the thick river woods, raising the hairs on the back of his head. *Reaper!*

"And, sir?" Rand asked.

"And I'm going back up the road a bit to make sure there's no pursuit."

Rand pushed the glasses back up on his nose and nodded. "Ten, fifteen minutes at most, sir."

"Patel. Hoboken."

They trotted over, Patel solemn at the tone in his voice.

"Hood," Valentine said, using Southern Command slang for a Reaper.

They took the news like experienced Wolves. Concern but not panic. Hoboken put his hand on the big parang at his waist.

It was back along the road away, somewhere at the top of the riverbank. It might just be watching, waiting for someone to trot off into the bushes to take a crap. Sure, it could wade into them and do a lot of damage, but how many dead pawns would make the Kurian controlling it think the sacrifice worth the loss of his knight?

But who knew what might be rushing to its aid.

Valentine and the Wolves slipped off into the brush, spread out by a few meters, preventing the Reaper from taking two at once if it decided to fall on them.

"Lifesign down," Valentine said.

Reapers hunted by seeking the emotional signal given off by intelligent minds. The Hunters had spent a good deal of time in mental training, learning to meditate their lifesign down until it was like background radiation.

Problem was, it was hard to forget that you were on the wrong bank of the river, with your friends about to leave, and a walking death machine lurking, probably as fast and strong as all three of you put together. At night Reapers were at the height of their lifesign-sensing powers. He hoped this one was concentrating on the throng at the riverbank.

Valentine quietly removed the stiletto from his forearm. If it grabbed him, he might get it through the eye or ear or jaw as it snapped his spine or tore into him with its foot-plus long, flanged tongue.

Purely a matter of chance which man it would target, but Valentine took the middle. A smart Reaper might strike there, hoping that the others at either wing would shoot at each other in the confusion.

They took turns walking, one going forward while the other two covered, the men behind giving soft clicks of the tongue when the first man could no longer be covered.

Something was wrong—the location. . . . Valentine cast about like a dog in a swirling breeze. No, it was to the side, too high.

He froze, gave a signal for the others to keep still as well.

Jesus, Mary, and Joseph—

It was up a tree, resting on a flattish branch above a deadfall that gave it a good view of the river and landing. But the silhouette was all wrong—the pelvis and lower limbs were turned around, like a bird's. The limbs were thin. Valentine had seen starvation cases that looked fat compared to this Reaper's limbs. Leathery wings like a bat's extended from overlarge arms and oversized fingers, now flaccid and hanging like a child playing superhero with a sheet pinned to his back and clutched at the fists.

A backswept forehead had a little plume of stiff hair to it, like a centurion's helmet.

Valentine must have startled, misstepped. The long, backswept face turned and cocked, just like a robin listening for a worm.

The eyes, the color of a dying sun, were cold and familiar.

Valentine shouldered the 18 Select and it launched itself off the branch with a spring of its rear limbs. A short, forked tail had more webbing leading to the legs. The thing could maneuver like a duck. It turned and Valentine loosed a burst.

It disappeared into the trees. Valentine got a glimpse of elongated ostrich toes as it disappeared. He hardened his ears and heard branches snapping.

"What the blue hell was that?" Patel asked, coming forward at a crouch. He scanned the branches above, as if fearing nests filled with little chirping Reapers.

"I don't want to wait to find out. Back to the landing."

Valentine's head wanted to disappear between his shoulders, turtlelike, the whole way back. It was far too easy to imagine the avian Reaper—if it was a Reaper—reaching down and knocking his head off with one of those slender legs like a perched cat swatting at a ball of string.

The men had fun stripping and destroying the trucks. They'd even used a tree limb to winch out one of the diesels. Patel made some flatbread on a greasy skillet while the strike platoon rested and let Rand's team do their jobs filling the boats. Valentine rode back on the ricketiest-looking raft, leaning against stacks of tires and boxes filled with headlights and radio gear as he watched the old houseboat's pontoons and netted masses of Ping-Pong balls scrape and roll through the water.

He could hear firing from downriver, a *kak-kak-kash* of small cannon that reminded him of the old *Thunderbolt*'s Oerlikon. He watched signal flares fired from the friendly shore, and a boat roared by with the last of the Wolf rear guard.

The sky was already pinkening.

Some of his men gathered at the far end of the boat, watching the hostile shore recede. As Valentine watched the southern half of the mighty river in the direction of the firing, he listened in on a member of his strike platoon and a member of the landing detail talking to a rafter as they were towed back across the Mississippi:

"The major is the coolest sonofabitch under fire I've ever seen, I'm here to tell. The bat-bastards came in and he stood up on the truck, just picking them off while grenades dropped all around."

"They can't train guts into you," another agreed. "He's tough."

Well, you can bungee yourself up so you can't run too.

Valentine was too pleased to correct them; besides, the shaggy hound had decided to hop up on the piled tires and deploy a rasping tongue on the cuts and scrapes courtesy of the Kentucky roadside growth.

All in all, it was a successful operation. A sniper had killed one of Moytana's Wolves and a Bear was missing in action. He'd last been seen roaring down after a blood trail in the assault on the river patrol docks. Gamecock was hopeful he'd wander back into camp in a week or so once he sniffed out a method to get back across the river.

The worst losses had been suffered by the Skeeter Fleet: A motorboat with three men had blown up during a riverine duel with river patrol craft. Their pictures had already gone up on the memorial wall at Backwater Pete's, a bar up the Arkansas River near the Skeeter Fleet general headquarters.

That was the hateful side of the Cause. A chance conversation leading to an opportunity to hit the enemy where he wouldn't expect. And at the end of it, when the excitement was over and the ineffable, afteraction halo faded, came the bill. All because he did his duty.

But his duty was also to turn this assortment of experienced soldiers (and the odd ex-sailor; he had two floaters in with his fighters) into a cohesive unit, to know which pieces functioned in what way under stress. They'd been over the river and back again together, in spirit, even if everybody hadn't crossed the Mississippi.

Now he had a team.

At the debriefing back at Camp Highbeam, the only person unhappy about the raid was Brother Mark. He looked strained and pale in the fluorescent lighting of the camp classroom that doubled as a conference room. He'd been out on one of his contact trips, negotiating with legworm ranchers, the resistance, and who knew what else.

"There is a plan, you know," Brother Mark said after asking questions about exactly where the fighting had taken place. "We don't need to be jamming sticks into the hornet's nest, stirring them up."

Valentine was a little dissatisfied too, when he told the story about the flying Reaper.

"Sure it wasn't just a real skinny gargoyle?" Captain Moytana asked. He'd written the letter about the dead Wolf and posted it to his folks that morning.

"I'll send a message to the Miskatonic about it," Valentine told the faces around the conference table. "I don't suppose there's a good artist somewhere in the brigade."

"One more matter," Colonel Seng said, his wide catfish face graver than usual. "The usual after-action leaves will not take place. I wish to intensify training. The whole camp is going to start route-marching exercises and war games. The orders and scheduling will be on your desks within two days."

Gamecock groaned. "My Bears expect their due."

"They're not your Bears, Lieutenant," Seng said. "They're Southern Command's. They'll get their chance at a short leave. So will all of you. This operation may begin sooner than anyone dreams."

Valentine intercepted Brother Mark as the meeting broke up. It was easy; he wasn't a popular man. Valentine didn't know if it was his fussy manner of speaking or the resentment of soldiers who had to work with a civilian's eye on them.

"Excuse me, sir," Valentine said. "Were you just with the rebels in the Virginias?"

"I can't tell you that, son."

"You've been there, though. You've told us that much."

"Yes," Brother Mark said, wary.

"Have you seen the Grog that's supposed to be with them? Leading them?"

"I don't know about leading. They definitely listen to him. He's sort of a mascot or good luck charm. They always perk up when he's around."

"What's he like?" Valentine asked.

"I suspect you know. I was briefed on your trip through Kentucky. Big. Leaner and less stooped-over than those thick-hides with the fangs. He can speak too. I've never met a Grog who can do that."

"The last time you saw him, was he well?" Valentine asked. Brother Mark should be able to answer that.

"Healthy as a horse. They call him the Uncle, by the way. I just remembered that. He's scarred, but the injuries are healed. Does that put your mind at ease?"

"You've— I'm very happy to hear that, sir. Thank you."

"Happy. I remember that. I'm jealous, son. Excuse me, I must attend to the colonel. Be true."

He turned away, hurrying to catch up to Colonel Seng, ending the conversation.

The brigade made practice marches interspersed with combat training. Jolla's command, including Valentine's company, was often matched against the rest of the brigade.

After one of these skirmishes, the Guard lieutenant colonel Gage sat Valentine in his command car, a beat-up old Humvee with an oversized bed and extra brackets that allowed it to double as an ambulance.

"Goddamit, Major, our boys are supposed to win. How are they supposed to build confidence when your glorified chicken wranglers burn a couple dozen of them?"

"Tell your junior officers that just because an area's been checked for mines, it doesn't mean I can't go back and replant after they've passed through," Valentine said. "My orders were to delay your march on Red Ridge."

Valentine wanted to add that if Daniels would keep his companies in closer contact, Valentine wouldn't have had time to mine their road, but that would be presumptuous.

"You could act a little more like Quislings. They always fall back in the face of superior numbers. They don't hunker down and let the first wave get past."

"I know, sir," Valentine said.

Gage cooled down. He'd obviously just been chewed on by Seng, who was pushing the brigade like a madman. "They still calling your guys the shit detail?"

"I haven't heard it in a while," Valentine said.

"Got to hand it to you, though. After the last time getting at those Grogs of yours with the auto 50s, everyone figured we hadn't run into your boys yet because they hadn't started sniping. Weren't you staff at one time?"

"Supposed to be. An old ghost caught up to me and I never made it."

"Sorry to boil up on you like that. I'm glad you'll be on our side when we march up-country."

As January turned to February, a big duffel bag arrived, labels and identifying inking scrawled all over it. It turned out to be all the way from Pacific Command.

Valentine read the letter in the waterproof courier pouch stitched onto the canvas:

Valentine,

After many wanderings your goods surfaced and I became aware of their existence. I promptly inventoried and dispatched them to Denver, courtesy of a liaison, and I'm confident they'll make it to Southern Command before too many more months pass.

Been seeing a lot of your friend Gide. She's got a mouth on her but she's turning into a dead shot witch of the woods. They're talking about putting me into GHQ up here and if that happens I might see about a ring for the end of those snake tattoos. She lost three toes and a chunk of buttock to a mortar round, so she's off the A-active list but is recovering nicely. She sends a kiss and wants to know if you're still musky. I won't be ungentlemanly and speculate.

Please accept your property with my compliments and apologies for the delay. What the hell is that thick leathery material, anyway? If you've got any to spare I'd like some for a jacket.

Yours in the Cause,
J. LeHavre, Colonel, Pacific Command

His old legworm leathers, gear, and sword had been wrapped up in a waterproof, but someone had made off with his boots either before it was turned over to LeHavre or along the road. Valentine wished their new owner's feet well.

The thief, if there had been a thief, missed a stiffened cuirass of cross-grained Reaper cloth, light and breathable and yet strong enough to stop a rifle round.

He looked at the sword. Some craftsman had put a new sharkskin grip on it—at least he thought it was sharkskin; it might have been roughed up big mouth—which was just as well as the old woven one had been getting ragged and bloodstained. He looked closer. There was a tiny little G inked just under the hilt cap next to the stitching. Now that he knew what to look for, he found a similar initial stitched just inside one of the interior side's many map pockets.

Nice to have a souvenir of his best memories of the Cascades.

Valentine noticed that she hadn't returned the old Steyr Scout. He didn't regret it—she'd probably make better use of it than he could.

With the company full up and the training proceeding as planned, Valentine found more time to study Seng's texts and notes from his term at the staff school. Seng was generous with his own time, translating cryptic notes if nothing else. Seng's graduation thesis, filling an entire binder, was on Winston Churchill when Britain was fighting alone during the dark years between the fall of France and Operation Barbarossa, when Germany launched her fatal attack on Soviet Russia. Valentine found the Seng thesis more interesting and readable than many of the historians he'd read in Father Max's old library.

He still felt his company lacked a certain spark of initiative that Southern Command's soldiers seemed to be born with. Or perhaps Valentine, with more experience in picked commands, was used to building a unit with a better grade of materials. Their instinct was to hand every problem up rather than improvise a solution and then report.

He took to sending out small units with simple tasks—find a backpack he'd placed in a ravine without being spotted by pickets—and then change their orders at the last moment and kill all radio communications. He and Patel would then lead a couple squads in a mock pursuit.

If they weren't bred to think on their feet, he'd train it into them.

The bright spot in the shakedown was Glass' improvement. He knew the men joked that in Ford and Chevy, Glass finally had some friends who shared his taste for communicating mostly in grunts. Glass wanted to try them out with grenade launchers or the new, ultralight knee mortars from a Southern Command inventor.

Valentine allowed himself one luxury (other than the occasional long shower with his gift soaps): He taught Bee to shine his shoes and polish his belt buckle and name tag on his A uniform. Bee was feminine enough to like things pretty, though he occasionally had to take the woven daisy chains of wildflowers off his pack or remove the mini-bouquets peeking out the gutter at the bottom of his pistol holster. Some of the other officers in the brigade asked him how he classified her—adjutant, aide, or spouse—but Bee's elephantine grace and gentility gave her a charm that assured her a constant stream of sweets and ribbons from officers "just passing through the trader stalls and thought she'd like this."

He'd even heard the Command sergeant major, the senior NCO for the brigade, refer to her as their "big beauty." She'd come a long way in the men's opinion since her arrival in a tutu.

For relaxation he played chess with Rand. Rand won most of the time. He was such a talented, cold player that Valentine wondered if he made intentional mistakes out of curiosity to see what his CO would do when presented with an opportunity, just to give his brain a new set of data points and challenges. Rand apparently never let anyone behind the shield of his professionalism, even when they chatted after their chess games about the progress of the company.

They weren't close, but he was as fine a junior officer as Valentine could ever want.

Then came the spring storms. The camp began to buzz. As usual, the men had somehow picked up that something was about to happen and soon, days before Valentine got his orders to report to a final briefing.

The camp grapevine proved to be right. All future leaves were canceled, the day trips into town ended, and last-minute munitions arrived, including a small supply of Quickwood bullets.

With the gear, the important men and women who came equipped with bodyguards, advisers, secretaries, and drivers began to arrive the next day. Valentine gave the same status report for his company three times in one day.

It would have been four but General Lehman cut him off as Valentine spoke to him in the base officers' club that never really got going. The dusty chairs, old movie posters, and license plates from the states making up the UFR all looked like they wanted to be put out of their misery.

"Javelin's under step-off orders, Major. Any reason your men can't go with it?"

"No, General."

"Heard good things about you. Gage says your men have been giving him hell playing OPFOR."

"That's kind of him, General."

"Not sure I like you training Grogs though. Sniffer dogs have their purposes, but you don't want them juggling grenades." He stopped, waiting for an answer.

"Of course not, sir."

An aide appeared and handed Lehman a flimsy. Lehman excused himself, scanned it, and nodded his head yes as he handed it back.

"They'll add a bit of verisimilitude to the, what is it, technical crew your men are supposed to look like."

"That's the idea, sir."

"A good one. Yours?"

"No, one of the Liberty recruits'. She's company clerk now."

"I don't trust ex-Quislings much farther than I can throw them. They caused us a lot of trouble before. Hope it works out for you. See you at the briefing tonight, Valentine. Dismissed."

The briefing, held in the guarded mess hall and using chairs begged and borrowed from every headquarters tent in the brigade, was mercifully brief. Which was just as well; the blackout curtains killed airflow as well as light. More than a hundred bodies burned a lot of calories over a couple hours. The tent quickly became stuffy.

Lehman opened it with a few words about how javelins were used in ancient warfare to strike troops behind the front ranks. Lambert and Sime and a few new faces were there, politicians most likely. In the throng of uniformed aides and assistants stood one man in hunting gear who took a lot of notes and a few pictures. Valentine guessed he was from the *Battle Cry*, Southern Command's military newspaper.

Conspicuously absent, at least to Valentine, were Brother Mark and Moytana's senior Wolf lieutenant. Rumor had it they were already in the Kurian Zone, somewhere north of Memphis.

What combination of diplomacy and guerrilla havoc might be already under way? If Valentine had had his choice of assignments for this operation, he would have been with them as well. But support and logistics would be critical in an operation this far from Southern Command's bases.

Seng gave some final instructions for the movement to Rally Base, the terminus for the operation's communications with GHQ and what would one day, hopefully, be a routing station for troops staging trips to or back from the new Freehold on the northern Cumberland Plateau and Appalachians.

The campaign map had a few new notations. Three Cats had been dispatched to Kentucky, spaced out along their line of march. Logistics Commandos had infiltrated in behind the Cats. Valentine wondered what they'd been told about Highbeam, or Javelin, or whatever false information they'd been fed in case of capture.

Lambert look strained. But she collected her old briskness for a few words to the assembled officers.

"Yes, this operation is a risk," she said. The junior officers and senior NCOs had just found out their true destination from Colonel Seng. The news was still sinking in.

"But the coal country of Virginia, and the legworms of Kentucky, are both key to the Kurian Order. Civilization needs electricity and the people living in that civilization need protein."

For a moment Valentine thought he was back in the Cascades, where denial of resources had meant grisly strategies involving civilian bodies stacked like cordwood, while Adler carried out his war against Seattle. He envied the men around him for a moment. To them, Lambert's words were just military jargon.

"They'll hit back hard when they figure out what you're doing. But if you can win that fight, it'll put cracks in the foundation of every Kurian tower east of the Mississippi. Remember that. Remember, also, that you're not alone, even in the darkest valley of fear. The people across the Mississippi hate the Kurians just as much as we do; they just don't get a chance to do anything about it. Is Javelin Brigade up for this challenge?"

Variations of "Sir," "Yes," and fighting yips broke out in the cafeteria.

"Send 'em back to hell," General Lehman said.

With that, the meeting adjourned, though Seng somewhat killed the theatrical mood by announcing a new series of meetings starting before breakfast the next day.

The columns marched out of camp in a drizzle. Valentine rode, but he stopped his horse across from the gate to admire the rare sight of Southern Command forces marching in step, swinging their arms in time, rifles over their shoulders.

"Good luck in Louisiana," someone called. Valentine wondered if he was a plant or just a camp civilian employee who'd picked up the rumor that they were heading south.

The general's color guard was present for the occasion. The pipes and drum set up a merry tune. Valentine thought it might be the hoary old sports perennial "Who Let the Bears Out?"—a favorite at basketball games.

110 *Fall with Honor*

"Next stop, New Orleans, Major," Rand called to him as his company wheeled to head south down the highway. He'd been coached to say it, and it sounded forced. Whatever his other strengths, Rand couldn't dissemble.

Valentine nudged his horse forward and took his place in the column at the head of his company. Their strange un-uniforms stood out so they marched at the rear, among the wagons, trucks, cook vans, and pack animals.

"That's a nice mule, mister," a woman's voice called from the crowd as Valentine walked the Morgan on the Malden road. Valentine recognized the voice.

He searched the crowd.

"Molly!"

It was her. Valentine saw a tan, full-lipped face. Her blond hair shone even in the blustery spring gloom. She'd made an effort with her face and eyes.

He hadn't seen her in four years. The emotional rush almost unseated him from the Morgan.

They'd once been intimate—no, that wasn't fair, they'd once been lovers and passable friends. He'd met her on a long courier mission to the Great Lakes, when her family had helped an injured comrade of his. He'd extracted her family from the Kurian Zone, and Molly as well, by a near miracle after she'd been arrested for the murder of an important Illinois mouthpiece. She'd become engaged to a Guard while he was in the Wolves.

Edward stood next to her in what Valentine guessed was his only pair of long pants, judging from the state of the knees. His dark, cowlick-filled hair looked like it had waged a morning-long guerrilla war against its combing. How old was he now? Six?

He'd lost his father before he'd been born, in Consul Solon's invasion. Graf Stockard was one of thousands missing in action from the "old" Ozark Free Territory.

Valentine turned his horse and got it out of the way of the marching column. Engines blatted and wheels creaked on by. He dismounted swiftly and Molly gave him a friendly hug.

"What in the world—"

"It's a long story," she said. "We made a special trip to see you off, Edward and I."

Molly had a small cap stuck in the belt of her overcoat. Valentine lifted it and checked the insignia.

"I purchase horses for Southern Command now. Do you remember

Captain Valdez from Quapaw? He got me a job as a wrangler for the equine department at Selection and Purchase. I got promoted last year." She patted the Morgan's nose. "I might even have bought your mount. It's about the right age and from Half-Day Farms."

"Raccoon's a good horse," Valentine said. "I don't understand. You found me through Logistics?"

"Oh, no. I was worried about you, after—after that business where you were . . ."

Her eyes had lines at the edges. But then she spent a lot of time outside. Up close, the blond hair looked a trifle brittle. She hadn't had an easy time of it either, raising a son on her own.

"Arrested," Valentine said, coming back to the road.

Edward seemed fascinated with the butt of Valentine's .45. His eyes hardly left it.

"I wrote a letter. I wanted to know about your trial. It took forever to get an answer. A junior secretary in civil affairs, a very nice corporal named Dots. I guess she saw it in a pile and she wrote an answer. It's those long-service corporals who are always nicest to work with, I find."

Valentine would have introduced her to Glass if he had the time. He reminded himself to add a private message to Lambert on his first report.

"I'll have to thank Corporal Dots. I—it's nice to have someone see you off."

"She sent me a quickie a week ago, saying that your unit was moving out. I wondered that she kept track of you. I bet she's got a bit of a crush on you. She said you had a very handsome file photo."

Valentine saw her eyes flit to his scar and then his jawline. "Must have been an old photo."

She hooked her cheek with her index finger and showed a missing molar. "The years haven't been kind to either of us."

"You could get that fixed."

"Thought about it. But I stick my pencil there when I'm testing horses."

"Good luck, Daddy," Edward said.

Molly grabbed him at the shoulder. "Edward! We talked about this."

Raccoon seemed to sway first one way, then another, as Valentine used the horse's neck to hold himself up. "What?" he thought he said. Maybe it was just a choked exclamation.

Edward went wide-eyed in recognition of his own wrongdoing.

"You can't break promises like that," Molly continued. She looked to her left. "Mrs. Long, can you make sure he doesn't run under a truck?"

Mrs. Long looked like she wanted to hear the rest of the conversation. "Yes'm," she said. She gave Valentine a dirty look as Molly pulled him away.

"Edward, do me a favor, watch my horse," Valentine said, passing the reins to the boy.

They dodged between trucks and made it to the other side of the road, just missing Tiddle roaring along the column on his dirt bike. A soldier with a clipboard near the gate gave Valentine a curious look but didn't move to intervene.

They got out of the way of traffic and stood under a yew.

"David—" she said, hard and quiet. "I'm so sorry about that. I've been stupid."

"Molly—it's not possible."

"Of course it's not possible. David, there's so much you don't know. About Edward's father."

Obviously there was, if Molly wasn't willing to call him her husband. . . .

"Molly, it's not my business. But how?"

"I told you, I was stupid," she repeated. "I . . . I didn't show you when you visited that time, but I've got a drawer with some pictures of you. That old scarf of yours you gave me that winter in Minnesota. Two paper clippings too, one showing you getting a decoration, or was it a promotion? It was while you were fighting in Texas. I keep the letters from you in there too. It's not like a shrine or anything. I've just always wanted you to do well with your Cause."

"I still don't see the stupid part," Valentine said.

"Edward got to the age where he got snoopy. He was poking around in the drawer and saw all the stuff they'd written about you. He said he remembered you being at our house, God knows how."

"He called me his father," Valentine said.

"Yes. I don't keep pictures of his father around the house. I thought, *What'll it hurt if I shave the truth a little?* If things had fallen together a little differently, you might have been."

Valentine, who'd calmly given orders with the gigantic shells of a massive Grog cannon called the Crocodile making the earth ripple beneath his feet, stood dumbstruck.

"Oh, it doesn't matter anymore." She wiped the corners of her eyes.

"Here," she said, passing him a packet extracted from her overcoat. "Three chamois. They're the best Texas kid I could find. I embroidered your initials into the corner. Not like my mom could do, but I did my best. You can use them for your boots or guns."

Valentine didn't know what to give her. The only piece of jewelry he owned was that brass ring acquired from Seattle. "Molly, I—"

"Sorry about Edward. I can tell him the truth."

"You know my name's under something of a cloud, officially."

"Yes. I had this reporter ask me about you, by the way. I wonder how he got my name."

"A reporter?"

"For the *Clarion*. His name's Qwait. Ever met him?"

The column had finally passed. Valentine felt the eyes of the small crowd who'd turned out in the rain focus on them. "No. It's not important. I'll leave Edward to your judgment. I'm honored, in a way." He paused. "I need to catch up to my men. I'll write you, if I get back."

"When you get back," she said. "You won in Texas. You'll do the same in Louisiana—or wherever you're really going."

Molly always was smart, or maybe just sensitive to lies.

He trotted back across the road and retrieved his horse.

"I'm sorry, Momma," Edward said.

"Edward, there's nothing for you to be sorry about. I should be saying sorry to you."

Mrs. Long stepped back, staring at him as though wishing to shorten him by at least the length of his shins.

Valentine wondered what he could leave Edward with. He opened a shirt pocket and took out his battered old compass.

"Edward, do you know what this is?" he asked.

"An officer compass."

"An officer's compass, yes. With one of these and a good map, you're never lost." He handed it to the boy and mounted.

"Thank you, Father," Edward said, wide-eyed again.

"He's got your hair," Mrs. Long said, approving for a change.

Molly tightened his girth. "You're good, Major," she said.

"Good God, man, kiss her good-bye," Mrs. Long huffed. "What's this world coming to?"

Molly blushed. Valentine had never kissed a woman from saddle-back before. It wasn't as easy as it looked in the movies; he almost fell on top of her.

"Uh. Thanks," Molly squeaked.

Valentine rode on in the tangled tracks of the column, trying to catch up. He passed a member of the general's color guard dumping rainwater out of his drumhead.

Irony. That's what it was. He had a daughter in the Caribbean who thought he was an uncle, and a son in St. Louis that ninety-nine out of a hundred would insist was an abomination and demand to be destroyed. Now this tousle-haired boy was calling him Daddy. Or Father, when he remembered his manners.

God is just, but that doesn't mean he lacks humor, Father Max used to say.

"Amen," Valentine muttered, clicking his horse into a trot.

Six

Breakthrough, western Tennessee, March: Operation Javelin and Colonel (later General) Seng's march to the Virginias, later to be studied and debated—turning point or footnote?—with good arguments on both sides, began with a masterstroke.

The thousand-foot Kurian tower at Mississippi Point had stood for two generations. Every now and then Southern Command would bring some heavy artillery forward and shell it for an hour or so, just to see the light show as mysterious rippling bands of violet rose and detonated the shells a mile from target. The scientists from the Miskatonic attending these shows tried to study the effect with their poor collection of instruments but always left flummoxed.

The Kurian in that tower controlling the Mississippi between Memphis and Paducah is called "the Goober-maker." Even the best Hunter, sneaking into the woods around that tower, slowly becomes confused and disoriented. The more cautious, or maybe luckier, stagger away, underwear sometimes loaded like a sopping, sagging diaper, wondering what their name is. Most recover their sensibilities and memory eventually.

The Miskatonic consider the Goobermaker a powerful Kurian, feudal lord to sub-Kurians stretching from the outskirts of Nashville to Memphis and into southwestern Kentucky. He makes claim to the river as well, extracting tolls for water traffic, and ever more exorbitant fees in auras for cargo cutting across his territory to the Ohio or the Tennessee when Southern Command gets the upper hand against the gunboats of the river patrol.

David Valentine always chuckled and dismissed his participation in the assault as being "on the bench—when I wasn't sitting in the bus with my helmet."

*   *   *

"Are you fucking kidding me?" Glass said on his return from the ammo dump with the last boxes of brass, lead, and smokeless powder for the .50s.

"'Are you fucking kidding me, sir,' Corporal," Valentine corrected. "You'll follow orders, just like me. No matter how ridiculous."

It was the last week of February and spring peeped through the twigs and breaks in the iron gray clouds as a bitterly cold storm blowing in from Canada exhausted itself somewhere over southern Missouri.

Their assault barge yawned before them at the end of a boarding plank. It was a Kurian transport for aura fodder, and someone had painted the inside a soothing pink. It looked like a giant mouth extending a sickly, rusted tongue held down by a twelve-foot depressor.

Valentine smelled of sandalwood. He'd treated himself to a long shower to relieve the jump-off tension.

He looked out at his company through the Halloween mask rubberbanded across his face. The soldiers looked like a bunch of burned matches, with tinfoil wrapped around their head except for eyeholes.

Glass submitted to having tinfoil wrapped around his head and spray-painted dull black. Patel helped him poke eyeholes and breathing apertures in it.

"At least it's warm," Glass muttered. His heavy-weapons Grogs already had their masks on. Some artiste in the company had formed tinfoil strands into horns on the Grogs' heads.

"Hey, Sergeant Major," a soldier called. "Shiny side out, remember? Glass's grouchy enough without getting brain bake."

"It doesn't matter," Patel said, securing Glass's headpiece with a rubber band at the forehead.

It wasn't a very good joke, but Valentine was relieved to hear it. The men smelled nervous, that sharp electric acid odor of anxiety.

Word had filtered up through the NCOs that some of the men were remembering what happened to Quislings caught fighting for Southern Command. The Kurians developed imaginative and painful manners of extracting auras from those guilty of such treasons.

Every Southern Command soldier knew that, if captured, they could probably expect to be shuttled to some work camp or other—they were young and fit, after all. Officers could expect a good deal of interrogation. Leading figures of the resistance, majors, colonels, and especially generals could expect a long period of wear and tear under drugs or blunter instruments before the inevitable show trial. Valentine could never find it in himself to condemn those captured in the Kurian Zone who confessed to plans ranging from blowing up hospitals to poisoning

Youth Vanguard bake-sale cookies, because the confession was un-doubtedly forced and false.

"We're ordered to load, sir," Preville said. Preville was a near-sighted company com tech with an old Motorola headset wired to the pack radio. He made do with some old round glass women's frames that didn't do much for his face. Valentine, through Rand, had insisted that he see a Southern Command doc and get some regulation glasses, but Preville liked how he looked in his lenses. The new ones hadn't shown up in time anyway.

Patel had overheard, so all Valentine had to do was nod.

"Load up and board! Load up and board!" Patel bellowed.

Word had it that General Lehman was watching the embarkation, going from formation to formation giving a last few words of encour-agement. He hadn't made it to Valentine's group.

Odd-looking and inhuman in the painted tinfoil that obscured hair and ears, they filed into the barge.

"Enjoy, guys," Valentine said. "This'll be the easiest part of the whole trip."

With Ediyak, the company clerk, and Preville trailing behind, Val-entine boarded. "Last on gets to be first on the Kurian shore," he said.

The Skeeter Fleet and Logistics Commandos who'd arranged for the barges had chalked all sorts of helpful messages on the inside. Val-entine could see two:

THANK YOU FOR CHOOSING
MUDSKIPPER CRUISE LINES
WE ACCEPT RESPONSIBILITY FOR NOTHING
BUT GETTING YOU OVER AND
HAULING YOUR BODY BACK

and

TETANUS SHOTS ARE RECOMMENDED
FOR ALL PASSENGERS

When the recently constructed loading doors closed, Valentine saw another.

NO POINT WORRYING ABOUT IT NOW

A single overworked tug, a temporary buoy, and various lines from smaller craft working together got them across, with some help from the Mississippi current. Someone discovered that knife hilts made decent drumsticks on the barge's side, and soon there were two dueling syncopations.

Bee stamped out a pretty good 4/4 base beat as she hung on to the drooping camouflage netting hanging across the open top of the barge.

Valentine wondered what the sentries on the other side of the river made of it all. A couple of sentries would get their sergeant, who would get an officer, who would probably call in an even higher officer, who would give the alarm.

This part of the operation was secret enough that even Valentine knew only the outline. His only orders were to get in column with the rest of Jolla's command and move out to the northeast along an old highway.

They splashed ashore in darkness, fiddling and adjusting the tinfoil headdresses as they waded in the slough between two sandbars, heading for blue signal lights on the shore proper. Upstream and down there were more boats and barges landing, and the riverbank echoed with the throbbing engine of the tug, the honking cries of outraged mules, and the low, firm voices of sergeants and corporals who could manage to make their softly spoken words carry through all the noise without shouting. Valentine saw lines of craft of all descriptions waiting to vomit out men and material.

Sailors and Logistics Commandos had set up lines, and netted bags full of gear came ashore like a parade of lumpy bats swinging in the wind. Someone had hung a portable radio from a tree, where it muttered out love songs in tribute to expectant and new mothers everywhere. In between the songs were tips on prenatal health and nursing given by a woman with precise, softly hypnotic diction.

The Skeeter Fleet's ships weren't manned by pregnant women. The men liked the songs, and if the Kurians sounded some kind of civil defense alert for western Kentucky, they'd hear it over the broadcast.

"Make to route green," said Preville at the com set. "The colonel wants us to take over for the Wolf pathfinders."

Valentine relaxed a little. That was according to plan as well.

"Break open a box of green chemical lights," Valentine told Patel.

He heard a crump of artillery being fired downriver. Southern Command was supposed to be bringing a trio of big guns across. Rumor said they were Harry, Hermione, and Ron, three old 155mm behemoths. Hermione was famous for having fired the first shot of the Archangel counterattack.

Southern Command was sending them into the Kurian Zone with the same long-range blessing.

He instinctively checked the big-numeral watch looped through his top buttonholes. Oh five twenty-eight. The detail would be of interest to some historian or other. Valentine hoped it wouldn't be a New Universal Church archivist collecting notes for a paper on the suppression of the Cumberland insurgency.

Valentine formed his men into rather ragged lines, wishing he could find a high spot and see the light show. The Goobermaker's strange defense had been described to him, but he'd never seen the effect personally. All he saw was the occasional flicker of a shell heading east through breaks in the trees.

He didn't hear any counterbattery fire. One would think that the local Quislings would at least have mortars in place to harass the landing by now. Perhaps they were as wary of the Goobermaker's woods as the Wolves and Cats.

Pairs of Wolves marked the path to the old highway, looking even dumber than Valentine's company with painted tinfoil topping their weathered buckskins. A trail up from the riverbank gave over to a little road, which crossed a bridge and passed through a wood before joining the old federal route. Valentine distributed his men in corporal-led units, supervising the placement of the glow sticks himself so that they'd be visible only to those coming up from the riverbank and following the trail.

The Wolves were glad to be relieved and hurried off in the direction of the firing.

It was a strange sort of KZ. As far as Valentine could tell, the Goobermaker made no attempt to build farms or settlements. He kept the old federal highway clear enough, though as they came into town he saw brush growing out of broken windows of otherwise fine brick buildings. The town looked like a decrepit old man with untrimmed eyebrows, ear, and nostril hair.

Jolla arrived and set up temporary HQ in an old primary school. As the rest of the support battalion showed up, he distributed the units so they'd be ready to move north.

"There's quite a show, if you want to go up to the school roof, Valentine," Jolla said. He'd ripped open a big triangle from his mask so it only half-obscured his face, making him look a bit like the Phantom of the Opera. "Just follow the power cords from the mobile generator."

Easily done. Valentine left Rand at company HQ with Glass and the heavy weapons Grogs and headed into the school, Bee trailing dutifully behind. Valentine had long since given up trying to get her to do anything but watch over him. Evidently he'd replaced Hoffman Price in her life in some manner.

He followed the cords up the stairs and to the roof, where the main signals team was working. Seng's chief of staff, Nowak, was throwing orders like hand grenades. She was a rather willowy woman with baby-soft skin, though that too was obscured by tinfoil.

Valentine brought up his binoculars, focused on the torchlike flicker six or seven miles away.

The Goobermaker's turret-snail tower, topped by what looked like a broken minaret, was aflame, sending a long spiral of smoke like a question mark into the sky.

Artillery shells landed somewhere in the hills well south of the tower, looking like distant lightning in the growing dawn, big horizon-shaping flashes punctuated by smaller bursts. Someone was putting up a steel curtain between the Goobermaker's lands and Memphis.

Southern Command was apparently giving everything it had in the eastern approaches to start them off.

"They did it?" Valentine asked, astonishment making him ask self-evident questions.

"Really and truly," Nowak said. She told the person at the other end to stand by. "Chatter says they've captured a Kurian alive. It may be the old bastard himself. They've sealed him inside a glass fish tank, and a couple Cats and a Bear team are hauling ass back for the river."

"Has that ever happened before?"

"If it had, guys like us wouldn't have heard of it," Nowak said in a tone that indicated she was smiling. "Of course, they're yakking about it almost in the clear. Might be a diversion trying to sucker in a big effort to recapture him, catch the patrol under our guns."

The sun was visible.

Valentine smelled food cooking. He suspected that if they moved out again, his troops, in their uniforms designed to confuse identification, might have to lead the way again. Best see if they could be relieved and get them fed, to keep their strength up for the next lap.

Valentine organized the distribution of hot chicory coffee and sandwiches for his strung-out platoons. Jolly had a quick meeting, showing the next route that they'd take as soon as a few more companies of Guards arrived, and set the next leg of the march to begin at noon in any case. Seng wanted everyone through the Goobermaker's lands and out the other end, heading for Kentucky, as soon as possible.

A tired-looking figure in black rode into camp on a lather-streaked mule. It was Brother Mark under a thick coat of dirt and dead twigs. He dismounted stiffly, handed his mount to a groom, and tottered to the field kitchen.

Valentine found a folding camp stool and brought it to him.

"You have my profound gratitude, son," he said, seating himself. "You wouldn't know if my baggage has been unloaded?"

"You need a change of clothes?" Valentine asked. Brother Mark smelled of sweat and smoke.

"My goosedown pillow. I've been on my feet or in my saddle since . . . is it Sunday already? Since Friday morning. I feel as though I could sleep propped up against that wall over there."

"I thought only the Wolves went over before Saturday night."

"Oh, I was well ahead of them. Meetings to attend. You can remove that ridiculous tinfoil now, young man. Not that it ever provided anything but psychological comfort."

Valentine would have liked nothing better—his skin felt itchy and he had sweat in his eyes—but decided to wait for official orders.

"Meetings?" Valentine asked, since Brother Mark seemed in a mood to answer questions.

He dipped a doughnut in his coffee and ate half of it. "Yes, concerning the settlement of the estate of the late Ri-Icraktisus. I beg your understanding—the Goober-maker, you boys call her. The Goobermaker's estate."

Valentine felt the ground beneath his feet tilt. "Who attended this meeting?"

"Some of the local Kurians," Brother Mark said, pulling off his boots and socks. "He was quite unpopular with the Nashville clan, and Memphis only just tolerated him because of his military acumen. When she switched over to female and started budding off her own clan, that was the last straw. The feel went out that Memphis was willing to withdraw her support. . . ." He rubbed a finger between his toes, sniffed, and made a face. "If I were in the old bishop's palace, after a night like that I'd take a steam with a pair of flexible fourteen-year-olds scrubbing me down. I'm reduced to cleaning my own feet. I wish I could indulge my humanist patriotism in a more comfortable manner."

"You're saying the Kurians ganged up on one of their own?" Valentine wasn't sure what he had a harder time believing: Southern Command helping other Kurians bring down the Goobermaker or Brother Mark, ostensibly a high Church renegade, meeting with other Kurians and returning alive to tell.

"Not so much ganged up as withdrew their minds from her contact, leaving her rather alone at a key moment. Once the conspiracy started, everyone wanted to join. There's an old proverb from the Silk Road: A falling camel attracts many knives."

"So the tinfoil was pointless?"

"Not pointless. Useless, maybe, but it did its job. Everyone was

122 *Fall with Honor*

afraid to set foot on this side of the river near that great tower. It gave the troops confidence. I understand the Bears were quite a sight, blowing open holes in the bottom of the tower with turbans of glittering foil wrapped around their heads."

"Those Kurians are not going to be happy when we march into Kentucky," Valentine said.

"Memphis or Nashville don't give two figs about the legworm ranchers. The only ones who claim control over central Kentucky is the Ordnance up in Ohio, and they're happy to cause trouble for them. They see it as removing two turds with one flush. Is that how you say it? I'm still not used to all this colorful cracker-barrel talk you fighting men use down here."

"There's a rumor that she was captured."

"No, one of her detached buds. Developed enough to inherit much of her mind. He may prove useful."

Valentine tried to digest that. "How do you meet—"

Patel walked up, using the help of his metal-tipped hickory cane. When in front of the men, he mostly used it as a pointer or to scratch maps in the dirt.

"Colonel Jolla's called for all the staff-level officers, sir," Patel said. "The route's been changed. Moytana's Wolves have captured a motor pool and fueling station. We're to move there at once."

Brother Mark finished his coffee. "Go and line your men up neatly, Major. I think I shall despair of my pillow and just sleep on my coat for whatever length of time God and Colonel Seng allow. Oh dear, it looks like rain. As if I'm not uncomfortable enough."

By nightfall they were almost out of the Goobermaker's territory, camped at the captured garage that reminded Valentine of the rig yard he'd briefly seized back in his days as a Wolf lieutenant. This one had no organic labor force, however, just a few mechanics and relief drivers who took a motorbus in from Memphis every day.

Just before setting off on the hard march for the garage, Jolla had ordered the men to discard their tinfoil and officially announced the destruction of the Goobermaker's tower.

Valentine wasn't able to determine which bit of news made the men cheer harder. But he was glad to feel air on his skin again.

The march out of the Mississippi camp marked the last time that Valentine's company stepped in ranks and files together for weeks.

Once out of sight of the river valley, they were put to work, scattered into details and squads gathering news and sustenance, watching road crossings, finding fords or paths, siphoning gasoline, and warning off wandering locals.

Two days later they crossed into Kentucky, following old Route 79. Patel and a platoon rode scout, traveling ahead or around the flanks to major intersections where they could idle beside a utility pole or beneath a bridge, quietly keeping watch. Glass and Rand stayed with the main body at company headquarters. Valentine switched between the scouts and the men riding with the Logistics Commandos gathering supplies.

Valentine was happy to quit Tennessee, mostly because it meant he wouldn't have to deal with Papa Reisling any more.

Reisling was an unpleasant individual, a former Logistics Commando who'd married and settled on the fringe of the Goobermaker's grounds north of Clarksville. He was a strange figure of a man, old yet hale, thick-haired but gray flecked with white.

He didn't like Valentine from the moment he first set eyes on him, when a local underground contact arranged a meeting. Perhaps it was due to Bee, who didn't like the look of the old Dairy Queen garbage nook where they met while Reisling's brother-in-law kept watch from the roof.

Reisling considered the entire Southern Command invasion of Kentucky—the first true offensive across the Mississippi in the history of that Freehold—a deep-seated plot to make his life difficult and bring the Reapers down on him.

"I can make a pork loin disappear, or ten pounds of flour and molasses," Reisling complained, showing Valentine a flyleaf from an old book scrawled with requirements. "But *this*. Two thousand eggs, powdered or fresh. Thirty pounds of salt. Six hundred chickens at the very least, and 'as many more as I can provide.' Fruit juice or dried fruit. Where am I supposed to get dried fruit by the goddamned barrel?"

"Nobody's going to die if you miss a few line items," Valentine said. "It's a great help to us to get anything. Every mouthful you provide means less that comes out of stores that we carry along for emergencies."

"Three weeks ago I was told to start setting aside food for a big operation. I thought it would be a company of Wolves. Got a pen of year-old pigs and two fifty-pound bags of beans the local production officer doesn't know exist. Thought I'd done my job and done it well. Then half of the goddamned Southern Command crosses over the river and stands here, mouths open like baby birds expecting me to stuff 'em."

Reisling's voice reminded Valentine of a transmission giving out, all grind and whine.

"Old tricks are usually the best," Valentine said. "Find a Church relief warehouse, loot it, and set it on fire."

"And have Church inquisitors questioning half of Clarksville? No thank you, Lieutenant."

"Major," Valentine said.

"That's why we're in the state we're in. Kids with momma's milk still on their lips throwing rank around."

It had been a while since anyone called Valentine "kid"—Brother Mark's "my son's" hardly counted; churchmen of his rank called everyone obviously beneath their age son or daughter.

"Just give us what you can. Even if it's just those yearling pigs and the beans."

"Harebrained operation you're on, Lieutenant—Major," Reisling said. "You want to fool the Kurians, you gotta go on tippy-toe. You boys are stomping into the KZ in clown shoes. They're going to slap down on you, hard."

"Just get us what you can. We'll be back tonight with a truck."

The supplies showed up, including a surprising quantity of eggs. The underground men who helped them load it said practically every family in Clarksville had given up little reserves of food they kept in case of shortages. Word had gone out that eggs were needed, and they came in straw-packed, ribboned baskets. Many of the eggs had been decorated using vinegar dyes, red and blue mostly, with gold stars stuck on.

God bless you, read the tiny, cursive ink letters on one.

But Reisling just stood with arms crossed in an old overcoat, watching them load.

"You'll get your food. The people here are going to pay for every bit. Mark my words."

Valentine could taste his grudge in every mouthful.

At the first camp in Kentucky, Seng had a ceremony inviting members of all the companies in his command to see him hand out commendations and medals. Most were going to the Bear and Wolf teams who destroyed the Kurian tower.

Valentine and Patel decided to send Glass and his Grogs under the supervision of Patel and Rand. Valentine wanted the rest of the brigade to get used to the sight of the Grogs, lest some nervous picket open up on them as they brought a cartload of pork back. He called Glass into the company headquarters tent.

"Send someone else, sir," Glass said. "That crap doesn't impress me."

"Glass," Patel said.

"Oh, he's free to talk," Valentine said. "You've got something against medals, Glass?"

"The right guys never get 'em, that's my problem."

Valentine felt he should reprimand Glass, but he wasn't speaking contemptuously of any particular person, just the practice in general. Valentine could hardly upbraid him for having an opinion and expressing it when asked. "Don't tell me you think that way about Colonel Seng too. He's got too many medals to wear, and probably deserves twice that."

"Only medal that means much to me is the combat badge. If you've faced fire, you've proved all you ever have to prove in my book. The valor medals look pretty, but valor's just another word for something getting screwed up. A well-run fight's where you throw so much shit on target what's left of the enemy crawls out begging you to stop."

As they camped in the quiet, greening hills of Kentucky the first day of April, Rand brought him the front page of the *Nashville Community Spirit* ("Giving a little good for the betterment of all" read the motto just under the rather imposing-looking font of the newspaper's logo).

Rand pointed to an article at the bottom of page one.

MISSISSIPPI SECURE AGAIN

Guerrilla WRECKERS STRIKE OUT! A full-scale raid on rail and river routes north of Memphis ENDED WITH A WHIMPER Monday. The last elements of the bandit incursion gave up or swam for their lives as LOCAL VOLUNTEER HEROES restored ORDER AND SAFETY to north GREATER MEMPHIS.

Security spokesmen affirmed that there had been unusually DESPERATE WINTER SHORTAGES IN TRANS-MISSISSIPPI. The attack failed utterly as a heavy barrage pinned them against the river. The barrage, which ALARMED PEACE-LOVING MEMPHIS FAMILIES, lasted only long enough to organize the COUNTER-ATTACK which SWEPT TO VICTORY against the banks of the Mississippi.

This paper is one of many voices happy to see GREATER COOPERATION BETWEEN MEMPHIS AND NASHVILLE SECURITY ZONES and looks forward to further SUPPRESSION OF TERRORISM.

The paper had helpfully printed a few blurry pictures on the second page of bodies lying along the edge of a dirt road and a group of men sitting cross-legged, with arms tied behind their backs.

"Skinny Pete showed up again. That boy makes a good living," Ediyak said, glancing at the pictures but not bothering to read the rest.

"Skinny Pete?" Valentine asked.

"That's what we used to call him. He's a little wisp of a thing from Alabama; looks like he's never had more than two mouthfuls of soup at one time in his whole life. He's always sitting there with his collar pulled up around his ears in the prisoner mock-ups, since he looks hungry as sin."

"Doesn't anyone else notice him?"

Ediyak shrugged. "I had to have it pointed out to me. It's not like you'd recognize him unless you're close. Sometimes he's grown in a scruff of beard, sometimes they shave him bald, sometimes he's in a wool watch cap. Anyway, that's his job. Go sit beneath a sign that says 'Clarksville, thirty klicks' and look like you got taken prisoner that morning."

Valentine had to chuckle. "They got the big story right. Just left out a few details."

"KZ papers don't print unpleasant facts. They disappear, like dust swept into a cement crack," Ediyak said.

"Civilizations are won and lost in such cracks," Rand observed.

Kentucky's hills exploded into spring colors, fireworks displays of wildflower and dogwood blossoms. Valentine took parties out to show them trees bearing wild legworms. The crawlers would stay in the branches, devouring bark, twig, and leaf alike, until they became so heavy they either snapped the branches or bent them until they were lowered gently to earth. Then they commenced grazing in their long, crooked furrows.

Valentine changed back into his legworm leathers, adding Velcro strips for Southern Command insignia. He had been dreading the Kurian reaction to their march with every step into Kentucky, waiting to see what shape the reaction would take. But the march covered miles with not much more difficulty than they'd experienced on the practice marches in northern Arkansas and the Missouri bootheel.

Every time he topped a rise, every time they took a bend, every time they broke out of forest or heavy brush and into pasture, Valentine expected to see them, campfires and tents and columns of motor vehicles. But the landscape remained as empty as it had when he followed Hoffman Price across Tennessee and into Kentucky.

Bee seemed happy to be back. When they cut legworm trails, little rises of plant growth and dirt that looked like planted furrows cut by a drunk plowing farmer, Bee urged him to follow. Some sense of hers allowed her to tell which way the legworm had gone, though unless the marks were very fresh Valentine couldn't make head from tail.

The legworm ranchers were a clannish bunch. Some sat you down and offered pie; others would chase you off with bird shot.

And that was just for a few wanderers crossing their grazing lands. Valentine wondered how they'd react to the appearance of better than two thousand Southern Command soldiers.

South of Bowling Green Valentine and a team of his men idled on a running pickup at dawn, keeping warm by sitting either in the cab or atop the engine-warmed hood. They'd been tasked with meeting a pair of Cats who were supposed to guide them into the legworm bluegrass.

The pickup sat beneath a power pylon. Birds, with their usual good judgment, had transformed it into a high-rise condominium.

The men passed around thermoses of sage tea and talked about legworms. Valentine told his story of a battle between two legworm clans he'd witnessed, with the gunmen on each side using their beasts as a cross between World War I entrenchments and eighteenth-century fighting sail.

Valentine left to take a leak. As he zipped up and turned from the back of the pickup, he tripped. As he fell, he noticed a binding-twine lasso attaching his ankle to the mufflerless exhaust system on the truck.

He fell face-first into spiky dandelion.

Two men jumped off the front of the truck, coming to his aid.

"You okay, Major?"

A shadow unfolded from beneath the truck. "He deserves it for splattering me with pee," Alessa Duvalier said. "I taped two grenades under your truck and pegged the pins to come out when you drove away. You clowns are lucky I recognized him."

"It got a distinctive left hook or what, sir?" one of the men laughed.

"I meant his leathers," Duvalier said.

Valentine cut himself free from the twine. "They pulled you into this operation? Gentlemen, this is Smoke, one of Southern Command's best Cats. I've covered more miles with her than any living thing."

"Thanks to you, I'm rated as one of Southern Command's expert Cats on the bluegrass," Duvalier said. "I've been working Kentucky since the fall, escorting that churchman around."

"He's cheery company."

"Never more so than when he's trying to stick a spitty finger inside you. Horny old goat." She put two fingers in her mouth and whistled, up-down-up.

Another woman, hair knife-cut high and tight into a cross between a mohawk and a mullet, rose from the ditch running along the road. She had legworm leather trousers and a poncho concealing what looked to be a military carbine. A camouflage bandanna added a festive touch to her neck.

"This is Vette, Val. She was blooded in Missouri. It's quieter there now, so Southern Command retasked her here because she was born in Bowling Green. Vette, this is Ghost. I went to Colorado and across Nebraska and Kansas with him."

Vette extended hands in fingerless gloves and gave a strong handshake. "Pleased to see you're still alive."

"If you watch him close when he walks, you'll see that he's had some near misses," Duvalier said.

"Hope you learn as much from her as I did," Valentine said.

"She's smarter than you when it comes to picking a fight," Duvalier said, running a knuckle down the scar on his cheek.

"So, what have you got for us?" Valentine asked.

"You guys have moved fast and hard. We're going to take you to sort of a feudal lord. He's got several tribes united under him."

"Including the old crew you ran with, the Bulletproof," Vette said. "I recognize the cut of your leathers."

"No other hints, Smoke?"

"You'll be relieved to know you're about to be reinforced," Duvalier said. "A third of Kentucky is mounting worm to fight."

One of the soldiers snorted. "Worm ranchers fight?"

"On our side, is what he means," another added.

Duvalier glared at the doubters. The fire in her eyes reminded Valentine of how pretty she was, when her real self peeped through the scruffy exterior.

"Six clans have come together," Duvalier said, nodding to Valentine's detail and shaking any proffered hand. "That churchman may like playing stinkfinger with the female help, but he's one hell of a diplomat. Every time things heated up, he calmed them down and got them talking again. It's as much his triumph as it is Karas'."

"Who's Karas?" Valentine asked.

Vette also shook hands all around. "He's a Bowling Green boy too. He's just what the Cause needs. A visionary."

*   *   *

The men of the brigade waited. With some fresh bread and Kentucky honey in them, they were in good spirits and chattering like meadowlarks. They lounged on a gentle hillside forming a natural amphitheater, warm in April sunshine that promised summer on the way.

During Valentine's training and time in the Bear caves of Pacific Command, he sometimes spent a few hours at night in the rec room. They had an LCD TV rigged there, and he watched old movies on disk. One Bear favorite was an old movie called *Highlander.*

While Valentine found it interesting enough, especially the sweeping images of scenery, he'd forgotten the movie until he saw Karas emerge from his vast tent. He immediately thought, *that's the Highlander!*

Karas had the same strong face, long hair, and impressive build, though the hair was stringier and the build wasn't enhanced by camera angle. He wore a big-pocketed waxed canvas coat that hung to midthigh and rather striking pants that were legworm leather on the inside and what looked like corduroy on the outside. His soft brown boots, with just a hint of felt showing at the top, made Valentine rather jealous. They looked durable and comfortable.

Followed by deputations from the six clans supporting him and by Brother Mark, who looked pleased for the first time since Valentine had known him, Karas approached an old pasture tree that had been butchered just that morning for firewood. Earlier in the morning Valentine had watched two men working a long saw cutting it off, but had wondered at why they went up the tree and sawed off limbs instead of simply felling it in the first place.

Valentine recognized the honey-colored hair of Tikka among the tribal dignitaries. She'd apparently assumed some role of importance within the Bulletproof.

Karas mounted the stump with the aid of a ladder. Valentine wondered how he'd look to the men in the pasture or on the lower slopes of the hill—a statue atop a column?

The breeze died down as if by command.

A leathery worm rider stepped forward. "Let the Kentucky Alliance take heed," he called in a formidable bass baritone. "Our chief is about to speak."

"This is a sight I've dreamed of for a long time. You all don't know how happy you've made me, marching to these quiet hills. It's been a long time since the Stars and Stripes has been carried openly, pridefully, across these hills. Let me formally welcome you as friends. A mite more valuable: as allies."

Southern Command's troops cheered that.

"Some of you went to school. I only had one teacher my whole life. A simple man. A plumbing contractor, before 2022. That man was my father. He taught me to ride. He taught me to shoot. He taught me to tell the truth.

"One day I was looking at pictures of animals of the world. I liked big cats, lions and black panthers and tigers. He told me that one tiger needed to eat as many as three hundred deer in a year. Three hundred! Of course, the tiger must eat them one at a time. No tiger kills three hundred deer at once."

The spring breeze contested the voice again, but Karas could project, though the men upwind were cupping their ears to catch his words.

"Imagine, though, if those three hundred deer could talk as we do. If they could take the tiger's tally. If they could organize against this tiger. If three hundred deer together hunted the one tiger, threw themselves against it, biting and goring and kicking, I reckon that tiger would never hunt again.

"We have one great advantage over the Kurians. Human beings naturally come together, the way water droplets find their way to pools. The Kurians like to remain individual drops.

"Divided, all we can do is crawl to the Kurians and lick their boots, begging not to be killed. Their tigers are the master of any one of us. United, we will hunt the tigers.

"I'm going to ask you to follow me east into the mountains. There we'll start the biggest tiger hunt you've ever seen. Then with the forces that are meeting there, we'll come back and start taking over town after town, county after county here in Kentucky. Can I count on the men of Arkansas, of Texas, of Oklahoma, Kansas, and Missouri? We're pledged to you, Wildcats and Gunslingers, Coonskins, Bulletproofs and Mammoths, and of course my own Perseids."

Valentine cheered along with the rest of them. If he understood it right, Javelin was now the largest operation against the Kurians since Archangel.

Lambert and Brother Mark and the rest had told them they'd have support of some of the legworm ranchers in Kentucky. He thought they meant foodstuffs and fuel; he'd never dreamed they'd be fighting at their side.

Why had they kept so much secret from the officers involved? To avoid disappointment if Karas turned out to be a windbag, full of bluster and promises? Or did Lambert feel it necessary to keep this from Southern Command's own higher-ups?

Valentine laughed at himself as Bee thumped him on the chest, not really understanding the reason for the cheering but enjoying the mood.

As the men and women roared their lungs out, thrilled that Kentucky wasn't just supporting their advance but coming to their side, he was considering the possibility of informants high up in Southern Command's officer list.

After the speech ended men and women of the Alliance handed out coins of brightly polished nickel, it looked like. They bore an imposing stamp of Karas in profile. The reverse had a five-pointed star with a 10 at the center and "TEN DOLLARS" written around the edge.

"The king's coin," the boy who handed Valentine his coin said. "Lot more where these came from."

"Long live the King of Kentucky, then," Ediyak said in reply. "What do you s'pose we can buy with it?"

Valentine examined the engraving. A faint halo had been etched around the profile. "A whole lot of trouble, if this man wants us calling him king."

Seven

Across Cumberland Plateau, April: It is a land of sandstone bluffs and old coal fields, swimming holes and iron bridges, old loblolly pine plantations run amok and new deciduous forests.

Almost every kind of tree found east of the Mississippi can be found here, mixing among each other and gradually reclaiming land from the pines, each occupying land according to water requirements, with chestnuts and shortleaf pines atop the ridges and poplar, black gum, and maples in the bottoms.

For much of the early United States history, the eastern escarpment served as a barrier to the gradual migration west. The tough bluffs running the southeastern border dividing Kentucky from Virginia served as a natural choke. Cherokee and Shawnee hunted the land until passages through the Cumberland Gap were mapped out and opened. Even so, the region remained somewhat wilder than the states north and south until the exploitation of coal and timber resources made the area profitable.

The picturesque sandstone gorges once drew photographers, and protect the homes of cliff swallows and bats, but to David Valentine that spring they were a frustrating maze dotted with dead towns so decrepit they reminded him of his first operations as a Wolf in the run-wild forests of Louisiana. Negotiating ridges and valleys meant weary hours of scouting and camping as the columns wound their way east through the twisting, turning cuts, where one mile of red-shouldered hawk flight meant perhaps three up and down and back and forth.

Luckily, it is a wild region empty of Kurian holds. Kentucky always has gone its own way, even in its uneasy relationship with the Kurian Order. Self-reliant to what some might call a fault, they saw off the first

*emissaries of the New Order in the chaos of 2022 with torch and buck-
shot, demanding to be left alone. Neither at war with the Kurians nor
cooperative with their Reapers, they bring coal to the surface and legworm grubs to market to trade for the goods they need. Every time a
Kurian tries to establish a tower in the Cumberland, he finds his Reapers hunted, his Quisling retainers ambushed and hanged, and the alleged rich prospect of Kentucky dissolving into a confusion of legworm
tracks and ash.*

*The tribes have formed a feudal society, quarrelsome when at peace,
uneasily united when threatened from outside. Every feudal society
needs a king to smooth the former and lead them in the latter.*

Karas' coins turned out to be only so much shiny dross when it came
to bartering with other legworm tribes. Valentine's company went back
to trading the crank-powered radios, rifles, and learn-to-read Bibles for
butter and eggs.

But the legworm riders did offer spare worms, rigged for hauling
cargo. Valentine's company received two, one to carry burdens while the
other grazed in its wake, with roles switched the next day. Every third
day the column rested now, to give the worms time to feed and recover.
For all their size, they could be delicate if mishandled or underfed.

As they passed the more settled central part of Kentucky, the land
became a patchwork of small towns and huge, clannish ranches. The
towns were controlled by "badges" but rarely saw a Reaper, though Valentine heard fireside tales of bounty hunters and human traffickers who
collected criminals and troublemakers.

Contacts with the underground dried up once they reached the ranch
lands. Though the soldiers broke into a few locked NUC storage rooms
in the dead of night, Valentine scanning for Reapers and his sharpshoot-
ers standing by with their blue-striped magazines in the rifles, they rarely
returned to Javelin with full carts.

Where no small, easy game were to be had, Valentine felt it necessary to organize a hunt for larger prey.

"This is what's called hitting them where they ain't," Patel said to
second platoon.

They were dispersed on a steep hillside overlooking a railroad cut.
Valentine stood between Patel and Glass, who had the Grogs' .50 set up
within a blind of machete-sculpted brush. Wolf scouts had relayed a
report of a lightly guarded cargo train heading north on the Lexington
track, and Valentine's company was dispatched to hit it if it looked like
it contained anything useful.

Below them, an engine and ten boxcars stood on a single track in front of a blocked bridge. The engine puffed like an impatient fat man.

Valentine stood above Patel, watching one of his Kentucky recruits talking to the engineer from the cover of a stand of thick redbud. A few other members of first platoon stood, looking at the blocked bridge. Another pair of soldiers, Rutherford and DuSable, whom Valentine considered his two coolest heads, stood at the back of the caboose, swapping some captured New Universal Church activity books and Lexington newspapers for cigarettes and what looked like a sheaf of mimeographed crossword puzzles with the guards in the armored caboose.

Whether the engineer wondered why some technical crew just happened to be blocking a bridge where trains were running yesterday, Valentine couldn't say. Crow, the soldier in question, was a good talker and had worked rail crew as a boy and into his early manhood.

The binoculars in Valentine's hands stayed steady on the armored caboose. Patel watched the gunner in the little bubble just behind the engine. They were woefully attentive to duty, experienced enough on the lines to know that any unexpected pause called for extra vigilance.

"Faces. In the boxcars," Patel said. "It's not cargo; it's fodder."

"Another load heading up for Cincinnati," Harmony, a Tennessean, said. "Blood money."

Valentine swiveled his glasses over a few degrees. His vision blurred for a moment as redbud intervened, and then he saw it. A pair of haunted eyes looking out through the bars, knuckles white as the prisoner hefted himself up to the airholes at the top of the car.

He did some quick math. Maybe four hundred human souls behind that puffing engine, bound for destruction.

"No point hitting it now," Glass said. "Nothing we can use."

Valentine ignored him.

"What caused you to get culled, cuz?" Harmony said as if talking to the prisoner. "Heart murmur show up on a health check? Forget to make a payoff? Screw up under the boss's eye on a bad Friday?"

A clean-cut young officer left the caboose. Another railroad guard trailed behind him wearing the harassed look of adjutants everywhere in any army. After a conference with the engineer, they approached Crow, who gestured for them to come and look at the bridge.

They walked out to the edge of the gorge, and Crow pointed to the pilings at the base of the bridge. A couple of the idling workers fiddled with the pile of shovels and picks at the edge of the road; another went back to a captured pickup with a freshly painted logo the platoon had been using, avoiding the officer.

A perfectly natural move.

Captain LeHavre always told him not to let the perfect be the enemy of the good. This would be as good an opportunity as they would get with this train.

Valentine looked again at the young officer, wondered why someone hardened by experience wasn't on this trip. Maybe he was fresh out of some New Universal Church leadership academy, telling himself that this winnowing, distasteful in the particular, helped the species in general.

Tough luck, kid.

"Give the strike signal," Valentine said. "Glass, have the Grogs hit the engine first, then the caboose."

Patel rose and made a noise like a startled wild turkey.

Rutherford and DuSable shoved the newspapers in their vests, reaching for the small, cylindrical grenades that hung within.

Glass made a face, but patted Ford on the shoulder and pointed at the engine. He and Chevy swung their .50 and aimed.

"Open fire," Valentine said.

The .50 chattered out its lethal *chukka-chukka-chukka* rattle. The glass of the cupola turned to spider-webbing and blood.

Crow froze up. One good shove and he could have sent the young officer headfirst into the gorge. Valentine silently implored him to move, but he ducked down at the gunfire.

Another of Valentine's men in gray denim, a thick-armed ex-motorcycle cavalry named Salazar, raised a shovel and bashed the adjutant with it as Crow still gaped. The soldier didn't have time to make sure of the adjutant, for the lieutenant had his pistol out. The flat of the shovel caught the lieutenant under the chin, tumbling him into the gorge.

Two hammering bangs, less than a second apart, sounded from the armored caboose. Plumes of dust spouted up from the ventilators on the roof of the caboose. Rutherford and DuSable crawled like fast-moving snakes toward the front of the train, sheltering next to the wheels of the boxcars, where the men in the caboose couldn't bring their mounted weapons to bear.

The Grogs shifted their .50 to the armored caboose, emptying the rest of the box of ammunition, punching holes around the firing slits.

"Third platoon, covering positions," Valentine told signals, who spoke into his walkie-talkie, shielding the receiver with his palm. "Second platoon, forward!" Valentine shouted over the firing.

They'd done it, and done it well, dozens of times in training. Now it was for keeps.

"Check fire," Patel roared, as a soldier paused to blast the caboose. "Check before you shoot. There are friendlies down there."

They did it well, moving all at once at a rush. Third platoon, higher on the hillside, moved forward to the prepared positions.

Valentine, half sliding down the steep hillside nearest the cut, landed and glanced at the front of the train. One of his men was already inside the engine compartment, waving off additional fire. At the bridge, there was nothing to see but Crow, kneeling beside the soldier who'd clobbered the lieutenant with the shovel, a bloody pistol in his hand.

Bee loped after him, one of her sawed-off shotguns in one hand and an assault rifle in the other, moving forward like a fencer with the assault rifle pointed at the caboose, the shotgun held up and back.

"Get Cabbage over to Crow," Valentine ordered as he approached the caboose. "He's not calling man down but I think Salazar is hurt."

Cabbage was the company medic, when he wasn't assisting the cook. Formerly a demi-doc in the KZ, he'd gotten sick of signing unfitness certifications.

"Cover the cars until we know for sure what's inside," Valentine told Patel.

People were shouting for help from inside the boxcars. Valentine looked beneath the cars, searching for explosives. He'd heard of the Kurians sending decoy trains lined with plastic explosive and claymore mines to take out guerrillas when someone hit the kill switch. This didn't look to be that kind of train, but it was best to make sure.

No sign of strange wiring leading from the caboose.

Valentine looked through one of the bullet holes into the armored caboose, saw a twitching foot. Rutherford slunk up beside him.

"I'm going in," Valentine said.

"Let me go first, sir," Rutherford said.

Valentine noticed blood running down from his forehead, already caking into cherry flakes.

"Rutherford, you wounded?"

"It ain't mine, Major. I got some on me when DuSable and I were checking for booby traps. It was dripping out of the caboose. The cars look clear. DuSable's checking the rest forward."

He was a cool head.

Second platoon had taken up firing positions, covering the caboose and the rest of the cars up to the engine.

There was some trouble with the caboose's metal door; it was either jammed good or latched from the inside. Valentine pointed to the hinge rivets and the second platoon entry man employed a monstrous four-gauge shotgun on the door. Then Bee smashed it open with her shoulder.

Rutherford slipped in, pistol held in a Weaver stance.

Nothing but blood and body parts awaited them.

Valentine checked the radio log. The set itself was as dead as the gunners inside the caboose, but there was a notation that an unscheduled stop had happened, with approximate location, and that the message had been acknowledged by LEX.

Lexington, Valentine guessed.

They opened up the boxcars, giving in to the pleading and pounding from within.

"Liberators," an old man in a black coat shouted. "They're liberators."

"That's better than 'shit detail,' " Ediyak commented.

They thronged around the soldiers, some in blue and yellow and pink clothing that looked like hospital scrubs woven out of paper fiber. In some Kurian Zones, they even begrudged you the clothes on your back when selected for harvesting.

"Please, stay close to the train. Don't wander off," Valentine repeated, walking up the line to check on Salazar.

Salazar had two bullets in him, or rather through him. The Quisling adjutant had opened up on him at pointblank, and Salazar still managed to half decapitate the Quisling before Crow finally fired his pistol.

Crow looked miserable, rubbing at Salazar's blood on his hands like Lady Macbeth.

"I think he'll live, sir," Cabbage reported. "Four neat little holes, two coming in and two going out. His left lung is deflated and he may have lost a big chunk of kidney, but that's just a guess without X-rays."

"Nearest machine is probably in Nashville," someone said.

They held an improptu officers conference while second platoon distributed food from the stores in the forward-most boxcar to the "fodder."

Valentine had to snap Crow out of his misery.

"Crow, forget it. I need you in the here and now, okay?"

"Yes, sir," Crow said.

"Salazar's either going to make it or not. You poured iodoform into the wound and applied pressure. The rest is up to him and the medics. Worrying about fifteen minutes ago won't cause him to draw one breath more. Answer a few questions for me, and then you can go back to him."

Crow took a breath. "Yes, sir."

"They got off a message to Lexington. What happens if guerrillas hit a train?"

"It depends on if the train is just reported overdue or if they called in that they were being attacked," Crow said, his pupils gradually settling on the group of men around him.

"Let's assume the worst," Valentine said.

"They'll send out an armored train and motorbike and horse cavalry, backed up by at least a few companies of infantry and some light artillery in gunwagons. There's never been more than a few dozen guerrillas here. Too many Kurian-friendly legworm clans."

"How do they track the guerrillas?"

"Reapers, usually. I've seen them get off trains myself."

"Reapers mean there has to be a Kurian controlling them," Valentine said. Or the strange organization known as the Twisted Cross, but ever since the Nebraska Golden Ones smashed their facility south of Omaha, there were only a few odd units of them scattered around.

"I was told there's a Kurian in charge of rail security who goes around in an armored train," Crow said. "I never saw him though, just his Reapers."

"Brave of him to venture out," Patel put in.

"Yes," Valentine said absently. He was wondering how Gamecock's Bears would like a chance at a Kurian on the loose.

"What about the fodder?" Patel asked. "We can't take these people over ridges."

"No, we'll have to use the train," Valentine said. "We've crossed over enough old tracks this week. Is there a line we could use?"

Crow scratched his chin. "Lessee, sir. There's an old spur that heads off east at first, hooks around more south. Skirts the south end of the Boonwoods. It fed some mines that went dry. That'll get us back toward brigade maybe even a little ahead of them."

By "Boonwoods" Crow meant the Daniel Boone National Forest, according to the legworm ranchers' description of Kentucky's regions.

"Yes," Valentine said, reading the doubt on Crow's face. "What's the problem?"

"Major, it's really overgrown," Crow said. "The engine has a brush cutter on it, but we'll have to go slow, move fallen logs and whatnot ourselves. They'll catch up to us easy, especially since it's obvious where the trail is leading."

"We'll blow track at the cutoff," Valentine said.

"That'll only slow them up for an hour or so," Crow said. "Their rail gangs can do anything but build a bridge in just a few minutes."

"I don't suppose there are any bridges."

"Lots, but they'll dismount and follow. If we even get that far. Somebody might have torn up track for scrap steel or used ties to build a cabin. You never know."

"We'll risk it," Valentine said. "At the very least these people will be no worse off than they were before."

*   *   *

Valentine joined Preville up at the ridgeline at company HQ, where he talked to Seng over a scrambler. Seng didn't sound happy about it. Valentine had been assigned to conduct logistical raids, not start small-scale guerrilla warfare on the Cumberland a week before they were due in Virginia, but Seng was too good an officer not to see a chance to bag a bunch of railroad security troops more adept at flushing guerrillas out of the tall timber than facing combined arms attacks.

"I've only got a few Wolves left at HQ. Most of them are elsewhere," Seng said, his voice crackly thanks to the scrambler.

"I'll try to keep the Reapers homing in on lifesign," Valentine said.

Then he broadcast in the clear to "Allegheny HQ" that they'd intercepted the train carrying "Doctor Faustus" and he was safely on the way back. Some lonely slob, probably working the transmitter out of some shack near Mount Eagle and creating nonsensical chatter between Seng's HQ and the mythical operations' headquarters, acknowledged.

That would give the Kurian intelligence services something to chew on for a while as they examined the manifests of those shipped north as aura fodder. Hopefully some selection officer would be chopped for a screwup that existed only in Valentine's imagination.

It also might give the impression of a quick, fast-moving raid. If half the pursuit forces headed into the Kentucky hills following their foot trail, that many less would be left to pursue the train.

The toughest part of getting going again was convincing the transportees to climb back into the boxcars. Valentine didn't blame them; the Kurians hadn't bothered to provide much in the way of food or sanitary services. They refilled the cars' big yellow freshwater jugs from a handy stream, and his troops shared out what rations they had handy.

Valentine sent Rand with the carts that would have carried off whatever goodies they could have raided from the train, plus the small amount of supplies they'd bartered or scavenged on this trip, back east toward headquarters. He put Crow up front and the wounded Salazar with company headquarters in the caboose, now freed of bodies but not the sticky, coppery smell of blood despite a quick swilling-out. Cabbage already had an IV going, with Salazar as comfortable as doping could make him.

Even better, the intercom with the engine still worked.

The train bumped into motion. Bee didn't like being in the train, for whatever reason. She clapped her hand over her head and made nervous noises.

Valentine had nightmares of meeting a high-speed relief train coming south head-on and had to make plans for the abandonment of their charges. But they made Crow's turnoff, and the rocking and clattering increased as they moved down the old spur line.

The terrain around here was too hilly for good legworm ranching, but herds of sheep and goats grazed on the slopes. They passed signage for old coal mines, saw the rusting, vine-covered remains of old conveyors and towers frowning down on slag piles tufted with weeds and bracken fighting for a precarious existence on soil that had accumulated in nooks and crannies. In some places more recent strip mining scarred the hills, leaving the Kentucky ridges looking like an abandoned, opened-up cadaver on an autopsy table.

They set up watches, allowing most of his men to rest. There was little enough left to eat.

Valentine didn't think much of their guide, a rather slow man in his thirties who thought that by "guide," his duties required telling old family stories about who got married in which valley, the hunting abilities of his preacher's astonishing coon dogs, and the time Len Partridge got his index finger blown off by Old Murphy for sneak-visiting Mrs. Murphy while he was off gathering legworm egg skin. Valentine did manage to glean that the Kurians still sent trains into this region in the fall to trade for legworm meat, though it was sandwiched into a story about a wounded hawk his cousin Brady nursed back to health and trained for duck hunting.

Luckily there were only brief delays due to downed trees on the tracks. The men moved—or in one case dynamited—the trees with high-spirited enthusiasm. The audacity of a theft of an entire train had been the highlight of the march across Kentucky.

But the sinking sun set him nervously pacing the caboose until he realized he was making the rest of the occupants nervous, and he distracted himself by discussing Salazar's condition with Cabbage.

They came to a small river and stopped to check the bridge's soundness, with Valentine thanking his lucky star that he had such a diverse group of ex-Quislings in his company. He consulted his map and saw that the river arced up into the hills where Seng was headquartered. Sheep and goats and several legworms grazed in the valley.

"The bridge'll hold, sir," came the report over the intercom. "We can take a span out with dynamite and slow up the pursuit."

Not the Reapers. They'd come hot and hard with men on horses, or motorbikes, or bicycles, homing in on the crowded lifesign in the railcars—

Valentine tapped the intercom thoughtfully. "I want a conference with all officers," Valentine said. "Give the refugees fifteen minutes out of the cars."

*   *   *

They traded the captured rifles and shotguns and boxes of ammunition with the shepherd families for a generous supply of sheep and goats. The shepherds and goatherds thought him a madman: He was willing to take kids, tough old billies, sick sheep, lamed lambs. Valentine was interested more in quantity than future breeding potential. He warned them that there'd be some angry Reapers coming up the tracks shortly, and they'd better clear out and play dumb.

Then he had his men load the animals onto the boxcars.

The toughest part was convincing Patel to leave the train with a squad of men to guide the hundreds of refugees into the hills.

"Do I have to make it an order, Sergeant Major?" Valentine asked. Valentine hated to fall back on rank.

"It'll come to a fight when they catch up to you, sir. The men will need me."

"I know the job now. I was lucky as a junior lieutenant. My captain put me with his best sergeant on my first operation in the Kurian Zone."

Patel relented and walked around to the remaining NCOs, giving tips and hurrying the loading of the livestock.

"Give 'em hell, billy goat legion," Patel said as he walked off with the crowds from the boxcars and into a hillside defile on the far side of the river. Patel wanted to put at least a ridge between the tracks and the life-sign he was giving off before nightfall.

David Valentine watched them go, silently wishing them luck.

The animals he'd purchased but couldn't fit into the train, he left behind to muddle the tracks. They'd fuzz up the Reapers' sensing abilities for a few moments, anyway. The smell of goats reminded him of his induction into the Wolves. Valentine wondered what he'd say if he could have a talk with that kid he'd been.

He thought of a young couple he'd noticed, clinging to each other in doubt as they looked back at the boxcars as Patel led them into the defile. How did they get selected for harvesting? Sterile? Passing out anti-Kurian pamphlets printed in some basement? The woman had mouthed "thank you" at him. That goat-sniffing kid would have written Father Max a long letter about those two words.

"It's worth it," Valentine muttered.

Valentine still had a few refugees: the old unable to make a long walk, the sick, and a few devoted souls who stayed behind to tend to them. He gave them a boxcar of their own just in front of the caboose.

Then they pulled across the bridge and dynamited the center span in a frosty twilight.

Valentine didn't hear any cheers as ties spun like blown dandelion tufts into the river. He had too many engineers in the attenuated company

who'd sweated over the calculations and effort required to build a
bridge.

The train squealed into motion again. Now the clatter of the wheels
passing over points was accompanied by the bleating of goats and bawling of sheep.

Now the question was whether they'd make enough of a lifesign signal to draw the Reapers. He had what was left of his company, plus the
refugees, plus whatever signal the sheep and goats would send.

He sent another message to Seng, reporting the destruction of the
bridge.

"Scouts confirm you are being pursued. Two trains out of Lexington. The rear is heavily armored with engines at either end. Coming your
way. Over," headquarters reported.

"A Big Boy might be managing the pursuit. Over."

"GC will attend to it," Seng's headquarters replied. "Instructions on
the way. Over and out."

Valentine slowed their progress to a crawl, both to check for track
obstructions and so they could easily see a messenger. He smelled roasting goat in the refugee car—with tarragon and cumin, it seemed. The
resourcefulness of soldiers in feeding themselves still found ways to
amaze him.

A mile later the intercom crackled. "Stopping. Rock slide."

Valentine swung off the caboose and took a look. His Cat-sharp eyes
made it plain. That ended it. Piles of sulfur-colored limestone had ended
the chase. This was no tree that could be sawn and rolled, or blown. The
rock slide would take his entire company working with beams, chains,
and the train engine to clear.

At least half a day, working in daylight.

The door in the next car opened. Valentine caught a whiff of the
improvised charcoal brazier they had set up under an air vent. Glass and
the Grogs were eating chunks of goat meat toasted on skewers made
from bedsprings. Other members of the company dismounted from the
train to take a look at the rock slide. Everyone shook their heads.

It was a tight little corner of Kentucky, Valentine decided, looking
at the steep hillsides to either side, the *braaak* of complaining sheep and
goats from the railcars magnified by the cut.

They'd come at least ten miles. Horsemen or cyclists would be
strung out, keeping up with the Reapers. Would whoever was puppeting
the Reapers risk them? Valentine wondered if there was a finders-
keepers policy for the rail security Kurian.

The hills around this cut would allow his troops to set up murderous cross fire. There'd be no danger of the men hitting each other; they'd be shooting down.

There was a slight upward slope to the rail line. Valentine thought of the wild cart ride he'd taken down Little Timber hill.

"Set up company headquarters back in that rock pile," he told Ediyak and Preville. "Try to make contact with the brigade."

"Yes, sir."

Valentine felt something tickling at the back of his scalp. He decided it was his imagination, fretting at the dark and the delay, with Seng still miles away. He put some men to work making stretchers from the rickety beds in the boxcars.

He posted Glass and the two Grogs in the rocks above at the source of the fall, having him take some illumination flares. The .50 would have a nice look down the cut from that point, and they could make a quick retreat over the ridgeline.

He put Rutherford and DuSable on the other hill, just above the caboose, with a machine gun taken from one of the train's mounts. He made sure they had pistols with Quickwood magazines loaded and ready.

Valentine posted himself with the majority of the platoon around the caboose. The cupola gun in the engine could cover a quick fallback and serve as a rally point in the rock pile.

Valentine posted Crow at the coupling between the engine and the boxcars.

He walked from position to position, checking the men, checking that nagging itch at the back of his neck that was turning into a doubt, stiffening the hairs there. He told Bee to stay in the caboose. She'd be an unpleasant surprise to any Reaper who clawed his way in.

There were Reapers somewhere off to the west. Or maybe it was the Kurian, reaching out with his senses, searching for his quarry.

Valentine heard a sudden burst of voices from company headquarters. He saw a flash of messy, knife-cut hair in the dim light from the LED bulbs lighting up the radio log.

Duvalier?

He clambered up the rocks, saw Duvalier putting away her sword into the walking-staff holder. He smelled sweat, rubber, and lubricating oil on her.

Ediyak's mouth was opening and shutting like a landed fish, and Preville trembled like his heart had been jump-started.

"Sorry, guys, had to make sure. Where's your major?"

"Right here," Valentine said, stepping across a rock.

She sat down on a rock and rubbed her thighs. "Three hours on a bicycle bumping along a railroad. The things my poor body does for you."

"That's it. I'm shooting for senior rank," Preville said to Ediyak, sotto voce.

Valentine offered his canteen and Duvalier cleared her mouth out, then drank.

"I wish we could have saved you a few miles. These rocks prevented it," Valentine said.

Duvalier unwrapped a piece of dried legworm jerky and took a bite. "Seng's got half the brigade on the way. The Bears and what Wolves he has left are on their way to the bridge you dynamited, along with some of the legworm troops. Karas gave another whoop-'em-up speech and sent them off hollering. There's a big file of legworms following this track too. They're tearing a bunch of new holes in their mounts, prodding them at speed."

"Any orders for me?"

"Just to let them know if you found some good ground for an ambush."

Valentine let himself soar a little. Seng saw an opportunity to sting the Kurians good and was grasping for the rose and not minding the nettles. Even if it drew lots of troops into this part of Kentucky, he'd be across another line of mountains by the time they could organize themselves.

"Can you help me here?" Valentine asked.

"Sure. Want me to brew up some of this Kentucky hickory nut coffee? Not like those cafés in the French Quarter, but it's hot."

Valentine smiled. "Not that easy. The Reapers could be here any time. I'd really like another trained Hunter up with my men. You could jam yourself between a couple of boxcars, wait for a chance to make a move."

"Me? I'm no heroic kinda fighter, Val. When bullets start to fly, I prefer to head the other direction."

Valentine touched her on the shoulder. "I know. Just this once. Please, Ali."

She looked off down the tracks and into the Kentucky night. "No, Val. I don't like the odds. Multiple Reapers, at night?"

Duvalier at least had the sense to refuse quietly. At most, Preville and Ediyak heard her.

Valentine wondered if she'd obey a direct order. Technically, Cats bore the rank of captain, but he suspected she'd tell him to get stuffed and bring her up on charges. "All right, how about a job more in line with your tastes?"

"I hope it doesn't involve climbing back on that bike."

"No, I want you to scout out a good, covered route away from the rails and up this ridge. Take Ediyak with you and show her it. If a Reaper starts sniffing around in our rear, take care of him, or warn me."

"That's more my style," she said, fixing a button on her coat. "Want some of this bug jerky? It's not half bad. I think these guys use molasses."

Valentine stomped down his vexation with Duvalier. "Ediyak, go with Smoke here. Don't worry, she's just marking out a line of retreat. She'll keep an eye on you out in the dark."

"Two eyes," she agreed, smiling at his clerk. Ediyak was rather good-looking at that. But then the kind of Quislings who ended up in the Order's services had better access to nutrition and grew up well-formed.

A soldier trotted up.

"Sir, Red Dog is acting really weird. He's hiding under the sheep and whimpering. Harmony says they used to have a hound that acted just the same way when there were Savio—mean to say, Hoods around. He told me to get you."

Valentine still felt disquieted.

He turned to Duvalier. "You'd better make your exit now, or you won't have an option anymore."

She gestured to Ediyak. "Direction is the better part of valor," she said. Ediyak picked up her rifle and checked it.

Valentine was beginning to suspect Duvalier liked to misquote Shakespeare just to bug him. He reached into a cargo bag and extracted a flare pistol on a lanyard and a pouch of flares.

"Don't get yourself taken," she said to Valentine. "One is my limit for heroic rescues." She gave him a quick buss on the ear, standing on tiptoe to reach, kissing lightly enough that Valentine felt like Peter Pan brushed by Tink's wings.

Then the Kentucky night swallowed her.

They were right about the dog. Valentine tried to tempt him out from under the train engine, but the dog bobbed his head and whimpered, tail tucked tightly between his legs.

"I know just how you feel, ol' buddy," one of the company said.

Valentine nodded and reached, opened a Velcro flap on his canvas ammunition harness. He extracted one of the blue-taped magazines, loaded it, borrowed some camouflage gun tape, and married a regular 9mm magazine to the Quickwood bullets.

Valentine walked up to his foremost pickets. He knelt, sent them creeping back to the main line, relieved in more ways than one.

They were out there. Reapers. Valentine's heart began to hammer.

Use it. Use the fear.

It woke him up with a capital awake. Each insect in the Kentucky night hummed its own little tune with its wings.

Valentine saw brush move. A peaked back, like an oversized cobra hood, rose from the brush.

Valentine felt its gaze. Every fiber, every nerve ending, came alive. He felt as though he could count the blood capillaries in his fingertips and the follicles on his scalp. Individual drops of sweat could be felt on his back. He opened the front grip on the gun, put the machine pistol tight to his shoulder—

The attack came from the hillside. Valentine heard a flap—*laundry on a line*. The gun went up without Valentine willing it and the muzzle flash lit up a falling, grasping parachute of obsidian-fanged death.

The next one was up to him before he could even turn to face it.

WHAM and the gun was gone, spinning off into darkness. Valentine fell backward, rolled, came up holding his sword protectively in front, noted coldly that the Reaper he'd shot was clawing at its chest, foot-long barbed tongue extended and straining.

The unwounded Reaper advanced at a crouch, a thin sumo wrestler scuttling insectlike in its squat. The inhuman flexibility of its joints unsettled. Your brain locked up in frozen fascination, trying to identify a humanoid shape that moved like a fiddler crab.

Valentine backed up a step, opening his stance and setting the sword behind, ready to uncoil his whole body in a sweeping cut when it leaped.

It sprang, taking off like a rocket.

BLAM! BLAM!

Shotgun blasts struck it, sent it spinning away as unexpectedly as a jack-in-the-box yanked back into its box as Valentine's sword sweep cut the air where it would have been.

Bee rose from some brush clinging to the small gravel swell the tracks ran along, other shotgun now held forward while she broke open the one she'd just fired with her long, strong fingers.

Valentine heard crashing in the brush as the shot-struck Reaper ran away. Valentine's instinct was to pursue. If it was running away, it was damaged and disadvantaged. He forced himself back to his senses and his men, sheathed the unblooded sword.

"Good work, Bee," Valentine said.

"Beee!" Bee agreed.

Officers' whistles cut through the darkness somewhere down the tracks that led toward the pursuing Quislings. Valentine located the sound. It came from the middle of a trio of tall robed figures in the center of the columns. Valentine saw movement all around them in the dim light.

Someone—Glass probably—had the sense to fire an illumination flare. The firework burst high, lighting up the steep-sided cut as it wobbled down.

The railroad cut was full of troops walking their bicycles uphill in two open-order lines up either side of the tracks, carrying their rifles at the ready so that the muzzles were pointed toward their open flanks rather than at their comrades.

Valentine backed up a few steps, fired another flare with his own gun as he retreated toward his line, more to highlight himself to his men. He drew a shot and then another from scouts the Quislings had sent forward. Luckily these troops didn't have nightscopes.

"Check fire, check fire. It's the major," someone shouted.

Valentine made sure Bee was following—she was backing through the brush like a living fortification between him and the advancing troops—and came up to his men. They'd stripped the boxcars of bed frames, thin mattresses, and water barrels and improvised a breastwork, shielding it with cut brush.

"Fire on my order. Single shots only, and take your time," Valentine said. "Pass the word. Single shots only. We're guerrillas, remember. All we've got are deer rifles and bird guns. Sergeants on up, have your pistols out with Quickwood magazines in."

Valentine trotted to the other side of the tracks, passed the word to the troops opposite the cut. As he was about to climb into the caboose, Valentine heard something skip and bounce through the dirt toward the fortification.

"Grenade," he shouted, embracing gravel like it was his mother.

It blew on the far side of the breastwork. The men began to shoot back, placing careful single shots. The machine guns from the caboose opened up and drew fire in return.

Did the Reapers know they were chasing nothing but sheep and goats yet?

More whistles, and the Quislings came forward at a rush, bright flowers of shotgun blasts cutting through the brush as the assault began.

He fired another flare and saw them coming, heads bobbing as they advanced, the foremost less than twenty yards away, covering each other with bursts of fire that pinged off the caboose or thwacked into the bed-frame breastworks. If they could be turned now . . .

"Fire at will!" Valentine shouted.

Gunfire roared into the night. Grenades bloomed and died, each one exploding more softly as the ears became overwhelmed by the noise. Valentine saw figures falling or diving for cover.

A Reaper ran toward them straight up the rail line, a satchel held in each hand. The Kurian animating the Reapers must have been either desperate or determined to overwhelm them in an all-or-nothing gambit. Bee fired and missed, and then tore up its robes with her second barrel. Valentine didn't need to wonder what was in the satchels, or see the digital seconds ticking down. God, his pistol was out there somewhere—

A sergeant, Troust—though the men nicknamed him Surf, as he combed his thick blond hair into a wave on his forehead—appeared beside Valentine and rested his 9mm on a step of the caboose, firing steadily, aiming with each shot. Valentine duly noted his coolness as though already composing the report.

The Reaper stiffened, leaning oddly, and started a throw, but the blood drinker's fingers refused to release. The momentum of the satchel toppled it, and Valentine saw the astonishment in its eyes.

Valentine saw heads rise as the Quisling soldiers scrambled out of the way of what was coming.

"Down!"

Valentine covered his ears and felt the weight of Troust come down on the back of his head. The satchel charges went off in twin booms that must have echoed in Georgia, and Valentine felt the world momentarily give way.

Surf let him up, the weird underwatery feel of the explosions' concussion sapping his strength and wits. A Quisling in a torn green uniform was at the barricade, staggering as he tried to climb over, and suddenly Valentine's backup pistol was in his hand and he shot, realizing as the bullets hit that he was killing a man trying to surrender.

More bursts of fire came from the darkness down the track. The gunfire seemed wrong. Those titanic blasts should have been an operatic blast at the climax of the fight, not punctuation in the middle of a long, deadly symphony. His flare hung on a tree downslope, sputtering as its light died.

More whistles, low and muted to his outraged ears. Valentine saw wounded men being carried back.

Had to do something to break up the attack.

"Empty the caboose," he told Troust. "Fall back to the rock pile as soon as the cars start moving."

Valentine crept along the tracks, sheltering from the wild high bullets in the wheels, Bee trailing him like a gigantic dog. He opened each boxcar door about halfway. A goat jumped out. The other livestock looked stupidly at him, jumping and quivering at each shot.

He climbed into the engineer's cab, told the soldier there to start the train backward, and hurried to the back door.

He found Crow still posted, moving the barrel of his rifle at every sound.

"I want you to uncouple as soon as the cars have a little momentum."

"While the cars are moving?" Crow asked.

"Yes."

The cars bumped into motion, their squeals curiously innocent after the noise of combat. Valentine gauged the train's speed.

"Now, Crow. Release!" Valentine shouted down from the engine.

Crow waited until the tension came off the coupling, then pulled it. Pressure cables for the car brakes hissed as the valves closed.

Valentine extended a hand and helped pull him back into the engine as the man working the controls applied the brakes. The rest of the cars pulled away, picking up speed on the slope.

"You did well, there," Valentine told Crow as the latter wiped his greasy hands on a rag.

The sheep and goats didn't like the motion and began to leap from the train. First a few goats, and then the sheep, all in a rush. Some went head over heels as they came off in a mass, a waterfall of wool and tufted hair. The goats' instinct was to head for high ground, and the more nimble goats made the escape up the hillside first. The sheep stuck together in bawling clumps.

Crow slipped and Valentine lunged, catching his arm. Crow's toes skipped on the tracks, sending up pebbles and dust. The train wasn't moving that fast, but the engine's tonnage could maim or kill even at a crawl. Valentine hoisted him into the engine compartment as the gunner opened up on some unknown target. Tracers zipped off into the darkness, zipping like hornets with meteor tails toward an enemy.

"Back up toward the rock pile," Valentine told the engineer, who applied brakes and sent the engine in the other direction. The gun overhead chattered again and Valentine heard casings clink into the canvas bags that prevented the spent shells from rolling around underfoot in the control cabin. Then, to the men at either side, he yelled, "Fall back! Fall back up the tracks."

Bullets rattled off the engine in reply. But the men began to move, NCOs tapping their charges on the shoulder and gesturing.

Valentine watched the spectacle of confused sheep and goats caught in a cross fire. Even experienced soldiers would hesitate to just gun down animals—there wasn't a man among them who didn't sympathize with the poor dumb brutes with little control over their fate, for the obvious reason that soldiers occasionally felt like sheep in that way—and Valentine's company used the confusion to scuttle back behind the rocks blocking the railroad cut.

The rocks were comforting in their thickness and sharp edging. There was good cover for shooting all along the fall; a crenellated wall on a medieval castle wouldn't have been more heartening.

The engineer and Crow leaped for the rocks, jumped over, and took cover, Crow leaving his rifle behind in his panic, the idiot. Valentine picked it up.

He tapped the gunner's leg. "C'mon. Leave it."

The gunner ignored him, emptied the weapon's box, and stood dumbly for a moment, as though waiting for someone to reload the weapon. Then he turned and looked down at Valentine with confused eyes. There was blood running down his face from a wound on his scalp.

"Out, back to the rocks," Valentine shouted, slapping him hard on the ankle.

The gunner finally left the cupola, slithered like a snake out of the battle seat and stirrups, and jumped out.

Valentine reversed the gears on the train one more time, clamped the pedal of the dead man's switch shut with a heavy wrench left for that purpose, and sent the engine puffing back down the tracks after the freewheeling boxcars, more to open the field of fire from the rock pile than anything. He paused in the doorway, suddenly tender about jumping, and leaped so that he landed on his good leg. He scrambled back toward the rock slide as sheep bleated in alarm at the engine picking up speed through their midst.

Valentine wished he'd thought to set some explosives in case a hero tried to jump into the cab to stop the engine before it collided with the boxcars.

The Quisling rail soldiers came up the cut one more time, but Glass and Rutherford and DuSable poured fire down the cut as the rest of the company took positions in the rock pile. More sheep and goats fell than men, but the return fire was inaccurate in the dark. Mortar shells began to explode on the hillside. The fire corrected, and a shell dropped into the rocks. Valentine heard a scream and he saw Cabbage run forward toward the blast, the big medical pouch bouncing on his hip.

Valentine drew his sword. The Reapers would come now, with the whole company listening to the sound of a man screaming his life out. Or they'd kill the men high on the hillside and then come tumbling down the grade like jumping spiders.

But he didn't feel them. The only cold on the back of his scalp was from the chill of the Kentucky spring night.

"They're coming! Brigade's coming," he heard Ediyak shriek from somewhere above.

Valentine felt a lump in his throat. He heard horse hooves and a motor from somewhere up the cut. The mortars shifted fire, sending a few rounds exploding back along the ridge, and then went silent.

Valentine saw a wave of soldiers pour over the ridgeline to his right, taking up positions to fire down on the railway Quislings. Every yard the enemy had fought for now meant a yard they'd have to fall back under fire from support weapons on the hillside. Valentine saw hands go up or men stand with rifles held over their heads, hurrying toward the rock slide to surrender.

His company ran forward to group the prisoners and relieve them of their weapons. Valentine saw one officer carrying the machine pistol he'd lost; he recognized the colored tape holding the magazines together.

Harmony relieved the prisoner of his souvenir.

Valentine felt dazed, half awake, with the smell of gunfire and smoke and livestock and sweat in his nostrils. The weird elation that settled on a man when he starts to believe he'd survived, won, picked him up and floated him back toward the foremost troops to report.

Seng, frowning, sat in the passenger seat of his Humvee, issuing orders into a headset.

"You caused me at least two days' delay, Major," he said in response to Valentine's salute. "More likely three."

"Yes, sir," Valentine said, wondering if he was in for a dressing-down.

"I'll take it," Seng said. "Gamecock's Bears and the legworm outriders are hitting the support train now, and the Wolves are raising hell with some artillery tubes at the crossing they set up where you destroyed that bridge. A captured prisoner says their Kurian Lord's in a panic, disappeared into some secret area of his command car."

One of Valentine's company trotted up and presented him with his recovered gun. It now bore a nice set of scratches on the barrel just behind the foresight, a souvenir of the Reaper's power.

Valentine begged off from the questions and congratulations to check on the wounded. Which reminded him: "I've got wounded, sir. Can we set up a field hospital here?"

"Of course. This ridge is good defensive ground. I'll establish brigade HQ here until all our, ahem, stray sheep and goats are rounded up."

The fight already had a name—Billy Goat Cut. Valentine heard one of his corporals relaying the details to a Guard sergeant deploying his men for a sweep of the battlefield to look for enemy wounded or hiding.

Duvalier wandered out of the hills with Ediyak trailing behind, his clerk looking like she'd just been through the longest night of her life. Duvalier carried a Reaper skull by its thin black hair.

"Found him lurking on the ridge, all dazed and confused," she said, sticking the skull on a rail grade marker with a wet squelch that sounded like a melon being opened. "I thought I'd solve his problem for him."

Just like a Cat. She did everything but leave it on the back step.

"Don't mess with that," a corporal warned a curious Guard. "You'll seize up and die if you get some of that black gunk in you."

"It's safe once it's dried," Duvalier said, rubbing some on her index finger and making a motion toward her mouth. Valentine slapped her hand down.

"Cut it out, Ali. What's the matter with you?"

"I wonder sometimes," she said.

Valentine's holding action was just one-third of the story. The Bears, Wolves, and assorted legworm-mounted troops had fallen on the support trains like hyenas on a pair of sick cattle.

Gamecock had found a piece of tentacle that looked like it came from a Kurian in the wreckage. It was already sealed in a specimen jar for eventual delivery to the Miskatonic.

Of course, there was no way to identify the remains positively. Valentine imagined the Kurians weren't above sticking some unimportant former rival or inconvenient relative in an aquarium marked IN CASE OF EMERGENCY, BREAK GLASS, so to speak, should a body ever need to be left behind while the Kurian stuffed itself up a hollow tree somewhere, or in the rear engine that managed to decouple and escape at full speed.

Moytana's Wolves had their own triumph, tearing up the artillery support hurrying toward the railroad cut. They were already working on chain harnesses so the legworms could haul the tubes up and down Kentucky's hills.

Seng was wrong about the delay. It took four days to get everyone organized, the refugees and the two men too shot up to move to a local brand.

Miraculously, Valentine had no one killed in the fight; his only losses were wounded—and the jibes from the rest of the expedition.

They crossed the Big Sandy into West Virginia. Special Executive Karas commemorated the occasion by having his legworm riders offer a banquet.

They sacrificed an egged-out legworm to feed the troops. For all their size, legworms didn't offer much in the way of edibles. The tenderest pieces were the claw-like legs themselves. They reminded Valentine of the shellfish he'd eaten in New Orleans and the Caribbean. The farther away you traveled from the legs, the worse they tasted. The riders assured him younger legworms were both tenderer and tastier, as were unfertilized eggs—"Kentucky caviar."

Legworm flesh barbecue was something of an acquired taste and depended greatly on the quality of the barbecue sauce. Southern Command's soldiery invited or shanghaied into attending chewed manfully.

Valentine ate his deep-fried with a lot of cider vinegar.

They put Karas' chair on another stump, this one only a foot off the ground at the high end of the picnic field's slope, but it still gave him a commanding view and a sort of dais from which to command his legworm-riding knights-errant.

Seng tapped Valentine on the shoulder. "Major, our ally heard about Billy Goat Cut. He wants to see you."

Gamecock and Moytana were there as well, along with a Guard captain whose command had taken a whole platoon of railway security troops prisoner. A small crowd of legworm riders and soldiers had gathered to watch events, while sneaky dogs, including Valentine's company mutt, raided unattended plates. Valentine saw Duvalier's freckled eyes in the crowd. She had a broke-brim felt hat pulled down almost to her knees and looked lost in her ratty old overcoat.

The leaders of the assorted clans of the Kentucky Alliance arranged themselves behind Karas. His handsome face smiled down at them.

Valentine saw Tikka again, standing next to her adoptive brother, Zak. Zak had a welt at the corner of his eye, but then it was a rare day when there wasn't a good fistfight in the Alliance camp. Kentucky men fought the way New Universal Churchmen golfed, as both a recreation and a social ritual.

"The major first," Karas said. "Congratulations on your brilliant fight."

"Brilliant" wasn't the word Valentine would have chosen. Brilliant commanders bagged their enemy with a minimum of shooting back.

Karas stood up. "A presentation is in order, I think. Bravery must be rewarded, just as treason must be punished."

"Bow," Tikka urged in a whisper that somehow carried.

Valentine wanted to tell her that the only time a Southern Command officer bowed was as sort of a preamble before asking a lady for a dance (Captain LeHavre used to say that it gave you a last chance to make sure your shoelaces were tied), but decided to cooperate in the interest of keeping the new allies happy.

"I dub you a knight of the New Kentucky Homeland," Karas said as he looped the medallion over Valentine's head. Valentine noticed that Karas' hands smelled like a cheap Kurian Zone aftershave called Ultimate, strong enough to mask a hard day's body odor in an emergency.

Valentine liked Karas a little better. No one with royal pretensions would walk around smelling like a blend of gasoline and window cleaner.

Valentine straightened again.

"Kentucky thanks you, son of both Southern Command and our own Bulletproof."

Kind words, but Valentine hoped he wasn't using the word Kentucky the way the Kurian in the Pacific Northwest used to be called Seattle.

While Moytana, Gamecock, and the Guard captain got their ribbons and medals, Valentine examined his decoration.

It looked like a piece of old horse show ribbon with a brassy circle at the end. Valentine looked closely at the medal. It was an old commemorative quarter glued facedown on a disk of brass—the Kentucky state design, rather nicked and scratched, but as clean and polished as elbow grease could make it.

Karas must be some kind of coin enthusiast. That or he was a student of the little common details that built a culture and a community.

Zak gave Valentine a discreet wave. His sister winked and moistened her lips.

The rest of the march had its share of difficulties. Valentine lost two soldiers of his company, whether through desertion or simple loss he never learned—they took bicycles into a town that allegedly had a good, safe market and never returned.

Seng was moving too hard to the northeast for Valentine to delay in searching for them. He led a detail in civilian clothes into town but could learn nothing.

Bee slept outside his tent like a dog. Duvalier brought home grisly trophies now and then—Quisling scouts, an unfortunate pimp who tried to drug her at a trans-Appalachian inn, a Reaper who'd lost a foot to a bear trap.

Word of Red Dog's Reaper-sensing powers spread, and Seng attached him to brigade headquarters as scouting and detection gear. The dog went out with Wolf patrols and nighttime picket checks. Red Dog's cheery enjoyment of his excursions rubbed off as they neared their goals.

There certainly were pleasures to the march. Valentine loved the vistas of this piece of country. The old, round, wooded mountains had a tumbledown beauty, and seemed to keep secret histories in the silent manner of aging former belles.

Valentine visited the Bulletproof camp and learned some of the ins and outs of the Kentucky Alliance. All the clans were powerful organizations, powerful enough so the Kurians kept watch on them and sometimes started feuds to prevent any one from getting too powerful. At least that's what Zak thought, expressing his opinion over some well-diluted bourbon at one evening's camp.

After a final pause that allowed Brother Mark and a pair of Cats to attend a meeting with the guerrillas and the underground, they marched to a map reference point and made camp on a defensible hillside. It was well watered, with a nasty rock pile to the north on one flank and a swamp to the south. Below, just visible between two lesser hills, was the town of Utrecht, seemingly chosen for its misty, mountain environs and the echoes of history in its name.

The representatives of the guerrilla army guarding the town seemed woefully undermanned, tattered but well-armed. The legworm ranchers mixed with them more freely than the Southern Command troops.

With Bee leading the cart horses and Ediyak sitting beside with the company fund, Valentine took a barter cart down into the valley and saw a better ordered group of men, perhaps in reinforced regiment strength, camped on another hill to the northeast of town. Thinking that this was the partisan army proper, he turned the cart onto a road skirting town and toward their pickets, and received yet another surprise when he saw tattered flags identifying the men as belonging to Vermont and New Hampshire.

"Who the hell?"

"I'll be damned. Those are the Green Mountain Boys," Ediyak said. "Jeebus, all that's missing is a complement of Kee-bec Liber-tay for us to have every Freehold east of the Mississippi represented here."

Valentine waved hello to a corporal's guard watching the road but the soldiers just stared at him, waiting for orders from their superiors.

They were good-looking men, wearing woodland camouflage, boots, leather gaiters, and a good selection of Kevlar. Most had 4x combat sights on their assault rifles. On closer examination Valentine saw what were probably masked gun emplacements on the hillside, and a headlog or two peeped out from covering brush at the edge of open hillside pasture. Anything short of a divisional assault on this hill, with armored car support, would be torn to bits.

Their tents weren't laid out in an organized fashion, but in little groupings that made their gently sloping hillside look like it had sprouted a case of green ringworm. Camouflage netting covered some tenting and mortar pits; others were open for the world to see.

"Dots, you magnificent bitch," Valentine found himself saying. *Good God, how did all this come about?* She'd played her cards very close to the chest.

His vision had come true—and then some. He'd imagined leading some Wolves and technicians to the aid of the guerrillas. Lambert had taken that idea and turned it into something for the history books.

It made him clammy just to think about it.

Valentine turned back into town. It was a rather old-fashioned main-street type of town, and every third building seemed to be named after somebody or other, nineteenth-century achievement emblazoned in Romanic letters in stone ready to bear witness to their greatness until wind and rain wore down even their gravestones.

The civilians were keeping indoors, were terrified, or had fled the gathering of forces. Valentine saw Southern Command uniforms mixing with the timber camouflage of the Green Mountain Boys, guerrillas in patched riding coats and legworm leathers, all meeting and talking and buying one another drinks. A trio of milk-shouldered girls in halter tops, plump and tempting, called out to the soldiers from the expansive porch of an old Victorian mansion just off the town square. Valentine wondered whether some entrepreneur had followed a regiment on the march and set up shop, or if it was a local establishment operating discreetly under Kurian eyes and now enjoying a quick gold rush of uniforms.

Bee whooped excitedly. Valentine saw a tower of faun-furred muscle, back to him, moving through the crowd in the middle of a complement of men with foxtail-trimmed ponchos hanging from their shoulders. Valentine felt his throat swell. He whipped the cart horses, hard, and caught up to the short column.

"Yo! Old Horse," Valentine called to the Grog's back. It ignored him, perhaps not hearing him in the noisy street. "Hey, Uncle!" Valentine yelled.

The men in back turned, and so did the Grog.

It had a long scar running up its face and a fang missing. An eyelid drooped lazily; the other glared at him, keen and suspicious.

It wasn't Ahn-Kha.

Eight

*The Allegheny Alliance, West Virginia, June: The campaign surround-
ing the great union in the Alleghenies near the town of Utrecht is one
more men claimed to be at than ever were. Or if not themselves in person, a brother, a cousin, an uncle or aunt—laid down like a trump card
when veterans get together to talk about their experiences in the Liberation. (Only writers of lurid exploitative novels title the fight against
the Kurian Order the "Vampire Wars.")*

*It's safe to say that Utrecht, West Virginia, had never seen such a
feast, even during holidays during the platinum age pre-2022. The
town square had a smaller square of groaning white-clothed banquet
tables set up within. The old pedestal in front of the courthouse that
had once contained a memorial to First World War veterans (replaced
by a statue of a Reaper holding a human baby up so it could look up at
the stars, and happily sawn off at the ankles the week before when the
"guerrilla army" occupied the town) had a new set of stairs, as well as
a platform and loudspeaker system for speechmaking. Most said Special Executive Karas had been working on a stemwinder for months,
looking forward to this moment.*

*For David Valentine, out of thousands readying themselves for a
party of special magnificence, the night held little promise.*

David Valentine drove the cart back into company headquarters,
fighting tears. All around the people were putting up colorful bunting
(red, white, and blue or yellow being the colors of choice, but some
folks were making do with tinsel and other old Christmas decorations).

Blueberries were in season, and Bee happily scooped out an entire
pie Ediyak purchased for her. Ediyak was whistling Southern Command

marching tunes, rather off-key. Every storefront had fresh baked goods for sale, and around the back door bottles and flasks and mason jars of liquor were being passed out in exchange for everything from gold or silver coin to overcoats, old eyeglasses, and boots.

Southern Command's officers and NCOs spoiled not a few prospective evenings by checking packs and ammunition pouches of those traveling to and from town.

Valentine pulled himself together enough to institute a liquor search of his own when he returned, and three bottles were emptied into the thirsty Allegheny dirt and Patel had new miscreants for latrine and garbage duty. Though he'd laid out his best uniform for the banquet, the prospect of a feast had lost all its luster and he decided not to attend. He checked in at headquarters and swapped purchases he'd made in town for twenty-four duty-free hours after the banquet. He wanted quiet and solitude.

Jolly was left in command of the camp. He said he'd heard enough speeches about Kurian tactics of fear never conquering the human spirit in his life. But he almost ordered Valentine to go.

"If anyone deserves a good feed, it's you, Valentine," he said. "You've kept us in fresh eggs and vegetables for three months."

Moytana saved him from being ordered to attend by appearing. His Wolf patrols were routed or posted, and this bit of Virginia was at peace, though they had intercepted some high-ranking Quislings scuttling north with a couple wagons of clothing and valuables, and Moytana needed orders.

Valentine, hearing that the brigade was still attending to basics despite the festival, went to the commissary and got a sandwich. He found a comfortable stump and watched the partiers depart. Seng led the way with several other officers, some with hardy wives and husbands who'd come along for the march, plus select NCOs and regular soldiers—the wounded or those deserving of special consideration. Music echoed up from the Kentucky hills.

He finished his sandwich. Tasteless, despite the fresh vegetables and mayonnaise.

Duvalier waited for him in his tent. She was reclining in his hammock, her boots off and her bony feet greasy with something that smelled of lanolin and mint. "What's got you down?" she asked, dropping a Kurian newspaper bearing a headline about a rail accident in Kentucky.

"I was in town," Valentine said. He decided to tell her. Talking might ease the heartache. Ahn-Kha's loss was real, fresh and raw again like a stripped scab. "I saw a Golden One. Thought it was Ahn-Kha. It wasn't."

She sat up. "That bites. I—I can't believe it. I heard the stories about him organizing the partisans."

"Ahn-Kha's not the only Grog who could organize a revolt. This one wasn't as well-spoken. I got about three words out of him," Valentine said. "He's probably wary of strange uniforms."

"This is still a big deal, Val. You helped make it happen. I remember you laboring over reports about Kentucky, when we wintered. You had a stack of papers the size of—well, you remember."

Valentine didn't say anything, willing her to be as miserable as he was.

"In a way, it's still Ahn-Kha's victory. You decided Southern Command could march across Kentucky, what with the Kurians few and far between in the legworm ranch country."

"I know."

"Look, I should just say it: I was an ass to you back then. You were killing yourself looking for Ahn-Kha. I thought you were wasting your time, tried to slap you out of it. Plus we fought about that baby Reaper. Is it doing well? Did you tame it—er, him?"

"Blake's well enough. Growing fast. I don't think anyone but Narcisse could have brought him up."

"Want to talk about Ahn-Kha some more?"

"No," Valentine said. He hated the celebration he was missing. It felt like a dance on the Golden One's grave.

"I've got a bottle," she said, patting one pocket on her long coat. "Want a drink?"

"I ordered everyone in camp searched," Valentine growled.

"If they can't locate someone, it's a lot harder to search them," Duvalier said. "You've got some good guys here, but they're not that good."

He could stand her company. She'd known Ahn-Kha almost as long as he had. "Pour it out. I don't want liquor in the camp. We'll arrange passes soon so people can go into town if they want to get drunk."

"I'll do no such thing. There's no swiping liquor. I had to buy that with some of Karas' funny money."

"Strange that they took his coin. Or did you offer a little personal bonus to get the booze?"

"Fuck off. I've blown a few sentries to get over a bridge or through a fence, but I'm no whore." She angrily shoved the bottle back into the coat.

Valentine retrieved his ten-dollar piece from his pocket. It was crude, and it had nothing more than the word of some jumped-up legworm rancher behind it. Maybe the citizens of Utrecht were swept up by patriotic fervor.

"I sometimes think we fight just to keep from falling in love," Duvalier said.

Valentine almost dropped the coin.

She rolled on her side, not the easiest thing to do in a hammock. "So, you going to dance with me at the glam-up? I'll get dressed. Ediyak has a civilian skirt and a top she said she'd loan me." She gripped the edge of the hammock and put her delicate chin over the edge, smiling like the Cheshire cat after a three-canary meal.

"I volunteered to stay in camp," Valentine said, shaking his head. "Speaking of which, my four hours starts soon."

"I'm not a fan of parties either. But I did go to the trouble of swiping some new underwear. Cute knit stuff, like lace from a fancy doily."

"Ali, these people are patriots," Valentine said. "It's not some KZ three-dollar store."

"I guess so. They're making a very patriotic profit on fresh bread and pies for the soldiers who liberated them."

In worthless coin, Valentine thought. Something about that was bothering him.

"Do me a favor. Stick close, okay? I want to talk to you when I get off."

"That sounds kinda perverted for sterling Major Valentine," she said.

With the tent next to empty, his duty time at brigade headquarters crawled. So he spent it roving. He walked the posts, checked the firewood and water supply, saw to it that no one had dug the latrines so they drained toward the food preparation area. The reserve supply dumps were still being built and a mini-backhoe was still at work digging magazines for their small supply of artillery.

Seng had chosen the spot for their new base well. Utrecht stood on the heel of a short mountain range, at a crossroads that would allow a shift northeast up either side of a mountain ridge, or to the southwest, and there were further cuts east and west, old roads and disused rail lines that were in poor shape but better than hacking one's way through woody mountains. At the last officers' meeting, Seng had stated that the first order of business would be a new survey of the area; Seng wanted to know every cow path and bike trail.

Valentine's company would probably be put to work improving old roads or creating connecting trails.

Valentine thought he saw the shape of the coming campaign. He guessed Seng hoped to imitate Jackson's Valley Campaign from the American Civil War near Winchester just on the other side of the Appalachians, as a matter of fact, popping in and out of mountain passes and sliding up and down roads to catch the Kurian forces unawares.

Even now Valentine saw some dozens of legworms being driven into a brushy area south of town, on the other side of a twisting, turning stream where he saw some old, collapsed roofs. Ever since the linkup with Karas's group of rebel tribes, Seng had his regulars learning to handle the creatures. Legworms didn't need much more width than a jeep, and they never got stuck in mud or hung up on a rock. He watched them feed their way into the tangle of bush and young trees. They'd soon have it grazed down into open country, potential pasture or field. Legworms were better than a Bush Hog.

Some of the goats he'd purchased back on the Cumberland Plateau had made the long trip. Valentine paused to scratch one. A few of the men were already developing a taste for goat milk. He wondered if they had anyone with cheesemaking experience in the brigade.

The wind was blowing sound away from the torchlit town, but every now and then when the wind died he thought he caught words punctuated by music.

At the end of his duty he made a brief report to Jolla, who was dozing in a chair in his office near the headquarters tent. He turned the duty over to Nowak and left, walking past Brother Mark's tent. Valentine's ears heard soft snores from within. The old churchman had pushed himself hard, riding ahead with parties of Wolves, setting up meetings and last-minute details for the unification.

He wondered why he wasn't at the party. Brother Mark, from what he could tell, led a rather Spartan existence. Maybe he didn't like parties.

Duvalier waited in his tent. The soft, comforting aroma of a woman in the canvas-enclosed air was more welcoming than the thermos of coffee she opened on his return.

Instead of some dripping trophy, she'd brought two big slices of cherry cobbler. She smelled faintly of sandalwood too.

"You snuck a little whiskey into this," Valentine said, trying the coffee.

"Just a tetch, as they say here. I think we deserve a celebration too."

Valentine sipped the coffee, thinking of Malita in Jamaica. The coffee had been real there. Had the emotional connection been fake? What was real and what was wishful thinking—on both their parts—in this little hillside tent?

Duvalier leaned on the tent pole, sipping hers.

"You used to joke all the time about sexing me up. I think you're the only man who crossed the whole state of Kansas with a hard-on."

"Twenty-three will do that to you. My balls did my thinking for me whenever you seemed approachable. You used to say, what was it—"

"Dream on, Valentine," they said in unison. They both giggled.

She kissed him, softly, on the lips. Looking up into his eyes, she smiled. "There's a grand alliance forming down there, helped along with liquor and barbecue. I think tonight's a night for dreams coming true."

It was so tempting. He could forget everything, thrusting into her. He could find oblivion in satisfying lust the way some men lost themselves in drink, or at the green gaming tables, or in swirling clouds of narcotics. So tempting. No more thoughts of Ahn-Kha's face, those curious townies peering at him from behind quilted curtains, the apparently bottomless supply of alcohol . . .

Valentine put his hands on her, tickled the back of her neck. "But we'd—"

The *krump* of an explosion interrupted him. The distant *pop-pop-pop* of small arms fire followed.

Duvalier's brow furrowed. "I hope that's fireworks."

Valentine grabbed his pistol belt and sword and poked his head out of the tent. No comforting bursts of fireworks filled the mountain valley, but there were red flares firing in the air above the Green Mountain Boys' encampment. He couldn't see the town, but the torchlight glow in the sky over it was almost gone.

"I've got to get to headquarters," he said.

"I know," she said. "Where do you want me?"

"If any of your fellow Cats are in camp, round them up and report to Moytana's headquarters."

The corner of her mouth turned up. "It was a nice moment, while it lasted."

"It was," Valentine agreed. He trotted a few feet over to company HQ as the brigade bugle sounded officers' call.

Rand was already up and Patel came into their two-pole headquarters tent carrying his boots and his rifle. Red Dog was running around, excited in the commotion but not looking at all frightened. That gave Valentine some comfort.

"I'm going to brigade," Valentine said. "Preville, come along in case I need a messenger. I've no news, other than that something's wrong. Assemble the men with full field kit and three days' rations. Make sure the reserve dehydrated food and ammunition reserves are handy. Get a meal into the men if there's anything hot handy."

They nodded. Patel just kept putting on his boots. Preville patted back some rather straggly hair over his ears that made him look more than ever like a revolutionary intellectual.

Valentine could rely on them. He hurried to brigade headquarters, saw Duvalier's head bobbing off toward the Hunters' collection of tents within the larger encampment. Lights died out all over camp, and she vanished as a lantern was extinguished. He tried to let the red hair take his regrets with it.

He beat Moytana into the headquarters by fifteen seconds. Others trickled in, way, way too many junior officers who missed the celebration thanks to privileges of rank. Nowak was speaking to someone over a field phone.

Major Bloom stood behind, looking like a pit bull waiting for the release. From her position, Valentine guessed she was the temporary senior for the Guards.

Jolla's balding head glistened. He kept wiping it with a handkerchief. "There's been some kind of disturbance in town. We don't know anything more than that."

"Observers report the firing is dying down. There's still some torchlight and lanterns in the town square, but the rest of the lights in town are out," Nowak reported.

"Are . . . are the lines to the Green Mountain contingent and Karas', er, headquarters functioning?"

"Not strung yet," Nowak said. "We're in radio contact with the Green Mountain troops. They're asking us what's happening in town, since we've got a better view. They got a walkie-talkie distress signal, it seems." She spoke with the flat monotone of someone operating on autopilot.

More officers arrived and Jolla silenced the babble.

"Defensive stance," Jolla said. "Let's get the men to their positions for now. Where's Colonel—oh, at the party, of course."

Valentine dispatched Preville to pass the word to Rand, met Moytana's eyes, and jerked his chin toward Jolla. As everyone filed out to get their men to battle positions, some of which were only half-completed, they were joined by Bloom and Nowak.

"Your Wolves haven't reported enemy formations?" Valentine said.

"No, Major," Moytana said. "Only thing out of the ordinary they reported was a lot of activity at an old mine north of here. Military-style trucks and command cars. Locals said it had been shut down for years and just reopened and was being garrisoned. Said it was because the guerrillas had wrecked a couple of other more productive mines and they had to reopen. Seng's got us keeping an eye on it, and a Cat is taking a closer look."

"You could hide a lot of men in a coal mine," Jolla said.

"Maybe the 'Green Mountain Boys' aren't really Green Mountain Boys," Bloom said.

"No, they're real enough," Nowak said. "Lambert and Seng were expecting them. We've had progress reports."

"Perhaps we should shift camp, Colonel," Valentine said. "Move closer to Karas' bunch and the Green Mountain Boys. Right now we can't support each other."

"In the dark?" Jolla asked.

"Old Wolf trick, sir," Moytana said. "If somebody's marked out our positions for artillery, might be better if they wasted their shells on empty space."

"I took a look at their positions this morning," Valentine added. "They've got a good high hill to their backs."

"I think the enemy would be firing on us already if they had our position," Jolla said. "We don't even know what's happened in town yet."

"We may soon, Colonel," Nowak said, ear to the field phone again. "Pickets are reporting Private Dool is coming in. He ran all the way from town. Says there's been a massacre."

"No one else?"

"Just Dool, sir. He said they took away his rifle and his pants."

"His *pants*? Get him up here," Jolla said.

Valentine had the uncomfortable sensation that Dool's missing pants was just the first oddly heavy raindrop in a storm to come. He could almost feel trouble gathering, like the heavy air in front of piled up thunderclouds. Like an animal, he wanted to get away or underneath something.

Dool showed up soon enough, shoeless and footsore, a blanket wrapped around his waist. Dool was a Guard regular who'd been wounded by a grenade in the cleanup action after the fight at Billy Goat Cut. He looked distraught. He still had his uniform shirt, though a blood splatter ran up the front to his shoulder like a rust-colored bandolier.

Jolla said, "Just give it to me, Dool. Don't worry about military form."

"Killed them all, sir. Colonel Seng and the rest, Roscoe next to me—they're all dead. They told me to tell you. Said that someone was to come into town to hear terms at dawn. They told me to tell you."

"They?"

"The fellers with the squared-off black beards."

"Like this," Moytana said, passing his hand just under his chin.

"Yessir, yes, Cap'n, that's just it."

"What's this, Moytana?" Jolla demanded.

Moytana cleared a frog from his throat. "It's the Moondagger Corps. Or elements of it. They all wear beards like that." Moytana's face went as gray as the washed-out ropes in his hair.

Valentine knew the name. Oddly enough he'd heard it from Duvalier when they were discussing recent events in Kansas. They were some kind of special shock troops used to quell uprisings and had caused the '72 operation in Kansas to fall apart before it even got going.

"Never mind that," Jolla said. "Tell us what happened. Take your time."

Dool hitched the blanket around his legs a little tighter. "It was a fine dinner, sir. Officers from the Green Mountain troops were across the square from us, and the legworm guys were around the statue and on our left. Guerrilla troops too, only now I think they wasn't guerrillas but turncoats. Like Texas and Okie redhands, only worse.

"Then King Karas, he gets up and starts one of those fine speeches of his."

A siren started up, interrupting him.

"Engine noise reported overhead. One plane," Nowak reported from the field phones.

A second drop. How long until they start to fall, hard?

"Is the HQ dugout done yet?" Jolla asked.

"It's just a hole at the moment, sir," Nowak said.

"We'll adjourn there."

The hole was only half dug. There weren't any floor-boards even. They squelched uncomfortably into the mud. It was deep enough so they could sit with heads below ground level. Nowak stayed at the head-quarters tent.

Some squatted. Valentine's bad leg ached if he did that for more than a minute or two, so he settled uncomfortably into the mud.

"Go on with your story," Bloom said to Dool.

"Here, sir?"

"Little else to do," Jolla said.

Except get the camp moving. Forward, back, just somewhere other than where the Kurians expected them to be. Valentine could hear the engine noise growing—a single prop, by the sound of it.

Observation planes. The herald of coming trouble.

Moytana was gnawing on the back of his hand again.

"Where did I leave off?" Dool asked.

"Karas's speech," Jolla said. "Do they really call him King Karas?"

"King of the Cumberland, some of those legworm fellers say, sir. It was a real good speech, I thought. Real good. He was just going on about mankind saying 'enough,' and there was this bright blue flash from the podium and he was just gone. Like lightning struck him, only there wasn't no bolt.

"Then the town square just sort of exploded, sir." Dool thought for a moment, as though trying to describe it. "Like a minefield wired to go off or something. Anyway, they blew up like mines. One went off right under the colonel's chair. I've always had decent reflexes, otherwise that grenade I tossed from the squad at the rail line would have been the end of me. Gunfire then, a real sweeping fire, and they started cutting down everyone. Women with serving trays and beer mugs—everyone. Only now that I think back on it, the guerrilla leaders clustered around the podium, they weren't blown up or shot; they were sort of clear from it in this little cement area with benches and a fountain. I think they all jumped in that old fountain. Wish we could have put a shell into it. The top half of the colonel was still sitting in his chair, tipped over, like. You know, like when you're at the beach and the kids half bury you in the sand, only it was real. I tried to drag Roscoe into some bushes but he was dead."

He paused for a moment. Valentine looked away while Dool wiped his eyes.

"All clear," Nowak called down into the hole.

Valentine noticed that the engine noise had died. They picked themselves up and returned to the headquarters tent.

Gamecock was there in full battle array, a big-handled bowie knife strapped to one thigh and a pistol on the other. Black paste was smeared on the exposed skin of his face and each bare arm. He had his hair gathered tightly in a food-service net.

"The whole Bear team's ready to go into that town, suh," Gamecock said. "I got twenty-two Bears already halfway up. We'll get the colonel back safe."

"Too late for that," Jolla replied. "I'm afraid he was killed in an ambush."

"Treachery, you mean," Bloom said.

"Then we'll pay them a visit to even the score," Gamecock said. "Just say the word."

Jolla tapped his hand against his thigh. "No, they're probably fortifying the town now."

"Sir, they told me to tell you what I saw," Dool said. "There wasn't anything like an army in town that I saw, just maybe a company of these bearded guys and the guerrilla turncoats."

Dool spoke up again. "The ones that surrendered, they took the prisoners and chopped their heads off. That big gold Grog was taking off heads with this thing like a branch trimmer. I thought I was gonna get chopped but it turned out I was the only one left from the brigade. Colonel Gage drew his pistol and was shooting back and they gunned him down, and a sniper got Lieutenant Nawai while he was wrestling with a redhand for his gun."

"And they told you we'd hear their terms in the morning," Jolla said. "I think we should wait."

"Wait?" Valentine said, unable to believe his ears.

"Way I see it, the fight's started," Gamecock said. "I think we can guess what their terms will be."

"Javelin's almost four hundred miles from Southern Command," Jolla said. "The locals were supposed to support us, and now we've found that they're hostile. How long can this expedition survive without the support of the locals?"

Gamecock sat down in a folding chair, took out his big bowie knife, and started sharpening it on a tiny whetstone.

Frustrated, Valentine felt like he was playing a chess game where his opponent was allowed to take three moves for his one. They'd be checkmated in short order.

"Longer than it'll last if we wait on what the Kurians have dreamed up," Valentine said.

"Javelin was named right, that's for sure," Jolla said. "Thrown over the front rank of shields at the enemy. If it hits, great. If it misses, the thrower doesn't expect to get it back. 'Sorry, General Lehman, we missed.'"

Bloom and Moytana exchanged glances. They both looked to Valentine. What were they expecting, a Fletcher Christian moment? Valentine wondered just what was said about him in Southern Command mess halls.

Valentine didn't want to think that Javelin's acting CO had his nerves shattered. Maybe he'd recover in the light of day.

Except by the light of day it would be too late.

"I'm willing to wait and hear what their terms are," Jolla said. "They may allow us to just quit and go home."

"Why would they do that?" Bloom said. "We're at the disadvantage now."

"Perhaps their real target was Karas. Kurian regulars are good enough when suppressing a revolt by farmers with pitchforks and rabbit guns. They're not as successful against trained troops. Except for in extraordinary circumstances, like Solon's takeover."

"All the more reason to pitch into them," Valentine said.

Jolla wiped his head again. "I'll go and see what they have to say.

Bloom, this is a little unorthodox, but I'm promoting you to command of the Guards with a brevet for colonel. Radio to Lehman's headquarters for confirmation and orders about how to proceed. Do you think we can get a signal through, Nowak?"

"So the radio silence order—"

"I think the Kurians know we're here now," Jolla said.

Nowak's face went red. Jolla shouldn't have snapped at her. Anyone might ask a dumb question under these circumstances.

"Thank you for your confidence, sir," Bloom said.

Nice of you, Cleo, changing the subject.

"You know the regiment and commanded them when Gage was away. If something happens to me, you're the best regular . . ."

Of what's left, Valentine silently added the unspoken words.

Valentine didn't know Southern Command military law well enough to know whether a colonel commanding could promote someone to colonel in the field, and frankly didn't care.

Nowak put down the handset.

"Colonel, I don't think you should go," she said, her face still emotionless. "Let me get their terms."

"They might pull one of their tricks," Jolla said.

"All the more reason for me to go," she said.

"Oh, Dool," Jolla said. "Why did they take your pants? I can see your shoes."

Dool tugged at an ear. "What's that, sir?"

"Your pants."

"I plain dumb forgot! They said to tell the brigade commander, 'Caught with your pants down.' I thought they were nuts. He was laying there dead in the town square. I guess they meant you to get it."

Jolla stood up. "Those were their words?"

"Yeah, caught with your pants down. I was to remind you."

"That mean something, sir?" Moytana said.

"It must just be a coincidence," Jolla said. "It's an old joke, goes back to my days at the war college. A dumb stunt I pulled."

"Has it come up recently?" Valentine asked.

"I . . . we were telling stories over cigars. Right after that fight at the railroad cut. Colonel Seng, myself, Gage was there, Karas, a few of the leaders from the legworm clans."

"I remember, sir," Nowak said. "The story about six-ass ambush. Five got away."

"And one didn't," Jolla said. "Forever branded as the one who couldn't get his pants up and tripped on his own belt."

"I wonder if there's a spy in our ranks?" Bloom asked.

"Dumb spy, to give himself away with a detail like that," Moytana said.

Or did the Kurians want everyone looking over their shoulder? Valentine wondered. They were better at sowing dissension than fighting.

The meeting broke up and Jolla ordered Valentine to check the defensive perimeter of the camp. Everyone was nervous, so he took the precaution of using the field phones to let the next post know he was on the way as he left each post.

He was checking the west side of camp when he saw a group of men. It looked like some sort of struggle. One had lit a red signal flare and held it high so the troops knew not to fire.

Valentine trotted up to the mob. They were mostly regulars from the Guard regiment.

"Stop, hold there!"

"Who says?" someone in the mob called.

"Shut it, you, it's Major Valentine," a corporal said. "Sir, we caught our spy."

The mob parted and two men dragged another forward, one holding each arm. He already had a noose around his neck. The man was folded like a clasp knife, coughing, clearly gut-punched—or kicked.

They raised his face, using his scant hair as a handle. It was Brother Mark.

"He was dressed all in black. Sneaking off."

"He always dresses in black," Valentine said. "Let him go; give him some air."

"He's the spy for sure," someone called, and the group growled approval.

Valentine wondered how word of "a spy" in camp had spread so quickly. Soldiers had their own communications grapevines, especially for bad news.

"God help me," Brother Mark gasped.

"Let's hope so," Valentine said. "Who arrested him?"

At the word "arrest" the mob stiffened a little. Valentine had used it intentionally, hoping that a whiff of juridical procedure would bring the men back to their senses.

Brother Mark groaned and sucked air.

"I guess it was me, Major. Corporal Timothy Kemper, Bravo Company, first battalion. Pickets under my command caught him sneaking out of camp."

The man in question came to his knees, grabbed Valentine by the sleeve.

"The pickets didn't 'catch' me," Brother Mark almost wept. "I hailed them and requested a guide to get me to Karas' encampment. For God's sake, tell him the facts, Corporal."

Valentine wondered if crying on bended knee got you off the hook in the Kurian Zone. Tears wetting his uniform coat cuff just left him feeling embarrassed for both of them.

"Stop that," Valentine said, backing away. "Karas is dead."

"I'd heard there was some kind of treachery in town. I thought I should see to our allies. I'm sure they're as frightened as we are."

The men growled at that again. For a man of the cloth and a diplomat, Brother Mark wasn't very good at communicating with ordinary soldiers.

"Who told you to do that?" Valentine asked.

"I thought it was my duty," he said, reclaiming some of his spaniel-eyed dignity.

"Your duty?" Valentine said, almost amused.

"My higher calling to unite—"

"Save it. You should have checked with someone and had orders issued."

"I've never had to ask permission to come and go, son." With the noose now loose around his neck, he rose to his feet, dusting off the plain black moleskin.

"Major," Valentine reminded him.

"I'm not sure where I fit in to your hierarchy."

"Under the circumstances it would have been wiser to get permission and an escort. Corporal, return to your pickets." Valentine picked out two men who made the mistake of standing a little apart from the others. "You two, come with me as an escort. I'll take our churchman to headquarters and see what he has to say. Consider yourself confined to camp for now, Brother."

"I must be allowed to visit the other camps. We must hang together, or as Franklin said, we shall all surely hang separately."

Valentine saw no point in engaging the churchman in a debate. They were already wasting time. Wasting words would just add insult to injury.

He took him up to the headquarters tent. Jolla had pushed two tables together and spread out a map of western Kentucky. He had the mission book, a set of standing orders that covered several contingencies, including loss of the commander and abandonment by the legworm clans.

Nowak was gone. Another officer was handling the communications desk—if a folding-leg table covered by a tangle of wires connecting assorted rugged electronics boxes could be called a desk—but if anything, headquarters was busier than in the first shock of the alert. Complaints and problems were coming in from all points of the compass. It was just as well that they weren't under attack, Valentine thought. The artillery spotters couldn't communicate with the mortar pits, two companies were trying to occupy the same defilade, leaving a whole eighth of the perimeter unguarded . . .

Valentine ignored the assorted kerfuffles and explained what he'd seen, and stopped. He let Brother Mark do the rest of the talking. Jolla apologized for the men being on edge.

"But you must give me orders to contact our allies, it seems," Brother Mark said.

Jolla scrawled something on his order pad and signed it.

"Do you think it's wise to just let him wander around, under the circumstances?" Valentine asked.

"I wouldn't be wandering," Brother Mark said.

"You're right, Valentine, and you just named your own poison. Go with him. They tell me the Reaper hasn't been built that can sneak up on you."

"Yes, sir," Valentine said, fighting a battle with his face.

"Besides, someone in uniform should be representing Javelin. Tell them that I've informed Southern Command of the situation and I'm waiting for orders. Until then I'm free to act as I see fit."

That'll reassure a bunch of nervous Kentucky worm-riders.

Valentine had heard rumors as a junior officer that the Kurians could befuddle key men through some sort of mental evil third eye, but had never attributed to mysticism what could be explained by stupidity. Jolla's sudden plunge into routine and procedure, when circumstances called for anything but, made him reconsider his old attitudes.

"You're a sharp instrument of good in His hands, my son," Brother Mark said. "Thank you for getting the noose off me. Those poor anxious men were rather letting their passions run wild on them."

Valentine decided he wanted the far blunter instrument of Bee along, just in case, so he delayed Brother Mark for five more minutes. He took Ediyak as well. Beauty sometimes calmed better than brawn. He grabbed some legworm jerky and peanuts and took an extra canteen. If the real fireworks began, they might be forced to flee in the wrong direction.

As they set out, Brother Mark graced them with only a single aphorism: "Let's be about God's work this night of fear and doubt." Then he stalked off toward the legworm campsites, taking long, measured strides, for all the world like a hero in one of DeMille's old biblical videos they liked to show on washed-out old 1080 screens in church basements on community night.

Valentine almost liked him. He couldn't say whether the renegade churchman was crazy, a true believer, or simply the kind of man who always stepped forward when necessity called.

He took care moving—God knows what might be prowling in the dark—with first Bee scouting while he made sure nothing was following him, and then swapping with the Grog.

The legworm clans didn't even have anything that could be called a camp. They'd gathered their legworms together into five big clumps, feeding them branches cut and dragged from the woods, with a few more grazing at the borders of their camps. Their sentries and picket positions were two-man pairs who lay behind clumps and lines of legworm droppings, the fresh deposits notched with little sandbags the size of small pistols supporting deer rifles. Behind the spotter/sniper positions more men stood ready to mount their legworms.

Valentine had seen the mobile breastworks that legworms provided in action before. The riders planted hooks and straps in the fleshy, nerveless sides of their mounts and hung off the living walls, employing their guns against an opponent, using tactics that combined First World War trench warfare with wooden ship actions from Nelson's day.

The legworm clans were quick to blame Southern Command for not properly securing the town. Valentine conceded the point. The Wolves had checked it out, and then the Guards conducted a more thorough search, but whatever soldiers had been posted at key buildings and crossroads were missing along with the rest of the celebrants.

"I told Spex Karas this whole affair would go wrong," the dispatcher of the Coonskins said. He glared at Valentine through his one good eye. The other was a milky wreck. "The Free Territories egg us into fighting with the Kurians. We're for it now. For it deep."

"It's not this young man's fault," Brother Mark said.

Valentine thought of correcting him. He'd urged Southern Command to explore an alliance with some of the legworm clans and support the guerrillas in the Alleghenies.

"Careful, Coonskin," a low female voice said. "He's Bulletproof. Might just challenge you to a duel."

Tikka forced her way to the front of the throng. "Welcome back, reiner. My life gets interesting whenever you show up."

"Hello, Tikka. Where's Zak?"

Valentine heard startled breaths. She replied in a monotone, "He was at the party."

"I'm sorry to hear that," Valentine said.

She thanked him quietly, looked around at the assembly. "I'm able to speak in my brother's place, with my dispatcher's authority. The Bulletproof won't quit. Won't throw down their guns. Won't run."

"I stand for the Alliance too," another called. Cheers broke out.

But they sounded halfhearted.

By the pinkening dawn, they were at the camp of the Green Mountain Boys and Valentine was growing tired. The New England troops took the precaution of blindfolding the party before letting them into camp. Bee didn't appreciate being blindfolded, so Ediyak offered to wait with her outside the lines.

The Green Mountain Boys still had their senior officer, General Constance, who'd begged off the party because of a broken ankle. He looked like Santa Claus without the beard, sitting with his leg extended.

"Thought we had a bit too much of an easy time getting here," Constance said. "Thing is, if a trap's been sprung, where are the jaws?"

"Have you decided on a course of action?"

The cheery, red-cheeked face frowned. "If I had, I'd be a fool to tell you now, wouldn't I?"

"I don't blame you for not trusting us," Valentine said. "We're all wondering what's going to go wrong next."

"They've got a twist on us, that's for damn sure," Constance said. "Masterful, suckering us out like this. Masterful. They've set us up. Now I'm wondering how they're going to knock us down."

With that unsettling thought, Brother Mark got a promise from Constance not to act without first consulting Javelin's headquarters.

Under blindfold again, they were led back to the pickets. But Valentine knew the sound of a camp being packed up when he heard it.

Full daylight washed them as they returned to camp. Valentine looked around at the hills and mountains of West Virginia, black in the morning glare. The only sounds of fighting were from birds, battling and defending in contests of song and chirp as squirrel-tail grass waved in the wind. How long before the shells started falling?

The Kurians usually came off the worse in a standup fight. But this was above and beyond, even for their standard of deviousness.

He checked Brother Mark back in, gave Nowak's adjutant a report of his estimation of the situation in the Kentucky and New England camps, and returned to his company. After passing along what little news he had, he entered his tent and slept. Bee sat upright at the foot of his bed facing the tenthole, snoring.

Valentine's first captain in the Wolves, LeHavre, once told him a story of a Kurian trick, where they emptied a town and filled it up again with Quisling specialists who pretended to be ordinary civilians. The Kurians had done something similar here, on a much larger scale, involving even the partisans and the underground. Or perhaps used agents posing as them.

Valentine dreamed that he was in that town, walking down the center of the main street, frozen statues on sidewalks and in doorways and shopwindows watching him, their heads slowly turning, turning past the point their necks would snap, turning full around like turrets.

"What brings you here, missionary?" one of the reversed heads asked.

Valentine woke to find Ediyak shaking his shoulder. "Some kind of emissary from the Kurians, sir. Thought you might like to see it."

"Is Nowak back?"

"I don't know, sir."

His platoon just coming off guard detail was skipping a chance for both breakfast and sleep to catch a glimpse of the Kurians' mouthpiece.

When Valentine got a look at him, all he could think was that D.C. Marvels had an evil twin. The mouthpiece rode in a jointed-arm contraption on the back of a Lincoln green double-axle flatbed wrecker, modified for high ground clearance. Loudspeakers like Mickey Mouse ears projected from either side of the truck cab, and a huge silver serving cover, big enough to keep a turkey warm, rested over the hood ornament.

What really caught the eye was the contraption mounted on the flatbed. Valentine thought it looked a little like a stick-insect version of a backhoe, suspending a leather wing chair where the toothy shovel should be. Gearing and compressors appropriate for a carnival ride muttered and hissed at the base.

Valentine marked an insignia on the truck, a crescent moon with a dagger thrust through it, rather reminiscent of the old hammer and sickle of the Soviet Union.

"That's an old camera crane, I think," Rand said, wiping his glasses and resettling them on his nose. "Big one."

The mouthpiece himself wore a plain broadcloth suit over a white shirt and a red bow tie, though the suit had apparently been tailored to fit a pair of football shoulder pads beneath. He wore a red-trimmed white sash covered in neatly arranged brass and silver buttons, with a few dazzling diamond studs here and there. Jewels glued into the skin sparkled at the outer edge of each almond-shaped eye. Close-cropped curly hair had been dyed white, fading down his sideburns to two points at either side of a sharply trimmed beard.

He flicked a whiter-than-white lace hankerchief idly back and forth, his hand moving in the dutiful measured gestures of a royal wave. With his right he worked the crane and the chair, rising and dipping first to one side of the flatbed, and then sweeping around the front to the other side.

"I am the Last Chance," the mouthpiece said. Valentine noticed a tiny wire descending from a loop around his ear to the side of his mouth. It must have been a microphone of some kind, because the mouthpiece's words boomed from the speakers, startling the assembled soldiers. "For credentials I present only the mark of my obedience and the tally of my offspring."

He lifted his beard. A silver bar, widened and rounded at each end in the manner of a Q-tip, pierced the skin at the front of his neck just above his Adam's apple. Then he made a sweeping gesture with brass-ringed fingers at the sash.

"The holy balance represents the duality of existence. Life and death. Good and evil. Order and chaos. Mercy and cruelty. Wisdom is knowing when to apply each and in what measure and Grace how to accept each in submission to the will of the gods, who see horizons beyond the vision of human eyes."

He gave his speech in the measured, rehearsed manner of a catechism. Valentine wondered how long it had been since the mouthpiece had thought about those words.

Valentine found Moytana standing next to him. "Silver buttons are children who entered Kur's service; gold are children who had children of their own who took up the dagger. The cubic zirconium means someone who died in the Moondaggers."

"Lot of kids."

"Tell you about it later," Moytana said.

"He doesn't look old enough to have brought up that many soldiers."

"They start fighting at thirteen or fourteen, whenever the balls drop," Moytana said as the mouthpiece blatted something about the kindness of the gods giving them a last chance.

"Who in this assembly of the disobedient is in authority to speak to me?"

He spoke in a stern but kind tone through the speakers, with a hint of suppressed anger, making Valentine feel like a third grader caught putting a frog in the teacher's pencil drawer.

"That would be me," Colonel Jolla said, stepping forward.

"I wonder. You have the face of one who has lost a bet. You look like—what is the phrase you swamp-trotting crackers use?—you look like the 'bottom of the barrel.' And not a good barrel at that."

"Where's Captain Nowak? Why hasn't she returned with your terms?" Jolla asked.

As the mouthpiece dipped, Valentine noticed a golden-handled curved blade with an ivory sheath resting in his lap.

"Oh, but she has."

He worked the joystick and swept his chair around the front of the truck, removing the silver serving cover. Nowak's head was spiked, literally on a platter, her insignia, sidearm, personal effects, and identification arranged around her head like a garnish.

"She chose not to let her womb be a nursery of my greatness. As in her arrogance she took the counsel of her head rather than that of her body's blessed womanly nature, we took the liberty of ridding her of its burden."

He swung his chair around, turned the winged leather. Valentine saw gold leaf painted on the exposed wood at the front and tiny Moondagger symbols painted precisely on the nailhead trim. The mouthpiece fixed his eye on Ediyak.

"I trust others will not be so foolish."

"You killed a soldier under a flag of truce?" Jolla said.

The mouthpiece laughed. "What new folly must I expect from men who would have women do their fighting? I made her an honorable proposal of motherhood. Let that be a lesson to you. Do not send women to speak in a man's place again. Besides, she is not dead, just free of the body whose duty she refused in the first place. Tell them, sexless one."

Valentine saw him press a button next to his joystick. Nowak's eyes opened.

"I live," Nowak's head said. "If you want to call it that." Valentine noticed her voice came through the speakers. Clearly Nowak's, though the words sounded forced.

Some of the soldiers backed away. The more ghoulish craned their necks to get a better view.

Nowak's eyes rolled this way and that. "Well, hello, Jolly. You look intact this morning."

Valentine searched for the mechanics of the trickery. You needed lungs, a windpipe, to speak. A head couldn't just talk. This was some bit illusion by a Kurian or one of their agents.

He just wished real-looking blood wasn't slipping out of the corner of Nowak's mouth as she spoke.

"Tell them our terms," the mouthpiece said. "You must remember. I whispered them to you often enough on the ride up as you rode in my lap. First, obedience—"

The eyes in the severed head blinked. "First, obedience to the order to lay down your arms and a solemn pledge to never resist the gods again," Nowak said. "Second, a selection of hostages, one taking the place of ten in assurance of future good conduct. Third, a return to the squalor of our bandit dens on the other side of the Mississippi, taking only from the countryside such as needed to sustain the retreat."

Her voice broke. "This is your only alternative to horrors and torments everlasting. The grave that gives no rest is my fate, for my willfulness," Nowak's head said, bloody tears running from the corners of her eyes.

The Kurian Order always provided plenty of evidence for your eyes. After a lifetime spent trusting your senses . . .

"You men may save your families by giving up your arms." A faint, low drumming carried up from the town. Must be some massive drums to make that deep a noise. "Women, shield your children from Kur's wrath by offering up your bodies to our commanders."

Valentine wondered at that. Was the mouthpiece so used to giving his last-chance speech that he failed to notice he was in a camp full of soldiers?

"Listen to him!" Nowak shrieked.

"You've got a long drive ahead of you, prance, if you want my boy," Cleo Bloom called from the back of the crowd. "He's six hundred miles away."

The chair rose and spun toward the sound. The mouthpiece fixed her with a baleful eye. "No matter. We'll simply take one from a town between here and Kantuck. We will let the mother know the willfulness, the arrogance, the insolence that demanded his sacrifice."

"Twisting tongue of the evil one, begone!" a commanding voice said in a timbre that matched the amplified speakers. Every head turned, and Brother Mark stepped forward.

Brother Mark stared at the head on the front of the hood and Nowak's features fell still and dead, the eyes dry and empty.

The chair descended again, sweeping forward just a little. The men next to Brother Mark retreated to avoid being knocked over. The two stared at each other, the mouthpiece's hand on the hilt of his dagger. Valentine sidestepped to get nearer to Brother Mark.

"Don't let this one fill your ears with pieties," the mouthpiece said. "He's expecting you to die for a cause. Futility shaped and polished to a brightness that blinds you to the waste. Honor. Duty. Country. How many millions in the old days marched to their doom with such platitudes in their ears? Wasted potential. It is for each man to add value to his life. Don't let wastrels spend the currency of your days."

The crane elevated him to its maximum extension.

"Our divine Prophet's Moondagger is still sheathed," the mouth-piece boomed through the speakers. The drums in town sounded in time to his pauses. "Do not tempt him to draw it, for it cannot be put away again until every throat in this camp is cut."

"We're volunteers," Valentine said. "We've all seen how lives are counted when Kur is the banker."

The crane lowered the mouthpiece.

Valentine stood, arms dangling, relaxed. He opened and closed his right fist, warming his fingers.

"Your face will be remembered. You'll regret those words, over and over and over again, tormented in the living hells."

"Can I borrow that?" Valentine asked. He whipped out his hand, raked the mouthpiece under the chin, came away with the silver pin— and a good deal of bushy black beard.

"Outrage!" the mouthpiece sputtered, eyes wide with shock. Blood dripped onto his white shirt.

Valentine, keeping clear of the extended crane arm, cleaned his ears with the silver pin and tossed it back into the Last Chance's lap, where it clattered against the curved dagger.

"Thanks," Valentine said.

"You'll writhe on a bridge of hooks. You'll roast, slowly, with skin coated in oils of—"

"Is that part of the living hells tour, or do I have to pay extra?" Valentine said. He called over the shoulder at the brigade: "That's how it always is, right? They hook you in with the price of the package tour, but all the worthwhile sights are extra."

The soldiers laughed.

"Here's my moon. Where's your dagger?" someone shouted from the back of the mob. Because of the crowd, Valentine couldn't see what was on display.

"You have until dusk to decide," the mouthpiece said, pulling his chair back toward the truck. The drumming started again.

The mouthpiece's flatbed rumbled to life. It backed up, turned, and rocked down toward the picket line. Some stealthy Southern Command hooligans had hung a sheet off the back of the flatbed, with

ASS BANDIT–PUCKER UP!

written on it in big block capitals.

The rest of the assembly laughed the Last Chance out of their camp.

Had this Last Chance ever ridden off to the sound of raucous laughter? Valentine doubted it.

Outside of the color guards and bands, no officer had ever quite succeeded in getting any two Southern Command soldiers to look alike in dress and hair, even for formal parades. They etched names of sweethearts in their rifles, sewed beads and hung tufted fishing lures in the caps, dipped points of their pigtails in tar, and stuck knives and tools in distinctly nonregulation snakeskin sheaths. But David Valentine had never been more grateful for their mulish contrariness.

Nine

Decision: One of the vexations with writing histories concerning the Kurians and their intentions is the lack of records as to their thoughts and plans. In previous wars, there were government archives, speeches, even laws and commands that offer some insight into enemy intentions. Debriefings of the captured and memoirs written after passions had cooled also offer particular, if limited, insights.

The Kurians left nothing like that.

At best, we have the guesses from those under them. Church archons, generals, civil administrators. Sometimes the order of events give some clue as to priorities.

For example, in the Appalachian Catastrophe in the summer of '77, some argue that the Green Mountain Boys (itself a misnomer, as many of their numbers were made up of formations active in upstate New York and even western Pennsylvania) were the real target of the ruse, for they were the Moondaggers' main concern. Others say they were attacked first because they had the shortest trip home.

Assorted lies, threats, promises, and deals from the Kurians are equally unreliable, for whether they were kept or canceled depended very much on the character of the individual Kurian lord and what sort of situation he found himself in when bargaining with his friends and enemies.

The reader, alas, is left to draw his own conclusion from events as experienced by the human side in the struggle. So were commanders in the field in that fateful summer.

The brigade HQ tent had an unusual number of soldiers buzzing around with the busyness of bees in a flower garden. They'd found something to do in its immediate vicinity, camouflaging lack of purpose with energy. Valentine told a couple of sergeants to find something to keep them busy.

The only idler seemed to be Red Dog, snoring after an anxious night at the fringes of the camp, whining whenever he was brought to the defensive positions facing Utrecht.

Bloom opened the meeting with her usual blunt style.

"Hit them hard now," Bloom said. "Can't let them just draw blood. We're in as good a shape as we'll ever be."

Valentine checked the corners and under the tables. If there was ever a good time for a Kurian agent to plant a bomb, now would be it. Some captains and Duvalier would be running the brigade.

"The same could be said of the legworm clans and the Green Mountain Boys," Brother Mark said. He looked exhausted from his efforts against the Last Chance and spent most of the conference with his eyes closed, rubbing his temples.

"What are your thoughts, Valentine?" Jolla asked.

"I wonder if they sprang their trap too early. Were I arranging a trick like this, I'd have these hills filled with my army. We'd be listening to the man in the whirly chair with one eye on the hostiles."

"Reliable troops have always been the Kurians' Achilles' heel," Brother Mark added. "They have their elite cadres and the Grogs, but they've had problems with mutinous formations unless they're carefully controlled and properly motivated. Church archives are full of it. In more ways than one."

Jolla turned a clipboard, showed them two pages of taped-together flimsies. "Southern Command has confirmed your promotion to colonel, Bloom. Congratulations. We should have a toast. Carillo, won't you bring in some glasses?"

"How about a rain check, sir," Bloom said. "Let's get the men moving before they have too much time to think about how far they are from home and family."

Jolla ignored her. "GHQ also promoted Colonel Seng to general in recognition of his achievement."

Carillo slipped in with a bottle of real black-labeled Jim Beam and a stack of thumb-high leaded glass vessels.

"Seng arranged for six barrels of very good bourbon for the men. The connection from the distillery gave us a few cases as a bonus. Came with a card, signed 'a patriot.' I wonder if he's sweating whether he left fingerprints on it. Pour everyone a neat, would you, Carillo?"

The meeting was taking on a dreamlike quality. Valentine knew the bourbon was real enough; one of his platoons had met the distillery smugglers.

"Gratifying as gratis liquor is," Brother Mark said, "shouldn't you be writing orders by now?"

"Keep out of solemn military traditions, Brother," Jolla said. "I'm still waiting to hear what the Green Mountain Boys intend to do."

"They intend to leave unless we *do* something," Valentine said tightly.

"I've made up my mind about that. First, the toast."

Valentine accepted his glass and pushed his hair back with his left while he tipped most of the liquor out with right, feeling a little like a cheap stage musician. He covered the glass with his fingers.

Jolla stood. "First, to the memory of General Seng. May his example inspire future generations of officers."

It's sure not inspiring the present generation, Valentine thought. *Seng wouldn't want us drinking to his memory. If he were still running the brigade, we'd be arguing with the Green Mountain Boys over whose rope would be used to hang the ringleaders of the ambush in town.*

"Now, I've come to a decision. After consulting with Southern Command and a careful assessment, I've decided our position here in West Virginia is untenable. Remaining here would seem to ensure our destruction."

That got their interest. The shifting and note taking ceased from everyone but Jolla's military secretary.

"We were misinformed—note that I say misinformed, not misled, Brother Mark—as to the support we would receive from the local populace. We've found plans drawn up against us. The enemy executed a masterful ruse and struck just as we were busy congratulating ourselves on our own cleverness."

The word "masterful" poked at Valentine. He'd just heard it—where? He needed to think.

Jolla didn't give him time. "My one hope now is that the Kurians will allow us to leave quietly. God knows, the Kurians prefer carefully controlled bloodshed. They don't like battles any more than we do."

"Sir," Bloom protested.

Jolla held up his hand.

"I've made up my mind. Now there's just a matter of choosing a route and an order of march. We'll need a strong fore guard and an even more capable rear guard if this operation is to succeed."

"There's no doubt that the guerrillas exist," Brother Mark said. "I've seen the reports of the damage they've done. For all we know, they're trying to reach us at this moment."

Jolla frowned. "In view of the situation we find ourselves in, perhaps you should leave retrieving the situation to the professionals. I'm sure we'll need your diplomatic expertise on the way home. Perhaps you could turn your thoughts to that."

Brother Mark returned to his chair and put his head down. Valentine saw his lips moving.

Valentine wondered at Jolla's manner. Did men in the midst of some kind of mental breakdown acquire a new vocabulary? The cadence and pronunciation were right, but the words seemed unusually fussy and chosen, as though they'd been preprinted. But the personality, the attitude, was Jolla! Gage would probably have slapped Brother Mark down hard. Seng would have turned a frowning fish stare on him until he withdrew his objection and apologized for intruding onto military matters. Jolla was the same polite, go-along-and-get-along self.

Valentine heard two flies turning pirouettes over a tub that held some dirty plates and utensils from the headquarters breakfast. An opportunistic spider was already at work on a web.

How far do your strands extend, Kurian?

"Now, Colonel Bloom will assume command of the regulars and be second in command in the event something happens to me. Valentine, I need a new chief of staff. Can your lieutenant take over your company?"

Valentine turned cold. He could just see the headlines in the *Clarion. Scraping the Barrel Bottom: Disgraced, Condemned Officer Organized Humiliating Retreat in Appalachian Disaster.*

"Rand's a good man, sir. As to me being the new chief . . . perhaps someone already from the headquarters would do better."

Jolla fingered the buttons of his field jacket. "In an hour like this, you're—you're saying no?"

"May we speak for a moment privately, sir?"

Jolla nodded. They both angled for a corner of the tent and spoke with their backs to the rest of the assembly. Valentine heard whispering behind.

"Sir, I don't have anything like the training. I've done my share of reading, but I haven't led military forces since Archangel. I'm a lieutenant who found himself with a major's cluster. Until Seng gave me his texts, most of the training and experience I had above the platoon level was leading Quisling formations, after a manner."

"You never struck me as the kind to crayfish when responsibility comes your way, Major. Of course, if you really believe you're not up to the job, I'll select someone else. If I didn't think you were the best man for the job, I wouldn't have selected you."

"Thank you for your confidence, sir. But . . ." Valentine grasped for the right words but they got lost somewhere between his brain and his larynx.

"I'll add a 'but' of my own. But, well, I need you right now, Valentine. The men like me well enough, but we need another Seng, God rest him, and I don't think liking me's enough. They need to believe in something. I've never been all faith and vision like Karas, or brilliant like Seng."

"Quiet plodders have won their share of wars, sir," Valentine offered.

"This war's over before it even got going. Turns out the Kurians have been one step ahead of us the whole time. The troops need to believe we'll get them out of this.

"Chief of staff isn't easy, I know," Jolla continued. "You'll be running your legs off. I've been in the service about as long as you've been alive, Valentine. I've watched the men when you're around. They look at you and then they talk. You wouldn't believe some of the stories floating around about you. They bring ideas and complaints to you. There aren't many in Southern Command—at least good ones—who can boast of that. Then there's that business with your nose, that tingle. Even if it's just luck, well, luck counts for something in life. Thirty years service proved that to me too."

Valentine's throat tightened. "Very well, sir. Then, as chief of staff, I'd like to propose taking one good crack at these Moondaggers before we leave."

"No. I'm certain we're outnumbered. Even a win could doom us. I want to keep the brigade intact. Let's save their lives for future use."

"As chief of staff, I'd like permission to coordinate our departure with the Green Mountain command and the legworm riders."

"Granted. Hope you don't mind working from Nowak's cubby. Now let's get back to the meeting."

Valentine tried to pay attention to the rest—the empty congratulations for himself and Bloom, the anxious silence from Brother Mark, who stared and stared and stared at Jolla as if he were studying some strange species of animal.

But all he could think about was how Jolla could be so certain that they were outnumbered.

Valentine broke the news quickly to Rand. Rand suggested some kind of farewell dinner was in order; Valentine left the details to him.

"Don't think I'm not going to keep riding your backs," he told the NCOs who gathered as the news spread.

"Congratulations," Patel said.

"More like condolences," Glass said. "He's been given command of the *Titanic* ten minutes after the iceberg."

"I don't want any of you to worry," Valentine said, hopping up into the bed of one of the company supply wagons. "Javelin's not about to surrender to the Kurians or anyone else. We're going back under our own terms, and God help anyone who gets in our way."

They cheered that. Spin, they used to call it. The idea of fighting their way back appealed a lot more than being chased out of the Appalachians with their tails between their legs.

Valentine waved Patel over.

"If you want a little garnish around your star," Valentine said, "I can appoint a new command sergeant major for the brigade. You'd be at the top of my list. Less hiking and more riding."

Patel smiled but shook his head. "Douglas is doing a good job, filling in for poor Reygarth. In any case, I am stuck shepherding a promising but raw lieutenant again."

"I'm sorry I got you into this, Nilay."

"You did not get me into anything. I had little to do at home but read the newspapers and remember. It is good to be out of the rocking chair and in country. This is my life; that was just waiting. You know, my knees have not felt so good in years."

"You're a hell of a wrestler, Patel, but you can't lie for crap. You always blink when you're lying."

"You could have told me this, sir, before I lost six months' pay in poker games back in LeHavre's company."

"Here's my last company command: You ride on the company legworm. That's an order. Hear that, Rand?"

"Yes, Major," Rand said.

"Rand's my witness."

He slept for an hour, and then summoned Brother Mark. "I think we need to pay a call on the Kentucky Alliance. It would be safer for us if we left as a group, or at least traveled parallel paths so we could support each other in case the Kurians have a follow-up trick. Not much we can do for the Green Mountain Boys, but Southern Command and the Kentucky Alliance can stick together."

"Your caution does you credit, but are you sure we can't change the colonel's mind? He strikes me as a man suffering from a shock. In a day or two he may be amenable."

Valentine shook his head. "I have my orders to follow. We're turning around and heading back. I've got to figure out how best to put that into effect."

"Seems to me the great flaw in your formidable, pyramidal military machine is that it depends too much on the trained monkey working the controls."

"As a civilian, you're allowed to express that opinion."

"Tell me what you think, Valentine. That's one of the reasons that I headed south when I left the Church. Your Southern Command sounded more like a band of brothers united by common cause."

"Colonel Jolla's orders will be followed, and that's that. Southern Command's got a bunch of handy, rarely used regulations just in case you try to interfere with his command. Most of them involve a noose."

"Don't you have a noose around your neck too, Major?"

"Just get yourself ready to visit the Alliance again."

At the Alliance camp, they found a rather more informal debate proceeding in a sort of corral formed by tied-down legworms. Riders sat on their animals, or hung off the sides, or gathered in little lounging groups in the center of the circle, each clustering close to their own clan.

"He told us all we had to do was go home! Matches my wants, so what are we waiting for?" a Wildcat asked.

"He also told us to throw down our long guns, Geckie," a man in a sagging, shapeless cloth hat yelled back. "I don't trust a man who makes me being unarmed part of the deal."

"You calling me a coward?" the one called Geckie yelled back over the heads.

"No, but it's mighty interesting that that's the first word that popped into your head, isn't it?"

"I don't care if you're head rider or dispatcher. You're challenged to a duel at your convenience, Gunslinger." Cheers and claps and whistles broke out, along with a few boos.

"Right now's pretty convenient to me. Fists until one man goes down."

"So much for the alliance," Brother Mark said.

"That Last Chance fellow said we could go. Who needs Virginia anyway?" a rider from the Wildcats shouted to general approval.

"West Virginia," someone corrected.

"You lousy bunch of cowards," Tikka told the Bulletproof and anyone else listening. She stepped into the center of a hostile circle. "You call yourselves men—more than that, Bulletproof men? I've never heard of such a bunch of sunshine strikers. Sure, when it looks easy you all want a piece of the fight. But when the fight comes to you, it's hook up and run. You wormcast. No, not even wormcast. The wildflowers grow prettier on wormcast. You're more like slag from one of the mines around here: dull, cold, and useful as dry dirt."

"You're the Bulletproof and the Bulletproof is you," a grizzled rider with the Coonskins responded.

"Not anymore," the new leader of the Mammoths said. "We're still the Alliance. We've had enough of their edicts and requisitions and demands. We've thrown in with the Cause and we'll finish with it or be finished."

In the end, they split into three parts.

The Green Mountain Boys headed north, hard and fast in a sprint toward friendly territory, leaving their heavy gear and a good deal of their supply train behind.

The Kentucky Alliance was the first to visit the abandoned camp and cleaned it out of the choicest gear like the first family back to the house of a deceased relative after the funeral.

The Perseids gave up outright. Bereft of Karas, they groped like lost children for a solution. Valentine watched them march and ride toward Utrecht and hoped the Kurians meant their promise not to harm any who gave up, for their sake.

The rest of the Kentucky Alliance turned for home in four separate columns. Valentine rode his Morgan hard from column to column, with Bee loping behind, and assured them that Southern Command's forces would come to the aid of any who were attacked, but the leadership looked doubtful.

And so the bright and shining dream of a new Freehold left for Kentucky. Though a bristling rear guard scouted for Moondagger troops who had yet to appear, Valentine couldn't help feeling they were abandoning the Virginias with their tails tucked between their legs, running from shadows.

Ten

Withdrawal: Directing a successful retreat can be as difficult as an advance.

Eastern Kentucky offers some advantages to Javelin and its legworm-riding allies. Mountain passes could be easily held against greater numbers—though this could be worked to their disadvantage as well, if the Moondaggers could slip around behind them. The mountains also serve as screens, and the clouds frequently trapped by the peaks hide them from aerial observation.

As Napoleon learned on his way back from Moscow, the most problematic of all is the threat a retreat poses to morale. A beaten army, like an often-whipped horse, lacks the dash and spirit needed to fight a successful battle. Any setback or check threatens a collapse of discipline and a rout. Understandably, the soldiers become shy of risk.

Worse, they come to see every mile of land as an enemy between them and their goal. Food, clothing, and shelter can be obtained at rifle point from the locals. Friction, any mechanic can tell you, is an enemy to speed and smooth function.

Worst of all, they might see the slower-moving elements as hindrances to the all-important goal of getting home. A retreating army will dissolve like sugar spread in the rain, lost to desertion and despair.

Valentine's earliest woe as chief of staff was handling the Kentucky Alliance. He couldn't order, he could only suggest. He had to ask for riders to watch their flanks, to take their mounts up mountains, to go ahead and seize passes and rickety old railroad bridges the vehicles could bump across.

At meetings with the company commanders, he forced himself to

bluster and threaten regarding treatment of the locals, up to and including hangings for crimes of violence. If the collection of captains and
lieutenants thought him a tyrant, drunk on newfound power, so much
the better. He'd be the bad guy, the glowering, uncompromising stickler
for regs, if it would keep the soldiers from doing anything to turn the
populace against his side.

And he made it clear that responsibility would flow uphill for once.

They found a sample of Moondagger mercy the third morning out,
planted right along the road they were using to retreat out of West Virginia.

They came to a clearing of freshly cut trees, with bits and pieces of
broken guns smashed over the stumps. A black and gray mound with a
charnel-house reek sat in a circle of heat-hardened ground.

Tikka, riding with a few Bulletproof at the head of the column, identified the bodies as belonging to the Mammoth clan, God knew how. The
unarmed men had been thrown into wooden cages and burned. From the
burned heads and arms forcing their way between the charred bars, Valentine guessed they'd still been alive when the fires had been set.

Looking at the clenched teeth behind burned away lips, Valentine
would have rather gone to the Reapers.

Valentine put his old company to work clearing the bodies and
burying them in the loose soil of the grown-over slag heap of a mine in
a mountain's pocket just off the road.

"Sorry, men," he said, a handkerchief tied around his face to keep
him from breathing ash that might be wood, clothing, or human flesh.
"The brigade can't march through this."

Brother Mark rode up on muleback to have a look and say a few
words over the departed. "This is their method, men," he told the parties at work moving the bodies. "They talk you into giving up your
guns, and without your gun what's to stop them from taking whatever
they want? Resistance is a guarantee of dignity and an honorable death."

"Come down here and help pick up these charcoal briquettes that
used to be hands and feet," a man said to his coworker. "We can have a
nice little talk about dignity."

"Enough of that, there," Patel barked.

Company scouts caught up with a disheveled trio hobbling bootless
up the road toward Kentucky. Glass sent Ford galumphing back to request Valentine's help with them.

They made a pathetic sight. One's eyes were bandaged, as were
one's ears, and the third had dried blood caked on his chin.

"We are the blind, deaf, and dumb," the blinded man said. Valentine saw a light band on his finger where a wedding band had been. The Moondaggers certainly weren't above a little theft. "Testament to . . . er—"

The tongueless man tugged on the blinded one's sleeve and said, "Ebbatren ob ah'oolisheh."

"Yes, testament to the foolishness of those who deny the evidence of their senses as to the supremacy of the Ever-living Gods. The Moondaggers did this for the good of others we might meet."

"You were with the Mammoth?" Valentine asked.

The tongueless man gave a groan, and took the deaf man's hand and squeezed it.

"There are only two kinds of people," the deaf man said loudly. "The graced and the fallen. We are warning to the fallen."

"Cutting them up's not enough," Glass said to a Wolf scout. "Had to take their shoes too. Cruel I understand, but that's just mean."

The Moondaggers probably wanted to make sure we caught up to them, Valentine thought, just as the Wolf voiced the same sentiment.

"Webb ub uss," the tongueless man said.

"Let us pass," the blinded one said. "We've said our words. Let us pass."

"First tell me what happened," Valentine said.

"Did you not see?" the blind man asked, his voice cracking.

Ediyak wrote something on a sheet of paper and handed it to the deaf man. He read it and looked at Valentine.

"We surrendered. We followed every instruction. They made us cut down trees and smash our guns on the stumps. Then they bound us in a line, and that's when they started working on the cages," the deaf man said, loudly and a little off-key. "They laughed as the fires started. I can still hear the laughter."

"Why did they pick you three?" Valentine added on to the end of Ediyak's note.

The deaf man took it and read. "We were chosen because we all knew the Kurian catechism."

"What's that?" Tikka asked. "I never had much to do with the Church."

Brother Mark cleared his throat.

"Who are they?

                    The wise old gods of our childhood.

"Where are they from?

                    Kur, the Interworld Tree's branch of Wisdom.

"When did they come?

                    In our darkest hour.

"Why did they come?

To guide mankind.

"How may we thank them?

With diligent obedience."

Brother Mark had tears in his eyes when he was done. He turned away.

"Your church gives orders for this kind of thing?" Tikka asked.

"Former church, daughter. Former. This most terrible sect of a misguided faith isn't spoken of much in the marble halls," he said. "But I fear they find them useful at times."

"Tikka, can you spare a rider to get these men home?" Valentine asked.

"I'll have to check with the veep," she said. "But the Mammoth have been friendly to us most of the time."

One more body turned up. A young woman from the Mammoth, stripped of her leathers and wearing a plain smock, dead from what was probably a self-inflicted wound to the abdomen. She'd gutted herself with one of the curved knives of the Moondaggers.

"Whoever lost his knife didn't want it back," someone observed.

Valentine wanted another talk with the Last Chance. Might be fun to chain one end of him to his flatbed and use his crane to yank pieces of him off.

"Try not to let it get to you, men," he said as the company reformed after disposing of the bodies. He sent word to headquarters that the brigade could move up the road again. "They did this to put a scare into you."

"Hope we get a chance to get scary on them," DuSable said, wiping ash from his forearms with a wet rag.

"Amen, Sab," Rutherford added.

"Remember the Cause," Valentine said. "We're the good guys. You're better than that."

DuSable straightened a little.

You're better than that, Sab, Valentine thought. He wondered how long he could keep the angry monster inside bottled up and channeled into duty.

Brother Mark, with the lower ranks dismissed from the officers' meeting, sat down wearily.

"I tried three different clans. They're terrified of helping us. Won't even take guns. The Kurians are promising destruction to anyone who gives us so much as a rotten egg."

"It's the reputation of the Moondaggers," Moytana said.

"Maybe we can tarnish it," Valentine said.

"The clans can get away with not resisting us. Claim they don't have guns and so forth," Brother Mark said. "But trade? Never. The Moondaggers are promising to obliterate right down to the infants any clan who helps us. All legworm stock is to go to whichever clan reveals their 'treachery.' They're filling wells with dead dogs and cats as we approach."

"A little boiling will take care of that," a Guard captain said. "It's food I'm worried about. I believe we've got rations for the rest of the week. Then we're eating grass like the horses."

"Two weeks on short. That's not enough to get us home. At least not intact," Bloom said. She sounded beaten.

"So that's it, then," Valentine said. "We can't go on. Not without food."

Brother Mark shook his head. "That's what they count on, my son. Despair. A victory comes so much easier when you are the one defeating yourself."

"An army marches on its stomach," Moytana said. "What do you propose to fill my men's bellies with?"

"They must march on hope."

"That's not much butter to put on a long slice of bread," Moytana observed.

The next day they woke to harassing gunfire from far-off batteries of the Moondaggers. The shots weren't being observed; they were falling wide by a half mile or more and not being corrected. But it unnerved the men, made them jumpy and scattered the way a coming thunderstorm puts rabbits underground.

Valentine gave orders to put a reserve on alert and hurried to the headquarters to find a medical truck parked there and his staff silent and nervous. Even Red Dog panted and crisscrossed from man to man, seeking reassurance.

"Colonel Jolla's dead, sir," the staff agronomist reported.

"Who can tell me what happened?"

"It's like this, sir," Tiddle, the headquarters courier, said. "I had the communications duty. Colonel Jolla came up to the rig and looked at the latest communications. Everyone was talking about the worm riders quitting on us.

"Well, sir, he didn't say much. Just stared—didn't seem to be reading the communiqués at all. Colonel Bloom arrived with a report about some civilian bodies we found. She was just telling him that they were trying to bring us food. Oh, Colonel Jolla wasn't really paying attention to what she was saying. He just sort of nodded. Looked like his mind was elsewhere, like he was having a phone conversation or something."

Tiddle looked miserable, the White Rabbit stilled for once. Valentine saw a bagged bundle resting in the back of the truck.

"Well, then we heard some artillery fire in the distance, the usual calling cards from the Moondaggers to let us know they're back there, and Colonel Jolla just sort of went white. He reached for his service pistol and started to bring it up to his head. Bloom grabbed for it and they started wrestling. She said, 'For God's sake, help me,' and then we heard the shot. We were moving toward Colonel Jolla but he was too fast for us. He put the barrel in his mouth and pulled the trigger. Awful mess, sir—" Tiddle pointed at the front fender of the jeep, and Valentine saw caked blood in the crevices.

"How's Colonel Bloom?" Valentine asked, calming Red Dog and himself by flapping the dog's ears.

"Shaken up. She's in command now."

Valentine sought out Bloom. The usually quick and decisive Bloom seemed suddenly doubtful, but it might be the flecks of blood still on her cuff and shoulder. Red Dog approached her cautiously, sniffing.

"We could try taking a crack at the Moondaggers, sir," Valentine suggested. "We might get the confidence of the worm clans back if we prove ourselves against them."

For a moment her eyes flared.

"Hmmmm. I don't know, Valentine. Southern Command doesn't want another Kansas on their hands, you know. I'm under orders to keep the brigade intact."

They'd continue the retreat.

Two days later Brother Mark returned from the Kentucky Alliance camp.

"They're quitting on us," he said. "That Last Chance arranged a secret meeting with some of their leadership. Wildcats are packing up. Some of the Gunslingers are leaving, going to start a new clan. Even the Bulletproof and Mammoth are hedging their bets, sending some riders back to reinforce their main camp. All we have left are the attenuated what's left of those two and the Coonskins."

He reached into his battered courier bag, brought up a black-labeled bottle. "They gave me a farewell gift. Were it were hemlock."

"You've done your best," Valentine said, waving the others off. He sat Brother Mark down in the chair farthest from the communications desk, and the rest of the headquarters officers gave them a wide berth. Being the CO's chief of staff offered a few privileges.

Brother Mark looked thoughtful, took a pull at the bourbon.

"They always start you off easy. After I took my first vows, they put me in a little schoolhouse, helping the Youth Vanguard with their reading, writing, and 'rithmetic. Cozy. And they had a full priest there for all the tough questions. If someone asked where their grandfather went, all I'd have to say is 'Let's go talk to our guide.' Then sit quietly while the full priest talked about sacrifice for the greater good.

"Then they moved me to the hospital. I'd just taken my second set of vows. Passed all my examinations with flying colors, by the way. Dead-even emotional resonance when presented with disturbing imagery."

Valentine didn't know what that was but didn't want to change the old churchman's loquacious mood. He'd only seen the church from the outside.

"Did hospital service change your opinions?"

"No, it took me a long time to wake up. Nightmares shouldn't be allowed to pose as dreams."

"I ran into one of those about a year ago," Valentine said. He still felt conflicted about the course he'd chosen in the Cascades. Valentine was not a believer in the revolutionary's morality, where the result justified the means. Could he have come up with a better way to get rid of Adler's bloody direction of Pacific Command?

Brother Mark broke in on his thoughts. "Again, they made it so easy. At the hospital I had a nice little office, and each patient went through a rubric while their medical needs were being evaluated. Took into account age, physical condition, skill set, community activism, and responsibility . . . and of course how involved the treatment might be and prognosis for recovery to full useful life. Above a certain score and they were treated. Below a certain score and they found themselves on the drop list."

He whispered the last two words, as though they were something shameful.

"Drop list," he continued. "Sounds innocuous, right? It meant they crossed over into the hands of the Reapers, of course. In a lot of cases the really sick people stayed at home or had quacks treat them, so we always talked to the school-agers about reporting any adults they knew who were sick. Spread of contagion and so on.

"There were scores in between the drop list and treatment. In those cases I consulted higher authority. I'd call the local senior guide and we'd talk it over. Sometimes I'd visit them. Later I found out my guide would phone the family and ask them to come into his office for a consultation. He'd tell their families that serious decisions had to be made about a loved one, and by the way, the residential hall is practically falling apart on the east side and everyone knows clergy aren't paid salaries . . .

"After a year there my senior guide started having me make decisions myself and then explaining them to him. I must have been good at it. He only overruled me once, in the case of a nephew of a brass ring who had cerebral palsy. They'd found some sinecure for him, and I suspect old Rusty had a big bag of money drop between his ankles under the table. With practice it got easier. I was able to tell myself it was for the good of the species. All the usual *Guidon* false analogies and circular arguments when it's not engaging in outright devil's advocacy. You wouldn't believe—or maybe you would. But I was destined for greater things."

"So when did you start to question your *Guidon*?"

"It might have been the time I went to the basement. There was an incinerator down there for medical waste and so on, and I was responsible for destroying certain records. Lost records are the bureaucrat's best friend when trouble pays a call, Valentine, and don't you forget it if you ever rise to a desk.

"Now usually I just dumped the files down the chute, but it was after normal office hours and for some reason I thought the incinerator might not be burning since we were on a winter fuel savings drive. I went down to check. The basement had its own cargo lift, otherwise you had to take the stairs, and there were two doors out of the lift. The first set, by the buttons, went to the incinerator. I'd always heard that only people who were dropped went out the back doors.

"I took the lift down to the basement because they were painting in the stairs and the fumes bothered me—we'd hit the natal goal for the year, and the doctors and nurses from the delivery ward were having all their faces painted on the landings—and I heard a sound from the other side of the back door as my exit opened. It was like . . . like a sander, a belt sander or one of those ones with the little round pads. I heard screaming."

"We'd always been told, you see, that everything was done to make death painless and worry-free, right down to the use of drugs to relax the person designated for recycling. I still hear that whirring noise and the screams, right to this day, like someone made a tape of it.

"I went to the incinerator and burned the old records and took the stairs back up. Though it almost choked me."

Valentine asked Ediyak to see if she could scare up some food, worried what the ten fingers of bourbon consumption would do to Brother Mark's nerve-worn system.

196   *Fall with Honor*

"You're a good boy, Valentine."

"Where did they send you after the hospital?"

"Education in Washington, DC, seat of the New Universal Church. The Vatican, Medina, Jerusalem, and the River Ganges all wrapped up around one green mall. Ever seen it? No, I suppose you haven't."

"No."

"Well, all the Church upper education schools and monuments are there. 'For the service of mankind,' they all say. Yes, each and every one of them. Sometimes in letters six feet high in marble.

"My six years there reaffirmed my faith in mankind's future. I took lots of classes on old wars, intolerance, racism, studied how mankind had been in a downward spiral and that the so-called Age of Reason led to anything but. I could recite the four controls *Homo sapiens* needed and wrote long essays on the correctly actualized person.

"Oh, and I had my great moment of fame, when I acted in an atrocity film. I got to play both a local priest bemoaning the slaughter of an entire town and a colonel who admitted giving orders to your terror operatives to poison water supplies feeding hospitals and schools. Different films, of course."

"Of course."

"I wondered if anyone would recognize me. Of course I had a full beard and an eyepatch when I was playing the captured colonel.

"They assured me my script was based on actual documentation. The problem was the colonel's testimony sounded quite similar to a film I'd seen three times as a Youth Vanguard. They always began and ended with an 'authenticated documentation' seal and statement. Of course, my films bore one too. I had to wonder. Since we were filming fake documentaries allegedly based on real documentation, I naturally began to have doubts about the veracity of the real documentation. Had it been based on the documentation in that film I saw sixteen years before? I wondered whether my transcribed testimony based on the real documentation might serve as further documentation for another film. Do you follow?"

"You lost me two documentations ago."

"Sorry." He took another drink.

Ediyak arrived with some flatbread sandwiches and a shredded-meat stew that didn't commend itself to close analysis.

They camped the next night with Valentine's usual caution, flanked by the legworm clan encampments, Coonskins to the south and the rest of the Alliance to the north, in a hummock between two higher hills. The hills sloped off to the west like unevenly cooked soufflés, and were situated above a good supply of firewood and water in an old crossroads town. His scavengers dug up a supply of wire in town. Old copper wire had any number of uses in a military camp, mostly in quick repairs. The only interesting feature was an almost paintless church with a steeple that served as a cramped observation post. Otherwise it was no different than any of their other half-dozen camps in the hills of central Kentucky.

Distant gunfire, a sound like sheets slowly torn under a comforter, woke him. He had his boots on by the time the camp siren went off.

The sound brought moisture to his palms and dried his mouth.

Only two events warranted that alarming wail: Reapers in the camp or a surprise attack.

The wail brought the camp together like drizzle turning into pools on a waterproof tarp. Individual drops of soldiers sought their nearest comrades and corporals with the same molecular cohesion of water. The fire teams called to the nearest sergeant or officer as captains passed word and gave orders.

Valentine needed to travel only forty feet or so to headquarters, Bee appearing like a genie summoned by the siren. He forced himself to go at a brisk walk, buckling on his combat harness. The first flares burst to the south as he did so, turning the twigs and leaves of the young trees on the slope into a lattice.

Bloom, who slept just off the headquarters tent, barked orders to a succession of couriers and confused junior officers.

"Legworms coming through the pickets to the south. They'll be on top of us in a few minutes," she said.

"Already over the south ridge," a corporal at a radio receiver reported.

"I'll take a look," Valentine said. He spotted Tiddle, the lieutenant with the motorbike.

"Your bike gassed up?"

"Yes, sir, always."

"Get to the Alliance. Tell them the Coonskins have turned on us. They're not, repeat, not to come into the camp. They'll get shot at."

"What about some kind of marking, so we can tell the difference?" Rand asked. He'd been hovering, waiting for orders for his company.

Valentine gritted his teeth. He should have thought of that.

"Good thinking, Rand," Valentine said. "Have them drape a couple of sheets over the side of their legworms, anything we can make out in bad light," Valentine told Tiddle.

"How do you know the others haven't turned too?" a Guard lieutenant asked. He looked like he should be leading a high school football team rather than a company. "You've got a direct line to the Bullet-proof?" he asked.

"He's got a line on that Alliance girl," Bloom said. "I'd reel her in, if I was you."

A few chuckles lightened the mood.

"Save it for the mess hall. There's no shooting to the north, is there?" Valentine said.

Tiddle ignored the byplay and Valentine heard the blat of the motorbike starting up.

"I'm heading for the OP," Bloom said, slipping a pack of playing cards into the webbing on her helmet. According to mess hall gossip, her father, a soldier himself, had given her the pack to aid passing the time, but she'd never broken the box's seal. Her eyes looked luminous in the shadow of the brim.

He barked at the communications team to set up a backup for communicating with the camp observation post, and then turned to Gamecock.

"Form your Bears into two-man hunter-killer groups. Give them explosives—a couple of sticks of dynamite will do. Have them keep to cover until a legworm comes near. Try to get the bang under the things. They're sensitive there."

"I've heard that. The middle, right?"

"The nerve ganglia's there. But if they can't get near enough to be precise, just under the thing will do. They'll reverse themselves."

Valentine braced the camp for impact. He relocated headquarters to the old graveyard behind the church, where there was a good wall and tree cover.

Artillery shells began to fall, hitting the motor and camp stores and the camp's former headquarters with deadly accuracy.

Of course the Coonskins wouldn't turn on their own—they'd coordinated it with the Moondaggers. Someone in the Coonskins had given the Moondagger spotters a nice little map of camp. Valentine wondered how the brand rank and file felt about the switch in allegiance. Sure, the leadership might decide to bet on the winning team, but what threats would have to be used on the men to turn their guns against erstwhile comrades?

Valentine climbed to the church steeple, so narrow it used a ladder instead of stairs. Bats had taken up residence in the bottom half, hawks higher up.

He felt a little like the proverbial candlestick maker trying to wedge into a shower stall with the butcher and baker. Bloom and her communications tech had a tight enough squeeze in the tiny cupola.

"Valentine, if a shell hits here now, it'll be a triple grave."

"Had to take a quick glimpse," Valentine said.

Bloom slapped him hard on the shoulder. "Moondagger troops are advancing behind the legworm screen."

Valentine watched the lines of crisscrossing legworms. The Kentuckians fought their worms differently than the Grogs of Missouri, who hurried to close from behind shields. He'd seen a Kentucky legworm battle before. The riflemen and gunners hooked themselves to one side of their worms and protected the beasts with old mattresses and sacks full of chopped-up tires on the other. Legworms were notoriously resistant to bullets, but machine-gun fire had been known to travel right through a worm and hit the man on the other side.

A new wrinkle had been added this time—classical siege warfare. The legworms zigzagged forward, acting like the old gabions and fascines that sheltered approaching troops and guns. Valentine could see companies of Moondaggers behind the worms, following the mobile walls as they moved down the night-blue slope toward the camp.

Muzzle flashes sparked on the worms' backs. The legworm riders were shooting, sure enough, but the fire wasn't what Valentine would call intense. More like casual target practice.

"Put some air-fused shells on the other side of those worms," Bloom said. "Slow those troops."

"South line wants permission to fire," the communications tech said.

"No," Valentine said. "Hold fire. Hold fire. Wait for the Moondaggers, sir. There's no artillery on our defensive line, sir. If the riders have spotted it, they're not telling the Moondaggers," Valentine said. "I think a lot of those riders are just play-shooting."

"If that's how you want to play it," Bloom said. "Don't fire till we see the whites of their eyes, eh?"

"They're almost on top of the Bear teams," the communications tech reported.

"And here comes the Alliance," Valentine said, looking north. The Bulletproof worms looked like fingers wearing thick green rings thanks to the tenting banding them.

"Pass the word not to shoot at legworms with the bands. They're Alliance," Bloom said. The communications officer complied.

"Go to the south wall, there, Valentine. Get a hit on 'em," Bloom said.

"Yes, sir."

"Where are those mortars?" Bloom barked.

Valentine hurried back down the patched-up ladder. He went forward, Bee gamboling like an excited dog. He checked his gun and magazines.

Mortar shells whistled overhead. Valentine hurried toward the flashes.

Bee looked at a sentry and Valentine identified himself to the nervous chain of command to the forward posts. Rifle fire crackled overhead.

"They're on top of us. Are we pulling back, or what?" an understandably nervous captain asked.

"The legworms are just cover for the Moondaggers," Valentine said. "They're making the real assault. Don't let your positions show themselves until you can do some real damage."

Gunfire erupted off to the right. Someone wasn't listening to orders or had been knocked out of the communications loop.

Valentine crept up to a stream cut that sheltered the captain's headquarters and took a look at the southern line. The men were sheltered behind low mounds of old legworm trails, patterns crisscrossing as though braided by a drunk, creating little gaps like very shallow foxholes. Atop hummocks of fertilized soil, brush grew like an irregular hedge. The other side had a good view of gently sloped pasture ground and the oncoming parallels of legworms.

A yellow explosion flared under one of the legworms. Gamecock's Bears struck.

Valentine looked to the east. The Alliance seemed to inch forward across the hillside, turning yellow in the rising light of the dawn, still kilometers away but coming hard. This was about to get messy.

Valentine heard another *bang!* of dynamite going off. A legworm, cut in two, hunched off in opposite directions.

"This is it. They're coming!" the captain said.

The lines of Coonskin legworms parted, crackling rifle fire still popping away atop the mounts, but the bullets were flying off toward the church and camp, not at the line of men pressed flat behind the bushy legworm trail.

Valentine took in the loose wall of men coming forward, more tightly packed than Southern Command would ever group an assault. Were they being herded forward? Valentine's night-sharp eyes made out a few anguished faces.

The Coonskin legworms angled off to the sides, retreating. The Moondaggers were revealed.

"Let 'em have it, Captain," Valentine said. "This is it."

"Open fire. Open fire!" the captain called. "Defensive grenades."

Gunfire broke out all along the line, sounding like a sudden heavy rain striking a tin roof. Screams sounded from the ranks of the Moondagger assaulting column.

Valentine saw a field pack radio antenna, an officer crouching next to it on the slope.

"Bee," Valentine said, pointing. "That one."

Bee swung her hockey stick of a rifle around and dropped him. Good shooting, that. Uphill fire took a good eye.

Rand reported in. Bloom had sent Valentine's old company up to support the line with Glass' machine guns.

Valentine issued orders for them to create a fallback line at the stream cut as though on autopilot. His mind was on the assault. The first lines fell under withering fire, hardly shooting back, and a second wave, better dispersed and disciplined, came forward.

Grenades exploded, deeper thuds that transmitted faintly through the ground.

The Moondaggers broke through and it was rifle butts and pistols along the line. Valentine realized he'd put his gun to his shoulder without thinking about it and fired burst after burst into the second wave, knocking them back like target cans. He ducked and slid along the stream cut as he reloaded.

Bee grunted and the hair atop her head parted. Valentine saw white skull. She ignored it and kept shooting.

"Medic," Valentine called.

Bear teams at the assault's flanks, like tiny tornadoes at the side-lines, bit off pieces of the Moondaggers that Valentine's line chewed up.

The Moondaggers fell back, tripping over their own dead as they backed away, shooting and reloading.

"Keep the heat on!" the captain called.

"Send back to Bloom: Repulsed. For now," Valentine ordered.

A medic was wrapping up Bee's head. He gave Valentine a thumbs-up. "Good thing this old girl doesn't set much store by hairstyle. She's gonna have a funny part."

"You all right, Bee?" Valentine asked.

In response she handed him four shell casings. Her tally, evidently. The ever-observant Bee was picking up habits from Duvalier.

Valentine sent Rand's company forward to fill the gaps in the line, just in case. He went up, keeping at a crouch behind the brush as he moved along the line. Snipers were trading shots across the battlefield as what was left of the Moondaggers' second and third waves retreated back across the south hill.

"We killed enough of 'em," a soldier said, looking at the carpet of dead from the first wave; the second wave wounded were still being hunted up from the brush.

"Yes," Valentine said. "Old men. Kids. Women even. The Moondaggers put some cannon fodder up front, and when the gamble didn't pay they kept the rest of their chips back. Those two don't even have guns. They gave them baseball bats with a railroad spike through the top."

"Those shits," a Southern Command soldier said. Another picked up one of the bats and examined it.

"Let's get a couple of their chips. To the ridgeline, men. Send back to Bloom: Have her put everything she's got on the other side of that ridge—that's where their real strength is."

Valentine felt a Reaper up on the ridgeline. It was probably assigning blame for the failure even now.

New gunfire erupted in the distance to the east as the Moondaggers and Coonskins attacked. The lines of legworms looked like fighting snakes, spread out on the hillside.

He sent word back to Bloom, asking for permission to attack. She gave it, enthusiastically. It was good to have Cleo Bloom in charge. She'd recovered some of her old spirit.

"We've busted up their face. Let's kick 'em in the ass," a sergeant called as the orders passed to advance.

Southern Command's soldiers went forward with their yips and barks like foxhounds on a hot scent. Gamecock saw what was happening and sent his Bears forward, flushing the snipers like rabbits.

Mortars fell on the other side of the hill, their flashes dimmer in the growing light. Valentine saw wild worms running off to the east, and the Bulletproof harrying the Coonskins. Hard luck for the Coonskins. Their halfhearted cover for the assault had aided in the repulse as much as the Southern Command's grenades and mortar shells.

Valentine looked behind. Bloom had better than half the camp moving up the hill.

They met strong fire on the ridge as the sun appeared, but the Bulletproof turned from their rout of the Coonskins to the east and put a fleshy curtain of gunfire against the Moondagger flank.

Valentine's assault expended the last of their grenades, pitching them over the hilltop. They captured two big 155mm guns which were being brought forward to complete the camp's destruction, complete with communications gear and a substantial reserve of ammunition.

Southern Command's forces secured the crest line, guns, and few prisoners who didn't blow themselves up with grenades and planted themselves. On that glorious reverse slope where the Coonskins had been camped, picked out for its suitable field of fire, they found the Moondaggers in disarray and falling back.

Valentine watched machine-gun tracer prod their retreat, leaving bodies like heaps of dropped laundry on the slope. Moondagger trucks, crammed with men hanging off the side, pulled off to the south.

If only they'd had real cannon instead of light mortars. The Moondaggers would have been destroyed instead of just bloodied. Valentine did what he could with what he had, sending shells chasing after the retreat, dropping them at choke points in the road.

Moytana's Wolves would give them a nip or two to remind them that they were beaten and running.

It wasn't a catastrophe for the Moondaggers. But it was enough. Valentine felt the odd, light, post-battle aura. He'd survived again, and better, won.

Seng's expeditionary brigade had fought its first real battle and emerged victorious.

They buried their dead, slung their wounded in yolk hammocks hanging off the side of the legworms, and pressed on. This time with lighter step and more aggressive patrols, half-empty bellies or no. It was still a retreat, but a retreat from victory, with honor restored.

Eleven

Crisis, August: Javelin's support slowly dribbles away as it passes through east-central Kentucky. The Alliance clans shift their families and herds away from the area of Southern Command's column as though they carry bubonic plague. The Mammoth depart to settle a private score with the Coonskins.

Only the Gunslingers and the attenuated Bulletproof remain at a reasonable level of strength, the Gunslingers grudging the Kurians the loss of their dispatcher at the ambush in Utrecht, and the Bulletproof through the force of Tikka's personality and a twinkling affinity for Valentine as a member of Southern Command.

The Moondaggers reappear, reinforced after their successful destruction of the Green Mountain expedition in Pennsylvania, this time in a motorized column, hovering just at the edge of the column's last rear guard's vision.

Valentine asked for, and received, permission to spend the day with the Wolves following the Moondaggers on their flanking march. Bloom had granted it halfheartedly, all the usual humor drained from her voice. Valentine wondered whether it was the strain of command—or was it the strange lassitude that infected Jolla consuming Javelin's new commander?

It felt like old times, with the odd addition of Bee's constant, protective shadow and a couple of legworms carrying the Wolves' spare gear, provisions, and camping equipment. Moving hard from point to point, one platoon resting and eating while a second went ahead, the tiny company headquarters shifted according to the terrain and movements of the enemy, small groups of wary scouts disappearing like careful deer into stands of timber and ravines.

All that had changed was the strain Valentine felt trying to keep up with them. He considered himself in decent enough shape, but a day with the Wolves made him feel like a recruit fresh out of Labor Regiment fell-running again.

Moytana himself was watching over the enemy whenever possible, a careful woodsman observing a family of grizzlies, knowing that if he made a mistake at the wrong moment, he'd be killed, partitioned, and digested within an hour by the beasts.

The Moondagger column resembled a great black snake winding through the valley. Or floodwaters from a burst dam, moving sluggishly but implacably forward. He could just hear high wailing cries answered by guttural shouts, so precise a responsorial chorus that it resembled some piece of industrial machinery, stamping away staccato.

Flocks of crows circled above. Valentine wondered if they were trained in some way, or just used to battlefield feasts.

The performance did its job. Valentine felt intimidated.

Valentine tried to make out the "scales" of the snake. All he could think was that the army was marching holding old riot shields over their heads.

"Umbrellas," Moytana said. "Or parasols. Whatever you want to call them. They've got a little fitting in their backpack frame for the handle."

"What's that they're—I don't want to call it singing—chanting?"

"That one's got some highfalutin name like the 'Hour of the Divine Unleashing.' Means they're going to chop us into stewing-sized pieces, in so many words."

Valentine saw some scouts on motorbikes pull to the top of a hill flanking the column. They pointed binoculars and spotting scopes at Valentine's hilltop. Valentine waited for a few companies to break off from the column to chase them off, but the Moondaggers stayed in step and song.

"They don't seem to mind our presence."

"They want us impressed. That's part of why they're chanting."

"You've heard that tune before."

"Yes. A small city called Ripening, in Kansas. Old maps call it Olathe."

"What went wrong in Kansas?"

"Everything. The operation made sense in theory. As we approached, the resistance was supposed to rise up and cause trouble. Cut communication lines, take the local higher-ups prisoner, blow up trucks and jeeps and all that.

"Problem was, it was kind of like Southern Command and the resistance set up a line of dominoes. Once the first couple tipped, it started a chain reaction. Sounds of fighting in Farming Collective Six gets the guys in Farming Collective Five next door all excited, and they dig up their guns and start shooting, which gets the guys at Four who've been sharpening their set of knives the idea that relief is just over the hill. So they start cutting throats. And so on and so on.

"Early on, seemed like we were succeeding beyond anyone's hopes. Wolves were tearing through Kansas knocking the hell out of the Kansas formations trying to get organized to meet us. Kurians were abandoning their towers in panic, leaving stacks of dead retainers behind.

"The way I understand it, the Kurians launched a counterattack out of the north, just a few Nebraska and Kansas and Iowa regulars. Typical Kurian ordering, from what I hear, futile attacks or defenses with rounds of executions in exchange for failure. Reapers started popping up along our line of advance, picking off the odd courier and signals post. That was enough to put the scare into a couple of our generals and they turned north or froze and right-wheeled, trying to establish a line with the poor Kansans under the impression that we were still coming hard west.

"Well, the Kurians must have got wind of our operation ahead of time. Maybe they even had, whaddya call 'em, agents o' provocation riling the Kansans up to get the resistance out in the open. They had these Moondagger fellows all ready to go in Nebraska, two full divisions plus assorted support troops like armored cars and artillery trains. Kansans started calling them the Black Death."

"I never saw anything like the Moondaggers when I crossed Nebraska."

"Oh, they're not from there. I guess they headquarter near Detroit with a couple of posts in northern Michigan, watching the Canadian border. Sort of a province of the Ordnance. That's one of the better-run—"

"I know the Ordnance. I've been into Ohio."

"They moved them fast, took them through the Dakotas on that spur they built to go around Omaha. At least that's what that Cat Smoke told me. She's the one who urged us to get to Olathe before it was too late."

Valentine didn't say anything. He let the words come.

"But once the Moondaggers started moving, they moved fast. On good roads they travel in these big tractor trailers made out of old stock cars stacked like cordwood. I've seen them riding on old pickups and delivery vans and busses, clinging like ticks to the outside and on the roof. They only do their marching when they're near the enemy, and then they pray and holler like that."

Moytana gestured at the winding snake.

"First they send an embassy of men from another town they've cut up, so the right accent and clothing and set of expressions is passing on all the gory details. I'm told their lives depend on getting the rebels to give up without a fight. Then they send in guys like our Last Chance to negotiate, get men to throw down their guns and quit, sneak off, whatever—then they make them prove their loyalty to the Kurians. Arm them with spears and one-shot rifles or have them carry banners in their front ranks so neighbor has to shoot neighbor."

He gulped. "Once they go into a town, well, they gut the place pretty bad. There are always a few Kurians in the rear, adding little tricks and whatnot, scaring the defenders. Outside of Olathe a rainstorm worked up and the Kurians somehow made it look like blood. I don't care who you are, Valentine—that'll rattle you, seeing blood run off the roof and pool in the streets. The Kurians get their pick of auras. The Moondaggers get their pick of women."

"You mentioned that before."

"Yeah, everyone from NCO on up in the Moondaggers has his little harem. Flocks, they call them. The gals are the flocks and they're the buggering shepherds jamming the gals' feet into their boots so they can't kick.

"That's the big thing in that outfit, breeding. A guy with a big flock, he's more likely to get promoted. They get decorated for the number of kids they've sired.

"Trick's getting started. You haul as many women as you can control home with you and start churning out babies. Seems the favorite age to grab is about nine to twelve. They don't eat as much, can't put up a fight, and they got all their breedin' years ahead of them."

"So making babies is like counting coup. What happens to the progeny?"

"Starting about five to eight they test them. I'm told one gets chosen to look after household when 'Dad' is away—almost always a boy. Toughest of the kids go into the Moondaggers, smartest go into the Church, the rest go off to labor training or get traded somewheres."

"Who controls the 'flock' while they're off fighting?"

"Dunno. Reapers, I suppose. Maybe the Church brainwashes some of the gals."

"You couldn't stop it in Olathe."

"No, it was just me and a squad of Wolves. We went through town after they pulled out. Found lots of bodies. And about a million crows eating the bits and pieces left in the streets. Moondaggers always like to chop a few up and stuff them back into their clothes the wrong way around, feet sticking out of shirtsleeves and heads where a foot should be. *For it is the blessed man who obeys the Gods and knows his place, for they are Wise; the man who claims for his head the mantle of god-hood is as foolish as one who walks upon his hands and eats with his feet.*

"They left three men alive. One with his eyes burned out, one with his ears scrambled with a screwdriver, and one with his tongue ripped out. Just like that trio from the Mammoths. They did a story on them in the *Free Flags*. Pretty sad picture to put on the front page. Did you see it? About a year and a half ago."

"I was out west at the time."

"Whole bunch of young women barricaded themselves into one of the New Universal Church buildings and killed themselves with rat poison. I found a note: *One kind of freedom or another.* Girl looked about fourteen. That Smoke, she cried a good bit. Wasn't a total loss. We found some kids their parents stuffed up a chimney. Poor little things. I saw pretty much the same story in three other towns. Now they're here."

Valentine, feeling impotent in the face of the river of men snaking south two miles away, picked up a dry branch and snapped it. "Now they're here."

"Yeah. I know what's coming too. They'll just harry us, tire us out, get us used to running away from them. They'll terrorize anyone who even thinks about helping us. Then when we're starved and exhausted, they'll strike. Least they won't get too many candidates for their flocks out of our gals. Southern Command's shoot back."

"That's just one division there. Where do you suppose the other two are?"

"We never marked more than two in Kansas. The other's probably harrying what's left of the Green Mountain Boys."

"How did you find all that out?"

"We picked off one or two stragglers. Some just didn't talk, recited prayers the whole time or killed themselves with grenades at the last second. Some of the NCOs wear these big vests filled with explosives and ball bearings. They'll pretend to be dead and jump up and try to take a few with them. Smoke went and found a boy in Moondagger uniform and took him prisoner. Couldn't have been more than eleven; his only job was to beat a drum after the prayer singer spoke. He stayed tough for about ten minutes and then broke down and started crying when she sorta mothered him. Heard most of it from him."

Valentine had a hard time picturing Duvalier mothering anything but her assortment of grudges. But then she was a Cat, and it was her job to get information.

They left the hilltop, mounted legworms, and conformed to the line of the Moondaggers' march. Scouts found a new wooded ridge with a good view of the highway and they repeated the process for another hour. Moytana took a break and started on a letter. Valentine watched the marchers and the opposing scouts. All Valentine could think was that the Moondaggers were experts at their particular brand of harshness. He wondered how long they could operate somewhere like Kentucky without—

"Sir, scouts have met up with a party of locals," a Wolf reported. "Armed. They saw us riding. One of them asked for you by name and rank, Major Valentine."

"Locals?"

"Hard to tell if they're Kentuckian or Virginian. Mountain folk. Careful, sir. I don't like the look of them."

Valentine put a sergeant at the spotting scope and Moytana abandoned his letter. They snaked down the slope to a rock-strewn clearing and Valentine saw five men in black vests waiting around a small spring-fed pond, boiling water. Valentine carried his gun loosely, as though meeting a neighbor while deer hunting.

Valentine approached. The strangers were lean, haggard men with close-cropped beards and camouflaged strips of cloth tying the hair out of their eyes. They had an assortment of 5.56 carbines with homemade flash suppressors and scopes.

Valentine didn't recognize any faces.

What he at first took to be a pile of littered rocks shifted at his approach.

A mass of straw canvas sitting with its back to him rose. It looked like a fat, disproportioned scarecrow made out of odds and ends of Reaper cloth, twigs, twine, netting, and tusklike teeth. A leather cap straight out of a World War One aviator photo topped the ensemble, complete with Coke-bottle goggles on surgical-tubing straps, though there were holes cut in the hat to allow bat-wing ears to project and move this way and that freely.

A face that was mostly sharp teeth yawned and grinned as a tiny tongue licked its lips in anticipation. The muddy apparition carried a strange stovepipe weapon that looked like a recoilless rifle crossed with a bazooka.

Bee let out a sound that was half turkey gobble, half cougar scream.

What? Valentine thought, feeling his knees go weak.

The mountain of odds and ends spoke. "Well, my David. What kind of fix do you have yourself in this time?"

When Valentine could see again, blinking the tears out of his eyes, he looked around at the two groups of men, Wolves and Appalachian guerrillas, both eyeing the astonishing sight of a man with Southern Command militia major clusters pinned on to a suit of legworm leathers crying his eyes out against the mud-matted hair of a Grog's chest.

"Our general ain't as bad as he smells," one of the guerrillas told a Wolf. "Talks a midge funny, but by 'n' by your'n gets used to it."

Ahn-Kha and Bee exchanged pats, scratches, and ear-cleanings as he and Valentine spoke.

"Did Hoffman Price turn up again?"

Bee turned miserable at the name and muttered into her palm, thumping her chest and pulling at the corners of her eyes.

Ahn-Kha made more sense of it than Valentine could, though he caught the words for "death," "lost," and "slave" in the brief story.

"I'm sorry to hear of his passing, my David. It seems to have worked out for Bee. You're her, um, liberator and dignity restorer. As far as she's concerned, you hung her lucky moon in the sky."

"I can't tell whether she's a bodyguard or governess. She's always about yanking me out of my boots at the sound of gunfire."

"Proving that she has more sense than you."

"Can I hear your story?" Valentine asked.

"Oh, it is a long tale, and only the end matters. I managed to get myself put in command of the Black Flags. I still wonder at it."

Valentine still couldn't resist asking. "Your injuries?"

"Healed, more or less. Though I urinate frequently. I use your old trick of dusting with pepper or peeing into baking soda, otherwise the dogs would probably catch on."

"What happened to the pursuit?"

"They thought they caught a dumb Grog driver. I was sold to a mine operator. There matters turned dark in more ways than the coal face. I did not care for their treatment of someone who was kind to me and began a vedette."

"Vendetta, I think you mean."

"Vendetta. Of course. My one-hand war grew."

"What are your numbers now?"

"I will not tell you exactly," Ahn-Kha said. "Not with all these ears around. The Kurians believe our army to number ten thousand or more. But they have multiplied when they should have divided."

"I don't suppose I can count on you at my side this time?"

"These men deserve my presence. I began their war, and I will see it through. This is a strange land, my David. Victory and defeat all depend on a few score of powerful, clannish families who run things in this part of the country. Everyone knows and is related to one or more of these families. It makes my head hurt to keep track of it all. For now, they endure the Kurians as best as they can, though there are one or two families who relish their high placement overmuch. But the others, if they believe that we will win, they will place their support with us."

They talked quietly for a while. Ahn-Kha was waging a canny war against these powerful Quisling families. His partisan "army" had the reputation it had simply because it didn't exist as a permanent body. Ahn-Kha would arrive near a town and his small body of men would gather a few second cousins and brothers-in-law, Ahn-Kha would issue arms and explosives, and they'd strike and then fragment again as the Golden One relocated to another spot.

Sometimes when they struck and killed some officer in the Quisling armed forces with a connection to one of the more powerful collaborators, they dressed him in the guerrilla vests and left him buried nearby where search dogs were sure to find him. This led to reprisals and mistrust between the Quislings, and the rickety Kurian Order in the coal country of the Appalachians was coming apart.

The Moondaggers, on their arrival, had destroyed a trio of the Quisling families under suspicion, creating bad feeling among the rest. If they were to be treated as guerrillas, they might as well join the resistance and hit back.

"You wouldn't be interested in a trip back to the Ozarks, would you? I've felt like a one-armed man since we parted."

"And I a Golden One missing the ugly half of his face. But my men need me. Though I started a revolt more by accident than intention, I must see it through."

"Forget I asked."

"Can I be of assistance otherwise, my David? In this last year my small body of men have become very, very good at quick, destructive strikes. Shall I bring down bridges in the path of your enemy?"

"It's the trailing end I'd like attacked. Do you think you can bust up their supply lines? I want the Moondaggers forced to live off the land as much as possible."

"It will not be difficult to find men to do that. They have carried off a number of daughters already. As I said, everyone here knows everyone by blood or marriage or religious fellowship."

Valentine felt an excited tingle run up his spine. Ahn-Kha usually underpromised and overdelivered. Ahn-Kha would tweak the tiger by the tail, and if the tiger was stupid enough to turn, it would find itself harried by a foxy old Grog up and down these wooded mountains.

"I can't tell you what this means to me, old horse."

"I have the easy end, my David. Kicking a bull in the balls isn't terribly difficult when someone else is grappling with the horns."

"They may deal harshly with the locals."

"They will find the people in this part of the country have short fuses and long memories, if they do so."

Ahn-Kha always was as handy with an epigram as he was with a rifle. Speaking of which—

"What in the world is that thing?" Valentine asked. "A shoulder-fired coal furnace?"

"My individual 75mm," Ahn-Kha said. "Almost the only artillery in our possession. Some clever chap in my command rigs artillery shells so they go off like rockets."

"You're kidding."

Ahn-Kha's ears made a gesture like a traffic cop waving him to the left. "Kidding? It is more dangerous than it looks. That is why I have the goggles. You are lucky you haven't seen me after firing it. My hair becomes rather singed."

They shared a simple camp meal of legworm jerky and corn mush. Valentine didn't even have any sweets to offer Ahn-Kha. If it had been in his power to do so, he'd have run all the way back to St. Louis to get some of Sissy's banana bread or molasses cookies.

If he could fantasize about running all the way, he could fantasize about bananas being available in the Grog markets.

"Sorry we don't have any molasses," Valentine said. "We're a long way from home."

Ahn-Kha extracted a small plastic jar of honey shaped like a bear, tiny in his massive fist, and squirted some onto each man's corn mash.

He quizzed Ahn-Kha on the capabilities of his guerrillas and their operations, soaking up his friend's opinions and experiences like a sponge. Ahn-Kha was doing his best to make coal extracted from these mountains as expensive in repair and garrisoning as possible.

As the Golden One told a story about the destruction of a rail tunnel, a report came in that the Moondagger column was turning again, this time north. They might have finally turned toward Javelin. They'd have to relocate again to keep it under observation.

They bolted the rest of the meal and washed their pannikins in the spring. Ahn-Kha wrapped up his jar of honey and stuck it back in a vast pouch on his harness that smelled like wild onions. Valentine gave him a collection of Grog guck scavenged from the men with promises to replace it with chocolate bars from the medical stores.

Valentine would always remember that tiny plastic honey reservoir, and the way Ahn-Kha licked his fingers after sharing it out. Would there ever be a world again where people cared about the shape of a container?

He hoped so.

When they parted he shook the slightly sticky hand again, felt it engulf his own. Fingers that could snap his femur closed gently around his hand.

"Good luck, my David. We will meet again in happier circumstances."

"You said something like that before."

"And I was right. Give my regards to Mr. Post and Malita Carrasca. And our smoldering red firebug."

The staggering weight of all that had happened since they'd last said good-bye left him speechless. Ahn-Kha didn't even know about Blake.

"I trust your judgment on that one, old horse."

"Major, we have to leave. Now, sir," Moytana said.

So much for the fleeting pleasures of lukewarm corn mash sweetened by a tincture of honey. Valentine considered requesting that "Resting in peace—subject to the requirements of the service" be emblazoned on his grave marker.

Ahn-Kha's ears flicked up. "I'll give you a little more warning next time so you can receive me properly." He pulled his leather cap a little tighter on his head and picked up his stovepipe contraption. "After all, as you can see, I am a distinguished general."

"I'll bake a cake," Valentine said.

"Heartroot would do. See if you can't get me a few eyeroots, would you?"

"Good luck, my old friend. I can't tell you how good it is to see you again," Valentine said.

"When matters are settled in these mountains, you will see me again. Chance is not yet done playing with us."

With that, he turned and loped rather heavily off to the east into the woods, his men running to keep up. Valentine wondered what another brigade, three thousand strong or more, of Golden Ones could accomplish if led by his old friend.

The column had turned for Javelin. They were mounting a small force on armored trucks. Valentine wondered what the urgency was and requested that they make contact with base.

"Javelin's hung up at a bridge crossing. I can't get a warning through—there's some kind of jamming," the com tech reported.

"Moytana, try to delay those vehicles. Avoid a fight if you can. Block the road with trees at some gap."

"I'll see what I can do, sir. Looks like they're taking several routes, though."

The Moondagger column had turned into a hydra. One head crawled up a ridge, trying to get to the next valley over. A second was turning northeast, perhaps to get around behind Javelin.

"Send your fastest messenger back to headquarters with a warning. I think we can guess their route well enough. I'll follow as best as I can."

"Yes, sir," Moytana said, calling for his runner.

A boy of sixteen or seventeen—so it seemed to Valentine—answered the call. He carried an assault rifle that made him look even more like a child playing at war. It was a good old Atlanta Gunworks Type 3.

"Here, I'll carry that back to brigade for you, son," Valentine said, wanting the gun's angry bark.

Valentine took a slightly different path on the long road back than the boy. He angled off to the west, to see what that column marching across the ridge intended to do.

There was plenty of daylight left. If the Moondaggers were daylight fighters, it was all the better. His men would worry more about inflicting damage on the enemy and less about what might be lurking in the woods.

He topped another rise, puffing. No one was there to see him take a knee and dig around for a handkerchief to wipe off the summer sweat. His pits and crotch stuck and chafed. Legworm leather breathed well, but there were limits to any material.

The westmost column looked to have found the road they were looking for. It wasn't in good shape at all, a broken surface with fully grown trees erupting from parts of the pavement. Of course men traveling on foot without heavy weapons could easily find a path. It looked as though the deer had already made one.

He checked his bearings and picked a target on the next ridge north in the direction of headquarters.

Valentine ran down the opposite side of his ridge from the column, firing first his machine pistol, then the deeper bark of the Type 3. Every now and then he broke up the sound with a longer burst.

The phantom firefight might just turn the Moondaggers aside from their path to investigate. How well they could track and read shell casings was anyone's guess.

What counted at this point was delay.

*   *   *

Valentine came to the Turkey Neck bridge, approaching along the eastern bank, and found chaos.

The river ran beneath deep, sculpted banks—Valentine guessed they were a flood prevention measure. Bluffs to the south frowned down on the slight river bend.

The old metal-frame highway bridge had been dynamited, quite incompetently, resulting in no more than the loss of some road bed and a few piles of paving. Bloom had sensibly sent several companies across to secure the far bank. But light mortar shells were now falling at the rate of one a minute all around the bridge area, keeping crews from covering the damage with timber and iron.

Legworms might be able to get across, but not trucks, vehicles, and horse- and mule-drawn carts. The brigade could cross, even through this shell fire, but would leave the supply train behind.

Valentine did his best not to anticipate the shells as he found headquarters, placed in a defile about a quarter mile from the east bank.

"Well?" he asked the first lieutenant he saw, ready to give someone a few choice words. Why wasn't anyone shooting back with the light artillery?

"Thank God you're here, sir. We've been under aimed artillery fire, sir. Cap—Colonel Bloom's wounded!"

"What's being done about those mortars?"

"They're trying to find a route north around the downed bridge. We're supposed to be set to move."

"On whose orders?"

"Not sure. You can countermand, sir."

"Why would I do that?"

"I think you're in command now, sir."

If he was in command, he might as well take charge. Valentine walked over to the headquarters vehicle, a Hummer bristling with antennae like some kind of rust-streaked insect.

Valentine studied a notated ordnance map. Pins marked the positions of his various companies. His jack-of-all-trades former Quislings were up waiting to assist the engineers in repairing the bridge.

He checked the bluff where the Moondaggers—if they were Moondaggers, and not troops out of Lexington or God knew where else—had set up their pieces. It was about a mile and a half south of the bridge.

"Set up an observer post, or better, two, to call in fire on those enemy mortars, if they can be effective. I'm going to the hospital."

He issued orders for defense of the temporary camp. He directed their tiny supply of anti-armor gear to the road that would most likely see the armored cars, and gave orders for everyone to be ready to move as soon as the bridge team could go to work. As soon as Moytana arrived, he was to take charge of the rear guard.

Then Valentine grabbed a spare satchel of signals gear, made sure one of the brigade's few headsets and a flare pistol rested in the holster within, and left.

The visit to the hospital was brief. It was the only tent the brigade had set up, mostly because of the big red cross on it. The only other casualty was what was left of a soldier who had a shell go off practically under him. The Moondaggers were dropping most of their shells on the bridge, either trying to keep the rest of the brigade from getting across or in the hopes of a lucky series of shots downing it for good.

Colonel Bloom seemed likely to live, at least long enough for the damage sustained by her pancreas to kill her. She sat up in bed, giving orders.

After hearing the medical report, he sent a messenger for Gamecock.

"Valentine, thank God you're here," she said, pushing away a nurse. "Silence those mortars, fix the bridge, and get the brigade across. These cutters want to sedate me and open me up. Don't let them stick anything in me until the brigade's safe."

"I think you should do what the doctors ask. I'll take care of the brigade. We'll wriggle out of this fix. The Moondaggers seem to be trying again."

"Yes, I heard the Wolf's report. Right before the world flipped over on me."

"Sorry about that, sir."

She looked like she was trying to smile. "Couldn't be helped. Don't worry about me. Go do your duty."

"If you'll let them get that shrapnel out."

She nodded. Then she opened one eye. "Oh, Valentine?"

"Yes, Colonel?"

"Get a hit."

He smiled. The old Bloom was back. "Their infield's in. I think I can poke one through."

Valentine found the doctor he'd first talked to.

"Have you ever tried transfusions from a Bear?" Valentine asked.

"I've read about some amazing results. But I believe it must be done quickly, while there's still living tissue and nerve impulses."

Gamecock arrived, breathless from a run across the bridge. His Bears were sheltering on the opposite side.

"What's Bloom's blood type?" Valentine said.

"O positive, suh," the doctor said. "Fairly common."

"Gamecock, get your Bears' blood type," Valentine said.

"I've kept up with the research too, Major," Gamecock said. "You might say I have needle-in experience. I spent a week at Hope of the Free hospital, passing blood to critical cases. They bled me white and kept trying to refill my veins with orange drink."

"I need an—no, make it two—two Bears with either O positive or O negative blood. Right away. Doctor, give Colonel Bloom a transfusion as soon as one can be arranged. Then a second in twelve hours. Is that clear?"

"If the Bears are willing, I am. I've heard stories about injecting one and getting your jaw rewired in return. I want willing and, more important, calm subjects."

"I'll watch over them myself, suh," Gamecock said.

"I'm going to need you for a few hours, Lieutenant," Valentine said. "We're going after those mortars."

"Did you take a look at that bluff, sir? It's a steep one. I'd hate to waste Bears taking it."

"The Moondaggers will have to prove they know how to hold off a Bear assault. I still think they don't know what to do about someone who fights back."

"It's still a steep hill. It'll look a lot steeper with bullets coming down."

"I know a way to get up it."

Valentine got a report from the artillery spotters. The height of the bluff made it impossible to accurately spot fire, so Valentine told them to save their fireworks.

"Infantry strength?"

"All we can see is perhaps platoon strength on this side. They're right at the top."

"Right at the top?"

"Yes, sir. I don't think they can see jack at the base of that hill."

They really didn't know how to fight. Or they just liked the view. No matter, Valentine had to take advantage of the error quickly, before a more experienced Moondagger arrived and corrected the matter.

The hardest part was getting one of the Bulletproof to agree to ride the legworm.

"Up that?" Swill, the Bulletproof veep in charge of their contingent, said. "If the footing's poor, you could roll a worm right over on you, especially if men are hanging on it in fighting order."

"I'll take mine up that hill," Tikka said, stepping forward. "I'm the best trick rider in the clan."

"There's trick riding and there's getting shot at. You don't know enough about the other," Swill said. "I'm not risking our senior veep's sister."

"So you told me. You're afraid to take your worms across under this shell fire. Watch this."

They did watch as she hurried to her worm grazing in some brush farther downstream. Digging her hook into its hide and using the spurs on the inner ankle of her boot, she mounted her worm and prodded it toward the bridge.

Swill ran in front of her worm and tried to divert it, looking a little like a rabbit trying to stop a bus. The worm nosed him aside, off his feet, and Swill threw off his hat in frustration.

"Watch those shells!" Swill yelled. "It'll rear back if one comes too close!" He turned back on Valentine. "The exec told me to keep her from doing anything stupid. Lookit me now. I'm going to have to go back and admit I couldn't keep a rein on one little female."

"Not the size of the dog in the fight, it's the fight in the dog," a handsome Guard sergeant detailed to the Bulletproof said. He rubbed his jaw ruefully. "That gal has her own mind about things."

Valentine sent a field-radio message to Gamecock to move his Bears toward the bluff, and then trotted up and joined his company, waiting for their chance to fix the bridge. They had all the tools and materials resting in the ditch next to the road.

"How's the shell fire, Rand?"

"Poor, if they're trying to kill us. I think they're just trying to keep us off that bridge. The fire's slackening, so I think they're running out of shells. Excuse me, sir, but is that worm rider crazy?"

"Feisty, more like," Valentine said, watching the legworm glide up the road on its multitude of black, claw-like legs, ripples running the length of its thirty-yard body as it covered ground. "Someone suggested she couldn't handle her worm."

Valentine watched Tikka fiddle with the gear on her saddle. She extracted another pole with a sharp hook, this one with a curve to the shaft.

"What's that for?"

"Legworms aren't very sensitive anywhere but the underside. She gives it a poke now and then to keep it moving."

Tikka aimed her mount straight for the hole. A shell landed near her and the legworm froze for a second. She goaded it forward again.

When it came to the hole in the pavement, she gripped the reins in her teeth, used one pole to goad her beast forward, and swung the other under what might be called its snout. It was where the food went in, anyway.

She poked it good at the front and it reared up, twisting this way and that. Tikka clung as another shell whistled down. It must have dropped straight through the hole in the pavement, because it exploded in the water beneath the bridge.

Tikka clung, shifted the forward pole down the legworm's belly, and then poked it again. It reared up, and she released the painful spur. It came down again, a good thirty legs on the other side of the hole. The legs over the gap twitched uncertainly, like the shifting fingers of sea anemones Valentine had seen in the Jamaican reefs.

"I didn't know they could do that," Rand said.

"I expect they can't, usually."

Tikka hurried her worm forward, a living bridge over the hole in the pavement. As she passed across, the beast's rear dropped into the hole, but with the rest of it pulling, it got its tail up and out.

Valentine checked his pack of signal gear again. How long until the Moondaggers got here?

"Preville, you've just been attached to headquarters," Valentine said. "You get to come on an assault with the Bears. Bring your radio."

"Er—yes, sir," Preville said, blinking.

"Red, then blue if we clear the hill. Understand?"

"Red, then blue," Rand repeated. "Got it, sir."

"Every minute counts. The opposition is on its way."

"They picked a good time to turn on us."

"I'm not so sure they picked it. The Kurians have long tendrils."

Valentine slapped his lieutenant on the shoulder and then ran up the extreme right of the bridge, Preville trailing, trying to run while folded in half. Another shell fell into the water. Valentine marked the glimmer of fish bellies bobbing in the current.

Someone downstream would collect a bounty of dead sunfish.

Tikka rested her mount on the other side, letting it graze in a thicket. Valentine watched brush and bramble and clumps of sod disappear into its muscular lipped throat. Valentine waved the Bears forward.

They came, three groups of four, in the variegated mix of Reaper cloth, Kevlar, and studded leather the Bears seemed to favor. Valentine even saw a shimmer of a chain mail dickey over one Bear's throat and upper chest. Their weapons were no more uniform than their attire. Belt-fed machine guns in leather swivel slings, deadly little SMGs, grenade launchers, assault shotguns, an old M14 tricked out with a custom stock and a sniper scope . . . never mind the profusion of blades, bayonets, and meathooks taped or clipped onto boots, thighs, forearms, and backs. Most of Gamecock's team favored facial hair of some kind. All wore a little silver spur around their neck—a team marker, Valentine guessed.

The Moondaggers, used to slaughtering rebellious farming collectives armed with stones and pitchforks, were in for a surprise.

"We're riding to the bluff. Can your worm hold them all?"

"It's young and strong," Tikka said. "As long as we're not riding all day."

Tikka unrolled a length of newbie netting from the back of her saddle, where it served as a lounger while coiled up. Gamecock's dozen picked Bears climbed uncertainly onto the creature.

"I've blown a few of these up but never ridden one," a Bear with a shaved, tattooed scalp said.

Another, who'd somehow stretched, teased, or sculpted his ears into almost feral points, wiggled his legs experimentally as he gripped the netting. "Not bad. Ride's smooth, like a boat. You could sleep while traveling."

"We do," Tikka said.

She kept them in the trees, keeping leafy cover over their heads whenever possible as they approached the bluff. The hills closed in between them and the riverbank. Then, suddenly, the steep slope was before them.

Valentine dismounted, carefully went forward, waiting for the sniper's bullet or the machine-gun burst. Every twig and leaf seemed to stand out against the blue Kentucky sky.

Nothing.

The Moondaggers had erred. Or at least he hoped they had. They'd put all their troops at the top of the hill, rather than on what was referred to as the "military crest," the line of the hill where most of the slope could be covered by gunfire. Even experienced troops had made the mistake before.

He trotted back to the head of the worm and tapped Tikka on her spiked boot.

"Still think you can get it up?"

Tikka winked. "I'm five and oh, Blackie. Wanna be six?"

"This isn't the time—"

She laughed. "I don't quit that easy. If I get you all up so you can cork those guns, you going to finally give me a taste?"

Just get it over with. "A three-course dinner."

"With dessert," she added.

"I think that's included in the price."

"Sir, how am I supposed to go red when an episode of *Noonside*

Passions is running at the other end of the fuckin' worm?" a Bear named Chieftain asked Gamecock.

They started up the hill, sidewinding on the long worm. Tikka found some kind of path, probably an old bike or hiking trail. The worm tilted.

A shot rang out.

"You all better side-ride—it's going to get nasty here," Tikka called.

"Can you keep the worm upright?" Valentine asked.

"Do ticks tip a hound dog? Grab netting."

The Bears slipped down the side of the worm facing downslope. Valentine heard bullets thwack into the worm, and Tikka shifted her riding stance, clinging on to the saddle and fleshy worm hide like a spider on a wall. Somehow she managed to work the reins and goad.

The mortars fired again, blindly, sending their shells down to explode at the base of the hill.

Valentine heard shouts from above, cries in a strange warbling language.

"Drop off now. They'll keep shooting at the worm," Valentine told Gamecock, seeing a cluster of rocks trapping fallen branches and logs.

The Bears scrambled for cover. Preville pulled out his field radio.

"Whenever you're ready, Lieutenant," Valentine said.

Gamecock took out a little torch and heated his knife. "Uh, sir, if I'm not mistaken, you're the brigade commander now. I don't think it's your place to be at the forefront of a hill assault. Let me and the Bears—"

"There's a good view from that bluff. The Moondaggers are on their way, and I need to assess the situation."

"Red up, red up," Gamecock cried.

Each of Gamecock's Bears seemed to have their own method of bringing the hurt, and with it the willed transformation into fighting madness that made the Bears the killing machines they were. One punched a rock, another stamped his feet, others cut themselves in the forearm or ear or back of the neck. A Bear, perhaps more infection-minded than most, made a tiny cut across his nose and dabbed iodine from a bottle on it.

Valentine heard fire following the worm.

"Time to fuck them up," the one with the iodine rasped, wincing.

Gamecock pressed the hot knife under his armpit, clamped down on it hard.

Preville looked around, gaping. Valentine knew what his com tech was thinking: *If this is what they do to themselves, what the hell's in store for the enemy?*

If Valentine wanted pain, all he had to do was think of his mother, on the kitchen floor, the smell of stewing tomatoes, what was left of his sister lying broken against the fireplace. . . .

Heart pounding, a cold clarity came over him. The next minutes would be either him or them. Doubts vanished. Everything was reduced to binary at its most simple level, a bit flip, a one or a zero. Life or oblivion.

Three . . . two . . . one . . .

"Smoke 'em up," Gamecock yelled.

A Bear from each four-man group pulled the pins on big, cyclindrical grenades. The senior nodded and they all threw toward where they heard orders being shouted.

Valentine smelled burning cellulose. The smoke grenades belched out their contents. There was a stiff breeze on the heights and the smoke wouldn't last long. Gamecock put two fingers into his mouth and whistled.

"Action up! Action up!"

The Bears exploded out of the cover like shrapnel from a shell burst, save that each piece homed in on the target line with lethal intent.

Valentine followed them through the smoke. Gamecock kept toward the left, where more of the hill and therefore more unknown opponents potentially lay, so Valentine went around the right, trying to keep up with the barking mad Bear with the clipped ears.

White eyes with a thick bushy beard appeared from the growth to the right—a Moondagger opening a tangle of branches with his rifle butt. Valentine swung his machine pistol around and gave one quick, firm squeeze of the trigger and the man fell sideways into the supporting growth, held up by a hammock of small branches and vines. He heard a shout from behind the man, a yapping, unfamiliar word, and fired blindly at the noise.

He followed the sound of bursting small arms fire up the hill.

The four-man groups divided into twos, covering each other as they went up the hill in open order and they vanished into the smoke.

"Target in sight. Grenades!" Gamecock's disembodied voice sounded through the smoke.

Bullets sang through the trees, tapping off down into the thicker timber, followed by the tight crash of grenades going off uphill. Valentine felt the heat of one on his left cheek as it passed.

Then he was through the smoke. A wide, bright green mortar tube sat, a bloody, bearded man fallen against the arms of the bipod, looking like a dead roach in the arms of a praying mantis. Just beyond, a severed head lay next to what had been its body.

A brief flurry of gunfire turned to cries and screams as the Bears did what they did best: close quarters fighting. Only it was closer to murder.

The Bear with the cuts on his nose was perhaps the most impressive of all. He grapevined through the position with only his .45 gripped carefully like a teacup, his body following the foresight like it was a scouting dog. Valentine saw him drop three Moondaggers spraying bullets from assault rifles held at their hips in the time it would take Valentine to clap his hands.

Valentine saw Moondaggers fall, blown left and right by shotgun blasts or gunfire. The men on the other side of the slope saw the slaughter and ran from their positions and into the thickest timber they could find while their officers fired guns in the air, trying to stem the panic.

By the time Valentine realized the top of the hill and the mortar positions were theirs, the Bears were already over the hill and chasing what was left of the Moondagger infantry and mortar crew down the gentler reverse slope. Gamecock recalled his team and sent them to the right to check out the rest of the hilltop. The Bear with the old M14 knelt against a moss-sided rock, squeezing off shots as he squinted through the scope.

A bullet came back and he sank down, reloading. He rolled to his right, fired three times, and then rolled back behind the rock. No shots came back this time.

Some bit of sanity recalled him to duty. Valentine posted Preville by the mortars and followed a path north, finding himself atop a limestone cliff with a good view of the river valley and the treetops they'd advanced under. He withdrew into cover and fired first the red flare and then the blue, but as the first went off he saw work was already started on the bridge. Rand had put the engineers to work as soon as he heard firing from the bluff top, figuring the mortar crews would have better things to do with Bears roaring up through the woods.

Valentine hurried back up to Preville and reestablished contact with headquarters. They connected him with Moytana, who reported the destruction of two armored cars. He'd delayed the center column, forcing them to come off the road and deploy, before retiring and leaving a screen of scouts who were giving enemy position reports as they fell back. The center column wouldn't reach the bridge for hours yet.

The long day would be over soon.

Valentine looked around at the dead being arranged by a couple of Bears in a neat row under the trees, their faces covered and arms and legs placed tightly together. Most of them had jet black hair and copper skin. Valentine recognized again the old game he'd seen so many other places—Santo Domingo, Jamaica, New Orleans, Chicago: elevate an ethnic minority to a position of authority, where their position and status depended on the continued rule of the Kurians above. More often than not, the more-visible middlemen took the blame for the misdeeds of those at the top.

Valentine counted heads. All the Bears were upright, including the four keeping watch to the south and west.

"Not even any wounds? Your command's not even scratched, it seems."

"Not exactly unscratched, Major," Gamecock said. "You left something behind, sir. Left ear. Lobe's gone."

Valentine reached up, grabbed air where the bottom of his ear should be.

"You could take up painting French countryside cafés," a better-read Bear laughed.

"Doberman can fix up your ears so they match," Silvertip said, pointing to the Bear with the docked ears.

"Want me to go look for it, sir?" Preville asked, perhaps desperate to get away from the combat-hyped Bears.

"You, with the iodine. Spare a little."

"Absolutely, Major," the bear said, exhibiting what was perhaps the deepest voice Valentine had ever heard in Southern Command.

"What's your name?"

"Redbone," the Bear said.

"Thanks, Redbone. Good shooting with that pistol. You don't give lessons, do you?"

"I can make time."

Valentine could turn the hill over to the Guard infantry now. With a few platoons posted on the bluff and some more companies spread out in those woods, the flanking column could bust itself to pieces in this manner, and every moment his forces on the west side of the river would grow stronger as men, vehicles, and legworms crossed, platoon by platoon.

With the brigade across and flanks well secured by river and limestone cut, the men could afford to relax and swap tales of skirmishes against Moondagger scouts. The Moondagger columns, discovering that Javelin had escaped the bridge choke point, skulked off for the sidelines like footballers who'd just given up a fumble.

The Wolves were coming in with reports that they'd turned tail.

"A mob. That's all they are," someone ventured.

"Like most bullies, they're toughest against people who can't fight back," Valentine said. "What happened to the third column?"

"Don't rightly know, sir," Moytana said. "Some of the scouts thought they heard explosions a mile or two to the east. The column turned toward them, then reversed itself, then turned back again east before it swung around south to where they were when we were first watching them. That's all they saw before it got dark."

The work of Ahn-Kha, perhaps, with ambushes or miscellaneous sounds of destruction getting the Moondaggers marching in a circle, chasing the noises of their own troop movements.

Valentine wondered what would have happened back at Utrecht if they'd united with the Green Mountain Boys. The Moondaggers had come to oversee a surrender, not wage a war. If only Jolla hadn't felt overwhelmed by the responsibility of command.

He'd leave the might-have-beens to the historians and armchair strategists. He had to check on his commanding officer.

For two days the column crept southeast as Bloom recovered from her taste of Bear blood. The doctors complained that it made her even more restive than usual.

The Moondaggers hovered in the distance, keeping in between the brigade and Lexington. Valentine wondered what sort of orders and threats were passing between various Kurians, high Church officials, and the Moondagger headquarters in Michigan. Bloom was soon up to half days in her jeep after one more Bear-blood transfusion.

Valentine, now that she was on his mental horizon, suddenly saw Tikka everywhere: giving orders to her fellow Bulletproof, cadging for strips of leather to effect repairs on tack and harness, giving advice to the cooks on the best way to quick-smoke legworm meat.

Perhaps it was just his libido, but she always seemed to be reaching, squatting, climbing, or bending over, the muscles of her backside tight in jeans and legworm-leather chaps.

She caught him coming out of the wash tent after dinner and revealed a glass flask tucked in her summer cotton shirt snuggled up next to a creamy breast.

Valentine had seen hundreds of liquor advertisements while paging through the tattered ruins of old magazines, but for all the tales of subliminal depictions of fornication in ice cubes, he'd rarely so wanted to reach for a cork in his life.

"I came here to collect on a promise," she said, taking the kerchief out of her hair and letting the caramel-colored curls tumble into a waterfall splashing against her shoulders. "Or are you going to Cin-Cin me out of my reward?"

What the hell. He should do something to celebrate his brief command of the brigade. Tikka seemed like five and a half feet of uncomplicated lust. He'd just have to make sure to use a condom for something other than keeping rain out of his gun barrel.

"Do you want to be seen walking into my tent, or will you sneak in under cover of darkness?"

"Let's go to mine. It's more secluded. I'm picketed to make sure the dumb things don't blunder into the stream."

"I'll change so I can blend in."

He buttoned his shirt and threw his uniform coat over his arm and went to his tent. While he put on his leathers, she refilled her pistol belt from the company supply.

"What in the world did you do to your rig?" she asked. "All your hooks and catches are gone."

"My maiden aunt Dolly was always complaining about the chips to her furniture. Kept snagging doilies at headquarters too."

She licked her lips. "I think I can tell when you're joking now."

"Good."

They walked through the knee-high grasses to the legworm camp, a little below the Southern Command encampment and closer to the stream. They wound through grazing legworms. On the hill opposite the stream, two riders sat on a mount back-to-back, keeping watch.

She beckoned him into her tent. Some tack odds and ends sat in a chest that opened out into shelves, and various ponchos and bandannas hung on a grate-like folding clothes tree. Her bed was a net-and-frame double with a rather battered-looking down mattress. It looked too rickety to support both of them.

"You should have taken better care of your leathers," she said, disrobing with a matter-of-factness that made Valentine remember a girl he'd once known in Little Rock. "You know, it's supposed to be the mark of a real well-suited pair of riders if they can do it without any punctures or lacerations. Kind of a good omen for their future together."

She had muscular buttocks and legs, good shoulders and a sleek, feline back. Her breasts, high and small and capped by determined, thumblike nipples, gave the tiniest of bobs as she danced out of her leathers. Their full firmness made her waist look even narrower by comparison.

"I could put some barbed wire around my nethers."

"Don't you dare," she said, coming forward and into his arms.

Her kiss was as wanting, hungry, and open as a baby bird's mouth. It had been so long since he'd had a woman press against him like this, her arms tight on his shoulder blades, he'd almost forgotten the delightful feel of breasts crushed against his chest, or a round hip just where his hand could fall as he tested the curves.

He lifted her easily and she laughed, pulling at his ears. She still had the day's sweat lingering between her breasts. It smelled like salt and sun and that powerful, caressing scent that women carried like a secret weapon for infighting. One of her heels pressed against the small of his back; the other rubbed the back of his leg. His pants seemed insufferably confining. They worked together to get him out of them.

She dropped to her knees, employed her mouth, but he hardly needed encouragement.

"Now. Hurry. God, I'm so fucking horny!" she said.

They didn't even bother disturbing the bed. The tamped-down grass was cool and smooth inside the tent's shade, and there was less chance of breaking it as she bucked and gasped under his thrusts.

After, she played with his hair. "God, that was good. I even forgot about Zak while you were doing that Morse code with your tongue. Why didn't we do this four years ago?"

"I had someone else then. Or I thought I did."

"That redhead? She could be pretty if she tried. And cut back on the attitude."

Valentine let her be wrong. He didn't want to talk about Malita and his daughter. In the rather formal, most recent letter, she'd been described as half monkey, half jaguar, climbing trees as easily as most kids walked.

Valentine felt strangely uncomfortable at the mention of Duvalier.

"We could try making up for lost time," he said, changing the subject. He reached for her.

So began a love affair carried out as discreetly as could be managed in a camp full of soldiers. Luckily Kentucky was full of glades, quiet hillsides, and swimming holes. Valentine had a tough time being spared from his duties, shorthanded as the headquarters was with their losses and Bloom still needing a long night of uninterrupted sleep. They had a magnificent yet lazy, four-hour afternoon fuck when Valentine had a midnight to four/ eight to noon watch.

Once she tried to use her mouth on him as he was supervising the empty headquarters tent—empty save for one sleepy radio operator with his back to them—and he had to send her back to the Bulletproof camp.

Good thing too, because Duvalier came in soon after. She extended her tongue at Tikka, disappearing into the dark in a disappointed flounce.

"That Reaper the Wolves thought they saw turned out to be a scarecrow," she said. "Some clever clod rigged it to a little track so the wind blew it around his cornfield."

She looked at his trousers. "You trying to win a blue or something?"

Valentine, embarrassed, finished zipping up.

"Odd that we haven't had more trouble with Reapers."

"They keep away from big bodies of men, at least if they're alert. Too many guns. Plus, I don't think the legworm ranchers like Reapers poking around in their grazing lands."

"Any problems between the Moondaggers and the ranchers?"

"I went into Berea right after they left and played camp follower. They left the townies alone. Of course, the Kentucks hid their girls and showed their guns."

"*Si vis pacem, para bellum*," Valentine said.

"No, these guys favor buckshot and thirty-oughts," Duvalier said. "Does the Atlanta Gunworks make the Sea-biscuit mace-'em? I never heard of it."

After his duty, he retired to his tent. He heard someone tap outside.

Probably Tikka, wanting to finish what she started in the headquarters tent. He rose and was surprised to see Lieutenant Tiddle standing there, looking freshly shaved and combed.

"What is it, Tiddle?"

"Can we talk, sir? Like, off the record?"

"Come in."

Tiddle rubbed his nose, looking like he was desperate to jump on his motorbike and disappear in a fountain of dust. "Major Valentine, that story you heard about the Colonel and Colonel Jolla ain't quite what happened."

"Excuse me?"

"We lied to you, sir. We sort of agreed about it. There was a struggle over a gun, sure, but it was Colonel Bloom's. When the shells started falling and Colonel Jolla was just standing there and started talking about surrendering while watching it like it was a rainstorm and not doing anything, she took command. He put his hand on his pistol and told her she was guilty of mutiny. The next thing we knew, they were fighting. Then we heard the gun.

"She was the one who put the barrel under Jolly's chin. Awful sight. We took another bullet out of Jolly's gun and put it in Bloom's."

"Why are you changing your story?"

"I—we all agreed, as we were treating Colonel Bloom, that whatever their fight was about, Colonel Jolla wasn't right in the head, ever since we lost the colonel. I remembered that story they taught in school about how the president wasn't giving any orders in 2022 and then he shot himself, and we decided that something like that was happening with Jolly."

Valentine decided Tiddle bore watching, in more ways than one.

"I'm still not sure why you're changing the story."

"Will this cause trouble for his family with line-of-duty death and all that?"

"No. Let's leave it be," Valentine said. "Conscience clear now?"

"The lie's been bothering me, sir." He sighed, and his face relaxed into the more agreeable expression Valentine had seen here and there around the brigade.

In Southern Command, if a court found that a soldier had been killed while in the commission of a crime under either military or civilian laws, their death benefits were forfeit.

"Don't worry, Tiddle. You did the right thing. Both times."

"How can it be right both times?"

"Good question. Why don't you think about it for a while?"

Valentine decided to forget everything Tiddle had told him, if possible. Whatever Bloom had or hadn't done, survival was their main concern now.

"Sir, if you don't mind me saying, there's one more thing that's worried me."

Trust established, Tiddle seemed intent on unburdening himself entirely. Valentine wondered if he was going to hear about Tiddle's loss of virginity to a cousin.

"Colonel Bloom, sir. She's been kind of distracted lately. Just like Colonel Jolla at the end. Absent, only half listening."

Valentine bit off a "Are you sure?" Stupid question. He had to act.

"I'll talk to her. Thanks for expressing your doubts, Tiddle."

"Whatever's going on, nip it in the bud now, would you, sir? I don't want to be known as the com officer who's had two commanders shoot theirselves."

"I'm not sure we should be in such a hurry to leave," Valentine said, trying to wash down a hunk of legworm jerky and sawdust at the next route-planning meeting.

"How's that, now?" Bloom asked.

"After their last try, the Moondaggers seem content to just nudge us along. They haven't made any real attempt to cut us off or even engage. Maybe they're licking their wounds from the last fight."

"Time is on their side, then."

"Not necessarily," Valentine said. "They're used to getting their way, and they're used to shoving around civilians when they don't. The legworm clans, they're not poor Kansas farm collective workers who don't know a rifle from a hoe. These boys can ride and shoot and they don't back down."

"They backed down easily enough back at the union," a Guard captain said.

"Now they're on their own land, though. I remember how startled I was, seeing Quisling uniforms walking around in Little Rock. Made me kind of mad. Felt more like a violation. I'm hoping the legworm ranchers will feel the same way," Valentine said.

"So what of it? They get jacked and take out a few Moondaggers in return. Does that help us?" Bloom asked.

"It gives the Moondaggers a new set of worries," Brother Mark said.

"The Moondaggers will respond the only way they know how. It could grow into a full-scale revolt. There could be advantages to that. Like better supply for us," Valentine said.

Moytana shook his head. "And disadvantages. There's a big garrison in Lexington and another in Frankfort. Right now they seem content to sit and not make waves."

"And the Ordnance, just over the Ohio," someone else added. "They've got a professional army. A lot of Solon's best troops came from there. If the Kurians there think Kentucky is up for grabs, they might make a move."

"We came across the Mississippi to establish a new Freehold," Valentine said, giving the table a rap. "I'd still like to do it. But I want it to be the ranchers' idea, not ours."

"Too risky, Valentine," Bloom said. "Javelin's low on everything."

"We win a battle and we might get more local support," Valentine said. "Right now they're just obeying the Moondaggers because they've seen that we aren't doing anything about them."

Bloom glowered. "Pipe down, Valentine. You're dancing toward a line marked 'insubordination.'"

"Sorry, sir," Valentine said, using the soothing tone that always worked with his old Quisling captain on the *Thunderbolt*.

The rest of the meeting passed with Valentine deep in thought.

He buttonholed Brother Mark as they left to get some dinner and look over the nighttime pickets.

"Is it possible that—that a Kurian agent is manipulating her? Sowing doubt, fear?"

Brother Mark's gaze looked even more droopy. He nibbled at a turnip. "The Kurians and their agents may play with your senses, just as the Lifeweavers do. I suppose you've . . . ahem . . . experienced . . ."

"The night I got this," Valentine said, rubbing the side of his face where his jaw hadn't healed right. "Speaking of night, it always seems like she's at her most timid then. Dawn comes up and she's almost her old self."

"Sunlight interferes with their abilities. If it is someone manipulating her, it would be like no agent I've ever heard of. That would put him—or her—on par with a Kurian."

"Then a Kurian—"

"No, they have to see, hear, smell—feel your aura, even, to be the devil whispering in your ear. Though I suppose they could work it through a proxy. Relay their mind through another, just as a Reaper becomes the Kurian when the Kurian is manipulating it."

"I haven't seen anyone touching her. She likes to pat you and slap you, locker room stuff, but that's never when she's making decisions. It's an 'at ease' thing with her to let you know you can relax."

"She's never slapped me," Brother Mark said in a tone that suggested he might enjoy the experience.

Churchmen. You never know.

"Anyway, I can't remember anyone going out of their way to make contact with her," Valentine said.

"Physical contact isn't necessary, you know."

Valentine straightened. "But you said—"

"An aura projects up to, oh, nine feet from the body. You didn't know that?"

"No."

"I saw it on a scanner once, during my education. An aura shows up on certain kinds of electrical detection equipment. It looked a little like the northern lights—ever seen them?"

"Yes, as a boy."

"It's an odd thing. A man missing his arm will still have the aura of his arm. It just looks more like a flipper. He can even move it around, to an extent, by working the muscles that used to work his arm. They could turn up the sensitivity of the equipment and show just how far an aura extends. Fascinating stuff. It's one of the reasons I don't eat cooked food. There's more aura residue clinging to uncooked vegetables."

"You don't say," Valentine said, wondering how to get the Brother back to the subject at hand. "Thank you for continuing my education."

"You weren't wrong—of course the connection is a good deal clearer when there's physical contact."

"How often would the Kurian have to make contact?"

"All I can do is guess. Different Kurians have developed different skills."

"Guesswork, then."

"Every few days. It's like a— Do you know what hypnosis is?"

"I saw a hypnotist once in Wisconsin. He was doing it for entertainment."

"It's like a hypnotic suggestion. Much of it depends on the will of the subject. With a strong-willed individual, I expect there'd have to be contact every day or two."

"Can you detect the connection?"

"Possibly. But I don't think our good commander would appreciate me hovering around her at headquarters, feeling the staff up until the hooded hours. I'd rather not have another noose put around my neck." He tugged at his collar, as if he could still feel the rope's abrasive coil.

"No sense wasting time," Valentine said. "Come to the headquarters tent for that glop that's passing for coffee. I need to talk to you about visiting the legworm clans anyway. Perhaps you can help with the snack table."

Luckily Valentine could lose himself in the detail of his position and his appetite's arousal as the food trays came in. As the nighttime activity commenced, his collection of officers gave Moondagger position reports from the Wolves and a Cat who'd single-handedly dispatched a three-man patrol, keeping one alive for interrogation. Clean bit of work, that. Valentine would talk that up with the companies as he passed through them on the march. Nervous pickets liked to hear that the other side suffered its own devils in the dark.

Bloom listened rather absently. She only spoke once.

"Send that prisoner back to the Moondaggers. Tell them if they'll leave us alone, we'll leave them alone."

A less Bloom-like order Valentine could hardly imagine. She earned her rank during Archangel by taking her company forward, hammering in the morning, hammering in the evening, hammering at suppertime (as the old song went) against Solon's forces at Arkansas Post to cut off the river.

Then there were more mundane announcements such as the discovery of leaking propane tanks in the mobile generator reserve—he'd put his old company on finding more—and the field kitchen was running short of cooking oil and barbecue sauce.

Legworm meat needed lots of barbecue sauce to make it palatable.

Valentine wondered if his opposite number in the Moondaggers was listening to his own briefing, worried over just what had happened to that three-man patrol and dealing with a shortage of hydrogen fuel cells for the command cars.

Brother Mark made himself useful. After giving his briefing regarding their allies' dwindling enthusiasm, he went about the room with a coffeepot, touching distracted officers and staff and asking for refills. Now and then he shrugged at Valentine or shook his head.

Valentine passed close and noticed that Brother Mark was sweating from the effort.

Tiddle took some catching, but Brother Mark finally managed to corner him and point out that his cuff and elbow were both frayed—Tiddle had spilled his bike with his trick riding. Valentine held his breath—he liked Tiddle.

Brother Mark sighed and shook his head.

"Perhaps it is someone not on the staff," he whispered, patting Red Dog's head as they passed. "Good God," he said, shocked.

"What?" Valentine asked, but he knew.

Brother Mark led him out of the tent. "It's the dog."

"How?"

"I don't know. Perhaps they've made some alteration to the animal, modified its brain. It seems a normal enough dog."

"It's the perfect spy," Valentine said. "It can't give anything away. Dogs won't break under duress and talk."

"You're wrong there, Valentine. I got a flash of something. A little of the Kurian's mind. I broke it off. I've had enough of *that* to last me more than a lifetime."

"How do we break the dog's hold on her?"

"A strong endorphin response. Alarm, maybe. An orgasm might be perfect."

Valentine could just picture Duvalier's reaction to that bit of line-of-duty cocksmanship. She'd herniate herself laughing.

"Regulations," Valentine said.

"You'll have to come up with something. Perhaps just explaining it to her, so she was conscious of it—"

"If there's some kind of connection between her mind and the Kurian, I'd like to use it, not break it. Play with the dog a little, see if you can get anything."

Brother Mark made himself ridiculous for a few minutes with Red Dog, wrestling and hugging it. Red Dog enjoyed himself and so did the churchman. Those passing in and out of the headquarters tent shrugged.

He returned to Valentine dusty and dirty. Valentine gave orders for Red Dog to be taken around to the sentries for the usual midnight Reaper check.

"What did you get?"

"A sensation. Cool and moist air. A glimpse or two through its eyes. The Kurian is high, over a small town on some kind of aerial tower. Fine view of these Kentucky hills. One odd thing about the town: There are train tracks running right down the center of town along the street. Shops and buildings to either side. Quite odd."

Valentine checked with the Wolves and had word back in ten minutes. There was a town to the north called La Grange that had train tracks running straight through town. Wolves on foot could be there before dawn if they pushed hard.

He had Gamecock alert his Bears.

"Can you just order an operation like this, even as chief of staff?" Brother Mark asked.

"No, I need Bloom's assent."

"I hope you get it."

"I will. I just have to get her back into the fight, somehow."

Valentine presented his plans for an attempt to bag the Kurian. He didn't know if the mind manipulating the dog was also directing the Moondaggers, but any chance to take out an aura-hungry appetite would be a blow for humanity.

Bloom listened impassively. "I don't think we should risk it."

Valentine slapped her. Hard.

"What in—"

"That's no way for a leader to talk. Especially not the Cleo Bloom who spearheaded Archangel."

"See here, Mister," she said, bristling.

Valentine's hand became a blur. The slap carried like a gunshot.

"I'm putting you under arrest for assault."

"You've lost your nerve, Bloom. Showing the whites of your eyes. And your teeth. All you need is a gingham dress and we'd have a minstrel show."

She gasped, swung for his jaw. Valentine took the blow. If anything, he was grateful for it.

"You couldn't do Morse code with a tap like that," Valentine said, tasting blood. "Try again, you alley ho."

"Mother*fucker*," she said, falling on him. They went down and it was a dirt fight of knees and elbows. He covered his face with a forearm as she rained blows down on either side of his head, right-left right-left right-left.

"Woo! Officers fightin'," someone called.

Cleo Bloom stood up, her eyes bright and alive. "Jesus Lord," she panted. "Jesus Lord."

"Feel better, Colonel?" Valentine asked.

Later, they talked about it in the dispensary as a nurse put cold towels on Valentine's bruises and dabbed his cuts with iodine.

"I figured pressure must have been building up in you somewhere," Valentine said.

"I don't remember feeling any kind of presence," she said. "I just had all these doubts all of a sudden. I thought it was because it was the first time I was in command."

"I'm sure that helped," Valentine said. "The Kurians know what they're doing. They attack when someone is most vulnerable. It's how they fight. No need to beat us if we beat ourselves."

"Boy, when it came out, it was like a firehose. I feel better than I have for weeks. I remember you were saying something about an operation?"

"We found the Kurian's temporary hideout. Dumb luck, really. It's in a unique-looking town, as seen from above. Of course there's a big radio mast, so it makes sense that he would be there."

"And we're waiting for what, exactly?"

"Your orders."

"Given. Let's get this brigade of ours back into the war."

"I'd like permission to accompany the Bears."

"No, I'll send that Duvalier. She's very good, and she knows the country. Besides, I need you here. I was looking at the map, and there's a nice notch in the ridge ahead. We could use a rest from moving, and I think with some flank security we could mess with the pursuit. The thought scared me before, but now I want to take a crack at them. They're so used to us running after brief holding actions, we might catch them strung out."

Valentine passed a busy, sleepless night. While Gamecock and Duvalier, guided by a trio of Wolves, headed for La Grange, Bloom turned the brigade and launched an exploratory attack on Moondagger reconnaissance following them up the road.

Then Javelin took a much-needed rest while waiting for the Bears to return. Scavenging parties found green apples and early squash to eat. The fall's first bounty was coming in.

The hours dragged as Valentine experienced the doubts of a man who'd rather be on the job himself than sending others into danger. He gnawed on an apple core, reducing it by tiny shavings, waiting for the parties' return. Bee sensed his mood and tried to comb out his hair and pick ticks.

They came in at dusk, one Bear short and Duvalier limping on a twisted ankle.

Gamecock, thick with smoke and dirt, gave a brief report, with Silvertip standing silently behind. Silvertip looked like he'd spent the morning wrestling mountain lions.

"Town had a Moondagger garrison, but they were living it up in the roadhouse at the edge of town," he said. "Sure enough, there was a little Kurian blister on the antenna, made out of whatever crap they use as tenting. They'd camouflaged it like an eagle nest."

Valentine had heard of some kind of specially trained bug that excreted Kurian cocoon.

"No Reapers?"

"The Cat took one jumping from a roof. She gave us the all-clear even with her bum foot. I sent the Bears right for the antenna with demo gear. There were some sentries but we disposed of them with flash-bangs and blades."

Valentine wished he could have been there. Or better yet, peering into the Kurian's eye cluster when it saw the Bears hurrying up.

"Did you blow the nest?"

"Yes, but it ran before then. Went sliding down one of the support wires or whatever you call 'em, suh," Gamecock said. "Gutsy little shit."

"You saw it?"

"No, Silvertip did. A Reaper hauled outta town like he was carrying hot coals. Silvertip managed to trip him up."

Silvertip. Big, brave Bear, that. "Very commendable," Valentine said, wondering if he sounded pompous.

"I don't train my Bears for dumb. Reaper running for the line like that? He looped a satchel charge on him. Of course, the thing animating the Reaper had us on his mind so he didn't notice. It dropped onto the Reaper's head and shoulders—looked like an umbrella collapsing on him."

"Looked back at me with all them eyes," Silvertip said.

"I don't think they're all eyes."

Silvertip shrugged. "Well, anyway, it was watching me take pot shots, carried like a baby with tentacles, when the charge blew. Reaper's head went straight up like a rocket."

"Best stick I ever saw, suh," Gamecock said.

"What happened after that?" Valentine asked.

"We knocked off three more Reapers pretty easy—sprayed fire into their shins and then took them out with explosives. The Moondaggers started tracking us on the way back, but the Wolves got a twist on them. Those boys are cruel but they sure don't know much about fighting."

*   *   *

All that remained was the decision about Red Dog. Valentine had him returned to his old company for a last meal together. He explained the situation and asked for a volunteer to shoot the poor hound.

"The whole brigade likes Red Dog, sir," Rand said. "Not the mutt's fault he's a Kurian spy."

"It's just a dog," Valentine said. "I'll kill it myself." He'd had to kill dogs before. Even gut them and stew them.

Glass stood up. "That Kurian's dead, right? Whatever connection he had is gone."

"Maybe the Miskatonic would want to study it," Rand said.

"It's too much of a risk," Valentine said. "One of you might fall asleep petting him and wake up kissing a fused grenade."

"I'll take the chance, sir," Glass said. "Like the lieutenant said, the Miskatonic should have a look at him. I'm stubborn and Ford and Chevy, well, I don't know that even a Kurian could make them much more confused unless there are bullets flying, food to be eaten, or a she-Grog around."

"What about you?"

"What, sir, 'n have me lose faith in the Cause? That train long since departed. Besides, I'd like to have a word or two with one of those Kurian sucks."

Valentine looked at Red Dog, utterly uncognizant of his peril but evidently just as happy to be with the old company as parked outside headquarters with the engineering gear.

"I guess one more ex-Quisling won't hurt. And I don't know how Glass' attitude can get much worse."

The men whistled and hooted and tossed scraps to the dog.

Twelve

The Banks of the Green River, September: The fortunes of Javelin are at their lowest ebb. Help from the legworm ranchers has all but dried up. Only the underground dares to make contact, informing Southern Command's forces where they've hidden supplies.

The trickle of foodstuffs, plus the usual resourcefulness of soldiers to find food even on the march, allows Javelin to stay together in body.

Its soul is another matter.

The Moondaggers have stepped up their harassment. They shift south and west faster than the brigade can move, herding the column north when it wants to go south.

It's too dangerous to send out patrols. Only the Wolves and Cats leave the column. Even Valentine's company keeps close, scavenging such towns and camps as they temporarily occupy. Even Vette, who grew up in Kentucky, was lost near Campbellsville.

The men are bearded, dirty, tired. Their rope may not have run out yet, but the tattered end is in view. Much of their artillery marks the line of retreat along the Cumberland Parkway, destroyed and abandoned as ammunition ran out. Wounded, sick, and injured are either hidden with the underground or carried along. The engineers, with their usual flair for improvisation, have rigged the legworms with yokes that allow them to carry wounded swinging from hammocks, a smoother ride for the injured than the ambulance trucks.

They're far from home, far from sound, and far from those dreams of becoming ranchers and whiskey barons. It's all they can do to keep moving, keep securing bridges and hill gaps, and keep the rear guard supplied in its endless leapfrogs while delaying the Moondaggers behind and at the flanks.

The Moondaggers may have begun the campaign as little more than a well-organized mob of killers, but they learned quickly under hard lessons.

Either that, or more experienced formations and commanders were sent to reinforce the division harrying Javelin. It seemed each day they grew more and more aggressive, bringing their route of march closer and closer to the brigade, sending small units to harass the flanks and rear.

The ranchers remained quiescent all around. If anything, it became harder to beg food from the brands. They either fled the brigade's approach or were found to be garrisoned by the Moondaggers. Scouts and the Cats heard a good deal of complaining about the Moondaggers helping themselves to supplies and paying with New Universal Church *Guidons* personally blessed by the Archon of Detroit. Or long harangues from missionaries asking for warriors willing to fight in the Gods' Holy Struggle.

"Holy Struggle to keep from taking him for a drag behind my worm," Duvalier reported an outrider from the Gunslinger clan grumbling. "He started talking about how my wife could be thrice blessed by faith, submission, and pregnancy."

They fought three skirmishes, and each time were forced to retreat by the Moondaggers bringing up reinforcements by truck. They dug in triple lines of entrenchments on good ground to move a little more north, until their line of march was north-northwest. The roads they needed to take came under long-range artillery fire, and the bridges and fords they wanted to use were mined or destroyed.

Then came the day when the scouts returned from the outskirts of Bowling Green with a special one-sheet newspaper speaking of a pitched battle in Pennsylvania. "Wreckers" (Kurian propagandists were growing tired of the word "terrorist"; with years of use it was losing its punch, so they were increasingly substituting "wreckers" when they discussed the Cause) out of New England had been soundly beaten. Over a thousand captured and the rest scattered in a panicked flight north. It was dreadfully specific in its maps and photographs.

"I don't suppose any of your old Church buddies are in these pictures," Valentine said to Brother Mark.

They went on emergency short rations that day. The legworm clans had stuck a wetted finger in the air and knew which way the wind was blowing. Even the Bulletproof began to suffer desertions. What was worse, sometimes they took their worms with them.

Valentine's company became a productive set of food thieves. They learned to filch from the edges of far fields, creeping in and digging up carrots and sweet potatoes and wrenching off a husk of corn here and there.

Valentine sat in the headquarters tent, eyes closed, listening to a news broadcast from Louisville. They were interviewing an author who'd just completed a new study on drug use among youth in the old United States. The main news had to do with a record harvest in the Dakotas, where farmers had overfulfilled their goals by sixteen percent. Locally all they reported was the opening of a new facility for freeze-drying legworm quarters.

He'd started listening because one of the communications techs reported hearing a blurb that train service between Nashville, Louisville, Lexington, and Knoxville had been suspended due to flooding. Militia units were being called up and deployed to save communities from the rising floodwaters.

The fall weather had been the one thing that had been kind to the brigade in their trip across Kentucky. Such an obvious lie gave Valentine hope that the legworm riders were attacking the lines.

They hadn't repeated the announcement.

Then Duvalier was tapping him on the shoulder.

"You know your plan to have the legworm ranchers fight the Moondaggers?"

"It's more of a hope than a plan," Valentine admitted.

"Well, maybe the Kurians are waiting for the same thing to happen to us. Or their generals, high Church people, whatever. A lot of them believe their own propaganda. They probably think we're stealing everything that isn't nailed down on this march. When we're not doing that, we're chopping down trees so we can stomp the baby worms."

"How did you come by this?"

"I sat in on a Church question night. Ever been to one of those?"

"I don't think so."

"They're pretty interesting. You write down questions and a priest picks them out of a box and answers them."

"That's a foolproof system," Valentine said.

"The questions smacked of being preselected. Right after a question about our column was another one asking what was being done about it. You haven't killed a bunch of Strongbows, have you?"

"No. We've been out of their territory for days. I don't think we even talked to any."

"Well, the Church is blaming it on you. Also some kidnappings in Glasgow."

"We never even saw the town. The Moondaggers had it occupied before we even got there. The kidnappings—they wouldn't be young women, by any chance?"

"Yes. They're kinda worked up about it."

Worked up. What would it take to push them beyond worked up?

He got an idea. An ugly, hurtful idea.

Are you a doer or a shirker, Valentine? What's the price of your honor? Is it worth more than the survival of your comrades?

Within an hour he was where the medical staff had unhammocked the patients and unburdened their worms.

Valentine looked at the three fresh bodies, good Southern Command men who'd traded in all their tomorrows for the Cause, hating himself. They gave up their lives for their comrades in the brigade. Would they object to their bodies being of further use?

"Doctor, I'm afraid I'll have to ask you for the use of three bodies."

"What do you have in mind, Major?"

"Nothing you want to know about, Doctor. They'll be treated respectfully, don't worry."

The Moondagger patrol never had a chance.

Reports from the legworm liaison said they were being supplied by the Green River clan.

Valentine chose the spot for the ambush well. He used legworm pasture along the most open stretch of road he could find, just east of a crossroads where other patrols might see and investigate smoke from three directions. A collapsed barn and an intact aluminum chicken coop stood opposite his position, off the road by about fifty yards.

His company, armed with the weapons meant for trade, backed up by Glass' pair with their machine guns, lay under piles of brush taken from legworm deposits, using the tiny hummocks of the snakelike legworm trails to rest their rifles.

With one squad left guarding his escape and evasion trail, he set up three parallel kill zones, anchoring their flanks with the .50s.

Once the men were in position, barrels down and hidden, he and Rand hurried around, laying brush across the groups of prone men.

The three-truck, one-car patrol was heading east, which struck him as strange. Better for him. They were coming off the rise six miles to the southeast, a good place to observe a long stretch of the Green River Valley.

They had a single antiaircraft cannon as armament mounted in the bed of a heavy-duty pickup. Just behind the cannon truck, the rest of the men rode in the beds of the armored double-axle trucks. Old mattresses and spare tires hung from aluminum skirting as improvised armor.

Valentine waited to detonate the mine until the cannon truck was over the old soda can that served as a marker. The mine, simple TNT under gravel in the potholed road, luckily went off right under one of the wheels and sprang the truck onto its side.

His men held their fire while the other vehicles turned off the road, facing the buildings at an angle. As the men dismounted to the side facing Valentine's line, he gave the order to fire.

"Antenna!" Valentine shouted.

The platoon fired on the command car. Valentine saw blood splatter the windows as the glass cracked and fell.

The .50 calibers completed the execution begun by rifle fire. The Grogs employed their guns like tripod-mounted rifles, firing single, precise shots, sniping over open sights.

Valentine went forward with his machine pistol, leading a maneuver team with Patel offering support fire. A shielded machine gun sprang up from the bed of the foremost of the trucks, almost like a jack-in-the-box as it unfolded, the gunner cocking it smoothly. Valentine fell sideways, shooting as he fell. The gunner made the mistake of swinging his weapon to shoot back, exposing himself to the riflemen.

Valentine watched invisible hands tug at the gunner's clothes and the gunner went down, shooting in the air as he fell. Through the gap under the truck Valentine saw two figures running for the old, half-collapsed barn. He took careful aim and planted bursts in one back and then the other.

The firing died down to single shots as the platoons made sure from a distance that the enemy was down. Valentine waved Rutherford and DuSable forward. They put their autoloading shotguns to their shoulders and stepped out. They took turns covering each other as they checked the cabins of the vehicles.

Valentine heard a shotgun blast, turned around.

"Thought he moved," DuSable explained.

"This one's wounded bad," Rutherford said.

Valentine nodded. He had to finish the job. They couldn't leave wounded behind who could tell stories.

Rutherford said, "Sorry, bro," and fired.

"Give up, give up," another bearded man shouted, holding his hands up as DuSable approached him.

DuSable ordered him to the ground. "Take him prisoner," Valentine said.

He had a sort of a long scarf about his neck. Valentine thought he might have been in the gun truck. He looked dazed but could walk. He wouldn't slow them up. Headquarters could figure out what to do with him.

"We're clear to this end, sir," Rutherford called, firing one more blast at a wet coughing sound.

"The easy part's over," Valentine said.

"I admire your definition of hard, sir," DuSable said, reloading his shotgun.

While scouts watched the road, the men worked in pairs, loading bodies into one truck. Then they backed it into the barn.

Valentine nodded to Patel. They both drew their knives and went to work.

Meanwhile Glass brought forward the dead bodies they had taken out of camp, now clad in legworm leather vests and soft boots such as the locals favored, and had the Grogs dig shallow graves for them near the road. They had assorted hooks and chains looped or stuffed in their pockets.

They hung some of the Moondagger bodies upside down from the rafters and cut their throats, letting the last of the blood run onto the barn floor. Then Valentine started cutting off beards.

He'd mutilated bodies before for effect in Santo Domingo. Then he'd only been risking his soul.

From what he understood of the Moondaggers, their retribution would be swift and merciless.

Valentine could picture the local reprisals easily enough. Moytana's description of their tactics had plenty of historical precedent. People herded into old church buildings and burned. Executions against town square walls worthy of Goya.

Who bore the responsibility? The agent provocateur or the troops? The Moondaggers would claim that if there had been no attack, there would be no reprisal.

Valentine took off another beard. Easier than skinning rabbits. No legs to deal with, just a long circular cut of the knife from one corner of the mouth, down the throat, and then back up to the other corner of the mouth. The bodies were still warm and he could smell their dried sweat. The cloying aroma of death wouldn't begin to rise for some hours yet.

For now they smelled like blood and diapers.

Rand was at the door of the barn, blocking the daylight coming through the gap between the truck and the post. "Sir, there's a radio in the command car that's still working."

Valentine stepped over to another body. "Put Previle on it. Have him listen to chatter and see if they know about the ambush."

Rand kept his eyes well above Valentine's waistline and the flashing knife.

"Will do, sir." Mercifully, he left without saying anything more.

Valentine's sense of honor wasn't taken word for word from the Southern Command *Officer's Epitome*. It was instead like a jigsaw collage from three or four different puzzles, all half-formed but recognizable pictures. Some came from his parents, others from Father Max, more from his training, a few from his experiences in the Kurian Zone.

Of course he'd done despicable things in the past. He'd bled men who had no more of a chance of fighting back than bound pigs, Twisted Cross lying in their tanks in a basement in Omaha. He'd tortured. He'd acted as judge, jury, and executioner over Mary Carlson's killers. He'd helped the overlord Kurian in Seattle wipe out Adler and his staff.

Each time one bit of his conscience or another had plucked at him, he'd burned with regret later thinking back on what he'd done, but necessity compelled and partially excused him.

But this time all of the jigsaw pieces agreed. This setup of the Green River clan stripped him of whatever scarecrow of his honor had remained.

He'd decided that the brigade's survival required a sacrifice. Of his honor. More important, of some members of the Green River clan. Wide-eyed children would be fed into war's furnace as a result of a ploy that couldn't even promise victory.

Or was it really for the brigade? *Do you need to be proven right this badly, David Stuart Valentine? Tip over the first domino in what you hope will be a series of massacres followed by ambush followed by another massacre, until these beautiful green hills run with blood?*

He'd have to shave with his eyes shut from now on.

"Maybe they were right about that shit detail stuff," a woman outside the barn said. Valentine made an effort not to place the voice to a face.

"I think I've gone crazy, Patel."

His sergeant major tossed a length of strong nylon binding cord over a still-sound rafter and hoisted a corpse by its ankles. Rigor was just beginning to set in.

"You remember Lugger, from LeHavre's old company?"

"Yes."

Patel fixed the other end of the line to the bare-beam wall. "She was on the Kansas operation. She saw what the Moondaggers did there—entire towns herded out into athletic fields and machine-gunned. She was on a scout and came into one of those ghost towns after. Saw Kurian cameras viding the bodies as guys posing as Southern Command POWs confessed to the killings. Sometimes they took out towns that weren't even in the fight—just did it to make a point."

"And?"

"These guys earned their killing. This," he said, looping a running hitch around another set of ankles, "is just interest on their deposit."

"What about the Green River clan?"

"David, worrying now will not alter the future. We must wait and see what happens."

Red Dog took the opportunity to relieve himself on a Moondagger tire.

Patel added, "The Moondaggers might wonder about a couple of large-caliber holes in their trucks and where a gang of legworm ranchers got a wireless detonator. Maybe we'll get lucky and they will see through this charade. They might stop dancing around, herding us, and try to settle things in one fight. I would very much like to see these bastards attack into overlapping fields of fire and proper artillery spotting."

"I don't think we'd win that," Valentine said.

"Perhaps not. But it would make a lot of people in Kansas feel better, knowing how many we took with us."

Valentine liked the picture Patel was painting. He wiped his knife on a Moondagger uniform and sawed off another beard.

"I wonder if they have the heart for it," Patel continued, hoisting the next body. "Despite all their shrieks and prayers and bluster. Is it all an act? They are at their most bloodthirsty when striking the defenseless. And do not forget, the legworm clans around here know how to fight and will not be as easily herded as populations brought up at the Kurian teat—"

"Major," a corporal called, not even poking his head inside the barn. "Preville's got some com traffic he wants you to listen to."

"Patel, can you finish up here?" *That's it, make it sound like a bit of carpentry.*

"Yes, sir."

Valentine left the half-collapsed abattoir gladly. The revolutionary's morality clung to his back, a heavier burden than any he'd ever carried while training with the Wolves.

The command car smelled like stale cigar smoke and blood. It had a side that opened up, rather like the hot-dog trucks Valentine had seen in Chicago, turning the paneling of the vehicle into a table and a sheltering overhang where the radio operator could sit out of the rain.

The radio had a bullet hole in it but somehow still functioned.

"Are they on their way here?" Valentine asked.

"Not sure, sir." He plugged in an extra headset and handed it to Valentine.

"I don't know some of the reports; they're in another language. All I speak is bad English and worse Spanish. But they're also communicating in English. I think that's their headquarters, here—"

"Group Q," a crackly voice said. "What is the status of the reprisal against the Mammoth?"

"Gods be praised, we are hitting them, brother," a clearer voice reported back. "There is much shooting. Q-4 is in their camp now. Sniper fire has delayed them dynamiting the remaining livestock."

Valentine smiled. Legworms took a lot of killing. He wondered if the Moondaggers knew just how long-lived a Kentucky feud could be.

"Is that you, Rafe?"

"No, brother, he has been wounded. Even the boys here can hit a target at two hundred meters. They vanish into the woods and hills and the trackers do not return."

"Where's that signal coming from?" Valentine asked, not familiar with this style of radio. "Is this Group Q in the Green River lands?"

"No, sir. Due north, a little northeast toward Frankfort. I'd say it's coming from the other side of our column. This is the channel the radio was on," Preville said, punching a button.

"Patrol L-6. L-6, you are overdue at Zulu," a clearer voice said. "Report, please. Patrol L-6, report, please. We are listening on alternative frequency Rook."

Valentine looked at the dashboard of the command car. A card with L-6 written on it stood in a holder.

"Guess they didn't get off a report after all," Valentine said.

They listened for a few more minutes. They heard complaints about blown-up bridges and roads filled with cut-down trees. A mobile fueling station had been blown up.

Kentucky, it seemed, had finally had enough of the Moondaggers.

"I want to talk to the prisoner," Valentine said.

The prisoner had a scuffed look about him. His eyes widened as he saw Valentine approach. Valentine looked down. His uniform was something of a mess.

Valentine cleaned his blade off on the man's shoulder.

"I'm not going to hurt you," Valentine said. "All I want is a news report."

"News report?" the Moondagger said.

"Yes. You know, like on the television. You've watched television."

"Allchannel," the Moondagger said.

Valentine smiled, remembering the logo from Xanadu. "Yes, all-channel. It's the Curfew News. Give me the highlights from Kentucky."

Realization of what Valentine wanted broke over his face like a dawn. He raised his chin.

"The worm herders. They fight with us. Our Supreme, he says to give a lesson, but from that lesson we must give five more lessons, and then fifty. So now we must call in many more re-erforcings. Much fighting everywhere—here one day, there another. I am diligent, I am peaceable, I follow orders only."

Valentine tried to get more out of him: places, clans, the nature of these "re-erforcings," but he was just a youth taught little more than to follow orders, line up to eat, obey his faith, and of course shoot.

"Let's get him back to headquarters. Give him a little food and water. He looks like he could use it."

"I pass my test," the prisoner said.

"Come again?" Valentine asked.

"The Gods, always they test us. Both with blessings and misfortunes. Either can lead you from the righteous path."

"On that, we're agreed," Valentine said.

"I was afraid that you would kill me and I would not be taken to higher glory by the angels of mercy. I still have a chance to make something of my death."

Valentine felt like slapping some sense into the hopeful, young brown eyes. *A little understanding, please, David*, he heard Father Max's voice say, sounding just as he had when Valentine complained as a sixteen-year-old about his first and second year students' haphazard efforts with their literacy homework. What would he have become, had he been raised on Church propaganda as though it were mother's milk?

He left the prisoner and his disquieting thoughts, and plunged into planning a route back to the brigade.

With the column under way again, Valentine sought out Brother Mark.

"Is confession a specialty of yours?" he asked.

Brother Mark took a deep breath. "It's not a part of my official dogma, no. But I believe in unburdening oneself."

Valentine sat. "There's a demon in me. It keeps looking for chances to get out. This damn war keeps arranging itself so I don't have much choice but to free it. I just came back from a little ambush in Green River clan territory. I did . . . appalling things."

"You want to talk sins, my son? You will have to live lifetimes to catch up to my tally."

"Killing wounded?"

"Oh, much worse. I believe I told you some of my early schooling and work at the hospital? Of course. After my advanced schooling they posted me to Boston. I did well there. Married, had three kids. All were brought up by their nannies with expectations of entering the Church in my footsteps. Poor little dears. There was a fourth, but my Archon suggested I offer her up. Parenting effectiveness coefficients for age distribution and all that. Middle children sometimes grow up wild in large families."

"I'm sorry. So you left after that?" Valentine asked.

"Oh, no. No, I gave her up gladly and took Caring out to dinner on the wharf to celebrate afterward. My bishop sent us a bottle of French champagne. Delicious stuff. I became a senior regional guide for the Northeast. The Church keeps us very busy there. There are a lot of qualified people employed in New York or Philadelphia, Montreal and Boston, and down to Washington. High tech, communications, research, education, public affairs—the cradle of the best and the brightest. They require a lot of coddling and emotional and intellectual substantiation. You can't just say 'That's the way it must be; Kur has decided' to those people. You have to argue the facts. Or get some new facts.

"So I became an elector. Myself and the council of bishops helped set regional, and sometimes interregional, Church policy. How old could an infant be before it could no longer be offered up for recycling? What was the youngest a girl could be and have a reasonable expectation of surviving childbirth? We listened to scientists and doctors, debated whether a practicing homosexual was a threat to the community even if he or she produced offspring. High Church Policy, it was called, to distinguish ourselves from the lower Church orders who spent their days giving dental hygiene lectures and searching Youth Vanguard backpacks for condoms. My glory days.

"They taught me a few mental tricks. Most of it involved planting suggestions in children to prove reincarnation, giving them knowledge they couldn't possibly have obtained otherwise. In an emergency I was taught how to induce hysterical amnesia. That's why amnesia is such a popular plot device on *Noonside Passions*, by the way. We've found it useful for rearranging the backgrounds of people who've engaged in activities that are better off forgotten.

"Better off forgotten," he repeated, taking another drink. "Then I lost my wife."

"I'm sorry."

"I was too. Caring was a wonderful woman. Never a stray thought or an idle moment. Her one fault was vanity. After the third child she put on weight that was very hard to get off. She wanted a leadership position in the local Youth Vanguard so she could travel on her own, and you had to look fit and trim and poster-perfect. She didn't want more pregnancies and of course you wouldn't catch me using black-market condoms, so she went to some butcher and got herself fixed.

"Of course matters went wrong and she had to be checked into a real hospital. Age and the source of her injuries . . . well, the rubric put her down for immediate drop. The hospital priest had more doubts about her case than I did. I signed her end cycle warrant myself. If there was any part of me that knew it was wrong, it stayed silent. I am almost jealous of you. You have a conscience which you can trust to give you pangs. Doubts. Recriminations. I've no such angel on my shoulder."

"Did you regret it later, then?"

"I'm not even sure I do now. She was so conventional, I'm sure she was happy to be useful in death. No, I didn't come to regret it. Not even after Constance, my middle daughter, killed herself rather than marry that officer. It was the strangest thing. I was at a rail station. A brass ring's mother had been put on a train, and he had enough weight to argue it with the archon, and he sent me, because as an elector and a regional guide I had enough weight to get someone taken off a train and the nearest porter who didn't genuflect promptly enough put on."

He took another drink.

"The next car had a group of people being put on. They had to know. There was one girl in a wheelchair. She must have been sixteen or seventeen. When you get to be my age, youth and strength take on their own sort of beauty, Valentine. She had so much of it she almost shone. I wonder what put her in that wheelchair. The lie that day was that they were going to work on factory fishing ships, but I think most of them knew what the railcars meant. This girl was laughing and joking with the others.

"Just an ordinary girl, mind you. Beautiful in her way. I looked at her tight chin and bright eyes, saw her laugh with those white teeth as she spun her chair to the person behind—she had a green sweater on—and I thought, what a waste. *What a waste.* Suddenly all the justifications, all the proverbs from the *Guidon*, it's like they turned to ash, dried up and illegible, at least to my mind.

"If only I'd learned her name. I want to write an article about her. Something. I want her to exist somewhere other than my memory. But if I give her a name—well, that just seems wrong. Any suggestions for what to call her?"

"Gabrielle Cho."

"That has a certain ring to it. Certainly, my boy. Someone special to you?"

"She was."

"Very well. She'll become a part of our documentation. We'll try to tell the truth as best as we can for a change."

"So a girl in a wheelchair you didn't know made you give up . . ."

"Twenty-eight years in the Church. What's counted as a good lifetime now."

"How did you make it out?"

"From that point on it wasn't hard to plan my escape. I had travel cards, staff, and best of all, I was in no hurry. I could choose my moment." He straightened his back, jamming a hand hard against his lower spine. Valentine didn't need his Wolf-ears to hear the creaks and cracks.

"How do you perform, what do you call them, powers?" Valentine asked. "Like at the Mississippi crossing, or when you connected with the Kurian through Red Dog?"

"It's not the easiest thing to explain. You've got to remember, everything you see, smell, touch, it all gets passed into your brain. You can't see certain wave-lengths, hear certain sounds, because your brain has no coding information. Much of it is simply planting new coding information into the target's brain. Of course the Kurians—and the Lifeweavers—can do the same thing. Every day, when they have to appear to us. It comes so natural to them they don't have to think about it any more than we do breathing."

Valentine nodded.

"As for me, it gives me a terrific headache. I hope your Cabbage fellow has some aspirin to spare."

Valentine watched Brother Mark totter off, wondering that the aging body didn't give in to despair.

Thirteen

The banks of the Ohio, October, the fifty-fifth year of the Kurian Order:
The long retreat ended somewhere southeast of Evansville.

The events of the first week of October 2077 are still a matter of dispute among historians. Clever shift or desperate flight? The Moondaggers juggled their forces with the energy and ferocity for which they were famous, cutting off each sidle by the spent Javelin brigade, shifting troops down the Ohio or up the Tennessee until the retreat ground to a halt near a small heartland city that seemed to grow more by virtue of nothing else within an easy distance than any particular advantage of situation or resource.

The Moondaggers accomplished all this even with their supply lines snipped and chewed, responding with harshness that to this day leads to a fall blood-moon being called a "Dagger's moon" all across Kentucky.

In a last gambit, the column turned almost due north, hoping the Moondaggers would not expect a movement toward Illinois. But the ploy failed and the Moondaggers found the brigade trapped on the south bank of the Ohio. Both sides dug in and prepared for the inevitable.

The camp is not well-ordered. Sandwiched in a fold of ground hiding them from both eyes in Evansville and the Kentucky hills, the only advantage to the position is that both flanks are more or less guarded by the river, and the rear is a long stretch of muddy ground pointed like an extended tongue toward Evansville between the loops of the Ohio.

A pair of the city's dairy farms are now under occupation. One serves as headquarters and the other as a field hospital. The previous night the brigade was lucky enough to catch a barge heading upriver. A *quick canoe raid by the Wolves later, the barge's engine was in their possession, along with the cargo. The raiders were hoping for corn and meat; instead they found a load of sorghum, sugar, and coffee.*

So the morning camp now smells of fresh coffee, well-sweetened and creamy, thanks to the dairy cows. The chance to get the brigade across in the dark and confusion of their arrival evaporated as Evansville's tiny brownwater navy took up positions and shot up the tug. So the men went through the tiresome task of building breastworks and digging ditches. Each man wondering if the long chase is done, if this is the last entrenchment.

Not enough are in any condition to care.

The men joked that they weren't in the last ditch, simply because the last ditch was full of muddy Ohio river water and collapsed every time they tried to deepen it.

This bit of river had one advantage, however. The Kurians who ran Evansville evidently feared attack from their neighbors up the Ohio or across the river in Kentucky, for the river loops in front of the city and the waterfront were a network of mines, obstacles, booms, and floating guard platforms that constantly shifted place. Only Evansville pilots knew the route that would take watercraft safely through the maze.

According to Valentine's Kentucky scouts, this was the one stretch of river where they wouldn't encounter artillery boats and patrol craft. The Kurians of Evansville clung tenaciously to their ownership of these river bends, squeezing every advantage they could from their control of the loops by exacting small tolls for passage up to the Ordnance or down to the Mississippi.

He thought it might just be possible to slip across the river and disappear into the woods and hills and swamps of poorly controlled southern Illinois, where at least he and the Moondaggers would be met by equally hostile Grogs in the form of the Doublebloods. But Evansville's flotilla of tiny gunboats and the news that more craft of the river patrol waited on the far bank downriver stifled that hope.

Touring the defensive positions with Colonel Bloom, exhausted and bloodless in the passenger seat of her command car and able to do little more than nod, he found himself giving in to despair. Their situation grew worse, practically by the hour.

The Moondaggers had reinforced their left, ready to defend his most likely breakout alley, and the Wolves reported sounds of troops being gathered for a knockout blow from the right.

A boxer's stance, poking him from the left as the right readied to lash out.

* * *

Valentine was woken from a sleep that wasn't amounting to much and requested to report to the command tent.

He entered, still buttoning his uniform coat thrown over his legworm leathers.

Several Guard officers had already gathered, and more were coming. Tikka and another grizzled legworm rider were taking turns slicing hunks of cheese with a knife and alternating bites of the cheese and hard biscuit.

All eyes were on a boy of thirteen or fourteen, stripped down to his underwear, who stood drinking a steaming beverage and shivering, with blankets wrapped around his bony shoulders and feet.

"Thought you'd like to hear this kid's story," Rand said. "We pulled him out of the river when we were setting fish traps."

"Pulled nothing," the boy said. "I swam the whole way."

"Story time," someone guffawed.

"When are you boys comin'?" the wet and muddy boy asked. He'd slicked his body with Vaseline or something similar to ease the swim.

"Coming?" Bloom asked.

"You're with the liberation, right? Underground says that all of Kentucky's rising. We're listening on the AM radio. Some of us made crystal sets. They took the transmitter at Bowling Green and are talking about all those Moondagger throats that got cut at their supply depot south of Frankfort."

"How do we know you're telling the truth?" Duvalier said.

The boy looked shocked, as if his long swim across the river should be proof enough.

"There's street fighting in Evansville. Some of the OPs came over to our side. Hit the downtown armory. We burned a representative when it ran into the mayor's city house. They're looking for its bones now."

"You say Kentucky is rising?"

"Of course. We thought you were part of that."

Valentine felt hope, real hope, for the first time since the catastrophe at Utrecht.

"Are we part of it?" Valentine asked Bloom.

"If we're not, we sure as hell will be by dawn," Bloom said.

"What else can you tell us?" Valentine asked the boy.

His eyes were so bright and white in the gloom of the headquarters tent, Valentine was almost hypnotized as the boy looked around. "Except for the river guard, there's not much in the way of troops in town, just some riot police holding the Kur Pinnacle. They called up most everyone they could trust from the area into the militia and sent them across the river. Hospitals in Frankfort and Lexington and Louisville are bursting with wounded. The Ordnance is mobilizing; they're skeered legworms'll be crossing the Ohio and into their state. My chief says to tell you that he's got boats and a couple of old barges. We can rig lines from the bridge and get you across if your guns can clear the river."

He was an intelligent youth. Valentine could see why they sent him. "What's your name, kid?"

"Jones, H. T. Youth Vanguard, but I'm only in it for the sports trips. Quit now, I hope. Vanguard service is just a rotten apple, shiny on the outside."

Bloom studied the brigade's defensive positions on her map. A few of the companies had been bled down to little more than platoons. A careful assessment of the mortar readiness status sheet would bring either tears or laughter. "Valentine, can we get one more fight out of the brigade, do you think?"

"I'll ask them," Valentine said.

Duvalier shook her head. "It's another gaslighting. This greasy little squirt's eyeing up a brass ring."

"Hey," the boy said, but Valentine held up his hand.

Bloom thought it over.

"Valentine, take your old company and go across the river and offer assistance. If we can catch a break in the city, safely tuck away our wounded. We can make that dash into Illinois and get to the mighty Miss."

"Define assistance, sir." Valentine hated to sound like he was crabbing out from under orders. "If it's to be combat to clear the city, I'd like a Bear team at least. If they're holed up in the manner this boy describes, I'll need demolition gear too."

"Just get over there and make an assessment. Use your judgment. We've got those two big guns we captured. Might as well use them for something other than blind fire on crossroads behind us."

They came across in the dead of night in an unlit barge, downriver, and marched through a muddy, overgrown tangle of long-dead industry on the riverbank to the west side of town.

Evansville itself burned and rattled with the occasional pop of gunfire.

Bodies hung from the streetlamps. One torn-frocked churchman still clutched his *Guidon* in the grip of rigor mortis as he twirled in the fall breeze.

He made contact with the local resistance, a trio of a butcher, a teacher, and the man who ran the main telephone office. All introduced themselves first as belonging to the Evansville Resistance Lodge.

What was left of the Kurian Order, with their few troops pulled out to fill gaps in the Moondagger lines and their populace burning and score settling, had retreated to the bowl-like bulk of the civic center.

The resistance had power, water—Valentine even passed a hospital with big, spray-painted triage signs for illiterates bringing in wounded. Barrows full of farm produce crept along the sidewalks, distributing food to small patrols and sentry teams. Charcoal-fueled pickups brought in gear—scavenged or improvised weapons. There were workshops fixing up firefighting equipment with bullet shields so that an assault might advance under cover of water sprayed into windows.

Parts of the city might be burning, but Evansville appeared to be functioning with a good deal more organization and energy than he'd expected. He met men who worked in machine shops and fertilizer plants.

Fertilizer plants could be converted to the manufacture of high explosives. How long would it take some of Evansville's workshops to convert to the production of mortar shells?

"We cut off their water and juice," the telephone office manager named Jones said. "Of course, I think they got a reserve. Some kind of emergency plan is in effect. A cop prisoner told us they had three days of water. That's how long they're supposed to be able to hold out in an emergency until help arrives from Indianapolis or Louisville."

"Who's left in there?" Valentine asked as Rand set up the fire control observation station and tested radio communications.

"Middle-management types who were in the militia," Jones said. "Local law enforcement. The Youth Vanguard Paramilitary Auxiliary. Go ahead, blow them out of there. Won't nobody miss them."

He got the nod from Rand.

Valentine had shells from the guns march up Main Street toward the civic center. The last one impacted just inside the barricade. He'd made his point.

Valentine examined the civic center and the pathetic assortment of cars piled up on the sidewalks around it, along with dropped bundles and half-unpacked trunks. Entire families had retreated to the security of the big building. In panic or by design, the Evansville Quislings had assembled a barricade out of the civilian and order-enforcement vehicles, stringing barbed wire through broken windows and between fenders.

Dead bodies hung here and there on the wire. Black birds shamelessly feasted on the detritus of desperate valor.

He couldn't blow the remaining Quislings out without killing their kids with them.

He couldn't drop 155mm shells on a bunch of kids and fill the approaches to the civic center with a mixture of dead civilians and his company.

That left talking.

One of the mob behind him sneezed and wiped his nose with a onionskin page from a New Universal Church *Guidon.*

Valentine heard a metallic *clang!* A string of men emerged antlike from a utility hole mid-street and made a dash for the civic center. Gunfire swept the street. Poor shooting—they only got one. The others made it to the safety of the barbed wire and vehicle necklace around the building.

He lay, groaning.

"Cease fire! Cease fire!" Valentine shouted, hoping that energy would take the place of training and military discipline. The gunfire died down.

"Go on and get him," Valentine shouted at the civic center. "Nobody's shooting. Just let us get to our people too."

"Really?" a voice from the dark maw of the main doors called.

"Absolutely, positively really," Valentine shouted back, feeling a little giddy at the absurdity of the question.

They dragged their man out of the street and the Evansville mob got their own. Some resistance men, pinned down beneath a school bus, took the opportunity to return to their own lines.

"Rand, I'm trusting you to keep things from getting out of hand. If someone takes a potshot at me, I don't want a sniper duel. We'll be back to trading machinegun fire in no time."

He unsheathed his sword and gave the blade to Rand. "If they drop me, give this to Smoke."

"Let me go, sir," Patel said.

"You're too slow a target. And Rand, it would be a tragedy if someone put a bullet through your double helping of brains. Colonel Bloom gave her orders to me."

Valentine walked out into the center of the street under a white flag tied to his sword scabbard.

"Could I speak to whoever's in charge in there? I represent the United Free Republics, Kentucky Military Assistance Expedition."

Valentine had been wondering what to call the forces across the river; the improvised name sprang from his lips without involving his brain, evidently.

They answered with a shot. The bullet whizzed by close enough for Valentine to hear it with his right ear and not his left. He was either lucky or the sniper was a bad shot. He forced himself to remain erect.

"Who shot?" a voice yelled from the darkness. "Tell that dumbshit to cut it out. He's got a white flag."

"Killing me won't give you another day of water and power in there," Valentine shouted, advancing toward the barricade. "It'll just start the fighting again. Don't see that's gotten you much so far, and there's artillery being set up across the river. How many shells is it going to take to collapse that big roof?"

Valentine wondered if there'd be an instant's realization of his folly if the marksman decided to put the next one between his eyes. Would that be better than having part of his face torn off, or a bullet through the neck?

The street hit him in the back hard and Valentine felt an ache in his chest. He never heard the shot.

Valentine felt busted ribs, burned a finger in the hot bullet embedded in the woven Reaper cloth on his vest.

It felt like someone had performed exploratory surgery with a jackhammer on his chest. Valentine felt content to lie in the street for a moment, holding up the white flag like a dead man with a lily. He let his Wolf hearing play along the other side of the barricade.

"Quit firing. I'll shoot the next man who fires."

"That's treason talk, Vole," another answered. "Kill-or-die order, remember?"

"The man who gave that order quit on us two days ago, you've noticed."

Valentine rolled to his feet.

"I'm trying to save lives, here," he called. He tasted blood.

The next shot went between his legs, but he made it to the cover of the bus barricading the main entrance. Barbed wire hung off it like bunting.

"I'm right here if anyone wants to chat." It hurt like fire to shout. "Does that kill-or-die order apply to your kids? Maybe we can get them out of there, at least."

A bullet punched through the far side of the bus. Valentine slid to put the engine block between himself and the sniper.

The bus window above him broke and fell in shards. Luckily it was safety stuff. Valentine heard more shooting, a deeper blast of a shotgun.

"We got the gunman, Terry," Valentine heard.

Valentine looked through the rear doors of the bus. Someone had cut a hole in the other side, offering egress through the barricade. He lurched in, marked a claymore mine sitting under the driver's seat, and decided that maybe entering the bus wasn't such a good idea after all.

He sat on the bus's entry step.

"I'm still ready to talk."

"We're sending a party out to talk under a white flag."

Valentine looked at the advertisements running along the roof edge of the bus. Church fertility treatments, infant formula, exhortations to join the Youth Vanguard, warnings against black market deals ("Profit to the enemy, Poverty for your friends"), and invites for the sick and halt to enjoy a refreshing sojurn to the Carolinas and the "best medical care east of the Mississippi." A photo of a smiling silver-haired couple in beach wear lounging in chaises under an umbrella, he with a cast on his leg, her with a cannula and IV hanging from a mount shaped like a flamingo, had a buxom nurse serving what looked like tropical drinks.

Visitors to Evansville were invited to see the Eternal Flame at Affirmation Park and add their names to the Wall of Hope for a small NUC donation.

The Kurian Order in microcosm.

Valentine heard movement from the other side of the bus. A trio of men, two in law-enforcement blue and one with a clean coat thrown over dirty collar and tie, entered one at a time. A cop went forward, yanked a wire from the mine, removed the detonator with a pocket screwdriver, and tucked the inert explosive under his arm. He had a huge nose that made his eyes look small and swinish in comparison. Valentine noticed numerous breaks in the greasy proboscis, a beak of scar tissue and whiskey veins.

"What do you have in mind, Rebel Rick?" the other cop said.

"Name's Valentine, major, Southern Command," Valentine said, learning to breathe with half his chest. He'd heal from this. He always healed, but always came back only to 90 percent. He wondered how many 10 percents he'd lost over the years.

"Cloth from a robe. That's why he's still alive," the man with the tie muttered to the other cop.

"I'm Vole, senior captain, Evansville Security and Enforcement," Big Nose said. "Emergency Militia Leader Albano, Temporary Mayor Bell."

"I was clerk of Resource Allocation," Bell said. "I never carried a gun or signed a retirement warrant my whole life."

"No separate deals!" Vole barked. "What's your offer?"

"No more fighting between you guys and the resistance," Valentine said. "That's my deal. Come out without your guns. I'll put any dependents under supervision of Southern Command personnel. They'll come to no harm."

"What about us?" Vole asked.

"That's up to you and the Indiana boys."

Albano purpled but instead of turning on Valentine, he elbowed Vole. "I say we hang him, just like they did with Sewbish. No more flags of truce—just delays the inevitable."

Vole ignored him. "Understand, Valenwhatever, we've got nothing to lose and orders to kill any rebel we can get our hands on."

"A hard rain's going to fall here, just a couple more days," Albano added. "A hard rain."

"I'm sick of that weather report, Albano," Bell said. "Where's that relief column out of Indy? Tommorow, tomorrow, always tomorrow."

"Shut up, you two," Vole said.

Bell ignored him. "Lindgren said the Moondaggers asked for it to cross the river into Kentucky to secure their lines for the retreat out of Kentucky. We're blood-piped. Let's refugee north to Indy. Even if a new guide comes, he'll have his own people. Better to start at the bottom rung somewhere else than get caught up in a reorg here."

"You willing to let us just walk out of here?" Vole asked Valentine.

"I'm sure that could be arranged," Valentine said. "If you turn over your weapons and gear intact. I'll try to make the local resistance see the advantage of getting their hands on your guns. But are you sure of the reception you'll get in Indianapolis or wherever you end up? You might be surplus to requirements. Someone's got to take a fall for a debacle in a city the size of Evansville. Might just be you all."

He let that sink in.

"Seems to me you men have two alternatives. Stay here and fight it out, waiting for help that's not coming, or surrender yourselves to your fellow Hoosiers."

"Six of one . . . ," Albano said.

Valentine coughed up a little more blood. "Fight or die, they told you. Take 'em up on it. Fight them for a change."

They blinked at him like sunstruck owls.

"Rengade and get picked off on some Reaper's manhunt?" Vole said. "Or get a stake pounded up my ass by a vengeance team? Painful way to go."

"I'm wearing what's left of one of those Reapers you're so scared of," Valentine said. He might be called a liar. Valentine looked at it as shaving the truth. "Join the fight against the Kurians. I lead a bunch of fighting men that's nothing but former Order. I can always use more men. You might get killed, but if you fall, you'll fall on the right side and you won't get recycled into pig feed. Once you've proven in combat, you're a new man, so to speak. We'll give you a new identity if you like."

Valentine was exceeding his orders and knew it. But if it would spare a mutual slaughter—

Valentine noticed that both sides had advanced on the bus, scraps of white tied to tips of rifles or held aloft at the end of bits of pipe fashioned into spiked clubs, trying to hear what was transpiring inside.

The resistance was more numerous, the Kurian Order forces better armed, facing each other across abandoned vehicles and curlicue tangles of razor wire. . . .

The Quislings looked a rough lot. Of course there would be the bullies, the cowards, and the lickspittles—the Kurian Order attracted such—but he had a tough, experienced bunch of officers now. They'd keep them in line.

The battered, big-nosed leader looked at Valentine with suspicious eyes.

"Trust comes hard, I know. I spent time under the Kurians myself. Don't they always garland their deals with a bunch of roses? What did they tell you before you joined Enforcement? Quick path to a cushy office and a luxury card? Any of that come true? I'm telling you you'll have it hard, but you'll be able to look yourselves in the mirror. No more bundling neighbors off into collection vans."

Valentine had no more words in him. He caught his breath, waited. The three exchanged looks.

"I want all this written up on paper with some signatures," Vole said. "And I want us to keep all our light weapons and sidearms. It's got to say that too. Every man gets a choice: join you, surrender, or walk out."

"Save us the effort of finding guns for you," Valentine said.

Valentine left a platoon of his company under Ediyak and Patel to organize the surrendered Quislings and returned across the river in a small boat, heartened. A barge would follow, laden with food, mostly preserved legworm meat rations marked "WHAM!—hi protein" in cheery yellow lettering. The barge would bring the wounded back, where the Evansville hospital could give them a bed and rest at last.

"That Last Chance feller paid us another call while you were across the river," Tiddle told him outside the headquarters tent as Valentine scraped riverbank mud from his boots. "Said he was giving us one more chance to give up before turning us into charcoal briquettes."

He called a staff conference and gave the good news to Bloom, trying to stay awake and alert. When it was done, he felt as tired as Bloom looked. She tilted her head back and closed her eyes. "We can get home."

He took a breath. Decisions like these were always easy, when, as Churchill said, honor and events both pointed in the same direction. "Hell with that. We've got a secure base in this country and they don't. Let's go on the offensive."

"With the brigade worn to pieces?" Bloom asked, looking as though Valentine had reopened her incisions.

"Now's our best shot, Colonel. If we can buy some peace and quiet to get things organized to support us in Evansville, we can cut river traffic on the Ohio and give some real help to the uprising in Kentucky."

"What happened to going home?" a Guard captain asked.

"Every time we've had a chance to run, we've run, and where's it got us? Javelin ends with a whimper as the men pile onto barges and motorboats under shell fire. If Javelin's going to die, I want it to die hard, trying to do what it was designed for: to establish a new Freehold. If we can take the Moondagger main body with us, Kentucky has a chance. We've got the technical people, even if they've lost a lot of their gear on the retreat. We've got the Wolves and Bears, even Smoke and a Cat or two."

"I wouldn't want to be up against this brigade," Gamecock said.

"Fingers around the enemy's throat and teeth locked on hide," Bloom said. "God grant me the strength to get out of this chair one more time. Valentine, will you help me draw up a plan for your clutch hit?"

"In this situation it'll be a simple one, sir," Valentine said. It was hard to say which emotion dominated, relief that they were turning at bay like a wounded lion, or anxiety over this last throw of the dice.

"If you do this, what's left of the Kentucky Alliance will be with you," Brother Mark said. "Believe it or not, we've still got riders from all the five tribes. Most are either Bulletproof or Gunslingers. Tikka's worked out some kind of command structure. Bitter-enders all. They want their ton of flesh from the Moondaggers."

I shot a javelin into the air, it fell to earth, I knew not where. . . .

Valentine kept the doggerel to himself. They could hardly move anymore, so they might as well fight. Where Javelin finally landed would—must!—be remembered. One way or another.

Javelin's camp was buzzing with rumor.

"I've got a message from Colonel Bloom, men," Valentine said, breaking in on breakfast. The men sat on their sleeping mats in neat rows, eating. He nodded to the commissary boy, and some of the kitchen boys brought out fresh hot coffee.

A few heads turned. Some in groups at the back kept eating. Others held out mugs for more coffee.

He climbed up onto the roof of cranky Old Comanche, the sole remaining truck. "We crossed the Mississippi to help the locals create a new Freehold," Valentine said.

"I don't know how you feel about it, but we came here to do a job. We ran hard across Kentucky on the way there, and then fought our way back. Our trail is marked by graves—some of ours, lots of theirs.

"Headquarters just received some startling news. Evansville's been taken by the local resistance. They've got barges full of grain, pork, medical supplies—everything we're short of. They're short of training and guns.

"On this side of the river Kentucky's as sick of the Moondaggers as we are. The legworm clans between Bowling Green and the Appalachians are fighting, hard. Not raiding, not burning a few bridges to give them some negotiating leverage with the Kurians. They're in it for keeps."

They stopped eating the keyed tins of legworm meat marked WHAM. That was something.

"The reason the city there fell that is that most of their militia's been impressed by the Moondaggers. What's left is willing to come over to the Cause.

"You've had some hard fights. You all know you've given it to the Moondaggers even harder. They're filling out those positions opposite with militia ordered to kill or die. Their division isn't even able to hold an entire line at our front."

A few of the men stood up, as though trying to see through the hill toward the enemy positions. That was something else.

"I think we can guess what they mean to do. Hold our beat-down brigade here until they can reestablish their lines of communication and supply, keeping their fingers crossed that we'll surrender. It's been three days. The Wolves keep hearing activity on the other side of their hills—why haven't they attacked? Last Chance told us that we'll die tomorrow. Let's shut him up for good. They're the ones worried about how much worse it'll get tomorrow, not us.

"I know what you're thinking: You've heard this story before. A populace rising, all we have to do is go help them, midwives to a new Freehold. I'm telling you what I've heard from the resistance. Maybe it's wrong, maybe it's lies, maybe they're trying to get us out of our ditches and into the open.

"Let's take them up on it. Put their money where Last Chance's mouth is. I wonder how often, in the history of the Moondaggers, they've been on the receiving end of an assault. Bears in the spearhead, Wolves snapping at their flanks, and a real assault by trained men coming in behind mortar fire.

"And a Cat opening up that asshole in the swinging chair," Duvalier said, suddenly beside him. "If you boys will loan me a couple of claymores from the front of your positions, I'll see if I can't plant a couple around the Moondaggers' headquarters."

"Whar's a little thing like you gonna hide claymores?" Rollings called. He'd come up with some lovely new boots, probably taken from a Moondagger officer.

Duvalier opened her coat, flasher style, showing her improvised harness with clips and holsters and knife sheaths, but the men whistled at what was under her tattered old T-shirt.

Valentine spoke again. "I've told you what I know. Maybe they're setting us up for another sucker punch, with everything, including the bodies hanging from lampposts in Evansville, a sham. Fine. I'm tired of running anyway. But I don't think it's another trick. I've got a feeling this is the day. This is the day when the tide turns. I'm asking you all to turn and fight with me. Our retreat's over." He considered his words to the Quislings across the river, decided they could be improved on. "From now on, it's forward. If we fall, we'll fall with honor."

Valentine stifled a few cheers before it became general by holding out his hands.

"Quiet, Javelin Brigade. Let's not do anything to spoil the surprise."

During the day they came under some distracting shellfire. They were 120mm mortars, Valentine knew, having become intimately familiar with the sound of mortar calibers on Big Rock Hill. If anything, it helped settle Valentine's mind. An army baiting them to attack by feigning weakness wouldn't waste resources on random harassing fire.

Duvalier made a quick scout of the enemy right that night. Valentine heard her report in the new assault headquarters, far forward, masquerading as an artillery observation post. They were close enough forward to draw sniper fire, so they had to keep their heads behind logs and brush.

"That greased-up kid is right about one thing. There's nothing but some nervous farmers and shopkeepers in front of you here, stiffened by Moondagger units behind. They pulled the best of them back to help with the disorder in their rear."

"How do you know that?" a lieutenant asked.

"I was close enough to taste splatter when one of them took a piss. I was able to pick up a couple of conversations."

Valentine could smell blood on her. "That's not all you did."

She wetted her lips. "They had a big machine gun backing up their line with a couple of our Moondagger friends manning it. Don't know if it was there to keep the men up front from running or not, but the loader was asleep and the gunner was jacking off. Couldn't resist a target of opportunity."

Valentine communicated her report, leaving out the story about the dead onanist, over the field phone. Bloom decided to put into effect the assault they'd begun planning after dismissing the boy for a meal and a return swim. They'd leave a skeleton line on the right opposite the Moondaggers and gather for the last effort on the left.

Duvalier shoved some legworm jerky in her mouth and had a cup of real coffee. "I'll take those claymores now, if you've got them," she said.

"Going to be a hero at last?" Valentine asked.

"No. I just like the odds. Their sentry positions out there are about as much use as a screen door in a flood. I'll plant the claymores in their headquarters dugout and wait for a full house. Just hope your guns don't drop a shell on me."

Valentine chuckled. "No ammo reserve. It'll be the shortest barrage in history."

She disappeared and he walked the positions, anxious. Especially after an illumination flare fired. Maybe Duvalier flushed a deer or threw a rock to get the Quisling militia looking in the wrong direction for her final wiggle through the lines.

He inspected the Bears. Gamecock had them in three circles. Chieftain already had his warpaint on. Silvertip was tightening the spiked leather dogskin gloves he liked to wear in a fight.

The Wolves had already left, half of Moytana's under his lieutenant's command to reinforce the right—just in case—and the other half to move along the riverbank and see if they could slip around between the Ohio and the Quisling positions on the left. Valentine authorized Moytana to start the action. The rest of Javelin would follow them in, with Gamecock's Bears leading the way.

Valentine's company was at the forefront. They'd creep forward and provide covering fire for the Bears.

"Thanks for the chance, sir," Rand said, squinting. One of the lenses of his glasses had been blown out and he'd filled the pane with a bandage. It was easier than keeping one eye closed all the time. "I won't let you down."

"Another dirty job," Valentine said to the men as they filed up.

Valentine gaped at Glass. His uniform was carefully pressed and he had a barbershop shave. More important, Ford and Chevy had fresh belts for the .50s.

"Where did you find .50 ammo?"

"That little redhead of yours dropped a couple of boxes off after her last scout. She's stronger than she looks."

"Nice of her."

"She said I was to kiss you when the attack started, sir."

"I see you shaved for it."

"Turns out Chevy here was some kind of trained servant for an officer. I started shaving and he got all excited, so I let him do it. Wasn't much of a beard anyway."

"Someone might mistake you for a soldier and shoot at you," Valentine said.

"Just want this war to be over one way or another. If we're hitting the Moondaggers with not much more than guts and bayonets, I thought I might as well look nice, just in case. And it won't end until we quit playing defense and start digging these ticks out of our hide. I caught a little of that speech of yours. I've heard the same before. Hope you mean it."

"I do," Valentine said. "But I'm just one major."

"With a death sentence, I heard. Stuff like that happens to a lot of the good officers. Cocker, who organized Archangel. We lost Seng in Virginia."

"Think there's a reason for that, Glass?"

He shrugged. "Troublesome animals in a herd get culled first. That's all I'm saying. Watch yourself, sir."

Ford and Chevy started blowing air through their cheeks because they were falling behind the other men. Red Dog gamboled, too excited, or stupid, to tell a battle was in progress.

"Take care of them, Glass," Valentine said.

Patel brought up the rear, walking with the help of his cane again. He nodded to Valentine, as though too busy to pause and chat.

Valentine trotted over to him. "I thought I left you safe over on the other side of the river."

"A lieutenant with a full company of Guard walking wounded is helping in Evansville now. They said there was to be a battle. This is my place."

"Not with those knees, Sergeant Major." Valentine said.

"Cool night," Patel said. "Fall's well on the way now. They're always bad when the weather turns."

"Don't go forward with the rest. I want the company on our flank, just in case the Moondaggers launch a counterattack from their positions."

Valentine had written the same to Rand, but he'd seen young officers get carried away with excitement before. "Find some good ground where you can hold them up."

"Yes, sir."

"That's all, except be careful."

"When am I not careful?"

"When you're throwing yourself on top of Reapers, for a start," Valentine said.

Patel shrugged, his eternal half smile on.

"Thanks, my friend," Valentine said. "For all you've done on this trip."

"Just doing what I always do," Patel said. "Seeing to it that young soldiers get to be old soldiers."

Moytana must have found a good target of opportunity, because Valentine, manning the forward post, heard firing from the riverbank. Well behind the titular Quisling line.

Valentine picked up the field phone.

"General Seng. Repeat. General Seng," he told command.

Valentine made a note of the time: 4:16.

Within a minute the brigade's last few shells came crashing down on the Quisling positions. He wondered if that militia had ever faced artillery fire before. Valentine remembered his first hard barrage on that hill overlooking the Arkansas and Little Rock. It made one frightfully aware of just how hard the enemy was trying to kill you, felt almost like a personal grudge.

Whistles sounded all along the brigade's right as the fire slackened— not by design but by lack of ammunition.

Valentine heard the bark of Ford and Chevy's .50s and watched Javelin go forward, Bears in the lead, the dirt and dust of the artillery falling on them like snow as three hard-fighting wedges pierced the militia positions.

He felt for the Quislings. Indiana stockholders who wanted more land for their herds, men who wanted to own a trucking company, boys told by their Church officiates that militia service was the path to security for their parents and siblings, a good mark for the family record. Rousted out of their beds, told to put on uniforms they wore six weeks a year, picking up unwieldy bolt-action rifles fit more for intimidating a mob than turning back Gamecock's raging Bears.

The odds and ends of the Kentucky Alliance urged their mobile fortifications into action. Just the sight of charging worms might be enough to send most of the Quislings running: They resembled a yellow avalanche moving uncannily uphill.

Valentine saw Tikka in their midst, expertly hanging off the side of her mount and using her saddle as a rifle rest. Their affair still sparked and sputtered along, though they were both too dirty, tired, and hungry to do much but quickly rut and depart like wary rabbits in fox country. Valentine wasn't sure he could even put a name to what they had, but it was something as natural as the fall Kentucky rain, and just as cleansing.

He thought of the artistic swell of her buttocks. Mad thought, with shells and bullets flying in at least three directions.   -

Bloom's command car bounced forward.

The Moondagger batteries joined the fray, but only a few shells fell, still heavies, hard to adjust to meet a fast-moving attack. Hopefully the tubes would be in the brigade's hands within a few hours. In the hands of trained spotters, they'd be handy against river traffic, especially if they had some white phosphorous shells that could be set to air burst.

The first reports began to come back to headquarters. The militia had simply dissolved into little groups of men lying on their faces, spread-eagle in surrender. There were reports of the Moondaggers doing as much damage to the Quisling militia as Javelin. The Wolves were finding trails blocked with bodies, shot by their alleged allies as they retreated.

It was Glass' kind of operation. No heroism required.

Valentine looked around the forward command post.

"That's a nice-looking province there," he said, pointing to some ground occupied by his company where they had a good view of the Moondagger positions. "Let's move forward. Signals, get ready to lay a new line. We're shifting operations forward."

He found Rand looking a little frazzled. "How's your first battle going?"

"It's a little more exciting than I'd like, sir," Rand said.

A wailing cry broke out from a shallow between the small hill of the observation post and the beginnings of Kentucky's rollers in the distance. A wave of Moondaggers poured up in a counterattack from the center. The phrase "gleam of bayonets" crossed Valentine's mental transom. The warrior poets were right—it is an unsettling sight when they're pointed at you.

Glass' machine guns cut into them but the Moondaggers ignored their losses, firing back wildly. They fell onto the outer edges of his platoon, fighting with curved dagger and rifle butt as grenades killed friend and foe alike. Bee was suddenly beside him, emptying her shotguns to deadly effect.

Then they were at the edge of the command post. Bee grabbed two bayoneted rifles thrust at her—Valentine heard her grunt as she seized the hot barrels—and poked the bearded men back, knocking them down like an angry mother snatching up dangerous toys. She reversed one rifle to have the long bayonet ready and used the other as a club to knock Moondaggers off their feet, sticking them like beetles on Styrofoam.

Rand fell without a cry, a bullet not caring that it cavitated one of the best brains Valentine had ever met.

Valentine, grenades bracketing him and vaguely bothered by the stickiness of Rand's blood on his face, did his best to cover Bee and Glass' gunners with his submachine gun. He reloaded, and only after emptying the gun again did he notice that he'd just wasted a full magazine of Quickwood bullets. Stupid!

Then a company of Guard engineers came forward, firing their light carbines, and it was over. Wounded Moondaggers, still lashing at their enemies with their knives, were shot and shot again until they quit crawling.

Bee poked at a loose flap of skin ragged from a bullet hole in her thigh like a child investigating a tick.

Valentine told Bee to put Rand in the shade of a beat-up medical pickup and get her wounds looked at, had Patel pull the company back together and see about ammunition supply, and then sent a bare report of the repulsed counterattack back to Bloom.

Javelin Headquarters was on the move to the old Moondagger positions.

"Sir, radio report coming in from the Wolves," Preville relayed. "The Moondaggers are running. Running! They're quitting and running hard up the highway to Bowling Green. Their legworm supports are going with them."

A lieutenant checked their large-scale map. "They keep heading down that highway, and they'll be getting into Mammoth country."

"Wonder what the Mammoth thought about the little catechism from those men the 'Daggers sliced up," Valentine said. "I wouldn't want to have my truck break down there."

"Wouldn't surprise me if they built a wooden cage or two," Patel said. "It's the end for them."

"Not the end," Valentine said. "Not even the beginning of the end." As Churchill might have put it, it was just the end of the beginning.

With the Moondaggers broken across Kentucky and perhaps beaten at last, a fatal crack in the foundation of the Kurian Order had been opened. Like any fault in a structure's foundation, it might not be easily seen or the danger recognized at first. But that first crack would allow more to appear, branching out until the whole edifice crumbled.

Even such an awful pyramid as Valentine had spoken of back at Rally Base could be undermined and brought down, in time.

Valentine hoped he'd live to see the fall.

WINTER DUTY

A NOVEL OF THE VAMPIRE EARTH

E. E. KNIGHT

To John O'Neill,
who keeps the heroic dream alive

Dies iræ! dies illa
Solvet sæclum in favilla
Teste David cum Sibylla!

—Requiem Mass
usually attributed to Thomas of Celano, c. 1200

One

The old Jackson Purchase, Kentucky, November of the fifty-fifth year of the Kurian Order: Summer and winter contest the season, with fall waiting on the sidelines as though waiting to determine a winner.

Gloriously warm, some might even say hot days give way to chill nights of thick dew and fogs. The trees cling to their leaves like bony old women chary of nakedness, and the undergrowth remains thick and green or brown.

A line cuts through the growth, trampled and torn into a furrow that circumnavigates only the biggest trees. A stranger to Kentucky of this era might conclude a bulldozer had gone on a rampage, but to natives the furrow is instantly recognizable as a legworm trail.

Capable of eating their way across country at a steady three miles an hour, or doubling that if the riders chain the jaws and scythes shut and prod them along with pokes to their sensitive undersides, the giant yellow caterpillarlike creatures provide a ride smoother than any wheeled conveyance. Especially considering the broken-up state of many of Kentucky's roads, cracked when the New Madrid fault went in 2022 and exploited by new growth.

The trail ends at a camp.

The two worms huddle next to each other in the cold, contracted as tightly as their segmenting allows. One would almost say "unhappily," were the odd, segmented creatures capable of anything as prosaic as happiness or its antonym. Their skin is never more reminiscent of old fiberglass attic insulation than this late in the year, when new winter growth turns the outer layer into tufts and tatters.

Each of the worms bears a pair of curious wooden yokes across its back, projecting from its sides like yardarms of a sailing ship. Each *pair supports full hammocks, two to either side of the legworm. A few more walking wounded limp here and there in the camp, bringing food and cleaning those in the hammocks under the supervision of a blue-uniformed nurse. The nurses look exhausted, having spent the day walking up and down the back of the beast with the practiced air of a circus performer, plunging a hook into a fleshy yellow tuft to drop down and check on a patient, offer water, or adjust a towel hanging so as to keep the sun out of the wounded soldier's eyes.*

The rest of the camp not on guard cooks, bakes, or sleeps dead-deep and dirty. There's always too much to do in a hospital train.

A thin strip of woodland and a slug-shaped marsh sit beyond the farthest picket, where a pair of figures lies on their bellies just below the crest of one of the low rolling hills of this quarter of Kentucky where it falls off toward the Mississippi River. Their prone bodies are pointed, like a pair of compass needles, at another camp, smaller in numbers but more spread out in size—a careless campsite, more interested in avoiding one another's smells and sounds than organization or security.

The watchers are male and female, though it is hard to tell by their hair or apparel. If observed from anywhere but atop them, they might be mistaken for a couple of dropped bundles of laundry. The female's long brown overcoat is so patched that the fabric takes the appearance of a camouflage pattern. A thin, freckled face and a fringe of knife-cut red hair can just be made out behind the bug eyes of a pair of mini binoculars. Her longer, leaner companion carries more weapons and gear. He's clad in an odd fusion of weaponry, pebbly leather, and slate gray uniform that looks more like the overalls a utility worker might wear, with thick padded knees and elbows. He's worn-looking from scarred face to pocked and scratched bootheels. In contrast, clean and silky black hair covers the back of his head in a luxurious fall down to his shoulders.

Her binoculars sweep from campfire to sentry, from thick-tired four-wheel vehicle to tent to trailer. She's counting, assessing, calculating risk and threat potential.

His unassisted eyes remained locked on a huddled group of figures in the center of camp. They're neither tied nor restrained; instead they sit behind a staked-out square of construction pegs and red twine, eating hockey puck–sized biscuits the color of gravel from a freshly opened box. Mothers have mashed and soaked them in water for their children; the others either break up the rations with fingers or bite into them, depending on the condition of their teeth. One of the stronger captives, a hulk with a pair of gloves over his ears serving as elephantine ear-

muffs, wrestles a heel of bread from a weaker, old man with a neat
goatee. Their guards do nothing to intervene. It's gone all too soon,
save for a few biscuits given up by the older specimens behind the
string to the mothers and children.

It's hard to tell exactly what the watching man may be thinking; he
keeps his face a careful mask. But a careful observer might note that
he's blinking more than his companion as he watches the huddled cap-
tives try to feed their children.

David Valentine suspected his eyes were glittering red in the dark,
like eyes reflecting a camera's flash in old pictures of wedding guests.
The night vision he'd had ever since becoming a Cat came with some
odd side effects. It was a gift of humanity's Lifeweaver allies in their
war against the Kurians, but a double-edged one. While his pupils could
open as wide as if under a pharmacological effect to let more light in to
the sensitive, and multiplied, rod-shaped cells beneath, that also left him
vulnerable to headaches when exposed to sudden glare and color vision
that was a little off from what most people experienced.

Though the tears interfered with his vision, Lifeweaver-improved
or not.

His light-thirsty eyes watched the strangers' nighted camp. The
sky might have been a pane of glass between Earth and the stars, and
the moon would be up in a couple of hours, when it would glow like a
searchlight.

They'd been lucky, oh, so lucky. Both parties had approached and
camped without cutting each other's trails, and only his train had bothered with a proper reconnaissance.

His wounded and their caregivers were settling down just on the
other side of a low hill and a stretch of soggy woodland between.

A meeting engagement, then. Whoever found out the most about
the other fastest would have the advantage. No sign of scouts discovering his wounded, or he suspected he'd see more action in the camp.

"Who do you think they are?" he asked the woman next to him.
Alessa Duvalier had trained him in the business of operating in the Kurian Zone.

"Poachers. Nomansland trash."

All the layers of clothing made them look like bloated ticks. A ratty
undershirt covered by variegated flannel with a Windbreaker over that,
and then an old military gear vest with ponchos in assorted configura-
tions pinned back but ready to rearrange if the strangely warm fall rain
started up again.

Headhunters returning from a successful raid, probably bound for

Memphis or Nashville. The Kurians had few scruples about stealing population from one another's territories. Human rustling could make a person rich.

In this case what the raiders were doing was a little less dangerous. They'd probably rounded up people displaced by all the fighting in Kentucky in the summer and fall, or perhaps caught escapees from some Kurian principality or other making a run for the Free Territory across the Mississippi.

Twelve poachers. Plus two kids and the women. That he and Duvalier could see. Maybe more in the tents or out of camp hunting or on errands. They were old-school with their transportation: a gas ATV, a few motorbikes, tough-looking mules and llamas, a knot of sleek brush ponies, and two trucks towing big horse trailers for their captives, riding like livestock on the way to the slaughterhouse.

Damned if he'd see them driven into those carts again.

But twelve. A job for a company of soldiers.

Or a small, very careful team. He had one of the best Cats in the business lying next to him. She'd volunteered for the operation in Kentucky last summer. He still wondered why.

Duvalier lowered the binoculars. The wide, light-hungry pupils turned on him. Valentine picked up a faint glitter in the darkness, like polished copper reflecting flame. "You're thinking about those scruffs."

Slang for future aura-fodder. Anything to keep from thinking of them as someone who might be a brother or a daughter.

"And if I am?"

"Will you at least let me go in first and shave the odds?"

Of course his orders said nothing about rounding up strays. He had to consider that if it went bad, his wounded could end up driven to the Kurians south or north of here.

The rewards in return for the risk didn't amount to much. The people who had the guts and resources and luck to make it to the Freehold often needed years of education before they were more of a blessing than a burden. Without someone to schedule every moment of their lives, they wandered like lost sheep or were taken advantage of by hucksters and con artists.

Their kids, however, took to the Free Territory like famished horses loosed in good pasture. The ones with memories of the Kurian Zone often made the best fighters in the Cause. They accepted the discipline and regulation and privation without complaint. They soon learned that the Quisling thugs who'd robbed and bullied everyone under their authority ran like gun-shy rabbits when put up against trained soldiers. Even more, the Reapers, instead of being invulnerable avatars of the local dread god-king, could in fact be hunted down and dynamited out of their holes and killed.

Colonel Seng, who'd led Javelin across Kentucky in the most skillful march into enemy territory Valentine had ever experienced, had once been one of those children.

The Free Republics could use another Colonel Seng.

But twelve. Plus two kids and the women.

He couldn't do twelve. Not all at once, not without running too many risks of a mistake. Duvalier might be able to, but it would take her all night in her methodical manner. But perhaps he could stampede them.

Two paces away, Alessa Duvalier lay swathed in her big overcoat with her sagging, flapped hunter's cap pulled down low. You had to look twice to be sure there was a person there rather than an old, lightning-struck stump.

Her eyes sparkled red, alive at the thought of cutting a few throats. Duvalier had a personal grudge against all Quislings. She'd selected Valentine years ago to become a Cat, tutoring him in sabotage, sniping, assassination, intelligence gathering—all the variegated duties that covert operations in the Kurian Zone entailed. They still bore faint, matching scars on their palms that sealed the odd bond between them, a strange blend of mutual respect and an almost filial blend of conflicting emotions.

"They'll send out scouting parties in the morning, sure as sunrise," Duvalier said.

"Bound to cut the legworm trail," Valentine agreed.

"We could nail the scouts headed our way."

"Which might draw more trouble, if this is just an advance party of a bigger operation," Valentine said. "Besides, it won't help those poor souls in the trailers."

Duvalier's mouth opened and shut again. "Let's skip the usual argument. I know you'll just pull rank anyway."

Valentine answered by stripping off his uniform tunic as she muttered something about crusades and hallelujahs and saving souls.

"We'll need someone good with a rifle," Valentine said. "Just in case they don't bite."

"That old worm driver, Brian something-or-other—he has that scoped Accuracy Suppressed. He hit a deer on the run with it. His kid's always carrying it around."

They ended up bringing the son—his name was Dorian—forward. The father came along as spotter. Dorian's father claimed the boy was just as good a shot, with better eyes. He'd already seen action that summer

and been blooded at what in better times would be called the tender age
of fifteen at the river crossing where Valentine had taken out a company
of Moondaggers with a handful of Bears. Dorian's swagger showed that
he considered himself a hardened veteran.

Valentine could just remember what it was to be that young.

He outlined the plan and had Dorian repeat it back to him.

"Steady now, Dorian. Don't pull that trigger unless they throw
down on me, or I signal. And the signal is . . . ?"

"You hit the dirt," Dorian said, even though they'd already been
through it once.

"Remember to check your target. I'll be moving around a lot in
there. Can do?"

"Can do, Major Valentine."

It felt good to run. Valentine enjoyed losing himself in his body.
Idleness left his mind free to visit the nightmare graveyard of his experiences, or calculate the chances of living to see another Christmas or
summer solstice, or think about the look on the old man with the goatee's face when his fellow prisoner ripped the heel of bread right out of
his hand. So he escaped by chopping wood, loping along at the old easy
Wolf cadence—even the rhythmic thrust of lovemaking.

Though the last left him feeling vaguely guilty for not being attentive enough to the woman.

Since they'd said good-bye to the Bulletproof leg-worm clan after
the battle across the river from Evansville, he had nothing but memories
of Tikka's vigorous sensuality and the musky smell of her skin. They
could be revisited at his leisure. Now he had work to do.

He had the sense that their affair was over, her curiosity, or erotic
interest, or—less flatteringly—the desire to cement good relations between Southern Command's forces and her clan being satisfied.

He crouched in a bush, watching the young sentry, who seemed to
be watching nothing but stars and the rising moon.

Valentine checked his little .22 automatic, which he usually carried
wrapped up in a chamois with his paperwork. Over the years he'd had
cause to kill with everything from his bare hands to artillery fire, but
he'd found a small-caliber pistol more useful than any other weapon. It
was quiet, the rounds were accurate at close range, and you could carry
it concealed. With the lead in the nose etched with a tiny cross so it
would fragment and widen the wound, it did damage out of proportion
to the weight of the round.

He wondered if the Kurians' death-machine avatars, the Reapers, felt the same electric nervousness when they stalked a victim.

Of course, in a meadow like this, in open country, Reapers did not stalk, at least not for the last few dozen meters. They acted more like the big, fast cats Valentine had seen loose in the hill country in central Texas, covering the distance in an explosive rush that either startled their prey into stillness or made escape futile.

Of course, in the city it was something else entirely. Urban Reapers were the trap-door spiders of many a ruined block, striking from a patch of overgrowth, a pile of garbage, or a crack in the ceiling. But he doubted these headhunters worked the cities. Too much law and order, even if the bad law and order of the KZ.

He turned his senses to the camp, trying to get a sense of the rhythms of the headhunters.

They were singing. Three of the men were passing a bottle, falling out and joining in the tune between swigs, taking turns improvising rhyming lyrics in old-style rap.

The sentry sat in a tree overlooking the bowl-shaped field and soggy patch, within hallooing distance of the camp.

The safety went back on the little .22, for now. Valentine guessed why they put the youth on watch. Young men had good eyesight, especially at twilight. He'd probably be relieved by a veteran for the late shift. The boy was alternately yawning and chewing on bits of long grass root, glancing back toward the camp for signs of his relief.

Valentine balanced the chances of the young man doing something stupid against the possibility of using the kid to get into camp armed with some bargaining power. If Valentine just approached the poachers, they'd have him facedown in the dirt until they secured his weapons, at the very least.

Valentine wormed his way up to the trunk from downwind, using a mixture of crawling and scuttling during the sentry's frequent glances back to look for his relief.

The relief sentry started his walk uphill to the lookout tree, holding a heavy, swaddled canteen by its strap.

Valentine loosened his sword and pocketed the automatic, grateful that he hadn't had to use it. He shifted to his submachine gun, double-checking the safety.

The boy, anticipating his relief, clambered down from the scrub oak. Valentine slipped up behind.

Valentine moved quickly, clapping a strong left hand over the kid's mouth and elevating the kid's wrist to his shoulder blade with the right.

"Don't crap yourself, kid. I'm not a Reaper. But I could have been. I want you to remember that when we get back to your campfire sing-along. I could have been. What's your name?"

"Trent. Sunday Trent," the boy sqeaked.

"Sunday? Like after Saturday?"

"Yes, sir."

"Knock off the 'sir,' boy. I'm not some local trooper you have to polish. They call me the Last Chance."

Valentine couldn't say why he picked the name. One of the Moondaggers had called himself that. An emissary sent to deliver threats and ultimatums, he hadn't intimidated the Southern Command's troops—the quickest way to get their backs up was to start making demands and informing them they were beat.

Valentine thought of tying the kid's hands—he had spare rawhide twine in a pocket, as it had lots of uses around camp—but settled for looping his legworm pick in the back of the boy's pants and prodding him along with the haft. Less aggressive that way and it kept Valentine out of elbowing distance in case the boy made a gesture born more of desperation than inexperience.

Being careful about others' actions as much as your own was how you stayed alive on Vampire Earth.

"Sunday, I need to talk to the boss of— What do you call yourselves, a gang?"

"Easy Crew, sir. Blitty Easy's Crew."

"Which one's Blitty Easy?"

"The one with the tall hat, sir."

Valentine thought of giving the kid a poke the next time he said sir.

"Call me Chance, Sunday."

"The one with the hat, Chance bo— Chance."

The use of names was relaxing the kid a little.

They met the relief sentry on the way, a man with no less than nine Old World jujus around his neck, a mixture of car manufacturer iconography and bandless watch faces. Valentine recognized a Rolex and Bulova dangling from gold chains. Valentine remembered some of the decorations as Gulf Coast Reaper wards.

"Keep your mouth shut, Sunday," Valentine said.

"That watch post has blind spots right and left," Valentine called. He kept Sunday Trent between himself and the sentry as they passed.

The relief looked distinctly unrelieved at the news.

"Hollup!" the relief called belatedly.

The camp was contracting like a turtle tucking in its limbs for the night. One of the poachers guided a captive to a tent, his hand firmly on the back of her neck. She didn't struggle—a pregnancy was a guarantee of life in the Kurian Zone, both as proof of fertility and for the sake of the new member of the human herd.

The gunmen stood up at Valentine's approach, swapping eating utensils for guns and clubs.

"Easy now, Easy Crew," Valentine muttered. "Just relax, Sunday. All I want to do is talk a bit."

Sunday led him into camp and people gathered, naturally curious about the stranger. Weapons were readied but not pointed.

Sunday pointed out the leader of the headhunters.

Valentine had to admire the big man's sartorial taste. From the dirt pattern on his extremities, Valentine surmised he drove the ATV. Valentine hadn't seen a beaver hat since New Orleans at least, if not Oklahoma, and this one had a lush shine to it that spoke of either recent purchase or tender care.

"Careful, tha, with that gun, stranger," Blitty Easy said. Everything on him looked bright and expensive, from the silver tips on his shoes to the diamonds fixed to the skin in the place of one shaved eyebrow.

"I'm here to talk, not shoot," Valentine said.

"Even shooting off your mouth can be dangerous around me, Injun Man," Blitty Easy said. "What's the matter, we grab somebody's heir? You the big tough man they sent to get him back. No, her back."

"I think bigger than that. I want the whole bunch. Leave the bonds. I want to present them wrapped up like a big bouquet."

Blitty Easy laughed. "You talk pretty big for a man with nothing but a dumb kid in his sights. You can shoot him if you like. Serves him right for letting himself get snuck up on tha in that tree."

"What direction you going, Sunday?" Valentine asked, poking the kid in the lumbar with the barrel of his gun.

"South. Mem—"

"Shuddup, Sunday," Blitty Easy said.

"South," Valentine said. "Good. You won't have to circle around to avoid us; you can just keep on track."

Blitty Easy stood up, thick legs holding up a stomach that jutted out like a portable stove. Not flab, exactly, but the heavy center of a powerful man.

Valentine walked Sunday around the circle of onlookers. Each took a step back as he approached and held his right fist cocked so his brass ring was at eye level. The circle of men and guns around him widened and spread and thinned as though he were rolling dough.

They eyed the submachine gun at his hip. Carrying a quality firearm like that openly marked one as either a tool of the Kurian Order or someone operating outside it. Easy's Crew maintained their well-armed independence by living on the fringes of the masquerade of a civilization beneath the towers.

Deadly as his weapon was, some would say the brass ring on his finger was the deadlier weapon. It was the mark of Kurian favor. A wearer was owed respect, for the fear and favor of the Kurians hung about the ring's owner like a king's mantle.

"Who do you think you are, threatening my crew?" Blitty Easy barked.

Valentine held his brass ring high. "Who am I? A man tested by the only law that lasts—that of the jungle. I speak three Grog dialects and have a foot pass for half the tribes west of the Tennessee and Ohio. I've watched Twisted Cross tubs open, ridden the cannonball St. Louis to LA, and flown with Pyp's Circus. I've sailed the Caribbean and the Great Lakes and Puget Sound, humped hills in Virginia and Baja, tickled lip from Albuquerque to Xanadu. I've won a brass ring and the power to put you all in unmarked graves. I'm your last chance, Blitty Easy."

Easy had a good poker face. "Why you bothering with us, then, Mr. Big Shot?"

"The Old Folks are interested in Kentucky right now. They don't want to see another state fall to the guerrillas. We're on our way to talk some sense into the more friendly locals. I thought my goons would have to forage for heartbeats, but you went out rounding up strays and did the job for us."

"We get paid for them?"

Valentine would have happily bought the lives, had he or his column had anything the brigands would accept.

"Payment is you just hand over your collection without going in the bag with them. My Old Man likes keeping brimful on aura when traveling, and they're not particular."

"He's bluffin'," someone called from behind Valentine.

Valentine whirled. "Kiss my ring and check it out. I don't mind."

A brass ring on its rightful wearer accumulated enough bioelectric charge to tingle when you touched your lips to it. Valentine found the sensation similar to licking a battery. His brass ring, fairly won in Seattle, was legitimate enough, and he usually kept it with some odds and ends in a little velvet bag along with a few favorite hand-painted mahjong pieces. Though he'd lost his taste for the game long ago, they still made useful tokens for sending messages to people who knew him. The only tarnish about the ring was the mark it had left on his conscience.

Valentine could tell the crew was impressed, even if Blitty Easy still looked suspicious.

"Or you want to test me some other way?" Valentine said, drawing his blade.

"Regular Sammy Rye, with that blade," Blitty Easy said.

"Steel without the talent to back it up's just so much butter knife," a man who smelled like cheap gin said, two younger versions of himself flanking him.

Valentine inflated his lungs and let out an unearthly wail. An imitation of a Reaper scream had worked once before, a dozen years ago, several hundred miles north in the hills of western Illinois. It might work here.

Movement and a bullet crack.

Valentine's reflexes moved ahead of his regrets.

The camp exploded into noise and motion, like a tray of ice cubes dumped into a fryer.

He knocked Sunday flat.

No rhyme or reason to the rest. The fat was in the fire and he had to move or burn. A hand near him reached for a chest holster to his right and he swung his sword and struck down in a sweeping blow. A shotgun came up and he jumped as it went off, spraying buckshot into the men behind him, turning one's cheek into red mist and white bone. A poacher put a banana-clipped assault rifle to his shoulder, and then his hair lifted as though an invisible brush had passed through it, and he went down, a thoughtful look on his face as he toppled.

Valentine rolled free, dropping his sword and reaching for the little submachine gun he'd carried across Kentucky twice as he ran out of the firelight. With a shake, the wire-frame folding stock snapped into place and he put it to his shoulder.

A bullet whizzed past, beating him into the night.

The poachers had pitched their tents in a little cluster, and he moved through them. A shaggy back with a bandolier—he planted a triangle of bullets in it between the shoulder blades, moving all the while, zigzagging like a man practicing the fox-trot in triple time.

Tent canvas erupted and Valentine felt hot buckshot pass just ahead.

Move—shoot, stop, and reload. Move—shoot, shoot; move—shoot, stop, and reload.

Blitty Easy's Crew was shooting at anything that moved, and Valentine was only one of several figures running through the night.

Turned out the twelve and then some could be taken without too much of a risk.

These weren't soldiers; they were brigands, used to preying on the weak. They popped their heads up like startled turkeys to see where the reports of the sniper fire came from and received a bullet from Dorian's

rifle. Pairs of men moved together instead of covering each other—
Valentine cut two down as they ran together toward the machine gun
pointed impotently at the sky.

Valentine saw a figure with long hair running, dragging a child.
Please, Dorian, don't get carried away.

There was only one headhunter Valentine wanted to be sure of. He
wasn't that hard to find; he made noise like an elephant as he ran through
the Kentucky briars and brambles.

Thick legs pumping like pistons, Easy made wide-spaced tracks for
timber.

A brown-coated figure rose from the brush as he swept past. She
executed a neat thrust under his shoulder blades.

The fleeing figure didn't seem to notice the quick poke. Blitty Easy
pounded out three more steps and then pitched forward with a crash.

Duvalier kicked the corpse and then waded through the brush to
Valentine, sniffing the beaver hat suspiciously as she passed.

"That was a good piece of killing," Duvalier said, wearing that old
fierce grin that made Valentine wonder about her sanity. She lifted a
coattail on one of the bodies and wiped off her sword.

An engine gunned to life and another shot rang out. The engine
puttered on, but he didn't hear a transmission grind into gear.

"This might be nice for winter." She tried the hat on. The size made
the rest of her look all that much more waifish, a little girl playing dress-
up. "Smells like garage gunpowder and hair oil, though."

They covered each other as they inspected the camp. The only one
left alive was Sunday. He looked around at the bodies, shaking like a leaf.

"They said it was good money," Sunday said. "Easy work. Easy
work, that's what they said. Easy crew. Easy work. Get rich, bringing
in rabbits."

Duvalier put her hand on her sword hilt, but Valentine took her elbow.

"He's just shaken up. We can let him go."

Valentine turned on the boy. "You load up a couple of those llamas
and go home to mother, boy. Kentucky's harder than it looks."

They circled around away from the bodies and checked the trailers
and the prisoner pen.

"We're turning you loose," Valentine said to the captives. "We're
heading west, all the way across the Mississippi. Any of you want to go
that way is welcome to file along behind under Southern Command
protection."

A few gasped. One young girl, no more than six, lifted one chained-
together leg as though asking for assistance with a fouled shoelace.

"There's got to be a bolt cutter in one of those trucks," Valentine said to Duvalier. "See if you can find it, Smoke."

He turned away and flipped the maplight switch on one of the running trucks, a high clearance pickup with the cab top removed and replaced by an empty turret ring. One of Easy's Crew leaned back behind the wheel. If you looked at the side of his head that wasn't sprayed all over the hood of the open-topped truck, it appeared as though he was sleeping.

"You want us bringin' our supplies, Cap'n?" one of the captives asked.

Valentine looked at the captives' rations. Blitty Easy's Crew fed their captives on the cheap, as you'd expect. Hard ration bread. Sticks of dried legworm segment divider—interesting only as chewing exercise—and sour lard, with a half-full jar of a cheap orange mix that tasted like reconstituted paint chips to drink. Though it did sanitize water. They'd be better off cooking the poachers for food, but of course Valentine couldn't suggest *that*.

It took a while to get them organized, to distribute loads on pack animals. He'd send a patrol back for the vehicles.

As he walked back toward Dorian's sniper perch with Duvalier, he refilled his submachine gun's magazine from a heavy box of 9mm rounds he'd found in one of the locked glove compartments. It had yielded easily enough to a screwdriver.

"What was that?" he demanded of Duvalier once they were out of earshot.

"A darn good killing," Duvalier said, showing her teeth.

"I said I'd make the first move," Valentine said. Was he more angry at the killing, or orders being disobeyed?

"You screamed, Val," Duvalier said. "I thought you were calling for help. I gave the order to fire. What's your malfunction, David? They were just border trash."

"Major, if you please."

Duvalier rolled her eyes heavenward.

"Just doing my duty," Duvalier said. "You even remember what yours is? We're supposed to fight them in as many places as possible, the 'fire of a thousand angry torches' or however that speech by the former Old World president went."

The mood passed, as it always did. Valentine was more vexed at himself than Duvalier. At least she had the guts to admit she liked killing.

Valentine took his mood out on the food snatcher wearing the stolen gloves as earmuffs. He got to arrange the bodies and see that each one's face was faceup but covered by a shroud of some kind.

Valentine felt better as they gathered Easy Crew's collection of aura-fodder and vehicles and brought them into camp. A sergeant gave the usual recruiting speech as they broke camp the next morning. Anyone who wanted to join the fight would head back west to the new Southern Command fort on the banks of the Ohio guarding Evansville from the Kentucky side. They'd have an important job right off, getting the vehicles back with the guidance of a detail from the sick-train.

They ended up with two. A fifteen-year-old boy with a lazy eye and a widow of forty-one who'd learned to use a rifle as a teen in the Kurian Youth Vanguard.

"I quit when my mom got sick in her uterus and they stuck her in a van," the volunteer explained. "Mom was right smart, could have been useful a hundred ways if they'd let her get operated on and recover."

Of course Sergeant Patel, the senior NCO back at Javelin, could make soldiers out of odds and ends of human material. There was always more work than there were hands.

More aura for the trip home. A prowling Reaper would spot their psychic signatures from miles away, even in the lush hills of Kentucky. He and Duvalier would have to team up every night and sleep in their saddles.

Four enervating days later Valentine had his wounded across the Mississippi. The Kentucky worm drivers turned homeward, their sluggish mounts willing to move only in the warmest hours of the day no matter how much pain they inflicted with the long, sharp goads.

The Kentuckians would stay on their side of the river. Valentine felt guilty saying good-bye and wishing them luck, they'd pushed their worms on through the cold until death was assured for their mounts. Without a group of others of their kind to coil with, in a knitted cocoon to protect the fall's eggs, the frost would take them like delicate fruit.

"These two are goners, I think," Dorian said as they made their good-byes. He'd been quiet ever since shooting six of Blitty Easy's Crew on that wild, clear night.

"We'll compensate you and your father somehow," Valentine said, signing an order and tearing it off from his dwindling sheaf of blanks.

"Wish they could give me back that night. The one with the shooting."

Valentine felt for the young man. Dorian had stepped across a terrible threshold far too young.

"You followed orders and did what had to be done, Dorian," Valentine said. "Better than thirty people are going to live to a fine old age because you're a good shot. Remember that."

The youth nodded dumbly, and his father nudged him back toward the high saddles.

Duvalier embraced him with one of her characteristic hugs, half handshake and half lover's embrace. She nuzzled the bristle on his chin.

"I'll see that they get back all right. Any orders for me back in Henderson?"

"Be careful. I think if the Kurians move on us, it'll be from the Ordnance. You could check the rail lines up that way."

"Can do," she said.

"I won't be gone long. I'm just going to give my report, see about supply and replacement, and return."

She slipped away as though bored with the goodbye, and Valentine returned to supervising the river embarkation.

Javelin had left Southern Command with bands playing and people cheering and tinfoil on their heads.

Its wounded returned under cover of darkness, hauled across the Mississippi in some of Southern Command's Skeeter Fleet—twin-engined outboards ready to make wake at the first sign of trouble.

No crowds met them on the western shores, just a deputation from Forward Operating Base Rally's commander at the edge of the Missouri bootheel.

Colonel Pizzaro looked incredulous when Valentine announced that he'd been returned with fresh from a hard-fought victory in Western Kentucky. Valentine handed over a sealed report to Southern Command from Colonel Bloom, now in command of what was left of the expedition to the Appalachians.

"Don't be stingy with the steaks and beer," Valentine said. "They walked a hard trail. They deserve a few luxuries with their laurels."

Pizzaro cleared his throat. "Tell me, Valentine. Don't hold back. How bad was it over there? Papers are playing it down or calling it a catastrophe."

"Could have gone better," Valentine said. "But it wasn't a disaster. We've gained allies, just not where we expected. I'd call it a major victory for the Cause."

"He's a good man, but kind of an oddball," one of Pizzaro's staff said to a corporal in a voice he probably thought too quiet for Valentine to hear. "Always full of fancy ideas about working with Grogs and stuff."

Pizzaro snorted. "Victory? Not according to the *Clarion* headlines. Or are you aiming for a nice long rest somewhere quiet with lots of watercolor paint?"

"It was a win for the good guys, Colonel."

"You're selling that at headquarters?" Pizzaro asked. "I wish you luck."

Two

Southern Command Mississippi Operational Area Headquarters, the second week of November: The architects who designed the Mall at Turtle Creek in Jonesboro would still recognize their structure, though they'd be surprised to see some of the renovations caused by war and necessity.

One of the anchor stores has been hollowed out and turned into a vast machine shop for the repair and renovation of valuable electronics, and the rest of the big box stores serve as warehousing. The smaller shops have been converted to training classrooms, meeting areas, offices, break rooms, a medical center with a pharmacy, even a kennel for the bomb sniffers and guard dogs. Only the food court is still more or less recognizable; if anything, it is a little more interesting, thanks to cases displaying unit histories, photographs, and citations. And some of the hardy palms planted inside by the builders have survived the mall's looting, deterioration, and restoration.

Most of the exterior doors have been welded shut, of course, and netting and silent antiaircraft guns dot the roof. Barbed wire encircles the parking lots scattered with buses, trucks, and staff four-wheelers and motorcycles ready for use and dispatch.

Of course, the polished floors are patched and the ceilings are being rebuilt in some areas to repair minor earthquake damage the mall received in 2022.

David Valentine, having passed through the security station and visitors' lobby taking up the old bookstore, idles with a yellowed copy of French military history on an upholstered chair that smells like cigars and mildew and body odor, his thumb smeared with ink for an ID record and his bad leg stretched out where it won't interfere with passersby.

He had enough pocket money for a bagel and a glass of sweet tea at the little café for visitors waiting to be met.
He fights off a yawn as he waits.
On the other side of the old store, security staff search and inspect those passing in and out of the headquarters, not a yawn to be seen. The Kurians have their own versions of Cats.

The ink had dried and the last crumbs of the bagel disappeared by the time General Lehman's adjutant appeared. The staffer might have been a living mannequin of crisp cotton and twill. Valentine felt scruffy shaking hands with him. All Valentine had managed in the washroom was to comb his hair out and wash his face and hands.

Perhaps it wasn't the chair that was so odiferous after all.

"You can just take that book if you like," the adjutant suggested. "It's all Southern Command library. I'm sure you know where to drop it."

"Thanks for the tip," Valentine said. Not that he needed it. He'd visited the quiet library and reading room in one of the mall's old stores to unwind after the quick debriefing he'd undergone on his arrival yesterday afternoon. Three paperbacks, one with a duct-tape spine—the illustration of the dripping-wet bikini girl on the cover reaching up to undo her top did wonders for circulation—were already stuffed into his duty bag beneath the reports and Javelin correspondence.

They'd talked about Javelin, good and bad. When Valentine gave them his assessment for the addition of Kentucky to the United Free Republics, his interviewers had exchanged a look that didn't strike Valentine as promising.

And he hadn't even begun to describe what he had in mind for his Quisling recruits.

He saved that for the end, and they told him to take it up with General Lehman the next day.

There was another wait outside Lehman's office, and Valentine switched to American history, a biography of Theodore Roosevelt. He was experiencing the Badlands with Roosevelt after the nearly simultaneous deaths of his mother and wife when Lehman's staffer summoned him.

When Valentine finally stood before the general in command of the eastern defenses, he was surprised to see a pair of arm-brace crutches leaning against the desk and the general's right leg encased in plaster and a Velcro ankle brace on the left.

"Bomb beneath my command truck," Lehman said. "Flipped us like a flapjack."

He looked paler than Valentine remembered, thin and strained.

"Let's hear it, Valentine," Lehman said. "Don't spare me; I know I sent you out there."

Lehman dipped his little silver comb in the water glass and commenced cleaning his drooping mustache in the methodical fashion a cat might use to clean its face. It was whiter and less bushy than it had been a year ago at the planning sessions for Javelin. Cover Lehman in dust and denim, and he'd pass for a cowhand straight off a Texas ranch, but he had precise, machinelike diction, weighing each vowel and consonant of his sometimes cracker-barrel phraseology. Valentine had heard that as a junior officer he'd been in signals, communicating with other Freeholds around the world.

"Should really make you a colonel, Valentine," General Lehman said.

"What about the confirmation vote?" Southern Command was allowed to run its own affairs within the confines of its budget—and parts of it even made money by engaging in civil engineering projects or restoring machinery—but promotion to colonel and above had to be approved by the UFR's legislature.

General Lehman nodded. "The *Clarion* would get in a huff and their chickens in the legislature would squawk in tune and the whole list would probably be voted down. They've had a field day over Javelin. You understand."

"I do."

"Of course, there's no reason we can't pay you like a colonel."

"Under the assumed name," Valentine said. Technically, David Valentine was a wanted man and couldn't draw pay, civilian or military. Not that it would do him much good if the pay increase went through. Few colonels got rich, despite their pay-draws twice that of a major. A colonel was expected to spend most of it on entertainments for his command, and most also gave generously to families of the command who'd lost fathers or mothers. A private who was good at scouring arms and medical supplies and selling them back to the Logistics Commandos could do better.

"There is one promotion I'd like you to make," Valentine said. "I'd like Sergeant Patel—his name is all over those reports—made a captain."

"Shouldn't be a problem. I've heard the name. Wolf, right? Twenty years or more."

Valentine noticed there were archival boxes all against the walls, and two locked file cabinets hung open.

"Moving to a new office, sir?" Valentine asked.

"That's one way to put it. You didn't hear about the election, then?"

Valentine didn't follow politics when he was in the Free Republics, beyond what filtered in to mess hall chatter and newspaper articles.

"There's been a change, as of the first week of November," Lehman continued. "President Starpe lost. Adding Hal Steiner to the ticket didn't help as much—"

"I'm sorry, General. Hal Steiner? From down south near the Louisiana border?"

"Yes. Of course, you've been out of the UFR. Sorry, it's all anyone's been talking about here. Steiner a friend of yours?"

"I met him as a lieutenant."

"Yeah, he's the one who helped keep all the Archangel forces hidden down in those swamps. The Concorde Party made a big deal about Steiner coming out of the KZ and treating Grogs like people, and between that and the bad news out of Kentucky and the Rio Grande, the New Federalists were plastered. Anyway, old DC is out and Thoroughgood is in. Once Lights's sworn in, he'll nominate Martinez to take over Southern Command, and I suspect the legislature will approve, though the Texas bloc will be voting against him, of course, because of the bad feelings about 'seventy-three."

A piece of Valentine's brain translated the political farrago.

Archangel, of course, was the operation that ousted Consul Solon and the Kurians from his brief hold on the Ozarks. In the chaos following, Southern Command seized much of Texas and Oklahoma and a patch of bled-dry Kansas.

The United Free Republics, after a messy birth, had divided into two parties, the Concorde and the New Federalists. Other than their slogans—*Liberty and Justice through Thoroughgood* for the Concorde, *Starpe Can't Be Stopped* for the New Federalists—he didn't know much about platforms and so on, though the perpetually dissatisfied *Clarion* supported Thoroughgood through its editorial page and its reporting.

"Old DC" was a nickname for President Starpe, not because of some connection to the old United States capital, but because he earned the nickname Danger Close as an artillery spotter during the tumultuous birth of the Ozark Free Territory. He'd infiltrate Kurian strongpoints and called in artillery fire literally on top of himself. His opponent, Zachary Thoroughgood, was a scion of the Thoroughgood family, owners of the Thoroughgood markets and a several hotels and casinos in Branson. They also controlled a brewery that produced a fine spruce-tip ale that Valentine's old CO in Zulu company had been fond of as well.

Valentine had first heard of Thoroughgood as a prosecutor who busted up criminal gangs operating from the borderlands and then for improving electrification and water supply across the UFR as a legislator. Thorough-good's friends and constituents called him "Lights," and Valentine had heard him called "Lights, Camera, Action" here and there, for he was famously photogenic and traveled everywhere with a photographer.

As to the "Texas bloc," Valentine knew that in the legislature there were constant fights between the representatives from the old Ozark Free Territory and the newer regions. Rules of seniority favored legislators from the Missouri and Arkansas areas.

General Martinez, of course, was an old enemy. Valentine had put Martinez on trial for the murder of a pair of helpful Grogs who'd followed him up from the Caribbean. Valentine had always suspected Martinez had, if not an entire hand, at least a pointing finger in his own arrest after the fight in Dallas that led to his exile from the UFR.

Lehman got up and dug around in a pile of newsprint next to a bureau with liquor bottles lining their little rail like spectators. He tossed down a copy of the *Clarion*.

STARPE STOPPED, read the headline.

"I suspect there'll be changes once Martinez takes over. I won't be running the Mississippi front and parts east. All these boxes and such, they're not me getting set to move out; they're from the new broom coming in. There's been a suggestion of malfeasance on my part over Javelin. Preservation of evidence and all that."

"How could you know it was all a setup? They fooled Brother Mark."

Lehman chuckled. "You've changed your opinion of him, then? Back when we were organizing Javelin, I got the impression he was a stone in your hoof."

"He grows on you. Even the men are starting to confide in him. He's like the grouchy instructor nobody likes but still remembers ten years later."

"Soon I'll be a memory here. If I don't get retired, I imagine I'll be checking locks on empty warehouses and filing reports on other reports that'll end up going into my superior's report. General Martinez and I don't piss in the same direction on any number of things, starting with Kentucky. He penned an editorial for the *Clarion* about Javelin, Valentine. Of course, all the paragraphs featured the word 'fiasco' with the same arguments, but then the *Clarion* only has two tunes in their hymnal. Everyone around here's tight as a turtle's ass with the soup pot bubbling."

"What are our chances of getting some reinforcements into Kentucky? Garrison and training duty, until they can get themselves organized."

"Somewhere on the short block between Slim Street and None Boulevard, I'm afraid, Major."

Valentine stood up. "Whatever's being said about Javelin, it wasn't for nothing. Kentucky's come in on our side, more or less. The Moondaggers, the ones who bled Kansas dry, they've left bodies scattered from the Ohio to the Tennessee."

"That was just the first wave, son. The signals and intelligence staff thinks something's brewing in the Northwest Ordnance. Beyond the usual dance of reinforcements for the river crossings, with armed rebellion just across the river and over Evansville way."

Valentine wondered about Evansville. Technically it had been the extreme southwestern tip of the Northwest Ordnance, which encompassed the old rust belt states of Ohio, Michigan, and much of northern and southern Indiana. (The central part of the state organized itself with the other great agricultural Kurian principalities in Illinois south of Chicago.) "All the more reason to send us at least something. Without their legworms, the clans in Kentucky lose their mobility and flexibility."

General Lehman leaned back in his chair, staring at the ceiling as he drummed his chest with his fingers. "Maybe they won't have any more luck in those hills than we did."

"A fresh brigade could make a big difference in western Kentucky. The old legworm clan alliance can take care of their ridges. With Evansville as a supply base, they have hospitals, fuel supplies, machine shops, factories. There's even a company that produces tents and backpacks."

"I hate half measures, Major. The way I see it, we either pull out completely or go all in and shove every chip we can scrape together across the Mississippi. I'd like to argue for the latter, but we're in flux right now."

"I've got an ad hoc battalion of Evansville volunteers—I guess you'd call them. There's more than that in western and central Kentucky. We could put the brigade back together and have near a division."

Lehman's comb went to work again.

"But right now, in Evansville, all you have is what's left of Javelin and your volunteers."

"The Kentuckians chased down the Moondaggers before settling in for the winter. Their legworms have to hibernate, remember. But the Evansville volunteers have the know-how for mechanized operations."

"Yes, the staff briefed me on that. You're proposing a sort of French Foreign Legion for ex-Quislings, am I right? They do a little bleeding for us, and in six years they get a new name and citizenship in the UFR. Quite a scheme."

"I realize I may have exceeded my authority in recruiting local support."

"That's what you were assigned to Javelin for: local support."

"To hear you tell it, my locals won't have anything to support much longer."

"All in or pull out, Valentine. I'm sorry to say it, but all in is just not in the cards this year. That leaves pull out."

"Can I at least get some matériel for my Quisling recruits? They're walking around in black-dyed versions of their old uniforms and using captured Moondagger guns. Not the best of rifles—they're mostly bolt-action carbines with low-capacity magazines. Fine for smoking out rebellious townies; not so hot when you're trying to bring down a running Reaper."

Lehman opened a notebook on his desk and jotted down a few words. "I'll see what I can do. I know some huge rolls of blanketing or bedding has shown up recently. Guns will be tougher."

"What about my offer to the Quislings, sir? Can you give me something in writing to back it up?"

"I'd be proud to. But honestly, Valentine, I don't think any of 'em will be around to collect. They'll either quit on you or be killed."

"Do you know something I don't, General?"

"It's been my experience that the top-level Quisling officers are excellent. Well trained, intelligent, motivated, cooperative. Their soldiers are brave enough. They'll stick where our guys will pull out a lot of the time. But you know as well as I that it's the quality of the NCOs and junior officers that define an army. I've not seen the Quisling formation yet that has outstanding sergeants. They're usually the best bullies and thieves in uniform."

Valentine swung through intelligence next. He had to place a call and be signed in by the security officer at the duty desk in the hall.

A corporal escorted him to Post's office. The corporal didn't even try to make small talk.

Valentine walked through a bullpen of people at desks and occupying cubicles, passing maps filled with pins and ribbons and whiteboards covered with cryptic scrawls on the walls, and arrived at an office beyond. Post these days rated his own adjutant, and Post's office was just beyond his adjutant's. There was no door between Post's office and his adjutant's, just a wide entryway.

Valentine knocked on the empty doorframe. Post beamed as he entered. There was a little more salt to his salt-and-pepper hair and a good deal more starch in his uniform, but then headquarters standards had to be maintained.

The last time Valentine had seen Will Post, his friend was lying in

his hospital bed after the long party celebrating the victory in Dallas
and the retirement of the old Razors.

Post sported a lieutenant colonel's bird these days. Even better, he
looked fleshed-out and healthy. Valentine was used to seeing him thin
and haggard, tired-eyed at the Chinese water torture of minutiae involved in running the old battalion, especially the ad hoc group of odds
and sods that had been the Razors.

When Valentine had first met him in the Kurian Coastal Marines,
his uniform bore more permanent sweat stains than buttons. Now he
looked like he'd wheeled out of an award-banquet picture.

"Hello, Will," Valentine said, saluting. Post, as a lieutenant colonel,
now outranked a mere major—especially one who usually walked
around Southern Command in a militia corporal's uniform. Valentine
felt embarrassed, trying not to look at the wheelchair. He'd seen it in
pictures, of course.

"Good to see you. What happened to your ear?"

Valentine had left a hunk of lobe in Kentucky. If he could find the
right man with a clipper, he should really even them up, even if it would
make him look a bit like a Doberman.

"A near miss that wasn't much of a miss."

"Sit down, Val," Post said. "I was just about to order sandwiches
from the canteen. They have a cold-cut combo that's really good; I think
there's a new supplier. Cranberries are plentiful now too, if you're in the
mood for a cranberry and apple salad. Our old friend Martinez has
made some commissary changes already." He reached for his phone.

"I'll have both. I've an appetite today."

Post, in his efficient manner, had seen Valentine's discomfiture and
acted to correct the situation.

While the Enemy Assessments Director-East called down to the
canteen, Valentine glanced around the room. Post's office had two
chairs and an odd sort of feminine settee that in another time and place
would have been called a fainting couch.

"How's Gail?"

"Good. She does volunteer work over at United Hospital. She's
good with me, with the wounded. She says she only does it to forget
about what she went through, but she could just as easily do that by sitting in a corner slamming tequila. Which is how I met her, way back.
Except she was reading."

Post's desk had too many file folders, reachers to help him access
shelves, coding guides and a battered laptop to have much room for
pictures. He had citations and unit photos—Valentine recognized the
old picture of himself and Ahn-Kha on the road to Dallas.

Ahn-Kha. Probably his closest friend in the world other than Duva-lier, and the big golden Grog wasn't even human. He was leading a guerrilla band in the Appalachians, doing so much damage that both sides were mistaking his little partisan band for a large army.

He'd seen that same shot on his visit to Molly and her son, ages ago. Ever since he'd brought her out of Chicago as a Wolf lieutenant, they'd been family to one another, with a family's mix of joys and heartbreak.

Odd that Post and Molly should both like that photo. Of course, the only other published picture of Valentine that he could remember was an old photo taken when he became a lieutenant in his Wolf days.

What Valentine guessed to be a map or recessed bookcase stood behind heavy wood cabinet doors complete with a lock. Nearest Post's desk was his set of "traveling wheels."

Valentine looked at the biggest picture on his desk: a family photo of his wife, Gail, and a pigtailed toddler. "I didn't know you had a child."

Post brushed the picture's glass with a finger, as though rearranging Gail's short, tousled hair. "We tried. It didn't work. The docs said they found some odd cell tissue on Gail's, er, cervix. Something the Kurians did to her in that Reaper mill, they think. We more or less adopted."

"Good for you."

"There's more. It's Moira Styachowski's daughter."

Valentine felt a pang. "I didn't know she had one."

"She's a pistol. Only sixteen months but we call her the Wild Thing. Jenny's all Moira. We were godparents, you see. And when that plane went down . . ."

They looked at each other in silence.

"Sunshine and rain, Val."

"I didn't know you two were that close."

"After you were hurt at the tower in Little Rock, we sort of hit it off. She found time for me while I adapted to rolling through life."

"You are rolling. A lieutenant colonel."

"I get a lot done. I'm more or less desk-bound."

Valentine wondered how much Post was leaving unsaid.

"Something to drink?" Post asked, opening a mini-fridge. "I have water, lemonade—er, wait, limeade this week—good old Southern Command root beer, and that awful cocoa—remember? I can order cof-fee. I don't keep liquor in the office. Best way not to give in to tempta-tion is to make it physically difficult."

"Any milk?"

The bushy, salt-and-pepper eyebrows went up. "Milk? Sure."

The food arrived on a tray, under shining covers, reminding Valentine of the amenities of the Outlook resort he'd visited, and partially destroyed, in the Cascades.

"Major David Valentine, drinking milk," Post said, passing a carton. "You getting an ulcer?"

"I'm surprised I don't have one. No, I acquired a taste for it out west, oddly enough. It's . . . comforting. Ulcer or no."

"You acquire one here. Anyway, East is more my area. Speaking of which, you owe me a serious Kentucky debriefing. Between you and the Green Mountain Boys, it sounds like you cracked the Moondaggers. What's left of them are back in Michigan, licking their wounds and singing laments."

"I'm not so sure it was us. They tried the 'submission to Kur's will' routine on the wrong set of locals. In Kentucky you can't just wheel into a legworm clan and drag off the sixteen-year-old girls. Those guys know how to make every shot count, and while you're driving around the hills, they're humping over them on their worms."

"Well, we're celebrating here. Those bastards painted a lot of Kansas soil red. We call the area west of Olathe the Bone Plain now."

Valentine remembered all the little towns he'd seen, crossing that area with Duvalier. Strange that the Kurians would shed so much blood. Living heartbeats were wealth to them.

They talked and ate. Post impressed Valentine all over again with his knowledge of Kentucky. And Valentine was grateful to forget about the wheelchair.

"Did Lehman give you the bad news?" Post asked.

"What's that?"

"Javelin plus the operation against the Rio Grande Valley. Southern Command is probably going to pull in its horns for a while. No more offensives. It's all about 'consolidation' and 'defensible resolution' these days. *We've won our ramparts back, let's be sure they never fall again,* and all that. We're going back on the defensive."

"That doesn't do much good for those poor souls outside the walls," Valentine said.

"We tried our damnedest. You should see all the workshops. There are more tires and artificial limbs than shoe soles. You remember Tancredi, from the Hill? He's there. He's got it worse than me—he's wearing a colostomy bag. Our generation's used up. I think younger, stronger bodies will have to see the rest through. We need a rest. You need a rest."

Valentine admitted that. He was so very tired. He didn't mind the stress of fights like that one against Blitty Easy's Crew. You aimed and shot, lived or died. It was being responsible for the lives and deaths of the men under you that wore your nerves raw.

Valentine was begining to think he wasn't cut out for that kind of responsibility. But then, if he didn't do it, you never knew who might take the controls. If you were lucky, someone like Colonel Seng or Captain LeHavre. But men like General Martinez rose farther and faster.

He covered the noisy silence with a sip of milk.

Post waggled a pen between his fingers. Optical illusion gave it a rubbery flexibility. The pen stopped. He gave the old turning-key signal Valentine remembered from their days conspiring together on the *Thunderbolt*. Valentine rose and closed the office door.

"I'm probably breaking enough rules to merit a court-martial here, Val. They've got you on the books as militia, sure, but that's about the same as civilian under our regs."

Valentine shrugged. He'd let go of the career long ago. He enjoyed the freedom of being outside the normal chain of command.

"A friend brought in your report, and I made a temporary copy and read it first thing. All these proposals of yours about aid to those ex-Quislings out of Evansville and eastern Kentucky? It's not going to fly. I doubt it'll even hatch, to tell you the truth. We're about to undergo a 'reallocation of priorities.' As far as Southern Command is concerned, Javelin was a disaster, and the less said and done about what's going on on the other side of the Mississippi, the better."

Lehman had given him the same impression, if not so directly worded.

Valentine shrugged. "We've friends in the legworm clans. We can operate as guerrillas. I'm only looking for a gesture of support. Some gear, boots, and a few boonies to train the men."

Southern Command's trainers of insurgent or counterinsurgent forces no longer wore the old US Army green berets. They'd taken to simple boonie hats, usually dressed up with a brown duck feather for NCOs, a larger eagle quill for officers.

"Not my area. I'd say take it to your friend in special ops, Colonel Lambert, but she's under a cloud right now. Investigation pending court-martial. Gross neglect of duty—Martinez is making her the scapegoat for Javelin. That giant staff of his has quite a few Jaggers."

Jaggers were Southern Command's military lawyers.

"Any more good news?"

Post spun, tossed his sandwich wrapper in the regular garbage pail. Security refuse went into a locked box with a slot at the top. "Lots. Well, not so much good as puzzling. We're getting odd reports from the underground, both in the Northwest Ordnance up in Ohio and the Georgia Control—they're very influential in Tennessee."

"I don't know much about the Georgia Control, other than that it's based in Atlanta. They make some great guns. Our guys will carry Atlanta Gunworks rifles if they get a chance to pick one up. Remember those Type Threes?"

Post nodded. "Good guns. 'A state run along corporate lines' is the best way to describe Georgia Control. Every human a Kurian owns is a share. Get enough shares and you get on the board of directors. Here's the odd feature: They let people buy shares too. By people, I mean brass ring holders, so I use the term loosely."

Valentine had to fight the urge to touch the spot on his sternum where his own brass ring hung from its simple chain. "I picked one up a couple years back. It comes in handy."

Post chewed on his lower lip. "Oh, yeah. Well, you know what I mean. Anyone who's served in the Coastal Marines is half alligator anyway.

"But back to the chatter our ears are picking up. Here's a helluva tidbit for you: Our old friend Consul Solon's on the Georgia Control board of directors. Would you believe it? Five years ago he's running for his life with Southern Command howling at his heels and half the Kurian Order wanting to see him dead for fucking up the conquest of the Trans-Mississippi, and damned if he doesn't wash up on a feather bed. The guy's half mercury and half Ralvan Fontainbleu."

Valentine chuckled. Fontainbleu was a nefarious importer/exporter on *Noonside Passions*, the Kurian Zone's popular soap opera. Valentine never did get the soap part, but operatic it was. Fontainbleu ruined marriages and businesses and sent more than one good man or woman to the Reapers. Oddly enough the drama was fairly open and aboveboard about the nature of the Kurian Order, though it towed the Church line about *trimming the sick branch and plucking the bad seed*. Fontainbleu was the particular nemesis of Brother Fairmind, the boxing New Universal Church collar who wasn't above busting a few heads to keep his flock on the straight and narrow. Valentine hadn't seen an episode since he returned from the Cascades—odd how he could still remember characters and their plots, relationships, and alliances. The desire to check up on the story plucked at him like a bad habit.

Back to Post.

"I had a feeling we hadn't heard the last of former consul Solon. What are the underground reports?"

"Scattered stuff. You'd think with Kentucky in turmoil the Kur would be grabbing pieces off of Ohio and Tennessee, guarding bridges and invasion routes, putting extra troops into the rail arteries north through Lexington and Louisville. But it's just not happening. To the north, the Ordnance has called up some reserves and shifted troops to support Louisville or maybe move west to hit your group at Evansville. But as for the usual apparatus of the Kurian Order, we're getting word of churchmen leaving, railroad support people pulling out. . . . If anything, they've pulled back from the clans, like they're a red-hot stove or something."

"Their troops in Evansville revolted. Maybe they're afraid the infection will spread."

"I'd like your opinion on that. What's Kentucky like now? Every legworm rider who can shoulder a gun shooting at the Kurian Order?"

"Nothing like that. The Moondaggers came through and just tore up Kentucky and hauled off any girl they could grab between fifteen and thirty. Really stirred the locals up. The place is in flux now; hard to say which way it'll go. They might just revert to their old semi-independence, as long as the Kurians don't aggravate the situation."

Post knitted his fingers. "We were hoping the Control was pulling back to more defensible positions and assuming there's a new Freehold being born."

"I don't think much will happen until spring," Valentine said. "That's the rhythm of the legworm clans. They settle in close to their worms for the winter until the eggs hatch."

Post nodded. "I wish I had more. You know the underground. They have to be very, very careful. What they get me is good; there's just so little of it. Kurian agents are—"

"Dangerous," Valentine said, rubbing his uneven jaw. The fracture hadn't healed right. A reminder of his encounter with a Kurian agent working for the Northwest Ordnance when he'd found Post's wife in a Reaper factory called Xanadu.

"Yeah," Post agreed. "I wonder how many we have in this headquarters. We tend to win the stand-up fights. Yet more often than not, they figure out a way to make it seem like a loss. Walk down the street in Little Rock—"

"And one out of two people will agree that Texas and Oklahoma were defeats," Valentine said. He'd heard about the famous *Clarion* war poll just after the Kansas operation, repeated endlessly in articles and opinion columns since. That had been the last operation he and Post had shared—a blazing offensive that tripled the size of the old Ozark Free Territory. But it just gave the *Clarion* more cities to report bad news from. "So what do you think I should do?"

"Get as many as you can back across the Mississippi," Post said. "We can use them here."

"And leave the legworm clans hanging? They threw in with us in Javelin."

"They might be all right. The Kurian Order needs that legworm meat for protein powder and cans of WHAM."

They exchanged grimaces. They'd both eaten their shares of WHAM rolls in the Coastal Marines. WHAM was a canned "meat product" produced in Alabama, filled out with bean paste, and sweetened with an uninspiring barbecue sauce to hide the tasteless, chewy nature of legworm flesh. *Three tastes in one!,* the cans proclaimed. The joke with WHAM is you got three chews before the flavor dissipated and you were left with a mouthful of something about as succulent and appealing as week-worn long johns. It went through the digestive system like a twenty-mule-team sled. *Three chomps and run,* the cook on the old *Thunderbolt* used to recommend.

It was a staple of Kurian work camps and military columns operating far from their usual supply hubs.

"There has to be some good news," Valentine said.

"Full list and details, or just bullet points?"

Valentine poured some more milk. "I need cheering up. Give me the full list," Valentine said.

"I won sixty bucks this week at poker," Post said. "It's a short list."

Valentine tossed back the rest of the glass of milk. "I think you're right about that ulcer."

Post's advice was absolutely correct. Javelin hadn't worked. It hadn't died; in a way it had won, dealing a deathblow to the vicious Moondaggers. But it hadn't worked out as planned. Give it up and move on, the way you folded when you drew into a promising poker hand and came up with nothing.

Except the pieces were scattered across Kentucky along with his bit of ear, and they included a big, hairy Golden One named Ahn-Kha; Tikka, brave and lusty and vital; and the former Quislings who'd put their lives and the lives of their families into jeopardy by switching sides. Southern Command had run up a big bar tab in blood.

The next day Valentine sat through a second series of debriefings with Southern Command personnel and civilians whose professional interests included the function and capabilities of the Kurian Order. He was questioned about political conditions of the legworm tribes and the organization and equipment of the Moondaggers. He even had to give a rough estimate of the population of Kentucky and the Appalachian towns and villages he'd seen.

He had to watch his words about the Kurian manipulation of Javelin's COs through a mutt they'd picked up named Red Dog, the strange doubt and lassitude that temporarily seized even as aggressive a woman as Colonel Bloom, who was back with what was left of Javelin in Kentucky just south of Evansville. It sounded too fantastic to be true, but he did his best to convince them.

Finally, a researcher from the Miskatonic queried him again about the flying Reaper he'd seen.

"You sure it wasn't a gargoyle?" she said as Valentine sorted through sketches and photographs. They had one sketch and one blurry, grainy night photo of something that resembled what he'd seen. She had the air of someone used to talking to soldiers who'd seen bogeymen on lonely watches.

It had been wearying, answering questions from people who weren't interested in his answers unless they fit in with the opinions they'd had when they sat down in the tube-steel office chairs. Valentine let loose. "I've seen gargoyles, alive and dead. They're strong and graceful, like a vulture. This was more spindly and awkward. It reminded me of a pelican or a crane taking off. And it wasn't a harpy either. I've seen plenty of those snaggletooths up close."

"Yes, I know." Valentine thought he recognized his thick Miskatonic file in front of her.

"So do you have a theory?" he demanded.

"The Kurians made Reapers by modifying human genetic code. They could have done the same with a gargoyle."

All very interesting, but he wanted to be back with his command.

His last stop on his tour of headquarters was Operations Support. General Lehman had come through with logistics: There was a barge on the Arkansas river being loaded with supplies for his new recruits and to replace the most vital matériel used up in the retreat across Kentucky. Valentine would accompany it back to Kentucky.

He picked up mail—presorted for the survivors of Javelin. Valentine wondered what happened to the sad little bundles of letters to dead men and women.

The mail had been vacuum-wrapped in plastic to protect it from the elements, but it still took up a lot of room, especially since the locals used all manner of paper for their correspondence. The mail office had a variety of bags and packs for the convenience of ad hoc couriers such as himself, and Valentine just grabbed the biggest shoulder bag he could find. Judging from the waterproof lining and compartments, it might have once been meant to hold diving or snorkel gear.

He made a trip to the PX and picked up some odds and ends: Duvalier's favorite talc, a bottle of extra-strength aspirin for Patel, and a couple of fifty-count boxes of inexpensive knit gloves. If there was one thing Valentine had learned over the years of commanding men in bad weather, it was that they lost their gloves, especially in action. He liked carrying spares to hand out.

Valentine needed peace, quiet, time to think. He caught an electric shuttle and wandered into Jonesboro and found a café by the train station—a family-owned grill with three gold stars in the window. He learned from photos and boxed decorations inside that they'd lost two sons and a daughter to the Cause.

He pleased the owners by ordering eggs accompanied by the biggest steak on the menu rather than the Southern Command subsidized "pan lunch." The steak was sizable and tough, but his appetite didn't mind, and the cook had worked wonders with the sautéed onions. The young waitress—very young waitress, make that; only a teenager would wait tables in heeled sandals—chatted with him expertly. Almost too expertly, because he didn't know any of the local militia outfits, and his equivocal answers made her wrinkle her trifle of a nose. How many single, lonely young uniformed men did she wait on in a month? He tried not to stare as she sashayed back and forth with iced tea in one hand and coffee in the other.

Whether she was family or no, it would be unseemly to ogle the help under the eye of the mother at the register clucking over her regulars like a hen and the muscular father behind the grill. He couldn't think with her friendly pats on the back of his shoulder as she refilled his iced tea, so he paid his bill—and left an overlarge tip.

The little park in front of the courthouse beckoned, and he was about to take a bench and read his mail when he heard faint singing. He followed the sound to a church where a children's choir was rehearsing and grabbed a pew at the back. Women and a few men sewed or knit while their kids screeched through the Christmas hymns.

Valentine watched the kids for a few minutes. Typical Free Territory youth, no two pairs of jeans matching in color or wear, rail thin and tanned from harvest work or a thousand and one odd jobs. You grew up fast here on the borderlands. So different from the smoothed, polished, uniformed children of the elite of the Kurian Zones, with their New Universal Church regulation haircuts and backpacks, or the wary ragamuffins of the "productives."

The boys were trying to throw one another off-tune by surreptitiously stomping one another's insteps or making farting noises with their armpits in time with the music; the girls were stifling giggles or throwing elbows in response to yanked ponytails.

The frazzled choral director finally issued a time-out to two boys.

Valentine thought better on his feet, so he remained standing at the back of the church, shifting weight from one foot to the other in time to the music like a tired metronome.

Pull out or go all in for Kentucky? Pull out or go all in for Kentucky? Pull out or go all in for Kentucky?

Valentine spent an evening enjoying a mock–Thanksgiving dinner with William Post and his wife, Gail. She looked strained by Valentine's presence—or perhaps it was the effort involved in cooking a turkey with the sides.

Jenny resembled her mother, white-haired and delicate-skinned. Maybe Valentine's imagination was overworked, but she crinkled her eyes just like Post when she smiled. The little three-year-old had two speeds, flank and full stop.

She was shy and wary around Valentine, standing in the protective arch of Post's legs, but she ate as though there was a little Bear blood in her.

The two old shipmates talked long after Valentine cleared the dishes away, Post had sorted and stored the leftovers, and Gail and Jenny went to bed. Valentine told the whole story of Javelin's trek across Kentucky, the sudden betrayal in the Virginia coal country, the Moondaggers and the strange lassitude of first Colonel Jolla and then Cleveland Bloom. He described the victory at Evansville, where the populace had successfully revolted, thinking that deliverance was at hand.

Valentine chuckled. "The underground was so used to parsing the Kurian newspapers and bulletins, assuming that the opposite of whatever was being reported was true, that they took all the stories about a defeated army being hounded across Kentucky to mean it was a victorious march along the Ohio. When the Kurians called up whomever they trusted to be in the militia to guard the Moondaggers' supply lines from the Kentuckians, they acted."

A cold rain started down, leaving Valentine with an excuse to treat himself to a cab ride back to the base's visiting housing. Post asked him to spend the night, but Valentine declined, though the accommodations given a corporal of militia couldn't match up to Post's cozy ranch-style. If he spent the night, they'd just be up all the while talking, and he wanted to get back to the logistics and support people about more gear on the alleged barge.

The "cab" showed up after a long delay that Post and Valentine were able to fill with pleasant chitchat. They shook hands and Valentine turned up his collar and passed out into the cold, rainy dark.

The cab was a rather claptrap three-wheeled vehicle, a glorified motorbike under a golf-cart awning that had an odd tri-seat: a forward-facing one for the driver, and two bucket seats like saddlebags perched just behind. The rear wheels were extended to support the awning and stabilize the vehicle. They reminded Valentine of a child's training wheels.

Valentine buckled himself in rather dubiously, wishing Post had offered him a drink to fortify himself against the cold rain. Another soldier, a corporal, slouched in the seat with his back to Valentine, his backpack on his lap and clutching the seat belt white-knuckled as though his life depended on it.

"Don't mind sharing, do you now, milly?" the driver asked.

"No. Of course not."

He gunned the engine, and it picked up speed like a tricycle going down a gentle grade. Valentine wondered why the other passenger was nervous about a ride you could hop off a few seconds before an accident.

"Of course you don't mind. Cheaper for both; gotta save fuel and rubber. Speaking of rubber, if you've a mind to expend one in service, I know a house—"

"No, thanks."

"I'm taking the other corp. It's right on the way."

That accounted for the nervousness. Worried somebody he knew would spot him. The awning wasn't like a backseat you could slump down into and hide. "Bit tired, thanks."

"Suit yourself. It's clean and cheap. Only thing you'll go back to the wife with is a bangover."

"A what?"

"Like a hangover, only your cock's sore instead of your head."

Valentine wondered what percentage the house gave the cabbie.

They pulled up to the house, a big old brick foursquare in the older part of town. Most of the houses here were vacant, stripped skeletons with glass and wiring removed, metal taken right down to the door hinges. The one remaining had either been under constant occupancy or been restored—Valentine couldn't tell which in the dark. It had a pair of friendly red-tinted lights illuminating the porch. Candles flickered from behind drawn curtains.

Seemed a popular place: A party of four was just leaving—

Valentine felt a sharp tug and his windpipe closed up. He realized a rope had been looped around his throat, and he was jerked out of the seat backward.

A quick look at looming figures framed frostily against the red porch light of the house. They had on ghoulish rubber Halloween masks. Then the ground hit him, hard.

The tallest and heaviest kicked him hard in the stomach, and Valentine bent like a closing bear trap around his neck. He opened his mouth to bite, but someone hauled at the rope around his neck, pulling his head away hard.

"David Valentine. You murderous, traitorous bastard. Been looking forward to this meeting," one of the masked men said.

"You hauled my little brother all the way across Kentucky to get him killed," another kicker put in.

Something struck him hard on the kidneys with a crack. "Few more officers like you and the Kur won't need no army."

Valentine roared back an obscenity and tried to get his hands up to fight the rope pulling his neck, but two of the attackers closed, each taking an arm above and below the elbow.

"All your idea. You and that dumb bitch from headquarters," an accuser continued.

"Cuff him good—he's slippery," someone with a deep voice advised from the darkness. He was too far away be delivering punches and kicks.

Or maybe his vision was going and it just seemed as though the voice was coming from a great distance. There were painful stars dancing in his vision like a faerie circus. Valentine felt kicks that might have just as well been blows from baseball bats, so hard were the assailants' boots.

"You've made enemies, Valentine. Now it's time to settle up."

The rain stung; it must be washing blood into his eyes.

"We don't like criminals walking our streets, bold as black."

They took turns punching him in the face and stomach.

"Grog lover!"

"Renegade."

"Murderer!" The last was a crackling shriek.

They added a few more epithets about his mother and the long line of dubious species that might have served as father. Valentine's mad brain noted that they sounded like men too young to have ever known her.

"You bring any of those redlegs into our good clean land, they'll get the same. Be sure of that."

"Hell, they'll get hung."

"Like you're gonna be—*huck-huck-huck!*"

"C'mon—let's string this fugitive from justice up."

They dragged Valentine by the rope around his neck. He strained, but the handcuffs on his wrists at his back held firm.

The old street in Jonesboro had attractive oaks and elms shading the pedestrians from summer heat. Their thick, spreading boughs made a convenient gibbet above the sidewalk and lane.

The noose hauled Valentine to his feet by his neck. His skin flamed. Valentine knotted the muscles in his neck, fought instinct, kicking as he strangled. The rope wasn't so bad; it was the blood in his eyes that stung.

Vaguely, he sensed that something was thumping against his chest. An object had been hung around his neck about the size and weight of a hardcover book.

One of them wound up, threw, and bounced a chunk of broken pavement off his face.

"Murderer!"

"Justice is a dish best served cold," that deep voice said again.

They piled into the little putt-putt and a swaying, aged jeep that roared out of the alley behind the red-lit house. With that, they departed into the rain. Valentine, spinning from the rope end as he kicked, bizarrely noted that they left at a safe speed that couldn't have topped fifteen miles an hour, thanks to the odd little three-wheeler.

Valentine, increasingly foggy with his vision red and the sound of the rainfall suddenly as distant as faint waterfall, looked up at the rope hanging over the branch.

For all their viciousness with boot tips and flung asphalt, they didn't know squat about hanging a man. And he'd purposely kicked with knees bent, to give them the illusion that he was farther off the ground than he actually was.

He changed the direction of his swing, always aiming toward the trunk of the tree. The rope, which his assailants had just thrown over the thick limb, moved closer to the trunk. He bought another precious six inches. Six inches closer to the trunk, six less inches for the rope to extend to the horizontal branch, six inches closer to the ground. With one more swing, he extended his legs as far as they'd go, reaching with his tiptoes, and touched wet earth.

The auld sod of Arkansas had never felt more lovely.

Valentine caught his breath, balancing precariously on tiptoe, and found the energy to give himself more slack. He got the rope between his teeth and began to chew. Here the wet didn't aid him.

His blood-smeared teeth thinned the rope. He gathered slack from his side and pulled. He extracted himself from the well-tied noose and slumped against the tree. There was a wooden placard hung around his neck, but he was too tired to read it.

Even with the rope—standard Southern Command camp stuff, useful for everything from securing a horse to tying cargo onto the hood of a vehicle—removed from his neck, Valentine could still feel the burn of it. He swept his hand through the gutter, picked up some cold wet leaves, and pressed them to the rope burn.

They might come back to check on his body. He lurched to his feet and staggered in the direction of the door of the bordello.

He missed the porch stairs, rotated against the rail until he tripped over them, and went up to the door on hands and knees. Blood dripped and dotted the dry wood under the porch roof.

His head thumped into the doorjamb.

"He's made it," someone from within called.

He didn't have to knock again; the door opened for him. He had a brief flash of hair and lace and satin before he gave way, collapsing on a coconut-coir mat and some kind of fringed runner covering shining hardwood floors.

"He's bleeding on the rug. Get some seltzer."

"Lord, he's not going to die on us, is he?" a Texas accent gasped.

"Uhhhh," Valentine managed, which he hoped she'd interpret as a "no."

"What if they come back to check on him?"

"They told us not to come out. Didn't say anything about us not letting him in," another woman put in. "He made it in under his own power."

"They still might do violence, if'n we help him. Toss him in the alley."

"Hush up and quit worrying while we got a man bleeding," an authoritative female voice said. "I've never refused a gentleman hospitality in my life and I'm too old to change now. You all can blame me if they do come back. Don't think varmints like that have the guts, though, or they would have watched till he was cold. Alice-Ann, iodine and bandages."

Valentine blinked the blood out of his eyes. The women were of a variety of ages and skin hues and tints of hair, mostly blond or red. He counted six, including what looked and sounded like the madam—or maybe she just catered to the certain tastes in experienced flesh. A gaunt old man moved around, pulling down extra shades and closing decorative shutters with a trembling arm. The doorman? He didn't look like he could bounce a Boy Scout from the establishment.

"Before you throw me out, could you please get these handcuffs off? If you don't have a key, I'll show you how to do it with a nail." The speech exhausted him more than the trip to the door. He put his head down to catch his breath and managed to roll over on his pack.

"Are you kidding?" a fleshy older woman said, showing a brilliant set of perfectly aligned teeth. "In this place? Standard equipment, hunneh."

They helped him up and took him back to the kitchen and performed first aid at the sink. Valentine embraced the sting of the iodine. It proved he was alive.

When he had stopped the flow of blood from face and lip, he looked around the homey kitchen. Baskets of onions and potatoes lined the floor, rows of preserved vegetables filled racks in the kitchen, and bulbs of garlic and twisted gingerroot hung from the ceiling, fall's bounty ready for winter.

The madam introduced herself as Ladyfair, though whether this was a first name, a last name, a stage name, or a title, she didn't say.

"There's a little washroom just off the back door, next to the laundry room and past the hanging unmentionables," the madam said as Valentine rubbed his free wrist. "You just make use of it. There's a flexible shower hose. Just the thing for a fast cleanup."

Valentine, feeling a little more human, realized he stank. An unpleasant presence was making itself felt in his underwear.

It's not just an expression. They really kicked the shit out of me, Valentine thought.

When he came out, a towel around his waist, he glanced into the front parlor and noticed that the porch light had been turned off. A thick head of hair looked through the heavy curtains from the edge of a window.

Valentine rubbed his sore neck. The attempted hanging wasn't so bad; the pain was from the hard jerks from the rope during the fight. He wondered if he had whiplash.

They presented him an old pair of generously cut khaki trousers and some serviceable briefs. "We have a little of just about everything hanging in the basement," Ladyfair said. "You'd think we were a community theater. We do everything but produce Shakespeare."

"I'm surprised you haven't. The Bard had his bawdy side."

"You just come back now when you're up to it. You seem like a better quality than that rabble, and a smart business is always looking to improve the clientele. Seeing as that disgrace took place right on my front lawn, I'll offer you a freebie when you're feeling more recovered."

"I appreciate you taking me into your house."

"Oh, it's not my house. We're a limited liability partnership, young man. Quite a few make that mistake, though. I suppose I'm the old lead mare of the house, though I'm still very much involved on the cash generation side of things. There are some that have learned to appreciate a woman without teeth."

She winked.

Bordello co-ops. What will they think of next? Valentine thought.

"Then I'm grateful to the whole partnership. Novel idea."

"Not really. I'm surprised. Your necktie party insisted you were a fan of professional gentlemen's entertainment. Said you used to visit a place called the Blue Dome. They said it was only fitting that you get hung up on the doorstep of a whorehouse, so to speak."

Valentine shrugged. "I don't suppose you could give me their names," Valentine said.

"You'll remember we haven't even asked yours."

"David will do," Valentine said.

"Well, David, if you want names, nobody gives a real name here. You should really hurry on. Mr. C, our banker and lawyer, is removing the rope from the tree, but if they come back . . ."

"Were they Southern Command?"

"They were in civilian attire but had fabric belts with those clever little buckles our heroes in uniform wear. One of them was drinking and kept talking about General Martinez and about how things are going to change for the better once he gets in, so I suspect at least some of them were."

A prettyish young "entertainer" came into the kitchen with the placard that had been hung about his neck. "You want this as evidence?" she asked with a strong Texas accent.

It was an ordinary wood bar tray, much ringed and weathered though carefully cleaned, with black letters burned into it:

**DAVID VALENTINE,
CONDAMNED FUGITIVE
LAW AND ORDER IS
COMING BACK TO THE UFR**

Whoever had done it hadn't bothered to pencil out the letters before setting to work with the wood burner. "Back to the UFR" was rather crowded together.

"David Valentine," Ladyfair said. "It sounds rather dashing and romantic, as though you should be riding around in a cloak, holding up carriages with a pistol and donating the booty to the peasantry."

Valentine probed his teeth, checking for loose gum line or a broken crown.

"I am fond of novels when idling in bed or tub."

Valentine wanted to keep the sign just for the interesting spelling of "condemned." Might make an interesting memento on his office door. Maybe they'd summed up his life better than whoever would write his eventual obituary—if he died where people noticed such things. Condamned.

"I've troubled you enough," Valentine said. "I suppose you've lost a night's business because of this. If you'll let me know what the clothes and bandages cost, I'll come by tomorrow to repay you what I can."

"Nonsense. Here's a card. If you do find those rowdies, give us a jingle. We'll give them a little law and order when we testify in court. Dumb sons of bitches didn't wear those masks when they were in our parlor waiting on you. I'd like to be able to point them out in court."

"Cheap too," the young Texan said. "Kept complaining about not being able to run a tab for their whiskey."

Valentine inspected his reflection in a little mirror next to the kitchen doorjamb. He'd probably have some horizontal scarring on the right side of his face to balance out the long vertical bullet furrow long since faded on his left. The asphalt had been sharp.

Well, he didn't have much keeping him in the United Free Republics anyway. Besides, he had mail to get back to Kentucky.

He might as well abandon the guise of a militia corporal; it wasn't doing him any good. He'd return to Kentucky in the leathers of the Bulletproof clan.

Three

Backwater Pete's on the Arkansas River, the third week of November: Pete's is the informal abode of the river rats—the brown-water transportation flotilla of Southern Command and the sailors of the quick-hitting, quick-running motorboats of the Skeeter Fleet.

Pete himself is long dead, killed during Solon's tenure for theft of Trans-Mississippi Combat Corps property and smuggling supplies to "guerrilla bands" during the Kurian occupation. His widow followed him to the Reaper-gibbet soon after (hardly a word had to be changed in the indictment or the sentence), but his brother survived Solon's occupation of Arkansas and rebuilt the old riverside bar.

Built of ancient gray cypress beams the color of a January cloudbank, part dockyard, part trading post, part gin mill, and part museum, Backwater Pete's is an institution. A new brown-water sailor who first sees the fireflies of tracer being exchanged at high speed while bouncing down the Mississippi comes to Pete's for his first drink as a real riverman. Newly appointed boat commanders and barge captains fete their crews there, and retiring master mechanics say their farewells beneath the pink and lavender paper lanterns and sensually shaped neon.

The bar is decorated with grainy pictures of boat crews as well as old Sports Illustrated *swimsuit models and* Playboy *centerfolds, immortal icons of wet-haired desire. Wooden models of famous Southern Command river craft—mostly pleasure or sport or fishing boats and tugs converted to carry machine guns and old rapid-fire twenty- and thirty-millimeter "bush guns"—rest on a little brass-railed shelf above the bar. The traditional mirror behind the bar is more a mosaic of shards now, having been broken in so many brawls and patched together with colored glass it now resembles a peacock splattered against a wide chrome bumper.*

Most newcomers say it smells like tobacco, recycled beer, sun-baked sweat, and mud fresh from a swamp where eggs go to die. The regulars wouldn't have it any other way.

On that warm night of a quick-fading autumn the bar saw a stranger. His clothing set him apart immediately: thick blue-black leathers that looked too oddly pebbled for cowhide but not stiff as snakeskin. He wore a small machine-gun pistol in a big soft holster across his midriff and a straight-bladed, sharkskin-handled sword across his back. Vambraces like a motorcycle rider might wear guard his arms, but odd bulges running up from the wrist suggest they might be offensive as well as defensive.

For all the weaponry, the high military boots with their lace guards snapped over, the scar descending from his right eye and fresh bruising to the left, and the long black hair tied back so it's out of his eyes, he doesn't look like he's after a fight. For a start, he looks tired: the haggard, leeched-out look of a man who has undergone prolonged stress. Then there's the odd hang of his jaw-line. A humorous tip to his jaw gives him a slight, good-humored smile.

"Cat. Or maybe a Bear," one of the grizzled river rats says to his companions dressed in more typical attire of soft white trousers and light canvas jackets, sockless in their rubber-soled boat shoes. They don't make room for the newcomer at the bar, river rats being as fiercely territorial as any Dumpster-diving rodents.

"What'll ye think a Hunter wants here?" a man with a patchy youth's beard asks.

"Someone to push up into a length of trouble," the oldster says, unaware of just how right he would turn out to be.

According to Southern Command tradition, Backwater Pete's served the best tequila on chipped ice in the Trans-Mississippi Free Republics. Not being an expert on tequila, Valentine opted for rum and tea, a concoction he'd grown used to during his sojourn in a Kurian uniform with the Coastal Marines.

The rum was of good quality, all the way from Jamaica. Valentine reread his accumulated mail over it while his mind subconsciously absorbed the rhythms of Backwater Pete's. A man in a bar had a choice to be alone, even if he could smell the sweat and engine oil on the man next to him, and he'd dumped his six new companions at a Southern Command billet-flop.

They were all the reinforcements he was getting, and he didn't like the look of them. Hatchet men sent to decide what was worth saving and what was worth discarding, plus one young doctor and an ancient nurse.

He savored his mail like a gourmet meal. The aches and pains from last week's wounds were forgotten in the excitement of mail.

He opened the one all the way from Jamaica first, wondering what tortured route it had taken to get to the UFR. Probably landed by some friendly smugglers on the shore of Texas, probably on the same boat that brought in rum, coffee, and fabric dyes. The Dutchmen from the Southern Caribbean were good about that sort of thing.

There was a picture of Amalee, dated six months ago and stamped by Southern Command's mails in mid-October, probably on the same boat that made the rum runs. She had deep copper skin and her mother's wide, bright eyes. She would be seven now.

Seven.

Nice of Malita to write. The letter was mostly of Amalee's doings and development and included a clipping from the Kingston *Current*, describing the exploits of Jamaica's "Corsairs" off the coast of Cuba.

Nothing from Hank in school—Valentine had made a call to make sure he still was in school. He was just getting to be that age where a boy notices all the interesting ways nature arranges for girls to be put together.

Molly wrote him as well. He had three letters from her, increasingly worried as the months of last summer went by.

He found a dry piece of bar and penned her a reassuring reply.

There was one more letter to write. It had to be carefully phrased. Narcisse up in St. Louis would have to tell Blake that there wouldn't be a visit this year. He'd have to see about sending a Christmas present.

It was hard to read Blake. Valentine still didn't know if Blake had strong feelings about him one way or another. Blake was always interested in new stuff. Was a visit from "Papa" a break from his usual routine and therefore a source of happiness, or was it more?

Valentine shouldn't have been this tired. Maybe he was slowing down with age. He hadn't bounced back from the beating he took outside Ladyfair's little cooperative. Served him right for continuing to wander from office to office and warehouse to warehouse, hunting up help for Kentucky and his old stored gear and their resident ghosts and memories.

David Valentine even had the dubious honor of a trip back to Southern Command's new GHQ at Consul Solon's old executive mansion atop Big Rock Hill to plead Kentucky's case with the outgoing commander in chief. One way or another, much of Solon's late-model communications gear survived or could be easily repaired, and old "Post One" didn't lack for office space and conference rooms.

The southern half of the hilltop, the old final trenches and dugouts, had filled in and greened over since being churned to mud by big-caliber rounds. The consular golf course was back in operation, and the red brick of the former college a beehive of clerks and radio techs. New, giant radio masts had sprouted both on Big Rock Hill.

They had stared at his cuts and bruises and listened politely but briefly. A few made noises about thanking him for his efforts in Kentucky. He endured another quick debriefing where he told the same story he told in Jonesboro with the same outcome.

It was time to take them back to Kentucky.

His efforts in Jonesboro and Little Rock hadn't been completely in vain. They'd given him the hatchet man team of "replacement" NCOs and a shipping manifest of matériel being loaded on a barge, though how Southern Command thought he'd get a barge all the way up the Ohio to Evansville was the sort of detail they had been vague on. When he asked, they said someone was "working the problem" and he could meet the barge at Backwater Pete's.

The manifest looked promising. Uniforms, or at least fabric to make uniforms. Cases of weapons. Explosives. Even recreational and educational materials for the new recruits.

Even more reassuring was the vessel and captain listed on the manifest. Whichever logistics officer they'd put in charge of "working the problem" knew his or her business.

Valentine had last seen the barge tied up on the Arkansas when Consul Solon was still running the Trans-Mississippi from his network of numbered posts. Valentine led his six new charges to the foot of the gangway and called up to the anchor watch.

"Permission to book a travel warrant?" Valentine asked the rumpled deckhand on watch, rubbing sleep from his eyes. The deckhand sauntered off to get the captain.

Captain Mantilla may have changed since Valentine last met him during Solon's brief hold on the Ozarks and Ouachitas. Valentine's memory of the man had diffused like a rewetted watercolor. But as the captain approached, Valentine noted the mat of hair and the quick, flashing glances that weren't suspicious, just indicative of a busy man with a lot on his mind—yes, it was him.

He stood there in gray overalls bearing a camouflage moiré of grease stains and a formerly white but now weather-beaten ivory skipper hat riding the back of his head as though bored with the job. Thick bodied with a bit of a pot, he still looked like a fireplug with a seven-day beard and a couple arms hanging off it.

"Have to ask my passenger," Mantilla said. "I expect she won't mind."

"Passenger? Since when do passengers give orders to captains?"

"Her charter." Mantilla jerked his thumb over his shoulder.

Valentine was shocked to see Dots—Colonel Lambert, officially—looking lost in a big patrol coat and a hat with the earflaps turned down, and fiddling with her dunnage as if deciding what to have handy and what to store below.

Valentine wondered if she was traveling not so much incognito as low-key, a simple officer looking for transport. Probably on her way to meet a Cat and a Bear team looking to raise hell in Mississippi.

"Sir," Valentine said, saluting. "I'm told this boat's headed for the Mississippi."

"Valentine!" Lambert said, brightening. "Not going back already?"

"Afraid so. Javelin needs these replacements. You'll take priority, of course. I'll go on once he's dropped you downriver."

Lambert cocked her head. Her usual brisk manner was gone; she looked like a traveler who'd missed a bus. Little fissures explored her formerly vital, cheerleader-smooth skin from the corners of her eyes and mouth.

"I think we're at cross purposes, Major. I'm joining your command. I'm headed to Evansville as well."

"Is there a new . . . operation?" Stupid words—she no doubt had to keep quiet.

"No, I'm joining up with what's left of Javelin. I suppose you haven't heard. My whole command was moved under one of Martinez's staffers. They were going to stick me in an office routing communications where the only decision I'd ever make is what to have for lunch. So . . . I volunteered to go to Kentucky."

"As what? If you don't mind my asking."

"I don't mind at all. They need a new full colonel out there to act as CO. No bright young officer wanted the job—Javelin's a dead end as far as Southern Command is concerned. I'm not so sure. Thought I'd be the one to be out there for a change."

Lambert had run a sort of special forces unit dedicated to helping allies in the Cause. Kentucky was the second trip she'd sent him on, and whatever had gone wrong in the wooded passes of the Appalachians wasn't her fault. "You've nothing to prove to any of us."

"The coffee on this tub's surprisingly good," she said. "I think the good captain has connections in every trading port on the river. Let's hit the galley and get some. Tell me more about these Quisling volunteers you recruited."

"I have some support staff looking for passage too. And mail, of course," he said, patting his oversized shoulder bag.

"That bag's a heavy responsibility," she said. "If the captain doesn't mind cramming a few more in, I won't object."

They asked Mantilla, who shrugged. "Fuck it. Cook will be busier, is all. I'm fine with it, ma'am," Mantilla said. "Your people do their own laundry and use their own bedding. I'm not running a cruise ship."

Valentine joined the chorus of "thank you, Captain's" from his charges.

"All you headed up to Evansville?" the sleepy mate asked.

"Looks that way," Valentine said.

"Tough run. Not many friends on the Ohio."

"Maybe I'll make some new ones," Mantilla said.

Last-minute stores of fresh vegetables came on board, and with no more ceremony than it took to undo mooring lines, the tug pushed the barge downriver into the narrow, dredged channel.

Valentine now knew why Mantilla's crew were somnambulists when they tied up. They worked like furies when the boat was in motion: throwing sacks of mail and unloading crates to shore boats along the run practically without stopping, nursing the engines, hosing wind-blown fall leaves off the decks, cooking and snatching food, and, most important, checking depth with a pole on the doubtful river. Mantilla's barge and tug was big for the Arkansas. Most of the river traffic was in long, narrow flatboats with farting little motors that sounded like fishing trollers compared to the tug's hearty diesels.

Valentine, feeling guilty for just watching everyone work, eating of their galley but toiling not for his bread, checked the matériel Southern Command had scraped up for his operation in Kentucky.

As usual, the promises on paper didn't live up to what waited in the barge.

There was plenty of material for uniforms: soft gray felt in massive, industrial rolls.

"I know what this is," Lambert said. "We took a big textiles plant outside of Houston."

"We'll have to sew it ourselves."

"It's light, and it keeps you warm even when you're wet. They use it for blankets and liners."

"What's it made out of?"

"Polyester or something like it. Everyone's talking about the winter blankets that Martinez is passing out made out of this material. But they're not talking about how he acquired them."

"What's the story?"

"Stuff comes from a fairly high-tech operation—a factory with up-to-date equipment and facilities. We captured it intact outside Houston. The ownership and workers were only too happy to start cranking out material for Southern Command as their new client. General Martinez wouldn't have any of it, though. He had them work triple-shifts cranking out fabric, and then when they'd burned through their raw materials, he stamped the whole product 'Property of Southern Command' and shipped it north. Factory never got paid and owner had no money to buy more raw materials, so it's sitting empty now instead of making clothes for Texans and selling uniform liners to Southern Command. But Martinez got close to a million square yards of fabric for nothing."

The weapons were painfully familiar to him: the old single-shot lever action rifles he'd trained on long ago in the Labor Regiment. They were heavy, clunky, and didn't stand up to repeated firing well. The action tended to heat up and melt the brass casings, jamming the breech. But it was better than nothing, and it threw a big .45 rifle bullet a long way. They'd be handy for deer hunting, if nothing else.

The guns kept turning up like bad pennies in his life.

"Don't look so downcast, Valentine. Check the ammunition."

Valentine opened a padlocked crate.

"Voodoo Works?" Valentine asked, seeing the manufacturer.

"Pick one up."

Valentine knew something was different as soon as he lifted up a box of bullets. He raised an eyebrow at Lambert.

"Yes, it's Quickwood. Testing found that the .45 shell was less likely to tumble and fragment. Only a couple of thousand rounds, but if you distribute the Reaper rifles to your good shots . . ."

She didn't have anything to say about the explosives Valentine uncovered next. They'd loaded him up with what was colloquially known as Angel Food, a vanilla-colored utility explosive that was notoriously tricky to use. The combat engineers used to say working with it kept the angels busy, thus the name. You could handle or burn it without danger, but it was quick to blow when exposed to spark. Even static electricity was dangerous.

For preserved food there was a lot of WHAM. Probably captured supplies taken off of Quisling military formations and now being repatriated to its native land. The WHAM had probably logged more time in service than many of his soldiers.

As to the training materials, they were mostly workbooks on reading, writing, and arithmetic: useful to many of the lower-level workers who escaped the Kurian Order functionally illiterate but not particularly useful to his troops.

For entertainment they had cases and cases of playing cards with the classic depiction of a bicyclist.

Valentine lifted one of the boxes and opened it. Inside, the cards were wrapped up like a pack of cigarettes.

"Strip poker?" he asked Lambert.

"Stakes aren't worth it, not with your face looking like that."

They laughed.

Valentine would have found it hard to put into words to say how relieved he was Lambert was joining them in Kentucky. She was the sort of person who did a good deal without drawing attention to herself. He'd come across an old quote from one of the Prussians, von Moltke something or other, that perfectly described her: *accomplish much, remain in the background, be more than you appear.*

But had she ever stood under shellfire before? History was full of leaders who were fine organizers but couldn't face what Abraham Lincoln called the "terrible arithmetic" of sacrificing some men now to save many in the future.

To be honest with himself, Valentine had a little trouble with his sums as well.

Later that night, as he fell asleep, he felt a slight, ominous tickle in his throat.

Valentine, thick-headed and sneezing on the flatboat trip downriver with his new charges, observed that you could mark the deterioration of civilized standards the closer you drew to the Mississippi by the signs along the Arkansas' riverbank.

He liked leaning on the rail, watching the riverbank go by. Mantilla had put them all in oil-stained overalls even dirtier than his crew's and beat-up old canvas slippers with strips of rubber sewn in for traction.

"Only because it's not barefoot weather, unless it's a sunny day," one of Mantilla's crew explained.

Back in the better-served counties with functioning law enforcement, there were polite notices not to tie up or trespass, bought at some hardware store.

Farther down the river, you had hand-painted boards up.

KEEP OUT! THIS MEANS YOU!

or

I'M TOO CHEAP FOR WARNING SHOTS

Then closer still to the Mississippi, the ownership left off with writing entirely and sometimes just nailed up a skull and a pair of crossed femurs at their jetty.

They left the last of the gun position and observation posts guarding the mouth of the Arkansas River at night and turned up the wide Mississippi with all hands alert and on watch.

Mantilla's men were experts with paint and brush and stencil and flag, and within a few minutes they had transformed the old barge with Kurian running colors.

Valentine stood on the bridge, drinking the captain's excellent coffee with Mantilla. They had a shallow draft, so the captain kept close to the Kurian east side as part of his masquerade. There were monsters on the river six times as long as Mantilla's little craft.

"You should have a little honey for that cold. Honey's the best thing. Colds are a real *suka.*"

Valentine accepted some tea and honey. As usual, he was in for another surprise. The tea was rich and flavorful; it made much of the produce in Southern Command taste like herb-and-spice dust.

"That's Assam, all the way from Sri Lanka," Mantilla said.

Valentine wasn't even sure where Sri Lanka was. To change the subject, he inquired about the dangers they might face on the river, motoring right up through the border of two warring states.

"It's a sort of truce at midchannel," Mantilla said, pacing from one side of the bridge to the other on the little tug. "Nobody likes to make a fuss, sinking each other's river traffic. The sons-of-whores military vessels will chase and shoot right and left, but the coal and grain barges pass without too much trouble. Of course, the Kurian captains are smart enough to do a little trade with our little luggers; a few tons of coal or steel given up here and there for a quiet run between the Kurian Zone and the UFR is a small price to pay. The bastards would rather pay up than fall in the *schiesse* with our side."

"Chummy."

"We stay on our side; they stay on theirs. Most of the time. Your little venture into Kentucky broke the rules. Our Kurian friends can't allow that to stand, you know. They'll strike back."

"It had better be with something better than what they've used so far," Valentine said as the Mississippi unrolled like a blue-green carpet in front of the little barge. "The Moondaggers were vicious, but they weren't much in a stand-up fight against people who could shoot back."

"They were supposed to take you quietly into custody. After a few culls, the rest would be exchanged back to the UFR in return for some

captured Texas Quislings or some other property the Kurians wished
not to lose. Your little rebellion in the Ozarks is getting too big for its
britches."

"Our little rebellion. You're on our side."

"Very much so. If I speak strangely, it's only because I know of
other rebels in other places and times."

The "and times" comment put Valentine on his guard. How much
did he really know about Mantilla? What did the captain's name mean
in Spanish again? Was it a cloak or covering of some kind?

Valentine wondered how Mantilla, a river captain, knew so much
about the fighting. You'd think he'd spend his time studying depth
charts and dealing with customs clerks and patrol boat captains.

With the usual methodical lucidity he had during illness, he thought
the matter over in the glorified closet that served as his cabin. He didn't
like being played, but unless Mantilla was an unusually cruel gamester,
he didn't think he was being toyed with. Instead, the barge captain
seemed to be trying to let him in on a secret without saying so directly.

He went to bed wondering just who, or what, their captain was. If
he was, say, a Lifeweaver, why would he be doing something as exposed
and dangerous as traveling up and down the rivers of the former United
States—and perhaps into the Caribbean and beyond as well?

The other possibility was that he was a Kurian who had gone over
to the side of his estranged relatives, the Lifeweavers, to help the humans, but that made even less sense.

There was a third option. Valentine had heard rumors, long ago in
his days as a Wolf, from his old tent mate that there was supposed to be
another kind of Hunter, another caste beyond the Wolves, Cats, and
Bears. Of course, it hadn't been much more than rumor. His old tent
mate had claimed that it was something the Lifeweavers tried to effect
in humans but that didn't work out; they all went mad and were locked
up in secrecy.

Then again, Valentine had met an old resistance leader in Jamaica
who'd been modified in some way by the Lifeweavers. She'd seemed
sane enough, even if most of the rumors about her were insane. She'd
offered some insight into his future.

She'd turned out to be at least partially right.

Valentine didn't know how there could be such a thing as precogni-
tion. There were so many variables to life. He'd seen too many lives lost
by someone being a step too late or a step too early.

He quit thinking about Mantilla. As long as he got them safely to
Evansville. Or to the mouth of the Tennessee in Kentucky, even. Past
Paducah.

He woke up to gunfire.

It alarmed him for an instant. The familiar crack put him atop Big Rock Hill and running through the kettles of south-central Wisconsin and in the dust of the dry Caribbean coast of Santo Domingo and with the punishment brigade on the edge of the minefields around Seattle, not sure of which and remembering each all at once in dizzy, sick shock. Then he remembered Lambert had told him that Mantilla had said she could practice with her rifle up by Missouri bootheel territory.

He put on his boots, grabbed a piece of toast, and went up on deck to watch.

Lambert, dressed in some washed-out, sun-bleached fatigues, was firing her rifle from the seated position, looking down the scope through a scratched and hot-glued pair of safety goggles. Valentine had seen the rifle's cheap cloth case when he came aboard and wondered what she had in there. He recognized the weapon: It was one of the Atlanta Gunworks Type Threes he'd become familiar with when Consul Solon had issued them to his ad hoc group posing as Quislings on the banks of the Arkansas. They were sought-after guns in Southern Command, basically an updated version of the old United States M14.

Lambert looked like she had one rigged out for Special Operations. It had a slightly longer barrel with a flash suppressor and a fine-looking optical scope, as well as a bipod that could fold down into a front handgrip. The plastic stock had a nice little compartment for maintenance tools and a bayonet/wire cutter.

The bayonet was a handy device. It had a claw on the handle that was useful for extracting nails and the blade was useful for opening cans or creating an emergency tap in a keg.

But he knew the weight and length of the weapon all too well. Lambert, for all her determination, found it an awkwardly big weapon to handle.

She was using it to pepper pieces of driftwood, old channel markers, and washed-up debris lining the riverbank. She clanged a bullet off of what looked like an old water heater.

"You're a good shot," Valentine said.

"It's hard to be a bad one with this thing," she replied, putting her eye back to the sight and searching for a target. "I wish it wasn't so goddamn heavy, is all."

"Try mine," Valentine said, offering her his submachine gun. It was a lethal little buzz saw, with an interesting sloped design that fought barrel-rise on full-automatic fire. Perfect for someone Lambert's size. He'd carried it across Kentucky and back.

Valentine looked at the serial number on Lambert's gun. Something about the stock struck him as familiar. An extra layer of leather had been wrapped around the stock for a better fit on a big man. He'd last seen this gun outside Dallas—

"This belonged to Moira Styachowski," Valentine said.

"Yes," Lambert said flatly.

"She gave you her old Number Three?"

"No. Colonel Post gave it to me. I wanted his advice on a good field rifle. He said something about Kentuckians knowing a good long rifle for three hundred years and counting, and that if I got desperate I could probably trade it for a working truck, optics being precious in the borderlands. I am thinking about trading it, though. It's a great heavy thing."

Post knew his guns. Odd of him to give Lambert too much gun. He'd made a present to Valentine of his first .45 automatic. Valentine had lost it, of course, but had replaced it with a similar version at the first opportunity.

Lambert fired off a few bursts with the entry gun, ripping up a blackened old post for a dock missing its planking.

"That's more my size," she said.

Valentine considered a lewd comment about a small size having its advantages in ease of handling, but decided against it. Lambert wasn't a flirt and had been his superior too long for it to feel right, even as a joke.

They each fired off a pair of magazines. The Number Three wasn't quite as handy as the Steyr Scout Valentine had gone west with, but the optics were better and it had another hundred meters on the carbine. It was a weapon that could serve equally well as a sniper rifle and a battle rifle. Valentine wouldn't care to use it for house-to-house street fighting, but for the woods and hills of Kentucky it was ideal.

"Want to switch permanently?" Valentine asked. "I'd love to get my hands on an old Number Three."

"Will said to sleep with it, or you'd steal it," Lambert said.

"Unless it has sentimental—"

"I'm teasing, Valentine. Will said I should trade it if I found something better. I like your gun more. But are you willing to—"

"Only if I'm not breaking up a love triangle between you two and the rifle." Valentine instantly regretted the words. Stupid thing to say.

"I think he'd be pleased as anything if you carried it," Lambert said. "He thinks you hang the moon, you know."

"Only by standing on his shoulders. While he bled," Valentine said.

The cheery intimacy evaporated.

"Let's shoot," Lambert said.

"Ever fired a gun in battle?" Valentine asked.

"During Archangel," Lambert said. "But I don't know if it counts. Our column came under fire at night. I bailed out and started blasting away at the gun flashes with everyone else. Turned out we were shooting at our own men. No one was killed, but two of our men ended up in the hospital."

"It happens," Valentine said.

"Post said when you were young, you lost someone close by accident like that."

"True," Valentine said.

"I'm sorry; was he not supposed to talk about it? He only told me to make me feel better about that night."

"I didn't know you two were that close."

"Oh, I might as well tell you. I facilitated his adoption of Moira's daughter after her plane went down. 'Facilitated' isn't quite the word. Stole, maybe. She was supposed to go to that special school where they're bringing up trans-human children."

"Trans-human?"

"It's just an official designation for people enhanced by the Lifeweavers. You never ran into it?"

"I've been out of the communication loop for a while now."

"Of course."

"Well, it's better than subhuman," Valentine said. "I've met a few civilians who'd use that word."

He decided to change the subject.

"When did Styachowski and Post get so close? During the fight at Big Rock Hill?"

"You mean Valentine's Stand?"

"The history books don't call it that."

"She knew him from that, obviously. She met him again when he was assigned to the assessment staff. He gave a very thorough report, and . . . Moira said she had a thing for the older, fatherly-looking guys. I was a little surprised: She never said anything about an interest—Well, that's neither here nor there. But I understand the appeal. He is good-looking. I got to know Post better through her. He told me some interesting details about life in camp with General Martinez, by the way. He knew Moira and I had been close and he said he wanted me to have her gun the last time we— I mean, the last time we met."

Valentine didn't know the extent of Post's injuries that confined him to his chair, didn't know how his marriage had been put back together or under what terms. None of his business.

Lambert was blushing. Valentine couldn't ever remember seeing her blush before.

"Does Gail know . . . about Will's connection with Jenny's real mother?"

"No. Moira said they ended it after you brought Gail back. It took them a while to figure out who each of them was and who the other was in the marriage. Will told me Gail had changed a lot out there, through her experiences. But he was determined to take care of her."

Valentine decided to pry. "Who's Jenny's father?"

"I—I . . . Moira said it was a man she met after the Razors broke up."

"None of my business. I wonder if Jenny's got a little Bear in her—or a lot. Some of the Bears get very randy after a fight."

"I've heard that," Lambert said.

"Whatever Moira had in her blood might have been passed to her daughter."

Lambert opened a little gear bag and began to clean the submachine gun. Valentine did the same with his rifle.

"But Bear parents don't always pass on their tendencies, I'm told," Lambert said. "Sometimes the kid's just a little feistier than most or heals bumps and bruises faster. Also, she's a girl. Don't female Bear fetuses miscarry?"

"I was told that it's adult women who tend to have heart attacks or strokes when the Lifeweavers try to turn them Bear," Valentine said. "I don't know about the children."

"Southern Command is still doing that breeding program. Because there are so few Lifeweavers."

Valentine nodded. He'd been part of that breeding program. Strange stuff. "I haven't spoken to one in ages."

"Knowingly, anyway. They're operating in secret these days, with so many Kurian agents around."

Boat trips leave you a lot of time to think. As Valentine played with his new rifle's butt and balance, trying to decide if he should add another inch to the butt, he thought about his friend.

Old Will. Well, not that old; he had a decade on Valentine at most, whatever his personnel file said. In the Kurian Zone you always falsified your birth date whenever you had the chance. Valentine pictured Styachowski running her quick fingers through Post's salt-and-pepper hair. So there was some hot blood beneath that cool countenance.

"Patrol boat signaling to board," the ship's speaker announced, breaking in on his thoughts.

Mantilla had warned all of them to expect this. The Southern Command soldiers were to go down and wait in the engine room.

Valentine filed down behind the rest of the hatchet men, new rifle and an ammunition vest ready—just in case.

Lambert hurried to catch up to him. "Mantilla wants us ready to go up top. He says he doesn't know this patrol boat. There may be a problem."

Valentine wished there was time to go forward into the cargo barge and get some of the explosives. No time.

He warned the young doctor and the old nurse to be ready, just in case, and had the hatchet men arm themselves and wait in the engine room. Orders given, he went up to the cabin deck just under the bridge. The portholes were a good size for shooting.

Valentine took a look at the patrol boat. Valentine didn't see the usual blue-white streamer of the Mississippi's river patrol, so he suspected it was from one of the Kurian towns. Maybe they were in search of bribes. But the craft had official-looking lights. It was a low, boxy craft and looked like it had a crew of three—sort of a brown-water tow truck.

He had a height advantage from the cabin deck.

The patrol craft suddenly sprouted a machine gun from its roof. The barrel turned to cover the bridge.

Valentine tipped a bunk and shoved it against the porthole wall. He didn't do anything as stupid as shoving the barrel out the window; he just kept watch.

The boat pulled up and lines were passed.

Valentine, flattening himself against the wall beside the porthole, watched two men and a dog come on board. The senior officer, judging from the stars on his shoulders, kept his hand on his pistol as he came aboard. He had a squinty, suspicious look about him, like an old storekeeper watching kids pick over candy tubs.

Captain Mantilla came down to greet them. The older of the two men looked shocked, perhaps at the captain's slovenly appearance. Suddenly, the officer threw out his arms and embraced Mantilla like a long-lost brother.

Valentine couldn't understand it, but it seemed like the crisis had passed. He watched the search team go forward.

He wrapped the gun in a blanket and stowed it and the ammunition vest in a locker. He didn't need to change clothes; like the rest of the passengers, he'd been wearing crew overalls so he could move around on deck freely without drawing attention from the riverbank.

Curious, he went out to the rail on the port side and watched Mantilla with the search team. They were doing a good deal of animated talking and very little searching. Even the dog looked bored and relaxed, sitting and gazing up at the humans, panting.

The patrolmen debarked. Valentine waited for the inevitable bribe to pass down to the senior officer, but a square bottle full of amber-colored liquor passed up to Mantilla instead.

The patrol craft untied and proceeded downriver. Mantilla's tug gunned into life.

As it turned out, they were boarded from the other side of the river an hour's slow progress from where they had met the patrol boat.

Valentine saw some soldiers, probably out of Rally Base, signal with a portable electric lantern and wave them in. By the time anchors had fixed their drift, a little red-and-white rowboat set out from a backwash, fighting its way through some riverside growth.

Two men were in it, a big muscular fellow at the oars who had the look of a river drifter who made a little spare money watching for enemy activity, and a magazine cover of a man with slicked-back hair.

"Permission to come aboard, Captain?" slicked-back hair called.

"Granted."

The baggage came first. A big military-issue duffel hit the deck with a whump, tossed up by the muscular man in the rowboat. It was followed by the would-be passenger. On closer inspection Valentine saw that he had a pencil-thin mustache, precisely trimmed to the edges of his mouth.

Which was smiling, at the moment.

"Good God, I was afraid I'd missed you. My river rat swore to me that your tug had passed yesterday. I thought a very bumpy ride had been in vain. Broke records getting to Rally Base."

"Let's see. Transport warrant. Letter of introduction, and permission to be on Southern Command military property. That's the lot. I was hoping to hitch a ride."

"This trip is chartered by Colonel Lambert," Mantilla said. "You'll have to ask her."

"Who are you?" Lambert asked from her spot at the rail.

"Rollo A. Boelnitz, but my friends call me Pencil. I'm a freelancer with *The Bulletin*. My specialty is actually Missouri but I'm eager to learn about Kentucky."

The Bulletin was a minor paper published near the skeleton of the old Wal-Mart complex in Arkansas. It was new—post Archangel and the UFR anyway. Valentine had never read it.

"Why Pencil, Mr. Boelnitz? Because of the mustache?" Lambert asked.

"No, at school. I always lost my pencil and had to borrow. It just stuck."

Lambert glanced at Valentine. "You wanted reinforcements. One pen a mighty army makes."

Valentine disliked him, maybe simply because of the way Lambert had perked up and thrown her chest out since this young icon came aboard.

"General Lehman suggested I join you," Boelnitz offered. "I was talking to him to get a retrospective on his tenure. He said a bit of publicity might help your cause in Kentucky, and the Cause on top of it."

Lambert examined his paperwork. "That's Lehman's signature. The permission to be on Southern Command property might have been overkill. Kentucky's neither fish nor fowl at the moment."

"Do you know what you're getting yourself into?" Valentine asked. "There's no regular mails between Kentucky and the UFR. No banks to cash expense vouchers."

"I was hoping for the traditional hospitality of Southern Command to members of the press. As to my stories, one of your men can transmit via radio. General Lehman said you are in radio contact twice daily."

That settled any issue about this being a put-up job. Radio security was about as tight as Southern Command could make it, involving scramblers and rotating frequencies. Lehman must have passed that tidbit on. Standard Southern Command procedure for brigades in the field was three radio checks a day. As theirs had to be relayed through Rally Base, they found it easier to do just two.

Valentine shrugged and gave Lambert a hint of a nod.

"Welcome aboard, Pencil. I hope you find the situation in Kentucky interesting," she said.

"But not too interesting," Valentine said. "We all had enough interesting this summer to last us till pension draw."

Boelnitz shook hands all around. It was hard to say which version of Pencil Boelnitz was more handsome: serious, expletive Boelnitz or grinning, eager-to-befriend Boelnitz. Valentine couldn't tell whether Lambert had a preference, either.

The bottle their patrol boat had given them contained some seven-year-old bourbon. Mantilla shared a glass with Valentine that night.

They sat in the captain's day cabin. Valentine supposed it was meant to be an office too, but the ship's records seemed to take up one thick sheaf of paper in various sizes, stains, and colors attached to a rusty clipboard.

A single bulb cast yellow light on the cabin deal table. Mantilla and Valentine sat with their legs projecting out into the center of the cabin as the captain poured.

"This is even better for your cold than honey," Mantilla said.

"It makes being sick a little more relaxing. The inspection today— what was that about?"

Mantilla leaned back and put his chin down so the shadow of the cabin light hid his eyes. "A formality, as it turned out."

"Thought you said you didn't know the boat."

"I didn't. But I turned out to be an old friend of the officer in command of the patrol boat."

"Were you?"

Mantilla chuckled. "For a little while. Today anyway."

"I thought you hadn't met him before."

"I never saw his face in the whole of my life. And you would remember a face like that. Like an asshole with pimples."

"What does that mean?"

"You know how a shitty bunghole seems like it's winking at you—"

"No, you never met him, but he knew you?"

"Major Valentine, let's just say that I'm an expert in letting people see what they want to see."

Valentine finished his glass of bourbon and tapped it. To be friendly, Mantilla tossed back his own, gave a little cough, and refilled them both.

"Let me tell you a secret about people, Valentine. They're really good at fooling themselves. They go through life jerking themselves off, complimenting themselves that they're seeing things as they are. Really it's wishing, like a little boy on a skateboard pretending it's a jet airplane. Some *chocha* says *no, no, no* but the prick she's with hears *yes, yes, yes.*"

"Or she's hearing wedding bells and he's thinking bedsprings. But I don't see how that gets a sealed bottle of bourbon out of a local river cop."

"He didn't want to come on board and find trouble. He was hoping for a friendly face. I gave him one."

"Just how did you do that?"

"Allow me to keep a few secrets, Major. I will say this. All it takes is the tiniest bit of a nudge. A shape in the shadows turns into an old friend. A crumpled old diner check turns into a valuable bill." He pointed to the sheaf of paper on the wall. "An old spreadsheet becomes a transport warrant."

"Sounds like magic."

"With magic, people are looking for the trick that is fooling them. What I do is give them a little help fooling themselves."

"Go on," Valentine said, interested.

"You're walking down a dark street and you hear someone following. *Merde!* When you turn around, would you rather see a policeman or, better yet, your neighbor following behind? But of course. As you turn, you hope, you pray, it is not a thug or worse. These men on the river, even the patrols, they do not want trouble. They like to meet bargemen they know, friends who bring the good sweet liqueurs of

Mexico and Curaçao, gold even, or silks from the Pacific Rim and Brazil that they have obtained in New Orleans."

Valentine took another mouthful of neat bourbon. Was the captain presenting him with what he wanted to see? Did he want to see an unkempt, out-of-shape boatman with a sweat-yellowed cap and grease stains on his knees and chest?

Valentine supposed he did. Older, weathered, an experienced man who'd lived long on the river and attended to his engines even at the cost of some mess, Mantilla had Valentine's respect. Even a little flab added to the secure image; Mantilla enjoyed his food. Then there was the keen, roving eye from the face Mantilla never quite turned directly toward you. Canny, with part of his mind on you, part of it on ship or river or weather. "Handy trick," Valentine said. "I don't suppose you could teach me the knack."

"When you work up the guts to look into your own mind and come to terms with what's living there, then you can come to me and speak of venturing into others' minds."

Valentine saw two more examples of Mantilla's trickery at a Kurian river station near Memphis when the captain stopped to pick up a few spare parts for his barge and some diesel for the motors, and then again outside Paducah, where their ship was inspected again. Two men went down into the barge hold ahead, and Valentine held his breath until they emerged, yawning.

Half a day later they approached Evansville and Henderson across the river. No bridge spanned the river anymore, but there were plenty of small craft on both sides. They scattered as the tug approached.

"Your boys close the river? Do I have to worry about artillery gunning for me?" Mantilla asked Valentine, who was standing with him on the bridge.

"No. Not a lot of traffic up and down the Ohio except food. We don't want to starve anyone. But I'd better go first in your launch and send some people down to the landing, just in case. We'll need all our motor resources to unload the cargo."

Valentine was met by a pair of Wolf scouts who took him up to an artillery spotter with a field phone. They'd made some progress with the communications grid in his absence. Perhaps his old "shit detail" had done the work. They didn't fight like Bears, but they had an interesting skill set. He called operations and reported the arrival of supplies from Southern Command. The hatchet men weren't worth calling reinforcements, so he called them specialists.

With that done, he returned to Mantilla's tug.

"We have some odds and ends needing transport back," Valentine said. "Sick and lamed men." Also a few who wanted out of it and were willing to take a dishonorable discharge to get away as soon as they could.

"Some might have to ride in the shell if there are too many. I'll need food for them, if there are many."

"That can be arranged."

"Then I'll be happy to offer transport back. In Paducah they will be surprised to see me again so soon."

"Captain Mantilla, once more I'm in your debt," Valentine said.

Mantilla pushed his hat back on his head. "It's my pleasure to aid a Saint-Valentine."

"It's just Valentine. As you can probably tell, I am about as Italian as I am Afghan."

Or does he know my mother was named Saint Croix? Valentine wondered.

"I've one more favor to ask. Do you know anyone on the river who can get a message up to St. Louis? There's a big church there that tends to the human population and the Grog captives. Slaves, I guess you'd call them. I have a friend near there that they help now and then."

"I'd be honored to bring a message to Sissy."

"Sissy?"

"Isn't that what you call Narcisse?"

"Do you know her?"

Mantilla dropped his chin so his eyes fell into shadow again. "Almost as well as you do, Major Valentine."

Four

Fort Seng: *Javelin landed and set up housekeeping within earshot of its victory against the Moondaggers on the banks of the Ohio.*

In the hills just outside of Henderson, which is now mostly a ghost town, a thickly wooded old state park is now more state than park. Named after the naturalist, the Audubon State Park has changed hands several times in the past year.

Briefly used as a headquarters by the Moondaggers, the park was captured by Javelin almost intact, complete with supply depots and communications gear.

They were attracted by the clean water, space, cabins, and utility buildings. Just off the highway, near the entrance of the camp, is a set of impressive stone buildings constructed from the plentiful limestone of the area's land.

The biggest building is reminiscent of a French château, a former museum complete with turret and gardens, broad patios all around, and decorative walls. Though long since stripped of its valuable Audubon prints, it still has pleasant, sun-filled rooms. The Moondaggers, hurrying up from Bowling Green to cut Southern Command off from its escape into Illinois, used its comfortable rooms as a headquarters and relocated the powerful Evansville Quisling who'd occupied the place to one of the two guest homes behind the pool patio. He and his family fled to the Northwest Ordnance as Colonel Bloom's columns approached.

Southern Command occupied the building with very little alteration. Of course the prayer mats and Kurian iconography had to go— unless the former were clean sheepskin or made of precious metals in the case of the latter. Southern Command set up a permanent hospital

*in the old staff quarters: The cooking area and numerous small rooms
fitted for two were ideal for the purpose.*

*The flagpole now bears Southern Command's five-pointed star and
the stylized white-and-red handshake of the Kentucky Alliance—
UNITED WE STAND.*

*Behind the estate house is a parking lot with an oversized lime-
stone gatehouse. That became the unofficial duty office and clearing
center as Javelin reorganized itself after their losses on the long retreat
across Kentucky and the battles with the Moondaggers. The rich Quisling's driver and mechanics once lived at the gatehouse, and he ex-
panded the place to add overnight accommodations for his friends'
drivers and a small canteen for staff. Javelin turned the canteen into a
recreation club and also a grill where any soldier could get a quick
bite, on duty or off.*

Valentine noticed the improvements to the camp as soon as he led
his party up past the small organized mountains of debarked supplies
on Henderson Landing. He checked in Lambert, his hatchet men and
medical staff, and Pencil Boelnitz under the watchful eyes of the sentries on the western side of the main highway's pared-down bridges into
Evansville. They walked up past artillery positions shielded by hill
from direct fire from the river, and communication lines strung to observers ready to order fire down on river traffic, but the Ohio was empty
that day.

As there was plenty of daylight left, Valentine sent the hatchet men
and medicos under gate-guide to their appropriate headquarters and
borrowed some horses to take Lambert and Pencil Boelnitz on a tour of
the battlefield where they'd attacked the Moondaggers. He showed them
where the guns were sighted, where the Jones boy had swum the river,
the spot where Rand had fallen.

Rand had to be remembered somewhere. Valentine described him
in detail to Boelnitz. Such promise, lost.

From the site of Rand's death Valentine could still see in his mind's
eye his old company's heavy weapons Grogs, Ford and Chevy, gamboling forward with one long arm to add speed to what looked like an un-
balanced canter, the other carrying their support weapons the way
regular soldiers tote automatic rifles.

"We saw them run," Valentine said, pointing out the final Moondagger line. "After all the tough talk about reprisals, roads lined with cruci-
fied, blinded, tongueless prisoners, men who'd be burned alive in cages,
they ran. They wept when they surrendered too, begged, wiped our
muddy boots with their beards."

"What did you do with the prisoners?" Boelnitz asked.

Valentine smiled. Perhaps his reputation had preceded him again. "Exchanged the foot soldiers for some of ours. The Moondaggers lied in some cases and handed over dead men—one or two still warm—in exchange for theirs. According to their philosophy, we're a 'gutter people' who can be lied to if it'll help defeat us. I think they forgot how much we gutter people enjoy kicking the asses of those who label us gutter people. Evansville is keeping a few more in their county lockup for trial. There are a lot of murders and rapes in Kentucky to be answered for. Still, wish we'd bagged a colonel or two. No offense, Colonel Lambert."

Lambert just turned up the corner of her mouth, lost in the hazy sunshine. Her eyes weren't interested, her questions perfunctory and polite.

The trees were as brown and bare as a tanned stripper gearing up for her big reveal.

"The big bugs got away, as usual," Valentine finished. He noticed that even the husks of the dead Moondagger vehicles had been hauled away. Probably melted down for scrap after every ounce of conductive metal had been torn out.

Valentine led them over to the old highway running south out of Evansville. Some of the buildings on the double-laned highway showed signs of occupation. A grease pit and a bar had opened up, and some mule wagons were parked in front of an old store. Valentine's ears picked up sounds of construction from within.

He wondered what the soldiers of Javelin were using for money. They'd probably picked up a lot of odds and ends on the retreat across Kentucky, or had looted watches and rings from dead Moondaggers— Southern Command turned a blind eye to some of the more ghoulish habits of her soldiers, especially after a victory. Valentine had seen ashtrays made out of Grog hands and rocking chairs with stretched, gray, fuzzy skin stapled to the supports, date and place of the former wearer's death inked discreetly into a corner of the leather.

After the tour of the battlefield, they turned east of the road and into the shadow of tall trees. Just outside the roadblock at the sentry post, with a fresh-painted sign identifying everything behind the gate as belonging to Southern Command and notifying all that trespassers may be treated as spies, a curious little vehicle stood. It was a cross between a chariot and a station wagon. The odd sort of tandem motorbike had a stiff bar leading back to a hollowed-out shell of a station wagon, its engine compartment hoodless and filled only with cargo netting.

A man in a rather greasy black suit, his white dog collar frayed and

holes at the knees and elbows, gave them a halloo. He had a pinched
look to his face, like someone had grabbed him by the ears and given a
good pull.

"Free doughnuts, fresh made today. Come right over—all are welcome."

Valentine glanced at the sentry pacing the gate barrier who'd
pricked up his ears at the singsong greeting. The corporal shrugged.

Valentine's eyes picked up lettering on the side of the souped-up
go-cart: NUCM-I.

"What do the letters stand for?" Valentine asked.

"I'll tell you as soon as you give your opinion of this batch. Ran out
of my own flour so I'm using the local stuff."

The doughnut he offered on a piece of wax paper was tasty. He'd
dipped it in honey.

Valentine had read somewhere or other that the Persians had given
the Greeks honey specially made from plants with pharmacological effects. He hoped that wasn't the case here.

"It's delicious," Valentine said, swallowing.

"I have iced tea to wash it down. Sorry it's not sweetened—the honey's scarce enough—but a dunk or two will sweeten her up." Valentine
noticed that the pastry giver addressed himself more to Boelnitz than
either Valentine or Lambert, despite the insignia on the uniforms. In the
Kurian Zone, it rarely hurt to favor the best looking, best fed, and best
dressed.

Lambert and Boelnitz each accepted a doughnut as well.

"You going to tell me about those letters?" Valentine asked.

"I'm with the New Universal Church Missions—Independent."

Lambert made a coughing sound. Boelnitz eyed his doughnut, hand
frozen as though the pastry had magically transformed into a scorpion.

"Don't worry, friend. I call all brother, whatever their affiliation or
uniform. My dunkers are wholesome as fresh milk."

Valentine guessed that the man had been living off of doughnuts,
fresh milk, and maybe a little rainwater and nutritious sun-and-moonshine
for a little too long. His skin had a touch of yellow about it, and the
greasy skin on his brow was blotchy. But it just made the eager stare in
his eyes more authentic.

"I don't want to sound like I'm threatening you," Boelnitz said.
"But aren't you afraid of, uh, street justice, so to speak? Some soldiers
don't like Universal Church lectures."

"A missionary must be prepared to take a blow. Die, even, as an
example of sacrifice."

"What, you give out pamphlets with the doughnuts?"

"No, though I have some literature if you'd like to read it. I have some good stories, written as entertainment, but they contain valuable lessons for today's questioner."

"Today's questioner is tomorrow's dinner, if he's not careful," Valentine said.

The missionary's face slid carefully into neutral. "Every potter's field has its share of broken shards. The just have nothing to fear. All this violence is wrong, wrong, brother. You Arkansas and Texas boys are a long way from home. Why not go back? The only land in Kentucky you'll ever claim is a grave if you continue down this path."

"Thanks for the doughnut," Valentine said. "It was delicious."

They checked in at the sentry post. Valentine nodded to the effusive "welcome backs" and signed in Boelnitz as an unarmed civilian. They issued the reporter a temporary ID. The men looked like they were willing to issue Lambert something else entirely. She was fresh and bright rather than thin and road-worn like the women of Javelin who'd made the long round-trip.

Lambert spoke up. "As a civilian you'll have to stay out of headquarters unless escorted. If you've written stories you need to transmit, just give them to me or the acting exec."

"I know security procedure," Boelnitz said. "All I need to be happy is a bed with a roof over my head. I hate tents."

"We'll see what we can do."

Lambert passed her reassignment orders to the corporal on duty to inspect.

"You have seniority on Colonel Bloom, sir," he said, tapping her months-in-rank line item.

"I'm not here to turn the camp upside down."

The pleasant walk through the woods to the headquarters building was fueled by a sugar rush from the honey and dough. Valentine's pack felt lighter than it had all day.

"Speaking of security," Boelnitz said, "that fellow outside the gate seems like a security risk. He's positioned to count everyone going in and coming out."

"The Kurians aren't usually that obvious," Valentine said. "I think he's just a nut, convinced that if he does something crazy enough long enough, the Kur will reward him with a brass ring."

"No harm treating him like a spy," Lambert said. "Best thing in the world is an agent with blown coverage who doesn't know he's unmasked. We can feed him all sorts of information. Low-grade stuff that's true for a while and then, when we really need it, false data to cover for a real operation."

"Voice of experience?" Boelnitz said. "Your operations in Kansas and the whole Javelin thing didn't work out that well."

"You don't know about the ones that were successful," Lambert said, shooting a wink Valentine's way.

The wink put a spring in Valentine's step. Lambert had been sullen and listless during the walk up. He'd been wondering at her state of mind, seeing herself cast into one of Southern Command's ash heaps. The river trip was just that, a trip. Now she must have felt like she'd washed up in a forgotten corner of the war against the Kur.

Seeing her energy and good humor return relieved him. Perhaps she'd just been anxious at having nothing to occupy her mind, the way a mother duck without any active ducklings to line up didn't quack or fuss.

A trio of soldiers on their way out of camp met them on the road. They straightened up and saluted in recognition of Lambert's eagle. Valentine could see that they had questions, but he waved them off at the first, "Excuse me, Major, is there any truth—"

"Can't talk in front of our new press representative," Valentine said.

"*Battle Cry* finally got around to sending a man over the river?"

"Not yet. Men, this is Mr. Boelnitz from the *The Bulletin*. You can call him Pencil if you like."

One of the soldiers asked what *The Bulletin* was.

"It's a small paper, new," Boelnitz said, looking a little abashed. "Published out of Fayetteville."

"Speaking of pen and paper . . . good news, men. I've brought the first mail. I'm bringing it to the all-call at the canteen for the company clerks to distribute."

The younger soldier looked at the other two.

"I don't want to wait," the senior said.

They turned around and fell in behind Valentine.

The first thing he did was stop at the big gatehouse and hand off the mail. His oversized carrier held nothing now but official correspondence for Colonel Bloom and a few small presents for his own staff.

With the mail delivered, Valentine's first duty was to report to his commanding officer.

Lambert turned up her collar and lowered the flaps on the hat. "Give Colonel Bloom my compliments, Major. I'll pay a call on her shortly, but I'd like to walk the grounds in mufti for the afternoon."

Valentine saluted and left her to her solitary tour. He gave orders to see to Boelnitz's quartering, and left him with a promise for a dinner where the reporter could meet some of the other officers.

The main building hadn't changed much on the outside since he'd last seen it. The comfortable-looking former museum and educational center, later an estate house, was designed to look like a cross between a mountain lodge and a small château. But once through the doors, he noticed new details. There was proper signage everywhere, a new map and roster behind a glass case, a duty desk instead of an officer making do with a bench and an entryway table that had been more suited for hats and gloves, and a proper communications center, probably servicing the new high mast rigged to the decorative gazebo behind the mansion.

"What happened to the face, Valentine?" Bloom asked after Valentine was escorted to her office.

"A difference of opinion in a brothel," Valentine said.

"Over a girl, I take it."

"My favorite there was old enough for false teeth."

Bloom chuckled and took from him her envelope of orders. The good humor bled away from her face as she read.

Colonel Cleveland Bloom took the news with professional grace. Or maybe it was just her instincts for good sportsmanship.

"I'm being benched," she said.

"Not benched, recalled. Someone has to bring the men home. They followed you most of the way across Kentucky. Southern Command must have figured you were the one to see them home."

"You'll stay?"

"They're giving me permission to orchestrate a guerrilla war."

She flipped through her written orders, found an attachment, scanned it.

"With what? They're not leaving you much. A communications team and a few hospital personnel to care for the wounded and sick who can't be moved. That Quisling rabble of yours will need more than that to be anything more than glorified POWs."

They'd had this argument before. Like most officers in Southern Command, she had a low opinion of the kind of men who the Kurians used to fill out the bottom ranks of their security and military formations. Thugs, sycophants, thieves, and bullies, with a few out-and-out sadists peppering the mix.

Valentine reminded her, "The shit detail used to be Quisling rabble. They made the round-trip with the rest of us. I don't recall the column ever being ambushed with them acting as scouts, at least until we bivouacked in the Alleghenies outside Utrecht."

"I'll leave you what I can, in terms of gear."

"Can I have a favor? I'd like to ask for volunteers to stay. I need gunners, technical staff, engineers, and armorers especially."

Bloom, when faced with difficulty, usually got a look on her face that reminded him of a journalist's description of the old US Army General Grant—*that he wears an expression as if he had determined to drive his head through a brick wall, and was about to do it.* "Don't know how Southern Command will react to that. You're talking about prime skill sets."

"They'll list them as Insurgency Assist. They'll still draw in-country pay. One day counts as two toward pension."

Bloom's mouth writhed as though she were chuckling, but she didn't make a sound. "By volunteers, you mean . . ."

"Real volunteers, sir. No shanghais or arm-twisting."

"Then good luck to you."

"Will that be all, sir?"

She looked at her orders from Southern Command. "They leave it to my discretion over exactly when I turn over command of this post to Colonel Lambert, though I'll maintain operational command of the brigade even while it's based here until it returns across the Mississippi. Seems to me there's just enough wiggle room for me to keep the troops here until you're convinced the base is functioning properly, from hot water to cooking gas to master comm links."

"I'll have a list tomorrow, sir."

"Anything else for me, Valentine?"

He had to choose his words carefully. "I told the truth about what happened, sir. I argued that we won an important victory, even if it wasn't the victory they expected. Southern Command's looking for a scapegoat. I expect they'll make Colonel Lambert and General Lehman take most of the blame. Lehman's being sent to a quiet desk and Lambert's out here. Be ready to answer for us, and for yourself."

"Thanks for the warning."

"Anything else, sir?"

"Is Colonel Lambert in the headquarters?"

"She's walking around . . . incognito, I suppose you could call it. She wanted to get a feel for the men and the place unofficially, before she takes an official role."

"I understand. If you come across her, please ask her if she'd like to have dinner with me tonight."

"Yes, sir. I'll pass the word."

Bloom sat back down to reread her orders, saying a few more words about hoping Lambert wouldn't mind eating late.

As Valentine walked toward his new formation's billet, he saw his hatchet men inspecting the vehicles in the motor pool. Of the long column of vehicles that had started out with Javelin, only one battered old army truck had survived the entire journey out of the large vehicles. The rest had been cannibalized to keep others going or lost to wear, Moondagger rockets, artillery, and mines, or accident. A few civilian pickups, Hummers, and motorcycles remained, looking like candidates for a demolition derby thanks to the knocks and cracks.

"Master Sergeant Brage," Valentine said, pronouncing his name as *Braggy*.

"It's *BRAY-zhe*, Major," Brage said, as irritated as Valentine hoped he'd be.

"Sorry, Sergeant," Valentine said. "Why the interest in the motor pool?"

"Orders, sir," Brage said, tapping his chest pocket. "We're to determine what's worth taking and what'll be left behind. My staff and I have final word. Our decisions are final and unalterable."

"I've seen my share of alterations to unalterable. May I see the orders, please?"

He handed them over with the air of a poker player laying down a straight flush.

Valentine read the first paragraph and then went to the next pages and checked the signatures, seals, and dates. He recognized the hand at the bottom.

"My old friend General Martinez. You're on his staff?"

"I have that honor, sir." With a wave, the rest of his hatchet men returned to work.

"Martinez has been honoring me for years now. I hardly feel it anymore," Valentine said.

"I'm sure you mean *General* Martinez, sir. Of course, whether I make the GHQ staff depends on my success with this assignment. I intend to leave no stone unturned."

"I wouldn't advise you to turn over too many stones in Martinez's staff garden. Not a pretty sight."

"I have to get back to work, Major. I'd advise you not to hinder me."

"Or what, Sergeant Bragg?"

"*BRAY-zhe*, sir. Anyone caught red-handed in the act of taking or keeping Southern Command property from its proper allocation, right down to sidearms, may be dealt with summarily," Brage said, sounding as though he were reciting. "That only applies in combat areas, of course."

"Of course. And if you want to see a combat area, Sergeant Bragg, I suggest you try to take a weapon from one of my men."

*   *   *

Javelin stood on parade, a great U of men. It reminded Valentine of his farewell to the Razorbacks in Texarkana, when they retired the tattered old flag that had waved over Big Rock Hill and been bomb-blasted at Love Field in Dallas.

Valentine read out the list of commendations and promotions. The men stepped forward to receive their medals and new patches and collar tabs from Bloom.

A delegation of civilians and officers of the new city militia from Evansville sat in chairs, watching. Valentine hoped they were impressed. All they'd seen of Southern Command's forces up to now had been files of tired, dirty, unshaven men lining up to receive donations of food, toiletries, and bedding from Evansville's factories, workshops, and small farmers.

Valentine had juggled with the schedule a little to get as many excused from duties as possible, but it was worth it.

He stepped forward to the microphone when she was done. "Colonel, with your permission I'd like to add one more name. If you'll indulge me, sir."

Bloom beamed. Her teeth might not have been as bright as Ladyfair's, but her smile was better. "With the greatest of pleasure."

Valentine spoke into the microphone, which put his voice out over the field amplifier, a device that turned your words into power-assisted speech that sounded a little like aluminum being worked. "Javelin Brigade, I have one more promotion. At this time I would like to recognize one of my oldest friends in the Cause.

"Top Sergeant Patel, would you step forward, please?"

Patel hesitated for a moment and then handed his cane to his corporal and marched out into the center of the U of formed ranks. Valentine couldn't tell if he was wincing or not. He marched without any sign of weakness in his old, worn-down knees.

"This man has been looking out for me since I was a shavetail lieutenant with his shoes tied like a civilian's. He helped me select and train my company, the shit detail."

The term was a badge of honor now, ever since their action at the railroad cut in Kentucky.

"Top Sergeant Patel performed above and beyond, crossing Kentucky and back on a pair of legs that are hardly fit for a trip to the latrine.

"I recommended, and Southern Command granted, a commission for Nilay Patel, elevating him to the rank of captain, with its attendant honors and benefits. He's been breveted over lieutenant so that our Captain Patel will never have to salute a sniveling little lieutenant with his laces half-undone ever again."

"You could have given me fair warning, sir," Patel said quietly. "Would have paid for a shave and haircut across the highway."

"Surprise," Valentine said out of the corner of his mouth. The amplified speaker popped out the *p* but nothing else. He spoke up again. "So be sure to save a seat for him on the barge home. He'll ride home in a comfortable deck chair, as befits a captain."

"Excuse me, sir," Patel said. "I'm not leaving before you and the company."

"We'll argue about it later, Captain." Valentine reached into his pocket. "These are some old insignia of mine. No branch on the reverse. They don't do that for Cats, or they put in a false one." He handed them to Patel, feeling paternal, even though his old sergeant major had almost twenty years on him. "Wear them in good health."

"Thank you, sir," Patel said, leaning over to speak into the microphone. Then, for Valentine's ears only, he continued: "It's good to feel useful again. Even if it comes with a little pain."

The fall weather turned colder and rainier. Through it all Southern Command's forces improved Fort Seng, rigging lighting and plumbing and communications throughout the fort. A double perimeter was laid out, though they didn't have the mines, lights, or listening posts to cover the entire length.

Valentine saw Boelnitz mostly around headquarters. He had a knack for finding something interesting going on and observing in the company of whoever was doing it, asking questions but keeping out of the way. The men felt flattered to be interviewed, as did some of the women—Valentine saw one long-service veteran giggling like a coquettish schoolgirl as they chatted. A couple of others looked at him with naked hunger, the way she-wolves might eye a dead buck strung up for dressing.

In the meantime, Valentine reintroduced himself to Bee, one of the three Grogs in camp. He'd rescued her and two others from the circus of D.C. Marvels before Javelin entered Kentucky, and he'd also known her years ago when she'd traveled as a bodyguard to a bounty hunter and trader named Hoffman Price. Big as a bull, she had arms long enough to go around him twice when she sniffed and touched and remembered who he was.

She'd apparently forgotten his existence but was equally delighted to reacquaint herself with him, and she soon fell into her old habit of trailing along somewhere in his wake with a shotgun and an assault rifle, both cut down to pistol grips, in holsters on her wide thighs, with plates of bulletproof vest serving as loincloth, vest, and mantle.

Each morning, Valentine visited the headquarters bungalow for his Quisling battalion. He had to split his time between his Quisling recruits and the main headquarters building, where Lambert needed him as she oriented herself to western Kentucky and Evansville.

His ex-Quislings were losing their baby fat, or their paunches, under Patel's double-time training. During the day, the mixture of tenting and barrack that housed his ex-Quislings—the men were building their own accommodations as part of the shake-down training—lay empty in the field behind the bungalow.

He'd chosen the bungalow not for its size or plumbing or available furniture—he liked it because it had a huge social room, a sort of living room–dining room–kitchen combined. He lined the walls of the big room with couches and stuffed comfortable chairs. Judging from the remaining books, the house had belonged to a gardener or a gamekeeper who'd worked for the estate's owner.

Valentine liked to hold meetings comfortably, with everyone seated and relaxed, usually in the evening.

This particular morning he found it in the hands of Ediyak—once a lieutenant but now a captain thanks to Rand's death. When he'd returned to Fort Seng she'd been across the river attempting to wrangle more supplies out of the Evansville leadership. She was a delicate-looking young woman, doe-eyed and usually buzzing with energy, who'd defected from the Kurian Order. The defection had been harder for her than most; she'd been involved in communications and intelligence, so she'd lived on an access-restricted section of her former base. She'd played a Mata Hari trick and arranged to date a general, slipping away from a resort hotel as her aged paramour slept. *I defected thanks to two bottles of wine and beef Wellington*, she was fond of saying.

Valentine liked his former company clerk, who'd first come to his notice when she came up with the gray denim utility-worker uniforms that allowed his company to roam Tennessee and Kentucky without attracting notice. Some of his command he respected, some he dealt with as best as he could, but he liked her as a person and found her company rewarding beyond the necessities. She was a little weak on assertiveness—she'd risen from private to corporal to sergeant to lieutenant and now captain thanks to assorted emergencies in the trek across Kentucky, and handled the detail work of each station with ease, but she seemed in a permanent state of finding her feet thanks to the constant promotions. She needed decent NCOs under her or the men would get away with murder, but she was bright and—well, "creative" was the word, he supposed. She sensed what he wanted with very few words of explanation from him.

"How's the organization going?" he asked her.

There was something theatrical about Ediyak. Maybe it was the big eyes in the thin face or her size. She made up for her small physical presence by moving constantly and gesturing. "After cutting out the unfit and the idiots, we're down to a hair over three hundred fifty," Ediyak said, swiveling on her chair and taking the roster off the wall for Valentine to examine. "The brigade's artillery stole some of the best and brightest, by the way. The culls are in a labor pool."

She rose and pointed to the large-scale local map. "Right now they're working on getting a better ferry in place between Henderson and Evansville. As you directed, I broke up our old company and made them NCOs over the new formations, five men to a platoon. So if you add them in, you have the makings of a decent battalion."

"Now tell me what's happened in the interwhiles," Valentine said.

"For a start, we're broke," she said, making a gesture that gave Valentine a pang for his mother: the *cassé* of French culture, a little motion like breaking a stick. "Evansville is a rat pile, and everyone's hoarding: food, fuel, everything from sewing thread to razor blades. Bloom asked, in her darling vigorous way, for the men to sacrifice 'valuables' or they'd have to do a thorough search of the camp to gather non–Basic Order Inventory that might be traded or sold. Of course the implied threat was that if they didn't contribute some gold and whatnot that they'd picked up on the marches, she'd search thoroughly for all of it.

"We had a few of our recruits go over to Evansville in search of a good time. Vole and a couple of his cronies. They never came back. I don't know if they deserted or the Evansville people quietly strung them up in some basement. I think the latter's more likely."

"Any good news?"

She slipped back to the desk. "Not much. Supplies are running short—food and dispensables anyway. The leg shavers among the women are sharing one razor between us."

"Opposition?"

"The Moondaggers are long gone. Kentucky doesn't have a Reaper east of Lexington, from what the Wolves tell us. Memphis sent up a couple of armored trains from the city, evacuated what's left of the Moondaggers and prominent Quislings in eastern Kentucky. The rest are holed up in the bluegrass region with what's left of the Coonskins. But anything that rides legworms is settling in for winter quarters, with the nights getting colder and their worms egging and piling up.

"Can I ask, sir, what's going to happen with us?"

"You're going home."

"We'll see about that."

"Just between you and me, Southern Command has written off Kentucky. They're sending some NCOs and transport to decide what's worth salvaging and what isn't."

"Lovely. There go our guns, sir."

"We'll see about that. By the way, Ediyak, where'd you pick up the *tschk* gesture?" Valentine asked, making the *cassé* breaking motion with his hands.

Ediyak's eyes widened. "The . . . oh, that."

"You grew up in Alabama, right?"

"Yes, sir. I grew up poor as dirt in a little patch of kudzu called Hopper where a girl was expected to be married at fifteen and nursing her way through sweet sixteen," she said, her accent suddenly redolent of boll weevils and barbecue.

"So you picked that up after you got out?"

"Yes, sir. Why so interested?"

"How did you get out?"

"Church testing. They had this extraordinary idea of putting me on the public broadcasts," she explained, her hand fluttering about her breast like a dove looking for a perch. "A sagging old Archon with my picture said I had the perfected look. If by 'perfected' they meant half-starved and iron-deficient, I'm guessing they were right. I went to school for two years learning about lapel microphones and makeup and pho-netic pronunciation, a dusty duckling among graceful swans, learning to dress and talk and give the appearance of being cultured even if I was to the outhouse born. Then they decided I didn't look right next to the other news broadcasters because I was too small. I tried out for *Noon-side Passions*, rehearsed with a few of the principals, but didn't get a continuing role. I did six episodes before they had me die in childbirth, giving my poor daughter to sweet little Billy, who'd only just learned to shave himself. They told me she'd grow up in no time and fall in love with him. They do get a little ripe on that show, don't they? But I'm get-ting away from the story of my brush with fame. I left the show and let myself be recruited into military communications."

"Is that where you saw the gesture? On the show?"

"I believe it was from a friend, a very good friend I made on *Noon-side Passions*: one of the writers, a Frenchman. He'd gone to an *école* something-or-other and was in New York picking up some tips for the French version of the show."

Relief washed down Valentine's spine like cool water. Ediyak didn't seem like the Kurian-agent type, but then Kurian agents that penetrated Southern Command spent years working at not being the Kurian agent type.

She had seemed discomfited about the mention of the show, though. Or the gesture.

At their first evening meeting after Patel's promotion that had leaped him all the way over lieutenant in a single, overdue bound, they held an informal party. Congratulations flowed along with some bottles of bourbon of mysterious provenance.

Alessa Duvalier appeared in the middle of the chatter and pours.

She didn't look agitated, just tired and with that pained look she wore when her stomach was bothering her. Valentine took her long coat anyway, noting the mud smears and the river smell on her. The waters of the Ohio didn't need a Wolf-nose to detect.

"Where have you been?"

"Bloomington," she said.

"All that way. By yourself?"

"I hitched a ride with a good old boy who trains fighting dogs. He was on the way to a match in Indianapolis. His truck got me there and back."

"You went to a dogfight?" Valentine asked.

"No, I skipped it. So did the dogs. But they weren't in fighting shape anyway. They'd just eaten about two hundred sixty pounds of asshole after I took the wheel."

"Why Bloomington?"

"We received an underground report that the Northwest Ordnance moved into a new headquarters, and I went to check it out."

"How did it go?"

"Maybe nothing; maybe not. Headquarters was for the Grand Guard Corps' Spearhead Brigade from Striker Division. From what my old Ohio boyfriend told me, that's the best of their best, unless you count their marine raiders on the Great Lakes. Armored stuff that usually is deployed at the Turnpike Gap in Pennsylvania against the East Coast Kurians. They may just be training, from what I could pick up in the bars. It may just be exercises to impress the Illinois Kurians and the Grogs."

"Where did you get the idea to go up there?"

"Brother Mark," she said, referring to the ex–New Universal churchman who was the UFR's main diplomat, more or less, east of the Mississippi. "The underground got word to him, Kur knows how."

"Where is he now?"

"Oh, back at Elizabethtown. The wintering clans are all sending delegates to this big conference to decide what to do next. There's talk that they might declare against the Kurians; others say they're listening to a peace delegation."

Valentine retrieved his mailbag and passed out a few precious gifts he'd picked up in the UFR for his officers and senior NCOs. He couldn't bring much, considering all the personal mail he'd had to carry for Javelin's survivors, but he had a new lipstick for Ediyak, aspirin for Patel, a clever chessboard with folding cardboard pieces for one of his corporals who was a chess enthusiast, and matching Grog scar-pins for Glass and his two gunners, Ford and Chevy. And, of course, the tin of talcum powder for Duvalier and her bootsore feet.

"Where'd you pick up the diaper bag?" Duvalier asked.

"This?" Valentine asked, looking down at the bag as though he'd never seen it before. "They said it was a mail pouch."

"It is, but even Southern Command doesn't take nine months to deliver," Patel said.

"Val, that's a diaper bag. I've seen plenty of them," Ediyak said.

"Diaper bag?"

"Southern Command, for use of," Duvalier said. "They gave one to Jules when she got out of the hospital after you inflated her."

"It's a messenger bag, Ali."

"No, sir, she's right," Ediyak said. "I saw plenty of them back at Liberty. It's a diaper bag. They came in cute pink and baby blue. You got green if you had twins."

"Doesn't say anything on the inside about diapers," Valentine said stubbornly. "Just a pattern number."

"Well, look it up in a supply catalog. It's a diaper bag."

"It's not a diaper bag," Valentine grumbled.

The women exchanged a glance and a smile.

Valentine continued to see Fort Seng's fixtures and equipment dribble away, allocated for return to Southern Command by the hatchet men, who were loading up the trucks as though they were Vikings loading their ships on an English beach for the trip back to the fjords.

He decided to make his stand at the artillery park when a little red-headed bird he'd put in charge of keeping track of their activities told him that was on the agenda for the next day. Valentine dressed in a mixture of military uniform and legworm leathers, complete with Cat claws, sidearm, and sword.

Bee, seeing how he dressed, took the precaution of adding a trio of double-barreled sawed-off shotguns to her array, thrust through her belt like a brace of pirate pistols.

With that, he headed over to the artillery park. Duvalier, who'd been lounging around headquarters on an old club chair in a warm, quiet corner, threw on her overcoat and followed him out the door.

Valentine fought yawns. He'd had a long night.

A copper fall day greeted him as he followed the marking stones and path logs serving as steps to the north side of the former park, where the emplaced guns squatted in a quarrylike dugouts area tearing up the ground around a trio of chicken-track-like communicating trenches linking the guns to their magazines.

Duvalier fell out of the procession as Valentine descended into the dimple in the natural terrain that served for the artillery positions.

Valentine saw Southern Command's artillerymen lounging around the fire control dugout.

Brage clearly wasn't the expert here; he stood apart while one of his hatchet men went over the guns.

"Good morning, Sergeant Bragg," Valentine said.

"That joke never gets old, does it?" Brage said. "What kind of getup is that?"

"New model Kentucky uniform."

Brage ignored him and looked over the guns. The three big howitzers were Moondagger heavy artillery that had been captured at what was now being called the Battle of Evansville Landing. The old Moondagger iconography had been filled in and modified with black marker to make a winking happy face—the dagger made a great knowing eyebrow.

Someone with fairy-tale tastes had named the big guns by painting the barrels: Morganna, Igraine, and Guinevere. None of the knights were present. Perhaps Arthur had led them off searching for the Holy Grail.

The squinty hatchet man artillery expert tut-tutted as he inspected the guns.

"Can't use these howitzers," decided the sergeant, whose name tag read *McClorin*. He gave Igraine a contemptuous pat. "Half the lug nuts are missing. Tires are in terrible shape. You'd swear someone had been at them with a knife. Can't have the wheels falling off. What are we going to do: drag them home, put furrows in this beautiful Kentucky grass? The state of these guns . . . You should be ashamed of yourself, Major— beg your pardon, sir. Those soldiers of yours playing cards all day?"

The grinning gunners looked abashed.

Valentine's oversized satchel pulled hard on his shoulder. Naturally enough, it was full of lug nuts and sights. They didn't clink, though. He had taken care to wrap them in pages torn out from the New Universal Church *Guidon*.

"Thank you, Sergeant McClorin. Thank you very much," Valentine said. "I will remember your name."

"Big-caliber guns are more trouble than they're worth. Need special trucks to haul them and a logistics train a mile deep thanks to those
shells. Our factories would do better to crank out more sixty mortars
instead of trying to hit these tolerances. A good reliable sixty's what
you need to hit-and-run in the field, or an eighty-one if you're looking to
make life miserable for the redlegs in some Kurian post.

"Besides, it never fails: We just set them up to cover the highway
coming down out of Memphis and the Kurians get word, and next thing
you know harpies as Hoods are coming out of the night like mosquitoes. No, sir. Fixed fortification guns are plain stupid."

Brage made a note on his clipboard. "Think you've put one over on
us, Major? Southern Command needs shells just as much as it needs
tubes."

You petty, petty bastard, Valentine thought. Good thing he hadn't
brought Chieftain or one of the other Bears along. Brage would be tied
into a decorative bow right about now.

Valentine pointed to Bee, who was digging for fat, winter-sluggish
worms in the wet soil at the top of the wood steps leading down to the
ready magazine.

"We keep the magazine under lock and key. All that work with con-
crete and reinforcing rods—we don't want it wasted with carelessness.
She's in charge of the key. Hate to think where she hides it."

"I can see the stories about you are true, Major," Brage said. "You'd
start a pissing match with a camel."

Duvalier was suddenly in the gun pit. She'd swung in on one of the
barrels like a gymnast and landed so lightly nobody noticed her.

The master sergeant reached for his pistol.

"Keep that weapon in its holster, Sergeant Bragg!" Valentine growled.

Brage lifted the gun anyway and Valentine slipped in and grabbed
his wrist, getting his body between Brage and the butt of the gun. The
master sergeant was stronger than he looked and put a leg behind Valentine, but as Valentine went down he twisted, getting his hip under
Brage's waist so the two touched earth together, still fighting for the
gun. Valentine somehow kept the barrel pointed at dirt.

Another hatchet man drew his gun. And watched it fall to the dirt,
his nerveless hand dropping beside him, twitching not from muscle action but from blood emptying from the severed wrist. Duvalier's sword
continued its graceful wheel as she pinned the next sergeant with the
point of her knotty walking stick. She brought the sword up, edge crossing the wooden scabbard with Brage trapped between as though his
neck were lard ready to be worked into biscuit batter.

Sergeant McClorin put his back to the gun he'd condemned, aghast.

"This is—" another hatchet man said.

The gun crews were on their feet.

"Shut up, Dell," the man with his neck scissored between Duvalier's scabbard and razor-edged sword blade said.

The sergeant who'd lost his hand had gone down to his knees and had picked up his appendage. He pressed the severed end to his bleeding stump, pale and growing paler.

Valentine put his knee into Brage's kidneys. "Call off your dogs and I'll take care of my Cat."

"Fuckin' trannies!" one of the hatchet men said. "Save it for the enemy."

Bee loomed from the top of the sand-and-slat wall, assault rifle pointed into the trench.

"Graaaawg?" she asked.

Depending on circumstance, the word might mean *help*, *need*, or *distress*. Bee put the barrel between the two unengaged hatchet men.

"Good, Bee. Safe," Valentine said, releasing Brage. "Medic! Call a medic," he shouted toward the fire control dugout. One of the audience ducked back inside.

"Beeeeee!" Bee agreed.

"I'll have you both on charges," Brage began.

"You drew first, Sergeant. I was defending a member of my command who posed no threat to anyone."

Duvalier looked Brage in the eye. "Just try it. Throw your weight around. Someone else'll be carrying that clipboard by the time a Jagger gets here, and you'll be scattered across the countryside in easy-to-carry pieces.

"You all heard me," Brage said, looking around for support. "She threatened me."

"Let it go, Brage," McClorin said. "Goebler's about to go into shock."

"I'm fine," the one-handed man said. "Should I put my hand in ice or what?"

"Keep pressure on the stump and put it above your head," Valentine said, ripping the field dressing he had taped to his weapon belt off. He picked up Brage's dropped pistol and tossed it up and out of the trench and then moved to help the wounded man.

Duvalier released her captive. He had a sizable stain running down his right leg. "You," she said, taking a quick step forward and holding her blade pointed like a spear. "The one who called us trannies. Come over here and lick your friend clean."

"Stop it, Ali," Valentine said. He turned his attention back to Brage. "I think you all might want to return to Southern Command now,"

Valentine said. "Colonel Bloom is perfectly capable of organizing a retreat."

"Not a retreat," Brage said. "A reallocation of assets."

As it turned out, there was no immediate fallout from the blood shed in the dirt next to Igraine. Valentine had a half-dozen witnesses ready to swear Brage threatened Valentine and pulled his gun first. All the rest that followed was necessary to prevent the death or injury of Southern Command personnel.

Only Pencil Boelnitz, who'd heard about the scene one way or another and regretted missing it, brought it up after Colonel Bloom's query was closed. Lambert shrugged and told him: Service with David Valentine gives no end of future anecdotes—but rest assured he's even tougher on the enemy.

Valentine kicked Duvalier's information about the new Northwest Ordnance movements up to headquarters at the next, and what turned out to be final, staff meeting.

"Not my problem anymore," Bloom said. "We'll be gone in a few days."

"Thank you for seeing the work to the fort through," Valentine said. The brigade had worked hard at finishing setting up Fort Seng as a working base—and, in a typical military irony, wouldn't be around to take advantage of the comforts they'd installed.

"Now that word's got out that we're doing a last dash home, everyone wants to get going as soon as possible," Bloom said. "You sure you don't want us to bury half that Angel Food around the joint, just in case you have to blow it up quickly?"

"We'll be able to handle that. Did I get any volunteers to stay?"

"Aside from your devoted shit detail, you have a couple skutty types who know they'll do time in the brig as soon as we get back to the Jaggers. Wouldn't trust them any farther than I could smell 'em."

"The Bears are staying, suh," Gamecock, the officer in charge of the three four-man Bear teams, said. "I took it up with the boys. Consensus is the Kurians are going to hit you as soon as the rest of the brigade leaves. They figure it's the quickest way to get back to fighting."

"How about the Wolves?" Valentine asked Moytana, the captain in charge of the Wolf company that had scouted for Javelin.

"I'm under direct orders to return," Moytana said. He had the slow, assured drawl of a long-service cowhand.

"What can you leave us?"

"That's up to the bone pickers," Bloom said, referring to Valentine's grim-faced hatchet men who'd been inspecting captured vehicles and gear since they arrived, sorting the salvageable wheat from the chaff that would be left to Valentine to make of what he would.

Valentine rubbed his fresh-shaven chin. "Since this is the last meeting of this particular staff, I feel like we should have something."

"A cake?" Bloom asked.

"I was thinking some of our friend's doughnuts."

"The nut at the gate?" Bloom's clerk asked. "They're good doughnuts, but you have to hear his sermonizing about Kur and the elevation of mankind."

"Might want to roust him for a few days, so he can't count us walking out," Moytana said.

Valentine and a corporal went to get doughnuts. They took bicycles down to the entrance to the base. Bee loped along behind. Some idlers were watching the Kentuckians build small, heat-conserving homes on the other side of the old Evansville highway running west of the base.

"Mind if we take a sack?" Valentine asked the missionary.

"One to a customer, sir. Did you read that literature I gave you?"

"Fascinating stuff," Valentine said. "I have eight friends. One to a customer means I need eight doughnuts."

"Oh, that makes sense," the missionary said, reaching into a shelf in his bakery van. "Did you get to the part about the select gene rescue and propagation?"

"No."

"A well-formed man like you would do well to try out. And don't worry. Less than three percent end up castrated."

"That must have been in the fine print."

"You know, this is an evil land. Best leave it to escape what is coming. The punishment."

"Punishment?"

"I take no joy in it. It's heartbreaking. But the fools will persist in their folly."

"True enough. How long will you keep handing out doughnuts?"

"Until it begins. There will be a sign, a sign from the sky. Beware the evil star! Take it to head and heart, friend and brother. There's a shadow of death over this land. It's flying closer and closer." He handed Valentine a bag so greasy that the paper was next to transparent and went back to scanning the sky.

"I don't suppose you know what direction the danger is coming from."

"The worst dangers blossom in one's own bosom. Look to your heart, friend and brother. Watch the skies, my friend and brother. Watch the skies!"

*   *   *

Lost in the sleep of the exhausted that night, Valentine dreamed he was back in Weening.

The last time Valentine had stopped in Weening, they were using the Quickwood tree he'd planted as a maypole, dancing around it every spring. One of the local preachers accused the family who organized the event of being druids.

Valentine had placed the seed there years ago. What Valentine wanted were some specimens of Quickwood tucked away here and there throughout the Ozarks, just in case—a Johnny Appleseed of resistance to the Kurians.

The tree he'd planted in Weening would be mature in another year or two, if what Papa Legba had told him on Hispaniola about the tree's life cycle was correct. It would be producing seeds for others to distribute.

That was the essence of his dream. The young coffee bean–like Quickwood seeds were dropping off the tree and rolling into the brush while he and Gabby Cho stood waist deep in the nearby stream. The seeds turned into scarecrows, and the scarecrows divided and turned into more scarecrows, all of whom stood in the fields and woods around Weening, all subtly turned toward himself and Cho as they shivered, naked and exposed in the river.

Five

"Repurposed." Southern Command doesn't call it a retreat, or abandonment, or evacuation. Word has come down from on high: What's left of Javelin is being "repurposed."

General Martinez calls it a part of his "new approach" to the war against the Kurians.

Admittedly, General Martinez was, is, and continues to be a controversial figure. What the precise proportion of malfeasance, malpractice, and misjudgment went into his tenure as the Southern Command chief general is the object of some dispute. There are still those who maintain that Martinez's only fault was to see to the welfare of the men under his command first and foremost, only fighting when it was absolutely necessary.

But a wise man knows that in life, absolutes vanish like a desert mirage, receding into an unknown distance before it can be quantified.

At Fort Seng, the men don't reveal much of their thoughts. They carefully pack souvenirs picked up on the march—both the conventional, like some of Karas' old Kentucky coin or one of the short, curved ceremonial knives of the Moondaggers, and the odd: buttons, bits of coal slag, commerce stamps with elaborate imagery, Kurian newspapers with their jumbled and misleading accounts of the fighting, bar coasters from the rail towns outside Lexington, even bits of legworm leather with dates of battles stitched into them. One musically inclined soldier has an entire portfolio full of sheet music. He was struck by how many of the same popular tunes were sung in Kentucky, with altered lyrics or harmonies to give the ditties a local tone.

"Gone-a-homer," an Arkansas tune reworded in Kentucky, was adopted by the troops and reworded again to capture the bittersweet

*nature of defeat—a defeat that meant you'd live to go home to spouses
and sweethearts. Beat, whupped, kicked out: These words weren't spoken aloud but found their way into the song.*

They were making vests and long johns out of the polyester felt
Valentine had brought. It was good-quality material, warm even when
wet and so light you hardly knew you were wearing it. They had some
doubts about durability, so they were adding coverings and liners made
out of old uniforms or Evansville tenting.

The workshop was churning out bush jackets and fatigue pants in
"Evansville timber"—a mottled camouflage that was a light bleach
wash of the dark uniforms the Evansville militia wore. Then they
dabbed it with two colors of camouflage in a vaguely leopard-spot pattern. Of course there were variations that came from a small group of
people working long hours at a fast pace. Sometimes it streaked and ran
into tiger stripes; other times the pattern was so tight and tiny it resembled a sort of houndstooth.

The end result might not have impressed a discerning Old World
eye, civilian or military, but Valentine was oddly proud. Once again,
the uniform was one of Ediyak's designs. A big overcoat with draw-
strings at waist and sleeves hung to midthigh. Beneath it was a padded
riding vest of the insulating felt and canvas with plenty of utility pockets, and beneath that their uniform shirts. Trousers had reinforced knees
and seats and a removable felt liner, but it turned out the buttons meant
to secure the liner weren't comfortable, so they were removed and replaced by hook-and-eye loops.

Boots were still a problem. Most of his recruits had come over in
civilian duty shoes, fine for the streets of Evansville but no match for
the tough field exercises in wet fall weather that Patel put them through.

Hobbled men were no use to anyone. Bad feet made men even more
miserable than bad teeth. Southern Command had little in the way of
spares after the retreat across Kentucky, so Valentine had to settle for
tire rubber "retreads" cobbled together with rawhide lacing, scraps of
webbing, and heavyweight canvas for breathability.

The men called them "Kentucky galoshes" and suffered through
the inevitable blisters and abrasions, but the footwear protected ankles
and kept off trench foot.

Valentine spent long hours recruiting from the soon-to-depart brigade.

A few NCOs volunteered to stay because they wanted to finish the
fight in Kentucky. Many were the best of Javelin, and Bloom crossed a
few names off Valentine's list, as she doubted she'd be able to make it

back to the Mississippi without them. Others accepted the extravagant promises Valentine made. One or two old soldiers elected to stick because they understood the devil in Kentucky and only God knew where they might be sent when they were "repurposed." Might as well spend the remaining time until land allotment or pension, riding herd on ex-Quislings.

Of course, beggars can't be choosers, nor can they expend much mental effort determining the motivations for those willing to help. Valentine was content to take names, get them approved by Bloom and Lambert, and then work out his battalion's order of battle—without having any of his volunteers "demoted," so to speak. He did this by creating an on-paper staff company.

One benefit of the rumors in Evansville about the departure of much of Southern Command's forces was a near panic about what might happen if the Kurians returned, especially with rumors about forces massing in Illinois, or Bloomington, or outside of Louisville for a dash down the old interstate.

So he had volunteers looking to join Fort Seng in any capacity—on the condition that their families would be able to come along if Fort Seng were abandoned. With food running short, Valentine couldn't accept all the volunteers, and even with enough to feed them he wouldn't be able to arm them, but he was able to fill out his uneven companies by taking, for once, the cream of the overflowing pail.

Bloom and Lambert both agreed that Southern Command needed some kind of send-off. The only point of contention was whether the piece that remained still be known as Javelin, or if the designation belonged to the brigade proper.

Bloom finally relented, mostly because Lambert had organized the whole party to begin with. If Fort Seng became a monument to the Cause's attempt to create a new Freehold east of the Mississippi and south of the Mason-Dixon, the tombstone might as well bear the proper name.

The headquarters staff kept the news of the celebration quiet to avoid raising expectations and just in case word traveled to the Kurian lengths of the river, either toward Paducah or in the direction of Louisville. No telling what the Kurians might choose to create in the way of their own farewell.

They detailed a few cooks to roast a pair of pigs and a lamb. Valentine spent the day in the field with his new battalion, returning to see beautiful paper lanterns lining the patio before the great estate house.

"The basement's full of that sort of crap," Bloom told him. "The guy who used to live here loved to throw a party."

Valentine's recruits stayed off to the side as Southern Command's soldiers occupied tables and chairs and benches. The two groups tolerated each other. Valentine's men oddly matched each other in the redyed uniforms they'd crossed over to wearing. Southern Command's troops had their patched fatigues, spruced up with their new medals and odds and ends picked up in Kentucky, mostly raccoon tails and legworm claw feet.

A band filled the chilled night air with noise. It was a merry-go-round collection of musicians as the players stopped to eat or drink and rejoined as the mood and tempo suited them.

Valentine listened to some soldiers warming themselves around a fire pit with even warmer spiked punch.

"Hope we get repurposed to Oklahoma or Texas—some kind of steer country," a corporal said. "If I never swallow another mouthful of those caterpillars, it'll be too soon."

"You're forgetting the good lean Kentucky horse meat, Corp. Meals fit for a dog."

A private leaned back, fingers interlaced behind his head as he reclined. "Soon as I get home to the wife, my johnson's being repurposed from peeing, that's for sure."

"Good woman, that. Puts up with that wood tick of a dick for more'n one night."

"What do you say, Williams?" one of the group called to a woman idly tossing cards into her helmet. "You think the bride said, 'I do,' knowing the triple-A battery Dalrymple here's sporting?"

"Size is for sluts. Give me a man with a quick tongue."

The men laughed, even Dalrymple. She added, "I meant interesting conversation, you lunk."

"Glad we're getting out of here. Only tongue you're likely to see otherwise would be out of a Reaper."

"Home alive in 'seventy-five."

"Worn-down dicks in 'seventy-six."

The chatter stopped when they noticed Valentine watching from the shadows.

"I miss the two-for-one whores of 'seventy-four, myself," Valentine said. Valentine headed for the barbecue spits, purposely altering his course so they wouldn't have to rise from their coffee and rolls and salute.

He found his old company headquarters staff passing a bottle of homemade wine, with vanquished soldiers tucked out of the way beneath their chairs.

Valentine wasn't feeling social. He passed in and out of the conversing groups, shaking hands and wishing well, never lingering to be included in a conversation.

He danced once with Bloom, who found his clumsy steps quietly amusing, and once with Lambert, who did her best to hide his offbeat lurches by holding her body so erect and stiff he had to move with her to avoid looking like he was trying to pull down a statue.

The Evansville group—"Valentine's Legion," some were beginning to call them, though Valentine himself corrected anyone who used the phrase—had an uneasy relationship with the Southern Command regulars. The average soldier had a low opinion of Quislings—they either ran from danger or knuckled under it when the Reapers hissed an order—and the soldiers preferred to keep thinking about them in familiar terms: as targets to shoot at or prisoners to be counted. So the ex-Quislings were relegated to the "back of beyond" at Fort Seng, a chilly field far from hot water.

If the goal of the celebration was to reconcile the two groups, the party was an unmitigated failure. But the two groups each ate well, albeit separately.

Brother Mark returned in the darkness. The man had a curious sixth sense about when to show up. If there was plenty of food and drink to be had, he was there. Yet he wasn't a social man. Like Valentine, he seemed to prefer hanging about the edges.

Valentine addressed a long table filled with his old shit-detail company. Many of them were wearing their new stripes and insignia for the first time.

"Be a lot more room for us once the others leave," Valentine said. "More hot water for everyone. We'll stick new recruits in your tent-shacks."

"Be good to have a home at last, sir," Glass said. His heavy-weapons Grogs were on guard duty while the men celebrated.

It was an unusually optimistic statement from Glass, but odd. He'd grown up in the Free Territory.

"We don't fit in," a corporal said. "Across the Mississippi, they put us in camps. Had to display ID all the time, wear prisoner clothes. Deep down it ain't life under the towers, but on the surface it wasn't that much different."

Valentine nodded. "You're changing that here and now. After you complete your hitch, you'll be as good as anyone else in the Republics, in the eyes of the law. You can settle wherever you like."

"Can we get our land in Kentucky?" Glass said. "Better land in some ways than Arkansas. People here aren't so hung up on where we came from."

"Not for me to promise," Valentine said. "There's Brother Mark. Ask him. He can go to the local government and see what they have to say. But they've been plenty helpful to us up until now, haven't they?"

"Reward's always over the next hill," Glass said. "Be nice if we could get something on paper."

Getting back across the river was much on the soon-to-depart contingent's mind. Valentine had men step up to say good-bye, shake his hand, or say a few hopeful words about wishing him success in the coming winter.

They gave him a present or two as well. One soldier gave him a flexible horsehide case for the new Type Three, having seen him practicing with it on the shooting range. Another gave him one of Karas' coins, the back carefully polished and re-etched with the brigade's designation and the dates of the Javelin's operational activity in beautiful copperplate hand.

As everyone settled down into groups after the eating and drinking, to smoke or play cards or show off valuables they were contributing to Bloom's "hopper" to buy supplies for the trip home (and for which they would receive a chit in return that, in theory, would restitute them once they returned to Southern Command, probably in near-worthless military scrip), a guard sergeant with the support staff loosened her belt and exchanged a few words with the musicians. Valentine didn't know her—she was one of the replacements—but he recognized the song as soon as the soldier with the fiddle began to draw his bow.

She sang:

> *The water is wide, I cannot cross o'er*
> *But neither have I the wings to fly.*
> *Build me a boat, that will carry tow,*
> *And both shall row, my love and I.*
> *A ship there is, and she sails the sea,*
> *She's laden deep as deep can be,*
> *But not so deep as the love I'm in.*
> *I know not if I sink or swim.*

The soprano had a rare voice, sharp glassy tones that carried through the night air. Valentine was reminded of the teenage thug who loved Beethoven in *A Clockwork Orange* who described a "sophisto" woman's singing like a rare bird who'd fluttered into the dive.

A huddled figure caught Valentine's eye. Alessa Duvalier was listening from just outside of the splashy colorful light of the paper lanterns, perched on a wall with her legs drawn up and clasped to her chest.

Valentine slipped across the party, moving in her direction, while the musicians played the refrain, allowing the singer to catch her breath and more listeners to gather. Even Valentine's own battalion broke off from eating.

> *I leaned my back on a proud young oak,*
> *I thought it was a trusty tree.*
> *But first it bended, and then it broke,*
> *And so my love proved false to me.*

He joined her on the limestone wall.

> *Oh, love is fair and love is fine,*
> *Bright as a rose, when first it's new;*
> *But love grows old, and sometimes cold,*
> *And fades away like the morning dew.*

"It'll never work, you know, Val," Duvalier said. "I thought you were smart about this sort of stuff."

She had that pungent, slightly cloying smell of liquor about her.

"Which 'it,' my friend?" Valentine asked.

"If you think I'm making another drunken pass at you, I'm not," she said. "I've sworn off men."

"Switching to women?"

"Ugh."

"You never could hold your liquor. You want some seltzer? The local stuff's pretty good. It'll settle your stomach."

She pinned him with her foot. "I haven't finished with you, Valentine. I figured when you recruited all these Quislings, it was just to have them make corduroy roads or clear brush or what have you. You really want to turn this bunch into a chunk of Southern Command? Quisling scum like that?"

Valentine switched to sign language. They could communicate in sign. They used to do it on their long assignment together as husband and wife on the Gulf Coast when Valentine had been working as a Coastal Marine. He could still use it but had slowed considerably. "Keep it down; some of the scum can hear you."

"I know their kind," she said louder than ever. "They're whipped, so they'll cringe and lick your boots for a while. First chance they get—*schwwwwwpt!*" She made a throat-cutting gesture with a sauce-smeared finger.

"It's my throat."

"Women fall for crusaders. It's a chance to be part of something big and good. That day out in Nebraska when you convinced me to go help the Eagles . . . I think I fell a little for you that day. A little. Lots of people get twisted by war, turned into something that's all sword and no plowshare. I like how you think of them." She waved her hand, gesturing vaguely to the northeast.

"But sometimes," she said, "you get all messed up about who the victims and the victimsizer . . . victimizers are. These bastards were stealing and busting heads of anyone who objected a couple months ago. Now you have them in Southern Command uniform. You told me once you spent two years hunting down the rapists of some girl you knew, or of the sister of some girl you knew. How many rapists are you feeding tonight?"

"None," Valentine said. He wondered if he should stick close to Duvalier tonight. Some of the men had heard her. While they wouldn't loop a noose around her and beat her up, they were perfectly capable of waiting until she passed out and then playing some sort of physical prank that would just make matters worse, especially if Duvalier woke up while someone was inking her face or filling her shoes with manure. "That's part of the deal I offered. Whatever their old crimes, they get a new identity the day they sign up."

"Like you're baptizing. Maybe the people who deserve a new life are the ones in Evansville, not these bastards."

"Maybe Evansville is happy to have them gone."

She didn't respond for a moment, and then she slumped against him. "Oh, Val, I'm so tired," she said, nuzzling his shoulder. "I'm more tired than I've ever been in my life. I want to sleep forever."

"Were you across the river again?"

"Yes. Checking some roads around Evansville in an old pickup. No sign of that armored Spearhead. But I can't shake the feeling something's going to happen as soon as Bloom marches her people out of camp."

"March out with them," Valentine suggested. "Take a break. You've been going hard for as long as I've known you."

"Can't. Every time I leave you, you do something stupid and I have to claw you out of it."

"I'd do the same for you," Valentine said.

She yawned.

"You'll sleep tonight. Where do you bunk these days?"

Duvalier had a habit of sleeping in strange spots: chicken coops, dog runs, little scraped-out hollows under rusted-out cars quietly going to pieces on the roadside. It was an act of security gained from long habit in the Kurian Zone: to not be where a Reaper might be poking around, looking for a victim.

"That's what death is, right? Just going to sleep forever. Unless a Reaper gets you. I wonder if the Kurians can mess with you, you know, even after death. Like it's hell or whatever."

"That's silly." Actually, it wasn't. Valentine had seen living bodies, suspended in tanks in a death that wasn't death, in one great, skyline-dominating tower in Seattle.

"They almost got me this trip. You think my luck's used up, Val?"

Maybe that was at the heart of her dark mood, drinking, and odd talk. "You're too smart for 'em," Valentine said.

Valentine escorted her up to his room at headquarters. Though the room had his name on a piece of cardboard taped next to the door, he rarely slept there, preferring to be in the little bungalow by the battalion.

"Remember crossing Kansas?" Duvalier said as they went up the wide stairs with big corner landings. "You were always up making breakfast. I woke up and there you'd be, frying eggs in a pan in bacon fat. Then you'd pour in some flour and make breading."

"It was to prevent you from dining out of garbage bins. The food's healthier when you cook it yourself. I suppose that's why I always fried it to hell. Fear of microbes."

"I thought it was delicious," Duvalier said, slipping out of her clothes. Which took a long time—she clothed her slight frame in multiple layers.

"Father Max used to say my cooking was made for Lent," Valentine said. He watched her undress. Not for pulchritudinous reasons; he wanted to make sure there was flesh on her ribs. She was a wanderer afoot, and the long miles left her scarecrow-thin. Valentine admired her knife-cut good looks, but wished she looked a little more like the sleek general's plaything she'd been during Consul Solon's occupation than the bony adolescent raising the sheet next to him.

"Make me breakfast, Val. Make me some breakfast."

"Okay. You stop talking nonsense and get some sleep."

"Next to you. Like the old days."

"Sure."

Valentine climbed into the bed. The queen-size mattress seemed extravagant, but then the estate owner considered anything under king fit only for the hired help.

He'd not lain naked next to a woman since the erotically mobile, lusty Tikka had gathered what was left of the Kentucky Alliance and harried the Moondaggers across Kentucky. Tikka had run through his inventory of sexual tricks, many acquired from an older Ohio doctor of highly specialized obstetrics, in a few marathon sessions that left her energized and Valentine exhausted but both happily relieved of the burdens of the Kentucky retreat during their few hours together.

Last he'd heard she'd returned to the Bulletproof. He hoped she was one of the delegates in Elizabethtown.

He felt some faint stirrings below the waist as Duvalier pressed her slight body against him, sighing contentedly. But the easygoing intimacy he and Duvalier shared wasn't physical, though they took comfort in the body heat and natural comfort of each other's frames when traveling together. Their intimacy might be compared to that of a brother and sister, but outside of black-cover gothic erotic romances, few sisters slept next to their brothers with pubic thatch tickling his thigh.

No, they were more like a veteran married couple, finding reassurance in each other's bodies, knowing that they'd wake up together or not at all—save that they'd skipped the sex that usually led to such complacency and gone right to physical reassurance.

The party went on until dawn and beyond.

The next day he accompanied Lambert across the emptied camp to headquarters. The trampled-down, dead grass where the tents had been set up turned the parkland into something resembling a chessboard.

They passed through to the CO's office. Bloom stood there, her files tied up in three big waterproof binders by her adjutant. She walked a little stiffly but kept the cane as more of an affectation than because she needed it for moving about the office.

They exchanged the necessary salutes.

"Fort Seng is yours. What's left of it, anyway," Bloom said. She turned a bit pensive. "Still wish I knew what they did to me when I got all scared," Bloom said. "I never once the whole time felt my mind was not my own. I was just dark and depressed about everything. Doubtful. That ever happens to you, tell somebody right away."

"How were you to know?" Valentine said. Lambert walked over to the east-facing windows and looked out at the Kentucky woods.

"Helluva way to fight: Make someone get so beat up about themselves they start thinking about taking their own life. I'd rather be shot at some more."

"I understand that," Valentine said.

"What ifs—you know. What if I could have been stronger, or figured out something was wrong with me. Does it make you not crazy if you recognize that you're sick in the head? I remember knowing I felt different. I thought I was just cracking under the strain."

"You did better than anyone would have expected."

"It was beautiful for a minute, wasn't it? When we showed up and found the Green Mountain Boys there. Colonel Lambert, you know you did all that. Too bad you couldn't have seen it. Oh, that was a good day."

Lambert turned back to face Bloom. "They fooled me just as much as they fooled you. Wish I'd been a little more careful."

Valentine wondered if his repeated requests to Southern Command for assistance to be sent to Ahn-Kha's coal-country guerrillas figured into Lambert's calculus when she'd decided on Javelin as Southern Command's next venture into the Kurian Zone. She knew Valentine, trusted him. Had he let her down? Maybe that's why she'd been so formal of late.

"I think the Green Mountain Boys were happy to see Southern Command arrive too," Lambert added.

"It's still the spot Javelin landed, as far as I'm concerned. I think we'll be back, one day." Bloom focused on Valentine. "I'm sorry, Val."

"Not your doing. I know you'd have stuck."

Bloom took a deep breath, brightened. "At least everyone's rested and refit. We'll make it the rest of the way . . ."

"Easy," Valentine said.

"I'd settle for hard. One twist away from impossible, even, just so long as I get them home."

Valentine stood flanking Lambert, watching the brigade walk out of camp under an iron gray sky. The soldiers moved in step—a rarity for the men of Southern Command, unless they were moving as part of a graduation class or parade review or under a general's nose.

Valentine expected the Kurians would let them return across the Mississippi. The Kurians liked to see defeated men live to tell their tales. It was the ones who'd beaten them they went after.

Men like his father.

It was hard watching the men he'd come to know on the long advance and the longer retreat file off down the road.

Of course, the few volunteers stayed on: some technical staff, communications people, and trainers helping transform the Quislings into something that could stand up to the Kurian Order. Even Galloby, the agronomist, had remained, waxing enthusiastic about learning more about legworm husbandry. He had some kind of idea about putting a special bacteria in the legworm's digestive tract and getting concentrated fertilizer from the other end. But while he put droplets into petri dishes and ran chemical tests, he advised Evansville on how they could do a better job growing their own food without the rest of Indiana to rely on.

Pencil Boelnitz also stayed, and Valentine wasn't sure how to feel about that.

The supply train left, and then some of the artillery Southern Command had brought in and were now towing out, and finally the rear guard departed, pushing burdened bicycles. Red Dog dodged in and out of their wheels to the turn into woods leading to the gate, then plopped down in the sun to pant.

"You ready for this, Dots?" Valentine asked Lambert, using her old military college nickname in an effort to lighten the mood.

"No," she said, looking around as if she were seeing the tree lines of Fort Seng for the first time.

Valentine chuckled. "Too bad."

"You're helpful."

"I'd be a lot more worried if you were more confident. What's my first order, sir?" Valentine asked.

Bloom's command car came roaring back into Fort Seng. Bloom hopped out before it even came to a stop, hauling with her a Kentucky "vol"—short for volunteer: a local who served in the loosest, most disorganized militia imaginable. Their only common element was a dark blue band around their baseball-style caps. Valentine smelled blood on him.

"The Kurians moved already. They didn't waste time. We aren't even out of camp yet," Bloom said. "I'm sorry I've got to leave passing you bad news. Evansville just hauled this guy out of his boat."

"Where?" Lambert said.

The vol spoke up. "It's lights-out for Evansville and Owensboro. A bunch of flying whatsits have taken over the power plant, and some Reapers and Moondaggers are holding the technical guys hostage."

Six

The banks of the lower Ohio: The Greenwater Infrastructure Support Plant—the former Elmer Smith Power Plant—on the Ohio River dominates the skyline for miles around. Or rather its smokestack does, a weathered, two-color pillar that resembles a Louisville Slugger (once produced a few score miles upriver) from a distance.

It is a quiet plant, generators thrumming away and a faint wind tunnel sound from the smokestack. The plant is active and confused only on days when thundering mountains of coal are unloaded. Once carried by barge, they're now brought by Kentucky's dilapidated railroad on captured trains, and irregularly at that. The Kentuckians break out the old joke that "these colors don't run anything but short."

The river is much changed since 2022. First called by the Frenchmen who explored it "La Belle Rivière," its banks are now coated with arteriosclerosis of trash and industrial waste. In more prosperous days the river carried a weight of cargo equal to that which passed through the Panama Canal: coal barges, oil, mounds of chemicals white or gray or sulfur-colored, grain, corn, soy, tobacco, and of course steel returning from the coal-fired furnaces of Pittsburgh.

The Kurian Order still dredges the river, off and on, to its usual main channel depth of nine feet. It maintains the locks that control the river as it descends the five hundred or so feet from Pennsylvania to the Mississippi junction at Cairo—where the few local Grog-traders are careful to correct your pronunciation to "Care-oh."

Now, in the warm-water outflow of the plant, tough carp and catfish survive the acidic, polluted river. The bass keep to their willow roots, stumps, and snags in their cleaner stretches of bank.

At this time of year, with the temperatures sinking lower and lower *at night, fog runs along the river most mornings, sending querying fingers into the riverside ravines. The foggy wall represents the new state of affairs along the river. Much of the north bank outside Evansville belongs to the Kurian Order; the south bank to the Kentuckians. When once they exchanged jokes about wool-headed Hoosiers and barefoot Kentucky hillbillies, now the locals steal and shoot.*

But around the power plant, the fog seems to cling extra thick, a shroud that suggests the unwary would do well to keep away.

They took the vol, who was named with a string of three personal names for first, middle, and last—John Robert Nicholas—into the main building, where members of Valentine's battalion were lugging boxes and setting up duty stations. Lambert escorted Valentine and the vol into her bare office, where a single box sat on her desk waiting to be unpacked.

"I want you to get them," Nicholas said, ignoring the bare decor. "You Southern Command people know how to deal with critters like that. We can make the soldiers jump when we have to, but this is beyond anything we can do without tanks and cannon and such-like. Don't belong on God's green earth, them things."

Nicholas shuddered. He raised his eyes to Valentine. "You'll kill 'em, right?"

"Private, Colonel Lambert's in command here," Valentine said. "Tell her how you ended up here."

Nicholas checked the insignia on their clothing. "That bird outranks that palm tree, right. I forgot. Our big bug is a senior sergeant."

"She outranks everyone on the base, Private Nicholas, so you're speaking to the right woman. Tell us what's going on."

Valentine went to the coffeepot, an expensive-looking plug-in model with silver handles and gold rings at the top and bottom that had probably been found in the house. Lucky it wasn't sitting in someone's knapsack. Or maybe it had been, and Bloom rescued it. In any case, she'd left it full of hot, delicious-smelling coffee for her successor.

The building had a pair of emergency generators, a portable gasoline-powered one and a fixed propane model, but Valentine couldn't hear either running. The power plant must still be putting out the juice, then.

"I'm to tell you that ya'll have a safe conduct pass out of Kentucky and back to the Mississippi for the next forty-eight hours, after which the skies themselves will fall on you. Those were the Tallboy's exact words, sir."

Valentine and Lambert looked at each other. The corner of her mouth turned up and Valentine shrugged.

"Now that you've passed the word," Valentine said, "tell us what hap-pened at the plant and what exactly attacked you. We need to know as much as you can tell us about what and how many and where they are."

Lambert called in a young man she'd selected as her clerk to take notes. When he was seated, she let Nicholas begin:

"Six I saw. They came in over the fence like— No, I should start at the beginning. I was part of the ten-man security team. We do three days on, then switch and get four days off, then four days on, you know—"

"Yes," Lambert said.

"Just there to keep an eye on the river, you know. We had an OP up the smokestack. We could see the Owensboro bypass bridge on one side—only bypass bridge still up west of Louisville, I suppose you know, sir—and Evansville on the other. Luckily it wasn't my shift to be up in the wind this morning. At dawn everyone got called out to look up be-cause there were these big things, like birds or bats only bigger than any turkey vulture you could even imagine. They were circling around the top of the stack. I think they drove Berk out. He started climbing down the outside ladder and they just harried him and harried him and he fell before he got to the first perch-rest. He fell and made a mess—spun as he came down and hit headfirst. We all ran inside after that and were look-ing out the windows to see what they were up to when the Tallboys came over the fence.

"Now that the plant's mostly automated, the people who work it just do maintenance on the machines and watch the load—never as much as the plant was designed to make, at least these days. That, and they work the loaders that keep the coal flowing—several people on that full-time. But those big fellers just came in and killed two of us right off the bat, and another jumped on Sergeant White, who was just trying to get away. The others herded us like dogs into the cafeteria and closed all the shut-ters. We just crowded in the center of the room while they circled. You ever had one of those things nipping at your heels, ma'am?"

"No," Lambert said. "All the Reapers I've seen have been dead."

"Let's hope that record remains unbroken," Valentine said.

"Then for no reason, one just reached in and grabbed a fuel man. At least I think he was—he was covered in coal dust. It fed on him. Got blood everywhere. I'd seen finished-up bodies a couple times, but this was the first time I'd seen one eaten in the flesh. Horrible sight. Most of us turned away. Figure I owed the poor soul that, you know? Someone said his name was Dewey," Nicholas added, looking at the clerk who was writing down his words.

"How did you get the message to give us?"

"After the one ate that poor coker, he grabbed me. That's where these bloodstains come from, his hands. The big pale bastard held me close, like he was going to dance with me."

The last dance, some called it.

"So the Reaper looked me in the eye and spoke, splattering flecks of blood on my face. I washed it off in the river, of course. Told me that you had time to quit Kentucky, forty-eight hours to leave with the rest of them. Of course, they had a message for the Evansville folks too. Then he carried me out like I was a toddler and chucked me in one of the commute boats the power plant workers use, and I got to Evansville as fast as the motor would take me."

"What are their demands to the Evansville people?"

"An exchange, they call it. Evacuation of Evansville. Anyone who wants to leave will be free to go into Kentucky. Then the south Illinois Kurians move in."

"I thought Evansville belonged to the Ordnance Kur," Lambert said.

"Must be some kind of deal they worked out," Valentine said.

"I don't know politics," Nicholas said. "I just wanted out of there."

They spent a few more minutes questioning him about numbers, and then they had him sketch out a map of the plant to the best of his ability. With that, they sent him to the small base hospital to be examined.

Lambert called her first staff meeting in the dining room of the big house. Moytana was there for the Wolves, waiting with the remaining platoon until Southern Command could send a replacement, Gamecock represented the Bears, and Captain Ediyak the rank and file of Valentine's battalion. Patel had charge of the base in the operations room. There seemed no getting rid of his former sergeant, for which Valentine would be everlastingly grateful. The door opened, and Brother Mark slipped in, looking tired and a little wild-haired. Valentine wondered if he'd been sleeping the previous night's party off.

"I was hoping to make this a friendly get-together," she began, ignoring Brother Mark, who was neither fish nor fowl in Southern Command but knew more about the Kurian Order than even the experts in the Miskatonic. "But the Kurians had other ideas. Word's probably gotten around the camp that they've moved against us already."

"Yes, terrible bombing," Brother Mark said.

"Bombing?" Valentine asked.

"The conference in Elizabethtown," Brother Mark said. "All the legworm clans sent representatives from the big towns to work out which way Kentucky's going to go. Franklin, Lexington, and Paducah aren't represented there, except by members of their underground. The town's been hit twice already, so you might say Kur is being represented after all. We're not sure if the planes should be part of quorum call or not."

"There wouldn't be a flying rattlesnake on the planes, would there?" Valentine asked.

"How did you know?"

"I ran into them in Dallas and again when I was out west. They're a remarkable organization. They can fly everything they need to a location, set up a small airport, and operate for as long as you can feed them fuel and munitions. They even can build simple bombs and so on if you give them high explosives and scrap for bomb casings."

"Brother Mark," Lambert said, "we're dealing with a separate event. The Kurians have seized the power plant that supplies Evansville."

"Which Kurians?" Brother Mark asked.

"Illinois, south of Chicago," Valentine said.

"Why should that matter?" Gamecock asked.

"I'm surprised you don't—," Brother Mark began.

"It's a binary problem with me, suh. Kurians are either dead, and therefore not a problem, or alive, in which case I try to make them dead."

"There's more to it than that," Brother Mark said. "To the Ordnance Kur, their Illinois cousins are practically enemies of the same degree as the people in Kentucky. To their minds, they're handing the city over to some 'neutrals.' The Ordnance wants the traffic on the river flowing free again. The Ordnance doesn't have much in the way of brown-water craft on the Ohio. They have boats from the Great Lakes, but they couldn't bring such substantial vessels to the Ohio without cutting them up into sections and reassembling them. And the rivermen in Memphis and Louisiana don't feel like raking the Ordnance's nuts out of the fire."

"Who's dumb enough to stick their nuts in a fire, I want to know," Moytana said.

Brother Mark harrumphed. "*Chest*nuts. It's a phrase going back to—"

Lambert rapped the table. "Let's get back to the situation at hand."

"Southern Illinois's no threat," Moytana said. "What forces they have are busy guarding against Grog raids out of the hills between the Ohio and the Mississippi, and the rest keep an eye on St. Louis. We could do worse. If the Ordnance decides to send that armored column that redhead wildcat claims is assembling and training there into Evansville, we wouldn't be able to stop them any more than the local leek cutters."

"Evansville has a hospital, workshops, manufacturers, horse farms, refineries for both ethanol and coal oil, factories even, never mind the agriculture—we need all that," Valentine said. "I'm not inclined to give it up."

"All those hospitals and factories and whatnot won't be much good if they blow up the power plant," Gamecock said. "You don't just pick up megawatt generators, you know."

"All the more reason to get them back," Valentine said.

"How do we do that against dug-in Reapers?" Moytana said.

"With enough covering fire, we can blow them out," Gamecock said, looking at the map.

"No, my guess is, despite wherever the hostages are, most of the Reapers will settle in near the generators or electronics—something we can't replace easily," Moytana said. Moytana's gray hair had turned a little whiter in the year Valentine had known him. "According to your vol, they're holding all the hostages in the workers' cafeteria."

"Logical," Gamecock put in. "Easy to feed them. Big enough for everyone to stay in one room, under observation. Warm and cozy."

"Packed in like that, a Reaper or two could kill them all in under a minute," Valentine said, remembering a "sporting event" he'd once attended in Memphis where a single Reaper executed ten men before a basketball shot-clock expired. Without the use of its arms.

"One problem. All those windows. We could put six Bears in that room in less than a second through those windows."

"Wolves can keep the gargoyles and harpies off of our backs. Bears take care of the Reapers. Power plant is back in our hands."

"If we can trust the map," Moytana said. "Someone needs to make a close reconnaissance before we plan anything. For all we know this is an elaborate trap—get all the Bears inside the place and blow it to hell. I think they want us to hit it," he continued. "They've probably got the whole place rigged. A ton of dead technicians, lights out in Evansville and Owensboro, and the resistance takes the fall."

"They're not that clever," Ediyak said.

"It doesn't hurt to act as though they are," Valentine said. "I'll ask Smoke about getting over there and taking a look tonight. She'll need transport."

"Better get her over here," Lambert said. "Where is she?"

"My quarters," Valentine said.

Lambert picked up the phone atop the table and gave instructions.

Most of those at the table found something interesting in the woodwork.

"My Wolves will drive her," Moytana said. "Light-duty truck, something inconspicuous."

"Any way we can get a twist on them?" Gamecock asked.

"Put the Whirlpool plant to work making generators," Brother Mark said.

"Something more immediate."

"There might be an easier way than assault," Valentine said.

"Head back to the Mississippi with the rest of the brigade?" Ediyak asked.

"No. Who's running those Reapers? We need to find the Kurian. Take the mastermind out of the equation and the whole thing will fall apart."

"He could be anywhere," Gamecock said. "We know there's no tower around, so it's probably hiding. When a Kurian wants to stay hidden, they're next to impossible to find."

"I don't think so," Valentine said. "He has to be near enough to the plant so he can control his Reapers day or night. Their range is limited to a dozen or so miles by day, maybe less. Kentucky is thickly wooded and hilly. He needs a high perch for good transmission."

"And one well guarded. Let's not forget what chickenshits they are, suh," Gamecock said.

Duvalier knocked and entered the room. She was wrapped up in one of Valentine's field coats. The table greeted her and she plopped down in a corner.

"Where on the river on the Ohio side is there a garrison?" Valentine asked the table.

Duvalier spoke up. "That's a pretty empty stretch, especially with Evansville in revolt."

"I say it's in a boat," Moytana said. "All it has to do is go over the side."

"In this weather?" Lambert said. "Kurians don't like cold. I think it would kill 'em. No, it's holed up. Brother Mark, could it be in the river somewhere? They look aquatic."

"That I don't know," Brother Mark said.

Lambert continued. "I was in a sort of a park that re-created their home planet—not Kur, which I think is warmer. It was quite warm, with shallow water."

"Boat still seems likely," Moytana said. "Mobile."

"No, it's high up," Ediyak said. "If it gets in trouble, it just launches itself into the air. They can glide for miles."

"How do you know?" Lambert said.

"I heard . . . before I defected over," she replied. "A friend in the underground told me he'd seen one glide away from a fire they'd started in his tower. He sailed off like he was in a glider."

Moytana was studying a map on the wall. "The bridge," Moytana said.

"Bridge?" Lambert said.

"New Bridge, the people in Owensboro call it. Just east of the city. Suspension bridge with two high pylons."

Lambert shook her head. "Too easy for us to get to."

"Not necessarily. Both ends are guarded."

"I've crossed it, a couple weeks back," Duvalier said. "North to south. I had a picture of a Moondagger and some letters, claimed I was looking for him. Smugglers bribe their way across all the time. One of the smugglers told me that it's actually harder to go north to south than the other way. Going north, they just check to make sure you aren't bringing weapons and ask about your business."

Moytana nodded. "The Kurians don't want their Ohio populace slipping across the river any more than they want Kentuckians visiting Ohio. That Kurian can get high enough so it's got a clear view of the power plant. The bridge and power plant can't be more than ten miles apart, I don't think. Clear line of sight, that is—not by road. Escape by air. Escape by boat. Escape by highway. It's perfect."

"Just guesswork," Gamecock said. "You know how many old cracking towers and water tanks and cell towers we've hit because somebody theorized that a Kurian just had to be there? All we came away with was a lot of rust on our gloves and birds' nests. I still say we wait for good, strong daylight and take out the Reapers. A Kurian's just a big bucket of ugly without his walking teeth."

"Not guesswork," Moytana said. "Our scouts have seen some new uniforms on that bridge recently. We've been paying attention because of this armored column reputed to be up from Bloomington way and it's the only intact bridge within sixty miles of Evansville. We keep a close watch on it through a telescope. There are some troops in big woolly overcoats that have showed up. All tall men in winter duty hats. They don't do anything; they just keep an eye on the Ordnance regulars. They look like high-level security types. Be easy for a Reaper to look like one from a distance, especially at night. He'd just pull his hat down and turn his collar up. We thought they might be there to clamp down on desertions or make sure smugglers aren't bringing necessities into Kentucky. But maybe not."

They worked out the details of Duvalier's reconnaissance, and Moytana took her out to find a pair of Wolf drivers for her. The nights were coming earlier and earlier, and they wanted to get her to the power plant by nightfall.

While Duvalier was off scouting the plant, Valentine spent an hour with his rifle and a weighted satchel on his back, training in an old grain elevator in Evansville. It had a similar-loading escalator that Valentine thought similar to the suspension cabling on the bridge, though the bridge's was larger and more graceful looking. He did a good deal of climbing on the inside of the elevator in the dark, getting used to the feel of hanging and climbing and resting. Then, when his muscles couldn't take the load anymore, he practiced balance work, using the gun as a balancing pole.

Duvalier returned the next morning while Valentine was sleeping. She was exhausted and smeared with coal dust and rust streaks. After everyone had gathered again, she gave a somnambulistic report, correcting a few details on the vol's map and delivering the unwelcome news that a platoon of Moondaggers now occupied the power plant as well.

"How do we get at the Kurian without it getting away?" Gamecock said. "In the time it takes my Bears to fight their way onto the bridge, it could escape."

"We don't even know it's there," Brother Mark said. "And even if it is there, it will in all likelihood be presenting itself as a garbage can or a loose wire hanging from a floodlight."

"Not in this weather, I don't think," Valentine said. "It'll be inside where it's warm."

"I might be able to find it," Brother Mark said. "There's just one difficulty, however. It would have to be communicating with its Reapers. Or even better, feeding."

"Is that all?" Duvalier said. "You let me in to the plant again, and I'll arrange that."

"How?" Valentine asked, unaccountably nervous at the idea.

"I'll know that when I get there."

"When will we attack the bridge? Strong daylight?" Lambert asked.

"No," Valentine said. "We'll need dark, with no moon. The bridge is too well-guarded for anything else."

"I don't like breaking up my Bears," Gamecock said. "They're too used to working together as a team."

"You won't have to," Valentine said. "That bridge is a job for a whole regiment—which we don't have—or one man. If he's there, I'll get him."

Duvalier stiffened. "Val, the last time you went off on your own wildcatting, it took me and a town full of Grogs to go get you back. Let me go."

"No, you're going to be busy at the power plant, getting it back in one piece."

They worked out a plan involving Duvalier, the Wolves, and the Bears creating a diversion at the power plant, while Valentine and Brother Mark made a try for the Kurian on the bridge.

*   *   *

The big basement in the Legion House—as the men were beginning to call it—was something of a treasure trove. Besides a spare generator and the new communications room (inhabiting what had been
before then a wine cellar; the precise climate control equipment was
kind to the electronics—and the operator), it had an old bar that was
now filled with boxes and odds and ends of the previous occupants, arranged like sedimentary layers in an archaeological dig. There were a
few holdovers from when it was a nature center: glass cases and displays. Valentine planned to empty them and return them to the "lobby"
behind the main doors, where they could post Javelin memorabilia.
Above that were the stored clothes from the owner and his family, elegant suits and dresses too delicate for his men to make much use of.
Then above that were piles of Moondagger clothing, uniforms and slip-
perlike footwear and odd Kurian icons, the most artful of which was a
wooden frieze of the curve of the Earth's surface in near-silhouette, as
though drawn from a picture taken from orbit, with a great nail like a
railroad spike driven through it. The spike had curious etchwork in it.
Valentine would have to have Brother Mark take a look at it when things
calmed down and see if he could make anything of it.

Valentine found an interesting, richly woven Moondagger outfit
that looked part prayer robe and part dress clothes and part military
outfit. It must have belonged to some high-ranking Moondagger, judging from the beautiful knitwork around the collar and seams and cuffs.
It had an attractive cummerbund or waist-wrap—he wasn't sure of the
word—of a flexible material like a bandage that had numerous zip
pockets. Inside, Valentine even found a little Ordnance currency.

Valentine had sought some decent attire from the ex-owner's ward-
robe, an outfit suitably impressive and redolent of status, but the
Moondagger robe-uniform might serve even better.

Luckily it didn't smell—some of the Moondagger stuff was now
rank and musty beyond belief.

With his clothes selected, Valentine and Brother Mark worked out a
rough timetable. It was a cloudy night, as had become usual as November wore on.

He and Brother Mark put together a small truck and a canoe, tying
it in the bed and on the roof and looking for all the world like they were
departing for a fishing trip.

Then it was a bumpy drive with Valentine, Brother Mark, and a
Wolf corporal at the wheel. He knew the roads, trails, and railroad cuts
for miles around and promised to get them to the other side of Owensboro—a town that was still more or less neutral. Wolf scouts had gone
into town, overcoats thrown over their uniforms but weapons carried

openly, and eaten at a diner with Ordnance soldiers at another table. They both paid their bills with Ordnance currency. Kentucky might be semi-free, but it was still integrated with the Kurian Order economically.

Discussion about the quality of the apple pie available in Owensboro or the amazing coffee at the Hitch had to be curtailed when they parked above the river. Valentine and the Wolf scouted and decided they were near enough to the bridge to make it a quick trip but far enough to avoid observation from the guards. Valentine and their driver set about untying the canoe while Brother Mark set out food and thermoses. They were all in for a long, cold night.

"Cold night," Brother Mark said. His breath steamed on the riverbank in the shadow of the bridge on the northeast side. They had left the Wolf back with the truck. "So much for our In—long-lingering summer."

"Indian summer, you mean," Valentine said. "Indian summer's a good thing, especially up among the lakes in Minnesota."

The Quisling guards didn't have any dogs on this side; Valentine was thankful for that. He'd heard barking up on the bridge at the guard change and briefly worried about patrols.

The bridge itself was elegant, a delicate-looking road bridge. Two tall pylons, one at the north end, one at the south, supported the bridge with a series of cables. They looked rather like a pair of matching spiderwebs, Valentine thought. The cables weren't tied to bigger main cables such as in more famous suspension bridges such as the Golden Gate. Instead they all linked to one of the two supporting pylons.

"You near enough?" Valentine asked.

"There's a Kurian on that bridge. That's all I may determine."

"What does it feel like?" Valentine asked.

"How do you mean?"

"The mental impression they give. Is it a voice, or thoughts?"

"It's like a chill. An open window on a still winter day in an otherwise warm room. Like the heat is leaving my body and flowing toward—it."

Valentine thought it odd that Brother Mark might be describing the cold tingle that sometimes came over him when he passed close to a Reaper.

"I just need to know where to go."

"Somewhere high, is my guess. They can sense longer distances that way without the clutter of animal and vegetable life."

Valentine looked at the riverbank. The Ohio was lined with refuse, mostly bits of plastic: bags, cracked bottles with blocky lettering advertising energy and stamina, cartons that looked like they were meant to hold eggs, chunks of foam clinging together like the chunks of ice Eliza hopped across to escape slavery.

There'd been a saying among the workers at Xanadu in Ohio—he'd learned it while digging ditches: *Flush it in Ohio, and it washes up in Indiana.* Valentine had taken it to mean that the less competent of the Northwest Ordnance were given duties in Indiana, but it appeared the phrase had a literal truth to it as well.

Owensboro, across the river, slumbered. There were burned-out ruins on the north side near the older of the town's two bridges. The closer of the two had long since collapsed—or been destroyed to simplify the border between Kentucky and the Indiana portions of the Ordnance. The "new" bridge was a little over a mile to the west, linking a bypass road that ran around the edge of what had been the suburban part of the old river town.

The Wolf had told him that Owensboro was a lively little town, popular with shady traders who brought Kurian Order products into Kentucky and returned with legworm hides, crafts, tobacco, bourbon, and marijuana. The big conference center practically in the shadow of the old bridge was still intact, the site of a bustling flea market on "Market Saturdays" every other week.

Valentine searched the bridge. He found what he was looking for even without Brother Mark—a little cocoonlike structure high on the north pylon of the bridge.

"There," Valentine said, pointing.

Brother Mark squinted. "I am afraid my vision is not what it once was."

Valentine handed him some binoculars. There must have been enough light for him to see, for he followed the delicate cabling of the bridge up to the north pylon.

"Temporary," Brother Mark said. "That, my daring Valentine, is the Kurian equivalent of a hammock-tent. Or the Kurian is very small and very young, a new bud off an old sire. Where else would he get multiple Reapers?"

Brother Mark muttered something else about budding in secret or an authorized increase.

"Is he there?" Valentine asked.

"I'm—I think so. There's some activity. As I said, it may be young. But it's able to control multiple Reapers at once. It must be a prodigy."

"All the more reason to kill it when it's young."

Brother Mark lowered the binoculars. "Savage."

"It's the truth, savage or no."

Brother Mark reached into his pocket and extracted a bandless watch. "Better get on with it, then."

Valentine changed into the black Moondagger robes and thick wool socks. He didn't have a beard, but if he tousled his hair right, it gave him a mad, Rasputin-like air that went with the Moondagger apparel. He didn't have the little curved knife many of them carried either; they were prized trophies for Southern Command's soldiers.

The robes had plenty of room in the sleeves to hide his Cat claws on their breakaway twine.

"Go back to the boat," Valentine told Brother Mark. "If you see a lot of shooting without the flare going off, just head back for the other side. If they loose the dogs in the woods, head back to the other side. If I'm still alive, I'll figure some way back, hopefully through Evansville. I'd rather not swim in this water if I don't have to. We'll have a frost by morning, judging from this wind, and I don't want to die of hypothermia thanks to wet clothes."

Brother Mark's lips writhed. "I'll do what I can to confuse matters."

"You'll do nothing. The Ordnance bridge guards are professional soldiers. I broke through a sentry point once and they chased me across half of Kentucky."

"No, I was referring to our friend in that oversized wasp nest. I have some . . . abilities where our Kurian friends are concerned, and if it's an inexperienced mind, I may be able to keep him occupied so you can approach with him unaware."

"I'm glad I decided to bring you along," Valentine said.

"Further proof that I'm good at what I do," Brother Mark said. "Hurry along now, daring Valentine."

Brother Mark was a man of deep waters—if he was a man. Valentine was beginning to wonder if he was in fact a Lifeweaver.

But he didn't have time to think about it. The Bears were scheduled to hit the power plant in two hours—or when Valentine sent up a green flare.

He took his Type Three out of the horsehide sleeve, checked the action, placed a magazine inside it, and tucked his Cat claws into the wide sleeves of the Moondagger uniform-robe. With that, he set off up the riverbank.

Valentine considered trying to bull his way through with his brass ring and the Moondagger outfit, but it looked like the sight lines for the guard posts covered the entire bridge. If he passed one they'd be able to see him all the way to the other.

Plus, there was a shadowy figure in the middle of the bridge that Valentine knew, without a doubt, was a Reaper. Undoubtedly there to guard its master Kurian in its nest high above.

So the easy way was out.

A Reaper, when alert and aware, was the most dangerous thing on two legs walking the earth. The eyes, ears, voice, and appetite of their Kurian, the avatars lived off of the blood of their victims. Terrifyingly strong and juggernaut tough, they were almost impossible to sneak up on, as they could sense a sentient mind nearby. As they fed, they passed vital aura, spiritual energies Valentine only half understood, to the puppet-master animating them. After feeding, the Reaper sometimes lapsed into a half-awake state. Some believed the Kurian became either insensible in the manner of a drunkard or preoccupied with savoring the vital aura—that was the time to strike. Or during daylight, when the sun's energy interfered with the connection between Kurian and Reaper.

If I can't go up from the top of the bridge, I'll take the bottom.

Valentine heard a dog growl up on the bridge as he approached. He froze.

There weren't sentries patrolling the base of the bridge on this side. But up by the lights there were guards pacing here and there, checking the approach to the bridge.

Damn, he'd have to get wet after all.

The Kurians and their poor habits when it came to keeping roads, bridges, and utility lines in repair served them badly at the new bridge. They'd strung power lines along the side of the bridge to bring electricity into southern Indiana from the Kentucky plant. Valentine took his shoes off and tied them around his neck, and then waded out into the river and took advantage of cracks in the cement bridge pilings to climb up to the power lines.

Luckily the high-voltage lines were well insulated.

Valentine dangled from the line by his gloved hands, swaying in the funneled breezes under the bridge as he moved out over the river a few inches at a time. It was exhausting business, and soon his fingers, forearms, and shoulders burned and screamed. He hung, rested, caught his breath, and went on.

Once well out of the security lights around the roadblock at the north end, he swung up his torso and quickly rolled across the pedestrian wall on the bridge and dropped to the side, pressing himself into the shadows, and lay like a dead thing.

He quieted his mind. The only way to get past one was to camouflage yourself, body and brain. The first thing he'd been taught after becoming a Wolf was how to box up much of his consciousness and tuck it away for safekeeping. Breathe in, breathe out, letting go of worry. Breathe in, breathe out, giving your fear to the air. Breathe in, breathe out, breathe in, breathe out, your body is nothing but a puff of air, flowing invisibly across the landscape. Valentine lost himself in half-remembered poetry, gone where all things wise and fair descend, moving toward "that high Capital, where kingly Death keeps his pale court in beauty and decay."

Breathe in, breathe out.

He watched the Reaper. There was something robotic about its motions. Was the Reaper idling? Perhaps the Kurian was concentrating on his Reapers at the power plant and ignoring his guard below.

The Reaper passed, and none of the bridge guards was eager to approach its perimeter. Valentine noted that in its passing, the Reaper's foot slapped the pavement of the bridge. One of its boots was missing the sole; on the other the heel was flapping.

This Kurian didn't take very good care of his avatars. Or it had just moved far, fast.

The guards left the center of the bridge to the Reaper. It paced like a trapped tiger, from the north side of the bridge to the south, crossing right lane to left, and then back from south end to north.

He looked up at the Kurian's nest. There it was, like a spider's egg sac in a hayloft, high and tucked out of the weather.

Sometimes it pays to take the hard way, Valentine thought.

Valentine got the rhythm of the Reaper's route around the center pylon. When it turned its back on him and began to walk away, he jumped up to the suspension cable junction with the bridge proper. He went to one of the suspension cables, looped a utility worker's harness over the cable, and began to climb hand over hand with wool stocking feet wrapped about the cold steel.

He moved up the cable like an inchworm. The belt harness enabled him to rest when he needed to catch his breath.

But it was a cold, bad climb. Numb fingers, couldn't feel his toes, aching arms and back . . .

He rested at the top, arm looped around a defunct aircraft warning light. Now it smelled like bat guano.

Off to the east he could see the power plant, lights illuminating the smokestack.

Valentine had seen Kurian cockleshells before. All he knew about them was that the paperlike material they were made of acted as both structure and climate control. For all he knew it was living cell material, some creature with no more ability to move or alter shape than an orange.

This odd bubo on the tower was about the size of compact car, perhaps the smallest such residence Valentine had ever seen.

He had considered bringing explosives on the venture, but the Angel Food was tricky stuff to work with, and Southern Command had departed with the good electric detonators. He might have to climb both ways only to have his bomb not work.

Valentine fixed a length of climbing line to the protective grid on the pylon-topping light and lowered himself to the Kurian's enclosure, rope looped around one leg and his waist.

The Kurian's nest was also a work of suspension. Two corkscrews of the odd material anchored it to the top of the pylon.

Valentine slipped on one of his Cat claws and slashed at one of the supports. The material was much tougher than it looked; it was like trying to cut wet nylon with a butter knife. Finally it gave way with a crackly groan.

Vision, air, sound—all cut off in an instant.

It was like someone had put a wet leather bag over his head. Seeing stars from it pressing against his eyes, he realized it must be the occupant.

Valentine had never been this close to a Kurian before.

He couldn't fight it without letting go of the rope and plummeting into the Ohio. If he reached up with his Cat claws, they'd go right through the Kurian, and he'd wind up scalping himself, or worse.

Consciousness filled with gluey sludge, he felt himself go dizzy and light-headed. The Kurian was taking over, denying him the use of arms and legs—

He settled for banging his head against the pylon over and over, hard. OUT OUT OUT! Valentine ordered the confusion.

Seeing stars, hardly knowing which way was up, Valentine felt his stocking foot slip, and he found himself upside down, suddenly free of the clammy, cold bag.

Something below spun as it fell through the night: the Kurian, looking a little like a torn scarf with sewn-on legs as it dropped lifelessly toward the river, pushed by the wind rather than riding it.

And then he realized he was dangling by one lucky loop around his leg, enervated and confused, a hammering sound in his ears.

Valentine found purchase on the Kurian's cocoon and dropped on it like a man poleaxed. The texture of the surface against his cheek felt like a dried, oversized spitball.

Except he'd done a little too good a job with his claws—the structure fell away. It fell slowly and silently, like a Japanese paper lantern might, catching air within. Or perhaps the material was a substance engineered to be near lighter than air.

The rope around his leg whipped this time like a startled snake. Valentine lashed out and grabbed one of the severed struts that had held up the cocoon. He plunged his Cat claws into it.

Hanging there, Valentine swung his leg, retrieved the rope, and hung again by two supports. Where were the damn rungs? Other side. Valentine didn't so much swing as roll to the other side, feeling with stocking feet for purchase. Finally the steel rung was in his hand and he could think again.

Valentine wondered what the goddamn thing had done to him. It felt like it was still hanging there. He waved his hand behind his back—nothing.

Despite the ladder, getting back down wouldn't be so easy.

Valentine was caught in the horns of what Duvalier had called "the assassin's dilemma." Early on in his training, she said that any fool could walk up and kill a target, provided you learned enough about its habits and grounds. The pro knew how to get away clean, or if not clean, at least alive.

If he fired the flare from here it would certainly be seen by the observers at the power plant, but the troops on the ground would wonder who'd fired it and why. But he couldn't delay until he could creep away; it gave more time for the hostage-takers at the power plant to figure out why the Reapers were acting so oddly and react.

No, Gamecock's Bears had to strike, and soon.

But Valentine had an unexpected ally. The Reaper, suddenly undirected and fearful, froze, looking this way and that. Did its master Kurian's final mental state—assuming they felt anything so prosaic and human as fear—remain in its brain psyche the way a flash left a white echo on the retinas?

The Reaper rushed toward the guards on the Indiana side of the bridge. Unfortunately for the men there, they were the closer contingent.

The first man it reached it just knocked aside with a sweep of the arm that left its victim turned around like a broken doll and twitching. It grabbed a man seated in a small, triangular armored car—was Valentine's crouched image, the last thing its master Kurian saw, reminiscent of the guard's position?—and pulled the man's arm out.

Valentine could hear the screams even high up in the wind.

It took a pull or two, but the Reaper got the man out of the car. The window wasn't big enough for the purpose, so the door had to come off, with the man's torso used as leverage.

Valentine checked his equipment and began his descent. Equilibrium and energy slowly returned, and he dropped the last ten feet to the base of the bridge.

Soldiers from the south side of the bridge were nervously peeping over the lane divider, watching the Reaper hunt their comrades like a loosed dog in a chicken run.

Valentine snuck up next to an Ordnance officer.

"Are you just going to stand here and let your men get shredded?" Valentine demanded.

The officer turned on him. "Waiting for— Who the hell are you?"

"I'm with Vengeance Six," Valentine said.

"What the hell's Vengeance—"

"Moondagger special operations," Valentine said.

"Then where's the beard and dagger?"

"It interferes with the disguise," Valentine said, hoping the man would see only a scarred man with dark hair and features.

"That's a nice Atlanta Type Three," an Ordnance NCO said. "I thought all you Moondagger types were issued Ordnance Columbus Assault—"

Valentine wanted to quit answering questions, and the best way to do that was to start questioning himself. "Captain, have you ever dealt with a rogue? They're unpredictable and very dangerous, worse than any rabid dog you've ever imagined."

"Glad to have you, but I'll need to—"

"Almighty, man, the thing's killed one of your men already. Let's work out who's subordinate to whom later. I need some light. A sudden burst of light always confuses them." Valentine passed him the over-sized plastic derringer that served as his signal gun. "Send up a flare, would you?"

"Sir, where did you come from?"

"New Universal Church School, Utica," Valentine said, giving the name of one of Brother Mark's alma maters. "When I point up, fire the flare."

"Who are you to be—"

Valentine whipped off his glove and flashed his brass ring.

"If you want to try to corral it, be my guest," Valentine said.

"After you," the captain said. The wild Reaper was carrying around the unfortunate driver's head, hissing at it like Hamlet speaking to the jester of most excellent fancy.

"Where the hell did he come from?" an NCO asked a lieutenant in an undertone that Valentine heard easily as he walked toward the Reaper.

"I hate these special operation types," the captain said. "They never let us know anything until we start catching hell."

Valentine trotted up the side of the bridge toward the north side, which was like a disturbed anthill as the Ordnance soldiers ran this way and that. Only three men stayed at their station: a group at a machine gun covering the roadblock on the bridge. They swiveled the muzzle of their weapon to aim it at the Reaper.

Valentine put his Type Three to his shoulder. He knelt and braced against a pedestrian rail between the bridge side and the traffic lanes.

He raised his left hand and waved his pointed finger skyward.

When the flare exploded into a green glow, the Reaper froze in its activities for a second, startled. Valentine, positioned so that even if he missed he wouldn't strike one of the few remaining Ordnance troopers on the other side of the bridge, squeezed the trigger.

The heavy round struck the Reaper squarely on the butt. Valentine doubted the bullet penetrated more than one layer of the strong, unearthly weave the Reapers used in their robes.

Reapers can scream when they want to. It's a high-pitched sound reminiscent of sheet metal tearing. The men at the crew-served gun, seeing Valentine shoot, opened up with their weapon as well.

Their target, probably frightened by the sudden light, pain, and noise, flattened itself under the fire and scuttled north like a crab and sprang off the bridge with an uncanny jump.

The men with the machine gun tracked it, spraying tracer off into the night. It cleared nine feet of Indiana-side fence topped by three foot loops of razor wire, landed, and disappeared into the darkness.

Leaving behind a heel from its boot.

"You're in a helluva lot of trouble, buddy!" Valentine yelled at the gunner. "I was about to put a round down its throat when you startled the bastard into fleeing."

"Thing was going nuts. What—"

"Now I have to chase it down in the goddamn woods. You know how dangerous that is, going into the woods after a wounded, pissed-off rogue like that?"

The green light began to pulse as the flare drifted down.

"You want us to sic the dogs on—" a corporal began.

"No, they'll just scare it. I'll have to hope it calms down enough so I can get a decent shot. And for Kur's sake, keep your men out of those woods. We've had enough bled for one night."

"Yes, er—"

"Get that gate. Unlike Jumpin' Jack Slash, I can't drop sixty feet and take off running. Is that a box of defensive grenades? Give me two. There's a good man. You never know."

Valentine hung the grenades on the Moondagger cummerbund and trotted off down the road. A pair of Ordnance medics went to work on the human wreckage left behind.

"Keep those dogs out of the woods," Valentine yelled at the officer, pointing.

He confused the officer just enough to get him to turn, and in that moment Valentine hopped over the rail of the bridge and dropped the twenty feet to the riverbank. Valentine took off into the Indiana woods.

He felt strange pity for the Reaper. What it remembered of its existence as a puppet of the master Kurian, Valentine didn't know. Would it be worse to awaken, confused and pained as a newborn, to a world of bullets and explosions all around and instinctive hunger that needed feeding, or to suddenly have control over your body again? Or was it something in between, where the Kurian gave his avatar ideas, needs, and desires, and let it carry them out with a little nudge now and then or a few words bubbling up out of the subconscious?

Valentine and Brother Mark rowed back across the river, fighting the downstream current that threatened to carry them within sight of the bridge. It would be light soon. There was a little highway stop with a good roof that the Wolves used to keep an eye on the bridge. They could warm themselves there and have a hot meal that would refresh them for the slow, bumpy ride home.

"What's that?" Brother Mark asked, pointing behind them.

Valentine put the oar across his thighs and looked over his shoulder. Something like a turtle's back was cutting through the current. Valentine saw a face come up for air.

"That," Valentine said, "is a Reaper head."

It wasn't swimming hard to intercept them; it was just following.

Valentine put his oar in the water and took six vigorous strokes while he thought. Then he set the oar in the bottom of the canoe and carefully turned around.

He took up one of the Ordnance hand grenades. It was the more powerful of the two used by their military, designed to be thrown from cover at an advancing enemy. Javelin had captured plenty from the Moondaggers, who used them to clear buildings.

"Hold up for a moment," Valentine said.

After a quick read of the yellow letters on the side to double-check the instructions, Valentine stripped off the red safety tape and pulled the fuse pin. The grenade whispered like a snake.

He knew better than to stand up in a canoe, so, kneeling and bracing as best as he could, he hurled the grenade at the following head.

It was a poor throw. It plopped short and detonated in a fountain of water with a rumbling roar that sounded like an oversized toilet flushing.

"Well done, my man," Brother Mark said.

"We'll see," Valentine said.

The last of the water fell and the head was still there, though it had halted and drifted with the current. It took a cautious stroke or two toward them again, letting the current put more distance between them.

"Not easily discouraged," Brother Mark said.

"Row hard," Valentine said.

Paddling hard enough to froth the river, with Valentine steering and Brother Mark puffing with the effort of providing power, they beached the canoe on the little brush-overgrown spit that they'd used to cautiously launch it a few hours before.

The Reaper scuttled up and out of the water sideways, like the crabs Valentine had seen on the Gulf Coast.

"Lord, oh lord, the thing's stalking us," Brother Mark said.

It had killed before but not fed. Valentine saw the yellow eyes, bright with something that was probably hunger in this cold, fixed on the slower-moving Brother Mark.

Valentine no longer felt sorry for the creature. The easy sympathy that came when he pictured it wandering the woods, confused and hungry, had been replaced by pale-skinned, black-fanged reality.

"Anything in your bag of tricks that lets you suggest something to a Reaper? Like going back across the river and trying the hunting in Indiana?"

Brother Mark closed his eyes, opened them, and then closed them again, this time firmly. "No, Major, nothing, I'm afraid. I get no sense of a mind there, not even a human one."

Valentine put his sights on it and it froze. It retained enough knowledge, then, to know what a pointed gun meant.

That made it more dangerous.

It slipped behind a tree with a swift step that cut the air like the sound of an arrow in flight.

"Shit," Valentine said.

He had one hope left.

A predator has a stronger survival instinct than most people credit it with. To the hunting cat or the pursuing wolf, serious injury is synonymous with death. If not defending young or scrapping with a challenger for territory, a predator will usually shy away from an aggressive display, especially if you can overawe it in size and noise.

Of course this isn't the case with all meat eaters. A wolverine or a bear will often welcome a fight.

He handed his remaining grenade to Brother Mark. "If it gets its tongue in me, toss this. They get lost in the act of feeding. You could run up and hang it off its back."

Valentine had lost a comrade in the old Labor Regiment that way near Weening, the night he killed his first Reaper. Weening still had the skull nailed to the town gate. The kids sometimes chalked words under it that appealed to a teenage sense of humor.

Valentine rolled up the Moodagger sleeves and slipped into his old, comfortable Cat claws. He advanced on the Reaper, arms spread wide.

It peeked from around the bole of the tree at him.

"Ha!" Valentine shouted. He swept one outstretched arm against winter-bare branches, stripping bark and crackling twigs.

"Ha!" Valentine shouted again, pantomiming a lunge as he approached.

"HA!" he tried again, stomping hard with his good leg.

If it came at him, he might still live. A good swipe across the nose might blind it.

The Reaper was dripping water from its robes but not moving. Nothing to do but go all in.

Valentine ran at it with a scream, and its eyes widened. It sprang away, running hard to the east up through the riverbank brush.

Valentine pursued it for as long as he could keep up the sprint and then lobbed a rock in its direction. His aim was better this time. The stone struck it in the leg and it jumped, crashing through some low-hanging branches and falling. It picked itself up and kept running.

"Yeah, you do that," Valentine puffed.

Valentine wasn't looking forward to the walk back to the truck. He'd have his rifle up and his sphincter tight the whole way, leading Brother Mark in wide circuits around anything big enough to hide the Reaper.

He had the funny feeling they hadn't seen the last of this fellow. And he'd have to pass the news to the Kentucky volunteers that there was a wild Reaper loose on their side of the river.

Just what the remaining Wolves and Bears would want to hear after the action at the power plant—assuming some catastrophe hadn't left the grounds of the power plant strewn with bodies.

They drove back to Fort Seng at a crawl, the vegetable-oil-powered diesel banging away in first and second gear over the broken-down roads. Valentine, exhausted and half-asleep in his seat, had the driver take them to the power plant first.

He was relieved to see a pair of Wolves step out and halt them on the last turn before the plant. They had to carefully go off road and route around a roadblock the Wolves had cut, unsure of the possibilities of a counterattack from the bridge and wanting to hold it up long enough for the Bears and Wolves—and one unpredictable Cat—to escape.

They found the power plant in Southern Command's hands and only lightly damaged in the offices, where explosives had been used to drive out the confused Reapers.

Valentine felt dwarfed by the immense architecture of the power plant and the towering smokestack. It seemed like a monument that would stand forever, like Independence Rock in Wyoming or the great Kurian tower in Seattle.

"Made angel food out of 'em, sir," Chieftain, the senior Bear NCO, said. He liked to decorate his uniform with feathers of various raptors—and a vulture or two.

Silvertip, another Bear who loved Kentucky and had decided to settle there and become a dealer in legworm leather, was partially undressed, sitting in the chill air and carefully scrubbing blood out of his studded leather with an old toothbrush. "Six," Silvertip said. "Don't remember ever taking so many in one day before."

"The Ghost did that," Chieftain said. "Shut down their master. Wolves saw the flare, certain enough, and got word to us. We went in and found the whole place in a tumult."

"Where's Ali?" Valentine asked. There were several leather-winged harpy bodies in a pile near the gate. Not enough for Valentine's taste, but they'd picked off a few.

"The Cat? I think she's sleeping in the kitchen."

There were Wolves near the exterior door, all asleep with bits of a meal scattered across the floor except one sergeant in deerskins quietly putting a freshly cleaned Remington back together. He pointed Valentine in the direction of the cafeteria.

The cafeteria had blood and black Reaper tar on the floor and a good deal of damage to the walls from bullet holes. The windows were broken where the Bears had come in.

Valentine found Duvalier in the kitchen, curled up between a steaming stove and a basket of potatoes. One of his Wolves was opening cans of tomatoes and pouring them into a vast soup pot.

She was sleeping cradling her sword stick, looking like a little girl snuggling with an anorexic doll. Valentine nudged her with a toe.

"Good job," he said as she blinked awake and yawned.

"You found the Kurian."

"Where we thought he was," Valentine said. "Just a little one."

"He was hungry enough."

"How did you feed him?"

"With the Moondaggers," Duvalier said, pouring herself some coffee from an urn. "It was like one of those *Noonside Passions* episodes I used to watch in New Orleans. I pretended to be a girl looking for her brother who was being held in the power plant, and this sergeant promised to get him back for me. The name I gave was for a dead man. Lying bastard. So he slobbered on me for a bit and then fobbed me off on a private to take me back to the gate where other family members were waiting, trying to shout messages to the men in the cafeteria.

"I played up to the private a little, the sergeant saw it and got jealous, and the next thing you knew they were fighting. Some officer-priest broke it up, took me away for 'counseling' and he started groping me five minutes later. I screamed bloody murder and the next thing you know half the Moondaggers were fighting with one another. I'll admit, I egged it on a bit by snatching a dagger and sticking it in the priest's kidney. The Reapers broke it up and killed two of them and hauled the bunch of us into the cafeteria. Then they lost it and started running around like chickens with their heads off. Next thing I knew the Bears were coming in the windows."

"Your feminine wiles have lost nothing over the years," Valentine said.

She snorted. "Dream on, Valentine. I think they put Chope or one of the other Church aphrodisiacs in that syrupy fruit juice they drink. I tell you, Val, there isn't enough hot water in the world to wash off the grubby fingerprints."

Seven

Owensboro, December: *Kentucky's third largest city, though a little smaller than nearby Evansville, has a vaguely Bohemian air to it. Long a riverfront town, Owensboro had its moments of fame: Its courthouse was burned by Confederate raiders during the Civil War, and once, at the turn of the twentieth century, it had been shaping up to be one of the pivot points of the new automobile industry before being eclipsed by Ford in Detroit. It was also notable for being the site of the last public hanging in the United States, that of Rainey Bethea for the rape and murder of a septuagenarian named Lischa Edwards in the 1930s.*

If Lexington is more bustling thanks to its status as a transport hub linking the Georgia Control and the rest of the middle and deep south Kurian Zones with the Ordnance and others to the north, and Louisville more industrious because of the huge legworm-rendering plants that turn quasi-insectoid flesh and a corn syrup sauce into WHAM!, Owensboro is proud of its cultural heritage. It prides itself on barbecue and bluegrass and, even in the reduced circumstances of the Kurian era, still manages to hold a few festivals a year dedicated to food and drink.

Now it is a popular watering hole for wealthy members of the Northwest Ordnance visiting from their vast homes and ranches in the delightful hills of southern Kentucky and the bluegrass outside Louisville. They enjoy the nominally illicit thrill of a visit across the river to dine and shop. The backdoor and under-the-table nature of the commerce along Owensboro's main street is the sizzle for goods that are often counterfeit, courtesy of the wily Kentuckians. The "Greek" olive oil is from Georgia, the "Colombian" coffee from Alabama, and the "Swiss" chocolate could be bought ten times cheaper in Pennsylvania.

*The gold in the quarter bars allegedly taken from Fort Knox is real
enough; the identifying stamps aren't.*

*The bourbon, musical instruments, and barbecue sauce is real,
however, as is the Kentucky weed. For some reason, plants that have
been grown from seeds that passed through the digestive tract of a legworm are considered more valuable.*

*The giant sassafras tree—according to the locals the largest in the
world—is still standing. It was recently the site of another public hanging, that of one of the Moondaggers from the nearby power plant who'd
gone over the fence only to be run down by the city's impromptu militia, mobilized to render aid to Southern Command in the return of their
plant workers.*

*The city is quieter than usual this December. Though often sub-
dued in the winter, this time around the city is in lockdown. It's not the
troubles at the power plant, or the revolt in Evansville, or the proximity
of the forces of Southern Command that has closed the bridge and
wharf to Kurian Order traffic. It is the great groups of strangers of all
varieties coming in, from long-haired legworm ranchers to statuesque
urbane females with gleaming leather courier bags and attractive wool
suits.*

*There's a good deal of speculation about who the strangers are.
The locals, for all their guitar picking and hurdy-gurdy cranking and
trucks with smuggling compartments over the axles, are keener observers of Kentucky politics than it might seem. They suspect that they're
playing host to the Kentucky Assembly but are willing to let history be
made before they start talking about it in the main street's many cafés
and bandstand joints.*

The Crucible Legion, as it was now being styled, had its first field
operation providing security on the streets of Owensboro. Valentine had
a standing order to put anyone who called it "Valentine's Legion" to
work filling potholes, and it didn't take many days of punishment with
wheelbarrow and shovel before the name disappeared.

Both the informal name and the formal request to go to Owensboro
had come through Brother Mark, who'd decamped without a moment's
rest to the Assembly at Elizabethtown and engineered its move to Owensboro.

Valentine and Lambert allocated two companies to the security detail, one to provide a presence on the streets in town and a second in
reserve just to the west, ready to move to the west bridge or travel on the
Owensboro bypass as needed. Valentine gave the street detail's command to Ediyak, and Patel's company had the reserve duty. Ediyak had

an intelligent charm about her that would mix well with civilians, and Patel could be relied upon to get his men from A to B in a hurry if it became necessary.

Valentine had little to do but get to know the town and keep his men from talking too much in the bars or being too high profile on the streets. The soldiers of the legion had the unusual orders to keep out of the establishments of the downtown they were guarding.

He felt odd patrolling a town not in Southern Command control, but as the Owensboro Emergency Council explained it, the delegates didn't trust some of the hotheads in the more vociferous clans not to try to storm the convention center and force the vote their way at gunpoint.

While the forces of Southern Command couldn't be called "neutrals" in Kentucky politics, they were famous for letting the civilians carry out votes without anything more than a soldier's fatalistic interest in the events of elected officials.

All Valentine's soldiers could do was provide an illusion of security. They stood in pairs and trios on the street corners and walked through the old town square and along the rusted, broken river walk. But if a file of Northwest Ordnance gunboats came chugging down the Ohio, all they could do was point the delegates to their designated bombproofs.

Of course, an illusion could be a powerful thing, as Valentine had learned at substantial pain in the Kurian Zone.

Owensboro had a police force, of sorts, who appeared to have one law for the town's residents and another for strangers and transients. Valentine had to keep in the good graces of the local police captain, his deputies, and his "detectives"—who, as far as Valentine could tell, were in charge of extorting money from the shadier local establishments.

The Kentucky Assembly met at the waterfront conference center that played host to Owensboro's famous flea markets. Instead of socks and shoelaces and genuine Japanese electric razors, they traded votes during the day and drinks at night.

Valentine set up his command post in the old town welcome center right on the main street, with a good view of his observation post on the old severed bridge over the Ohio that ran into the center of town. The welcome center had become a sort of lounge for restaurant and accommodation touts and cabdrivers. The touts and drivers were so busy with the Kentucky Assembly in town, they had no need of a place to sit out of the weather and swap lies about their clients, and Valentine had moved in without any protest.

Brother Mark came in on a coal train with a few other delegates, including Tikka, now dressed in an impressive mix of cotton, legworm leather, and riding boots that made Valentine think of a dashing flying ace of the First World War. She looked Valentine levelly in the eye and shook his hand before excusing herself.

"That bright young woman's building an army for Kentucky. Or an Army of Kentucky, though they haven't settled on a name," Brother Mark said in admiration.

"I hope word doesn't get out."

"Kentucky is turning into the proverbial tar baby for the Kurian Order," Brother Mark bubbled. Valentine wondered if he was drunk. Perhaps it was the stimulation of so much social intercourse, running from faction to faction, picking up on the queer electrical currents that run through political assemblies. "They're like Br'er Fox, getting stuck in the tar."

"I think the version I heard had Br'er Rabbit getting stuck. Br'er Fox wins one for a change," Valentine said.

"Well, either way the analogy is sound. Every time the Kurians try to attack Kentucky, they only get themselves stuck in worse trouble. They sent the Moondaggers in after us, and they perpetrated outrages against a people that tend to pick up their guns and let the lead fly until the point of honor is settled. Just when matters were beginning to calm down, they tried their gambit at the power plant. Now all of Kentucky is talking about that over their back fences and cracker barrels."

"I've yet to see a cracker barrel my whole time in Kentucky," Valentine said. Brother Mark had a city man's habit of cornpone clichés to make his points about the rural folks.

"Yes, yes, well, you know what I mean. But they're stuck in worse now. The bombing of Elizabethtown is another example. It united the delegates just as it chased them out of the city. Half were ready to break off and go home until the bombs started falling."

"And delivered them right into our lap," Valentine said.

"You're a victim of your own success, my daring Valentine," Brother Mark said. "All Elizabethtown spoke of the way you handled the power plant difficulty, and that smothered the idea of moving to Bowling Green or Danville. When planes hit the conference center unexpectedly again in a night raid, they decided to relocate in secret to Owensboro. We picked up two more leg-worm clans and several of the towns in the south. The only major holdouts are the towns in the Cincinnati-Louisville-Lexington triangle, but you can hardly blame them, practically in the shadow of all those Kurian towers."

There was still a pretense of an assembly going on in Elizabethtown, complete with press notices. A radio broadcaster calling himself Dr. Samuel Johnson—Valentine had no idea if that was his real name or not, but he felt as though he should know the name—continued to report jumbled details and play recorded interviews allegedly obtained in Elizabethtown over what was probably Free Kentucky's only computer–telephone line hookup. Of course Kurian agents were hunting all around Elizabethtown for the site of the assembly, probably so it could be targeted for bombing again, but for now the decampment to Owensboro and the new swearing in of delegates at the high school basketball court had remained a secret.

They kept an "underground special" radio in Valentine's city headquarters for listening to Dr. Johnson's daily report. Valentine, who was right in Owensboro with the Assembly meeting only around the corner from him, knew more about how the debate was progressing from a transmitter in Elizabethtown than he did from local reports.

Odd world. But he'd noted that before.

There didn't seem to be much for his security team to do. In the end, his one great contribution was to take Pencil Boelnitz off the hands of the Assembly security team. He snuck into the Assembly once, was warned off, and was escorted out. When he got in again the very same day, the Assembly sergeant at arms demanded that he never see Boelnitz's classic profile again.

Valentine had the journalist put under guard and walked back to Fort Seng.

Even Brother Mark wouldn't update Valentine on the real progress of the debate. Valentine plied him with food and had Ediyak cut and style his hair—strange duty for someone with captain's bars, but she was as curious as Valentine about the progress of the debate and was willing to play sort of a Mata Hari with comb and straight razor.

"Sworn to secrecy, I'm afraid," Brother Mark said, wincing at the amount of gray exposed at his temples. "Everyone's afraid of an opinion getting back to the Kurians. There's a rule, until the actual Assembly vote, that none of the voting on motions and so on is to be recorded or reported."

"But Dr. Johnson's sources keep giving him a 'sense of the Assembly,'" Ediyak said, applying a little Macassar oil (Owensboro style—probably cooking oil with a little dye).

"Dr. Johnson is not necessarily accurate in his reports," Brother Mark said. "Remember, he's also reporting that they're meeting in an 'undisclosed location outside Elizabethtown.'"

"Well, that's true after a fashion," Valentine said. "About eighty miles outside Elizabethtown."

"Why didn't they do this last summer?" Ediyak asked.

"Karas was operating on his own hook with his own allied clans," Brother Mark said. "But some of Kentucky supported him and started putting together a democratic assembly, on paper at least. The Assembly is almost feudal, going back to the traditions of the Magna Carta. This is a collection of powerful and influential men and women. Kentucky's nobility, you might say."

"You wouldn't know it by how they're spending in town," Ediyak said.

"They're afraid to show their faces. If you see a man hurrying down the street with his collar turned up and his hat pulled down, I guarantee that's an Assembly member."

Brother Mark was willing to brief them on general parameters of the debate. There were three broad factions in the Assembly, the Old Deal Caucus, the Militant Independents, and the All-Ins. According to Brother Mark, the future of Kentucky would be determined by which way the Militant Independents voted.

"Hard to say what'll tip the balance," Brother Mark said. "The Kurians seem to have finally figured out that threatening Kentucky is causing more problems than it's solved."

The debate was raging among the people as well. Dr. Johnson, when he had no news to report, read letters and notes from a few phone calls and even news reports from overseas. Of course there was no knowing just how much the good doctor was editorializing, but the vast majority of the messages he read were in favor of Kentucky declaring itself against the Kurians, though there were mixed feelings about whether they should join the United Free Republics or no.

The United Free Republics, as it turned out, suddenly developed a diplomatic interest in the situation in Kentucky.

A civilian of Valentine's acquaintance named Sime arrived with more than a dozen security men and aides dressed in the ordinary buttoned, collarless shirts and denims, corduroys, and moleskins of the Kentuckians.

Valentine could only gape at the motorcade. He hadn't seen vehicles like this since driving Fran Paoli's big Lincoln out of the Ordnance on Halloween night. The one at the front was marred by a big brush cutter. The passenger van at the rear bore a medical red cross. All were excessively dirty, however.

Sime checked in at Valentine's security office on a blustery afternoon. At the moment, Valentine didn't have anything but oatmeal and hot apple cider to serve his elegant visitor.

Valentine wasn't sure how he felt about Sime. In some ways they were similar: in age, melting-pot heritage—Sime a dark chocolate and Valentine a native bronze—and general height and build. There were contrasts: Sime was smooth-skinned, Valentine scarred; Sime bald, Valentine long-haired. Valentine found Sime's usual scent of sandalwood and gentleman's talc appealing.

More important, every time Valentine became involved with Sime, Valentine seemed to end up in deeper difficulty. Now Sime was giving him the additional headache of keeping tabs on one of Southern Command's bigger political bugs.

Sime idled in the lobby, after requesting the Kentuckians for an opportunity to speak on behalf of Southern Command. Perhaps for power-play reasons of their own, the Assembly put him off for a day.

"You wouldn't have a shower in here somewhere?" Sime asked Valentine. He had an entourage of sixteen, personal security types and drivers and communication staff.

"There's hot water in the washroom. Best I can do. You're going to have difficulty finding accommodations in town, unless you want to squat in a rat run or take charity. You're welcome to stay on base, but it's a two-hour drive to Fort Seng."

"We can sleep in the vehicles. They're rigged for it."

"I don't suppose they're rigged to carry medical goods and antibiotics. We could really use some."

"Yes, we'll spare what we can. I've brought you the latest ravies vaccine too."

"New strain loose?"

"You'll have to ask the doctor. I believe it's just this year's booster," Sime said.

"We could really use a doctor at the post."

Sime pursed his lips, and Valentine knew the man well enough to know when his patience was wearing thin. "I thought you had support from Evansville."

"It's a small manufacturing city, and even that's not much good without raw materials. I don't want to strip the town of what little they have for their own people. And it helps to have a doctor who has to obey orders."

"Personnel isn't my specialty. Remember, I'm not here to support your guerrillas or *légion étrangère* or whatever you're running here."

"What are you going to tell the Assembly?" Valentine asked.

"What do you think I'll tell them?" Sime asked.

"A rousing speech promising the friendship of the Free Republics, as long as that friendship doesn't get measured in bootheels over the river," Valentine said.

Sime had a good poker face. No tells gave away whether he was angered or amused. "I may just surprise you. I hope you come and hear it."

"I'm afraid they won't let me in."

The lips tightened again. "The man handling security for the town? I'll see what I can do."

"Seems to me everything you've been involved in has been a disaster for Southern Command," Valentine said. Sime's smooth exterior made Valentine want to stick a pin in him just to see if he would pop. "Kansas, Javelin . . . what about the offensive in the Rio Grande Valley? Your handiwork too?"

"You earned your dislike, Valentine. Maybe one of these days you'll grow up and realize I'm in the same fight as you. I can't swing a blade and I shoot like a cross-eyed man and I'd be dead in a week if I had to eat preserved ration concentrate and WHAM! But I know people and I can read my audience."

"Bet that comes in handy when a Reaper tears the roof off your house."

"Maybe I'm better equipped for fighting the kind of battles the Kurians wage. They don't put—what's that phrase?—shit on target. They'd rather make their target give up and go home, or do a deal that swaps a few lives, a few towns, for a generation's security."

He stared at Valentine. Valentine recognized the challenge and tried to meet his eyes, held them for a long moment, and then found an old lighting fixture over Sime's shoulder suddenly of great interest.

Perhaps he had been unfair to Sime.

"Like you, I'm ready to make sacrifices for victory," Sime continued. "I was ready to give you up to get Kansas. And if I could trade your life for a different outcome in Kansas, I would, like a shot."

"The feeling's mutual."

"Would you, now, if it came to it?" Sime said. "If you could get the high country of Kansas back for us by just putting that pistol to my head and squeezing the trigger, would you?"

Valentine took his hand away from his belt and crossed his arms.

"It's never that easy," Valentine said.

"Your father would have."

"You knew him?"

"Not firsthand. But I know the history. He was what we called a plantation burner. Left a lot of scorched earth—and scorched bodies—behind. But it made the Kurians pull out of most of Missouri. I won't argue the results. I'm sorry if he told you different, but that's the truth of the matter."

"He never told me anything at all."

"You a fan of football, Valentine?"

"I know the basics, but I never had much time to follow it."

"I'm a big fan. We have some fair mud leagues running the spine from Little Rock to Texarkana. I'm a Buzzsaw man, myself."

Valentine had overheard enough sports talk to be conversant. "I've heard of them. I think they won the championship a few years back."

"Two seasons ago. Every good team needs what I like to call a hatchet. With the Buzzsaws, it's a linebacker. It's the crazy mean player, the guy who puts people down for a game or two. So instead of covering assignments, the opposing team's eyeing the hatchet, wondering who's going to be broken next. Bad sportsmanship? Maybe. But I've learned something before I started shaving my gray hairs. Most good organizations have a hatchet or two to do the dirty work."

"I see."

"You'd make a pretty good hatchet. You have the right name, anyway, thanks to your father's, well, fierce reputation."

Valentine shrugged. The gesture made him feel like a hypocrite—a shrug from a subordinate always annoyed him—but he was only too happy to use it himself with the slippery Sime. "I always thought of myself as more of a screwdriver. Always being used for jobs other than the one I'm designed to do."

Sime was good to his word. An Assembly ID showed up for Valentine the next day. Though he had to report to the Assembly's own sergeant at arms to get his picture taken with a Polaroid and have a card made.

The Assembly itself was run by the Agenda. That office was held by a woman, thin and wan and brittle-haired; she looked like a cancer victim. Brother Mark introduced Valentine to her. She greeted him gravely, made a polite mention of the power plant and said she hoped Kentucky would support his command in the manner of allies who'd bled together, and then she moved on to other business.

Her handshake was a frail one.

"You are no doubt wondering," Brother Mark said. "Some kind of cancer, but it's not public knowledge. She's doing her best to get through the Assembly before it claims her."

"Brave woman."

"From a great old family in Lexington," Brother Mark said. "Our good Agenda believes that however this goes, the Kurian Order is going to extract their revenge on whoever leads the Assembly. She intends to die quietly this winter and deny them the satisfaction."

Once the formalities were taken care of, Brother Mark showed him around the pre-22, poorly lit convention hall, which smelled like musty carpet and popcorn to Valentine's sensitive nose. A lectern platform stood at one end, with most of the folding chairs around more-or-less arranged to face it. On the platform was a lectern with its own podium and a small desk just above a discreetly placed recorder's station.

The Kentuckians, a smattering of representatives from the Evansville area, and even a delegation from the rebels in West Virginia—he'd hoped Ahn-Kha would be among them but the golden Grog would have stood out among the men like an elk in a goat herd—had gathered into three distinct groups.

As Brother Mark explained it, the biggest faction in the room was the Militant Independents. A mixture of legworm clans and burghers, these Kentuckians believed that Kentucky now stood in a position of strength to negotiate with the Northwest Ordnance north of the Ohio and the Tennessee Kurians and the Georgia Control to the south. They had a provisional charter drawn up that declared Kentucky a self-governing territory with a promise not to engage in operations outside its old United States borders, nor to shelter fugitives or guerrillas.

"The fugitive law is the real sticking point," Brother Mark said. "Almost everyone in the legworm clan has a relative or an in-law who fled the Kurian Zone. They'd be grandfathered in, of course, but there's sympathy for escapees."

"How do they know the Kurians will go along with it?"

"I suspect there's already been some back-and-forth. Rumor has it a top-brass ring fixer has been negotiating in Louisville."

Valentine had heard of "fixers" before: trusted human intermediaries who handled difficulties between the various Kurian Zones. Without their intervention, the Kurians would eliminate each other in the snakepit world of high-level Kurian politicking.

Was there a conference going on in, say, Chicago or Cleveland or Atlanta, with Kurian representatives meeting to determine what to do about the chaos in Kentucky? He hoped some stealthy Cat had managed to worm her way in to listen. Or better yet, plant a thermobaric bomb.

Next in size among the groups at the Assembly was the All-Ins. These delegates represented the legworm clans gathered under "King" Karas last summer for Javelin and their supporting towns, the thinned-down remainders of the Kentucky Alliance who'd done much of the fighting in the destruction of the Moondaggers. They'd already beaten the Moondaggers and were expecting the other delegates to join them in a rebellion well-started, to their minds.

The Old Deal Caucus was the smallest contingent but, not surprisingly, the most polished and best turned out. They represented Kentucky's Kurian-occupied cities and those with financial interests in the

Kurian system. They had their chairs in a circle in the far east corner, mostly talking among themselves.

Of all the delegates, these men and women from the Old Deal Caucus may have been the most courageous, to Valentine's mind. Their lives, and probably those of their families, would be forfeit if the Kurians learned of their presence here. The more hard-line rebels considered them only a baby step away from being open collaborators, and Valentine's sharp ears picked up one of the All-Ins saying that they should hang the lot of them.

Whichever way the Assembly ultimately voted, Valentine suspected that these delegates would suffer the most.

Maybe it was just ego, the desire to show Valentine that there were victories to be won in the political arena as well as on the battlefield, but Sime had facilitated Valentine's credentialing on the day he was scheduled to address the Assembly on behalf of Southern Command.

Sime, looking like a walking advertising poster for skin toner, stepped to the podium as the Agenda introduced him from her little desk. Sime's aides had cleared away the Styrofoam cups and the scribble-covered scraps of provisional resolutions and vote-counts littering the podium and the stagelike platform. Much of the audience quieted—not just hushed voices and close-together heads, but true attention. Evidently all were interested in what he had to say.

"Thank you, Madam Agenda," Sime said.

"I come before you as a friend of liberty and an open enemy of the Kurian Order.

"This Assembly is now addressing the most vital question in human history. What is the future of our species?

"There are those who counsel for surrender. Certainly, deals may be struck with relative ease. Either the Northwest Ordnance or the Georgia Control would be happy to hand out a few brass rings, sign elaborate guarantees, and offer the usual Kurian promises of better food, housing, and medical care in exchange for the Kurian Order policing of criminals and troublemakers. Are there any voices who consider this their preferred option?"

The Assembly didn't produce so much as a cough. Had it been night, Valentine suspected he could have heard crickets outside.

"The next option is an understanding with the Kurians such as you lived under these past decades: the emasculated autonomy trading produce for peace before your martyred hero, Mr. King Karas, declared himself against our oppressors."

Several members stood up and began to applaud. Valentine recognized them as members of Sime's entourage, sprinkled about the assembly. The others who joined in on the recognition of the dead hero's name looked enthusiastic enough, but Valentine felt a little sickened by the planted enthusiasm.

Sime nodded solemnly, looking toward the circled chairs of the Old Deal Caucus. "The rightness of his decision, I think, is not questioned by anyone in this Assembly, even if the outcome was not all that we in the Free Republics hoped would come of our alliance.

"Are there any who think that all the blood shed across Kentucky between the Alliance clans and Southern Command's forces was wasted?"

"Madam Agenda," a delegate said, upon being recognized and permitted to speak. "The representative from through the woods and over the river forgets that Kentucky is more than just legworm ranchers. There are farms, mines, towns, and cities. Not all of us suffered reprisals. Even with the troubles up north, the Nashville Kur left us in peace, and the Georgia Control even pulled back from the borderlands."

A white-haired oldster cleared his throat. "Maybe the vamps don't know which way we're jumping, or even whether we're gonna jump, and they don't want to startle us. It's the sitting frog that's easiest to catch."

The Agenda pounded her gavel at her own small desk at the edge of the stagelike platform. "The delegate from Bowling Green will keep order."

Sime asked for permission to continue his address, and she nodded.

"There is a third alternative, one pursued by the Ozark Free Territory throughout its history, though we have recently been joined by Texas and much of Oklahoma and part of Kansas into the Free Republics. It is both the hardest and the easiest course: that of resistance.

"I say hardest because it means fighting, funerals, constant vigilance, loss of precious blood and matériel. Empty bellies in winter and blistered hands in summer. It has long been said that freedom is not free, but in the United Free Republics we've learned that those who desire freedom pay a bill more costly than the alternatives of supplication or cooperation. Freedom is a more exacting taskmaster than any Kurian Lord."

Sime had worked up a good head of steam. Valentine realized why he survived as elected leaders came and went. "Yet it is also the easiest choice, for we can meet the terrible reckoning with a clear conscience that we remain human beings, dignity intact, our births and deaths ordered only by our Lord on his Eternal Throne.

"We will not be chickens in a coop or pigs in a pen. No, we're the wolves in the forest, the bears in their caves, and those who would have pelts made from us must beware.

"While our cause is yours, I must tell you that for the moment, all that Southern Command can promise is that we will tie down as many of the enemy forces as we can on our borders. We've suffered grave losses recently. We need a few years' respite to catch our breath before taking the offensive again. All I can offer the Assembly is moral support and what our forces near Evansville are able to recruit and train."

The Assembly hid their feelings well, but Valentine could see consternation in the All-In faction.

They applauded, politely, and Valentine could only imagine the reception Sime would have received if he'd promised a whole division of Guards, complete with an artillery train and armored-car support.

"I'm glad you didn't overpromise," Valentine said later as he and Sime watched Brother Mark go from group to group to exchange a few words with the faction leadership.

"It's the New Realism, Valentine."

"Putting 'new' in front of anything as tenuous as a word like 'realism' sounds like an excuse rather than a strategy."

"Nevertheless," Sime said coolly, "I have to work within the parameters of the possible, just as you do."

"And you agree with this New Realism?"

"Of course not. We can't beat the Kurians playing defense."

Either Sime was an unusually artful liar or he'd finally revealed something of himself beyond an official presence. "Something's been bothering me for years," Valentine said. "I hope you don't mind if I ask."

"Shoot," Sime said.

"I've met a lot of men who shave their skulls, but your head looks . . . polished. What's your secret?"

Sime's face broke into a wide smile. He flicked his forefinger down his nose. "I'll loan you my razor and we can go over to a washbasin—"

"On you it looks distinguished. I would look like a mental patient."

"If I let my real hair grow, I'd look much older. Be proud of yours. Not enough gray yet to dismay the twenty-year-olds."

"I never had luck with twenty-year-olds, even when I was twenty," Valentine said. "Where will you go next?"

"You know that joke the Denver Freehold tells about the UFR, don't you?" Sime asked.

"What's that?"

"*Too near for a penal colony, too big for an insane asylum, and too fractious to be a nation.* I heard a similar joke in the Mexican desert, just not so family friendly in language. I'll return to our insane penal colony nation."

"Can't say that I like you, sir. But I'm glad you're with the team," Valentine said.

"The feeling is mutual," Sime said. "By the way, did you enjoy that soap?" The first time they'd met, when Valentine was sitting in prison awaiting trial for the murder of some Quisling prisoners, he'd complimented Sime on the unique smell of his sandalwood soap. Sime had presented him with a supply before the launch of Javelin. Valentine found its aroma relaxing, especially when worked into a fragrant lather in a steaming field-tub of water, and had used it frequently during the retreat whenever they paused long enough for a hot bath.

"Sadly, yes. Used it up last summer."

"I've a spare bar. I'll drop it by your fort on the way out. Oh, I'm taking Moytana back with me. The new broom wants a large reserve of Wolves ready to be shifted at need, and Moytana's due for an important promotion. Besides, his replacement has arrived."

Rumor had it the Assembly would vote before the first day of winter. Valentine found a reason to hang about the convention hall, hoping to run into Brother Mark in one of his circuits.

Valentine enjoyed the late fall air, chill but sunny. It reminded him of the Octobers of his youth in Minnesota. He wondered if the chill was characteristic of Kentucky this time of year.

A rather decrepit legworm stood facing the river. It was bare of all baggage, of course. Even the heavy saddle chair had been stripped off, and sheets of plastic tarp protected the legworm from the wind. Battle pads were on the side facing the street, with VOTE FOR FREEDOM = VENGEANCE painted on the mattresslike panels in Day-Glo colors.

Valentine felt for the legworm. In cold weather, their instinct was to gather in big heaps, forming domes that warmed and protected their eggs as living nests.

This dilapidated old creature had hide hanging off every which way and looked clearly uncomfortable on asphalt, glistening probes out to smell the air.

Valentine marked an ancient plastic refuse container holding a mix of leaves and refuse, probably from the quick cleanup of the convention center. Valentine picked it up and dumped it under the legworm's front end.

Where was the legworm's pilot? He could at least feed his beast.

"Wonder which end is worse, sometimes," a delegate said as he puffed politely nearby on a cigarette.

The legworm happily sucked up the refuse. Paper would be digested as regularly as the crackling leaves.

Valentine looked down its torn, perforated side. Skin was falling away in patches from—

Nature abhors regularity, and something about the pattern on the legworm's side facing the building disturbed Valentine.

Valentine quit breathing, froze. Sixteen holes in the legworm's side. He lifted a piece of loose skin, saw stitching in the legworm's hide.

He looked around, kicked some more refuse under the legworm's nose. He marked rings around the light sensors that passed for eyes. The creature wasn't old; it was ill cared for and badly fed. It had clearly been ridden on very little feed recently.

The legworm's anchor detached with a casual press to the carabiner attaching the drag chains to the fire hydrant serving as a hitching post.

"You!" he called to the smoker on the corner of the main drag. "Get everyone back from this side of the building. This worm's a bomb!"

When is it set to go off?

Valentine unsheathed his knife and prodded the creature in its sensitive underside.

Valentine crept along, keeping low in the gutter, moving the legworm along with shallow stabs. Clear fluid ran down the knife blade, making his hand sticky.

The legworm angled left, drawing away from the building as it slowly turned from the conference center, tracing a path as gradual a curve as an old highway onramp.

Duckwalking made his bad leg scream with pain. Valentine waited for the cataclysm that would snuff his life out like a candle in a blast of air.

The hungry legworm hit some of the overgrowth at the end of street. What had once been a pleasant river walk had largely collapsed into brush and small trees. The starving legworm settled into a hurried munch.

Valentine, launching off his good leg, used a saddle chain to swing up and over the beast and dashed for the convention center.

Whoever had spread the alarm didn't do a very good job. Several delegates, their ID cards whipped by the wind, ran out the doors on the worm's side.

"Not that way," Valentine yelled, waving them toward the main street.

Koosh! Koosh! Koosh! Koosh!

Valentine had his face in the pavement. Later, he was told by witnesses that some kind of charges had fired out of one side of the beast like cannons firing in an old pirate movie. Most of the charges fell in the Ohio, detonating in white fountains like a long series of dynamite fishing charges. Valentine, deafened, felt the patter of worm guts all around.

When the thunder stopped, he stood up. The worm had been opened messily, mostly in the direction of the river. Part of the northwest corner of the conference center looked like it had been struck by artillery fire.

Troops, police, and citizenry were running in from all directions. Valentine went to work getting help to the figures knocked off their feet or staggering around in a daze, turning chaos into order.

Valentine felt something squish and slip underfoot as he directed the confusion. He glanced down, expecting a brown smear of dog feces, and realized he was standing on a length of human intestine.

Incredibly, within a few hours of the blast the Assembly had reconvened.

"They are ready to vote," Brother Mark said. "They've excluded all non-Kentuckians from the Assembly."

Valentine saw the Evansville delegates decamp en masse for the beer halls and wine gardens of Owensboro—if you called a wood-paneled interior with a couple of potted palms a garden, that is.

"Which way do you think it'll go?" Valentine asked.

"Our, or rather, freedom's way, praise God. You know, that bomb ended up being ironic. It was obviously meant to blow the Assembly apart, but it ended up pulling them together. Another foot stuck well into mouth on the part of the Kurian Order. The one man killed was named Lucius F. B. Lincoln, by the way—a delegate from Paducah. A good name for today's entry into Kentucky history. He ended up doing more for the Cause by dying than we'll ever do, should we both live out our threescore and ten. The Assembly's all talking to one another again. I think they know those shaped charges would have torn through the Old Dealers or All-Ins without discriminating according to political belief."

"That's a hard way to put it," Valentine said.

"It's a hard world. I tell you, Valentine, that bomb couldn't have worked better if we planned it and one of our Cats had done it herself."

"You don't think we did, I hope," Valentine said.

"I don't know that we're that clever."

"I'd say ruthless," Valentine said.

"Oh, mass manipulation isn't all that hard," Brother Mark said. "I had whole seminars devoted to it. We're herd animals, Valentine. One good startle and we flock together. Then once you get us going, we all run in the same direction. There's a lot of power in a stampede, if you channel it properly."

"Perhaps. But it can also send your herd right off a cliff," Valentine said, "the way our ancestors used to hunt buffalo. Saved a lot of effort with spears and arrows."

"You're a curious creature, son. I can never make out whether you're a shepherd or a wolf."

"Black sheep," Valentine said.

"No, there's hunter in you."

Valentine nodded to some relief sentries, and said to them, "When the post has been turned over, head over to the diner and get some food. Kentucky is buying our meals, for once."

He turned back to the old churchman. "When I was inducted into the Wolves, the Lifeweaver warned me I'd never be the same. I'd be forever sundered from my fellow man, or words to that effect. I was too keen to get on with it to pay much attention."

"It's a bargain most of the men in your profession make, and it's a very, very old one. War changes a man, separates him from someone who hasn't seen it. You're both exalted and damned at the same time by the experience."

"What about you?" Valentine asked. "You've seen your share of fighting."

"Oh, I was damned before I saw my first battlefield."

Valentine was organizing his soldiers to block nonexistent traffic two blocks away from the convention center, using old rust buckets dragged into position as roadblocks.

Mr. Lincoln, the only man killed, had been running to jump in the river when the charges in the legworm went off. There was some bickering when his underage daughter, who had accompanied him to the Assembly, was given his place in the voting. Some said her sobs swayed a few critical votes.

He heard the commotion, the yells and firearms being discharged after the vote was tallied.

Some security. There weren't supposed to be firearms in the conference center. Well, Valentine's men were responsible for the streets; it was the sergeant at arms of the Assembly who'd been negligent. That, or after the bomb attack, they'd allowed the delegates to arm themselves.

Valentine sent a detail under a formidably tall Texan to get the delegates to unload their pieces and opened up a line of communication to Lambert at Fort Seng, which could radio relay to Southern Command.

Tikka herself was the first out of the convention center. She had a red streamer tied to the barrel of her rifle. The streamer matched the flame in her eyes.

"The vote was 139 to 31!" she said, leaping into Valentine's arms and wrapping her hard-muscled legs around his back. Her lips were hot and vital. "Five blanks in protest," she said when she was finished kissing him. "Cowards."

"For the Cause?" Valentine asked.

"I wouldn't have run otherwise," she said. "I want to fuck, to celebrate. You had a hand in this."

"That's all I can afford to put in at the moment. I'm on duty."

"Isn't part of your duty to maintain close contact with your Kentucky allies?"

"The closest kind of cooperation," Valentine said. "But we've just had a bomb explode, and no one seems to have any idea who brought a forty-foot legworm into town and how it was parked next to the Assembly."

She slipped off. "Too bad. May I use your radio? I want to communicate with my command."

Energetic Tikka. Denied one piece of equipment, she'll requisition another.

Valentine nodded and led her to his radio operator. Tikka almost bodychecked him out of his chair in her eagerness to put the headset on. Valentine knew he should really get it confirmed and look at an official roll count for his own report, but he trusted Tikka.

Valentine noted the time and vote on his duty log, and carefully covered the page so the cheap pencil (taken from the narthex of a New Universal Church, where lots are available to write "confessions," which were, in practice, accusations against a relative or neighbor) wouldn't smear. You never know what might end up in some museum case.

"Yes," Tikka said over the radio. "Put Warfoot into effect and open up the training camps." She pressed her earpiece to her head. "Oh, that's a big affirmative. Couldn't have gone better. Lost one delegate, but every cause needs a martyr."

Valentine, when he later considered her words over the radio, wondered just how large a role Tikka had in Mr. Lincoln's martyrdom. He hoped Tikka was just being her usual, brutally direct self. What he'd seen of the birth of the Kentucky Freehold was bloody enough, without adding deliberate political murder to the tally.

Eight

The Kentucky Freehold: Births are messy endeavors, biological or political.

Even the name "Kentucky Freehold" could be considered a mess, because the territory under control of the Assembly didn't include her two most populous cities, but it did include a few counties in Tennessee between the Big South Fork and Dale Hollow Lake and the chunk of Indiana around Evansville.

In that winter of 2076, the Kentucky Freehold voted into existence by the Assembly was a name only. There wasn't even a cohesive idea behind the name. There was no constitution, no separation of powers, no way to raise money nor legitimate channels in which to spend it. In the weeks after the vote, the Assembly adjourned to their home clans, towns, estates, and businesses to work out quick elections of delegates to the new freehold legislature.

The one piece of business the Assembly did manage to conduct was to vote into existence an Army of Kentucky. The A-o-K, as it came to be known, was to receive all the "manpower or material necessary to effect a defense of the Kentucky Free State," but who was to give what was left to the parties concerned.

As to the Southern Command forces in Kentucky, the Assembly reasoned that forces at Fort Seng were installed to help Kentucky—and help, to the Assembly's mind, would flow like water through a pipe from Southern Command's little force to Kentucky.

Fort Seng was full of new arrivals.

Valentine thought he was dreaming when he met the first of them as he led his companies back from Owensboro. A handsome young black man in Wolf deerskins emerged from cover at a good overwatch on the highway running east from Henderson to Owensboro.

"Frat," Valentine said. "You can't be— You're Moytana's replacement?" It wouldn't do to hug in front of all the men, so he settled for an exchange of salutes and handshakes.

Valentine hadn't seen him in years, since he'd discovered him in Wisconsin living with Molly Carlson's family. Though they'd never served together beyond the events in Wisconsin, Valentine's recommendation had won him a place in the Wolves.

The commission Frat had earned on his own.

"Major Valentine. Welcome back. We've heard the good news about the vote," he said in a deeper voice than Valentine remembered. He wore lieutenant's bars, and had dark campaign stripes running across the shoulder fabric on his ammunition vest.

Valentine hopped out of the truck, tossing his diaper bag on the seat. He'd decided he liked the bag; he always seemed to be carrying paperwork, and it also comfortably fit a couple of spare pairs of underwear and an extra layer or two in case it turned colder.

Frat eyed the bag. "Heard you were dead, Major."

"I heard the same about you," Valentine said. "Frat," Valentine said again. It wouldn't do to stand dumb-struck, so he fiddled with his glove as he pulled it off. "Lieutenant Carlson, I mean."

"Good to see you, sir."

"Wolf replacements arrived, then?"

"My platoon, from the reserve. We were part of the regimental general reserve. We scouted for the Rio Grande operation, came home dog-tired and thinking, *Job well done.* Got the bad news once we reached Fort Smith. Men still wanted to go back and volunteered—but they sent us here instead."

"Moytana was a good officer. You can learn a lot from him, even if it's just by a quick changeover briefing and by reading his paperwork. I'll see if I can get a few of his Wolves to remain behind to orient your Wolves."

"Thank you, sir. Actually, I was glad to hear I'll be serving with you. Not exactly again, but . . ."

"I know what you mean. It's good to see you too, Lieutenant."

Valentine wondered why Frat was still only a lieutenant. Of course, he was very young, and the Wolves had nothing higher than colonel, so there were only so many spaces on the rungs to climb.

"I stopped in to see Molly on my way to Jonesboro," Frat said. "She sends her regards. I have a letter from Edward, but, well . . . you know."

"I know." Valentine found himself looking forward to reading it.

Strange, that. He had a biological connection to a girl who barely knew he existed, and an invented fiction connecting him to another man's son. Life liked playing jokes with his feelings, rearranging relationships like an old magnetic poetry set.

"I'm not the only new arrival. My platoon guided in some civilians. Well, quasi-civilians, but I'll let herself explain it to you."

Valentine and Frat swapped chitchat the rest of the way back to Fort Seng. Frat made a few inquiries about Valentine's command. There were the most incredible rumors floating around Southern Command about his organization: They were all convicted criminals under death sentence, choosing service instead of the rope, or Valentine had an all-girl bodyguard of legworm-riding Amazons, or he was building a private army of freebooters who were stripping Kentucky like locusts of everything from legworm egg hides to bourbon.

"Southern Command scuttlebutt," Valentine said. "How I miss it."

Back at Fort Seng, Valentine observed some new vehicles in the well-guarded motor lot. The vehicles were an ill-matched set compared to Sime's quick-moving column and looked better suited for extensive off-road operation. They had extra tires and cans marked "diesel," "gas," and "water" mounted on them.

He reported to Lambert first, who only told him that they had a new set of headaches for the battalion but that it might work out to the benefit of the Cause in general and the battalion in particular. Then he drank a large, cold glass of milk—it was goat's milk; cow milk had run out—and went out to observe the arrivals.

They were equally interested in meeting him. Frat offered to introduce him to the visitors.

The gathering looked like a small, well-armed gypsy camp filled with people in neatly mended surplus uniforms that had a sort of broken double ring stitched on the shoulders.

If Valentine had been forced to describe the woman following the corporal walking up to him, he would have said "statuesque." Her face, under a bush hat with the brim stuck up on the left with a jaunty feathered pin, might have been molded alabaster. He put her age as fortyish or a very youthful-looking fifty, though her eyes danced with an ageless sparkle, blue ice on fire. She wore a long leather skirt and steel-tipped jodhpur boots with thick canvas half chaps, and she evidently knew enough about uniforms to pick him out as the ranking officer.

"Visitor in camp, Major," the corporal reported. "Mrs. O'Coombe, with a Southern Command travel warrant."

As Valentine introduced himself, she shook his hand. The almost challenging grip and steady eye contact marked her as a Texan.

Valentine knew the name O'Coombe. The family owned the largest cattle ranch in the United Free Republics—some said it stretched beyond the official borders. Now that he had a name, he even recognized the emblem on their fatigues, the Hooked O-C. They were said to be fabulously wealthy. At least as such things were measured in the Freehold.

"Mister Valentine. I've read about you on several occasions, as I recall. You're just the man I want to see about my venture into Kentucky."

She said the word "Mister" with such polite friendliness, he had no business correcting her. But her use of the word "venture" put Valentine on his guard. Was she some kind of wildcatter with an eye toward opening up a trade in legworm leather?

"I have here, Mister Valentine, a letter from the president himself. President Starpe was a good friend of my late husband's. He dined on our ranch on three occasions while in office and was a frequent visitor before."

She reached into her hacking jacket and removed a folded manila envelope. The letter within had a foil seal over a red-and-blue ribbon, with the outgoing presidential signature and a notation indicating it had been transcribed by his personal secretary.

After noting that it was simply addressed to "Officer, executive, or mariner commanding" and contained some polite words of thanks, Valentine read the meat of the letter.

> *Please offer whatever aid and assistance to Mrs. Bethany O'Coombe you consider practical. The retrieval and return of any and all of our wounded left behind on last summer's retreat would be, in my opinion, invaluable to our cause as well as the morale of the forces of Southern Command.*
>
> *Mrs. O'Coombe is a personal friend of mine. She can be trusted with Southern Command information and matériel relevant to her plans, and her signature would be accepted on any equipment voucher if she requests the use of any device or machine. I would consider it a singular favor for you to offer her any assistance that does not materially endanger your other duties.*

A crusader. Valentine had seen a few in his time, dedicated to relieving Southern Command of the evils of drink or the dangers of professional women and syphilis. This woman was clearly here to do more than give a few speeches, take a few oaths, or show some slides of tertiary cases. Were these vehicles a specialized medical train to care for the few wounded that remained in Fort Seng's small hospital?

"I would be delighted to accommodate you, Mrs. O'Coombe. Please tell me, how may I be of service?"

She looked around before answering. "I understand that during the battles of this summer, some wounded were left behind with such of our Kentucky allies who could be trusted with their safety. I would like to help recover them. From what I understand of your expertise, Mister Valentine, you have a good deal of experience going in and getting people out of difficulty. I've hoped that you could aid me from the first I heard."

"Why here, Mrs. O'Coombe? As a Texan, I'd think you'd be more interested in the Rio Grande Valley. More troops were involved in that action, I believe. I suspect there are more wounded scattered around southern Texas than we have here. We had the advantage of legworms, you see. All but our worst cases could be moved while remaining in their beds—or hammocks, rather."

"I have a personal interest, Mister Valentine. I recently learned my son was among those left behind as your column retreated from the mountains." Her gaze wavered a little, and Valentine saw what he suspected to be tears. "I have come to get him back. I should like you to guide me across Kentucky. As you're the one who left our soldiers scattered across the Cumberland, I expect you would be the one best able to help me retrieve them."

Frat stiffened a little at that.

"I would suggest that you speak to my commanding officer, ma'am," Valentine suggested.

Lambert heard Mrs. O'Coombe out and invited her to enjoy what hospitality Fort Seng could provide while she considered the matter. Could she perhaps return this evening, for dinner, and there they could discuss the matter in detail?

Mrs. O'Coombe was much obliged and said she'd be delighted.

Valentine was curious, a little aggravated, and anything but delighted at Lambert's response.

"You're not considering sending me across Kentucky as a tour guide for that stack of grief, I hope, sir," he said once Mrs. O'Coombe had left the building.

"I'm certainly inclined to let her have you," Lambert said. "Apart

from wanting our wounded back and safe, the gratitude of the Hooked
O-C is well worth having. I expect she'll be as influential with the new
president as the old."

"I didn't even know her son was with us," Valentine said. "Usually
Southern Command tells us when we have to deal with a scion of the
carriage trade. Quietly, but they tell us."

"Someone slipped up," Lambert agreed. "Noble of him to volunteer.
Mom passed down something besides Texas sand."

Valentine didn't have a number one uniform worthy of a formal
dinner with Lambert and their important guest. His least-patched ensemble was the militia corporal's uniform he wore when traveling in
Southern Command, but that had bloodstains on it now, and no effort of
soap or will could eradicate them.

He settled for the Moondagger robes he'd worn the night he knocked
the young Kurian out of its tree, with his leaf clipped on the collar and
a Southern Command tricolor pinned to the shoulder.

David Valentine wasn't one to stand in front of a mirror admiring
himself, but he had to admit the Moondagger robe-uniform suited him.
The various shades of black complemented his skin and dark hair and
made his perfectly ordinary brown eyes look a little more striking when
set in all that black. His old legworm boots gave him some dash and
swagger with their silver accents. The scars on the left side of his face
had healed down to not much more than big wrinkles and a pockmark,
and the old companion descending his right cheek looked more like the
romantic scarring of a dread pirate than the stupid souvenir of nearly
having his head blown off.

The dinner was held in the conference room, complete with a white
lace tablecloth and candlesticks.

It turned out he needn't have worried about his appearance. Colonel
Lambert had invited an eclectic company to her dinner.

Mrs. O'Coombe was there in her same field skirt and little lace-up
boots, only now garbed in a silken blouse and a— Valentine couldn't
find the word for it. Stole? It was a leather half vest that went around
behind her neck and hung down in two narrow pleats in front with
bright brass emblems. All Valentine could think of was sleigh bells on
a horse.

Fort Seng's three Logistic Commando wagon masters were there as
well, two western Kentucky specialists and one more they'd hauled all
the way to the Appalachians and back. They smelled faintly of stock
animals and sweat, but they'd combed their hair and flattened it with oil.
Patel wore his new legion-style captain's uniform and had polished his

two canes. That was a bit unlike Nilay Patel; he was more the type to grit his teeth through an evening of aching knees and retire with a bottle of aspirin. Lambert looked trim and neat as one would expect, her hair brushed and shaped by a dress clip for the use of female officers. And finally Alessa Duvalier stood next to the fire, warming her backside and dressed in a little black outfit that must have been liberated from the basement, perhaps from some formal ball of the great man's daughter. A red bra peeked from behind the low-cut front. Valentine vaguely thought it was a sartorial faux pas, but Duvalier's red hair, spiky and disarrayed as usual, made it work.

Odd assortment. If Lambert wanted to impress Mrs. O'Coombe, why not invite Captain Ediyak with her model-cheekbone looks and polished Eastern manners? Why not Gamecock, who had a courtliness all his own behind the braids and scars, smooth as his rolling accent, that showed off some collective unconscious vestige of the grace of old South Carolina?

Brother Mark, the other obvious candidate, was off on a junket with the Agenda from the late Assembly. Or, more correctly, the soon-to-be-late Agenda. They were arranging for the establishment of a temporary government in Kentucky, and the ex-churchman wanted to plead for an office devoted to relations with allies in the Cause.

Valentine joined Duvalier at the fire.

"What the hell is that, Val?" she asked, fingering the finely patterned knit trim on the top robe.

"It's the nicest thing I have that fits me. Some Moondagger's dress-up outfit."

"I've seen those before," she said, her voice hardly more than a whisper. "That's what they wear when they have a date with a Reaper. They treat it like a wedding."

Valentine searched her eyes for some hint of a joke. She did sometimes put him on.

"No joke," she supplied.

"Well, it's still an attractive ensemble," Valentine said. "I like how it looks, so what the hell."

"Your funeral," Duvalier said.

Lambert finished making her introductions, and everyone sat. Valentine sat opposite Lambert with Patel on one side and Duvalier on the other, with the Logistics Commandos near them. Mrs. O'Coombe was in the place of honor to Lambert's right.

Patel fiddled with his array of silverware. "Which is the one to clean the grease from one's lips, Major?" he asked quietly.

"You can dip your fingers in the fingerbowl and touch them to your lips when you're done eating," Valentine said under his breath.

Lambert, as host, got the Logistics Commandos talking about their difficulty finding even food staples, with Southern Command currency worthless here and what was left of Colonel Bloom's booty pile diminishing rapidly.

"They want gold, or Kurian bank guarantees, or valuables for trade," one of the Kentuckians said. "We're out of all the usual stuff we trade. Our depots don't have dynamite or two-way radios; not even paper and ink or razor blades."

"The vote didn't change nothing," his friend added.

"We could send a few Wolves with the LCs on their next run, sir," Patel said. "Give them a choice of Southern Command scrip or lead."

Valentine was tempted. "No."

"Been done before, Major," Patel said.

The dishes came out. It was a meager dinner, "ration beef" and seasoned patties made from falafel and corn that would probably be allocated to the pigs on Mrs. O'Coombe's ranch.

Lambert spoke up. "We're trying to teach these recruits that just because you've got a uniform and a gun, whatever you can grab is not yours for the taking. We have to set an example. Tighten our belts."

"We'll be eating our belts before winter's up, at this rate," the third Logistics Commando said.

"Mister Valentine," Mrs. O'Coombe said. "I couldn't help overhearing your conversation regarding the supply difficulties. I'm traveling with a substantial amount of gold and Kurian Bills of Guarantee."

Duvalier choked on her apple juice.

"I've dealt on both sides of the border often enough to know that one needs hard assets and negotiables to overcome certain bureaucratic difficulties."

"Excuse me, madam, but where did you get bills?" Valentine asked. Bills were certificates guaranteeing "employment, useful or otherwise" for a set period, usually five or ten years. They were extremely difficult to forge. Some said the seals acted in much the same manner as a brass ring, and they were very valuable in the Kurian Zone. Many an old-timer would trade his entire life's accumulation for a five-year certificate.

She read Patel's scowl. "If you think I trade cattle on both sides of Nomansland out of greed, you're wrong, sir. I sometimes find it useful to bribe for or buy what I cannot obtain in the Free Republics."

If she was in a giving vein, Valentine did not want to spoil her mood with accusations. He tapped Patel in the ankle. "Of course we'd be grateful for your assistance. What can you spare?"

"I can give you six thousand C-coin in gold and six Kurian five-year bills. You will, of course, sign a promissory note that I may redeem back at Fort Smith for their cash value, assessed per Logistic Commando fair market pricing of whichever month is current when I turn them in."

Southern Command, perpetually starved for precious metals, would be thrilled to have Mrs. O'Coombe show up demanding hundred-dollar gold coins by the roll. Frontier posts kept gold on hand for smugglers coming out of the Kurian Zone with antibiotics or computer chips or hard intelligence, and they'd be loath to part with it for nothing but a promissory note from a written-off outpost.

How would the loan change the status of Mrs. O'Coombe on the post? The men would learn she was buying their corn-meal and chickens and bacon, one way or another. Suppose she started issuing them orders, as though they were her bunkhouse cowpunchers?

"Dangerous to be traveling with that much gold, ma'am," Patel said, breaking in on Valentine's thoughts. Obvious thing to say. Perhaps Patel was buying him time to think it over.

She smiled, dazzling white teeth against those pink lips. "More dangerous than Reapers, Mister Patel?"

The men had to be fed, one way or another. The only other option would be to go in and take it at gunpoint, and they weren't pirates. At least not yet.

Valentine weighed his options. Once Kentucky got itself organized, Fort Seng would petition for support from the Assembly. Though Valentine wondered if his forces, being neither fish nor fowl, so to speak, would find themselves divested of support from both the rebels in Kentucky and his own Southern Command, especially once General Martinez took over and instituted his new "defensive" policies.

Mrs. O'Coombe waited, her hands clasped decorously in her lap. She'd only nibbled politely at the meager fare.

"Madam, I accept your very generous offer on behalf of my men," Lambert said, her train of thought arriving at the decision platform.

"Always willing to help the Cause, Colonel," Mrs. O'Coombe said. "Now, Mister Valentine, perhaps you will attend to the matter of facilitating me in the effort of finding my son. I would like your advice on routes and what sort of personnel we should bring."

"A complicated question, madam," Valentine said. "It depends on supply capacity in your vehicles, what sort of fuel they need . . ."

Duvalier hummed quietly:

> *The choice tan, the bought man,*
> *Prisoner 'tween golden sheets . . .*

It was a pop tune from just before the cataclysm in 2022 and had been prominently listed on most barroom virtual disc-jockey machines.

Patel let off an explosive fart and excused himself, but it stopped Duvalier's quiet amusement.

Well, if Valentine was going to take her gold, he'd get more for it than butter and eggs. Valentine hemmed and hawed his way through the conversation about the trip to recover her son—and others, of course—and as usual struck upon an idea while his brain was busy fencing with Mrs. O'Coombe.

Valentine escaped Mrs. O'Coombe the next day, pleading that he had to go into Evansville to see about purchasing supplies.

Evansville had an impressive city hall thanks to the region's ample limestone, but it reminded Valentine of a church with long-dead parishioners. Most of the offices were empty.

They should have used the empty rooms for the overflowing waiting room. Luckily, his uniform brought him right to the attention of the city's governor.

How they arrived at that title Valentine didn't know then, but he later learned that since Evansville considered itself a different state than Kentucky even though it was now part of the Kentucky Freehold, by definition it should have a governor as chief executive.

In this case the governor was a former member of the underground named Durand. Professor Durand, actually; he ran a secret college devoted to preserving classical Western education from the tailoring, trimming, and alteration of the Kurian Order.

He reminded Valentine a bit of Trotsky in his dress and glasses, minus the brains and the talent and the vigor.

"Can I help you, Major Valentine?" Durand asked. He was sorting papers into four piles on his desk, and he glanced up at Valentine as he stood before his desk.

Valentine would have sworn in court that he recognized some of the documents from his last visit three weeks ago, before the action at the power station, when he unsuccessfully pleaded for the Evansville provisional government to purchase supplies for Fort Seng.

"You've done so much already, Governor," Valentine said. "I'm simply here to pay my respects before we depart. A last duty call before I plunge into getting the camp relocated."

"Depart?" Durand asked, looking vaguely alarmed and suddenly less interested in the paperwork on his desk.

Valentine examined the walls of the office. A few corners of torn-off Kurian NUC enthusiasm posters remained between the windows.

"Yes, the fort will be relocated. For security reasons I can't disclose our destination, but the town's leadership has made a most generous offer, and strategically it makes sense—we'll be closer to the center mass of Kentucky, able to operate on interior lines. . . . You know the military advantages."

"But . . . the underground has word of an armored column north of here. Cannon, armored cars, riot buses, gunabagoes . . ."

"Yes, how is the city militia progressing in its training? The key is to brush back the infantry support. Then it's much easier to take out the armor."

"You've made so many improvements to your camp, I understand. Hot water, electricity . . ."

"Perhaps your militia can relocate and take advantage of all our hard work. True, that would mean a longer response time if you needed them to deal with, say, some airdropped Reapers."

"What is this other town offering you?"

"Offering? I'm doing my duty, Professor, not engaging in bid taking."

"Surely Evansville has its advantages. The textile plant, the appliances, our phone system . . ."

"All are superior to central Kentucky, I grant you," Valentine said. "But my men are running short on eggs and dairy and fresh meat and vegetables. The new town has offered to supply us amply. I have to consider the health and fitness of my men."

Valentine took out some of the gold coins Mrs. O'Coombe had so generously offered. "Of course, we'll have more difficulty purchasing building materials, tenting, plumbing supplies, munitions, uniforms, and such in Kentucky. After I've finished here, I will visit the marketplace and see if I can't have a selection packed and ready for transport."

Durand's eyes watched the jingling coins. "We've had something of a food crisis here, as well," Durand said. "It appears to be easing since the vote to declare openly against the Kurian Order. We've been neglectful of our protectors across the river. Now we could easily restart the flow of foodstuffs. I expect a boat full of chickens and eggs could be put across in no time."

Valentine took out a piece of paper. "We'll need this every week." He passed the grocery list to Durand.

"Basic staples shouldn't be difficult. But chocolate?"

"Some of my soldiers have a sweet tooth, but I imagine most of it will end up in the stomachs of Evansville's beautiful young women."

"You drive a hard bargain, Major. Is this quite ethical? Extorting the people you promised to protect?"

"Evansville's delegates voted to support the armed resistance to the

Kurian Order in men and matériel. I've most of the men I need. My material needs are small compared to the army they're trying to build outside the Kurian Triangle. You might consider yourself lucky."

"It appears we are bound to be symbionts, Major. I'll see to the deliveries of your foodstuffs."

"Then we shall be happy to remain in our comfortable and beautiful surroundings, with the congenial company of Evansville and Owensboro," Valentine said.

"I'm sure," Durand said. "I feel as though I've been played like a harp."

"If that column comes roaring south out of Bloomington, you'll be glad we stayed, or you might end up playing your own harp, sir."

He didn't want to go on Mrs. O'Coombe's expedition. He wished Moytana were still present; it would have been a much better assignment for a group of experienced Wolves.

It took a direct order from Lambert to get him to agree to do it.

They talked it over across her desk. Lambert had a policy that in private, when seated, you could talk to her without military formalities and treat her as a sounding board rather than a commander. It was a tradition Valentine had always followed with his own subordinates. Valentine remembered picking it up from Captain LeHavre. He wondered if Lambert had acquired it from Moira Styachowski.

Or did it come to Lambert from Valentine, in a roundabout way?

"Take whoever you like, just none of my captains," Lambert said, signing a blank ad hoc special duty personnel sheet and passing it to him.

Damn. So much for Patel. He could have ridden the whole way.

"I was thinking two Bears. Ali." As a Cat, Duvalier was considered a captain in rank, but Valentine suspected Lambert didn't need to hold on to her. "A Wolf scouting team."

"Medical staff?"

"They have enough to do here. Our patroness said she has her own medical team."

"Why don't you take Boelnitz too," Lambert said. "He's been making himself a nuisance here. I don't know if he's filed a story yet."

"Maybe he's working on a novel," Valentine said. He observed that Lambert's desk was as clean as an Archon's shaving mirror. Lambert managed to do a tremendous amount of work—she was in the process of reorganizing Fort Seng from the top down—but there was no evidence of it except for a three-drawer file cabinet and a brace of three-ring binders. Her clerk was always buzzing in and out like a pollen-laden honeybee, keeping the binders updated.

"I'd hate to be away if that column moves south," Valentine said.

"We'll just call you back," Lambert said. "Mrs. O'Coombe can delay them with a pillar of fire, and then spread her arms and part the Tennessee for us to get away."

Valentine couldn't say why he didn't like the idea of leaving Fort Seng. How do you put disquiet and restlessness into words? Normally he'd look forward to picking up his men and getting them on the road home—that sort of thing left a better aftertaste than surviving a battle.

One more thing bothered him. Red Dog had appeared a little nervous of late, always looking around with the whites of his eyes showing and hiding under tables and stonework. He'd even been dragged out from under the defunct hot tub in the estate house's garden gazebo.

Red Dog had been a tool of the Kurians in the retreat across Kentucky, when one Kurian had somehow linked through the dog's mind to Javelin's commanders at headquarters. If Red Dog was nervous, Valentine was nervous.

"Nice work at the dinner," Valentine said. "I think when Mrs. O'Coombe had to eat what we've been living on, it encouraged her to part with her gold."

"I just think she's a deeply decent person," Lambert said. "You don't often meet one of those."

"I met one back at the war college in Pine Bluff," Valentine said. "A little stick of a thing, always dotting *i*'s and crossing *t*'s."

"And I remember a shy young lieutenant who was always looking at his shoes and talking about the weather when he should have been asking me to a dance," Lambert said.

"We were both too busy, I think," Valentine said.

"And now we're in a fort where Southern Command rules on down-chain, up-chain, and cross-chain fraternization will be strictly observed. And not 'strictly' in the fun, blindfold and handcuffs sense, either."

"Dirty Bird Colonel," Valentine laughed. "Hands off."

"That goes for your captain, too, Major."

"Nilay Patel and I share a love that cannot—"

"You know who I mean. I don't want Boelnitz returning to his paper with an episode of *Noonside Passions* ready for action."

"Yes, ma'am. But rest easy: Ediyak didn't earn that rapid rise the hard way."

Duvalier waited a beat. "You're impossible, Valentine. Anyway, let's keep it zipped up for once, shall we?"

"As long as you restrain yourself with Boelnitz. You've made time for how many interviews?"

"I don't recall him being in the chain of command," Lambert said. "And if he were, I'd just have my clerk make a new page minus his name. But point taken, Valentine. Honestly, the only thing I want to get intimate with is that hot tub, if Prist and Toyonikka get functional again."

Nine

Civilian and military relations: Southern Command has a long history of "turnouts" to offer assistance to civilians in need. Their ethic might almost be described by the words "protect and serve."

Bases always serve as a temporary haven for the lost, dispossessed, or desperate. The men and women in uniform know they depend on the civilian populace for food and support. There are endless tales of whole camps going hungry to share their rations with hard-up locals and their children.

In return, civilians do what they can to provide for soldiers on the march, act as spare pairs of eyes and ears, and put in extra hours as poorly paid labor levies doing everything from laundry to garbage burial.

Especially in frontier areas, the soldiers are the only law and order around. While they can't treat criminals as combatants, they do have the power to hold someone until they can be turned over to civilian authorities—and the farther out the base, the longer the wait for a marshal or judge riding circuit to appear.

More important for this period in the turbulent history of the Middle Freestates, they can provide escort for vehicles, trains, and watercraft.

For all Valentine's reluctance to join Mrs. O'Coombe's famous and tragic trek to recover her son, the rest of Fort Seng worked like demons to prepare her group and vehicles for their journey. "Home by Christmas," the men said to one another, hoping that ten days on the road would suffice to recover the men Javelin had left scattered across Kentucky.

Each soldier could picture himself left behind somewhere. They

*provisioned and checked and armed the already well-equipped vehi-
cles. For the average man in the ranks, letters from the president and
connections in the general headquarters staff were remote facts, like
the Hooked O-C straddling much of southern Oklahoma and northern
Texas. What they understood was that the cots bolted to the inside of
the trucks and vehicles would bring home those who'd been left behind—at least those who survived their injuries and the sweeps of
Javelin's trail by bloodthirsty Moondaggers.*

He met O'Coombe's team on a warm December day. Valentine
hadn't seen vehicles like these since the drive on Dallas, and these specimens were in much better condition.

They sat there, not exactly gleaming in the sun but looking formidable in their grit and mud streaks.

Mrs. O'Coombe introduced him to her right-hand man, an ex-Bear
named Stuck. Valentine hadn't met many ex-Bears. It seemed you were
either a Bear or you were a deceased Bear; the ex-Bears he'd met were
all so badly damaged they couldn't stand up or hold a gun.

Stuck had all his arms and legs and sensory organs intact. All that
seemed to be missing was the bristling, grouchy Bear attitude. He was a
big, meaty, soft-spoken man with a wide, angular mustache.

Stuck took Valentine down the line. He introduced Valentine to the
wagon master, Habanero, a tough older man, thin and dry and leathery
as a piece of jerky. He had a combination hearing aid–radio communi-
cator that he used to issue orders to the drivers in the column.

"Ex-artillery in the Guards," Stuck explained as they left to inspect
the vehicles. "Used to haul around guns. Deaf as a post but knows engines and suspensions and transmissions."

First, there was Rover, the command car. It was a high-clearance
model that looked like something out of an African safari, right down
to a heavy cage around the cabin. Extra jerricans of water and gasoline
festooned the back and sides, spare tires were mounted on the front and
hood, packs were tied to the cage, and up top a pair of radio antennae
bent from the rear bumpers and were tied forward like scorpion tails.
The command car had a turret ring—empty for now.

Stuck said there was an automatic grenade launcher and two bins of
grenades in the bay.

Then there was the Bushmaster. The vehicle was a beautiful, rust-
free armored personnel carrier, long bodied with a toothy grin up front
thanks to heavy brush breakers. An armored cupola sat at the top, and
firing slits lined the side. Valentine saw canvas-covered barrels sprout-
ing like antennae.

"Teeth as false as Grandpa's," Stuck said.

Stuck glanced around before opening the armored car's back.

The vehicle was under command of a thickset homunculus. The man looked like he'd been folded and imperfectly unfolded again. Scarred, with a squint eye and an upturned mouth, his face looked as though some-one had given his unformed face a vigorous stir with wooden spoon. Even his ears were uneven.

Valentine recognized him. "I know you, don't I?"

"Yes, sir, thanks, sir," he said as they shook hands. "March south to Dallas. We was just ahead of your Razorbacks in column with the old One hundred fifteenth. I drove a rocket sled."

A vicious-looking dog that seemed mostly Doberman sniffed Valentine from next to the driver.

Hazardous duty, since the rockets had a tendency to blow up in the crew's face. Southern Command had any number of improvised artillery units. Crude rocketry was popular because the howling, crashing projectiles unnerved even the most dug-in Grogs. Someone said it was because the rockets made a noise that sounded like the Grog word for lightning strikes.

Valentine suspected it might be the other way around—that the Grogs started calling lightning strikes after the sound effect from the rockets.

"Dover—no, Drake. Your crew pulled my command car out of a mud hole outside Sulphur Springs."

"That we did, sir."

"Serves me right for taking the wheel. I never was much of a driver."

Stuck spoke up. "Drake here is on her ladyship's—Well, we call them the ranch's sheriff's deputies. He keeps law and order among the hands and their families."

"Not popular work, sir, but it pays well," Drake said.

"Quite a dog you have there," Valentine said, looking at the beast's scarred muscle. "Can I pet it?"

"You can, sir, but I wouldn't advise it. I don't even pet him."

"How's she drive, Drake?" Valentine asked.

"Like steering a pig with handlebars shoved up its ass, but it'll get there and back," Drake said.

"Riot control platform, isn't it? I've seen these in Illinois."

"That it is, sir."

Stuck opened the small access hatch in the larger back door. "We've got it rigged out to carry injured in comfort."

The tunnellike inside was full of twelve folding bunks attached to the walls of the vehicle, as well as seats along the walls: cushioned lockers. The bunks blocked some of the firing slits but not the cupola.

The machine guns looked more frightening from the outside, thanks to the big barrels. Inside, they were revealed to be assault rifles rigged out with box magazines. Still, firepower is firepower.

"What's up top? A broomstick?" Valentine asked.

"Oh, the gun's real enough," Drake said. "Twenty millimeters of lead that'll turn any breathing target into dog meat, from a Reaper to a legworm."

"Dogs know better than to eat off a dead Reaper," Stuck said.

Next in line was the Chuckwagon. It was a standard military truck with an armored-up cabin, a mounted machine gun at the back, and a twin-tank trailer dragging behind. The paint job and new tires made Javelin's venerable and road-worn Comanche look like the tired old army mule she was. The Chuckwagon towed a trailer with two big black tanks on it.

The hood was up on this one, and a plump behind wiggled as a woman in overalls inspected the engine.

"Ma," Stuck shouted. "There's someone needs meeting."

"Busy here."

"You're never that busy. Come out of there."

A plump, graying woman hopped down from the front bumper. She wiped her hands and gave a wave Valentine decided to interpret as friendly gesture instead of sloppy contempt.

"This is Ma, one of the ranch's roving cooks. Ex–Southern Command and ex–Logistics Commando, she's our expert on Tennessee and Kentucky."

"Really only know it to the Tennessee River, but from the Goat Shack to Church Dump, I've been up and down her. My specialty was likker, of course, but I traded in parts and guns too."

Valentine nodded. "I'll put you to work on this trip. We need medical supplies and—"

"'Scuse me, sir, but I don't know medicinals; never had much of a mind for 'em. Too easy to get stock-shuffled or wheezed or lose it all in the old Bayou flush. Easier to spot a true rifle barrel or bourbon from busthead."

Finally, there was the Boneyard, a military ambulance truck. It had the same basic frame as the Rover, with a longer back end and higher payload bay. A bright red cross against a white background decorated its hood and flanks.

"Doc and the nurse are helping out in your hospital," Stuck said. "The driver's name is Big Gustauf, old Missouri German. My guess is he's eating. Never was a Bear as far as I know, but he's got the appetite of one."

Valentine paced back up the column and found the matriarch who'd assembled all this to bring her boy home. "I'd like to congratulate you on your column, Mrs. O'Coombe."

She offered a friendly tip of the head in return for the compliment. "When we were young my husband and I ranched right into Nomansland," she said. "Hard years. Dangerous years. I knew what to bring on such an expedition."

"I hope your care obtains results."

"That's in God's hands, Mister Valentine. All I can do is my best."

"God usually fights on the side of the better prepared," Valentine said.

"I don't care for your sense of humor, Mister Valentine, but as an experienced soldier I suspect you've earned your cynicism."

"Your son didn't serve under the name O'Coombe, did he?" Valentine asked.

"No, he didn't want to be pestered for money or jobs for relatives," Mrs. O'Coombe said. "He served under my maiden name, Rockaway. Sweet of him, was it not, Mister Valentine?"

Valentine made a note of that. He'd have to check the roll call records and medical lists to learn which legworm clan ended up taking care of him. They had left only a handful of wounded behind who seemed likely to survive, and even then only in areas controlled by their allied clans.

"How much do you know about Kentucky?" Valentine asked.

"My sources say there are many off-road trails thanks to the feeding habits of the legworms. I wanted vehicles that could use poorly serviced roads and even those trails."

"How did you get vehicles like these together?" Valentine asked. When he'd first seen her, he wondered if she'd hired mercenaries. They knew about moving off-road with a column of vehicles. They had plenty of tow chains and cables ready to offer assistance to the next in line or the previous. He noticed the various trucks' engines had cloth cowlings stitched and strapped over them. The cloth had an interesting sheen. Valentine suspected it was Reaper cloth from their robes.

"Get them? Sir, they're from our ranch. We control property that covers hundreds of square miles. The ranch wouldn't function without range-capable wheels."

"Where do you ride?" Valentine asked Stuck.

He lifted a muscular, hairy arm and pointed to a pair of heavy motorcycles with leather saddlebags and rifle clips on the handlebars. "Me and Longshot are the bikers."

"Where's Longshot?" Valentine asked.

"Up here," he heard a female voice say.

Valentine looked up and saw a woman in old-fashioned biker leathers sunning herself atop the Bushmaster. She zipped up her jacket. "I'm the scout sniper."

She had strong Indian features, dirtied from riding her motorcycle. There was a clean pattern around where she presumably wore her goggles. You wouldn't necessarily call her "pretty" or "beautiful." Striking was more like it, with strong features and long black hair that put Valentine's to shame. "Comanche?" Valentine asked.

"Hell if I know. Tucumcari mutt: little bit of everything. You?"

"North Minnesota mix," Valentine said.

"Hey, want to see me feed these beasts?" Stuck asked.

Valentine nodded.

He walked over to the Chuckwagon's trailer. It had big twin tanks that Valentine had assumed were powered by gasoline or diesel or vegetable oil.

Longshot hopped down, and Stuck opened a latched cooler strapped on a little platform between the tanks. Two buckets rested inside. A ripe fecal smell came out, so powerful it almost billowed. Valentine watched Stuck and Longshot, apparently oblivious to the odor, each lift a bucket and pour it into one of the tanks.

"Everyone pisses and shits in the old honeybucket," Stuck said. "Food scraps are good too, especially carbohydrates."

Stuck took a leather lanyard from around his neck. Valentine noticed a Reaper thumb on it, interesting only thanks to an overlarge, pointed nail capping it. The lanyard also had two keys. Stuck used one of them to open a locked box on the tanker trailer and took out a plastic jug of blue-white crystals with a metal scoop sunk in.

"This is my job. I check the test strips and seed."

He extracted a long dipstick from the fragrant tank, wiped it on a piece of paper about the size of a Band-Aid, carefully placed the test paper in a clip, and held it up to a color-coded, plasticized sheet. Nodding, he made a notation on a clipboard that rested on the box's hinged cover.

"The Kurians guard this stuff like the Reaper cloth factories," Stuck said, leveling and dumping three roughly teaspoon-sized portions of the granules into the larger scoop.

"I've seen those factories," Valentine said. "Or one of them, anyway, in the Southwest."

"This tank's just about done," Stuck said. "Takes about thirty-six hours to do three hundred fifty gallons. Then we refill off this tank while we fill the other with waste, or pig corn, or melon rinds, or what have you. In a pinch, these engines can run off of kerosene, regular diesel, or even waste cooking oil, but this stuff's easier on 'em, and Habby doesn't bitch about changing gunked-up fuel filters."

Valentine watched him dump the crystals into the conversion tank.

"Always makes me wish I'd learned more science and chemistry and stuff, instead of just getting good at taking Reapers and Grogs apart," Stuck said.

"So where did you get that stuff? I've never even heard of it," Valentine said.

"The Great Dame is friends with some big bug in Santa Fe. He's playing both sides of the border, scared there'll be a reckoning if Denver Freehold and Southern Command pair up and hit the Southwest. He's a honcho in transport. Keeps trying to propose, but she shoots him down."

"What's your story, Stuck?"

"I was never cut out for military life, even as a Bear. Hurry up and wait, hurry up and wait. Drove me crazy. Stand here, look there, turn your head and cough, bend over and pull 'em apart. Not my lifestyle at all. Mrs. O'Coombe keeps me busy out in the open where I'm alone, riding from post to post checking security. No one to piss me off that way."

He looked up from the mix. "Longshot, get over here," Stuck said. "What do you think of this color?"

"More water," she said.

"That's what I thought. Thanks."

She hopped down and bumped into Valentine.

Valentine found himself looking into the reversed-raccoon eyes of the girl. The face mask had left an odd pattern on her features. Dusky and dark, she reminded him a little of Malita, save that Longshot was a good deal shorter.

"You must love your bike," Valentine said.

"I was out scouting east of here this morning," she said.

"Longshot gets bored easily," Stuck said, watching her grab a washcloth and towel and head for the camp's showers. "She's a retired guerrilla from down Mexico way. Met her during Operation Snakebite. She's ridden at my side ever since."

"Full partnership, or limited liability?" Valentine asked.

"Nah. A Reaper yanked my gear off when I was captured in 'sixty-six. Didn't hurt as much as you'd think, but about all she does is keep me warm."

Valentine had a hard decision to make, and after consulting Lambert, he presented it to Mrs. O'Coombe the night before their scheduled departure.

"I'm afraid I'll have to commandeer your doctor for Fort Seng, Mrs. O'Coombe. Our remaining doctor is exhausted. He's worked seven days a week for over a month now."

"And just who do you suggest will look after my son or any wounded we recover?"

"We'll take our nurse. If they've lived this long, I doubt they'll need any more care than that."

"I'm sorry, Mister Valentine, but this is one time I must tell you no. I don't like the idea of traveling with wounded without a doctor."

"A nurse should be sufficient for travel," Valentine said. And that was that. He had rank, after all, and it would take months for Mrs O'Coombe to get her friends to exert their influence for or against him. And by then he hoped to have her son back.

Valentine passed the word and names for an officers' call and then arranged for food to be sent up to what was now being called the map room. Next to the communications center, it had formerly been a game room. Lambert had altered it so it featured everything from a large-scale map of Kentucky to an updated map of the Evansville area, river charts, and even a globe Lambert had colored with crayons to reflect resistance hot spots against the Kurian Order.

Lambert was a whirlwind. Somebody had a screw loose if they had just cast this woman aside as part of a political housecleaning.

Gamecock was there representing his Bears, Frat for the Wolves, and Duvalier just because she saw the others gathering and wanted to grab a comfortable armchair. Patel was present, of course, and Colonel Bloom's new executive officer, a Guard lieutenant who'd distinguished himself at the bridge where Bloom had been wounded on Javelin's retreat.

"You looking forward to your trip, suh?" Gamecock said.

"We won't be touring. I don't care how well equipped and crewed she is. If she's recovering Southern Command forces, we need Southern Command along. I think she's sailing into trouble."

"Isn't she a bit old for you, Val?" Duvalier asked.

"You can come along and keep an eye on me," Valentine said. He hadn't yet told her that he wanted her to as part of his command.

"No walking, I hope," Duvalier said, with a light laugh that did Valentine's spirits good. She'd been so moody lately. "Twice back and forth across the state is enough for me."

"Who would you like to bring, sir?" Patel asked.

Valentine looked at his notes. "I'd like to take two Bears—Chieftain and Silvertip—four Wolves, and a nurse."

"Who's bringing the beer and barbecue?" Duvalier asked.

"Do I have to remind you that this is an officers' call, Captain?" Valentine said, using her titular rank.

"Then I'll join the tour," Duvalier said.

"Call it a survey, call it a reconnaissance in force, call it a recovery operation. Call it anything you like. It's my intent to have a mobile force of some strength who knows how to deal with Reapers. With the legworm clans encamped for the winter, they'll be so many sitting ducks for whatever vengeance Missionary Doughnut is talking about."

"Goodwill tour it is," Lambert said. "Our friend out front has never made much sense. Seeing some Southern Command forces in Kentucky's heartland will do the Cause some good, in any case. And let's not forget our outgoing president's letter. If I go myself, I'll consider my duties discharged."

"Can I go with my Wolves, sir?" Frat asked. "I'd like to see a little more of Kentucky."

Valentine looked at Lambert, who nodded. "Glad to have you along, Lieutenant. Thanks for volunteering. You'll save me a lot of legwork."

Duvalier snickered at that. Valentine wondered why she was so merry this morning.

Alarm.

Valentine came out of his sleep, heart pounding, a terrible sense that death stood over his pillow.

The Valentingle.

He hadn't called it that at first. If he thought about it, he might have remembered that he once called it "the willies" or "the creeps." The name came from his companions in the Wolves, who learned to trust his judgment about when they were safe to take refuge for the night—what hamlets might be visited quietly, whispering to the inhabitants through back porch screens.

Whether it was sixth sense, the kind of natural instinct that makes a rabbit freeze when a hawk's shadow passes overhead, or some strange gift of the Lifeweavers, Valentine couldn't say.

But he did trust it. A Reaper was prowling.

Valentine slipped into his trousers and boots almost at the same time, tying them in the dark.

He grabbed the pistol belt hanging on his bedpost. Next came the rifle. Valentine checked his ammunition by touch, inserted a magazine, chambered a shot. He slung on his sword. Oddly enough, the blade was more comforting than even the guns. There was something atavistic in having a good handle grip at the end of an implement you can wave about.

Duvalier would say that it wasn't atavism. . . .

Valentine hand-cranked his field phone. "Operations."

"Operations," they answered.

"This is Major Valentine. Any alerts?" He swapped hands with the receiver so he could pull on his uniform shirt.

"Negative, Major Valentine."

"Well, I'm calling one. Pass the word: alert alert alert. I want to hear from the sentries by the time I get down there."

The communications center lay snug in the basement.

Valentine looked out the window. The alarm klaxon went off, sending black birds flapping off the garbage dump and a raccoon scuttling. Emergency lights tripped on in quick succession. They were perhaps not as bright as Southern Command's sodium lights that illuminated woods on the other side of the parking lot, but they had precise coverage that left no concealing shadows on the concentric rings of decorative patio stones. The old estate house had quite a security system.

A shadow whipped across the lawn, bounding like a decidedly unjolly black giant, covering three meters at a stride, a dark cloak flapping like wings.

Reaper!

Could it be their old friend from the Ohio? The clothing was different, it seemed. The other one hadn't even had a cloak and cowl when he'd last seen it, and it seemed doubtful that a wild Reaper could attain one.

Valentine, in more of a hurry to throw off the shutters and open the sash than ever any St. Nick–chasing father, fumbled with the window. He knocked it open at the cost of a painful pinch to his finger when the rising pane caught him. He swung his legs out and sat briefly on the sill like a child working up the nerve to jump, rifle heavy across his thighs.

Valentine had no need to nerve himself, but he did want one last look at the Reaper's track from the advantage of height. Would it angle toward the soldiers' tents or the munitions dugout? Kurians had been known to sacrifice a Reaper, if it meant blowing up half a base.

It did neither. It headed straight for the woods south, toward the river.

Valentine jumped, felt the cool night air rush up his trouser legs. He landed on his good leg, cradling the rifle carefully against his midsection as though it were a baby.

With that he was off, settling into his old Wolf lope, the bad leg giving him the port-and-starboard sway of a tipsy sailor or perhaps an off-balance metronome.

He cast about with a coonhound's frantic anxiety at the edge of the woods. The tracks were there, hard to see in the deep night of the woods. Only the Reaper's furious pace allowed him to find the tracks at all.

Valentine searched the woods with his hard ears. The wind was smothering whatever sounds the Reaper made—if it was in fact running and not just trying to lure him into the woods.

Deciding on handiness over firepower, Valentine slung his rifle. Drawing his pistol and sword, he tucked the blade under his arm and began stalking into the woods with the pistol in a solid, two-handed "teacup" grip, searching more with his ears than his eyes.

His footfalls sounded like land mines detonating to his nervous ears. Of course, anyone venturing into thick woods after a Reaper would be a madman not to be nervous.

Motion out of the corner of his eye—

Valentine swung, the red fluorescent dot on the pistol's foresight tracking through wooded night to . . .

A chittering raccoon, blinking at him from a tree branch.

Valentine lowered the pistol barrel.

In a cheap horror movie, this would be the moment for the Reaper to come up behind. Valentine turned a full circle. The woods were empty.

A half hour later he'd traced the tracks to an old road running along the bank of the Ohio River above the flood line. Above what was technically the flood line, that is; the road showed evidence of having survived at least one flood. The Reaper could have continued on to the river or headed down the road in either direction. It might even have stashed a bicycle somewhere—a Reaper could reach a fantastic speed on two wheels.

Now all that was left was the grim accounting. Perhaps the Reaper had grabbed some poor sentry and terrified him into giving an estimate of their reduced strength once Bloom had departed. There'd be a name to report missing and fear in the camp.

Such a loss would be worse to take than an ambush or a firefight, where at least the men could feel like they shot back. A single man's death after so many weeks without a casualty worse than a broken ankle would loom all the larger over dinner conversation.

It took three hours for word to come back to the alarmed operations center: all in-fort personnel present and accounted for, from the most distant sentry to the cook stocking potatoes in one of the basements against the winter.

One other person had caught a good look at the Reaper, and Valentine and Lambert heard the story from a shaken-up mechanic named Cleland, brought in by Frat, who'd found him crouched on the unpleasant side of a board over a pit toilet and helped him out. Cleland was up late winterproofing a pump, went to the cookhouse for a hot sandwich and coffee, and saw a tall figure standing silhouetted against one of the security lights.

"Just looked like he was trying to keep warm, wrapped up. Didn't notice how tall he was right off as I was headin' up the hill, you know."

Valentine's nose noted that Cleland hadn't done the most thorough job cleaning up before giving his report.

"Standing in the light?" Valentine asked.

"Turned toward it, more like. I saw something in its hand."

"He needed light," Lambert said, looking at Valentine. "It's a dark night."

"Could you see what it was?" Valentine asked.

"Piece of paper, maybe. It shoved whatever it was into its cloak when it heard me. Damn thing looked right at me. Yellow eyes. Nobody ever told me how bright they were. A man doesn't forget that. Don't think I ever will."

"What then?"

"I ran like the devil. Or like the devil was after me, more like. Dodged through the transport-lot and jumped into the old latrine."

"You can go, Cleland," Lambert said. "Get a drink if you like at the hospital. Medicinal bourbon."

"What do you think?" Lambert asked Valentine after Cleland left.

Valentine looked at the alert report. "They found a garbage can overturned by the cookhouse. Could be raccoons again."

"A Reaper snuck onto the base to go through our garbage? Not even the garbage at headquarters; a can full of greasy wax paper and coffee grounds?"

Valentine had the same uncomfortable feeling he'd had on his first trip into the Kurian Zone, when he learned that one of his charges had been leaving information for Kurian trackers.

"A message drop," Valentine said.

"Possibly. People go to the canteen at all hours. It's a good spot. Almost everyone's there once a day."

"That means—it could be anyone."

"In a camp full of Quislings," Lambert said.

"Not anymore . . . at least I hope not," Valentine said.

Lambert lowered her voice. "They turned on their superiors once. We have to consider the possibility that they'll do it again. How many of them are above going for a brass ring and an estate in Iowa?"

* * *

"Will you take tea with me, Mister Valentine?" Mrs. O'Coombe asked as Valentine passed through her minicamp on a blustery afternoon with blown leaves rattling against the Rover's paneling. "You look chilled."

Valentine had no need to be anywhere. The column was waiting for a report from the Kentuckians about the status of their wounded left behind, not to mention offical permission to move through the new Freehold with an armed column. "Yes. I would like to talk to you."

"Tea elevates any social interaction," she said, placing an elegant copper pot on the electrical camp stove running off the generator. Valentine admired the long spout and handle. The decorative top had elaborate etching.

She opened a tin and spooned some black leaves into the holder at the top of the pot.

"You'll forgive me—I make some ceremony of this," she said. "Teatime was always my time on the ranch. Even my husband, God rest him, didn't disturb me if I closed my library door."

She poured.

"Tea is the smell of civilization, don't you think?"

Valentine sniffed, briefly bringing the old mental focus to his nostrils. Not a strong scent, even to his old Wolf nose. Just wet leaves and hot water.

"Not much of a smell." Valentine said. "I've heard people put, er, that oil, berge—"

"Bergamot," she corrected. "Yes, Earl Grey. A classic. Not that hard to make. Are you a fan of teas, Mister Valentine?"

"I used to drink some good stuff in New Orleans. Lots of trade there. I had sage tea in Texas. I trade my whiskey and tobacco rations for tea, the Southern Command stuff."

"Dusty mud," she said. "These are real leaves, from China and India."

They drank. Valentine sniffed again, letting his Wolf's nose explore the pleasantly delicate aroma.

"No, it's not a strong smell," she said. "But then civilization isn't a strong presence either. The whole idea is the sublimation of coarser practices. Yet when it disappears—just as when your cup is empty—you'll notice its absence more. Receiving mail is an ordinary experience until it doesn't show up for a week; then its interruption is keenly felt."

"We'd like nothing better than weekly mail out here."

"How is the bond tour going, Mister Valentine?"

"Poorly, I'm afraid. These Kentuckians keep their gold close. We've had some donations of whiskey, boots, and craft goods that we might be able to trade for butter and eggs, if we come across a farm wife in a patriotic mood. You'll see that on the road."

"I am anxious to get started. I wish to see my son again."

"You know, there's a chance we may never find Corporal O'Coombe." Valentine thought it better not to list all the reasons—sepsis, an illness, discovery by Moondaggers sweeping across Javelin's line of retreat looking for those left behind to take and torture . . .

"I've prepared myself for that eventuality, Mister Valentine."

"You seem like a woman used to getting her way. I hope we'll be able to complete our sweep and bring back a few more of Southern Command's own."

"My staff and their vehicles are entirely at your disposal, sir. Our agreement still stands. I am allowed to search for my son; you are allowed to bring back any you have left behind. If we cannot find news of my son, all I ask is a finding that he's been killed in action so that his memory may be honored accordingly."

Valentine would be glad to have Mrs. O'Coombe's crew out of his graying hair. Her precious doctor was always asking for better water, more sanitizer, more hands to pick up shifts changing bandages and bedding.

In the end, Mrs. O'Coombe's doctor came along after all, but only after the remaining Javelin doctor personally spoke to Valentine and explained that having a doctor along might mean the difference between a continued recovery and a setback as they moved the wounded.

Though Valentine wondered how much of a specialist Mrs. O'Coombe's doctor really was. He went by the unimaginative moniker of "Doc" and seemed more like a country sawbones than an expert in difficult recoveries, though his nurse, a thick-fingered Louisiana-born woman named Sahita, had the serene, slightly blank look of an experienced caregiver. Sahita looked at the entire world through narrowed eyes and seemed naturally immune to chitchat, responding only in monosyllables if at all possible to any conversational efforts.

Valentine and Frat did a final inspection before boarding the vehicles. Food, clothing, gear, guns. Everyone a first-aid kit, everyone a tool for finding food or making shelter.

Frat had a big shoulder bag over his arm as well, stuffed with maps and battered old guidebooks to Kentucky. Valentine was rather touched by the imitation, if that's what it was rather than coincidence.

Though Frat had avoided choosing a diaper bag for his miscellany.

Inspection complete and vehicles pronounced ready, they boarded their transport and put the engines in gear. Despite his misgivings, Valentine was relieved to be on the move at last. The sooner they started, the sooner he could return.

The vehicles rolled out of Fort Seng in column order the next morning.

The motorcycles blatted out first, followed by Rover with Valentine riding shotgun and Mrs. O'Coombe in back, looking for all the world like an annoying mother-in-law in a comedy of the previous century. Duvalier slumped next to her, head pillowed on her rolled-up overcoat, already settling in to sleep. Bee had reluctantly taken a place in the Bushmaster behind but soon amused herself by unloading magazines, cleaning the bullets, and reloading the magazines.

The rest of the camouflage-painted parade followed.

Valentine had a big, comfortable seat, and there was a clip for his rifle in the dashboard. A clever little map or reading light could be bent down from the ceiling, and there was even a little case in the seat for a pair of binoculars or maps or sandwiches or books or whatever else you might desire on a long trip.

For such a wretched, ungoverned, miserable place, the Old World sure put a lot of thought into conveniences, Valentine thought ironically. Of course a New Universal churchman would counter that the conveniences applied to only one half of one percent of the world's population.

Habanero the wagon master controlled the wheel and gearshift in Rover, his earpiece in and a little control pad on his thigh that allowed him to radio the other drivers. He gave Valentine an extension so he could plug in to listen—and to speak if he had to.

In the cabin of Rover, Valentine felt his usual isolation from the outside world when riding in a vehicle. While he enjoyed the comfort and convenience, you lost much of the appreciation of landscape and distance, proper humility before wind and weather.

Of course he couldn't overlook the advantages an engine and wheels gave when you had two hundred miles to cover in search of your scattered wounded. The pleasant, ten-minute walk to the gate took but a moment in Rover.

"Slow here," Valentine said as they approached the gate and the doughnut-selling missionary.

"You need to install a drive-up window," Valentine yelled from his rolled-down window. He'd been saving up the jibe all morning.

"Wise of you," the missionary said. "Oh, it's you, my brother and friend. I'm glad you've decided to bow to the inevitable. But time runs short! Hurry! Go like Lot and his wife and do not look back."

"Sorry to disappoint," Valentine said, getting out to claim a final doughnut for the road. "We're not leaving. We're just off to do a little touring. Would you recommend the Corvette museum in Bowling Green or the Lincoln birthplace?" Behind, he heard Duvalier get out, yawning.

"I weep for you," the missionary said. "You're all dead, you know. A reckoning is coming. Weeds have sprouted in Kentucky's green gardens, and it is time for the gardeners to replant. But first, the scythes and the cutters. Scythes and cutters, I say."

"They better be sharper than you," Duvalier said. "It's a sad—"

"Wait a moment," Valentine said. "What's this about, you? What scythes, what cutters? I don't believe in visions unless they're specific."

"Oh, it's coming, sir. Sooner than anyone expects." He looked up and down the column. "You have one final chance to repent. Turn west and follow the sun. If you turn east, by your actions is Kentucky doomed. You sow the seeds of your own destruction."

"Shut up, you," one of the Wolves yelled from the Chuckwagon.

"Want us to gag him with his own pastries?" Frat called to Valentine.

Valentine held up his hand, halting the Wolves in their tracks. "How does a man like you come by such intelligence?"

The doughnut missionary grinned. He passed a finger down his nose. "I prayed and I learned over many long years. But I too had faults: pride and greed and lust. I was cast out to make my way among the heathen. But they did not take all my gifts. I still have my vision."

"False prophecy. I've seen no portents. Red sunsets before the Kurians ever move, my mother always told me. Long red sunsets and dawns, with blood on the clouds."

"Whispers on the wind, you poor soul. That's how I know. Whispers on the wind."

"Would that the wind were a little clearer."

"I hear voices, you poor lost soul. See visions. Visions! Oh, they break the heart."

"I'm sorry you're so burdened. How long have you carried that cross?"

"Had them since I was little. Born in a Church hall, the New England Archon's own retreat it was, but a grim place and nothing but lessons from the time I took my first step. That's no way to serve the gods, no sir, not for me. I ran away as soon as I could climb over the wall and never looked back. Took up with some relief and reassurance workers and then signed up for the missions, first in group and then alone and with only faith and my poor wit. Been warning souls away from folly and death ever since."

Valentine took out his pocket notebook. "How long before our day of judgment? I'd like to make some preparations. Will, disposition of assets, and so forth."

"That I can't tell you. Soon, though, sir. Soon. This will be a cruel winter, and many won't live to see the spring. I say again: Repent now and leave Kentucky!"

Valentine decided he'd heard all the detail he'd ever hear from the doughnut missionary, and he climbed back into Rover.

"Why do you let that thing carry on so, Mister Valentine?" Mrs. O'Coombe said. "It insults every faculty of taste and reason."

"The men like his doughnuts," Valentine said. A few had hopped out of the column to claim theirs. Valentine saw Frat hurl his into the man's face as they pulled away.

Mrs. O'Coombe snorted. "I heard a little of him on the way in. I wouldn't give one of his clots of dough to one of my dogs. Sugar and lard. Mark my words, Mister Valentine, he's trying to clog their arteries or give your men diabetes. Now, tell me, should we turn east immediately, or should we go south and pick up the old parkway?"

Ten

The Discard Run: Winter is the quietest time of the year in Kentucky. The locals retreat to the hearth and their livestock to barns (or to great intertwined piles, in the case of the legworms), and the frequent rains and occasional snow accumulation keep people close to home unless emergency forces them to travel. It is a time for neighbors and small towns to get together and enjoy the indoor pursuits of the season: the final steps in the canning and preserving of the harvest, pursuit of courtship or friendship, sewing circles, and hand tool swap meets.

The column was sped on its way east by two factors. First, they did not have to forage for food or fuel, though where it was available, they were able to buy more with Mrs. O'Coombe's gold. Second, the Kurian Order no longer existed outside Louisville, Lexington, or the crossriver suburbs of Cincinnati—none of which the column was interested in visiting. There were no checkpoints to route around, unwatched fords to find, or patrols to look out for. The only thing their motorcycle scouts had to do was report the condition of the roads or cuts or trails ahead.

Valentine, always willing to see a glass half empty when anything having to do with the Kurian Order was being discussed, maintained that the ease on the eastbound leg would just mean that much more difficulty on the westbound.

Luckily, he couldn't imagine just how right he was.

Lambert had sent word to the clans through Brother Mark of the proposed route tracing the retreat of Javelin, with instructions that any of Southern Command's surviving wounded be made ready for travel and certain frequencies be scanned for radio contact.

They hadn't left many behind, at least many who were expected to live more than a day or two. Valentine doubted they'd need half the bed space that had been allocated in the Bushmaster. Either the soldiers would be recovered enough now to sit, or they'd be beyond medical attention.

Once in the Nolin and Green River Valleys, in this manner they picked up three of their wounded who'd escaped death by their wounds, secondary diseases, or the vengeful Moondaggers who'd followed in Javelin's wake.

The soldiers they picked up, eager to thank Valentine for their collection, were introduced to Mrs. O'Coombe, the true sponsor of their deliverance.

Valentine decided he liked her a little better when he saw her attend to the soldiers they were accumulating. It wasn't an act for the benefit of anyone, especially Valentine, who seemed to have as natural a knack for aggravating her as a piece of steel has for striking sparks when struck by a sharp piece of flint or quartz. She tended to them in a mix of Christian compassion and patriotic fervor. Nothing was too good for those who'd lost so much in the pursuit of the Cause.

He began to enjoy the trip. The cold weather invigorated him, if anything, and apart from delivering anecdotes about the retreat or advice on routes, he had little to do. Mrs. O'Coombe made all the strategic decisions for the column, and the mile-by-mile operations were handled by wagon master Habanero.

Frat was a superb scout, though Valentine was beginning to see why he was still a lieutenant. He wanted to do everything on his own. Run every risk, shoulder every burden, scout every town, be the first through every door. Valentine was impressed with his courage.

Had LeHavre ever said anything like that about his own eager young lieutenant out of the wilds of northern Minnesota? Of course, LeHavre had brought Valentine along differently, keeping him back rather than sending him forward until he found his feet among the men and in the responsibilities of his platoon.

Bee slept outside, snoring softly, her head pillowed on her shotgun. She'd arranged her mane—Valentine could never decide whether Grog hair should be called "mane" or "fur"—into a star to show off the wound she'd received when the Coonskins turned on the Kentucky Alliance.

She was proud of her wound, issued at his side like a stamp of bravery. Valentine wondered just when whatever debt Bee decided she owed him for freeing her would be paid off. She was mysterious about her loyalty, and Valentine's rough-and-ready Grog gutturals weren't up to discussions of intangibles.

But Frat could hold up his end of any conversation. The boy, who'd once possessed a wary, quiet intelligence, had turned into a well-spoken man.

Valentine waved Frat in, heard his report, and then had him sit on one of the tiny camp stools. His long legs made him look a little like a frog ready to give a good loud croak.

"What's with the big bag, son?"

"Saw yours and sort of admired it, sir. All these maps are a hassle."

"I used to carry them rolled up in a tube."

They chatted for a while. Valentine asked about his officers' training, and they shared memories of Pine Bluff. Frat accidentally mentioned a brothel that was either new or had escaped Valentine's notice in his days as a shy, studious lieutenant.

They laughed at their mutual awkwardness. Frat, for admitting that he took a trip upstairs as a rite of passage (always on the house for a Hunter on his first visit, it seemed), and Valentine for living so sheltered a student life that he was unaware of its existence.

Sometimes, their conversations turned serious.

"You ever heard the theory that the Kurians keep the Freeholds in business? That they have allies at the top of our military and government?" Valentine said.

"Well, sir," Frat said. "I think this might be a conversation that wouldn't stand an Honor Code examination."

"The 'sir' stuff only counts when we're standing up. I want your opinion. Disparaging and doubting our superiors is a fine old American tradition."

Frat thought for a moment. "It's something men like to shout after a defeat. They cry, 'Betrayed,' and run. Makes them feel better about running way, or keeping out of it to begin with. If the game's fixed, there's no sense putting any skin into it."

"You've put some thought into this already," Valentine said.

"There was the exact same argument when we got back from Kansas all bloodied, kind of. What's that saying? *Never attribute to malevolence what can be explained by stupidity.* Something like that."

"I heard it as *malice*. Interesting that we agree on that. Of course Kur has a few agents in the Free Republics; they'd be fools not to, and we're not fighting fools. Where'd you get that cry, 'Betrayed!'?"

"Those Shelby Foote books you gave me about the Civil War when I signed up."

"Ah, I'd forgotten about that." Valentine had thought the volumes would teach Frat some useful lessons about leadership in adversity.

"If you ask me, Kansas wasn't malice or stupidity. They just got lucky. The whole Moondagger army was training for a run at those Grogs in Omaha. But you know that."

Valentine had a lot of former friends there. Last he heard, after a big battle the Grogs had retreated up the Missouri River Valley and were now finding friends among the Nebraska ranchers he'd met when looking for the Twisted Cross with Duvalier.

"Actually I don't. I was out of the country at the time."

"Kansas was bad. One of the places I was reported killed, as I recall. My platoon was ambushed and I made it away with only two men. I think the others were captured. We tried to follow and see if we could help them escape, but—they were the Moondaggers, you see. Someone told me that Moondagger priests can channel aura to a Kurian just like a Reaper, and in return they get special powers, just like Wolves do, kind of. That's one of the reasons I volunteered to come out here, to get another crack at them."

"What's left of the ones that operated in eastern Kentucky are back in the Bluegrass region, licking their wounds, last I heard, under the protection of a clan called the Coonskins, who betrayed the Kentucky Alliance. The ones who chased us across western Kentucky have been scattered. Not many survived the massacre on the road to Bowling Green. I would have liked a few officers as prisoners, personally, but the legworm clans had women and children to avenge."

"We're heading near there, right?"

"Yes. Corporal O'Coombe was dropped off in the Rolling Fork Valley southwest of Louisville. But we don't want to tangle with them or the Coonskins. Not with two motorcycles and four transport vehicles."

"Isn't the size of the dog in the fight—" Frat began.

"Why aren't you a captain, Frat?" Valentine asked.

"Most of the fights I've been in since Archangel have been losing ones. In Kansas I lost a platoon. Rio Grande was a disaster, or turned into one a long time after I left. Maybe third time's the charm. Seems to me if I'm in charge of a permanent group of Wolves operating in Kentucky, I oughta be a captain at that."

"You're at the damp and sticky part of the bottom of the barrel in Kentucky, you know, Frat. Southern Command has written us off."

Frat listened to the wind for a moment and poked the center of the fire. "They wrote your boys off on top of Big Rock Hill too. They asked me to contribute to a memorial service for you and those Razorbacks when we lost communication when that big gun started blasting you. We got a big speech about how you bought us time and we had to make it count."

Valentine remembered the earth quaking with each fall of Crocodile's monster shells. The poor, maddened dog who had to be shot; the numbed, desperate man who wandered out into the churned earth to seek disintegration in one of the blasts.

"Let's forget that for now," Valentine said, taking his map out of his diaper bag. "Here's where I'd like you to scout tomorrow. . . ."

With that, they lost themselves in operational details until it was time for Valentine to check the sentries before turning in.

A clear, cold night on the banks of the Rolling Fork with the temperature dropping enough for men to sleep curled up with a fire-warmed rock . . .

The Valentingle came hard, so hard that Valentine thought he was ill until he recognized the familiar prickling on his scalp, the feeling that every molecule in his body was lining up to be counted. Valentine was almost nauseous with the alarm.

What the hell is approaching camp? What from hell, make it . . .

Valentine fumbled at his pocket, found the chain, and put whistle to mouth. "Alarm! Take your posts," Valentine yelled.

Something wicked this way comes.

Valentine heard the engine on the Bushwhacker come to life. Clicks and clatters of magazines being sent home sounded all around like crickets.

Valentine found his Type Three and put in a red-striped Quickwood magazine.

"Frat has a visitor. He's coming in with a parley," one of the Wolves said, shining a flashlight on himself as he approached through the brush. "It's a freak-Reaper—with a flag of truce."

Valentine recognized what he saw prodded along by Frat, a forage bag over its head. It was taller, more spindly than most Reapers, and its tightly wound apparel had tufts of fur at the edges. Great wings were folded at its side so they stuck out behind like a pair of curved swords, and it paced with torso bobbing and head bobbing, knees reversed like a bird.

He'd seen something like this before, perched on a limb, watching him load his column back onto boats after their gun raid into Kentucky.

A big scallop-shaped pouch hung from its waist, loose and empty, but apart from that it bore no weapons or other obvious gear.

"Ranks only, please," Valentine said to the gaping men. He glanced up at the clear sky, looking for other fliers, and then addressed the newcomer. "I will keep you blindfolded. No reason for you to look around."

"It is in your nature to quiver in fear." The creature had a high, faintly squawking voice, as though a goose were talking, rather than an ordinary Reaper's breathy whisper. Though softly spoken, the high-pitched words carried through the night like the notes of a flute.

"He knows how to get things off on the right foot," Chieftain said, his twin, gracefully curved forged-steel tomahawks at the ready.

"Those wings give me the loosies," Ma said. "I hate a bird you can't eat."

Bee brought up her big Grog gun and used a tree branch to rest it on with the sights lined up on the Reaper.

Valentine guessed that her gun wouldn't kill it, but it'd tear off an almighty big piece on the way through. The Reaper looked fragile. He wondered if the Kurians had built it to be proof against Quickwood, and was tempted to test it. Give Boelnitz something colorful at last: gunning down an emissary under its flag of truce.

Valentine looked at Mrs. O'Coombe, who had drawn herself up to her full height, hand resting on a pistol belt she'd strapped on. She nodded to Valentine.

"What do you have to say?" he asked.

"We are—how would you understand it?—an important branch of a larger tree concerning itself with affairs in North America. We of like mind are fond of you humans—such a mix of greatness and folly, with your charming notions of assistance to those outside your name. They call us the Jack in the Box. We've done our best to research the source and are somewhat confused, for we have nothing to do with hamburgers and French fries or a winding musical toy."

Its speech had an uncanny sound to it, as though the words were being forced through a vocalization apparatus ill-suited to English, yet it was easy to comprehend the words. Valentine wondered of the bird thing was making noises of the appropriate length, and the Kurian was speaking directly to their brains.

"Let's hear him whistle 'Pop Goes the Weasel,'" Silvertip said quietly to Chieftain.

"Still, there," Valentine called over his shoulder. "Lieutenant, wrap a handkerchief over that bag. I get the feeling he's looking right through it."

Frat threw his rain poncho over the Reaper's head.

"That's better."

"Indeed. We can't smell you anymore, just this musty fabric. What do you use for waterproofing, apart from grotty, bacteria-gathering mammal oils?"

"Reaper blood," Chieftain said.

"What is your real name, Jack in the Box?" Valentine asked.

"Silence, renegade. Return the brass ring you so ill-advisedly carry or we will say no more."

They all stood in silence for five full minutes—Valentine timed it with his watch.

"Perhaps we should start breakfast," Valentine said.

"Return the ring!"

"I earned it fairly. If you want it, try to take it."

"This is one of your flags of truce!" Jack in the Box's avatar said.

"Then speak your piece," Valentine said. "Do you want to surrender to us?"

"I come to offer a bargain. I like the people of this land: their independent streak, their enjoyment of hearty meals and entertainments, their work ethic—but most of all their adaptability. From a few escaped legworms running wild they have built an entire civilization, using them alternately as a food source and transportation and warcraft. They even use the skins of the eggs. No Grog dared penetrate a legworm nest with fresh spawn wriggling about, yet they send teenagers in to snatch the material from under living scythes."

"So you admire the state," Longshot said. "So do I. But I'm not making demands of people who never did me or my kind any harm."

"It is for the superior to arrange the affairs of the inferior. I only choose favorites to improve."

"Leave if all you want to do is argue and waste my beauty sleep," Duvalier said. "I don't have time for this."

"Quit arguing with the thing; it gets us nowhere," Valentine said. "Let's hear it, then."

"That Kentucky be placed under our protection. We will not take one life from your Alliance lands. Not one. No tribute, no flesh of worm or cow or goat—all we will ask is that it remain strictly neutral in the contest between civilization and progress on one side, and atavism and greed on the other."

"Civilization and progress—" Frat began.

"Oh, you only lack the experience of years, boy."

"You lack the experience of who you should be calling boy," Frat said, reaching for his parang.

"Are we done here?" Valentine asked. "You're giving your offer to the wrong people."

"Mankind has always been a herd. Well, two herds. The larger of the two are the dullards, the grotty masses with their simple pursuits of sex and drink and sport. They are easy to keep and thrive with a minimum of animal husbandry. But among you there is an elite, who appreciate art and culture. It's only the passions of youth that seek the physical gratification rather than the mental that has kept your race from progressing out of its current stage. A little more selective breeding and you would have made the leap to thought-energy manipulation on your own. We will fulfill that potential. But we have the time to see it through. Give us a few more generations."

"Baloney," Valentine said.

"You've been among our better vanguards of the new *Homo sapiens lux*, David Valentine. Have you not seen it with your own eyes?"

Valentine thought of Fran Paoli—no, that made him too uncomfortable. What about the officers Solon collected? Even at the time Valentine admired them. Intelligent, energetic, committed, organized. Cooperative as ants, brilliant as artists—they came so close to establishing their order in rebellious territory captured only a few months before. . . .

Yes, Valentine had admired them.

How had Valentine's memory latched onto Consul Solon's team so quickly? He'd spent years in the Kurian Zone, and his more recent time with, say, Pyp's Flying Circus was more pleasant to consider. Did the Kurian know what mental cards he was holding? Captain Mantilla had said that one's opponents were almost too eager to give the game away, seek the most comfortable mental path.

Was the Kurian putting a few illuminated markers on that path?

"We would almost take it to be universal," Jack in the Box continued. "On the Grog's world they became two distinct races, the golden and the gray, in their terms."

"Eloi and Morlocks," Chieftain said. "Only you feed on both."

"Does the same apply to your *Dau'wa*?" Valentine asked, using the old Lifeweaver name for the renegades who practiced vampirism.

"On Kur, the weak and the stupid were consumed long ago," Jack in the Box answered. "The most resourceful of us survived. Then they went after one another. But it provided the necessary lessons. We are all sprigs of a few hardy family trees, tested and tested again."

"Tested or twisted?" Valentine asked.

Who are you, Jack? Some Kurian who came off worse in a contest, looking for a safe place to hide? Valentine played music in his mind as he listened, mental chaff against the Kurian exploring his mind. Childhood nursery rhymes worked well, like the one employed by the Bears in the northeast to calm themselves down. *The itsy-bitsy spider . . .*

"Where would you put your tower?" Duvalier asked.

"We had in mind the Lincoln birthplace. The architecture is pleasing, the location central yet out of the way. It would suit us."

"How many 'us' would that be?"

"We are the only one. For now. But if the time comes, I may have others of my kind take refuge with me. The deal would remain the same. All we ask is to be left alone and for this land to remain neutral."

"Is there an 'or else' attached?"

"There always is. We have intimations of what our brethren are planning. Only my intervention can stop the whirlwind that is about to sweep across this land."

"This isn't for us to decide," Valentine said. "You need to speak to the Kentuckians."

"Events are not altogether in my control, either. I came to you in the hope that you would have that apostate who goes by the name Brother Mark persuade them into wisdom rather than folly. Our brethren are disappointed in the foolish gesture your cousins made in Owensboro. Tell your Brother Mark that Gall has been specified for Kentucky."

The creature reached inside its robes, and Valentine saw fingers shift all around from trigger guard to trigger—save for Duvalier, who's sword appeared with a *snick*. It produced a white, capped cylinder about the size of a dinner candle high for all to see, and then dropped it at its feet.

"You men like to have matters set down on paper. I give you paper."

"Thanks anyway. We've rolls of it," Duvalier said.

"Perhaps that's for the Kentuckians to say," Mrs. O'Coombe said. "It's their land."

"So entertaining a discussion," Jack in the Box said. "We almost forgot to offer a compliment. Brilliant gambit in Owensboro. You are worthy of your name after all."

"Gambit?" Valentine asked.

"Yes. The bomb. Blowing up some of your own. You won your goal, but the herd you stampeded is heading for a cliff. Keep your workmanship in mind in the coming days as the bodies pile up and this beautiful, rich land becomes a waste."

"We'll take you along to meet the Assembly," Valentine decided.

"No, I know that trick as well. You think you'll use our avatar to locate us."

"Maybe we won't give your avatar a choice."

"All I have to do is have it hold its breath. These flying forms are frail. Their hearts explode if deprived of oxygen for long. But that would be a shame. You will have no way to give an answer."

Valentine hated to admit defeat. "How shall we answer you, then?"

"We will be in touch. But if you ever wish another audience, simply tie a bedsheet on top of one of these vehicles. They will be observed. We will send a messenger."

So, the Kurian knew all about their vehicles. They hadn't seen its silhouette flying around in daylight, so it must search for them at night. Well, there were ways to hide vehicles and disperse lifesign.

"Be vigorous, Valentine. Do not delay even one day. We do not make empty threats; we choose the time and the place of their being carried out. The seeds of the destruction are already planted. My brethren only need to give the signal for them to sprout. You, Valentine, shall be the agent of this land's destruction. It will be your responsibility. The question is, of course, can you handle the responsibility? Can you handle responsibility?"

"You talk too much," Frat said. "The major's under orders, like the rest of us."

"Negotiating such an arrangement, even if the Kentucky Assembly is interested, would take a lot of time," Valentine said. "If this whirlwind is as imminent as you claim, you had better delay it, or you'll find yourself taking refuge in a wasteland."

The bird thing cocked its head. "Keep in touch."

Valentine nodded to Frat, who gave it a vigorous turn. He walked it out of camp.

Valentine turned to Habanero. "Wagon master, see if you can raise Fort Seng on your radio. We need to find out where Brother Mark is."

He turned to the owner of the biggest property in the Free Territory. "Mrs. O'Coombe, I'm sorry, but the needs of Southern Command and Kentucky will have to delay finding your son."

She tore her eyes from the strange strut of Jack in the Box's avatar. "But you said tomorrow we will be in the territory where he'd been left."

"We'll get there. Just not tomorrow."

She drew herself up. "Mister Valentine. I equipped this convoy with the best communications equipment I could find. The transmitter alone is worth one of my barns and its resident livestock. Are you telling me it is not adequate to pass along a message that may or may not be an empty threat?"

"Brother Mark may need transport to whatever responsible parties can decide what to do about this."

"Are you giving me an order?"

"If I have to," Valentine said, careful to keep his rifle under his arm as the camp began to line up behind their respective leaders, the Bears and Wolves with Valentine, the drivers and mechanics and security men and medical staff with Mrs. O'Coombe. Stuck just stood up and stared at Valentine.

Duvalier hopped up on top of the Bushmaster. "Cool off, all of you. I don't know who or where this Jack-in-the-off is, but we start throwing down on one another, he'll be laughing until the robins come back."

The camp broke into a dozen separate arguments over the reality of the threat:

"If a Kurian told me my dick was on fire, I wouldn't look down and give him the satisfaction."

"They always give you a last chance."

"So this Kurian makes peace with Kentucky. What about the rest of them? It's all well and good to be neutral, but others gotta respect it or it don't mean jack."

"It's like a game to the Kurians," Stuck said to Valentine's Bears. "Sometimes their threats are empty; other times they are carried out to the last degree and beyond. They keep us guessing and on edge."

"Just good poker," Chieftain said. "Sometimes you can win a pile on the cheap, if you know how to bluff."

"I have Fort Seng, five-five," Habanero said from the radio.

Valentine walked over to the parked Rover. So much for sleep. "Tell them to get Colonel Lambert on the line. Wake her up if they have to. We need to talk."

You never knew how much of a Kurian threat was illusion and how much was steel. They were like magicians, always diverting attention from the operating hand.

Valentine put a steadying grip on Chieftain's arm. The Bear's hair had risen on top of his head. Valentine had known Bears who turned purple when readying for a fight, or whose eyes lit up like a pair of flares, or who turned into snorting, steaming, turf-tearing bulls. He'd never seen one give himself a war headdress before. Valentine had always assumed that Chieftain's name came from the Bear's characteristic tomahawks.

"Eloi and Morlocks?" Valentine asked, by way of calming him down.

"I could never much stand reading, Major. But I liked that H. G. Wells guy. Except for *Food of the Gods*; that one was just too weird."

"But maybe the most topical, considering tonight's conversation," Valentine said. But to be honest, he'd skimmed it too when he was thirteen.

"I read my share of the stuff when I was a boy," Valentine said, remembering the long winters in Father Max's library. He'd once thought it profitless idling, but it gave him a truer picture of the world before the cataclysm in 2022 than he received through bits and pieces of the reworked histories of New Universal Church photo-studies children in the Kurian Zone received.

Valentine had sat in any number of New Universal Church lobbies, waiting for free cocoa or bread issued in exchange for attending a short lecture. He'd paged through photograph after photograph of poverty, devastation from war, death by starvation and disease, every horror imaginable and most of them featuring children as victims.

In the Free Territories most of the history the kids learned had to do with the post-2022 resistance and the crimes perpetrated in the Kurian Zone. It was taken as a given that the Old World was a pleasant idyll. One side showed ugly pictures of a hell; the other painted fair, vague portraits of a heaven.

Valentine believed the reality to be a blend. Perhaps whether you lived in heaven or hell depended more on your mental attitude than anything.

Back to the present. *One of the drawbacks of aging*, Valentine thought from his venerable age of having recently turned thirty, *is a tendency to dwell on the past*. Living in many of his memories would mean a waking nightmare. Better to think about the future.

With that thought firmly in mind, Valentine examined the baton the flying Reaper had brought. Mrs. O'Coombe's crew was already calling it "Mothman."

The baton case looked like polished bone, possibly a femur from a preadolescent human. Valentine didn't know bones well enough to determine. Besides, the joints were sawn off where the tube had been threaded and capped.

He buried the cylinder and its caps. No telling what the Kurian might have planted in the baton in the way of location devices. For all he knew there could be an audio-video transmitter.

The offer itself took up only one paragraph. There was no signature or date. The paper had a watermark that looked vaguely like a stylized depiction of an eclipse—a ring of faintly red fire, offering just enough of a glow to read the letters in darkness. Perhaps that was the Kurian's version of a commitment.

Valentine touched it with a first-aid kit's tweezers.

A FAIR OFFER OF A SECURE FUTURE

—it began, and went on to outline the same deal the Reaper had spoken of. Autonomy for Kentucky save for the Kurian bridgehead at Louisville—a fair exchange for Evansville—provided it remained neutral in the war.

Frat returned, looking thoughtful, and stowed his rifle and gear. Valentine waved him over to the radio, where he was waiting to see if Lambert could make contact with Brother Mark—then perhaps he and the old churchman could have personal communication.

The lieutenant looked like he'd aged a year since Valentine had last seen him. Had the Kurian figured out a way to siphon off a little aura? He'd decided some time ago that that was what had happened to him at the Owensboro western bridge.

"How'd that thing ever find you, Frat?" Valentine asked. "Did it just flap down?"

"I thought I heard an engine—aircraft, maybe—and went up a hill so I could find a better listening spot.

"It gave a chittering sound from a tree above. I looked up and there it was. I thought my number was up. But it had a white hand towel in each mitt and waved them."

"You shouldn't go poking around alone," Valentine said.

"What, some good ol' boys around here will bend me over and make me squeal?"

"That's a dream date compared to what a Reaper might do to you." Frat shrugged.

"Frat, one more thing. Did it have anything in that bag?"

"I searched it. Nothing but dog hair and stank. I think that was a ration pouch. Maybe some toy poodle got packed as its lunch."

"Didn't seem like the kind of creature that could fly far to me."

"Maybe the engine noise was from an aircraft, dropping the thing off."

Valentine nodded. "We had a little argument over the management of the column while you were gone. We're going to get Brother Mark."

"Before we get Mrs. O'Coombe's son? Hope you know what you're doing. She seems like a useful woman to know, if you ever decide to turn civilian and take up private employment."

Eleven

Central Kentucky, January: The locals have a saying: "You have to come here on purpose." This is the fastness of Kentucky, the region that stretches southeast from Louisville to the Tennessee Valley. It is a bewildering maze of knobs, gullies, streams, ridges, choked at the swampy bottoms and backwaters, breezy and cool and clear atop the region's many ridges.

The meadows, breathing in the shadows of the ridges, are the gut of the country. So rich in blackberry bramble and cherry, with grasses that grow indefatigably in summer and only a little less lushly in the brief winters, the meadows support dairy cattle for the landholders and such an abundance of deer that even the region's skilled hunters hardly trim the population.

Winters here pass mild; snow blows across several times a year but melts quickly. Even the songbirds seem to be resting between mid-December and February; all the greens and browns fade and blend together and everything looks washed-out and dull.

The water is the same, winter or summer. The hills are rich in wells and springs, all flowing with clean, crisp, limestone-filtered water tastier than any city tap could produce. Underground flows and seeps have worn away the region's limestone, honeycombing it with sinks and caves famous, dangerous, and unknown.

The people are clannish in the best sense of the word. Interlocking circles of families spread news, offer support, celebrate marriages, and mourn deaths at the many little churches dotting the region. They are fiercely independent, even from their fellow Kentuckians: the city folk outside Cincinnati and Louisville, the flatlanders of the more gentle hills to the west (not that they don't range their legworms there and maintain good relations with the Jackson Purchase locals), or the Appalachian mountain folk. In past decades some were moonshiners and marijuana growers; later they ran Internet start-ups and were artisans. They were the first in Kentucky to learn how to wrangle legworms, to study their herds and breeding cycles, unafraid to learn from even the smattering of Grogs in southern Indiana, becoming elderly veterans of the battles following the cataclysm in 2022 in worm riding and harvesting.

They use the many caves and holes to hide their weapons, their precious machine tools, their spare radios, and even explosives.

This is the heartland of the old Kentucky Alliance that accompanied Southern Command's Javelin into West Virginia. Now what's left of that fellowship is reorganizing itself into the Army of Kentucky—at least that's the formal name on the documents coming out of the government. The worm riders, wintering their mounts in the protective heaps they form around each year's eggs, are now a group called the Line Rifles and organized into three troops: the Gunslingers, the Bulletproof, and the Mammoth.

Men like to have something or someone to follow. Sometimes it's nothing but a favorite song; other times a bullet-torn flag. In the case of the Mounted Rifles of the Army of Kentucky, their standard is a warrior queen.

Young and beautiful in her full bloom, with a mane of hair flowing and alive as a galloping horse's tail, she wears her authority the way another woman might wear a favorite hat, only taking it out for special occasions and drawing all the more eyes because of it. She's a natural atop a legworm or a horse, and she designs and sews her own uniform from egg skins she's harvested herself, bearing a pistol that belonged to her father and a pair of binoculars presented to her by the old Bulletproof clan chief she grew up calling her leader.

Her words were the ones the Kentucky Alliance listened to on the long retreat back from the Appalachians, when many were discouraged and wished to go home. Her voice gave the order for the counterattack on the banks of the Ohio that sent the Moondaggers running. Under her leadership they chased the bearded invaders all the way to Bowling Green.

She has her hands full at the moment. There's a white-hot blood feud with the old Coonskin clan, who betrayed the Kentucky Alliance on the long retreat, dividing cousin against cousin, uncle against niece. What's left of the Coonskins have taken on the Moondagger faith, and members of the Mammoth troop are forever disappearing for weeks at a time while they avenge some sister or cousin.

As if that's not enough, the newly constituted government of Kentucky is still getting itself organized. Volunteers come in unequipped, untrained, and irregularly, hungry and in shoes with old pieces of tire serving as soles, adding to the food supply problem even while they wait for a rifle.

Valentine's luck was in. As it happened, Brother Mark was also in the Karas' Kentucky Alliance heartland. They managed to get a fix on each other over the radio and agreed to meet on Gunslinger clan ground.

What was left of the old alliance welcomed them into the Gunslinger camp squatting for the winter in the ruins of a megachurch near a group of their worm piles outside of Danville. If not cheering, exactly, there were shouted halloos and greetings and excited children rolling around and bumping like marbles.

The camp was unsettling in one manner, though. It seemed to be devoid of men between fourteen and forty. All Valentine saw were boys and old men. He knew the Gunslingers had suffered losses during the summer's fighting, but he had no idea they were this grievous.

There were plenty of horsemen and vehicles and guns in camp, however. Tikka was there with a column of her all-Kentucky army, and Brother Mark had arrived with a few members of the Assembly and their staff.

"Lots of mouths to feed, mouths that didn't do any planting or weeding or varmint shooting this summer," one of the cooks grumbled as he spooned soup into variegated plastic containers.

Valentine presented Mrs. O'Coombe to the temporary leader of the Gunslingers, an old woman who'd long served as an advisor to their clan's leader. Mrs. O'Coombe quivered like an excited horse as she asked about her son.

The Gunslinger leader asked the camp doctor, who stepped up and cleared his throat. "I have good news for you, madam," he said. "Your son is alive and well. I saw him not four days ago."

"May I see him, please?"

The temporary clan chief shook her head. "He is with our muster. They left to meet the Coonskins on the Kentucky river some ways north of here. Corporal Rockaway is serving with the new army's artillery."

"But—he is a soldier of Southern Command," Mrs. O'Coombe said. "He has four years left. . . ."

"An informal arrangement," the Gunslinger said. "He's still in what's left of the Southern Command Guard uniform. Settle, ma'am; settle. He's just along so we can show strength if they try another decapitation attack. Fine boy you raised."

"It's that Last Chance," Brother Mark said. "Raving about some kind of apocalypse that's going to hit Kentucky. Sad thing is, he's getting a few converts."

Valentine fought his body. It wanted to be up and in action, chopping wood or clearing brush for kindling if nothing else.

"We've had a lot of townies flee to Coonskin territory," the clan leader said. "Mostly people who drew breath thanks to the Kurian Order anyway, so good riddance to them."

"If you would provide me with a guide—," Mrs. O'Coombe said.

"Sorry, ma'am. I hate to say no to a worried mother—I have four myself and one grandchild—but it's a clan rule. When a fighting man is away, no parents, no children, no spouses until the fighting's over."

"But there is to be no fighting," Mrs. O'Coombe said.

"We hope not. As I was saying, our people end up worrying more about their families than the enemy, and they get themselves in trouble that way. But it looks like you brought a few gunmen of your own. If you want to send them up with a message to your boy, they're welcome to join young Tikka upcountry. Until then, I'd like to offer you our hospitality."

Gunslinger hospitality was meager with all the visitors in camp and the holidays emptying larders.

Everyone was talking about the peace conference between the Gunslingers and the Coonskin–Moondaggers northeast of them in the Bluegrass proper. The idea that Kentucky might be allowed to just let the bodies lie and stop the raids and counterraids that had been going on ever since the Moondaggers marched across Kentucky, burning and kidnapping, gave everyone hope for an early spring without gunfire exchanged in Kentucky's tangled dells.

Valentine had the disquieting feeling that their hopes would be in vain. This cease-fire might be the final calm before the storm.

The reinforcements were already pulling out of the Gunslinger winter camp to join the others to the north. Tikka's Army of Kentucky were dressed like scarecrows in everything from denim to black-dyed sports uniforms, but most sported new winter hacking coats in a uniform deerskin brown, *A-o-K* stenciled on the shoulder. Behind them were guns and commissary wagons. Valentine hadn't seen such a mule train since the campaign in Dallas. The animals looked fresher than the men.

Tikka greeted Mrs. O'Coombe's lined-up staff and Valentine's Southern Command additions. She and a few members of her staff took a quick appreciative look at their bikes and vehicles.

"How are you keeping these beasts fed in the backwoods?" one of the men in a new-looking uniform with a coonskin on the outside of his muffler-style field-jacket collar said.

"We burn organic," Stuck said.

Someone on the staff muttered to a friend about outsiders buying corn oil when there were hungry mouths this lean winter. The comment wasn't meant for him, so Valentine didn't react.

"I don't suppose we can count on that APC up at the peace conference," Tikka said to Stuck.

"We've got a few of our own wounded to take care of. It's mostly a hospital truck."

"Then how about lending your doc and that medical wagon, in case there's a fight."

"I'll ask Mrs. O'Coombe," Stuck said, and walked off.

Habanero was pointing out modifications to the suspension as Tikka walked Valentine back toward the road north.

"You want to join us and see the fun?" Tikka asked.

"The man I'm looking for is up there already. Yes, I'm glad to accept your invitation."

Tikka faked a stumble and knocked into Valentine with her shoulder. "On duty again, I'll bet."

"I'm not sure how to categorize what we're doing at the moment," Valentine said. "Civilian liaison, I suppose."

"Figures. I wouldn't object to a quick liaison under a blanket, but this time I'm the one with a bunch of men expecting me to have my pants on at all hours. Besides, your redhead's looking at me like I'm selling New Universal Church Bibles door-to-door."

Valentine turned around and saw Duvalier sitting cross-legged on the hood of the Chuckwagon, warming herself on the engine. She threw her leg over her sword stick and rubbed the handle in an obscene manner.

"Thin little thing," Tikka said. "I remember her now; she's the one who comes and goes. You should buy her a good Kentucky ham."

"She's always looked like that, but she still puts in thirty miles a day of walking when she has to." Valentine wanted to change the subject. "You know, I don't think I've congratulated you on your new post."

"I delivered one big victory, and now I get cheered everywhere I go. They keep saying they're going to appoint a general-in-chief for the A-o-K, and I wish they'd get on with it. I'm shooting from the hip from the time I get up until the moment I pull off my boots—when I get a chance to sleep, that is. I was brought up to keep the Bulletproof's worms from getting rustled and our stills from getting stolen, not to do this commanding general stuff. Speaking of which, if the men don't see me in my command truck, they won't keep closed up properly. I'll see you on the banks of the Kentucky, David."

Stuck remained at the Gunslinger winter camp. Where Mrs. O'Coombe went, so did he, a hulking shadow. At the moment he sat pillowed between Longshot's thighs as she rubbed oil into his scalp and massaged his temples, looking like a monkey grooming her mate.

"What's that all about?" Duvalier asked Valentine.

"Bears get twitchy if they don't let off steam somehow. That's how brawls start: Bears with nothing to use as a way to vent."

"Like chopping wood?" Duvalier asked.

Valentine stared at her. He'd never thought of it beyond satisfying exercise.

"You sure you don't want to come up to the peace conference?" he asked.

Duvalier poked him with her elbow. "Snore. There's an interesting craft market in Danville, they say. Maybe I'll visit that. I picked up some real gold braid in Indiana. I'll skip a few days of you making goggle eyes at your bowlegged worm rider."

Valentine decided not to ask how she'd acquired the braid. "I'm not sure how to make 'goggle eyes,'" Valentine said, and then regretted it instantly. A lot of times Duvalier said nonsensical stuff just to provoke him.

"You know, Val, you're just a big plaything to her. A doll with really nice hair and a dick."

"What a shame I missed Christmas morning."

"That's it. I am coming along, if only to keep you from embarrassing us."

The banks of the Kentucky were thickly wooded at the slight bulge that passed for a lake designated as the border between Gunslinger and Coonskin territory. Behind the banks were the river-cut hills, scarred with limestone cuts and patched with tufts of wood like an old man's hairline.

They could see on the other side of the river the observation positions of what was presumably the Coonskin force, no doubt here to safeguard their own negotiators.

Valentine's binoculars weren't much better than his eyes at that distance, but with the help of one of the A-o-K's telescopes, he could get a look at individual figures. He recognized the dark battle dress and red dagger sheaths of the Moondaggers.

"The Coonskins have formally united the Moondaggers," Brother Mark said. "May they live to see the error of their ways and have regret come to wisdom."

Frat took a long look at the foes he'd heard so much about. "Religious nuts, huh?"

"If you call worshipping Kurians a religion," Valentine said. Frat turned the eyepiece over to Boelnitz. He turned the knob back and forth, sweeping across the camp, and then made a few notes in his leather journal.

"Some of 'em like the lifestyle, I guess," the Gunslinger observer said. "No tobacco, booze, or red meat but all the wives you want."

"They've been calling themselves the Kentucky Loyal Host lately," a Gunslinger in an officer's slouch hat said.

"Fancy-sounding word for 'traitor,'" Silvertip observed.

Their long search ended in a matter-of-fact fashion. Valentine and Frat were escorted to Corporal Rockaway, raised O'Coombe, where he was setting up mortar positions on the hillside above the river.

"Your boy Rockaway—or O'Coombe, or whatever his name is—he's involved in this. He may be on one leg and be wearing a diaper, but he's a heck of a fire director and trainer for our captured Moondagger artillery," one of Tikka's captains said as he walked them along the ridgeline.

And making a bad job of it, too, to Valentine's mind. The artillery's position could be observed from across the river.

Valentine remembered Rockaway as soon as he saw the face, but there had been changes. He limped worse than Valentine and seemed to have lost weight everywhere but his midsection. He was a rather plain-looking, freckled young man with sandy hair and a delicate chin like his mother's. He seemed lost in the big service jacket the A-o-K wore, but he still had his Southern Command helmet. Valentine was surprised someone hadn't talked him out of it when he was left behind. Javelin ran short on helmets long before they hit Evansville.

"Did you pick out these emplacements?" Valentine asked as others kept trotting up to Corporal Rockaway for instructions.

"Orders," Corporal Rockaway said. He had some of his mother's Texas accent too. "We're supposed to show our teeth so there won't be any funny business like at Utrecht. Hey, Doc. What the heck are you doing all this way?" O'Coombe's doctor stepped forward. "We've come a long way to bring you home. I'm glad to see you well. When we'd heard—"

Rockaway smiled, which much improved his face. "Hell, Doc, well's a relative term. You put my first diaper on me, and I'm here to tell, I'm back in diapers now and will be for the rest of my life. Some emergency patching to the digestive tract, they said. And I have to drink lots of water to help things along. But I can still fight; I just leak a little doing it. I like fighting these Moondagger sons of bitches. If everything— Well, tell Mom not to worry."

"You can tell her yourself when this is done. She's back with the Gunslinger camp," Valentine said.

"She came all this way too? Devoted of her. When the news came about my older brothers, she just tightened up her mouth and hung black crepe around their pictures and made big donations in their names to the Rear Guard Fund."

Valentine had no business getting involved in family dynamics. He jerked his chin at Frat, and they excused themselves.

Once they were out of earshot, Frat said, "Heart's in the right place but the kid doesn't know much about setting up a battery. If anything goes down, he's making it easy for the Moondaggers. They're not all cross-eyed and stigmatic, I don't suppose."

"Not hardly," Valentine said, remembering the sniper's bullet that had sprayed Rand's brains all over headquarters.

Valentine spotted Tikka emerging from a knot of hilltop woods, walking the ridgeline. Corporal Rockaway limped up to her, and they spoke for a few minutes. Tikka pointed as she spoke, both toward the ridge on the other side of the river where the Coonskins and the Moondaggers were encamped, and behind, where the rest of her train was presumably approaching and deploying.

Once again, she made a show of strength, putting some of her vehicles and horse wagons in plain view on the hill.

She was kind enough to invite Valentine to accompany her to the peace conference. All she asked was that he wear one of the A-o-K field jackets and a hat, and keep to the back with his mouth shut.

Duvalier managed to work her way into the party too. Boelnitz tried to get permission to come along, but Tikka insisted that he stay back on the riverbank.

"Remember what happened the last time we were invited to a conference?" Valentine said.

Tikka grinned fiercely. "As a matter of fact, we're very much hoping for an encore."

"Without legworms? Won't you be at a disadvantage?"

"They'll be assuming that, yeah."

*   *   *

VIPs arrived in cars and passenger trucks; the Gunslingers and Bulletproof and a smattering of other old Alliance soldiers on horseback or in wagon trains. Many arrived via old-fashioned shoe leather.

They met out on the small lake, a widening in the Kentucky River separating Coonskin land from the Gunslingers.

Valentine felt like he'd read about a peace meeting like this before, but he couldn't place the exact circumstances.

The two sides rowed out to a pontoon houseboat anchored midlake. There, on the sundeck atop the houseboat (after both sides verified that neither had filled the living quarters with gunmen), they met.

Their forces lined the tree-filled banks to either side of the river. Valentine didn't understand the fascination. There was little enough to watch.

He wasn't important enough to go up on the top deck with the Kentucky or Coonskin principals. But he could listen from the base of the ladder facing the west side of the river.

There were introductions, neither side being particularly gracious beyond the grace required of opponents who were used to shooting each other on sight. If the Gunslingers were colder in their formalities, it was because they'd suffered more outrage at the hands of the Moondaggers.

In many more words than the Reaper's avatar used, they offered the representatives of the Kentucky Assembly essentially the same status as Jack in the Box had spoken of: a neutral Kentucky, running its own domestic affairs but leaving the outside world to the Kurians. The Agenda and Tikka were no more inclined to welcome the proposal from some Moonskin mouthpiece and a few traitors than they were through Valentine's birdlike Reaper.

"Glad to see you admit we whupped you out of Kentucky," Tikka said.

"We stayed only long enough to chase Southern Command out," a Moondagger responded. "Then we returned to our allies."

"Formerly *our* allies," Tikka said. "They turned on us; they'll turn on you someday. Remember that."

"You are the traitors," an educated Kentucky accent said. "The Kurians indulged you, and you paid them back by aiding terrorists and wreckers and murderers—"

"There is a reckoning coming!" one of the Moondaggers began to shout thickly. Valentine recognized the voice at once, their old blustering friend Last Chance. "A reckoning! This land, long peaceful—"

Ha! Valentine thought. Last Chance wasn't at the battle between the Bulletproof and the Wildcats a few years back.

"—needs to be cleansed of the filth that has washed into it. Intruders! Interlopers! Troublemakers! Trouble they brought, and death will be their reward—or something worse than death."

Duvalier made a fist and flicked out two fingers toward Last Chance with her thumb slightly up—the American Sign Language version of "asshole."

"That's not how you go about negotiating in Kentucky, beardy," the new Agenda for the Assembly said—the previous one was too sick to make the journey to the river. "You want to deal with us, you tell us what you offer and you let us make up our minds. You don't threaten."

Valentine liked the new Agenda already. Later he learned he was a man named Zettel, though most called him Mr. Zee. Formerly the clan chief of the Gunslingers and a friend of Karas, Mr. Zee, Valentine had been told, came from a family who'd once owned quarries and he'd grown up covered in limestone dust.

"We'll consider your offer and give you an answer tomorrow. Here, on the boat again. Shall we say noon?" Agenda Zettel said.

"There can be only one answer," the educated voice said. "The other doesn't bear thinking about. We both love Kentucky too much to see it turned into a graveyard."

Duvalier looked up at the sky, shivered. She edged closer to Valentine and stuck her hands in his pocket.

"We could go up there and kill all of them," she whispered. "Pay them back for Utrecht."

Killers who don't like killing never last long. They become drunks or careless. Duvalier liked it, as long as her targets were Quislings, the higher up in the social hierarchy the better.

Valentine had a dark part of him that liked it as well. The shadow that lurked inside him chose its time and place to be satisfied.

"The Assembly can make up its mind. It's their choice. Let's not make it for them."

A few more words were exchanged upstairs about day and night signals.

They departed. Valentine put one hand in his pocket and gripped Duvalier's with the other, making sure she accompanied him to one of the boats heading back for the Gunslinger shore.

They waited in line and ate like the rest of the Gunslingers and A-o-K troops. Chieftain and Silvertip were going back for thirds when Tikka interrupted and asked for a moment with Valentine. They stepped out of earshot.

"Mr. Zee's meeting with the Assembly representatives is civilians only, so I thought I'd track you down and talk to you."

Her dark good looks were suited for a chill Kentucky night. She sparkled like a bit of Kentucky's bituminous coal. Valentine knew that all you had to do was touch a match to her and she could generate a whole evening's worth of warmth.

"What reply should we give, in your opinion?" Tikka asked.

"Why should my opinion matter?" Valentine asked.

"I trust it, for one," Tikka said.

"I'm . . . uneasy. Everyone in the Kurian Order seems to be shouting 'surrender' or at least 'keep out' at Kentucky. I can't make sense of it. I don't mean to denigrate the land or the people, but it's not like Kentucky is filled with industries they'd miss and resources they can't get anywhere else."

"There's the coal," Tikka said. "And the Cumberland's the easiest route to the east coast in the South."

"Perhaps they are more worried about invasion than we thought. I can't help but feel there's something here very important to the Kurian Order."

"What? We know about what they did here; they weren't at all secretive about it. There are no big tracts of the country that are off-limits. A few towers in Lexington, a few more in Louisville. The legworm meat? The big plants up in Louisville fill boxcars with canned protein every day. I was told some of it even gets traded overseas."

Valentine tried to keep his mind on the possibilities in the Kurian strategy, rather than the possibilities behind Tikka's uniform shirt buttons. "Without food it's hard to grow your population. Maybe that's all it is: They don't want to lose their free-labor butchery."

"Perhaps its just geography. If Kentucky becomes a Freehold, the Free Territory extends from the foothills of the Appalachians to Mexico. That's a lot of people and a lot of resources, more than many countries in the world have." Tikka worked her fist into her palm. "The Assembly said that they wanted to hear from me before they make their final decision. Whichever way I go, I think the rest of the Alliance will follow."

"That's quite a responsibility."

"Well, if someone else made the decision and I didn't agree, it'd drive me straight into a froth."

Valentine smiled at her.

"I think we should tell them to make like a frog and boil. I'm sure they want us to disarm, get complacent, and then they'll give us the works anyway."

"It's happened before," Valentine said, meaning both throughout human history and in relations with the Kurian Order.

That night the reunited elements of the Kentucky Alliance held a celebration. All along the hillside impromptu bands started up their fiddles and guitars, or raucous parties rolled out the barrels of beer and casks of bourbon.

The locals knew how to live well. Any excuse for a celebration. The sentries and flankers were out and paying attention to their duties, so it wasn't all revelry.

Valentine didn't join in. He was tired from the trip and worried about what the Kurians were hatching in their towers, and he was in no mood for carousing—especially with negotiations at an impasse and an enemy army just across the river.

Chieftain and Silvertip were content to load up with food and settle down by Valentine and Duvalier.

"In another time," Duvalier said, "all we'd be worried about now is keeping New Year's resolutions. High-carb or lo-carb diets." Duvalier had the pinched look of someone on a no-food diet, but then her stomach gave her difficulty under the stress of field cooking.

"I've plenty of resolve. I just hope I'm granted the strength to see it through. Then another generation will get to worry about their carb intake," Valentine said.

"I don't know about that," Silvertip said. "I don't think the old world's ever coming back. Good riddance to it."

Chieftain stood up. "Not this speech again. I'm going back for seconds. I'll have fourths by the time he's done."

Silvertip gave him an elaborate double-index-finger salute. "You just don't know wisdom when you hear it. I say it's all got to come down. Everything: Kurian Order, the Free Territories. Let's say we beat the Kurians—we're not just restoring the United States as it was. There's Grogs settled all across in their bands from the swamps in North Carolina through Indianapolis, St. Louis, the Great South Trail and then up Nevada and out to Oregon. We just going to put them on reservations? Exterminate them? The Kurians have ruined half of mankind and impoverished the rest. Southern Command's handed out land right and left. Suppose some relations show up with old deeds saying it's theirs?

"It's all gonna get burned down, and then maybe the decent folks will rebuild civilization. The honest and diligent and talented will find others of like mind and start setting up again. It'll be ugly for the Kurian herds, but maybe their kids or their grandkids will be human beings again. That's why your legion's bound to fail, beg your pardon, Major.

"In the end, we'll be thanking the Kurians. They gave us a challenge and we'll end up better for it, the way a forest fire helps the trees thrive. Gotta burn away the rubbish once in a while."

Valentine disagreed but knew better than to get into a heated argument with a Bear. Most of Valentine's command would be "rubbish" in Silvertip's taxonomy. Time would tell.

Chieftain returned with a piece of newspaper filled with honey-dipped apple slices. "He give you the *world's got to burn down* speech?"

Valentine bedded down with the sounds of music and celebration still echoing from the hillside.

Duvalier shook him awake in the predawn.

"There's something brewing across the river. Can you hear it?"

Valentine went to the riverbank. There was still enough night air for the sound to carry; his Wolf's ears did the rest. A steady crunch and soft clatters and clanks like distant, out-of-tune wind chimes sounded from the screen of growth and trees across the river.

Frat was already at the riverbank, on his belly with a pair of binoculars to his eyes.

"You thinking what I'm thinking?" Valentine asked.

"We're about to get served by the Host," Frat said.

"Run to the A-o-K headquarters and tell Tikka that they're coming."

Frat passed the binoculars to Valentine and took off.

Flashes of light, like distant lightning, lit up the eastern riverbank ridge. Valentine saw the red lines of shells pass overhead.

They landed among the mortar tubes and wagons parked on the hillside.

"Those rotten bastards," Silvertip said, roused by the smell of action. "May they all rot in Kurian innards, or whatever happens when they dine."

"I have a feeling it's about to become unhealthy in these trees. We'd better fall back to the hill," Valentine said.

He made sure of Duvalier and his weapons and pulled everyone out of the woods, turning them south so they moved parallel to river and hill until they made it outside the box of artillery.

The Host executed their attack well. Valentine grudgingly granted them that. Artillery shells exploded in the vehicle park and all along the artillery line, sending up plumes of black-rimmed gasoline explosions. Smaller secondary explosions from readied mortar shells added to the dirt in the air.

Branches and undergrowth up and moved on the opposite bank, as though the Birnam Wood suddenly decided to move a few yards toward the Ohio.

Boats shot through the gaps in the riverbank growth. Lines of the Host—it looked as though most were Moondaggers—splashed into the water and then fell into the boats, where they picked up paddles and began to paddle madly across the river.

The pontoon boat seemed to spark, and suddenly smoke began to pour out of its windows and lower doors. Strange gray smoke, to be sure, but it did its job obscuring the river.

"I know that smoke," Valentine said. "Ping-Pong balls and match heads. Like ten thousand or so."

The smoke billowed and spread under the influence of the wind, advancing toward them at an angle like a flanking army.

Valentine was of the opinion that many battles were won or lost before the first shot was fired. One side just did a better job of getting more force into a position where it could strike than the other. Such was the case here.

The Kentucky Alliance could see it as easily as he could and decided to get while the getting was good, as a few of their own artillery shells fell blind into the mass of smoke.

"Let's get out of here!" Frat shouted.

"Bastards. Let me at 'em," Chieftain said.

"You'll fall back with the rest of us," Valentine said, grabbing the giant by the shirt collar and dragging him back.

Silvertip, not yet full of battle fury and able to think, yanked Valentine so hard in the tug-of-war with Chieftain's anger that the potential daisy chain broke. Valentine had to check to see if he left his boots behind. Bee did a three-limb galumph up and into the smoke.

As Silvertip dragged Valentine up the riverbank slope, he observed that the Moondagger artillery fire must have been heavy and accurate. The smoldering Alliance vehicles had been burned beyond belief.

With a scattering of fleeing Gunslingers, Valentine joined the route away from the riverbank, running as though hell itself followed.

Another Kentucky disaster to add to his list. At least Southern Command wasn't involved with this one, and at best it would be a minor, two-paragraph notation in the newspapers.

Valentine made it over the hill, and suddenly the trees were thinner and he was into pasture.

He pulled up. A long line of foxholes and headlogs and machine-gun nests stood before him. Behind there were piles of logs and the A-o-K's few armored cars.

This was no slapdash last line of defense but a prepared position. It was obviously quickly done. The fire lanes were imperfectly cleared and the knocked-over trees didn't have their branches trimmed as they should have, but it provided ample if imperfect cover for the reserve.

An A-o-K sergeant took Valentine back to Tikka's headquarters. Valentine heard regular reports of strength and direction coming in from observers on the ridge—she'd scared up a field-phone system from somewhere. Probably captured Moondagger equipment.

The Host came over the ridge in three attacking waves with a skirmish line trotting hard out in front, whooping and yelling. Their cries of victory as they drove the last few Alliance members like rabbits turned into confused alarm as they realized what they'd just stuck their head into.

An old trainer had once told Valentine that fire-fights won by just putting more SoT—shit on target—than the other guy. With the lines of riflemen backed by machine gunners, who were backed by light cannon and .50 calibers on the trucks and improvised armored cars, the Kentucky Alliance was throwing a pound of shit for every ounce hurled back by the dismayed Moondaggers.

The Gunslingers and Tikka's A-o-K had a deadly effect. Valentine saw limbs of trees and entire boles fall in the holocaust sweeping across the Kentuckians' front. What it did to the enemy could only be imagined.

They fell in rows, replaced by more men pouring up and over the hill.

"Get on up there," an Alliance captain shouted, pointing at the advancing Moondaggers.

"Go on then," Valentine called to Chieftain.

"About fuckin' time. Aiyeeeee!"

The Bear ran forward, spraying with this double-magazined assault rifle. When he emptied both ends of ammunition, he planted the gun on its long bayonet and drew his tomahawks.

Valentine settled for employing his Type Three. Duvalier, hugging a protective tree trunk like a frightened child gripping its mother, used Frat's binoculars to spot for him. Valentine squeezed shot after shot out, picking out officers for the most part.

Duvalier also seemed to be going by beard length.

They weren't men; they were funny targets in dark uniforms and hairy faces. A beard on a field radio fell. A beard firing a signal flare—down. A beard setting up a machine gun on a tripod to return fire—knocked back into the grass.

Shouts and whoops started up from the Gunslinger and A-o-K

lines, and a second wave of riflemen went up and forward, passing through and over the first wave, who covered them with fire laid down on the retreating Host.

Chieftain raged among a group of Moondaggers who'd found a wooded dimple in the landscape from which they returned fire. Pieces of men flew this way and that as he swung and stomped and swung again.

The forward motion stopped at the crest of the hill. The Kentuckians threw themselves down and began to pick off retreated targets.

"Let 'em have it," yelled Rockaway into his field radio from his new hilltop post.

Mortar shells whistled down into the trees at the riverbank, detonating in showers of splinters or foaming splashes of water.

A Kurian machine gun opened up on Rockaway's position, guided by his antenna. Valentine dropped to a knee and returned fire with the Type Three.

"Silvertip, try to do something about that gun" was the only order Valentine gave that day that had anything to do with the progress of the battle. He felt like a bit of a fraud, watching shells detonate on the western riverbank among the Host's boats. Maybe Southern Command needed Kentucky more than Kentucky needed Southern Command.

"Pre-ranged fire missions," Rockaway said. "Hope they brought a lot of tweezers."

The Kentuckians ended up with a few prisoners and a lot of big canvas-sided motorized riverboats.

As the battle sputtered out, Valentine found Tikka.

"Brilliant retreat and counterattack," Valentine said.

"Oldest trick in the book," Tikka said.

"I didn't know you'd studied Scipio Africanus, Tikka."

She frowned. "I'm not big on astrology. No sir, I learned all my tactics reading Bernard Cornwell. It's an old Wellington maneuver: Get on the reverse slope out of the line of fire, and then blast away when the Frenchies come over the crest, and advance to throw them back. We just didn't blast them quite as much as they approached; we wanted them to scatter a little bit as they advanced."

"So you swapped out the artillery and vehicles last night during the party," Valentine said.

"Too noisy for you? That was the idea. To cover sound while we were building the fortifications. We parked old wrecks and set up black-painted fence-post mortars to replace the real ones."

"Would have been nice to be let in on the secret. I might have been able to offer a few suggestions. We have some experienced snipers in our group. They could have trimmed the Moondaggers down by a few more."

"I'm sorry, Valentine, but after Utrecht I'll never trust Southern Command's security again."

Valentine must have had an air of command about him, because all through the day members of the Gunslingers who'd fought with Javelin across Kentucky kept coming to him for orders, probably out of habit more than anything. Whether to bind prisoners or just march them with their hands up. What to do with captured weapons and equipment. How to organize a search party for a missing officer. Valentine issued advice rather than orders and sent a constant stream of problems to Tikka's headquarters on the ridge.

For just being an observer, he had an exhausting day.

That night he found Boelnitz scribbling away with the remains of a meal around him as Chieftain and Silvertip told war stories about the fighting in Kentucky.

"You should know better than to ask Bears about a fight," Valentine said to Pencil. "To hear them tell it, the rest of us are just there to keep the fried chicken and pie coming while they do all the fighting."

Boelnitz chewed on his pencil, apparently not hearing.

"So, how's the story coming, Boelnitz?"

Valentine had to repeat himself before the journalist looked up from his leather-covered notebook.

"Story? Not the one I was expecting, Major."

"You're getting some good tall tales out of these two, I hope."

"Kentucky's been interesting enough, but I don't know if my editor will want travelogue. I wish I had the guts to go inside one of those legworm tangles and get a few pictures, but the locals say that until the worms are born, it can be dangerous."

"That's right," said a nearby Gunslinger who'd plopped down to listen to the Bears spin their yarns. "Make any kind of disturbance and they'll snip you in half easy as you might pull a weed."

"To be honest, Major Valentine, I was expecting you to be a little different, more of the legend and less prosaic. Where are the raids into the estate homes in Indiana? You haven't even interrogated any of those Moondaggers or the Kentucky Host or whatever they call themselves to see what's in store for Kentucky."

"The Kurians never tell their foot soldiers their plans. They like to keep everyone guessing, including the other Kurians. I wouldn't be surprised if the reason they're so desperate is because they're afraid Atlanta will just end up taking over Kentucky the way they have much of Tennessee.

"Besides, if you were expecting a war in Indiana, you need men for that kind of job. Our ex-Quisling recruits need training. Most of them are experienced in handling weapons and vehicles and equipment due to a smattering of law enforcement or military duty, but they've got to learn to act as a team somewhere less predictable than a city street. More important, learn to trust one another and their officers. Trust doesn't come easy to someone brought up in the Kurian Order. They're so scared of making a mistake that they all stand around waiting for orders, and then for someone else to go first. There's a story for you."

"Problem is," the neighboring Gunslinger said, "they ain't even human in anything but shape. All the spunk's been bred right out of them, the way a team horse reacts different from a Thoroughbred lead mare or a wild stallion."

Valentine spent the next forty-five minutes on and off the radio. Frat had returned by then, having volunteered to scout across the river, looking thoughtful. After he secured his rifle and gear, he sat down by Valentine, eager for news.

"Where's the Kentucky Host?" Valentine asked. "Run out for more ice?"

"Left the party early," Frat said, milking the joke. He became serious. "Are we going down an evolutionary blind alley, sir?"

"Where does that come from?"

"They left some of their literature behind. There was a magazine I hadn't seen before, comparing various kinds of testing before and after the Kurians came. Of course the article proves there's been improvement in human mental acuity after their arrival."

"An article saying it doesn't make it true. Don't read Kurian intellectual porn; it's all lies anyway."

Frat dug around his satchel and tossed the magazine at Valentine's feet. "Well, I thought it was interesting.

"We're more moral than the enemy, right?" Frat continued. "Isn't that a hindrance? They'll do anything to win. We won't. Doesn't that make them the 'fittest' in a Darwinian sense?"

"Fittest doesn't mean strongest or most brutal. Loyalty confers an evolutionary advantage. So does sacrifice. You get all this from those traditional morals the brutes dispense with. Mountain gorillas trample strangers. That's about as brutal as you can get. For all I know, mountain gorillas no longer exist."

Frat looked down. For a moment he seemed to be summoning words, but they never made it out.

They convinced Rockaway to leave his guns and return to the Gunslinger camp. Now that the A-o-K had arrived, there were some experienced artillerymen to take over the mortar sections in any case, but he was still strangely reluctant, even though he admitted he hadn't seen his mother in years.

Tikka finally ended up ordering him to leave. "Show some consideration for your poor mother," she said.

So they rode back with Doc and his nurse in the Boneyard. The medical workers were more exhausted than even the Bears, having worked on the wounded of both sides in the late Battle of the Kentucky River.

They were not the first to arrive back at the Gunslinger camp, so the news of the victory on the riverbank, and the losses, had already been absorbed, celebrated, or mourned.

Valentine, wanting to be a bit of a showman, had the driver back the overloaded Boneyard back toward the little circle of Mrs. O'Coombe's convoy. Valentine and Duvalier hopped out of the cab, and he opened the doors for the assembled Hooked O-C staff.

"Mrs. O'Coombe," Valentine said, "your son."

The effect was spoiled somewhat by the fact that Chieftain and Silvertip were dressed only in their rather worn-through underwear.

"We've come some way to find you, Corporal Rockaway," Valentine said. "I've brought a familiar face."

The corporal jumped down out of the back of the ambulance medical truck.

"What's the matter, Mother?" Corporal O'Coombe said. "Sorry to see me still breathing?"

It wasn't the reunion between a son who served under his mother's name and his devoted parent that Valentine had imagined.

Mrs. O'Coombe stiffened. "You know I'm pleased to see you alive, Keve. Please be civil in front of your fellow men in uniform. Don't disgrace the uniform you wear."

"Respect the people beneath the uniform too, Mother."

"If you're going to be this way, perhaps we should talk in private."

"Do you have something you want me to sign, Mother, now that you've recovered from your disappointment that I'm still alive? Produce it. You know I'm not interested in running a ranch, however large."

"I'm glad your father isn't alive to hear this."

"Yes, yes: *The good sons died, the bad one lived. God must have a plan; all we can know is that he gives burdens to those strong enough to handle them.*"

Rockaway turned to Valentine. "My mother probably left out a few details. Like that the ownership of the ranch was willed by my father to his sons, and Mother only would own it if we were all dead. What is it, Mother? Do you want to sell off some of the land, or riverfront, or water rights?"

She extracted some surveys and a blueprint from her bush jacket. "I am building a home for the disabled in the Antelope Hills, on the Canadian River. I need to deed the necessary acreage to Southern Command."

Rockaway didn't even look at the papers.

"I'll do you one better, Mother. I'll sell you the whole ranch—lock, stock, and the old man's cutest little whorehouse in Texas—for a grand total of one dollar. I'll accept Southern Command scrip if you aren't carrying your usual smuggler's gold."

"That's very generous of you, Keve, and I am happy to accept. The problem is that you'll have to do this in a UFR courtroom, in front of a judge. My beloved husband's will was most specific on points of ownership."

She turned toward Valentine and the others. "You probably think I'm a grasping, conniving woman. Nothing of the sort. It's just extremely hard to run a business interest of this size when you can't enter into contracts without the owner's approval, and the owner is seven hundred miles away from a lawyer, a notary, and witnesses. My son, as you can see, is uninterested in a business that provides a quarter of all Southern Command's meat and that employs a permanent staff of over a thousand and seasonal help three times that."

"I'm only sorry I didn't sign it over to you two years ago," Rockaway said. "But I was seeing Arbita and she didn't want me to give it up, and for my sins I listened to her. But I'll sign it over to you now, Mother."

"So you'll return to the UFR with us?"

"If that's what it takes for me to be able to live my life in peace, do my job, and marry who and where I choose, I'll take the trip."

So the happy reunion wasn't quite so happy, at least as far as Mrs. O'Coombe and her son were concerned.

Brother Mark needed a ride back to Fort Seng. A wounded Gunslinger named Thursday was also going that way, as he wanted to recover over the winter at home with his family in a town called Grand Junction on the road back. His brother-in-law was supposed to drive out to the Gunslingers and pick him up, but his brother-in-law had flaked. Again. O'Coombe and Valentine's command had passed near it on the way up, and Thursday promised it was just over a ridge from their route home, on an old federal route in reasonably good condition.

They packed up the four vehicles. Valentine made sure Bee had all her odds and ends. Traveling with a Grog was a little like taking a child or a pet on a journey: You needed to make sure you remembered favorite toys, snacks, and clothing.

Thursday wasn't much of a guide. He spent a lot of time examining map, compass, and map again before giving instructions that proved to be guesswork. Valentine could have done just as well with an old road atlas. Thursday's wound was a piece of shrapnel to the buttock, or so he said, and he rode on a special pillow. Valentine wondered if he wasn't really suffering from aggravated hemorrhoids.

His instincts improved once they crossed a small river and he claimed to be in home territory.

"Grand Junction's not even an hour away, now. Three more big ridges and we're there. We could use a garrison of you Southern Command boys, now. There's a marketplace and even a bank that trades Karas' old currency for the new government scrip. Some riders came in a while back and tried to rob the town, but we shooed them off."

Valentine said, "Most of Southern Command's back across the river. All that's left are some training and technical personnel."

"That's Southern Command all over. They claim they swing the biggest dicks but always come up short when belts hit the floor."

A flake struck the windshield like a bug. A big piece of almost-sleet, it sledded down on its own melt.

"I guess winter's here," Valentine said, by way of breaking the tense silence.

In his winters south of central Missouri, Valentine had softened in his attitude toward cold weather. Winters weren't a matter of life-or-death survival, with desperate, predawn to post-dusk fall efforts to stock up on enough fuel, food, and fodder to get yourself and the livestock through to spring—an almost unimaginable span of time away. Winter was a season of rest, refit, and relaxation.

The horizon closed in as the real snow started, following behind the big flakes like a wall of Napoleonic infantry advancing behind their pickets.

Valentine didn't like the look of the big, soft flakes. When they first appeared they fell idly, spinning and drifting in the wind, but minute by minute they thickened, aligning themselves in a single, southeasterly direction.

"Better slow down," he told the driver. "Turn on the running lights. I think we can quit worrying about aerial observation."

"Hope we don't have to do too much off-roading in this," the driver said. "Wish the locals took better care of the roads."

"Legworms make their own roads," Thursday said. "We like it nice and run-down. The Ordnance doesn't risk their axles bothering us." He chuckled. "This is Kentucky. We just don't get that hard weather. Even the sky takes it easy here. This'll blow over in no time."

Twelve

*The Storm, January, the fifty-sixth year of the Kurian Order: Though
rare, heavy winter weather sometimes burdens Kentucky. Blizzards
have been known to dump enough snow to form formidable, chin-high
drifts where the snow is pushed and channeled by wind and terrain,
and once in place, the snow is surprisingly tenacious when protected
by hill or tree from the sun.*

*The storm that winter of 2076 became a byword for bad conditions
for generations after. To anyone who survived it, nothing that hit Kentucky in the future could compare to those wild weeks in January when
the sky seemed determined to alternately freeze and bury the state.*

*The Moondagger prophet from the houseboat on the Kentucky
River might have smiled in satisfaction as white judgment fell. Some
said the real reason for the bad weather was the Kurian desire to see
Kentucky's populace gathered together yet isolated, the better to be
stationary targets for what bloomed like Christmas cactus in the thick
of storm and gloom.*

The storm and the night dragged on.

The snow waxed so heavy that night that they couldn't see more
than fifteen or twenty feet in front of Rover. The headlights reflected
back so much light from the snow they did more harm than good, so
they drove using the service red guide lights. The motorcycles were useless in this weather, so Stuck and Longshot stopped and hung them up
on the side of the Bushmaster. Fortunately, Thursday had put them on
the right road for once, and all the driver in the cramped Rover had to
do was stay on it.

With the storm raging outside, reaching Grand Junction became not just a matter of convenience but a necessity. If they pulled off and camped, everything would take three times as long thanks to the weather, and no one would have a comfortable night.

"Still can't believe about the Coonskins," Thursday said. "They were good men. Had many a meal with them when we all rode for Karas. The Moondaggers must have threatened them with something awful."

"Haw," Habanero said. "I'll bet every head in my share that no one threatened them with anything more than having to come home to six wives."

"That's how the Kurians get you," Longshot said. "Giveaways. That's how they took over in the first place, my old man always said. They showed up—and, sure, they offered food and fuel, but there was more than that. They offered structure and freedom from having to think for yourself."

"I'm sure that's just what people in an earthquake-hit city wanted," Thursday said. "What the hell you talking about, Habby?"

"It's like that story about how to trap swamp pigs. Ever heard it?"

"No," Thursday said.

Valentine had. Habanero had all of five parables, and the pig one wasn't nearly as good as his story about the frog and the scorpion. Mostly because that one was shorter.

Mrs. O'Coombe read her Bible by map light.

"Well, seems that down in the Congaree swamp in South Carolina there was a whole passel of pigs running wild. Now, pigs are smart. Every now and then a hunter would go in and try to get one, but most came back empty-handed, the pigs were so wary and wild.

"Well, a strange feller came into town and said he was going to get them pigs. Of course all the locals about laughed him out of town, but he ignored them. Instead he went and bought himself a couple fifty-pound bags of corn.

"Every day he went into the swamp and poured some corn on one of the pig trails in a nice woodsy spot. Well, of course the pigs came along and ate the corn. It was free, after all. Easier than rooting up grubs and tubers.

"After a few days, with the pigs showing up regular for their feed, he put a few beams down in front of the corn, and he watched them eat from a distance. Just wood on the ground, easy for a pig to hop over, and none of them minded making that jump to get at that corn. Then he started building a fence for a stockyard. He always made sure there were plenty of ways in and out for the pigs. They were a little nervous of the construction—one or two hightailed it right back into the swamp—but the rest were getting really used to that corn, so they went in.

"Now gradually he shut off the entrances and exits, kept watching them from nearer and nearer, and made it tougher and tougher for the pigs to go in and get the corn, till all they had was a little gap to squeeze through. But darned if they didn't squeeze through and gobble till every last bit of the corn was eaten.

"Only one time, when they were done, the pigs saw that there was no way back out of the pen. He'd blocked it up.

"They got their free grain still. 'Nother day or two, anyway, before a big ol' livestock trailer pulled up, and they used sticks and dogs to herd them pigs right into the trailer. Didn't cost him much: a few big bags of corn to convince them pigs there was such a thing as a free lunch."

"So that's what they're doing to us Kentuckians, you think?" Thursday asked.

"I don't know if the Kurians are smart as that man down Congaree way. But the Kurians are big on advertising their wares as free, aren't they? Sometimes I think the scariest words in the American idiom are 'no obligation.' Of course, sometimes they stick in an 'absolutely' 'cause that one more lie just pushes people right over the edge into stupid."

They only knew they entered Grand Junction once buildings appeared on either side of the road.

"I know just where you should park, Habby," Thursday said to the wagon master at the wheel. "There's a grain mill just the other side of town. Not one of those claptrap corrugated iron things—real stonework. Abandoned now because of the lack of juice. We grind grain with a couple oxen these days, the old-fashioned way."

Valentine looked out the window. He was used to seeing gutted storefronts, but one of the buildings that had a hole in the front looked like it had received recent damage—the splinters in the door were white and fresh.

"I wonder how long we'll be snowed in here," Duvalier said from the bench she had to herself at the very back of Rover. "Charmingly dead."

"What's that?" Habanero said suddenly into his mike.

Valentine plugged his own headset in, uneasy. "What happened?" Mrs. O'Coombe said.

"Ma in Chuckwagon says she just hit a person."

"Good God," Mrs. O'Coombe said.

Valentine's earphone crackled: "—maybe it was just a big dog. But he came leaping, trying to get on the back of Bushmaster, and slipped. Under my wheels before I knew it. We bumped over him."

"We should stop," Mrs. O'Coombe said.

"What kind of fool runs into a line of trucks in this weather?" Thursday said, his face unholy in the dim light of the console.

"Must have been a dog," Habanero said. "Shadows are weird with all the reflections."

"Here's the mill," Thursday said. "I'll get it open for you, and then I'll check in with our sheriff and let him know you've arrived. As long as that wasn't him Ma ran over."

He laughed at his own joke, but no one else did.

The mill looked like a staggered tower, in levels going back from the street rising to a sloped roof on the top floor like an old ski jump.

"Always thought this building would be great to live in if you could gut and rebuild like they used to. Left just here, Habby," Thursday said. "Don't think you can get more than the first two vehicles parked inside. The loading dock's only made for one truck, really. There's plenty of space around the side with the train tracks."

Habanero turned on Rover's lights. A metal gate broke the pattern in the stone sides of the mill. Thursday climbed out and met his dancing shadow at a crank handle.

Turning the handle, he raised what had probably once been an electric door.

Thursday lost his footing. Mrs. O'Coombe took a sudden breath at his fall.

Or not a fall. Thursday disappeared under the half-raised gate with a scream.

"What the hell!" Habanero said.

"Wagon master, get ready to reverse and get out of here," Valentine said.

Habanero began to speak into his microphone.

Valentine grabbed his rifle out of its seat-back clip and stepped outside.

"Valen—" Duvalier began, but he slammed the door.

He ducked down, looking into the dark of the old grain elevator. Rover's lights cast beams through that were cut off by the half-closed door. A pair of hands, Thursday's, were reaching out of the darkness and clawing in an effort to crawl back to Rover—but something was holding him back.

And hurting him. Thursday was screaming like a man being slowly dismembered.

Valentine wished he had a light clipped to the barrel of the gun. He looked around at the column but could see nothing but the whirling flakes and the columns lights.

The Type Three pointed from his hip at the gate, he went to the crank for the door gate. He extended his arm and gripped the freezing-cold metal. Tendons tight, he managed to turn the wheel with one hand while he kept the barrel of his rifle pointed at the growing gap between tracked door and ground.

Thursday's hands were twitching spasmodically now, and as more and more light bled into the mill, the rest of him was revealed.

A piercing shriek in his ear. Ali was out of the car, a pistol in hand and a sword stick under her arm. Valentine had never heard her shriek like that—the noise must be coming from another.

Ragged two-legged forms appeared in the white bath of the headlights. Gore-smeared mouths testified to a recent, messy feast.

Ravies!

Valentine had encountered the disease on his first independent command in the Kurian Zone.

Ravies was a disease of multiple strains, first used in 2022 to help break down the old order, and used here and there since whenever the Kurians needed to stir up a little chaos. On his trip into Louisiana as junior lieutenant of Zulu Company in the Wolves, the Kurians reacted by gathering up some of the indigenous swamp folk and infecting them with the latest strain.

Valentine took them down with four quick shots. Red carnations blossomed on their chests and they staggered in confusion before crashing to the ground, dead.

As a member of Southern Command, he'd been inoculated against the disease, but you never knew how current your booster was. Valentine had a theory that they were sometimes injected with nothing but some colored saline solution to give them confidence before going into the Kurian Zone, so they wouldn't panic if faced with the disease, spread by bite and gouge and gush of arterial blood.

It didn't take a special shot to the brain or anything like that to kill a ravies sufferer, as some people thought—though if you wanted to live to go home and kiss your sweetheart again, you made damn sure you put some lead into center mass, for a ravies sufferer felt no pain. Indeed, he or she felt nothing but a desire to rend and tear.

Valentine realized Duvalier's scream had been answered, in a muffled and echoed manner, from farther up the street in town.

Hopefully those who shrieked the responsorial were confused by the muffling effects of the snow as to where exactly Valentine's column was.

Valentine fiddled with his Type Three, took out the bayonet, and fixed it at the front of the rifle. He worked the slide in the hilt, extending the blade to its full length.

He pounded on Habanero's window. "Alert everyone: There's ravies in this town and God knows where else," Valentine said. "Get Rover and the Chuckwagon inside. We can block the main door with the Boneyard and stuff the Bushmaster in the truck entryway. Toss me a flashlight."

Valentine took a green plastic tube handed to him and clicked on the prism of long-lasting LED light. A beam one-tenth as powerful as Rover's, but much more flexible, played around the inside of the grain mill. Nothing else was drawn out of the shadows by the bouncing light, so Valentine satisfied himself that the grain elevator was empty of everything but corpses.

For now.

Judging from the smell, the locals used part of the old grain tower as a smokehouse.

Grain mills always reminded Valentine a little of churches. They had the same shadowy, steeplelike towers, tiny staircases up to balconies and antechambers, and of course the important platform at one end. In mills, that was where grain could be ground into feed or flour.

With blood and pieces of Thursday scattered on the floor, the phrase "dark Satanic Mills" from Blake's Jerusalem floated through Valentine's mind. Valentine pulled the corpses out of the path of the vehicles and waved the Rover in.

Thursday had done them one favor before his untimely death. He had guided them to a well-built structure. Limestone gave decent insulation, and it was as strong or stronger than brick.

Mrs. O'Coombe jumped out of Rover. "Mister Valentine. If there is the ravies virus in town, shouldn't we drive on—"

"If the weather were clear, that would be my choice," Valentine said.

Habanero nodded from the window. "He's right; we're lucky to have gotten this far."

Frat and his Wolves needed something to do. Valentine sent them up a short set of steps and into the mill's office to look for messages from the town's inhabitants.

"No noise," Valentine said.

"Put Rover over there," Valentine told the wagon master, indicating a corner by the old loader equipment. "Get Chuckwagon in here."

"The medical wagon is more valuable," Mrs. O'Coombe said.

"Right now the fuel in Chuckwagon's trailer is the most important thing," Valentine said. "And we can all get a hot meal. We can refuel Rover, Chuckwagon, and Bushmaster, and then put Chuckwagon outside and bring Boneyard in."

Mrs. O'Coombe blinked. "Very well. You are thoughtful under

stress, Mister Valentine. I admire that. But I still think we should hurry on, weather or no weather."

"You could make yourself useful by refueling Rover," Valentine said to Mrs. O'Coombe, urgency consuming his usual polite phrasing with the great lady.

"Snow's killing the sound," Stuck said, entering the mill. He had a skullcap of snow already. "Ravies are drawn to motion and sound. They won't see us or hear us even if the town's full of them. As long as there's no shooting."

Habanero spoke into his comm link. Valentine heard the Chuckwagon backing outside.

Bee, who was riding in the Chuckwagon to give her two-ax-handle-wide frame elbow room, hopped out and trotted to Valentine's side, sniffing the blood in the air.

"Easy now, Bee. It's okay," Valentine said. How much she got from syntax and how much from tone he didn't know, but she went to work arranging the bodies neatly head to toe. She put Thursday one way and the ravies victims Valentine had shot the other.

Stuck was at the gate entrance, a big gun in a sling across his chest. Valentine had to look twice, but he recognized it as an automatic shotgun. He wondered where Stuck had acquired it and where it had stayed hidden in their travels—the weapon in his arms was easily worth its weight in solid silver. It was one of the few weapons that didn't require a tripod and that could kill a Reaper with a single burst of fire.

With the Chuckwagon parked, its trailer well inside, Valentine had Habanero tell the driver of the Bushmaster to back up the APC through the gate and into truck dock. It would fill it, perhaps not as tight as the Dutch boy's finger in the proverbial dike, but close.

Backing up the Bushmaster was no easy matter—the driver didn't have the usual rearview mirrors. Rockaway was at the top forward hatch, passing instructions to the driver.

Figures flashed out of the darkness, barefoot in the snow.

"Get inside, get inside, get inside!" Valentine shouted to Stuck. "Habanero, Bushmaster needs to clear the gate and get in the loading dock. Have Boneyard pull forward and wait, buttoned up tight."

Valentine heard a scream. Rockaway lit up the night with his pistol, firing at the ravies running for the Bushmaster.

Another charged out of the snow on his blind side. Valentine swung to aim, but the ravie jumped right out of his sights and landed on Rockaway, biting and pulling.

"Keve," Mrs. O'Coombe screamed from the doorway.

Rockaway emptied his gun blind and over his shoulder into the thing biting him.

Chaos. Everyone shouted at once, mostly to get the gate down.

"How the hell do you shut this door?" Stuck hollered.

"Inside!" Valentine yelled to Stuck. He was fumbling around with the wheel Thursday had used to raise the gate.

The Bushmaster rumbled through the gate.

A flash of brown and Duvalier was up on the gate rails. Duvalier had leaped nine feet in the air and now hung from a manual handle, trying to bring it down with her slight weight.

Valentine finally thought to look on the side of the wall opposite the crank and saw a pawl in the teeth of a wheel. There was a simple lever to remove it.

The compressed thunder that was the fire of the automatic shotgun licked out into the night, turning snowfall orange.

"Cease fire," Valentine shouted. If the Bushmaster opened up with its cannon, it would draw every ravie for a mile. "You'll just attract more. Habanero, tell the people in Boneyard and Bushmaster to turn off lights and engines—don't fire. Don't fire!"

Habanero repeated the orders.

The smaller door on the back of the Bushmaster opened, and Boelnitz jumped out, pulling a bloody-shirted Rockaway out, and the two ran for the mill.

Panicky fool! The fear of ravies caused just as much damage as the sufferers.

A shirtless figure tore out of the darkness. It didn't so much as tackle Boelnitz as run over him. It pulled up, as though shocked he'd gone down so easily.

Rockaway fell on his own.

Stuck took a quick step from the door crank and swung with his rifle butt, cracking the ravie across the back of the neck. It turned on him, swinging an arm that sprawled Stuck.

Valentine aimed the Type Three and put two into the ravie's back. It went down on its knees. Boelnitz, stunned, crawled toward the door and the safety of the mill's interior, lit by the headlights of Rover and Chuckwagon. Stuck picked Rockaway up by his belt and almost threw him through the door like a bowler trying for a strike.

"The hell's the matter with you?" Stuck said, kicking Boelnitz toward the mill. "Why didn't you stay in the APC?"

Valentine let loose the lever on the pawl, and the door, still with Duvalier hanging on it as she tried to force it with her leg, descended. Valentine stopped it high enough so a man could still enter at a crouch.

Stuck rolled in and sighted his gun to cover Bushmaster.

Valentine dragged Boelnitz in.

"Dumbshit didn't shut the door on Bushmaster," Stuck said, swinging the barrel of the auto-shotgun and pressing it to the thick, soft hair on Boelnitz's head.

Mrs. O'Coombe hugged her bloody son. "My God, my God . . . ," she kept repeating.

Valentine kicked up the gun barrel, and Stuck head-butted him in the gut.

Duvalier dropped from above, landing on Stuck's shoulders, and wrapped her legs around his back. She put her sword stick across his throat.

"Okay, okay," Stuck said. "Get 'er off!"

"Close the door, somebody," Valentine gasped as they untangled themselves.

Mrs. O'Coombe worked the lever and the door rattled down at last.

A pair of hands thrust themselves under the gate. Mrs. O'Coombe pushed the pawl back in, held it there.

Metal bent at the bottom of the gate as though a forklift were being used to pull it up instead of a pair of hands. The bottom of the gate groaned and began to bend.

Duvalier's sword flashed and sparked as it ran along the gate bottom, leaving severed fingertips lying about like dropped peanuts.

"The pawl, ma'am," Valentine shouted. Rockaway reached for it. Mrs. O'Coombe broke out of her reverie and extracted it.

Valentine stomped the handle hard. The door slammed shut.

"You better?" he asked Stuck.

The ex-Bear nodded.

"I'd forgotten how much I enjoy noise and danger," Mrs. O'Coombe said to no one in particular. "Very little, to be precise."

"You wouldn't have really shot me, would you?" Boelnitz said, picking himself up.

Stuck took a deep breath. "Maybe not me, but the Bear sure as hell was about to."

Boelnitz looked at Valentine. "Thank you. I owe you."

"Valentine, what the hell was that?" Stuck said, pointing at the fingers on the ground.

Valentine ignored him, tore open his own tiny first-aid kit, opened the little three-ounce flask of iodine, and poured and dabbed it into Rockaway's bites and scratches.

"Doc says they're nervous in Boneyard," Habanero reported as

Valentine's heartbeat began to return to normal. "It's not exactly an armored car."

"Get Doc in here at once," Mrs. O'Coombe said. "My son's been bitten."

"I'm not opening the door until things quiet down out there," Valentine said. "This is the best we can do."

"What the hell was that?" Stuck continued, shaking his head. "Have you ever seen a ravies case like that?"

"They were . . . like Bears," Duvalier said. "I've never seen anyone bend steel like that, except a Bear."

"Maybe it wasn't human. Maybe they've got a more human-looking Reaper," Valentine said, looking at the fingers.

"A Reaper would have just torn through it," Duvalier said. "Trying to lift it is a dumb way to get in. Reapers are smarter than that."

"Everyone needs to eat as much garlic as possible," Ma said from the Chuckwagon as she sorted through her stock. "I'll make a poultice for Keve."

"That's an old wives' tale," Stuck said.

"Well, I got to be an old wife by following old wives' tales, so you'll eat your garlic."

Valentine had heard dozens of folk remedies supposed to ward off ravies. Eating asparagus was one of the stranger ones.

Getting iodine into a ravies bite right away was the only one the Miskatonic people said worked. Iodine and a quick broad-spectrum antibiotic within a few minutes. The latter was a good deal less easy to come by in the Kurian Zone.

Instead of reminiscing, he should be refueling Rover and getting the Boneyard in, and then they could take care of Bushmaster. Everyone should get a hot meal and catch some rest too, and he'd better see how the Wolves were doing battening down the office in front.

So much for the responsibility-free tour of central Kentucky.

As it turned out, Doc snuck in the front door with his bag, moving extremely quietly. He cleaned Rockaway's wounds and gave him two injections, one for the pain, the other an antibiotic.

"Contact with Fort Seng," reported Habanero, who hadn't quit listening to Rover's radio since pulling it into the mill.

They'd rigged lanterns in the mill. Valentine had considered running the tiny portable generator to spare the vehicles' batteries but decided against it. A storm this intense couldn't last much longer, not in Kentucky.

He took a deep breath to wake himself up and put on the second headset.

"Major, we're getting reports of ravies outbreaks all across the Mississippi plateau," Lambert's voice crackled at the other end of the radio. "Report position and status, please."

"Grand Junction. We've just had a brush with them, sir."

"Repeat, please."

"We've fought a skirmish. Two casualties." Technically they'd just lost Thursday, but Rockaway had been bitten. . . .

"Major, I'm hearing strange reports about this strain. The infected cases are unusually strong and ferocious."

"I won't vouch for the ferocious, but they are strong, exceptionally strong. Like Bears."

"Are there other outbreaks in Kentucky you know of?"

"No, sir. This is the first we've seen of it. How are things at base?"

"Quiet. No sign of it. A new patrol has just gone out to check Owensboro. We've lost contact with the town."

"Orders?" Valentine asked.

"Get back as quickly as you can. The underground has informed us that that armored column has moved south from Bloomington and is now outside Owensboro. They've been shelling the city."

"We'll be mobile as soon as the weather lets up," Valentine said.

"Good luck," Lambert said. "Report when you're moving again."

"Wilco. Signing off."

"Signing off."

"We were lucky, I think," Stuck said. "I'll bet there is only a handful of ravies left in this town—mostly ones who were torn up in scrapes with them and succumbed to the infection."

"Lucky?" Boelnitz said, looking at Rockaway, who was being tended to at the far end of the mill by Doc.

"I said we," Stuck said. "Not him."

With time to think and a hot cup of Mrs. O'Coombe's tea inside him, Valentine realized the Kurians had played a brilliant double cross in Kentucky.

Or perhaps it was a triple cross, if you considered the attack on the Kentucky River position a double cross. He almost had to admire the genius of it. If the attack on the A-o-K had routed the principal body of armed and organized men in central Kentucky, the Kurians would have been in the position to act as saviors when the ravies virus hit. The New Universal Church could show up en masse, ready to inject the populace with either a real antiserum or a saline solution, all the while persuading the populace of the advantages of returning to their semiprotected status in the Kurian Order.

As it turned out, the attack failed, but it also served to concentrate their enemies. With the storm raging, they wouldn't be able to spread out and contain the virus to a few hot spots. Instead, the A-o-K would suffer the agonies of men knowing their families were threatened and unable to do a damn thing about it. Given the brief existence of the A-o-K, it might dissolve entirely, like salt in a rainstorm, fragmenting into bands of men desperate to return home.

The one patch of light in the snowy, howling gloom was that Kentucky wasn't the earthquake-and-volcano-ravaged populace of 2022. The legworm clans were armed to the teeth—man, woman, and child—and were used to living and working within the confines of armed camps organized for defense. Ravies bands fought dumb. They didn't coordinate, concentrate properly, or pick a weak spot in their target's defenses—except by accident.

Valentine didn't like the look of Boelnitz. He had been pale and quiet ever since the madness between Bushmaster and the gate.

Worried that the journalist might be going into shock from stress alone, Valentine squatted down next to him.

"Something for your notebook at last," Valentine said, noticing that the paper under his pencil was empty. "Don't let it bother you."

"The wounded in Bushmaster. They saw O'Coombe's boy was bitten. They said he had to go out, or they'd shoot him. I think they meant it."

Boelnitz looked at his notebook. "When I said I owe you, I meant it. I owe you the truth," Boelnitz said. "I've been flying under false colors, I'm afraid. Here."

He handed Valentine the leather notebook with a trembling hand and opened it to a creased clipping.

"It's one thing to write about wars and warriors and strategy," Boelnitz said. "It looks very different when you're looking down the barrel of a gun. Or up one."

Valentine read a few paragraphs.

It was always a strange sensation to parse another's depiction of oneself, like hearing someone describe the rooms in one's own home, bare facts attached to memories and emotions but as artificial and obvious as plastic tags in the ears of livestock. Valentine took in the words in the *Clarion*'s familiar, sententious style and typeface with the unsettling feeling of reading his own obituary:

> The terror of Little Rock during the late rising against Consul
> Solon, David Valentine has created a career that makes for exciting,
> if disturbing, reading. Trailed by a hulking, hairy-handed killer
> bodyguard named Ahn-Kha, Valentine is a man of desperate

gambits and vicious enmities without remorse or regret. The corpses of gutted, strung-up POWs and murder to followers like the Smalls . . .

Valentine couldn't read any more.

"I only showed that to you because I can't reconcile the figure described in Southern Command's archives, at least the ones I was given clearance to see, and *Clarion*'s articles with the person in the flesh. I just thought it was time for a little honesty. Pencil Boelnitz is a fiction; it's the name of my first editor, the English teacher who helped us run the school newspaper. My real name is Llewellyn. Cooper Llewellyn."

"You thought . . . you thought that if I knew you were from the *Clarion* . . . what? I'd run you off base?"

"Something like that."

"I have to say, I like Pencil Boelnitz better. He seemed like the kind of guy who'd observe and relate what he observed without trying to psychoanalyze a man he'd known for only a few weeks."

"You've a right to be mad. But there's a sign up at the *Clarion*: *Anyone can transcribe. A journalist reveals.*"

Valentine chuckled. "I can't see why your paper is so beloved for its editorial page, if that's the best they can do. It's easy to come up with something like that for any profession. *Anyone can disrobe. A stripper profits.*"

Thirteen

Ravies.

One of the most terrifying weapons in the Kurian Order's arsenal is the disease that makes man revert to a howling beast, a lizard brain seeking to kill, feed, and, yes, sometimes even procreate.

How they remove all the higher brain functions, leaving the lower full of savage cunning and reckless determination, only their elite scientists would be able to say.

The fear of a ravies outbreak is one way of keeping their human herds in line. There's such a thing as civilizational memory, and the human strata of the Kurian Order have been taught that only timely arrival of help from Kur stemmed the howling tide that threatened to wash away mankind in the red-number year of 2022. They instinctively know that without the protection of the towers, the screamers might return.

Anyone who's heard the dive-bomber wail of a ravies victim in full cry has the unhappy privilege of hearing it repeated in nightmares for years to come.

Of course in the Freeholds, they know that ravies is just another Kurian trick up one of the sleeves of a determined and ruthless creature with more limbs than can be easily counted on a living specimen.

Folk remedies abound, all of them nearly useless. A bucket of ice-cold water is said to distract a sufferer long enough for you to make an escape. If you suck a wound clean while chewing real mint gum mixed with pieces of pickled ginger, onion, and garlic, you'll never catch an infection from a bite. Pregnant women are naturally immune—this particular canard leads to all manner of bizarre remedies as others seek the mystic benefits, from drinking breast milk to pouring umbilical cord blood into a fresh wound. And, of course, that the only sure way to stop a ravies sufferer from getting at you is to shoot them in the head.

Of course, anyone who's ever emptied a magazine into the center mass of an oncoming screamer knows that they go down and stay down when suffering sucking chest wounds, cardiac damage, or traumatic blood loss.

No, the only facts absolutely known about ravies is that it is a disease that affects brain tissue and the nervous system. Sufferers don't feel any pain and are hyperaware, ravenous, and irritable, and if they are startled or provoked, they will try to rend and bite the source into submission and an easy meal. Heart rate and blood pressure both increase. Most brain-wave patterns decrease, save for the delta, the wave most associated with dreams, and beta, which increases during anxiety or intense concentration.

Many wonder why the Kurians, usually so careful with lives and the aura that might be harvested, allow whole populations to be reduced by the disease.

David Valentine had two theories. One is that ravies encounters shocked and wore down professional military types—no one enjoys gunning down children and preteens who, under ideal conditions, could be easily kept away with a walking stick or a riot shield until they drop from exhaustion. It took David Valentine months to quit hearing the screams in his sleep following his first encounter with ravies near the Red River in 2065. The other is that sufferers were harvested like everyone else in the Kurian Order, with the disease simply adding flavor to the aura thanks to the unknown tortures of body and mind.

Stuck was right, as it turned out. There weren't many cases in town. As they switched vehicles for refueling from the trailer, only one more ravie attacked, and Frat brought her down with a clean head shot.

They prepared to leave the mill once there was full daylight.

"We're going to try to keep moving to make it back to Fort Seng without another stop," Valentine told the assembled vehicle chiefs in the mill. "We'll take on rescues of anyone alongside the road until the vehicles are at capacity."

"Isn't that dangerous, sir?" Chieftain asked. "They might be bit. And if we lose a vehicle, who'll end up walking if there's no excess capacity?"

"And what about that kid?" Silvertip put in. "He's been bit."

"He's in Boneyard, with his mother and Doc keeping an eye on him," Valentine said. "At the moment he's not symptomatic, not even trembling, so the iodine may have got it or Southern Command's last year's vaccination may work against this strain. In any case, they'll keep him sedated. As for rescues, if we lose a vehicle, we'll travel overloaded and chance the fine."

One or two got the joke and laughed.

"One more thing: Let's break out the winter camouflage. We're still soldiers, and we still have eyes in the sky watching us and enemies to fight."

The winter camouflage was mostly old bedsheets and fancy tablecloths cut into ponchos, and extra felt that could be wrapped around your shins and tied with twine to create extrawarm gaiters.

Valentine changed the route order. Bushmaster would go first in order to clear drifts. Rover would follow, and then Boneyard and Chuckwagon brought up the rear. The two Southern Command Bears would ride in the Chuckwagon, as they'd most likely be attacked from the rear by ravies running on foot—Valentine had never heard of a ravie driving.

They wouldn't use the motorcycles at all, not with the snow and this strain of ravies that could leap the way they'd seen at the mill gate. Longshot volunteered to ride in the open atop Bushmaster so she could stand up and look over drifts, but Valentine told her to keep warm out of the wind.

So they pulled out. Valentine chalked a rough mile marker of empty circles on one of the roof struts of Rover. Every ten miles, he'd mark one off.

As they pulled out of Grand Junction and made it back to the old federal highway, he filled in the first of the twelve circles.

Three circles filled.

With room in Rover thanks to Mrs. O'Coombe being in Boneyard, Brother Mark now rode shotgun and Boelnitz, desirous of keeping away from Stuck, crammed himself into the backmost seat. Valentine sat behind Habanero so he could consult his maps and speak into the driver's ear, Duvalier next to him.

The snowfall had stopped, but the wind still threw up enough snow to make visibility bad and kept the convoy to less than five miles an hour.

The heavy cloud cover made for gloomy thoughts.

"Anything from the A-o-K on the radio?" Valentine asked as Habanero worked buttons to tune it.

"No, sir. Got some CB, just some lady looking for her man. Says she's scared."

"Take her position and tell her we'll report her if we can get in touch with anyone," Valentine said.

While Habanero spoke on the radio, Duvalier nudged in closer to him.

"I wonder if this is it for Kentucky, then. How widespread is the virus, do you think? Think they hit the Republics too?" Duvalier asked.

"If it's a tough new strain, seems a waste not to do as much damage as you can. Either way, Southern Command needs to know it's here. Any luck with the radio?" Valentine asked Habanero.

"Maybe atmospherics are just bad," Habanero said.

"What do you mean, if this is it?" Brother Mark said, balling his fists on the dash. "Kentucky survived the ravies plague in 2022 when nobody knew what was happening. They'll survive this. People are more prepared for this sort of crisis now."

Valentine looked at mile markers on the truck top. "Someone told me once that the Kurians were handling both sides of this war, and if they ever became really worried about us, they'd just wipe us out."

Brother Mark sighed. "Of all people, Valentine, I'm surprised you would consider such nonsense. Why would they want the Freeholds? We run guns into the Kurian Zones, broadcast news, and give people a safe place to run to, if they get away. They can't want that."

"I don't know," Valentine said. "Having a war going on can be handy. You can blame shortages on it, deaths, tell folks that the reason the days of milk and honey are a long way off is because there's a war to be won first. And its a convenient place to send ambitious, restive men who might otherwise challenge Kur."

Brother Mark locked his knuckles against one another. "I don't think so. Unless they are keeping it even from the Church. I rose fairly high before my soul fought back against my interest, and many times I handled communications for my Archon. I saw nothing to indicate that was true."

"Maybe they wouldn't trust such an important detail to written communications."

"There are five-year plenaries attended by a majority of Archons from around the world. None but the Archons attend. They depart with masses of facts and figures—not that the thick binders of data do them much good; you cannot trust the statistics of a functionary whose life depends on pleasing the boss with the totals in a report. But when the Archons return, there are sometimes a few promotions or a new Church construction project—ordinary activities."

"I wouldn't mind dropping in on one of those and changing the agenda," Valentine said. He glanced at his map again. Two more miles and he could fill in another circle. "Where are they held?"

"The location is held secret until the last minute. Probably because of vigorous, ambitious young men such as yourself with similar ideas."

Valentine always smiled inside at Brother Mark's description of him as a wet-behind-the-ears kid.

"Let me see. . . . Since I entered the Church it has been held at Paris, Cairo, Bahrain, Rome, and Rio de Janeiro. Not that there aren't important churchmen from Indonesia or middle Africa or the subcontinent; I believe the Archons simply like to see a few sights and shop."

They saw their share of sights on the drive, descending from the Mississippi plateau in central Kentucky.

Valentine would rather not have seen any of them, and it took a while for him to forget them.

As the wind died down and it turned into a still winter day, they saw smudges on the horizon, barns and houses and whole blocks of towns burning.

They saw cars and trucks with doors torn off and windshields punched in, blood splattered on the upholstery and panels.

The column passed huddled figures along the side of the road, sitting in meager shelter afforded by ruins of houses and ancient, rusted shells of cars and trucks. Many of them had frozen to death, fleeing God-knew-what blind in the night. When the column saw a figure floundering in the snow, waving its arms, they slowed and shouted. If it shouted back in English, they let them climb into the back of the Chuckwagon.

If not . . .

Target practice, Chieftain called it.

For the ravies, the snow worked against them.

Valentine tried to turn his mind off, not think about the future. The old Kurian trick might just work again. If that armored column massing outside Owensboro came into Kentucky and plunged into the heartland of the state—and the Kentucky Alliance—bringing order by killing off the diseased and dangerous, the Kur might just be hailed as heroes. At the very least they'd have little difficulty seizing key road junctions, towns, and rail lines. The disease-ravaged A-o-K wouldn't be in any kind of shape to contest the matter.

His own command would be hounded out of the state, and Southern Command, instead of having a quietly neutral bunch of legworm ranchers, would have a full-fledged enemy with access to some hard-to-stop cavalry.

*   *   *

Five circles filled in . . .

"I think I've got a Kentucky contact, sir. Major Valentine, they're asking for you by name. You know somebody called Ankle?"

Ahn-Kha! Even Duvalier bolted awake.

Valentine put on a pair of earphones and cursed when they wouldn't adjust fast enough.

He heard his friend's deep, slightly rubbery tones speaking: ". . . very short of ammunition. Before I lost contact with friends in the Shenandoah, I was told they had military roadblocks in all the principal passes, and there were reports of aircraft flying in the mountains."

"How are you, Old Horse?" Valentine asked, his throat tight.

"My David, can it be that you are caught up in this too?"

"Afraid so. What's your status?"

"It goes . . . hard, my David. There are so few of us left. I sent some of the men away so they could see to their homes and families. I only hope I did not delay too long. We are— Well, best not to say too much over the radio. But a good-bye may be in order."

For Ahn-Kha, always quick to make light of burdens, to talk like this, it turned everything behind Valentine's stomach muscles into a solid block of ice.

"Don't draw attention to yourself. They seem to be drawn by light and noise," Valentine said. "You haven't been bitten, have you?"

Static came back, or maybe the Golden One was laughing and shaking the mike. "Oh, yes, many times. Fortunately I seem to be immune. I wish I could say the same for the rest of my brave men. I will not say more. We have made some hard choices, hard decisions, and more hard decisions are coming. As you said, we too are aware that they are drawn to sudden sounds and sharp flashes and—" His words were lost to static. Habanero adjusted the dial. "We've used blasting explosives to try to draw them up into the mountains, away from our populations. We have, perhaps, been too successful. One might walk across the throng using heads like paving stones. Excuse me, there is some commotion. I must sign off."

"Good luck," Valentine said, wishing for once he had Sime's tongue for a phrase worthy of his old friend.

Valentine watched Boelnitz, an earpiece for the radio in one ear, writing furiously and transcribing the Grog's words.

"Who's writing this passage? Pencil Boelnitz or Cooper Llewellyn?" Valentine asked.

"I don't know, Major. All I can do is try to be accurate about what I'm hearing."

"I hope you're getting it right, sir. That's the hulking, hairy-handed killer I know," Valentine said.

Boelnitz drew away, pencil trembling. Valentine realized he was snarling.

Seven circles filled in . . .

They were getting closer to the Ohio now. The land became less hilly and was filled with more old farms. Someone sprayed the column with gunfire as they passed. It caused no casualties, but Valentine wondered if the person shot because he or she suspected they were from the Northwest Ordnance, or if they shot because they suspected they were Southern Command.

Out of the hills, the drifts grew less and less and finally disappeared entirely. The snow hadn't been as heavy in this part of Kentucky. Valentine put Rover back at the head of the column, but the ice patches were still treacherous.

"Major, Doc says we should pull over," Habanero said, acknowledging a signal. Valentine had taken his headset off so he could think about Ahn-Kha.

"Why?" But Valentine could guess.

"He wants you to look at Rockaway."

Valentine didn't want to stop for anything. "He's symptomatic?"

"Doc just wants to pull over."

Valentine signaled for a stop. Everyone took the opportunity to get out and hit the honeybuckets.

Valentine went to the Boneyard. The nurse silently opened the rear hatch. A red-eyed Mrs. O'Coombe nodded to him, her Bible stuck in her lap, a finger marking her place.

"Well, Doc?" Valentine asked.

He shook his head. "He's symptomatic. Starting to shake."

"You have him sedated?"

"Yes," the nurse said.

"What's the usual medical procedure for ravies?" Valentine said.

Doc sighed. "Ninety percent of the time, they're quietly euthanized. Some are kept around to try various kinds of experimental medications. They don't feel pain, from what we can tell by brain-wave function and glandular response. Oh, and early cases are important for study to develop a vaccine. That's where the booster shots come from. Too bad he missed this last series, issue date October. We should have thought to bring some."

"I want you to end this, Mister Valentine," Mrs. O'Coombe said.

"End this?" Valentine asked.

"I can't watch him suffer."

"He's not suffering, is he, Doc?"

Doc agreed, "Not while the sedatives hold out. Even when they wear off, provided we can keep him in the bed, I'm not sure suffering is the right word for what he'll be going through."

Valentine wondered how much of the patriotic, Bible-reading charity act of Mrs. O'Coombe was real. With Keve Rockaway/O'Coombe dead, she'd own the vast ranch her husband had built.

"Any decision about your son's health I'll leave to the Doc."

Doc said, "I work for her ladyship, I'll remind you, Valentine."

"A rich woman outranks the Hippocratic oath?" Valentine asked.

"Major," Doc said. "Please. I'm in no hurry. I'm just wondering if I'll still have a job if I ever make it back to the Hooked O-C."

"Do what you can, Doc," Valentine said. "Anything else?"

"One more thing, Major," Doc said. He took out a little powder blue case. "In my younger days, before I settled down to bring babies into the world and plaster broken bones and dig bullets out, I was a researcher.

"This is a perfectly ordinary piece of medical technology from fifty years back. Nowadays I use it for interesting butterfly pupae and leaves. It instantly freezes and preserves, like liquid nitrogen without all the fuss and bother.

"I've been taking samples of Keve's blood as the disease progressed to see how his body's fighting it, and to see just how the ravies virus is attacking and changing him. It could be useful to Southern Command in developing a serum for a vaccination." He handed the case to Valentine.

"I'll get it back across the Mississippi as soon as I can," Valentine said.

Mrs. O'Coombe caressed her son's head.

"Keep an eye on her, Doc," Valentine said.

"Understood." Doc lowered his voice. "In all honesty, Major, she does love her son. She loved all her sons. Deep down, I think she was really trying to get him back home, but make it his idea."

Valentine stepped out of Boneyard. "Hey, Major," he heard one of the Wolves call. "There's a plane flying around north of here a few miles. Two-engine job. Looks kind of like it's circling."

Valentine wondered if the plane was part of Jack in the Box's operation. How did he fit in with the divine judgment of war, famine, disease, and death to Kentucky?

Which reminded him. He called Frat over. "Frat, how are you on a motorcycle?"

"Decent, sir. I used one to get around in Kansas."

"I want you to courier something important back to Fort Seng for us. And, if necessary, get it all the way back to the Mississippi—but that'll be for Colonel Lambert to decide."

"I don't want to leave you in the middle of this mess," Frat said.

"You'll do as I ask, Lieutenant. If you want to be addressed as captain in a week, that is."

"Captain!" Frat grinned.

"A platoon of Wolves this far outside Southern Command is supposed to have a captain in charge. I hope you'll be it."

"Not as easy as it sounds. But we should get a sample back to Southern Command as soon as possible."

They gave Stuck's big motorcycle to Frat. Frat grabbed his rifle and his bag and very carefully put Doc's sample freezer in a hard case. Doc added a final blood sample and a note before packing it on the bike.

Valentine shook Frat's hand, and the young man tied a scarf around his face. "I'll get it through, sir."

Valentine wondered just where that Ordnance armored column was. Their own vehicles would be simple target practice for a real—

"Frat, even if we don't get through, these blood samples need to. They're more important to Southern Command than everything in this convoy."

"Understood, sir."

He watched the youth rumble off, trying not to think of his own misadventures as a courier. Maybe somewhere on the road Frat would meet another capable young teen, the way Valentine had long ago met Frat. Part of being in service was helping train talented young people to take your place.

By the time Frat had left, the plane had taken off too, flying back to the north—probably across the Ohio in just a few minutes.

Valentine tried to raise Fort Seng to inform Lambert that Frat was on the way, but he couldn't make contact. With one more thing to worry about, Valentine returned to Rover and put the convoy in motion again.

"See if you can find a road turning north," he told Habanero. "I'd like to see what that plane is up to."

"Looks like a flea market that broke up quick," Duvalier said.

Valentine wouldn't forget the sight of the body field as long as he lived.

Even as an old man he'd remember details, be able to traverse the gentle slopes dotted with briar thickets, stepping from body to body.

You had to choose route and footing if you didn't want to step on some child.

Judging from the injuries and old bloodstains on the bodies, these were ravies victims. Some had torn or missing clothes, and all had the haggard, thin-skinned look of someone in the grip of the raving madness.

"What killed them, Doc?" Valentine asked.

"My guess is some kind of nerve agent. That accounts for some of the grotesque posing. Whatever it was, it happened quickly." He knelt to look at a body. "Notice anything funny about these?" Doc asked.

"There's nothing funny in this field," Duvalier said.

"Strange, then. Look at the ravies," Doc said.

Valentine had a tough time looking close. This was like peeping into a Nazi gas chamber. Though he felt a bit of a hypocrite; he would have turned the Bushmaster's cannon on them if they'd been attacking his vehicles.

"I don't—" Duvalier said.

"The hair," Doc said. "Ears, chins, eyebrows, arm hair. Worse on the men than the women, but everyone but the kids are showing very rapid body hair growth. A side effect of this strain of ravies, perhaps?"

Valentine let the doctor keep chattering. Valentine wondered where the pilot of the little twin-engined plane was now. *Enjoying a cup of coffee at an airstrip, while his plane is being refueled?*

"I don't think they really knew what was happening," Doc said. "Ravies does cloud the mind a bit."

"Wolves found something interesting, sir," Chieftain reported, looking at a deerskin-clad arm waving them over.

The vehicle tracks were easy to find and, sadly, easier to follow. They stood at the center of the field, in an empty space like a little doughnut hole surrounded by bodies.

"Okay, they drove in, or the ravies found them here," Doc said. "Then when the ravies were good and tight around the vehicle, those inside slaughtered them all in a matter of minutes."

"This one was still twitching," Valentine said, looking at a victim who'd left gouges in the turf. "I think he tried to crawl toward the truck."

Chieftain said, "Maybe it was a field bakery van or a chuck wagon. Food, you think? Baskets of fresh bread hanging off it? They look hungry."

"Ravies does that," Doc said. "You get ravenous. It's a hard virus on the system. The body's usual defense mechanisms—fatigue, nausea—that discourage activity during hunger are overridden."

Valentine wondered what could attract such throngs of ravies, yet keep them from tearing whatever made those tracks to bits. His own

column would probably have need of such a gimmick before they returned to Fort Seng.

Nine circles filled in . . .

Maybe it was the sun in their eyes as they drove west. Maybe it was
error caused by driver fatigue. Maybe it was the speed. Valentine was
anxious to move fast—there was less snow on the ground, and they had
a chance to be back at Fort Seng that night.

They dipped as they passed under a railroad bridge, much overgrown, and suddenly there were ravies on either side of them and the
headlights of a big armored car before them.

It wasn't an equal contest. Rover folded against the old Brinks truck
like a cardboard box hitting a steamroller.

When the stars began to fade from Valentine's eyes, he heard an-
gelic strings playing. For a moment, he couldn't decide if he was hallu-
cinating or ascending to a very unoriginal, badly lit, bare-bones heaven.

Valentine looked out the spiderwebbed window and saw tattered
ravies all around, cocking their heads, milling, either working themselves up to an attack or calming down after one.

Then he saw the big armored car, and it all came back to him.

The music was coming from the armored car. Chopin or someone
like him.

Valentine prodded Habanero, but it would take more than a friendly
tap to revive him. He was impaled on the steering column like a butterfly on a pin.

Duvalier opened her door and fell out, still gripping her sword cane.
Brother Mark seemed to be unconscious, blood masking his face, with
a similar stain on the window.

Valentine heard an engine roar, and the armored car backed up. He
waited for it to rev up, roar forward, and crush what was left of Rover.

He took his rifle out of its clip and climbed out. The least damaged
of any of them, Boelnitz or whatever he called himself crawled forward
and out.

Boneyard came forward to their rescue.

The music suddenly died. A new tune struck up, a harsh number
welcoming them to a jungle with plenty of fun and games.

The ravies didn't like the sound of the music. They began to spread
away from the armored car in consternation.

Boneyard's driver came out of his cab. He slammed the door as he
climbed down.

The ravies heads turned, looking at him.

"Careful," Valentine said.

Boneyard's driver put his gun to his shoulder and fired at the speaker atop the armored car.

Which showed initiative but not very good judgment.

A pair of teenage ravies came running, as though the spitting assault rifle was an ice cream truck's musical bell.

Bushmaster bumped off road and gave them covering fire, Silvertip at the turret ring with the 20mm cannon.

Like sand running out of an hourglass, more and more ravies sprang into violent motion, running toward the vehicles.

Nothing to do about it now.

Valentine went around behind Rover, set his rifle on the rear bumper, and began to fire into the ravies. Machine guns and cannon tore into them.

Regular troops would have scattered or taken cover on the ground. Not these men, women, and children. Most of them went for the Bushmaster: It was the biggest and—

"Chuckwagon," Duvalier shouted in Valentine's ear, pointing.

A mass of ravies hit Bushmaster like an incoming tsunami. They tipped it, perhaps by accident, in their fury to get at the noisy guns.

Valentine pulled Brother Mark out of Rover and threw him over his shoulder in a fireman's carry. A ravie with a mustache gone mad sprang around the corner.

"Uungh!" Duvalier grunted as she opened the ravie from rib to hip point with her sword. She spun and took a child's head off behind her.

Chuckwagon pulled up next to Boneyard, forming a V by having the front bumpers just meet.

"Leave them, leave them!" Mrs. O'Coombe shouted to the Boneyard's driver. "Get me out of here!"

Silvertip extracted himself from Bushmaster's cupola. But he'd left an arm behind, crushed against the autocannon. He tottered a few steps toward the tattered crowd beating at the driver's front window, studded leather fist raised, and toppled face forward into the snow.

Valentine set down Brother Mark between the two big trucks.

He brought down three approaching ravies, clicked on empty, and changed magazines.

But there was still fighting around Bushmaster.

Longshot climbed out one of the side doors, now a top hatch on the prostrate APC. Her bike was strapped there. All she had to do was untie it and right it. Valentine watched, astonished, as she gunned the engine, laid a streak of rubber with the back tire as the front stayed braked. She released and shot along the armored side of the Bushmaster, flew off its

front, and knocked a ravie down as she landed. Sending up a rooster tail
of snow, she tore off east.

"That coward," Mrs. O'Coombe sputtered. "There were wounded in
there."

A figure tottered out from around the back of Bushmaster, looking like a doomed beetle covered by biting army ants. Bee staggered
under the weight of a dozen men, women, and children. She shrugged
one off.

All Valentine had left for the Type Three was Quick-wood bullets.
He loaded and used them, sighting carefully and picking two off of Bee.

Bee writhed, throwing off a few, breaking another with a punch,
crushing a head, removing an arm.

But there were too many, clawing and biting.

Bee dropped under the weight.

Valentine saw her agonized face through the mass of legs.

Valentine lined up his Type Three, ready to put a bullet in her head.
Bee opened her mouth—

To bite an ankle.

Valentine only hoped he could end with such courage.

With the bayonet, mes enfants. *It's nothing but shot,* Valentine
thought, quoting one of the heroes of the Legion he'd read of thanks to
the headquarters library.

Valentine had never used a rifle bayonet for anything but opening
cans since training. But he extended the one on the Type Three.

Valentine charged, yelling, his vision going red in fury and despair.

The ravies bared their teeth.

Valentine threw himself into them, lunging and wrenching and club-
bing. A hand like a steel claw grabbed his arm, and he responded by
giving way to the pull, throwing himself into the opponent. He clubbed
the butt of his gun into the ravie's face again and again.

Another lunge and he lifted a young man off Bee like a kebab on
his bayonet skewer.

He noticed Duvalier next to him, slashing like mad, killing anything that approached her like a bug zapper firing cold steel bolts.

He got Bee's arm around his shoulder and dragged her up. She
managed to rise.

A storm of gunfire cut down the ravies in his way back to the V
between Boneyard and Chuckwagon. Stuck stood atop the Bushmaster,
firing his assault shotgun. Chieftain stood at his back, removing fingers
and hands from ravies trying to climb atop the wreck.

Valentine realized he was bleeding but he felt no pain, fighting
madness coursing through his nervous system.

He stumbled into the Boneyard, almost carrying Bee, rifle dangling by its sling and .45 pistol in his hand now.

"Graawg," Bee said, tears in her good eye, the other socket a gory pulp, pointing to bloody divots in her shoulder.

"Doc, you got a shot or something you can give her?" Valentine asked.

"I'll fix her up."

Valentine waved Stuck over.

"No, wounded inside!" he shouted, gesturing at the Bushmaster beneath him.

He emptied the shotgun into the remaining ravies all around.

Pkew!

A red blossom appeared in Stuck's shoulder, and he toppled off the APC.

Valentine looked back at the musical armored car. A rifle barrel projected from a rivet-trimmed slot in the front passenger-side window.

He could see the grinning faces of the driver and gunner behind their armored glass.

"Chieftain, take out those fuckers!" Valentine shouted.

The Bear nodded and disappeared.

Stuck, despite the rifle wound, was still swinging. He had a knife in each hand and used them like meathooks, plunging the blades in and pulling his opponents off their feet.

"You want a piece of me? There's plenty left, you assholes! Reapers and Grogs left enough for yas!"

Stuck led the remaining ravies down the road, shouting and gesticulating even as his steps grew more and more erratic.

While Stuck attracted ravie attention, Chieftain was dragging something away from the Bushmaster. Valentine realized it was the 20mm cannon. The big Bear, hair bristling up like a cockatiel's, righted it, braced it with his legs, and pointed it at the armored car.

Valentine looked at the armored car. The faces in the cabin weren't smiling anymore.

Krack! Krack! Krack! Krack! Krack!

The thick glass of the armored car had five holes with little auras of cracks all around, and blood splattered about on the inside.

And still the music played on.

Valentine—covered in quick-and-dirty bandages and iodine, injected with Mrs. O'Coombe's expensive Boneyard antibiotics, and feeling like he'd been taken apart and put together by a drunk tinker—investigated the musical armored car.

The back door was unlocked. After the cannon fire had killed the men in the cab, whoever was back there ran off into the growing dark.

There were a lot of dials and switches and electronic equipment, a screen and a controller for a camera at the back, and a blinking little box that one of the Wolves told him held all the music the system played in digital form.

Most of the music was soothing light classical, according to the computer-literate Wolf. "I guess they were attracting those Woolies by playing calming music," the Wolf said, giving this strain of ravies a name that was soon in wide use both officially and unofficially.

"It must soothe them," Doc said.

"And attract them at the same time. Must have been what they used to gather them . . . so the plane could spray them. That's how they killed them off," Valentine said, words finally catching up to his guesswork.

They fiddled until they had music playing and put some gentle Mozart up. A few ravies, wandering back from their final encounter with Stuck, shuffled up to the truck to listen.

Valentine gave orders that they weren't to be harmed. More important, they weren't to be disturbed by any aggravating noise.

They were prevented from engaging in further speculation by the arrival of a company from the Fort Seng battalion.

They were on bikes, Captain Nilay Patel wobbling unevenly at their head.

"The cavalry's a little late to the rescue," Valentine said with an effort. He had at least three bloody ravies bites, bound up in stinging iodine.

"The cavalry is having a hard time biking on melting ice," Patel said. "It's Colonel Lambert's idea, sir. We were leading a party of civilians out of Owensboro with the full battalion in field gear. There's a whole Northwest Ordnance column of trucks and motorcycle infantry and light armor getting set to cross the bridge where you got that Kurian."

"And you were heading toward them or away?"

"Trying to keep as quiet as possible as we got away, obviously, sir. That fury on a motorcycle came roaring up and said you'd had some difficulty. Colonel Lambert sent me back for you and Captain Ediyak ahead with the dependents, and then organized the rest into a Mike Force to support either if we ran into trouble. She's a better than fair tactician, sir."

"Where'd you get the bicycles?"

"We found them in a warehouse in Owensboro. Ownership seemed to be a matter of some dispute, as they were meant for transport to a purchaser in the Ordnance, but said trader was in no mood to fulfill his end with ravies in town. Colonel Lambert made him a generous purchase offer."

"What was that?" Valentine asked, but he suspected he knew Lambert's bid.

"He could ride along with the rest of the civilians, provided the bikes came as well." Patel looked at the stuporous ravies gathered around the musical truck. "What are we going to do with this lot?"

"Give them back to the people who created them."

"An excellent idea, sir, but just how do we do that?"

"We're going to need some noise, Patel. A whole lot of noise."

"I'm sure that can be arranged. Music or—"

"I have three vocalists in mind," Valentine said. "My radio's wrecked. Can you put me in touch with Fort Seng?"

They cleaned out the armored car's cab and brought the engine to life. Valentine put Ma at the wheel, as she understood both the armored car's controls and the volume and direction controls on the loudspeakers. Valentine had them turn down the road toward Owensboro. According to Patel, the city had been hard hit by ravies.

Bee with her Grog gun, the techie Wolf, Boelnitz for the sake of his story, and Chieftain just in case rode in back. Valentine road shotgun, squeezed onto the seat with Duvalier, who was clinging to him like a limpet.

"I'm worried about those bites," she said. "First sign of trembling, you go into handcuffs."

Valentine wondered if the bites were taking their toll. He was so very tired. But he had to see this through before he succumbed to either exhaustion or the disease.

They passed through the beltline of the city and drove among the Woolies like wary naturalists intruding on a family of gorillas. They thronged thicker and thicker around the armored car.

Suspicious, bloodshot eyes glared at them. Nostrils flared as the Woolies took in their scent.

"A little more soothing music," Valentine said.

Ma fiddled with her thumb, rolling it back and forth across the ancient, electrical-taped device. Harsh, synthesized music blared.

The Woolies startled.

The music hushed, stopped. A big Woolie, his mouth ringed by a brown smear of dried blood like a child's misadventure with lipstick, lurched toward the speaker, head cocked.

Ma said something under her breath—Valentine had no attention to spare for anyone but the big Woolie—and a soothing cello backed by violins started up.

The speakers ratcheted up, filling the main street with noise.

More Woolies emerged from alleys and doorways, some dragging dead dogs or more gruesome bits of fodder.

"They like that," Duvalier said, peering out a firing slot.

"Just like the Pied Piper," Valentine said. "Now to teach Hamelin a lesson."

Soon his followers filled two lanes and the verge to either side of the highway leading out of Owensboro and to the east.

They found a slight hill from which they could see the bridge and watch the fireworks. Valentine signaled Ma to stop the soothing music.

Valentine's trio of iron throats opened up. Guinevere, Igraine, and Morganna began to sing, and their notes fell upon the highway in brilliant flash and thunder.

The ravies ran toward the bridge.

"There go the Woolies!" one of the artillery observers reported over the radio. The Wolf's moniker had spread quickly.

The forces of the Northwest Ordnance had removed their barricades and some of the fencing to allow the invasion force to rumble across the bridge, its formation undisturbed. The Woolies found no resistance to their rush.

Panic struck the soldiers of Ohio's elite force. Immunization or no, an inoculation wasn't proof against one's injection arm being yanked out of its socket.

Valentine, having seen the destruction visited on Kentucky, rejoiced at like medicine being distributed among the "relief" forces parked in a long file along the highway.

He heard the drone of an engine. A plane hove into view.

"Bee!" Valentine said. He formed his hands into wings and had them crash.

Bee grinned from among her bandages, licked a bullet, and slid it into her big Grog gun. She put the gun to her shoulder and raised the barrel to the sky, as though it were a flag. The barrel began to descend as smoothly as a fine watch hand, lining up with the approaching plane, which had turned to pass directly over the bridge so that its flight path matched the north-south span.

It was a two-engine plane. She'd have to be quick to take out both as it passed over the bridge.

The plane dove, seeming to head straight for them. It hadn't started sprinkling its nerve agent yet, not wanting to lay it on their own forces.

Bee brought the gun barrel down, down, down, humming to herself. She fired.

The plane didn't so much as wobble. It continued its pass, remorseless. Valentine waited for the fine spray of nerve agent that would lock up heart and limb—

The plane shot over their heads, wingtips still, level as a board, engines roaring and flaps down, following a perfect five-degree decline to hit and skip and cartwheel into the woods of Kentucky.

Valentine heard firing from the other side of the bridge. A gasoline explosion lit up the low winter clouds.

Valentine tried to tell himself that he was killing two birds with one stone, not slaughtering civilians to confuse a military offensive.

"I know what the editorial in the *Clarion* would be," Boelnitz said. *"Southern Command Uses Bioweapons in Indiana Massacre."*

Valentine was inclined to agree: both that they'd use the headline and that the headline was true. But you had to give the enemy whatever flavor of hell they gave you. "Of course, you could add some picturesque color thanks to your firsthand experiences."

"Hell with them," Boelnitz said. "You know, the publisher used to tell me, 'It's always more complicated than a headline.' That's only so much bovine scat one can tolerate. Our headline here is pretty easy. 'Victory.' They should have offered, instead of threatened."

"I hope we can remember that," Valentine said. "You know, Llwellyn or Boelnitz or whatever you want to call yourself, Kentucky could use a newspaper. It's one of the building blocks of a civilization. What do you say? Want to bring the first amendment back to Kentucky?"

Boelnitz smiled. "I have a feeling that as long as you're here, there'll be no end of stories."

Fourteen

Fort Seng, February, the fifty-sixth year of the Kurian Order. The snow has melted and the winter has returned to normal. Old-timers are predicting an early spring, perhaps to balance the fierce January weather.

The losses of Kentucky are great and still being counted. But the damages from the ravies virus could have been much worse. As it turned out, the snow that the Kurians hoped would freeze Kentucky's population in place while their disease swept across the wooded hills worked against its spread rather than for it—the towns hardest hit by the virus were contained by the weather, rather than the reverse.

It was a meager, hard winter, but it is ending. The shortages and bitter cold are fading as new winds blow and new supply lines are created. Old, tattered uniforms are traded in for the new pattern, and equipment and weapons improve as equipment is gleaned and reconditioned from the fight near the Owensboro west bridge.

Also, there is the knowledge that they won a victory against the best that the Northwest Ordnance could muster, even if the ravies victims paid the tab on that victorious banquet.

Valentine never suffered even a quiver from the ravies bites.

Had the iodine and antibiotics worked? He didn't know. It hadn't done Keve Rockaway any good. When last Valentine heard, Rockaway was an invalid on the huge ranch straddling the Texas–Oklahoma border country. His mother had retired from public life to nurse him, and the real leader of the ranch was the new ex-Bear named Chieftain. Mrs. O'Coombe had arranged for three hundred head of first-class beef cattle to be brought to Kentucky in exchange for a few legworms and men with the experience to breed them. According to her, the ranch encompassed a good deal of wasteland that might support legworms.

She even spoke of establishing a horse farm or two nearby. Southern Command always needed fresh horseflesh.

But that was trivia. Valentine wondered how Southern Command had managed to have an effective vaccine to a strain of ravies that had never been deployed. Or perhaps it was just a very, very happy accident that Southern Command's latest vaccine was also proof against the Kurians' newest weapon.

So many questions that needed answering.

"I do have one piece of good news," Lambert said one morning at a meeting with Valentine. "We're in radio contact with the Bulletproof through the Army of Kentucky. They said a certain oversized yellow Grog of old acquaintance staggered into their camp pulling a cart full of kids. He had pink ribbons tied to his ears and a teddy bear riding between his ears."

It was the best news Valentine had heard since Narcisse's reply to the letter he'd had Mantilla deliver. She and Blake would await his instructions about joining him in Kentucky, once he arranged with a river rat for properly discreet transport. "Ahn-Kha is alive?"

"A little chewed up, they said. Their chief promised to send him here just as soon as a worm can be saddled this spring."

Valentine wondered if he was dreaming. If he did see Ahn-Kha again, he'd send him right back to his people. The Golden Ones had been driven out of Omaha and needed a leader of Ahn-Kha's caliber.

Lambert decided to celebrate the victory with a grand review of her battalion. It couldn't be said that they'd fought a battle, but they'd performed effectively in the field, keeping the ravies off while they protected Owensboro's civilian population.

Valentine recovered fast, as he always did, and managed to stand through the whole review.

They formed the men up, four companies strong plus an almost equal number of auxiliaries in an oversized "support pool."

The Southern Command "remainders" stood in a quiet group off to one side, watching the ex-Quislings in their polished boots and fresh uniforms.

"Our new regimental flag, my friends," Valentine said, pointing to a banner flying overhead. Even though they were a smallish regiment.

The flag couldn't be said to be fancy. Valentine had worked out the design with Ediyak, now in charge of the headquarters platoon.

He'd loosely based it on an old Free French flag. It was red and blue, with a big white five-pointed star dividing it at the center and large enough to touch the edges of the banner with its top point and bottom two feet. A little black pyramid with a Roman numeral I in silver filled the bottom-center between the two legs of the star.

With the flag flying, Lambert began the speech Valentine had written, largely cribbed from a military history book he'd swiped from Southern Command's service libraries.

"Legion soldier, you are a volunteer, serving the Cause of freedom with honor and teamwork.

"Each legion soldier is your brother in arms, whatever his origin, his past, or his creed. You show to him the same respect that binds the members of the same family bloodline.

"You respect the traditions of these United States. Discipline and training are your strengths. Courage and truth are the virtues that will one day make you admired among your peers and in the history books.

"You are proud of your place in the legion. You are always orderly, clean, and ready. Your behavior will never give anyone reason to reproach you. Your person, your quarters, and your base are always clean and ready for any inspection or visitor.

"You are an elite soldier. You consider your weapon as your most precious possession. You constantly maintain your physical fitness, level of training, and readiness for action.

"Your mission is sacred. It is carried out until the end, in respect of the Constitution, the customs of war, and law of civil organization, if need be, at the risk of your own life in defense of these ideals.

"In combat you act without passion or hatred. You respect surrendered enemies. You never surrender your dead, your wounded, or your weapons.

"You consider all of the above your oath and will carry it out until released by your superiors or through death."

Ediyak modeled the new uniform. The cut was similar to his old shit detail company's utility-worker uniforms, right down to the tool vest, the padded knees and elbows (a simple fold of the fleece made for light and comfortable cushioning), and the pen holders on the shoulder. The outer shell was a thick nylon-blend canvas of Evansville tenting, the inner the soft fleece so generously supplied by Southern Command. The color was a rather uninspiring, but usefully muted, rifle green. She'd daubed hers with gray and brown and black into a camouflage pattern.

Valentine tried to read their faces. Were the men standing a little taller? He could tell Lambert's speech, the new flag, and the new uniform had their interest and attention.

*   *   *

He spent two frantic days trying to make contact with the Bullet-proof. He wouldn't believe the news about Ahn-Kha until he heard his old friend's voice.

In between haunting the communications center and helping Patel and Ediyak evaluate the new NCOs, he was asked to visit Doc. Doc had stayed behind to research the new strain of ravies the Kurian Order had deployed that winter. Despite the gray hair and the bent frame, he'd been putting in long hours seven days a week. He'd spent an inordinate amount of time on the radio, mostly advising communities how to prevent cholera and deal with an isolated ravie found here and there, half-starved and confused. The challenge had reawakened the committed researcher who'd lost himself on the Hooked O-C ranch.

Valentine walked over to the hospital—formerly the servants' quarters for the estate. The patients had small, comfortable, climate-controlled rooms. They'd turned a former garage into an operating room, and the old office into an examining room and dispensary. Doc had taken one of the little patient rooms for his research. What little equipment he had, he'd brought with him to begin with.

"Major Valentine, a moment of your attention, please," Doc said. He stood in his office, rocking from the waist. Doc kept eyeing Valentine's sidearm.

Valentine was expecting another request for nonexistent microscopes or a culture incubator. "Sure, Doc. My time is yours."

"May we speak privately? I have some analysis to show you. I would not want my . . . theory—theory, mind you—to become a subject of common discussion."

"I'd like nothing better," Valentine said, and shut the office door.

Doc went to his closet and opened the door. On the inside he'd pinned up a map of Kentucky. He flipped on a bright track light that placed a spot of light on the map when the door was all the way open. The glare made Valentine's head hurt and he felt a little nauseous as Doc invited him over to look at Kentucky, covered in incredibly tiny notations.

"Doc, I've been meaning to ask: Wherever did you learn to write that small?"

"My father was a hog man, Major. He didn't like to waste good feed money on paper. So I learned to take notes in the margins of my class-mates' discards. By the time I was studying biology at Jasper Poly—"

"Never mind. I didn't know you'd been tracking our trip to get the O'Coombe boy so closely," Valentine said, looking at the map.

"But I haven't," Doc said, shoving his hands in his pockets, where they went to work like two furiously digging rodents as he rocked.

"This is an epidemiological study. With ravies, geography is a strong predictor. Ravies sufferers naturally seek water, whether for sustenance or its cooling effect. Given no higher attraction, such as noise or a food source, they will find water and then follow small tributary to larger river, rather in the manner one is taught to find civilization if lost in the outdoors.

"Of course, my information is sketchy and mostly based on radio reports. But the dates and places of outbreaks show a curious track, don't you think?"

Valentine did think. It followed the arc of their path through north-central Kentucky.

"Always forty-eight to seventy-two hours behind us. Grand Junction. Elizabethtown. Danville. It always started in places we'd visited. We've been a four-wheel Typhoid Mary through Kentucky, Major Valentine."

"Someone's infected but not showing symptoms? They shook hands with a Kentuckian and spread the virus without knowing what they were doing? I thought ravies didn't pass through casual contact; you had to break the skin or eat contaminated food or some such."

Doc shook his head. "Even if it had been via casual contact, it spread too fast. No, the contact network for any one of us is not wide enough, not for this kind of effect in only forty-eight hours. There were multiple infections. It had to be placed in a food source or water supply."

Valentine startled at the implication. "You're saying someone in our column spread it intentionally."

"I'm saying that is what my analysis indicates. My sourcing may be faulty. There might be a statistical anomaly, as our communications with Fort Seng relied on relays with stops behind us, so the data points are naturally skewed to cover our trail. But there were no alarms from outside, say, Bowling Green or Frankfort, as you would expect from a population center that wide."

"Why would the Kurians use us? You'd think trained harpies or—"

"I'm no strategist, Major."

The Kurians would want to use the forces of Southern Command to make sure Kentucky would know who to blame for losses. Give every family a grievance.

Suddenly Valentine knew who'd spread the virus, and where he'd got it from. The sudden realization made him so sick he staggered to Doc's sink and vomited.

Valentine wiped his mouth. Double cross, triple cross, cross back . . . Kurian treachery was like a hall of mirrors. Somewhere a vulnerable back was showing to plunge the knife in. No doubt there were

Kurian agents dropping a few broad hints, revealing a few interesting details, in minds willing to believe the worst about outsiders. Bears weren't well understood even in the UFR. Many a regular citizen heard only of howling teams of battle-maddened men killing anything that moved. He could see an average Kentuckian believing Southern Command had brought a contagion into their land, probably by accident. But the dead were still the dead.

The winter wind blew dead leaves and freezing rain in confused swirls. Valentine didn't like freezing rain. It magically found crevices— the collar, the small of the back, the tops of your shoes—hitting and melting and leaving you wet and cold.

He'd summoned Lambert, Duvalier, Ediyak, Gamecock, and Nilay Patel to the old basement of the estate house. They'd cleaned it out and were in the process of turning it into a sort of theater that could show either movies or live plays.

It could also serve as a courtroom, if need be.

Frat stood before him, his bright new bars shining.

"Why'd you do it, Captain?" Valentine asked.

"Do what, sir?"

"Betray us," Valentine said.

Frat's eyes went wide and white. "Wha— I don't understand."

"I had that big satchel you carried, the one like mine, tested. There was some spilled preservative in there and a hell of a lot of ravies virus in the preservative fluid. What did you do? Put it in the water supply of the towns we visited?"

"We're going to have to handle this ourselves," Lambert said. "If it gets out in Kentucky that we were the vector that spread the disease . . ."

"I'll do it," Valentine said, speaking quickly as his voice fought not to break, go hoarse, choke off the words. "I brought him into Southern Command. I'll take him out."

He shoved Frat to his knees and pulled the old .45 out of its holster. A gift from another man he'd brought over from the Quislings.

Or did he hate Frat for playing the same trick he'd so often played: infiltrating, striking from within? Being better at the deadly game?

What kind of hold did Kur have on Frat's mind? They found a bright young boy, trained him, and then sent him out among decent people like the Carlsons—probably to learn more about the underground in the Kurian Zone, the mysterious lodges Valentine had heard mentioned now and again. Surely Frat was bright enough to see that life in the Freehold was better than that in the Kurian Zone. What did they promise, life eternal? Did fourteen-year-old boys even consider questions of mortality?

"It's an ugly truth, Frat. Shit rolls downhill. It's hard to stand in front of a superior and say, *We threw the dice on this one—and lost.* Someone must be to blame. You made the blame list."

Did Frat, miserable and shaking, know how like brothers they were? An accident of birth put Valentine in the woods of the Boundary Waters, Frat in some Chicago brownfield. If Valentine had been raised up in the Kurian Zone, would he have answered the bugle call of the Youth Vanguard, done his damnedest on the physical and mental tests?

Valentine stepped behind him. His .45 had never felt so heavy.

"I want my second chance," Frat said.

"What?" Lambert said. Valentine froze.

"You heard me," Frat said. "I'll put up my right hand and take the oath. Put in my years, just like the rest. Wash all this shit away."

"He's helped kill thousands in the clans," Duvalier said. "Whole families wiped out. You can't just let him walk away from that like a wet Baptist."

Valentine wondered. A highly trained ex–Kurian agent could be a valuable asset. Had Southern Command ever taken one alive? If they had, he wouldn't know about it.

But the virus Frat spread had killed thousands. Even though it had backfired on the Kurians, there were men, women, and children all over Kentucky who'd died in the madness, from the disease itself or the stress brought on by the change, or in the fighting.

"Let him live and you'll lose half of Kentucky."

Frat raised his right hand. "I freely and of my own resolve . . ."

Valentine had to make a decision. Is an ideal—a collection of words that makes everyone feel cleaner, purer—worth anything if you can just discard it at will? He'd promised every Quisling who came over a new future if they sweated and suffered and risked for the Cause.

Suppose Frat meant it and was ready to put his obvious talents to work for the new Freehold coalescing in Kentucky?

Valentine had squeezed his conscience through the keyhole of a technicality before. He pressed the pistol to the back of Frat's head, but the man who'd helped him rescue Molly Carlson went on speaking with only the briefest of pauses.

He couldn't do it. Cowardice or compassion?

He pulled back the gun.

"If you're going to take that oath, take it on your feet, Frat."

"Don't be a fool, Valentine," Lambert said.

"You want to shoot him?" Valentine asked. "Go ahead. It's not so easy to do."

"She's right, Val," Duvalier said. "Quisling snot'll turn on us first chance he gets. You can't change him no more than you can train a scorpion to quit killing beetles."

"Maybe," Valentine said. "But I'm also an officer. That little hearing we had may have returned a verdict, but it wasn't sent to headquarters for confirmation. I'm ready to suspend the execution on that technicality, barring an emergency that requires me to carry out the sentence.

"We're both hung men, Frat. We'd have nooses around our necks in civilized lands. But we're still kicking."

Frat looked off at the eastern horizon. "I'm not afraid of that gun. It's those motherfuckers who need to be afraid. They said they'd protect me."

"The piece of shit doesn't give a damn about the damage he's done," Patel said. "I'll stagger all the way to Little Rock if I have to, to get that sentence confirmed."

"I was following orders," Frat said. "Same as you all when you burned out Louisville. Or when the resistance killed every trustee on my block. Even my grandmother and my little sister. We all got sins worth a stone or two."

"He's joined up. He'll follow a better set of orders from now on," Valentine said.

Valentine needed air and light. He walked across the grounds of Fort Seng, Duvalier trailing carefully in his footsteps like Piglet tracking a Heffalump.

They paused on the little hill sheltering the guns and looked at the old manor house. Some soldiers were putting in new military-strength block-glass windows, yet another in the hundreds of odd jobs needed to turn an old park and former estate home into a proper military base worthy of a new Freehold.

A warm wind took over from the confused air, a fresh new gust from the southwest. The sleet fled, turning into tiny, blowing drops of rain.

"I'm ready for this winter to be over," Duvalier said, turning her face toward the wind to take in the warmth on her freckled cheek.

"Not yet," Valentine said. "There's a lot to do before spring."

About the Author

E.E. Knight was born in Wisconsin, grew up in Minnesota, and now calls Chicago home, where he abides in domestic felicity with his family, and assorted pets. He is the author of the Vampire Earth series.